GODS OF MYTH AND MIDNIGHT

Seeds of Chaos
Book 3

AZALEA ELLIS

Join the Inner Circle**

Become part of the Inner Circle.

Instantly receive a free copy of *Gods of Smoke and Stars*, a Seeds of Chaos novella.

https://www.azaleaellis.com/newsletter

I will send you new release updates, exclusive content like pre-release or deleted scenes, as well as news about giveaways or contests I'm doing (signed paperbacks, posters, etc.) and other cool stuff I think you might enjoy. Sometimes I tell weird stories about my life.

Support me on Patreon

https://www.patreon.com/azaleaellis

Read along chapter by chapter as I write the next book in my current series, with early access chapters not available elsewhere, plus exclusive short stories and bonus chapters, and even audiobooks.

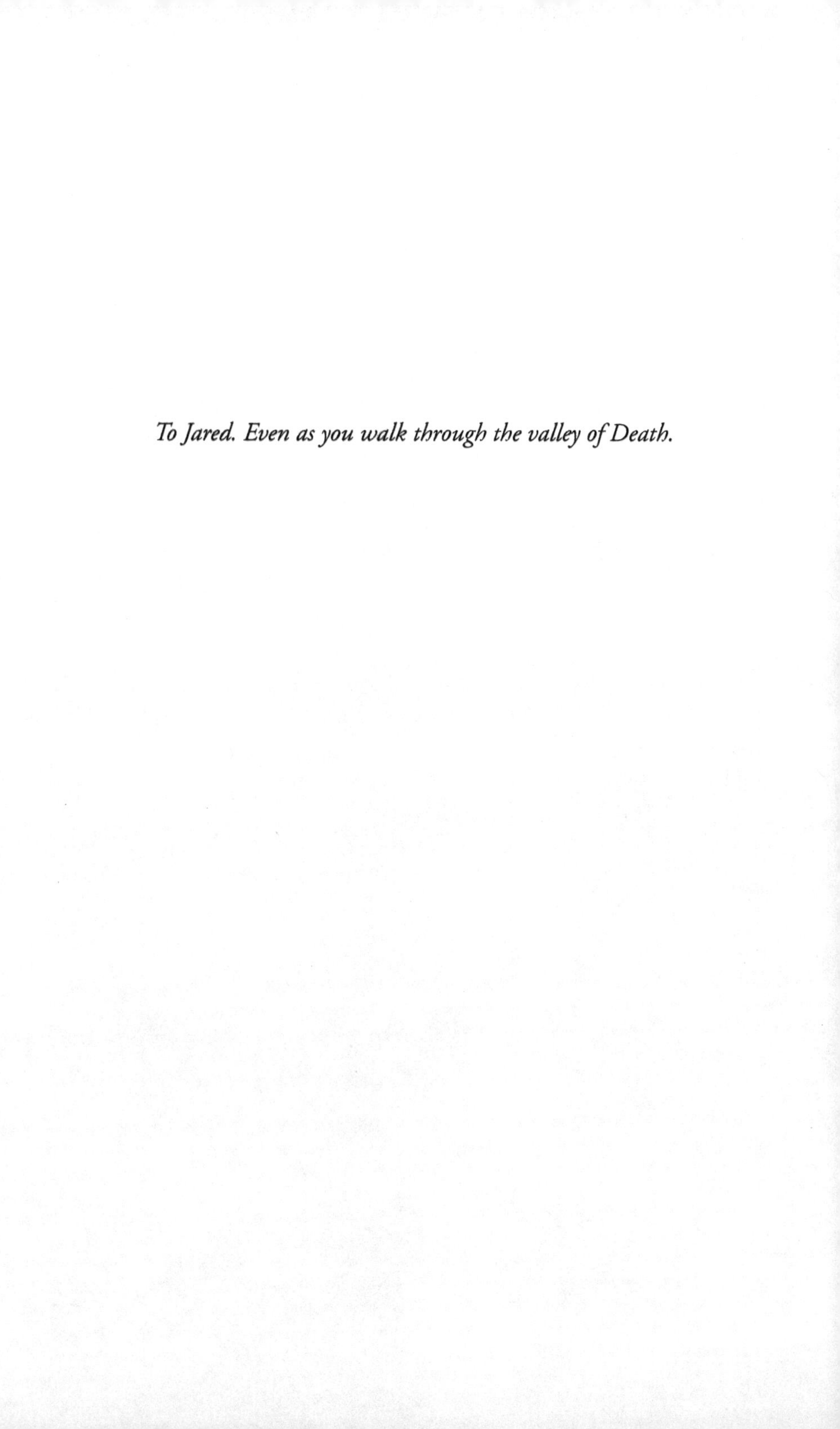

To Jared. Even as you walk through the valley of Death.

Chapter 1

Betrayal is the only truth that sticks.
— Arthur Miller

A TINGLING WAVE spread through my body, each thud of my heart sending blood rushing through my ears with a drum-like thunder, till it drowned out all other sound. Queen Mardinest had just declared war. On Earth. I drug my eyes away from the screen, where ships were still flying through the array, and looked at her.

She was already staring at me, as if she'd anticipated my response. When our eyes met, she gave me a slow, predatory smile, and dipped her head in a shallow bow.

I drew in a shuddering gasp of rage, and the tips of my fingers quivered. But my claws did not extend. That tingling wave rocked through me again, and, completely against my will, I relaxed. My body moved without my consent, like a puppet on strings.

The sudden lack of control was disorienting. I grew dizzy. I pushed against the relaxation, a reflex as quick as catching yourself when you start to trip. Instead, my body stayed calm, and my face settled into a mask of sober dignity.

Wraith lashed out of me, sending my awareness exploding through the room as I searched for the source of the attacking Skill. The glow of power coming off all the Estreyans present was bright enough to obscure any individual person. However, most of them were looking at the screen. A few reporters had gathered their wits enough to turn back to the queen and my team, and the eyes of the guards on the outskirts of the room roved, but only a few of them showed the flaring glow of an active Skill.

As my mouth twitched involuntarily into a subtle smile, my awareness climbed upward to the inward-facing balcony looking down on the main floor of the throne room.

A blonde Estreyan man, wearing a circlet similar to the one around Torliam's head, stood there staring at the dais below, power blazing from him.

A Window in front of my face made my heart sink.

—I CAN'T MOVE, AND I CAN'T USE MY SKILL. SHE MUST HAVE
PLANNED THIS.—
-ADAM-

I reached for Chaos, but after a surge of Seed-glow indicating Skill use from the man on the balcony, my mental grasp slipped off of my own power. A few thin wisps of dark-tendriled destruction grated against my armor before dissipating, ineffectual and unfocused.

The reporters had regained their composure and turned their attention, and recording devices, back to the queen and my group. The ensuing barrage of shouted questions struck a blow to my already frazzled concentration.

As the last of the ships left Estreyer through the array, Queen Mardinest raised her hands to the room, motioning for quiet.

One of the kiddos let out half a whimper, quickly choked off.

I sent a Window to all the members of the team with VR chips, which only excluded Torliam and Birch.

—WE'RE BEING CONTROLLED. IT'S THE GUY ON THE BALCONY
ABOVE US. I CAN FEEL HIM FIGHTING BACK WHEN I TRY TO ACT.
—
-EVE-

—HE CAN'T BE STRONGER THAN ALL OF US, YEAH? WE JUST
GOTTA BUST THROUGH.—

-Jacky-

—Good idea. He can't keep this up forever.—
-Eve-

I turned Wraith on my teammates.

Gregor flickered for a fraction of a second as he tried to activate Shadow and failed.

Blaine's suit whirred softly as if preparing for action, but he did not move.

Zed's fingers trembled as if reaching for something, though I didn't know if he was trying for his gun or his Skill.

Birch managed to kick up a wind before our controller's power clamped down on him.

Torliam's body language was as calm as my own, but when my awareness brushed against his skin, I could feel his pulse running fast through his neck.

He shuddered minutely, and his muscles spasmed, even as my own grip on Wraith slipped away.

My attention frayed and my sensory ability regressed to the limited capabilities of my physical body. The man above was clamping down on his control of me, apparently.

Once the room was suitably hushed, Queen Mardinest ran her gaze over the assembled reporters, shoulders thrown back in arrogant pride.

I reached for Chaos again. My mind seemed to fumble stupidly, and I got so little power that it wasn't even visible beyond a faint haze close to my skin.

"My people have been working tirelessly to uncover the extent of the atrocities committed by the Earthlings," she said. "We discovered much. They have stolen our technology and used that to come to our world in secret, petitioning *our gods* for power."

A murmur of outrage welled up in the rapt crowd.

"They jailed and tortured a member of the royal family." She took a deep breath, and, even behind her, I could feel the force of her presence, a righteous kind of anger that encouraged my heart to pound.

"They have taken the Sickness and mixed it with another disease meant to weaken us. In doing so, they have created a new horror. Their weapon, cruelly tested and grown in their own people, will destroy our blood-borne power so that we are as weak and feeble as them, and as if that were not violation enough, it will infect those who receive it with the taint of the Sickness, *purposefully.*"

Was that how Chanelle had been infected? Through the meningolycanosis? But I was pretty sure NIX had no idea about the Sickness. I drove the distracting thought away and continued to struggle for command of my body and my Skills as my teammates did the same.

Up above, the man with the circlet pushed back, but my awareness spread out from my body a little further each time, and the air around me writhed with little gusts of warmth created by Chaos.

"These brave warriors have agreed to go through the array to Earth to neutralize this threat before it becomes even greater. In doing so, we also save the Earthlings from themselves. They are too foolish to realize that the Sickness can never be a true ally, and will turn on their own people just as it attempts to drag us down into ruin."

She paused, and my Skill sensed her eyes flick upward to the spot where our puppeteer stood. "We will not allow their madness to reach our world, to hurt our loved ones and our children. They will not destroy us. We will not rest till their depraved leaders and Sickness-infected warriors are ground to dust." She bowed crisply, her body held stiff.

After a pause, she straightened. "Questions shall be accepted by my son Reglium, who has returned from his diplomatic endeavors to lend his aid in this time of need." She gestured to the stairs leading down from the balcony which grew out of the wall behind us.

The man in the circlet descended, then cut across the room toward us. He entered my field of vision as he walked past, stepping onto the dais to stand by his mother.

I raged against his control and felt the hair on the back of my neck tremble from the restrained power tingling in the air around me.

He almost stumbled, but caught himself, breathing a little too hard.

My body stood, along with the others on the team, except for Adam, and bowed to the reporters.

Queen Mardinest lifted a hand in silent farewell and walked away. She stepped through the subtle door behind her throne, which led into a nondescript hallway.

I followed her, my face still refusing to twist into the visage of snarling rage I demanded.

My eyes caught on Adam's for a moment. He was white-faced with pain, being carried between Blaine in his mecha suit and Torliam. Without access to his Skill, he had no way to move on his own. I took small comfort in the fact that Reglium obviously couldn't control our Skills enough to use them, only suppress our ability to operate them.

I stumbled as the door closed behind us. My body continued to move under Reglium's control, but it grew clumsier as we walked further from him and the throne room.

What was Queen Mardinest's plan? It seemed obvious she couldn't keep us under direct control indefinitely. Sure, she'd kept us from speaking out against the invasion of Earth and made it seem like we agreed with her decisions. But she'd made an enemy of us in doing so. Which meant she thought she could handle us as an enemy, despite our recent success in killing a god and the political power that had gained us.

—Is she taking us somewhere to kill us?—
-Gregor-

—No. Don't worry. She would never get away with that. She's going to *threaten* us. She needs our cooperation.—
-Eve-

***

QUEEN MARDINEST LED us to a nearby room with a thick stone door and no windows. Four Estreyans waited inside, one woman and three men. They bowed to her when we entered.

I sensed the glow of their power and knew we couldn't win against them easily.

The door closed behind us with an ominous finality, and I almost fell on my face as Reglium's tingling Skill released my body. My claws slid out as I regained my balance.

Adam jerked his arms away from Blaine and Torliam, spilling ink from a cartridge at his waist. The ink swirled up and wrapped around his legs and torso, supporting and stabilizing them, then sprouted eight spider-like legs to hold him aloft.

Blue mist wafted off Torliam as he took in the waiting Estreyans and then looked to the queen. He spoke in his native language, his words deliberate and tightly controlled. "What are you doing, Mother?"

Jacky grew to match my height and a little more, stepping up beside me with a quick glance to make sure she stood securely in front of the kids.

Blaine's mecha suit loaded ammunition into the arm thrusters.

"I am doing what must be done," Queen Mardinest said, her clenched fists nearly white with tension. "The humans are helping the Sickness to destroy us all. I will stop it, even if I must raze that vermin-infested planet to the ground." Her voice dripped with vitriol. "I will not allow you to stand in my way."

Torliam shook his head. "We, too, wish to stop the Sickness! Why are you acting against us? We could have spoken of this—"

She slashed her hand through the air, and he clenched his jaw shut. There was no Skill at work to silence him, only her authority and the granite-like hardness of her expression.

I ran my eyes over the other Estreyans in the room. To be there, Queen Mardinest must have believed they could subdue us. We were strong, but I couldn't unleash Chaos' full destructive capabilities while trapped in a room with my teammates, and I knew that we still weren't a match for a group of elite Estreyan warriors. "Is diplomacy not an option?" I said. "You have assaulted my team without warning, without an attempt to come to an understanding. Have you done the same to the humans of Earth?"

"*We* are humans," Blaine said, his voice steady. "Earth is our home, and we are the very solution to that Sickness you so want to eradicate."

Queen Mardinest laughed.

Birch growled, a low rumble I could feel as he pressed himself against my leg.

"There is no cure to the Sickness." Her voice held no doubt, and I knew things were about to get worse. "The best of us have been trying to find an answer, for thousands of years. The Sickness is now defeating even the gods. And what can you do? You killed the God of Knowledge, yes. Do you now know how to cure the Sickness? If so, show me this miracle. You have infected among your own teammates, surely you would heal them if you could!" She slashed her hand toward Chanelle and the kids, who stood half-hidden at the back of the group.

I steeled myself against the crushing power in her words. "I do not have the cure, that is true. But I also have one gift remaining from the Oracle, and we have not yet found the Champion. Who, if I may remind you, is likely on Earth. It is the reason your son came to my planet in the first place."

She spat on the ground.

Torliam flinched, as if she'd slapped him. "Mother. There *is* hope. The Goddess of Testimony and Lore has marked us. Eve is a descendant of the line of Matrix. We have defeated a god." Torliam's voice shook. "I knew you did not believe me before, but I have *proof* now."

She turned to Torliam. "My son, I know you do not want to believe this. However, I realized when your sister Tonila died that there is no future for our world. How many times have our people found some new hope, only for it to be crushed? It is a cruel game."

Ah. Well, that changed things. If Queen Mardinest did not believe in a cure to the Sickness, there was no incentive for her to ally with us, no influence we could use to adjust her actions.

TORLIAM STARED AT HIS MOTHER, blinking a little too fast, as if trying to understand what he was seeing.

"So why did you act like you believed?" Adam burst out.

"I could not do otherwise, unless I wished to kill you all before word of your presence spread. As a ruler, it cannot be said there is any possibility of curing the Sickness which I do not attempt. It is not expected for these attempts to truly succeed. I needed to buy time and political goodwill for myself. You are my son," she said, her voice softening only a little as she looked at Torliam. "I did not wish to have you killed, though I did not believe any of you would survive your ill-conceived attack on the God of Knowledge."

I narrowed my eyes, the tips of my claws scraping against my armor. "But we're still alive."

"Indeed. This puts me in a difficult position. I still have no wish to kill you, if I do not have to. Nevertheless, I cannot allow you to interfere with the ruling of my people, or to try to stop me from doing what must be done out of sentiment for your parent race or fanatical belief in something that will never be."

I knew we'd finally arrived at the threat. She *couldn't* just kill us, not while we were so high in the public eye.

She gestured behind her, to the Estreyans who hadn't yet called attention to themselves. "These warriors are bound to me in *blood-covenant*. They are loyal to me, and me alone. They will be your new guards and escorts, along with my son Reglium. You will do my bidding as loyally as they, or I will be forced to kill you all. First, I will reveal to the public that the Sickness has infested members of your team." She let out a sharp bark of laughter. "Ironically, that is even the truth. I will *show* the public your crazed frenzy as it takes over your minds and bodies, just as I *showed* them your calm acceptance of my leadership today. You will have no choice in the matter. That is, if you do not succumb to the Sickness on your own. Each of these warriors has been picked specifically, their abilities chosen to ensure you will not defy me. Ni," she pointed to the woman, "will keep track of you at all times, San and Shi are fighters so mighty you will not stand against them long, *if* you manage to somehow escape immediate death in an attempt to defy me. And Ichi…"

One of the Estreyans, a man slightly paler than seemed healthy, stepped forward.

"He has the ability to transport any living being he can see to any point within the many levels of Estreyer." She snapped her fingers.

Ichi nodded, and in the space of a blink, I was underwater, pressure crushing down on me. The breath left my lungs, drifting away in bubbles barely visible in the darkness. Wraith pushed out sluggishly through the liquid, and found my teammates around me.

Torliam's blue mist expanded to encircle us, and ink spilled into the water around Adam, and then we were back in the stone-walled room.

I dropped to my knees, gasping for air. The water dripped onto the stones beneath me.

Gregor was in his Shadow state, and he pushed forward to stand beside me, his daggers held threateningly above me.

I rose to my feet, letting Chaos boil out an inch or so over my skin and armor, the tendrils of smoke-like darkness writhing like angry snakes. "Sam?" I said, grabbing Gregor's shoulder and urging him back. He didn't need to protect me.

Zed's fingers disappeared into the air and the water on his hand turned to ice, but he glared at the four guards and Queen Mardinest, then withdrew his hand, letting the rip to the Other Place close.

Jacky had grown until her head brushed against the ceiling. She snarled, and Ichi raised his hand to her.

I placed a hand on her side and shook my head silently. We couldn't afford to turn this into a real fight.

Jacky turned and smashed her fist into the wall. Stone flew outward from the point of impact, the sound thunderously loud in the small room.

Queen Mardinest still stood where she'd been before the threatening display of power. "You are cunning, Eve-Redding, and you are all very resourceful as a group. Perhaps you will find a way to survive all that. So I won't take any chances, if I need to kill you. Ichi will transport you directly into the Voids of Tartarus. Since you are an Earthling, you may not know what that is. Suffice it to say, *nothing* that enters has *ever* left."

Sam touched the others, and after a short second of examination each, sent a single nod my way. At least no one had been seriously injured by that little stunt, though I noted that Sam returned to Adam, who was white-faced and trembling. The crushing pressure of the ocean depths on Adam's mangled spine must have hurt like hell.

"My people may cry your names in the streets now, but if they knew you harbored the Sickness, they would call instead for your bodies to be cleansed beyond ash with a fire as hot as the sun. If you force my hand against you, I will ensure they mourn only the loss of a few more victims of the Sickness."

"And if we comply?" My voice was hoarse.

She gave the most humorless of smiles. "I will allow you to be your own destruction, over time. You will be seen continuing your attempts to cure the Sickness. You will act as diplomatic envoys to those who wish to meet the godkiller. You may even petition the minor gods for Bestowals, though no more of my warriors will die on your behalf while you do so. However, do not think I am unaware of your true nature, Eve-Redding. You will plot and scheme within your heart, seeking to sting me with deadly poison when my attention is diverted. I know this, because I can sense it within you even now."

She stepped forward. "The line of Aethezriel did not always rule. Did you know that? I wrested this crown, and with it my seat of power, from another family before me. They had many secrets. Now, I am known as a *warrior-queen*, and the *blood-borne* ability the people know is my godlike skill with the blade and bow. Yet the ability that gained me this crown, and the one which allows me to keep it among the *skirling*-infested court members who wish it for themselves, is my sense for the secrets of others."

I did not step back from her, even as I sensed the glow of her power tugging at my body and repressed a shudder.

"It is necessary that I keep this power secret, both so that it might be used against those who are unaware, and so that my enemies cannot use the instinctive fear of one's secrets being revealed against me. I can smell the things you keep hidden like the misty ghost of an idea. It has always been enough. If I believe you plan to become my enemy in any way, I will be forced to act against you." She stepped back, but didn't bother to smile toothily like I might have done. She was serene, confident in her own power without the need to revel in it.

"Mother. We need not be enemies." Torliam's words were choked, but he held himself straight and with dignity despite the water still dripping from his hair. "Even if you do not believe in us, or that the prophesied cure exists, we might still prove you to be wrong. Let us go to Earth, so that Eve may find the Champion, and bring him back to Estreyer."

She scoffed. "This one," she pointed to me, "is only using you. The Champion is not on Earth. He is dead, and has been for thousands of cycles. I will not allow one as treacherous as her the potential to ally with our enemies, which she has already done once, before she discovered the power you might provide her in their stead. You will remain on Estreyer. I will give you time to reconcile yourselves with the new order of things. I have many demands on my attention. Return to your assigned quarters. Ichi may relate to you your duties henceforth as you walk."

One of the other Estreyans stepped forward and opened the door behind us, seemingly unperturbed by the threatening stares of my teammates.

When the queen motioned dismissively toward the open doorway, they glanced at me. I nodded, and they filed out, along with three of our four new guards.

Jacky glared at one of the guards and feigned a lunge toward him, grinning when he flinched, and then swaggered off down the hallway.

I moved to go with them, but the queen placed her hand on my shoulder.

Torliam stopped, frowning, but she waved him on. "Go. Eve-Redding will not be harmed. I merely wish to speak with her a short while longer."

"I am in blood-covenant with her," he said, the words heavy with an insinuation I didn't quite understand. "It is the duty of the line of Aethezriel to guard and serve the line of Matrix."

Her hand tightened on my shoulder, and before she could retort, I spoke. "It's alright. I'll speak with her, and meet you in a little while."

I could almost hear the creak of his jaw as he clenched his teeth together, but he nodded and walked off after the others.

Queen Mardinest waited an uncomfortably long time with her hand silently on my shoulder, undoubtedly used to the superior eavesdropping senses of the Estreyans. Then, she leaned in and murmured into my ear, the warmth of her breath tickling me. "I know your secret. You are a desperate liar and a charlatan." She breathed in deep, an exaggerated sniff. "I do not know how you managed to convince my son these sparkling gifts mean you are all tied into the destiny of a savior, but I know that you came to the both of us with lies. Every time someone spoke of curing the Sickness in your presence, I smelt the hint of it. When you returned, I understood. You meant all along to kill a god, but it was never anything to do with altruism. There was *never* any Bestowal offered, either of a cure or information leading to one. There is no cure for the Sickness. We are in agreement on that, I believe. But if your precious team-mates, and my son, were to learn of your duplicity, I do not think they would be so understanding as I."

Chapter 2

There is no passion so contagious as that of fear.
— Michel de Montaigne

THE HALLWAYS, normally spacious and bright, seemed to close in on me. I walked with the remaining guard, one of the warriors, following the same path the others had traveled ahead of me. I took deep breaths, but it didn't feel like I was getting enough air. The world spun, and I reached out to brace myself on the wall.

I found myself staring at my left hand. It was an alien thing. The fingers were a little too long, and one too many of them grew out from my palm. If it were just the darkened skin, or the hardened, scale-like segments stretching out from under the armor at my wrist, I would have still been able to look at the hand and think of it as my own. But the shape of it had changed altogether.

I clenched my fist and brought it down to my side, closing my eyes. "Get it together," I mouthed to myself, hoping the guard hadn't taken too much note of my moment of weakness. After successfully surviving the fight with the God of Knowledge, I'd still been adjusting to the changes in myself and my life. I hadn't yet figured out my new path going forward. This development, and its possible ramifications, had given me whiplash when I was already struggling for balance. But I was adaptable. I had to be.

Queen Mardinest's threat to reveal my duplicity was meant as another layer of binding around me, but it was only effective if I gave it power. If she tried to expose me to my teammates, I could just *lie*. After today, they wouldn't trust her over me without *damning* proof, especially with so much evidence to the contrary. Even if the original quest had mentioned nothing about curing the Sickness, after that it was like the world was bending itself into contortions trying to make my lie into truth. Whether it had succeeded in making me what I claimed or not, I wasn't going to let my teammates die to a curable disease. She'd been wrong. I believed in a cure to the Sickness. I'd create one, even if I had to form it out of the very ether or the bones of my enemies.

Unfortunately, things had just gotten a lot more difficult. If the god with the cure was on Earth and not Estreyer, we'd need to bypass the queen's new authority over us. *Without* getting tossed into the Voids of Tartarus.

The image of ships flying through the array asserted itself in my mind again. War on Earth? What did that even really mean? If she was trying to eradicate the meningolycanosis, Queen Mardinest would go after NIX, right? Except I knew they had more than the one base, and other countries might even have their own versions. And NIX was part of the government, at least to some degree. One which had been preparing for just such an invasion for the last seven or eight years.

This couldn't end well.

A small "Mrrp?" drew my eyes, and I saw Birch peeking around the corner ahead. He padded over to me, bumping his forehead into my knee.

"You waited for me." I reached down and ran a hand over his head, giving him a few scratches behind the ears and at the base of his wings. When the guard motioned impatiently at me, I started to walk again.

Birch kept his shoulder pressed to the side of my leg in silent support.

He let out a grumble that was half growl, ears flicking around alertly while keeping his hostile gaze on the warrior walking slightly ahead of us.

"Yes. This was a very unfortunate development," I said. I couldn't understand cat speech, but his body language and tone of voice were usually enough to get a good idea what he was trying to convey. When they weren't, he could communicate telepathically with skin contact.

I took a deep breath and let it out slowly. I hadn't yet met a truly unsolvable problem. This would be no different.

We couldn't trust Queen Mardinest. We were a threat to her, and would become even more of one if we made progress in curing the Sickness. If we stayed under her control, there was no future for us. Some of my team would die from infection, and once the rest of us weren't so beloved, it wouldn't be so hard for an "accident" to kill us all. She'd insinuated as much to our faces.

She had gotten too used to getting what she wanted. It was time we served her a healthy dose of disappointment.

WE ARRIVED at a part of the palace I hadn't explored before, on ground level. I pushed Wraith ahead to sense my teammates, who milled like a small swarm of angry ants outside a door with runes carved into it, across from an open room with metal melted into the floor in a complicated diagram and some lounge-type furniture. I could hear them arguing in semi-hushed voices before I even turned the corner.

"I am not responsible for my mother's actions," Torliam growled.

"You're the freaking *prince*! You can't do anything about this?" Adam said.

"I am the youngest, I am a son, and I am not even favored enough for my mother to attempt to rescue from imprisonment and torture! Only people too ignorant to know better think I have any political power!"

"If not for you, pushing Eve to be your 'chosen one' and then telling your mother all about her and that people tried to kill the kids, we wouldn't be in this situation at all!"

"If not for me, Eve would be dead!"

I rounded the corner to see blue mist rise and lash at the air around Torliam futilely. Both he and Adam turned to look when I arrived, and I wasn't sure if Gregor's huge sigh of relief was for my wellbeing, or for the end of the argument. I frowned at them, and Torliam, at least, seemed abashed.

The queen's new watchdog Estreyans stood in the open room across from the door, doing something with the rune-carved floor. If I had to guess, it had something to do with locking us into the adjacent room, which was undoubtedly a cell to keep us from escaping or doing anything rash. So much for the new, fancy bedroom I'd been assigned.

Adam's ink carriage skittered around on its legs, turning him to face me. "What did she keep you behind for?"

Torliam scanned me with his eyes. "Are you unharmed?"

"How can she *do* this?" Kris said. "Earth is our home. She knows we're from there, and she acts all supportive to our face, then suddenly—"

Gregor squeezed her hand, and she cut off.

I resisted the urge to let my claws slip out and bare my teeth at my guard as he moved past me to join the others. I settled instead on a stony glare. It wouldn't do to seem *too* complacent, after all.

I rubbed my neck, trying to release some of the tension there. "She took the opportunity to threaten me in some more detail."

One of our guards opened the door and shooed us into the large, windowless room. It had a few bed mats spread directly onto the floor, and there was a small walled-off area I assumed to be a bathroom. The ceiling glowed, mimicking the brightness of the world outside.

I noted more metal runes and designs sunk into the stone and felt the muscles around my eyes tighten with stress. I let my awareness swirl out into the open room behind us. When the female guard, Ni, who now sat in the middle of the design carved into the floor, let out a slow breath, I felt the buzzing barrier in our new windowless cell snap to life and couldn't help but flinch.

Displayed on the surface of one of the tables outside I caught a blurry image of the room and us within it. They weren't incompetent, it seems.

Adam paced back and forth on his ink spider. "Is the Estreyan justice system corrupt enough that she can really get away with this?"

"Well, obviously she can," I said, flopping onto one of the thin bed mats and rubbing my palms across my face.

He moved to loom over me like some horror-film amalgamation of spider and man. "What are we going to do?"

"There's nothing we *can* do. Just try to get some rest while we have the opportunity. I know *I* need it."

Adam frowned, exchanging a look with Zed. "We just got threatened and blackmailed into servitude, and you're too tired to talk about it?" His eyebrows raised high, and his voice tightened, growing angrier as he spoke.

—They're watching?—
-Adam-

I suppressed my smile as I read the Window message. He'd understood exactly what I was going for. I sent my response to everyone who had a VR chip, and hoped that Torliam, who didn't, wouldn't push the issue.

—Yes. We'll talk when it's too dark for them to see, since we'll need Torliam's input on this.—
-Eve-

Outwardly, I pressed my lips together in an expression that reminded me of my mother. "There's nothing we can do about it, is there? We can talk in a couple hours, once *I've* had some time to wind down. If *you* want to keep that stick up your ass till it gives you a heart attack, be my guest."

Sam's eyes were wide. "Guys, uh, we're all a little on edge right now. Let's just take a deep—"

Adam rolled his eyes and whipped off toward the other corner of the room, lowering his body onto another of the bed mats while pointedly not looking at me.

Chanelle sat next to me, her gaze tracking with the lucidity it sometimes lacked. "Do you have any food?" she said in a small voice.

I dug some fruit and dried meat out of my pack, grateful that I'd carried it with me even to the queen's announcement out of ingrained, paranoid habit. As she began to eat, I took out the Oracle's final gift and fiddled with it. With mental commands, I sent Zed a Window.

—We're trapped in here by some sort of energy barrier that's flush with the walls. Investigate it, as innocently as you can. It's okay to act curious, that's normal, but they'll be watching me specifically to make sure I'm not planning an escape.—
-Eve-

Zed moved to the wall and pressed his palms against it. It produced an audible zap, and he jerked back in surprise, shaking his hands.

Torliam paced back and forth and he clenched and unclenched his fists. "This cell is meant to hold prisoners of significant strength. It has been modified with a barrier powered from the ritual circle in the room outside. Nothing will leave this room."

Zed poked the wall again. "Not even air?"

"I doubt they mean to kill us. The air will refresh itself through the orb on the ceiling." Torliam gestured, barely sparing a glance toward it. He caught my eye for a second and seemed to notice something in my expression. He stopped pacing.

Zed narrowed his eyes, lowered his hands to hang at his sides, and poked a finger into the air surreptitiously. His finger disappeared. I felt the pinprick spot of cold seeping through the tiny rip he'd created in reality.

Outside, the woman in the middle of the circular diagram gasped, then hunched over. "It's sucking too much power!"

I kept my face expressionless and pushed Wraith through the opening Zed had torn, into an almost perfect replica of the room we stood in. Except, in the Other Place, there were no bed mats on the floor, and the doorway was empty of the stone door keeping us enclosed. The buzzing barrier still existed, though.

Another guard moved to the gasping woman's side in concern.

Ichi stared at her for a few moments, then strode toward our cell.

—They're about to open the door. Act natural.—
-Eve-

As soon as the door opened, the barrier broke, in both the real world and the Other Place, and the woman straightened with a sigh of relief.

"What are you doing?" Ichi snapped, his eyes tracking over us.

Zed poked the wall again lazily, then looked up at Ichi. "Oh, hey. Since you're here, could you get us some food? I'm thinking maybe some cheesy bread?"

"I want meat," Jacky said slowly, enunciating the Estreyan words carefully.

Ichi glared at the two of them, looked around again, and slammed the door shut with a shuddering *boom*.

Zed turned to Jacky. "He didn't acknowledge our food order. Do you think he'll manage to get it right?"

Gregor huffed. "Maybe they're trying to force us to resort to cannibalism."

We passed a couple hours with talk, trying to seem as natural as possible, which meant being angry and worried while also not acting as if we planned any betrayal.

"Do you think Mom is safe?" Zed asked, propped against the lightly buzzing wall with me on my bed mat.

Sam and Chanelle both turned toward us at his words, no doubt wondering the same thing about their own parents.

My claws fumbled, dropping the puzzle band into my lap. I retracted them and clenched my left fist together to conceal the extra finger from my sight. "I hope so," I said. "Even if we did try to hide our families, once NIX had us back in the system, they shouldn't have had as much trouble as they did finding them." I sent them a Window for the remainder of my response.

—We'll search for them when we get back to Earth. Ironically, it's probably best for us if NIX managed to find them after we left. Unless they're holding them hostage.—
-Eve-

—So we're definitely going back to Earth?—
-Zed-

—We have to.—

-Eve-

Aloud, I said, "We'll have to talk to Queen Mardinest about it. Maybe she'll help us find them." I resisted the urge to put obvious sarcasm into the words, despite the ball of anger that rose up in me.

I thought back to the last time we'd gone to NIX, an Estreyan group of warriors coming along as an incentive for Commander Bragg to agree to our demands. My heart thumped with sudden, sickening realization. I turned my head to stare at Zed. We'd gotten meningolycanosis and their research on it, but I'd never thought to ask for more of the nanite booster my brother needed.

"How much of the nanite paste do you have left?"

Zed didn't answer at first, fingering the spot at his waist where he kept the vial-like containers. "A couple weeks. Maybe three, if I stretch it out and don't mind feeling a little sick."

I was silent. This was my fault.

He pressed his lips together. "I thought, once we were finished with the God of Knowledge, I'd have time to bring it up. Blaine could probably make more, with access to a lab. I never imagined something like this would happen."

"Blaine *can* make more." The words were just as much to reassure myself as for Zed. "We'll make sure he gets the chance to do so."

I meditated to pass the time till we could talk more openly, examining my body and the castle around us. Jacky played with Kris and Gregor, Blaine fiddled with a piece of his armor that kept shooting sparks despite his intense glares at it, and Adam worked on the ever more intricate, fractal tattoo growing from his wrists up to his shoulders.

Fretfully, I browsed through my VR chip's Windows.

PLAYER NAME: EVE REDDING
TITLE: BEARER OF TESTIMONY
CHARACTERISTIC SKILL: SPIRIT OF THE HUNTRESS,
TUMBLING FEATHER
LEVEL: 38
SKILLS: COMMAND, WRAITH, CHAOS, VOICE

STRENGTH: 23

LIFE: 76
AGILITY: 32
GRACE: 28
INTELLIGENCE: 32
FOCUS: 24
BEAUTY: 16
CHARISMA: 33
MANUAL DEXTERITY: 10
MENTAL ACUITY: 29
RESILIENCE: 70
STAMINA: 36
PERCEPTION: 33

My official level hadn't changed since we broke from NIX, since it was determined by them and only noted the number of Seeds they'd awarded, not my actual Attribute levels, which could be increased through training.

If NIX had wanted to forcefully push me to this Attribute level, they would have had to award me almost four hundred Seeds. Granted, I had planted a huge number of stolen Seeds in my healing-related Attributes. Still, I knew the self-sustaining growth of Attributes through training was probably why NIX decided to create a lot of Players rather than just loading up a handful of people with their limited Seed supply. Sure, they probably created or enhanced their Thinkers via direct Seed influx, but for the rest of us, NIX wanted the Skills more than anything, since superhuman physical abilities could only take you so far.

Someone could have Attributes much higher than mine, but it didn't matter if I caught them with Chaos. Then again…if I couldn't manage to catch them, even a godling-class Skill could do nothing.

CHARACTERISTIC SKILLS

TUMBLING FEATHER (KINETIC CLASS): INCREASES GRACE AND AGILITY. IMPROVES SENSE OF BALANCE AND MOTION. SKILL EFFECTS WILL EXPAND AND STRENGTHEN WITH PLAYER GROWTH.

SPIRIT OF THE HUNTRESS (SPIRIT CLASS): INCREASES GRACE, AGILITY, PERCEPTION, FOCUS, BEAUTY, AND STAMINA. NAILS EXTEND AND SHARPEN ON COMMAND, ALONG WITH PHYSICAL RESTRUCTURING OF HANDS AND FEET. FEET PERMANENTLY AUGMENTED FOR INCREASED PERFORMANCE. INCREASES CHANCE TO LAND ON FEET AFTER A FALL. AGGRESSIVE TENDENCIES INCREASE. SKILL EFFECTS WILL EXPAND AND STRENGTHEN WITH PLAYER GROWTH.

SKILLS

COMMAND (MUNDANE CLASS): ALLOWS LEADER ACCESS TO THE TEAM MANAGEMENT WINDOW. LEADER CAN COMMUNICATE WITH TEAM MEMBERS THROUGH GAME WINDOWS AND ACCESS BASIC GAME INFORMATION OF TEAM MEMBERS.

WRAITH (PROJECTION CLASS): INCREASES PERCEPTION. SENSES EXTEND BEYOND THE BODY, GIVING A COMPREHENSIVE UNDERSTANDING OF SURROUNDINGS, AND MARKING AREAS OR BEINGS OF POWER ACCORDING TO DEGREE. SKILL EFFECTS WILL EXPAND AND STRENGTHEN WITH PLAYER IMPROVEMENT.

CHAOS (GODLING CLASS): LATENT ASCENSION POTENTIAL. GIVES ACCESS TO THE PRIMORDIAL POWER OF THE GODDESS OF CHAOS.

VOICE (SOVEREIGN CLASS): INCREASES CHARISMA. ACTS AS A BEACON FOR BEINGS OF POWER. ALLOWS PRESENCE AND WILL TO BE IMPOSED ON SURROUNDINGS. SKILL EFFECTS WILL EXPAND AND STRENGTHEN WITH PLAYER IMPROVEMENT.

When the ceiling had been dark for several hours to match the world outside, and the screen displaying us to our guards showed nothing but darkness, I knew it was time.

Silently, we gathered in the center of the room.

Adam spilled ink on the ground, and with a silently mouthed "Animus," it rose up around us in a protective sphere of darkness.

"We need an anti-eavesdropping buzz, if you'd be so kind," I whispered, my words barely more than a breath on the air.

Torliam heard me without difficulty, and blue mist wafted out from him ever so faintly, setting the surrounding air to vibrating with pseudo white-noise.

"I'VE IMBUED the barrier with as much intention to block sight as I can," Adam said. "It might help, even if one of them can otherwise see through walls."

Blaine turned on one of the lights on his mecha suit so we could all see each other.

I raised my eyebrows, testing the ink barrier's resistance. "Good job."

One side of Adam's mouth quirked up into a smirk, and he gave Torliam a pointed look.

Torliam crossed his arms across his broad chest and turned away.

"So what the *hell?*" Jacky burst out, clenching her fists.

Blaine pushed his glasses up. "I have to agree. This is a completely unacceptable outcome, Eve. I will not give up on the search to find the cure."

"Not only that," Adam said, with a glance at Torliam. "But your mom's going to kill us, the first chance she has."

"We've gotta kill her first, then, no?" Jacky said.

Torliam snorted. "Did you not see the guards? Or realize that my mother is no simple pleasant face for the royal crown to frame? She is a *warrior-queen*, with both sword and tongue." He looked around at the others, then uncrossed his arms, looking down at the palms of his hands. "I...did not know she would do this. If I had known..." he shook his head. "How else were we to get the forces necessary to attack the God of Knowledge? We needed her alliance. Nevertheless,

Adam is right. She may be my mother, but…I cannot help but wonder how soon a horrible 'accident' will befall us."

"You are merely stating the obvious," Blaine said. "I am more interested in solutions than recriminations at this point, though recriminations are surely warranted." He gave me a pointed look.

I met his gaze until he looked away. "We're obviously not going to keep working with, or for, her. But we don't have much time, and it won't be easy." I ignored Jacky's small whoop of excitement and continued. "Tell me about this Skill for sniffing out secrets, Torliam. Did you know about it?" If he had, it was gross negligence that he'd never mentioned anything.

"I grew up knowing my mother was incredibly insightful. It was as if she could sniff guilt, but that does not mean I never escaped blame for something. I was also at times blamed for something I did not do. I have been thinking on this issue, and I believe there is a solution of sorts. She may know when a secret is being held, perhaps even be able to tell when it weighs most heavily on your heart, but I believe she may only make thoughtful deductions as to the *nature* of this secret. Perhaps, we could hide one secret within another?"

"A lesser rebellion to mask the greater," I said aloud, nodding as ideas spun to life in my head. Torliam's assessment of his mother matched what little she'd revealed to me about how her Skill worked. "Hide the unexpected within the anticipated." I caught Adam's look of irritation and everyone else's confusion, and clarified, "I'm pretty sure she's expecting, even hoping, for us to act out, so she can smack us back down even harder and make sure the lesson has really set in. At the least, I'm sure she doesn't believe this situation is *sustainable.*"

Torliam's eyes widened. "She did not so much as ask us to state our agreement to her terms. As sobering as this Ichi's Skill may be, that seems…reckless. An Estreyan's word is their bond. Perhaps she does not trust a human to hold any honor, but as it is, it seems she does indeed not expect our current arrangement to last for any length of time."

The words put a cold weight in my stomach. If we didn't act now, while the situation was hopefully still malleable, it might be too late. I needed to put myself in a position of strength. But how? If I denounced the queen, she would retaliate both physically and politically. With nothing to lose, there was nothing to stop her from siccing Ichi on us. Plus, denouncing her put *both* of us in political hot water. Once that hand was played, she would still be queen and have the power to hurt us, but our own influence—which came in part *from* her—would be greatly diminished.

I could try to ally with one of her enemies as a shield against retaliation, but I would need to find someone powerful enough to match her, and then try to keep the plan secret long enough to meet with them and ensure they could counter her plans. Even then, I would potentially be stepping into a situation just as treacherous as the one I'd be leaving.

We could try and kill her, but surely she'd be prepared for that. I glanced at Torliam. Would he agree to murder his mother? Even if she had betrayed us, matricide, combined with regicide, still had to be a big deal. Probably better not to bring it up unless I could find no other workable option.

If I could just buy some time… My eyes widened. "She can't just kill us right away because she's already tied her name to ours so thoroughly. The public eye is on us. We can't fight back overtly without fear of reprisal, but she also can't simply remove that link, either. I just need to make sure she *can't* sever it easily. So what's her plan for our next move? What did Ichi tell you guys?"

Blaine was the first to speak. "We are to visit a monkish temple, to learn from them their method of avoiding the Sickness."

Torliam's jaw clenched. "The monks do not speak, and devote their entire lives to enlightenment. Out of one hundred that would usually fall to the Sickness, only ninety of their number succumb. The method, if there is any beyond mere coincidence, is unknown, and has remained that way since the temple was founded. We are not meant to learn from them. It is merely a way to remove us from the public eye for a time."

Blaine pushed his glasses up. "It may be prudent to mention that Queen Mardinest is not entirely wrong about the danger NIX poses. However, this may in fact be a boon to us. I took some time to examine the medical reports that we 'obtained' from NIX along with the meningolycanosis samples which we used against the god. There is a strong correlation between those infected with meningolycanosis and those who show physical signs of the Sickness, and at the later stages, cannibalism."

"You're saying the meningolycanosis is a consistent infection vector for the Sickness?" I said. "If a 'wolf' with the disease bites someone, they're likely to spread it to their victim."

"Oh, gods help us," Torliam said when Blaine nodded. "How is this a boon?"

"As far as I know, this is the first time the vector for the spread of the Sickness is trackable. Perhaps, if we are able to research what makes the meningolycanosis such a convenient carrier, we can better understand the Sickness itself, and take a major step towards curing it."

"That is, ironically, good news," I decided. "But we still have to get out of here to do anything about it." I resisted the urge to pace back and forth within the crowded sphere of darkness. "She wants to take us out of the public eye and find a way to dissociate herself from us. So we need to mix her image up with our own like ink in water, and publicize the hell out of it."

Zed nodded "That means we need a reporter or three. Shouldn't be hard for the godkiller."

Adam's ink construct wavered and then disintegrated under him, and, if not for his quick reflexes in creating another, he would have dropped to the floor. "But that still only buys us time."

I smiled toothily, uncaring that perhaps I didn't seem as regal as the queen. "Time enough to subtly discredit her, or cast doubt on her good intentions toward us. Time enough to find some other way out from under her thumb. Time enough to maybe figure out how the Seal of Nine is actually meant to come into play, or where we might find the Champion on Earth. Time enough to figure out how to *get* to Earth without her stopping us or getting killed in the meantime."

Zed gestured to Torliam. "You can find anything with your Tracker Skill, right? Could you find a missing god?"

"Given enough time, I believe my Skill will lead me to anything, as long as I understand what it is that I am looking for. Which…may be a source of difficulty. I do not know in what detail and to what depth I need to understand the thing I am searching for. I have not had the Skill long enough to experiment with it."

"Great!" Adam scoffed, throwing his hands up.

"Don't gotta get so worked up," Jacky said. "We're in a tight spot right now, but one way or another, we always find a way to bust through, no?" She looked to me.

Adam followed her gaze. "No offense, Eve, but we barely manage to scrape through even when we do have a plan. And sometimes, we lose more than we win."

I felt the significance of his words clearly. We'd been struggling against seemingly insurmountable odds from the beginning. We'd won when it should have been impossible, but along the way China had died, Zed had become a Player, the kids and Chanelle were infected with the Sickness, a powerful alien species had declared war on Earth, and we were now being blackmailed into submission. Not exactly a great track record. "I understand," I said, trying to *think*, to come up with a solution that wouldn't backfire on us. "The Oracle's third gift might help us figure out our next move. But I'm not sure how quickly I'll be able to solve it. In the meantime, we need to work on keeping the team safe—"

Torliam's eyes widened dramatically, and he straightened, drawing our attention. "There is a way to gain information about the prophecy of the Spark, and the Seal of Nine."

"Why didn't you mention this before?" Adam snapped.

Torliam grimaced. "This method usually…always ends in death, and it is extremely forbidden. I did not previously consider it a viable option. But I believe we would be fine. Probably."

I flinched as a Window flashed into being in front of my face, opaque enough to block out my view of my teammates.

THE SPIRE OF PROPHECY
TRAVEL WITH THE OTHERS BOUND BY THE SEAL OF
NINE TO THE SPIRE OF PROPHECY AND ENTER PAST
THE GUARDIANS.
COMPLETION REWARD: KNOWLEDGE
NON-COMPLETION PENALTY: IGNORANCE

"Err, does this method happen to involve traveling to the Spire of Prophecy?" I said.

———

Chapter 3

———

You cannot run away from a weakness; you must sometimes fight it out or perish. And if that be so, why not now, and where you stand?
— Robert Louis Stevenson

TORLIAM'S EYEBROWS RAISED. "You have heard of it?"

My eyes flicked over the words again. So the Oracle hadn't renounced me after all. I'd had my suspicions, after we succeeded in dispersing the God of Knowledge and cleansing him of the Sickness. She'd been playing some twisted game of reverse psychology, not actually trying to teach me how to lose. It didn't endear her to me any further. "I just got a quest to go there."

"Is it from the Oracle?" Sam said. "Maybe she can help guide us out of this mess."

"To the place that '*usually always*' ends in death?" Adam drawled, raising his eyebrows.

Torliam kept his attention studiously focused on me, but his voice was chagrined. "Well, yes. The Spire is a place where those who are the subject of prophecy may gain glimpses of the workings of the universe, as it pertains to their place in it."

"This is not a good thing!" Blaine said, the tendons in his neck standing out as he clenched his jaw. "Based on my knowledge of our past experiences with the Oracle, let me guess the contents of the quest. We must go to this Spire of Prophecy, and, upon arriving, place ourselves in mortal danger? She has already betrayed us before. Have you forgotten how she sent us to the Goddess of Testimony and Lore, trapping even the children in her games? Or how she turned against us in the final battle against the God of Knowledge, attempting to remove Eve from the quest given to her, and leave all the rest of us to die?"

"The gods have their own agendas," Torliam said. "Many times, those may not align with the wishes of us mortals. But in this case, I have no doubt that the Oracle wishes to cure the Sickness. Is that not also what we want?"

"If only staying alive and going along with the Oracle's crazy quests were mutually compatible," Adam said.

"Exactly my point," Blaine said. He turned to face me directly. "The Oracle's goal might be to stop the Sickness, and I want that too. But she has proven she does not care if we die along the way, if it increases her chances of success."

"That's true." If I were the Oracle, I'd undoubtedly act the same. Sometimes, sacrifices had to be made to reach a goal. It's just that I might choose the specific sacrifices differently than she would, because I cared about my team members more than the myriad people I'd never met, whose lives didn't converge with mine. "But the kids have the Sickness. Chanelle has it. Maybe others of us do, too, and don't even know it yet. The problem is, we don't have any better alternatives. The Oracle knows what we need to do to fix this, whether or not she cares about us. She's our best bet."

"I think we should go," Zed said. "It's too big of a risk not to go, and like you said, Blaine, we're kind of flailing blindly right now. We need answers to some questions before we try to fix all this."

"But the Sickness must follow the rules of nature, even if the discovery of Seeds and 'gods' does change our understanding of science. That means one person can't hold the answer secret forever. We do not need her." Blaine's jaw clenched repeatedly, but his tone wavered, almost as if he was pleading with himself.

"Do you really think we can 'science out' the answer ourselves, before it's too late?" Adam said.

Blaine spun toward him, already glaring.

Adam held up a hand to stop him from speaking. "I know you'll try. I also know this conversation is pointless, because you won't risk being wrong. We'll do our best to protect the kids and keep them away from whatever danger might arise. We're not just going to rely on the Oracle to solve this. Anything and everything that might help, we're going to do. But this is part of it. We have to go…and it's not like the kids will be any safer *separated* from us. Not under these circumstances."

Blaine was silent for a long moment. "You are not wrong," he finally said. "I cannot truly remove them from danger."

Jacky walked over to Blaine and nudged him with her shoulder. "We're just gonna have to help them get strong enough that they can handle a little danger on their own, yeah? That's the only real way to protect someone."

Adam rolled his eyes and turned to Torliam. "How do we get to this Spire, then? I'm sure your mom won't let us go. Unless she decided a visit would be a good excuse to kill us off believably."

Torliam raised a deliberate eyebrow. "We may travel there by ship. However, seeing as she has access to Ichi's Skill and can transport us about the world in an instant, there is no reason for her to allow us access to a ship."

"No reason except politics," I said. "I don't think that will be a problem. And once we have access to both publicity and a ship, we'll have access to the arrays, and everything gets a lot easier. So we need a reporter who's willing to ask the questions we want to answer, a ship with enough eyes on us that nothing can go wrong, and a plan to tie it up in a bow perfect enough that Queen Mardinest can't stop us without cutting her own neck. To make this work, we need to know what you know. Start off with everything you can remember about our new guards and your brother Reglium."

OUR SCHEMING WAS INTERRUPTED by one of the watchdogs checking in on us. I'd kept Wraith active, so we had barely enough time to scramble back out of the many-times renewed ink bubble and to our respective bed mats.

Still, by that time we had a plan, and we wasted no time implementing it. It was likely the queen would want to see us again the next day, and if she did, she would almost certainly discern enough of our plans to ruin them. We didn't have time to wait.

Adam tried to get an ink construct out of the room, but there was no opening in the barrier for it to slip through.

Instead, we ended up using a combination of Wraith and Summon. Kris' marionettes were halfway across the castle, but with some concentration that was firmly within Wraith's range. Kris hadn't experimented much with Summoning a spirit into a body she couldn't see, but we knew she could do it. So I curled up with the girl inside another concealing ink bubble and talked her through the mental travel to the room where her marionettes were, describing the setting in as much detail as possible.

The Summoner Skill granted her a vague ability to sense the bodies of marionettes even when they were empty of a spirit, and along with her imagination of the path I described, it was enough for her to reach out to the one next to the table in her bedroom. She was sweating and pale by the time the distant marionette twitched with seeming life.

I resisted the urge to cheer as I sensed its metal body climb shakily to its feet. It took a few steps across Kris' bedroom and grabbed the Estreyan datapad lying on the desk. The marionette jerked around at first, touched several commands at once, and altogether flailed like someone trying to thread a needle with a foam noodle after guzzling an entire bottle of vodka. But with painstaking slowness, and plenty of correction, she was able to operate the datapad through her artificial servant.

Some whispered instructions from Torliam guided her in sending off a few messages to various important contacts, flagged as urgent correspondence with his royal code. The people on the receiving end would get the messages, middle of the night or not.

There were no obvious signs of surveillance on our old rooms, but the danger of being caught was enough to wind us all into a state of quivering tension.

Finally, when a few more hours had passed and dawn arrived, we knew we could wait no longer.

Kris began to move her marionette through the halls and out onto the palace grounds, with my help to avoid notice from the early risers, mostly servants. As it moved closer to her, its jerky, puppet-like movements smoothed out, and her labored breathing grew easier. She had it hide inside a large bush outside the closest outer wall to us, and could only hope no one noticed it.

Torliam began to do some sort of martial kata, blue mist wafting off him and through his armor. It illuminated the room, both for us and the guards outside keeping track of us through the display screen.

Adam grumpily pushed his upper body up from his bed mat. "Some of us are still trying to sleep. Do that some other time."

Torliam continued to move, his power now causing gusts of winds to buffet the room. "How long do you puny humans need to sleep? Your lives are too short to waste a moment. Consider me to be doing you a courtesy."

I couldn't help the upward twitch of my eyebrow. He was laying it on a bit thick.

Adam spilled ink, the liquid supporting his torso and legs and sprouting spider legs beneath him. "Doing us humans a courtesy?" His voice rose into a yell. "You're just like your damn mother!"

Outside, the Estreyan guards shared a look with each other. The woman who had been powering the barrier was now on monitor duty instead, and Ichi sat within the circle.

"I am *nothing* like her!" Torliam roared, face twisting with anger as his glow increased and his hair blew outward from his head.

Birch growled at Torliam, puffed out his wings and fur, and, with a shriek, unleashed a gust so strong it literally blew the huge man off his feet and into the wall.

Torliam cushioned himself from the stone with a gush of his own power.

As soon as Torliam hit the wall, Zed's fingers dug into an invisible crack in the world, just enough to open the room up to the Other Place.

Ichi grunted, then began to pant. "It pulls too much power, again!"

Torliam recovered from Birch's attack easily and lifted his hand for a retaliatory strike.

Adam dashed ink out into the air with a dramatic arc of his hands, and it burst into a barrier that cut off most of the room from Torliam, shielding the rest of us away from his attack. The barrier also happened to cut us off from the faint dawn light of the ceiling where the monitoring device was, and thus from the sight of the guards outside.

"Coward!" Torliam yelled. "Come and face me!"

Zed pulled the rip wider, and grey light spilled out of it.

A careful check reassured me the guards' display showed only black ink over most of the room.

I stepped through the rip gingerly, one foot and then the other, careful not to touch the edges just in case. The cold was *biting*, more like a full body blow than a mere temperature change. But I didn't die. I motioned for the others to follow, tucking my hands under my armpits and trying not to make any sounds of pain as I hurried toward the doorway, where the barrier rippled and buzzed despite being untouched. Little pieces of gray fluff lay on the floor around it, like dust accumulated by static electricity.

Chanelle's vacant look cleared as Jacky helped her through the rip. "Wow. Please tell me this is only temporary."

The female guard looked between her fellow, gasping on the floor as the Other Place affected the barrier, then back at Torliam, the only visible figure within the cell. "We must stop him," she said. "They have somehow damaged the barrier again, when the tailos attacked him."

"Damnation," the remaining guard said, but he nodded. They rushed forward, hands ready on their weapons, and opened the door. As soon as they did so, the buzzing barrier around the room in both the normal world and its counterpart cut out.

I lunged into the hallway of the Other Place through the doorless opening, turning to face the place where the guards stood in the real world.

As the rest of the team, except Torliam, rushed out of the cell, I pointed to a space in the air, and Zed opened up the nearest rip in the world with a grunt.

I looked through the little portal into warmth and color, and reached my hand through. As Adam's ink barrier dropped, and Torliam threw himself backward toward the larger rip, my clawed, too-long fingers pierced into the back of the female guard's neck.

She barely had time for a gasp before Chaos ate into her, tearing apart skin, muscle, and bone between my fingers, leaving me holding a still-disintegrating mush as I tore backward. She was the one who could supposedly track us. Not anymore.

Torliam made it through the opening to the Other Place, and, with an exhale from Zed that hung visibly frozen in the air, the large rip inside our cell closed itself up again.

As soon as my hand was clear, he closed the second, smaller tear, and we ran. The Other Place looked like a replica of the palace, though a few of the smaller pieces of furniture and almost all the doors were missing, the color was completely washed out, and the vague grey light seemed to suffuse the air rather than emanating from any specific source.

It would have been fascinating, if the cold hadn't been so savage.

Gregor stumbled, and I picked him up, hugging him to the already-cold armor covering my chest as I pushed ahead harder. "It's almost over." I puffed, my feet slapping into the painfully cold stone and scoring little claw marks with every step.

"What *is* this place?" Blaine asked, squinting against the cold until his frost-laden eyelashes stuck together. His suit was wheezing more than normal, and I assumed it struggled to continue, just like the rest of us.

"There!" I pointed to what would have been a window looking out onto the grounds in the normal world, but here was just an empty opening in the outer wall of the palace.

We hurried through it, and with trembling hands, Zed opened another rip.

I jumped through with Gregor, and the others followed immediately. I collapsed onto my knees, coughing as I sucked in heaving breaths of the sudden warmth, painful in its intensity. I allowed myself a few moments of recovery, then forced myself to stand. I looked around and met the shocked gaze of one of the gardeners, clippers frozen in his hands as he looked at us. "We have to move," I said.

Both Blaine and Chanelle were woozy to the point of dizziness and required support to move. As we stumbled off through the grounds toward the outer wall and the main city, I watched with Wraith as the gardener moved over to the spot we'd appeared from. He waved his hands through the empty air with wide eyes. Maybe it was the adrenaline making me loopy, but I couldn't help but gasp out a laugh.

WE RAN through the streets at first, then hid for a little while to recuperate and measure the response to our escape. I used some water from my pack to wash the blood and little chunks of meat off my hand as thoroughly as possible, suppressing a shudder at the origin of the sticky red coating. Without the female guard, Ichi wouldn't be able to teleport himself or anyone else right to us. And both Ichi and Reglium required line of sight to affect other people with their Skills, so, as long as they didn't know where we were, we'd bought ourselves time.

After a short recuperation, we hurried toward the airbase. I knew Queen Mardinest would be able to track us eventually. We didn't have the resources or preparation to avoid that. But, if things went according to plan, soon it would be too late.

As we neared the huge, flat patch of land that was their equivalent to a civilian airport, the mammoth cylindrical ship taking up most of the launch pad came into view. It looked more like a shelled clam than most of the other Estreyan ships, which tended to take the forms of more maneuverable "sea" creatures like crustaceans or stingrays. People scurried around it, obviously preparing for takeoff.

Adam's mouth fell open. "You can't be serious. We're supposed to escape in that thing? It doesn't look like it could out-fly a chicken!"

Torliam shrugged, a very human gesture. "It is meant for comfort over long distances and pleasure journeys, not speed."

I spoke before Adam could continue. "It doesn't matter if it's fast. We care about the people inside, not actual escape capabilities. That *is* the right ship?" I turned to Torliam, my eyebrows raised. If I were honest, I, too, felt a little underwhelmed by the cow of a ship.

"My mother has been foisting off half her duties onto me for the last few days as she dealt with or avoided the passengers of that ship," Torliam said, drawing my attention back to the bags under his eyes. "The leader of the Panacean is aboard, as well as dignitaries from a few of the smaller countries and a couple people rich enough to think they'd get an audience with Queen Mardinest and her godkiller if they came along."

Jacky grinned up at me, bouncing lightly on her feet. "There's no *way* she messes with us when all those people are watching."

I nodded vaguely, looking around till I spotted the other recipients of the late-night, urgent messages we'd sent out. "There," I said, jerking my head toward the group of reporters milling about the edge of the takeoff pad. Their broadcast equipment and looks of excitement labeled them clearly. Some of them noticed our group in return and pointed the pen-like recording devices in our direction. "Let's go," I said, checking my posture and facial expression for proper camera-readiness.

Torliam sent me a pointed look, and I nodded reassurance. My Charisma wasn't high enough to lie convincingly on camera, not when people with Skills in lie-detection would be watching the three-dimensional recording taken by the cameras once we got closer. Whatever I said had to be at least a version of the truth, if I didn't want to be caught.

We strode up to the group of reporters as confidently as possible, ignoring the double takes and stares from the workers preparing the fat clam-ship for takeoff. I gave a shallow bow and they shined their recording devices toward us with quivering anticipation. "Thank you for meeting us here today—" I cut off, as movement at the edge of my vision caught my attention, and Wraith identified the person peeking around the corner of a building out onto the airstrip as Reglium.

"Shields!" I snapped, jerking my head toward Adam.

He responded with lightning-quick reflexes, well-conditioned in the art of creating almost instantaneous barriers at the slightest provocation.

One of the reporters actually screamed, as the ink engulfed them along with us, their recording devices now emitting the only light within the barrier.

"They're already here," I said. "They must have been waiting, anticipated our next move." I resisted the urge to curse. Queen Mardinest was intelligent. It wasn't such a leap to assume we'd be trying to escape from the capitol via ship. If she'd been able to deduce which way we were moving through the city, either from surveillance or the occasional civilian spotting, it would be easy to get Reglium in place before we arrived.

And what better set-up to make us look crazed with the Sickness than in front of a group of hastily assembled reporters rabid for the next news on the godkiller?

The only redeeming fact was that I didn't sense anyone *besides* Reglium, and he needed line of sight to control his victims.

"Change of plans," I announced, to both my team and the reporters. "We have reason to believe that a faction of people who do not wish us to continue trying to cure the Sickness—I suppose you could call them *allies* of the Sickness—are attempting to stop us. We must board the ship *now*, and you all are coming with us. You may be in danger if we leave you behind unprotected."

Chapter 4

I felt myself on the edge of the world; peering over the rim into a fathomless chaos of eternal night.

— H. P. Lovecraft

MOST OF THE reporters stared in shocked silence as Adam directed the shields centered in space around his body to move along with our large group toward the ship. A couple were cognizant enough to ask questions, but I ignored them.

We shuffled together up the ramp to the grand door, which opened into the side of the ship. Once inside, Adam blocked off said doorway with ink, then moved to shove his hands into the guts of the electrical control pad beside it. "Eugh," he said, since some of those guts were a bit more biological than electrical. Still, a few experimental pulses of electricity from him and a flutter of his eyelids as he activated his Hyper Focus and Electric Sovereign Skills at the same time, and the door behind us slid closed, ignoring the cries of the workers still outside. "It's locked," he said.

One of the reporters shoved his shining tube camera toward me. "Who are these allies of the Sickness pursuing you, Eve-Redding?"

Torliam gave him a glare, and the other man stepped back. "This ship cannot stay here any longer," he said. "We must also deviate from the acknowledged flight path." He left unspoken that if Ichi knew where we were, even if that happened to be a thousand feet above the planet and flying through the air, he might still be able to teleport himself, and perhaps others, to us. Torliam didn't even wait for me to respond, instead motioning for Blaine to follow as he sprinted off along the curved hallway.

I ran after the two of them, with the rest of the team and then the reporters following behind. "Prepare for emergency takeoff!" I yelled, as we passed what seemed to be one of the ship's staff.

He jerked around to watch as we rushed past, blurting out, "Eve-Redding?" and then cursing as he fumbled the platter he was carrying, sending food flying everywhere.

Jacky grabbed a slab of meat before it could hit the floor.

I repeated the warning as we passed through a common area with row upon row of safety seats, where most of the civilians seemed to be milling around. I slowed a little and directed the reporters to strap themselves into a seat.

"Can you give us some insight into this emergency situation?" one of them asked.

I continued after Torliam without answering.

He led us to a large command room and shooed one of the uniformed employees away from the main control console. He turned to the man in the most centralized seat. "Captain. On behalf of Eve-Redding and our people's fight against the Sickness, I am commandeering this ship. You are relieved of duty."

The man swiveled in the large chair, his eyes taking the group in with a single assessing sweep. "There are civilians on board," he said. "This is not an appropriate ship for any military operations."

Adam grabbed the other man, the one Torliam had shooed, his spider-legs invading the Estreyan's personal space a little too close for comfort, judging by the look on the other man's face. "We need to send a message to the queen. Open the secure communications system."

Torliam didn't back down. "There is no choice. Step aside, Captain."

The captain's jaw clenched, but he relinquished his seat and nodded at his underling, who'd looked to him for guidance. The flight crew left the control room to us, some more reluctantly than others.

Torliam sat in front of the console and got immediately to work. The ship started to rumble sub-audibly as he activated the flight systems. Then Torliam sent out a message to the passengers and other employees through the intercom. "This is Torliam of the line of Aethezriel. We are commencing emergency takeoff. Please find a secure location."

I sat next to Adam as he worked the communications system. "Everybody, strap in," I said to the rest of the team, then followed my own advice.

"We will be gone before the queen's people have time to react, with my skill as a pilot and a small dose of luck," Torliam said.

Adam finished with the console and nodded to me. "You're connected. One-way only, secure as I can make it."

The control room fell silent, except for the ambient sounds of the ship straining against gravity. I took a deep breath and leaned forward, typing out a message on the unfamiliar Estreyan console as quickly as I could.

We have escaped. You may be prepared to retaliate either in punishment for our disobedience, or to remove our perceived threat to you entirely. I caution you, stay your hand until you watch the upcoming news broadcasts. The world will watch along with you, and it is far too late to stop dispersal of my talks with the reporters. Any movement against us will only tighten the noose around your own neck. Do not misunderstand. We have not attempted to destroy you. However, if we see a hint of further aggression on your part, or come into contact with any we find suspicious or threatening, you have given me the perfect idea for retaliation and defamation. Any threat to us will be declared a carrier of the Sickness, and their removal called for immediately. You have been given a reprieve. Do not be the cause of your own destruction.

I sent the message.

UNDER TORLIAM'S GUIDANCE, the ship climbed and continued to climb, till even its huge form might have been confused for a bird or a small speck in the sky. "We will continue for a couple more

Earth-hour lengths at this height," he said. "I have turned off the location beacon on the ship, but people may still track our flight by sight or use a Skill to deduce our destination. We must remain watchful."

I nodded. It was time. "I'm going to talk to the reporters. I need the rest of you to make sure the passengers are alright and keep them subdued if necessary."

Jacky gave me a thumbs-up as she swallowed the last of the meat she'd rescued earlier and tossed her head in a way that would have flung her hair around if it wasn't cut in a short pixie style, since most of it had burned away during our fight with Ifkana's assassins.

Kris nodded seriously, the single marionette she'd brought with us rising from its crouched position at the far side of the room. "We'll handle it," she said, shoulders back and chin thrust up.

Adam renewed his ink harness and legs with a huff and a tremble that he quickly suppressed. "I'll make sure no one is broadcasting our location, either purposefully or not."

—DON'T PUSH YOURSELF TOO HARD.—
-EVE-

He read the Window, shot me a harsh glare, and skittered out of the room without another word.

Chanelle looked vacant again and didn't respond when we spoke to her, so we left her strapped into the chair where she sat.

Torliam turned away from the controls for a moment. "Remember, your Charisma levels." It was a covert reminder not to lie. Did he think I had so much trouble telling the truth?

Back in the room with the rows of harness-seats, the reporters talked dramatically into their cameras about the "unknown danger," "allies of the Sickness," and their inclusion into the "emergency escape with the prophesied Eve-Redding." Altogether, they seemed much more excited than afraid. Was that a good thing, or bad?

Chatter from both the reporters and the alarmed civilians died down when I entered the room. I sat down in one of the few open chairs across from the reporters, in full view of the rest of the occupants. "I will give your interview now," I said. For what I was about to say, the more witnesses the better. It would make it harder for

Queen Mardinest to extricate herself from the consequences. The reporters had been told clearly that certain avenues of questioning were off limits, so as long as the interview went smoothly, the payoff would be even higher. I'd sent the threat to Queen Mardinest. Now it was time to actually back it up with something, even if all I had to fight with were words.

Cold sweat trickled down my back. I spoke before they could start hurling questions at me again. "My power can defeat the Sickness. Even so, it is not what we need. It is a weapon and a shield, not a cure. For that reason, I and my team will continue to search for the Champion of old, the god who can cure—truly cure—the Sickness, whose blood runs in my veins in some small measure."

When I paused, the reporters called out questions, each one talking over the others. In the background, the ship's passengers watched the interview with avid fascination, chattering amongst themselves and calling out the occasional question, though they were drowned out by the loudness of the reporters.

"Did the God of Knowledge show you where to find the Champion?"

"Many experts do not believe this god exists. Do you have proof otherwise?"

"Do you feel your search for the Champion is in danger from the people who forced this emergency flight away from the capitol?"

I met their eyes, but continued to ignore their questions. "Part of the reason I've come to this ship is to talk to the leaders of the Panacean and the other dignitaries aboard. Current policy is to immediately kill any infected and attempt to sterilize them and their belongings with fire. These laws were implemented to mitigate the crazed destruction someone carrying the Sickness may enact if allowed to degrade until death, as well as attempt to stop further spread of the disease. I believe that for the first time, there may be a better way. There are still those who do not believe we may ever defeat the Sickness. There are those who have lost all hope of a better future. These people are wrong. I will find a way not just to stop the Sickness, but to remove its grasp on those who have already succumbed. My team and I will return your loved ones to you, themselves in mind and body once more."

I paused, and the reporters jumped in like excited puppies.

"Do you plan to enact new policies for dealing with the infected?"

"How long do you estimate this search for a cure will take?"

I shook my head. "I don't have the authority to enact new policies, but I do hope to open communication about a better way to preserve lives while my team and I continue our search." Vagueness was key in avoiding a lie, but I hoped I wasn't laying it on too thick.

Before I could take a breath, they continued.

"Will you be calling on further warrior forces to aid you in your quest?"

"Eve-Redding, you were forced to kill the God of Knowledge when you discovered he had been infected. If even the gods are succumbing, what do you base your belief that a cure is possible on?"

I kept my face calm and confident while I tried to figure out how to walk the fine line between truth and fiction. "First, the God of Knowledge is very much 'alive.' I simply dispersed his physical manifestation. I acted somewhat like a fever, burning out the Sickness, quite literally. I was given a boon in exchange for cleansing him, and had previously received three gifts from the Oracle to guide us on the path. My team has received Bestowals from both the Goddess of Chaos, and the Goddess of Testimony and Lore. Yesterday, I spoke with Queen Mardinest about my plans to stop the Sickness, and we discussed those within the very palace who I know to be touched by it."

My words were bait, and they bit down eagerly.

"Can you release any information about those within the palace who have the Sickness?"

"Queen Mardinest previously refused to have her daughter cleansed when Tonila was diagnosed, leading to the current law that does not allow pardons for those sentenced to death because of infection. Does this hold any connection to any new policies you may plan to enact?"

"I will not comment on my knowledge of the infected unless it becomes necessary to protect my team." There. I'd insinuated people with the Sickness might be a danger to us, and that if so I'd reveal their identities. "Normal contact with an infected person has no proven correlation to the spread of the disease." Unless they had meningolycanosis and decided to bite you, but that wasn't *normal* contact. "Before symptoms begin to show, they themselves may not even realize they have it. They are just like you or me. I will not condemn any infected to an even earlier death, because it does not matter! When we are finished, those people may be healed. So I say to you, do not lose hope. Do not turn to fear, anger, and thoughtless violence. Those affected by the Sickness are not our enemy. The Sickness itself is our enemy." Voice added a faint reverberation to my words, and when I paused for effect, most of the reporters didn't jump back in with questions immediately.

Unfortunately, one of them did, visibly steeling himself before he spoke. "How do you feel about Queen Mardinest's declaration of war on your birth world? Does the invasion of Earth factor into your plans?"

My jaw tightened, despite my attempts to seem unfazed. Questions about the invasion had been clearly marked as off-limits to all the reporters we contacted. Unlike Earth, Estreyer didn't have even nominal freedom of the press, but there was enough that news companies not directly sponsored by the crown of a country might speak against its leader's actions. This reporter must have been an independent, or hailing from one of the countries Queen Mardinest didn't control, and decided that we couldn't stop him once he'd already asked the question. Unfortunately, he wasn't wrong.

But how was I supposed to answer him without lying, and also keep from cementing Queen Mardinest as my mortal enemy? "I don't believe the invasion of Earth is the answer to either world's problems," I said. That was honesty. Now, time for misdirection of a sort. "For one, the bans on using the arrays were placed for seemingly sound reasons. However, I am not the ruler of this land, so it is not my place to make policies." Would my response stand up to scrutiny? I hoped so, for the sake of any fragile armistice that might remain between the queen and me.

I could see the reporters slavering to ask more penetrating questions, so I tossed out the sparkly distraction I'd been planning all along. "I realize there is no time to waste. While our abrupt departure from the capitol was primarily meant to ensure our safety, we are taking the opportunity to pursue another goal as well. I have received a new quest from the Oracle." The tension grew palpable as a wave of excitement spread throughout the room. I held up a hand to stop their questions. "I cannot relate the details of this quest for fear that our enemies may try to stop us before we are able to complete it, but we are acting toward its objective even now." It was true. By Torliam's estimates, we'd be to the Spire in another few hours. "Coincidentally, you have been brought along on this quest. For this reason, I must end all recordings now. The interview will be broadcast from the secure console of this ship, and, after that, information must remain concealed until our quest has been completed and we part ways."

I COULD SMELL my own sweat. I shifted uncomfortably, glancing out the huge viewing window built into the common area of the passenger ship. Hopefully, the passengers crowded in a half circle around me weren't offended. My sweat smelled different than I remembered. Maybe the sharper, less musky and more citric scent was a product of my Perception changing after Chaos burned away and remade such a large portion of my body, or maybe that same metamorphosis had altered me enough that I just didn't smell quite human anymore.

I fended off questions about my interview from the civilians and tried to ingratiate myself with them and the various dignitaries who spoke to me. I resisted the urge to flinch back and release my claws as a large man swung a paw-like hand around to pat my shoulder, almost as heavily as Jacky might.

I looked around, hoping to find an escape path, and caught Adam's eye. He'd grumbled about the "idiotic lack of security" inherent in letting all the passengers stay free. I agreed with him to a degree, but the whole point of commandeering the passenger ship and talking to the reporters was to stay in the public eye and ensure our popularity protected us.

Now, though, he was grinning as a group of Estreyan women crowded around him. He unbuckled some of the armor over his arms to show off his tattoos. The cooing of his fans was audible, and I had to consciously keep from rolling my eyes as he allowed them to reach out and touch his tattoos. I guess he'd changed his mind about fraternizing with the civilians.

I turned away, feeling vaguely irritated, and looked instead out onto the abandoned Estreyan city far below, making vague sounds to pretend I was still contributing to the conversation around me. I knew their population had been greater once, and I'd been to Trials where I walked through the remnants of their civilization, but the sight reminded what it really meant. The Estreyans were dying out.

I turned and caught Jacky's scowl. She'd been backed into a corner by a man who towered over her. Despite her expression, she did not meet his eyes, and her hands were tightened into fists.

He reached out to clamp his hand around her shoulder, and, as I focused past the general chatter, I caught him saying "tiny little thing."

"Excuse me," I said to the group surrounding me. "There's an issue I have to deal with." I walked away without waiting for a response.

Jacky's face twisted with an expression I couldn't quite decipher when she saw me, but I thought at least some of it was relief.

I clamped a clawed hand around the Estreyan's wrist, where it was pressed against the wall and trapping Jacky in the corner. My heart pounded, and my lips twitched with the urge to bare my teeth at him.

His head jerked around to face me, and after a few silent seconds where I didn't move, he flushed. "Do you need something?" He yanked his arm away, and I let him, since it also freed Jacky.

She moved to stand beside me, glaring at him directly now. "I told you to leave me alone. If you're gonna try and start something, *I'm* gonna finish it."

The man looked around at the increasingly large audience we were drawing and flushed even darker. "Do not pretend I am some scoundrel. We were merely speaking, and you found my attentions pleasant. You encourage me in private, and condemn me before the eyes of others? These are the actions of a—"

Whatever he was going to say was cut off, as Sam tiptoed, reached up, and clamped onto the back of the man's neck from behind, not so dissimilar to the way I'd killed the female guard earlier that morning. This time, the man merely choked as his eyes rolled back in his head. He collapsed into Sam's arms, almost knocking him over with the impact, and was carefully lowered to the ground.

"I coulda handled him," Jacky said.

Sam nodded at her. "I know. But you shouldn't have to. He made an enemy of all of us as soon as he decided to act as less than a perfect gentleman toward you. I just decided I was too angry not to solve this particular problem myself." He stood, and looked around at the gathered crowd, raising his voice but losing some of his projected confidence. "Er, Torliam, as the current captain of the ship, has ordered a return to the secure seats. We'll be engaging in some maneuvers that may cause severe turbulence and, um, loss of gravity."

The ship's staff groaned and scurried around picking up loose trays, food, and any of the other items that weren't already attached firmly to the floor.

Sam heaved the unconscious Estreyan onto his back, then, straining a little under the weight, carried him away. "We've got about five minutes. I'll strap him down in the brig and be back soon," he puffed out, cheeks flushed from exertion.

I helped herd the passengers back to the safety seats, then escaped to the control room, where most of the team was already strapped in. Torliam was navigating the flight console with intense concentration. In front and slightly below the ship stood two huge trees, so tall they towered over everything in sight, so old they'd turned to stone.

I moved to strap myself in beside him, but an insistent grunting made me turn my head.

Chanelle jerked in her seat, her face twisted into a rictus scowl. She clawed at the straps holding her down, nails catching the skin around them and drawing blood.

I lunged toward her, grabbing her hands to stop her from doing any more damage to herself. "Are you alright? What's wrong?" I sent a Window to Sam, even as I examined her myself.

—Something's wrong with Chanelle. Hurry here as quick as you can.—
-Eve-

She looked up at me, with none of the vacancy her gaze sometimes held. "Let me go, you bitch! You can't control me. I'll rip your throat out!"

I jerked back from her, more out of surprise than fear. "What—" I snapped my head around and extended Wraith, searching for Reglium.

Adam tossed up shields around us without my even needing to say the word.

"Agh!" Torliam said, moving frantically to pull up the view from the forward window, which had just been blocked off with ink, onto a screen in front of him.

Chanelle started laughing as she finally managed to unfasten her safety straps.

Wraith found no sign of Reglium, or of his Skill reaching out to Chanelle, and there was no line of sight to anyone outside the room.

"She's not being controlled," I said with a sinking heart.

———————

Chapter 5

———————

That which we had we still possess,
　　Though leaves may drop and stars may fall.
　　— Ella Wheeler Wilcox

SAM BURST into the room and Adam opened up a space in the shield for the other boy to get through to us.

"I hate you!" Chanelle screamed, the sound echoing off the ink around us and ripping through her throat hard enough to make her start coughing uncontrollably.

Sam reached out to her, holding her arms to her sides as she continued to cough and fight against him. The self-imposed scratches on her skin transferred to Sam and quickly healed, and he coughed a bit as he healed her throat.

"I do not believe this is mere emotional reaction," Torliam said, confirming my fears. "I do not know her character as well as you might, but her words seemed deliberately hurtful and destructive. It is a hallmark of the advancing Sickness that one's mental and emotional connections to that which was once important to them are destroyed and twisted. The Sickness made my sister tell me that she had never loved me, well before it made her try to eat my flesh to sustain her own life."

"And that is what you believe is happening to Chanelle?" Blaine said, seemingly undisturbed.

"It is common. The Sickness is an agent of destruction. Not only physically. Once the will of the host is gone, the mind lingers without the self."

I turned toward him, "What do we do?"

Torliam shook his head. "There is nothing we can do. This will pass, with time, and come again more frequently as she succumbs to its sway."

Adam let the ink shield drop and flopped his head back against his seat. "Wonderful."

Gregor and Kris both stared at her, and though they didn't say anything, I could see the fear on their faces. How long, till they too lost themselves like this?

I suppressed a shudder. "Put her to sleep," I said, watching Chanelle's muscles strain against Sam's grip as she cursed at him.

Someone else walked through the door to the control room. My claws slipped out, and I took an aggressive step forward before I realized who it was.

The former captain's eyes roamed across us and then out over the viewing window. "What is going on here? I cannot in good conscience allow you to place the wellbeing of my passengers in continued danger. It is imperative they arrive at their destinations on time, unharmed, and *unharried*." He straightened his back, moving his glare between Torliam and me.

Sam moved the now-limp Chanelle into her chair and strapped her back in.

The captain frowned as he watched, but his gaze was quickly drawn to the front viewing window and the two fossilized trees we traveled ever-closer to.

"If you do not wish to be thrown about, I recommend you take a seat," Torliam said, tilting the huge, fat beast of a ship forward and down.

The captain's eyes widened as the angle of descent kept increasing, and he and I both scrambled forward to strap ourselves in.

Torliam sent us all the way into a screeching dive, aimed right between the trees. "Hold on," he warned.

I clamped my hands down on the edge of my chair's seat as my stomach tried to float up out of my mouth.

Kris let out a muffled shriek around clenched teeth, and Gregor slipped into his Shadow state, while Sam cursed repeatedly under his breath and kept his eyes squeezed shut.

Jacky laughed the whole way down, whooping as if she were on an amusement park ride, till Adam snapped at her to shut up.

A cacophony of screams resounded from the safe seating area where the passengers were secured.

From morning brightness, the ship passed between the two trunks, and came out on the other side into twilight.

Torliam leveled out the ship's flight, and as my eyes adjusted to the sudden change, I saw we flew even higher above the ground than we had been, despite just diving what had to be thousands of meters. The terrain was flat instead of hilly, and grew a sea of what looked like dark blue grass.

I stretched out my awareness, but we were moving so fast they were already beyond my reach.

As if reading my mind, Adam pulled up the view from the rear of the ship on one of the screens near him. The screen showed only more of the twilight and waving grass, not the stone trees I'd been expecting. I saw no sign of whatever portal we'd just passed through.

Blaine put his glasses back on his face and squinted through them. "Did we just pass through an array?"

Torliam snorted. "No. We merely traveled to another layer of my world."

"Traveled to another layer… In the same way that foggy, airborne current carried us from the main layer to Testimony and Lore's domain? How many layers—" Blaine's eyes widened, and he seemed to lose his train of thought as Torliam angled the ship upward again, and more of the sky became visible.

No sun hung in the sky. A faint glow rose out of the earth itself, creating the illusion of twilight. Above, we looked into space, so clear and seemingly empty of atmosphere that the stars shone like flickering fires in the sky. They made so many points of light, I felt sure I was seeing all the way to the edge of the galaxy. The stars shimmered with every color I could imagine, and some that I wasn't sure I'd ever seen before. I could barely breathe past the wonder.

The usurped captain's voice broke my fugue, grating against my ears as it rose into a pseudo-screech. "Is this the level which holds the Spire of Prophecy? Access to the Spire is forbidden! It is my duty to shepherd the passengers of this ship safely! I cannot allow you to place them in danger." He leaned forward from his seat next to Torliam and tapped frantically at the console.

Torliam lashed out with a hand, slamming his fist into the other man's jaw.

The captain slumped over, unconscious.

Sam sighed. "Should I move him to the brig, too?"

I nodded, then leaned back and kept looking at the stars.

WHEN HE FINALLY SPOKE, Torliam's voice was hoarse. "We have arrived. In the interest of caution, I will land the ship before we fly too close to the Spire. We may approach slowly on foot, the better to avoid causing a disturbance."

Blaine nodded. "Perhaps it is time for Eve to make another speech, to mitigate any more issues from the other passengers as they become aware of our location and mission."

In the far distance, the grassy plains ended, shifting into stony ground interspersed with chunky rocks that seemed to be growing up from the earth. Beyond that, the rocks grew bigger, turning into boulders, and then into a large hill. Or maybe a small mountain, depending on how far away it actually was.

A tower speared through the mountain, so tall it looked like it actually pierced the sky. The only clouds in sight obscured its top, roiling around it like multicolored marshmallow fluff. The whole thing glowed bright enough to obscure the light of the stars above and around it.

Torliam set down the huge ship on the edge of the grassy plain, where the blue vegetation began to give way to stone.

Following Blaine's suggestion, and a few tips from Torliam, I did give a speech of sorts to the passengers and reporters, though they weren't allowed to record any of it. I explained where we were, what we were doing, and reassured them that they were safe, with Blaine staying behind to pilot the ship if necessary. I assured them we would not bring them any closer to the distant Spire and the danger it presented to those who were not the subject of prophecy. I was beginning to regret the decision to surround the team with watchful eyes. I could tell, when they looked at me, they saw something else, some idea of a person they'd made up, like a character in a storybook. The expectations and the weight of their attention were wearying.

As we prepared, Blaine grumbled about the necessity of staying behind with Chanelle, despite Torliam's assurances that the Spire wasn't dangerous to any who were truly the subject of prophecy. With the Seal of Nine from Testimony and Lore, there was no doubt of the kiddos' inclusion in that small number.

Gregor finally rolled his eyes at his uncle. "You're not being rational. We're part of Eve's new quest, so we have to go. The Oracle wouldn't have mentioned us if we weren't supposed to enter. Also, even if something were to happen, it's not like we're helpless." He slipped into his Shadow state and brandished his long daggers, then resumed corporeality. "Remember?"

Blaine conceded with moderate grace. "Even so, I will be on standby to pilot the ship in emergency takeoff, if necessary. Send me a virtual message immediately if anything goes wrong."

Kris' marionette crouched down so she could climb up and ride atop its metal shoulders, while Torliam opened one of the smaller doors in the ship's hull. I thought I was prepared, but the cold hit me like a blow.

I hunched my shoulders and stepped out of the ship. There was no ice or snow, and though it grew blue, the grass looked lush and healthy, so I hadn't been expecting the frigid temperature.

We walked for a long while. The closer we approached the glowing spire, the more massive and imposing it appeared. We stopped at the first big boulder we reached, the silent tension surging as we each read the message chiseled into its surface.

BEWARE, MORTALS DRAWN IN IGNORANCE. DEATH
COMES TO THOSE UNNAMED IN PROPHECY.

We shared grim looks with each other, but continued on past

several variations of the same warning message carved into the ever-larger stones around us. Though still far away, I could feel the power of the towering edifice licking across my skin like a warm wind.

When we passed the first skeleton, a four-legged creature that had seemingly curled up and never stood again, we skirted it silently.

After that, there were more.

I let my claws slip out and my vision sharpen as we grew nearer. "Something…is flying around the tower."

Adam squinted. "That glowy stuff?"

"Yeah." I strained to see more clearly. The glow coming off the edifice wasn't just amorphous light as I had thought. A host of gigantic, tadpole-shaped forms teemed around the tower and the strange clouds. My eyes had trouble distinguishing what they were, and when I focused too hard on trying to decipher what exactly I was seeing, a spike of pain shot through my head. It looked like they were made of refracted light, all the colors of the stars weaving through their ever-changing fractal bodies. They wound through the tower and around it, swimming through the air so close to each other it was almost impossible to distinguish one form from another. I looked to Torliam. "Do you see them?"

"I see them."

"See what?" Sam asked, his voice a little too loud as he swiveled his head to see in all directions.

"They are the guardians of the Spire," Torliam said. "Your weak eyes should be able to perceive them once we draw closer."

I was so focused on said guardians that I almost stumbled over another set of bones. This one was humanoid, and huge. An Estreyan.

I shared a grim look with Adam. Jacky caught my eye and nodded, letting me know she'd seen and understood the need for us to be on the lookout against danger.

The remnants of death grew more frequent as we neared the base of the mountain. The guardians swooped over and around us with nerve-wracking speed as we climbed, their glowing forms forcing me to close my eyes at times. One swam straight through my body, almost knocking me off my feet. I felt it in my brain as it passed through me, bursting into jagged-edged pain, as if each fractal edge was slicing me from the inside. Constantly shifting, searching my mind, it found my memories of the Oracle, of Testimony and Lore, and funneled itself through that space. It came out the other side smooth and coherent. I turned to the others, but they were unharmed, if now sporting headaches similar to my own.

Jacky glared at the receding guardians, Kris whimpered and hunched in on herself, and Zed looked like he was about to throw up.

When we reached the doorway at the bottom of the tower, the guardians swooping around us flew off to mingle with the others, plunging through the Spire and the clouds like cotton-candy ghosts.

"We must go up," Torliam said.

I turned my head for a glimpse of the ship waiting far behind us, beyond the stones. "Time to find the lost god." I stepped through the doorway.

A WINDING STAIRCASE STRETCHED UPWARD, lit only by the occasional open window cut into the stone of the outer wall. I was wary at first, but grew calmer as we climbed. The higher we went, the more I found myself losing track of time, or how many steps I'd taken through the darkness since passing the last stone window. When I noticed myself walking past the same single, small window for what felt like several minutes, I turned to ask Torliam if this was normal, and discovered I was alone.

My stomach clenched, but when I looked again I saw the others, except they faded in and out of my sight as they moved.

Jacky walked past me and I held out a hand toward her. "Wow," she said, even as she brushed against me and I barely felt her, like she was half ghost. "Can you see me?" her voice sounded like it was coming from a faraway place.

"Yes," I said.

She nodded and continued up the staircase. I exhaled slowly. They were okay. Whatever this was, my teammates were all still there. I turned and continued walking with them, making sure that none of them disappeared for good, even if I couldn't always see them.

Finally, the stairs opened onto a large cylindrical room. The stone here was cut open to the outside at seemingly random intervals and the light didn't travel right. There were patches of brightness and alternating darkness in the wrong spots—some too bright, others too dark. I had trouble focusing on exactly what was incorrect about the physics, especially as I watched the ghostly forms of my teammates wander around, fading in and out of reality.

I stepped into the room, and, as if they'd been hanging in the air, invisible to me simply because I wasn't the right angle to see them, lines of light scattered through the air like lasers through dust, rainbow bright.

QUEST COMPLETED!

Ahead of me, a faint image of Kris atop her marionette reached out and touched something I couldn't see. Her eyes rolled back in her head and her eyelids vibrated eerily, but she quickly snapped out of it and stepped back, shocked, and didn't seem harmed.

I stepped further into the room, blinking as space shifted around me. Slowly, I reached up and brushed my fingertip against one of the nearby threads of light. I gasped, arching my back like I'd been hit with a charge from a defibrillator. My vision went black, along with the death of my other senses. I was cut off, alone with only my mind for an unknown amount of time. Then, things showed themselves to me.

I saw a vast planet, with colonized surrounding moons and futuristic sprawling cities. A darkness bubbled up and made something visceral and instinctive inside me want to scream in terror, or curl up in a ball and hide. People died in rippling waves, like slow-growing mold spreading over the surface of the planet.

The vision cut to a young man, watching this with the same sense of horrified understanding I felt. He screamed, as he was branded with the same symbol I wore in the skin of my throat. He walked beside a group of forms I couldn't quite make out. He clenched his jaw in determination, and the scene skipped through time. I saw him speaking, always. Healing someone with a supplication, commanding an army to kneel, making a peer crumple and cry with his words, and a woman's eyes sparkle with devotion. The scenes grew more disjointed and staticky as he continued to speak and twist the world to his will, growing ever-crueler as the madness of power overtook him. The gods rose up to smite him down, and then my senses returned with a suddenness that was overwhelming. The colors were too bright and eye-wateringly saturated. I could smell the metal of my armor mixed with my sweat, and taste the saliva in my mouth.

I stared at the strings of light, then brought my hand up to touch the crystal at the base of my throat. There had been another bearer of the symbol before me, though it seemed his Skill had been much stronger than my own. What did this mean?

I reached for another string, this time prepared for the disorientation. I saw people, a horde of them that stretched out as far as the eye could see. My perspective changed, and I stood among them. They turned to look at me as one, staring blankly like some creepy hive-mind robots. I frowned as that vision ended, too quickly. Perhaps Torliam would be able to help me decipher the symbolism of the visions after this was over.

I took a few more steps, the room shifting around me as I did so, and reached out for a new strand of light. This time, I saw a man with hair like smoke. No. It was *Chaos*—rising from his body in dark-tendriled wispiness. He reached into the ground with his power and pulled out a tree of gold that unfurled before him and grew black fruit. The scene flickered, and I watched as he screamed before a giant, bigger than any god I'd ever seen, made of lava and smoke. Chaos devoured the man, even as he molded it into a flickering sphere of darkness that warped the world around it. The vision stopped, as quickly as it had started, and it left me dazed. Behelaino had spoken of a progeny before me, someone else she'd given the Seed of Chaos to. Was that him, or was I seeing a god, another physical manifestation of Khaos itself?

The next strand showed me a different man. On his forehead was the same glowing symbol I wore at the base of my throat. He spoke words of the future, and his words were true. Then he spoke words that had not been true, and the future bent to meet them, but in doing so, his words erased his own existence.

I jerked back from the light as soon as it released me, feeling dizzy with the dreamlike understanding that had been forced into my brain.

The next strand showed me another bearer of the same symbol. A woman, her silver hair cut short to show the smoldering seal glowing golden from the back of her neck. She walked through raindrops, cutting them apart with daggers made of molten gold. She sliced the air, and it shattered before her, as her blades cut through the bonds that held the pieces of the world together. Death followed her every step and her followers found death one by one. She walked alone, when there were none left to walk beside her, and then her blades found her own throat and cut the fragile bonds that held her own life.

I stumbled back and fell. How many others had there been, before me? I tripped into another thread. This one showed me a shadowed form, walking in darkness. With a wave of their hand, a universe bloomed. Another wave, and it died, morphing into glitter dust that fell from their fingers to the floor.

Once that vision had passed, I picked myself up off the achingly cold stone, and stood in a beam of light from one of the windows. It threw refracted rainbows across my skin as the guardians outside swam through the air. "This is surreal," I whispered to myself. My words echoed around me, and I shuddered, though I wasn't sure if it was from the cold or the unnerving situation.

With a breath to steel myself, I reached for another strand of light. Maybe, if I saw enough of them, I would be able to figure out how they all fit together. The vision took over my senses, but this time it hurt. My eyes ached as I watched the *shattering*, the separation, the inky razor of the rift severing pieces of what was once a whole into what was no longer. I caught a glimpse of the void from the corner of my eye and jerked myself back, forcefully cutting off the vision and my connection to that particular strand of light.

I stared at it in horror, knowing that I didn't understand what I had just seen, but that I never should have seen it in the first place. I raised my right hand to my cheek, touching the wetness under my eye, and drew away fingers tinged crimson.

The rainbow fractal light from the window drew my attention again, but this time the guardians had dispersed enough for me to see through them. On the edge of the horizon, as far as I could see, little moving dots were swarming. I activated Spirit of the Huntress, sharpening my eyesight even further as my claws unsheathed themselves from my hands and feet. The little dots on the horizon were monsters —tons of them—all different types, flying, running, skittering toward the tower.

The hair on my neck rose up in dread, then the quest Window bloomed in front of my eyes.

RUN
RETURN TO THE SHIP WITHOUT BEING DISCOVERED.
COMPLETION REWARD: AVOID ATTACK
NON-COMPLETION PENALTY: BATTLE

Chapter 6

The moon split in half
   and the stars crumbled,
   falling like fireworks
   into the sea.
   — Christy Ann Martine

I WAVED AWAY the virtual display and leaned forward, thrusting my head out the tall tower window to look back the way we'd come. The monsters' indistinct forms rose over the horizon from every direction and grew quickly larger. Some looked like huge bats, others, deformed, earthbound dragons, others still, gigantic beetles that tunneled through the air instead of the ground.

I drew back and looked around for my teammates, who were still walking around experiencing visions of their own. I waved my hands in front of Adam's face, but his eyelids were fluttering in the midst of a vision, and he didn't see me. Instead, I sent a Window to the entire team, warning them of the danger.

Adam jerked back and then blinked at the air in front of his face. He turned to me and nodded sharply.

Torliam didn't have a VR chip, but when I passed my hand through the tip of his nose, I got his attention and, with pantomime and some faintly heard words, conveyed our situation.

I herded the others down the stairwell ahead of me and counted them off to make sure no one was left behind. I don't know how long it took us to get down and out of the Spire, but every opening in the stone we passed showed the monsters grown closer.

We burst out the doorway at the bottom and threw ourselves down the steep mountainside, once again able to interact with each other and the world as normal.

I reached out to Gregor, and he turned to Shadow, climbed onto my crouching form, then resumed corporeality between my backpack and my back so he wouldn't be left trying to keep up on eight-year-old sized legs. He clung like a monkey. "Hurry," he said.

The fractal behemoths above swarmed like bees whose nest had been disturbed, some of them flying out to meet the oncoming wave of monsters.

One of the beasts slammed into a low-flying guardian from the side, ripping apart the lines of light and sending the being hurtling toward the ground in hundreds of glowing pieces. The monster collapsed, dead. But there were many more to take its place.

In the distance, the passenger ship struggled up from the ground, disturbed dirt swirling out and around it.

The construct Adam rode dissolved under him.

I saw him reach for an ink cartridge, too slow to save himself from a tumble. My toes dug into the ground as I attempted to swerve closer, but my momentum, augmented by Gregor's weight, was too much for me to get to him on time.

Instead, Kris' marionette snagged Adam by the neck of his clothes and kept him aloft.

He winced, white-faced at the pain being tossed around must have caused him, but nodded at her gratefully. However, when he poured out more ink from one of his cartridges, the dark liquid dribbled out and seeped into earth without taking form. He bit back a curse.

"Jacky!" I called.

"I've got him," she said. She swung his arm over her shoulder, but was too short to lift him entirely off the ground.

Torliam stopped her, pulling Adam instead onto a misty blue slab, which hovered just over the ground. Torliam fastened him securely down and pulled Adam behind him like a dog with a sled.

We raced toward the ship, Birch creating a wind at our backs to push us on even faster.

The guardians flew around at seemingly impossible speeds, orbiting farther and farther away from the Spire, pushing their forms through the monsters and leaving their bodies outwardly unharmed, but motionless on the ground.

"None who are not the subject of prophecy may come here and live," Torliam shouted over his shoulder by way of explanation. "The body will remain, but the mind is destroyed."

Unfortunately, even modified humans aren't built for real speed. Torliam was the only one of us who stood a chance at getting away, and he was purposefully pacing himself, not leaving the group behind.

The ship hadn't yet reached us by the time we met the fastest of the monsters. Blaine had to avoid the guardians, too, and seemed to be having trouble maneuvering the ungainly vessel around their racing forms to get to us.

A Window popped up in my peripheral vision, telling me I'd failed the "RUN" quest. I batted it away. No time for distractions.

Birch yowled, running next to Adam with his teeth bared. His fur was all fluffed out, and he extended his wings to make himself look even bigger as he screamed in threat to the monsters barreling toward us.

I translated my awareness into a map Window and broadcast it to the rest of the team. It would give them the location of every monster and human in my range, updated as fast as I could keep up with it. Greater battlefield awareness would make a big difference.

Some of the monsters ran past us without notice, but not all of them. A four-legged monster slammed its paddle-like tail into the ground, using it as a fulcrum to change its direction frighteningly quick. It shot straight at Sam, who was the slowest of us and thus bringing up the rear of the group.

Sam almost tripped when he tried to dodge, but he managed to stay upright, and ran a hand across the monster's side as its speed carried it past him.

It slapped its tail on the ground again and spun back toward him, unaffected by whatever effect he'd sought to impart through skin contact.

Bullets flew through the air with a *whoomp*, as Zed turned back for a couple seconds and shot toward the monster. Two of his three shots hit, while the third flew harmlessly overhead. The rounds impacted against its side and exploded, tearing chunks out of it.

Blackened veins were visible across thick, pale flesh. The thing's eyes jerked wildly this way and that, but it didn't react at all to the pain, and I noticed oozing sores on its underbelly. It reminded me of the spider-monkey creature we'd seen when we first came to Estreyer with Torliam.

"Careful, it has the Sickness!" I shouted to Sam.

The monster snorted and tossed a look Zed's way, but he was already running again. It ignored him, focusing back on Sam, who it had effectively blocked off from the rest of us and the safety of the ship.

Sam stopped. Even my Wraith Skill couldn't decipher exactly what he was saying with all the other distractions going on around us, but he muttered something that might have been, "Oh, shit," over and over again.

"He needs help!" Adam screamed, his voice breaking as he was jostled by Torliam's makeshift stretcher.

Jacky slowed, turning back toward our trapped teammate.

—GO! I CAN DO THIS.—
-SAM-

She hesitated, looking to me.

I nodded, and we continued on without Sam. My guts lurched within me, and I wasn't sure if it was fear or something else making me feel so queasy. Sam may not have been a fighter, but he was deadly all the same. If I didn't accept his assurance, and we went back to try and help him, it put the rest of us in even more danger. Still, it felt wrong, running while he stood still.

The monster seemed to grin, its blue-purple tongue, grotesquely swollen, lolling out of its mouth like a nightmarish dog. It sprang for him.

Sam didn't evade quickly enough, and its jaw caught his arm up to the elbow.

"Oh, god, no," I gasped.

He screamed, bracing himself on the ground. Then, Sam's arm moved along its side as they moved past each other. At first, I thought that the creature must have completely severed his arm at the elbow. Then, the monster's flesh sagged on the side he was touching, like a wax figure left too close to the fire.

A scream gargled out from the monster's half-collapsed throat. Sam kept moving, till its entire side was sliding toward the ground in a goopy mess. Finally, he drew his arm out of the flesh of its hind leg.

Its other set of legs scrabbled and flailed uselessly, the horrific, gargling whine of pain never stopping for breath.

Sam's skin was raw and bleeding where its teeth had first caught him, and he kept it cradled close while he resumed his sprint, pushing to catch up before another monster could attack.

More monsters turned, some of them attacking, some just running alongside our group.

Torliam, at the forward point of the group, smashed his fist through a bug-like creature's carapace, barely breaking stride. A wave of his Skill knocked a tight flock of metallic birds out of the sky. He leapt through the air with Adam trailing on his slab. His feet smashed into the bulging stomach of a winged creature, and he used its broken body to bat aside another monster. He was clearing the way for us, but it still wasn't quite enough.

The ground started to rumble, and the monsters running beside and chasing after us drew farther away, creating a circular clearing around us.

I stretched out my awareness. Another monster must be coming, something large enough to shake the ground, but I sensed nothing. I took the chance to look around physically, in case it was too far away for Wraith to reach. Nothing. Nothing big enough for what my instincts told me was coming, at least. The smaller pebbles on the ground jumped, like water droplets on a vibrating drum.

I slammed Wraith downward, pushing it through the earth as a horrible suspicion burst in my mind. My senses barely reached the edge of the fast-moving creature before I was screaming out to the others, a Window reinforcing my words. "Scatter! Something's in the ground!"

The earth bulged beneath us, a hill as big as a house forming as something pushed up through it, like a tongue through bubblegum.

I shoved desperately away from it, throwing myself toward the edge of the growing hill.

Gregor screamed in my ear, squeezing so tight around my neck I struggled to breathe.

The creature burst through, its cylindrical body stretching toward the sky. It had no eyes that I could see, only a single maw as big around as its worm-like body, and full of rows and rows of pointed teeth overlapping each other all the way down its throat.

"Wyrm!" Torliam shouted, his voice barely audible over the crashing earth.

Most of us moved far enough away that the wave of dirt and stone facilitated our escape, pushing us outward and away. I rode the dirt avalanche, stumbling a few times, jumping to avoid being overtaken and buried.

Kris wasn't so lucky. She was stuck on the mound as it rose, caught on the edge of the creature's gaping maw. The earth crumbled beneath her marionette's feet as it tried to push away, but it didn't have the leverage to get her to safety.

Gregor screamed again in my ear, almost deafening me. I didn't blame him. He could see what was about to happen just as well as I could.

I threw myself back up the cascading earth wall, trying to rise instead of escape. It was useless. I was too far away, and there was no time. None of my Skills could help me here. I yelled, Voice pulsing out of me and into the earth, through the side of the primordial creature. It changed nothing.

Sky-blue shot toward Kris from the other side of the crater, and my heart skipped a beat as I willed it to arrive on time. It reached them, spreading out below the marionette's feet like a disk. The blue shield stilled in the air, and the marionette touched down, bending its knees to absorb the force of its landing without throwing her off.

She scrambled up to crouch atop its shoulders.

The maw rose around them, obscuring my line of sight, but not Wraith's senses.

All my attention was focused on them. Kris gave a sobbing gasp of effort as she pushed herself and her Skill to the limit. The marionette *heaved*. Its joints cracked and popped, and it lifted them.

The maw closed in on them, thousands and thousands of stabbing teeth surging toward Kris and her marionette.

THE MARIONETTE FLUNG itself away from the grinding maw, and, as it reached the edge of its leap, Kris threw herself off, arms outstretched toward the sky. One of her legs scraped the edge of the maw as it closed behind her, tossing her sideways, out of control. The metal of her marionette shrieking as it crumpled and broke to the monster's teeth.

Jacky was closest to them, her body already bigger than Torliam's, with speed to match. She dashed toward Kris' falling form, her Skills pushing her forward much faster than I could move, fast enough to actually make a difference. She caught the girl before she could hit the ground, the combination of Gravitational Autonomy and Struggle helping to break their fall. They still hit the ground hard, and tumbled from there, but Jacky kept Kris tucked against her chest, protecting the girl with her own body.

Up ahead, Torliam dropped Adam's stretcher and ran toward the downed duo. He threw up a shield around them, and I let out a gasping sob of relief, almost dizzy from the crazed pounding of my own heart. I hated being so helpless.

The wyrm surged forward and tunneled back into the ground as easily as if it were made of water, the length of its tubular body flowing out of the first hole and down into the second.

I pointed Zed towards Adam, stranded on the blue sled of Torliam's power, and we met there. At a run, we grabbed the handles of the makeshift stretcher and continued on.

"I'm out, Eve," Adam said. "Wasted it all on riding around all day, should have saved some strength for when it really counted."

"Not your fault," I puffed out, panting too hard to say more. "We're almost to the ship." I shot a glance behind us to the Spire, where the monsters were now attacking the tower with extreme prejudice, falling to the attacks of the guardians without care, their numbers overwhelming both the guardians and the integrity of the stone edifice itself.

Sam drew even with Zed and I. "They're coming," he gasped.

Birch ran at our heels, his Skill once again creating a much-appreciated thrust of wind at our backs. The cub stumbled over his own feet, but picked himself up and kept running, ears laid flat to his head.

The ship lowered itself toward the ground, a few hundred meters ahead, crushing a few of the larger monsters who didn't get out of the way in time. Almost there.

But Sam was right. The monsters had been holding back as they waited for the wyrm. Now it was safe for them to attack.

Torliam's Skill flashed again and again, blue light spearing out in attack after attack, both holding off the monsters from Kris and Jacky while they found their feet and shooting forward toward us to help keep a path open to the ship.

I pushed my legs faster, pulling on the stretcher with one hand as the other made sure Gregor was securely latched to me. We ran around the edges of the wyrm-created craters, but the ground was still broken up and uneven, and I knew by the suppressed grunts and the way Adam's knuckles were clenched white that the sharp jerks and bumps hurt him. I disregarded it, because we had to get to the ship as quickly as possible. A little pain was nothing compared to our lives.

I felt dizzy, but I wasn't sure if it was due to lack of air or because of my panic.

At first, I thought I imagined the clopping sound. Then it grew louder, coming from all around like distorted, echoing hoofbeats.

The creature appeared in front of me, barely an outline to my Wraith Skill, till it became visible in a wave, like its body was being filled in with the rushing surge of a dark, misty ocean, from one side to the other.

Some spray touched my lips. It tasted like salt.

The huge horse looked over its shoulder at us, tossing its head, its mane half-ephemeral. It had eight legs, four in the front, four in the back, and its black eyes held a deep malice.

I recognized danger when I saw it. I raised my hand from Gregor's leg, guiding Chaos out of my depths and driving it toward the creature. My power reacted eagerly, and I could feel it almost gnashing its teeth in the desire to rend.

When Chaos touched the eight-legged horse with tendrils angled like claws, the creature burst apart like water upon a rock, leaving only a splash and a briny smell behind.

Zed's two bullets, shot a little too slow, blasted through empty air where it had been, and on into the distance. He gave me a sheepish smile, and we ran again.

The clopping sound came again.

"Seriously?" Zed gasped, panting.

I sensed it as the horse ran *through* us, but I was too slow to move away, too slow to even warn Zed, Gregor, or Adam.

It surged into being again, appearing in the air around us, inside of us. In an instant, my body was drenched, and my stomach, lungs, and throat were filled to bursting with saltwater. It pushed painfully against my insides, as if trying to invade my organs, muscles, and blood vessels. I could taste it, feel it, the sea-spray, the deep crushing ocean, and the moonless night. When the horse stepped forward and away, its water surged with it, yanking at our bodies. The monster broke apart into a splash of water again.

I dropped to the ground, convulsing as the brine spewed out of my nose and mouth. I scrabbled desperately at the dark blue grass crushed beneath me, trying to spit up enough water from my lungs that I could draw breath again. My body screamed for air, my head already throbbing.

Eventually, I got enough space to draw breath, and from there to cough up more of the saltwater. My insides burned, and I knew there was damage. Hopefully nothing too bad, nothing Sam couldn't fix.

I stood up, still hacking up fluid, and turned Gregor upside down so the liquid would exit his body more easily. The ship was so close. But still too far.

Adam and Zed were both still conscious and my brother stumbled to his feet, grabbing the handle of the sled. We pulled, straining toward the ship, only a couple hundred meters away now.

Ahead of us, a bird half the size of a man, with talons longer and more segmented than my fingers, dropped toward Sam.

Birch bared his teeth at it, creating a gust of wind sharp enough to knock it into a tumble. It crashed into another monster, which immediately turned on the bird and tore it apart for the offense.

The clopping came again.

Adam scored a line into his forearm with his butterfly knife and mumbled "Animus," and the blood spilled out into a mass of crimson tentacles, just in time to catch on the eight-legged horse as it formed around us. The tentacles detached from Adam's arm, hanging in place in the air behind us, the sea horse caught within their grasp. Adam slumped, his eyes rolling back in his head.

I thought he must be conscious still, or his Animated construct would have disappeared, but he didn't even have the wherewithal to try and stop the blood running from his arm.

Behind us, the creature struggled with the tentacles. Then it splashed into nothingness, only for the clopping sound to come once more.

Gregor sobbed in my ear.

I ran for the ship, every other breath ending on a wet, ragged cough.

Beside me, Zed stumbled.

I felt it as the creature's incorporeal form began to move through us again, but there was nothing visible outside me yet, nothing for me to attack, no way for me to protect myself.

Gregor released his hold from me. His legs kicked out at my back, sending me sprawling to the ground, and him backward through the air. He slipped into his Shadow form halfway through the jump, his body rotating as the horse formed around him. Hands as dark as midnight drew twin daggers.

He switched back into corporeality while inside its belly, the daggers rending as he whirled. He hit the ground hard.

The creature burst apart all around him, but this time spewed more water than it seemed its form could have contained, a gushing fount that crashed down on the boy.

I scrabbled forward on my hands and knees into the rushing water, grabbing the back of Gregor's shirt and pulling him away, lifting his head into the air. I turned him upside down again, holding him by one ankle and pounding on his back.

Liquid spewed out of his mouth, this time tinged pink with blood. He began to breathe again as soon as his lungs had cleared, but his eyes stayed closed.

I laid him down next to Adam on the blue half-stretcher, then Zed and I ran for the ship again.

Sam killed a monster ahead of us, and Zed and I had to swerve to avoid its carcass.

A flash of blue light accompanied a clap like muted thunder to my right, as Torliam used his Skill to literally crush a group of monsters into the ground on one side, while on the other side battling a striking snake bigger around than he was, with his bare hands.

Many of the monsters, eyes wild and bellies distended, had turned on each other, attacking and feasting on the flesh of other members of the horde, but too many were still focused on us, chasing after us as we hurtled toward safety.

At some point, Jacky's enlarged form had passed us again and reached the ship, holding Kris in her arms. Blood was streaked over them both. I wasn't sure whose. A door on the side of the ship opened, and they disappeared inside. Torliam stayed outside to keep a path open for us. Sam and Birch shot through, and finally Zed and I, with our two passengers.

As soon as the end of the sled was through the door and Torliam had backed inside, Jacky slammed a hand into the panel beside the door to close it.

Dull thumps reverberated through the hull as monsters slammed into the side of the ship.

Torliam ran ahead to the control room, and we followed at a slower pace, ignoring the screams of fear traveling out from the room where the passengers had strapped themselves in. Hopefully, they hadn't caused any problems for Blaine in the time we were gone.

Blaine had moved aside immediately so that Torliam could take over the main control seat, and was hovering over both Kris and Gregor, muttering frantic recriminations against himself, and me, for allowing them to be placed in danger again. How could I have known this would happen? How could anyone have predicted this?

We strapped our injured into the bolted down seats of the control room so Sam could tend to them without any danger of them further injuring themselves if the ship was badly jostled.

The ship rumbled beneath us as it slowly lifted off.

I dropped limply into a chair next to the big viewing window, looking out onto the Spire as it collapsed on itself. Stone crumbled and crashed, dust billowed, and the remaining guardians tore through the space it had once occupied as if maddened. Below us, monsters teemed around, some of them still attacking the ship.

Then, they scattered.

My back stiffened. "Wyrm!" I snapped. "Below us!"

The ship lurched as Torliam forced it higher, and Kris cried out in pain.

The wyrm burst upward in a colossal spray of dirt, its thousand-toothed maw gaping open, growing larger and larger as it approached us. I knew it was impossible, but it seemed as if it would swallow us whole, ship and all. Instead, it grazed the bottom of the ship, its teeth hooking in, piercing and tearing at the hull.

Alarms sounded inside as the ship lurched. The passengers and flight crew screamed again. Torliam's hands flew across the controls, and we lurched once more, then began to rise again as the wyrm fell back to earth, pieces of our ship in its mouth.

We were all silent, waiting to see what would happen.

It tunneled back into the ground like a fish into water.

"Nothing vital is damaged," Torliam grunted, most of his attention still on the controls.

Those of us still conscious let out a collective sigh of relief.

Then, the ground below us burst upward again.

"We're too high now," Jacky said, her hands pressed against the glass. "It's not gonna reach."

The creature kept coming, more and more of its body shooting out of the ground, till it was fully extended. It still didn't reach us.

Another sigh of relief gusted out of me, and I felt lightheaded. I'd forgotten to breathe, in my worry.

YOUR AGILITY HAS INCREASED!

Then, both of the wyrm's sides burst apart in a sprawling eruption of flesh and fluid, all down its length. Hundreds and hundreds of wings ruptured outward, each of them too small to lift something of its size. But they flapped together, at first frantically, and then with a synchronized rhythm. The wyrm's fall halted.

Below us, the monsters tore ravenously at the flesh falling from it, and then at each other.

The wyrm began to rise.

"*Of course* it can fly," I said, slamming my head against the glass.

Chapter 7

The sea has neither meaning nor pity.
— Anton Chekhov

AS THE SHIP got up to speed, we drew ahead of the wyrm, displayed now on a screen which showed the rear view from the ship. "Even this great cow of a ship should be faster than the wyrm. We may not completely escape it, but it shall not catch us," Torliam said. "For the moment, in any case."

"What do you mean, for the moment?" Sam said, his hands on Gregor's chest.

"A wyrm never stops growing. They adapt to the needs of their situation, constantly. If it cannot keep up, it will become faster. Our ship cannot do the same."

I bit the inside of my lip, letting the pain help to push me past exhaustion. "So we need to escape quickly. Can we go back through between those two trees, to return to Estreyer's main level?"

"That door is not open from this side. There is another, but it will take longer for us to reach."

"Let's not waste any time, then."

"More importantly, how badly are my kiddos injured?" Blaine said, leaning over Sam and the kids with his hands twitching like he wanted to be doing the healing himself.

"Gregor's condition is the most critical, but he'll be fine. He's got some, umm, internal bleeding. I've already relieved him of the injuries, and now I'm just forcing the blood clots around his abdomen into his stomach for digestion. He can cough out the blood in his lungs," Sam said.

Gregor did just that, sitting up and coughing harshly till a few mucous-red globs came up, then breathing normally again. "I saved you, Eve." His voice was smug at first, but then he jerked and looked around till he saw Kris. "Are you okay?"

She nodded, her lower lip trembling a little. "Sam already healed me. Just some cuts, and my arm was broken so I have to be careful with it now. But I just realized I left Moose back in my room in the castle. I forgot to grab him when we were leaving!"

Gregor exhaled, then rolled his eyes. "Your stuffed animal will be fine. It's not like it cares that you abandoned it."

She glared at him and turned away with a huff.

Adam was still unconscious, because there was nothing Sam could do about the backlash from overusing his Skill. Sam had already healed the minor internal injuries and the new damage Adam had done to his back wound with all the jostling.

"Do the guardian-things feel pain, do you think?" Sam said. "I wish we could have helped them."

"We would have been eaten just to help some tadpoles made of light," Gregor said. "Do you want to get killed?"

Zed waved his hands at the two of them dismissively. "I think the more important question is, what just happened? Why did all those monsters decide to suddenly attack?"

"Those creatures are not native to this level," said Torliam. "Very little made of flesh and blood can survive here."

"So how did they get here?" I asked. "And *why*?"

"The Oracle planned this," Blaine said.

I hesitated, but shook my head. "No, I don't think so. She did send us here, but when the monsters showed up, she immediately gave me a quest to escape."

"She *can* see the future, Eve," Sam said.

"Exactly," Blaine said. "Every time we listen to her, she leads us into danger. We might already be on Earth, if not for this diversion."

I snorted derisively. "And there isn't danger on Earth? Aliens just started a *war* there. Besides, I don't think the Oracle can actually see the future, the way you mean. She told me she sees possibilities, likelihoods. Maybe this wasn't supposed to happen. Because what's the point of leading us here, just to get us killed by monsters?"

Jacky pursed her lips. "I don't think the monsters were there for us. They attacked the Spire. Maybe we just happened to be in the way."

I touched the crystal at the base of my throat. With a few mental commands, I brought up the VR chip description of the Voice Skill again.

VOICE (SOVEREIGN CLASS): INCREASES CHARISMA. ACTS AS A BEACON FOR BEINGS OF POWER. ALLOWS PRESENCE AND WILL TO BE IMPOSED ON SURROUNDINGS. SKILL EFFECTS WILL EXPAND AND STRENGTHEN WITH PLAYER IMPROVEMENT.

"You may be right. Remember, part of my Voice Skill is to act as a beacon to 'beings of power.' I mean, they might have attacked us anyway, but we know it makes nearby monsters more likely to attack. Still, the timing of this, and the total destruction of the Spire, is really strange."

Blaine rounded on me. "The question of what exactly went wrong can be discussed at a later date. I am more interested in what transpired before your untimely interruption. Was this detour worth it? Did you learn valuable information, or anything that will help us cure the Sickness?" His tone was aggressive, but I could tell by the set of his shoulders that really, he was just desperate for a positive answer, but waiting for disappointment.

I ran my fingers over the warm crystal melded with my skin again. "I...don't know." I turned to Torliam and raised an eyebrow. "There were others with this same symbol before me, though the Skills they got from it seemed to be varying magnitudes of power above my own. I saw a few things that I didn't really understand the significance of, as well. For instance, it showed me someone using Chaos, and I think he might have been the mortal Behelaino gave a piece of her Seed to before me. I also saw other, stranger visions that might have been real, or might have been symbolism like the visions I get from the Oracle. I was hoping you could help decipher them."

He frowned. "The Spire was brought with us from the old world, in the exodus. It has been outlawed for generations. I had thought it would give us clarification of the path we must walk to complete the prophecy, but I, too, received only visions of the past and other's failed attempts to cure the Sickness. I believe I know of the woman who held my symbol, previously… Heldra the Victorious? Her Skill always lead her to the answer she sought, and yet she failed all the same. I believe you humans call this a Pyrrhic victory. There is mention in the history books that some believed her to be the subject of prophecy, destined to destroy the Sickness, but it is considered a myth. What else did you see?" He looked around at the others.

Jacky clenched her fists. "I saw a monster. He'd been a man, but he couldn't stop growing stronger, even when the strength had mutated and consumed him and he wished he'd die instead."

Birch let out a scratchy mewl and pushed his nose into my hand. An image burst through my mind. A woman with light purple skin, like the color of a sunset through storm-clouds, raising her arms to make the skies writhe with wind and anger. Hail the size of boulders crashed down from the clouds, crushing the army arrayed before her. Birch pulled back and blinked his inner sideways-closing eyelids, which looked a little disturbing combined with his green irises and human-shaped pupils.

"He saw a purple woman, controlling the weather," I said.

The others relayed varying versions of the same thing. Past counterparts to their symbols, the Sickness in action, and visions of strange, fantastical things they didn't understand.

"What does this mean?" I turned to Torliam.

"I do not *know*. I can only make guesses." Torliam's voice was strained, and he stood from his seat, letting the ship fly itself as he paced back and forth with long strides. "I know not how the Spire of Prophecy truly works. Perhaps these visions were indeed meant to aid us in our quest, in some way. Why else would the Oracle encourage our visit?"

"Maybe we're just not thinking about this the right way. We all saw the Sickness, and past versions of the Seal of Nine with different powers. That's relevant information. Prophecies are things that *can* come true, but how exactly they do so could be any number of ways, right?"

He rubbed his jaw, fingers smoothing through the short beard there. "Yes. Additionally, there have been many, many 'prophecies' about our struggle against the Sickness, the great battle. There is little way to verify the veracity of a prophecy, unless it comes from one such as Testimony and Lore."

"When I spoke to the Oracle during the battle with the God of Knowledge, she told me that I was *one* possibility for a cure to the Sickness. Not the only one. What if the gods have been doing this, over and over, for millennia? Creating new Seals of Nine, and when they die, waiting till the legends or rumors fade away and then trying again? And," I stood up, sweeping my eyes over the symbols of the others, "each variation is similar. 'The Summoner, the Gale, the Gifter. The Tracker, the Struggle, the Shadow. The Black Sun, and the Veil-Piercer.'" I quoted Testimony and Lore, during our Trial with her. "'One for each of the greater Trials.' So maybe it was trying to hint to us the ongoing theme of the resources they've given others, what we're going to need to find the cure. The other visions probably have some relevance, too, even if we don't have the framework to understand them."

TORLIAM FOUND it disturbing that he'd been unaware of previous, legitimate subjects of prophecy meant to cure the Sickness. "Research into the Sickness, the god, and the cure… I have made it my life's work. And yet, how did I not realize this was happening? When possible agents of prophecy were mentioned, they were always discredited. It seemed obvious, that none could have been legitimate, as the Sickness still plagues us. In my shortsightedness, I did not think of any other possibility."

"You weren't the only one, I'm sure." I meant the words as a consolation, but he just shook his head, eyes closed.

Zed fiddled with one of his specialized guns, its pieces spread out in his lap as he cleaned them carefully. "Well, it's not like it really matters, right? We knew finding this god wasn't going to be easy, and that we got these Skills for a reason. Even if it has happened before, this is just more confirmation of that. It doesn't change anything. We still have to get to Earth. That's where the god is, right?"

Torliam opened his eyes. "Yes, I believe so. You are correct, Zed. We can only forge onward."

We were all exhausted from what felt like one of the longest days I'd ever trudged through, but I sucked it up and took Torliam and Sam with me to talk to the civilian passengers again, who were all extremely alarmed and speculating amongst themselves. None of them had been seriously harmed during our travel to or escape from the Spire, but a few had minor bumps, bruises, or pressure injuries from the restraining straps or when the ship's maneuvers had thrown a couple loose items about.

I sent Sam around to heal those injuries, figuring he'd gotten a healthy dose of healing stored up from the damage he'd done to the monsters, and the return of the people's goodwill was likely worth some of us healing our own small injuries naturally. It might even force our Resilience to level up, which could only be a good thing in the long run.

Still, a lot of people were disgruntled and even downright angry. I focused on Voice, wondering if its Charisma-boosting effects could act as crowd-control when directed properly. "Thank you for your patience, and your participation in our fight against the Sickness." Voice didn't activate, but I resisted the urge to groan aloud, and continued speaking. "Your cooperation has allowed us to enter the Spire of Prophecy, as was the will of the Oracle, and receive visions to aid our quest against the Sickness. When we stand together, who can stand against us?" Voice finally thrummed through the air as I spoke the last words, and I raised my fist in the air in sincere triumph.

Some smiled, and others cheered. The angriest of the bunch weren't persuaded to cheerfulness, but they only grumbled to themselves a little.

"What have you learned from the Spire of Prophecy, Eve-Redding?" one of the reporters asked. The woman held out her empty hand as if pointing a camera toward me. When she realized, she blushed and dropped her hand back to her lap, but still looked at me expectantly.

The gaffe reminded me that without any cameras to catch me in the act, I was safe to lie. Not that I actually needed to, in this case.

"Torliam originally went to Earth on a quest to find the lost god, the Shaper and Molder who stands as Champion against the Sickness. He found me, instead. Now, we return to Earth to search for that Champion." I ignored their stunned silence and the questions that quickly followed. "You'll have normal use of your ship back shortly." I left to go back to the control room, leaving Sam and Torliam behind to deal with any other issues.

In the hallway outside the control room, Adam lay on the floor, propped up against the wall awkwardly, his legs sprawling into the walkway.

"Adam! What happened?" I hurried to his side, kneeling down beside him. My hands reached out for him, but I didn't know where to touch or how to move him without making things worse, so they just kind of hovered.

He was so pale he looked almost green, and sweat stood out on his temples, matting his curly hair down. He still found the energy to scowl at me. "My fucking back is broken. What do you think happened?"

I could guess. He'd run himself into the ground earlier with overuse of his Animus Skill, which was the only way he had to get around without help. When he'd awoken, he must have decided to use it again despite his exhaustion, and it failed him. "I can help get you back to the control room, and we'll call Sam to come take a look at you. What were you thinking? You just passed out from Skill overuse. You should be resting."

He slapped my reaching hand away, fairly spitting with anger when he spoke. "If you really want to help, why don't you use the only Skill that *can* actually help me, and *do* something about it? This is torture, Eve! If it was you going through this, you'd understand." He panted, then slumped back against the faintly rippling wall.

"Adam, I… It's not that I don't want to. Trust me, if I could fix you with Chaos, I *would*."

"You could try, at least," he said in a low voice. "I wouldn't mind if my back changed, got alien-like, like your arm. As long as I could walk again."

I clenched my jaw, as the muscles of my neck grew achingly tight. "Adam, I told you. I don't know how to do that. When I unleashed Chaos on the God of Knowledge, the information he had implanted in me released itself, all at once. I got an overwhelming amount of information about how to use Chaos to destroy a god and the Sickness contained within. But most of that knowledge faded. I don't know if he always meant it to do that, or if my brain is just literally too stupid to retain clear comprehension of how the Skill works."

I stopped until he met my eyes again, then spoke slowly. "I was literally dying when Chaos finished things off. It was out of my control already, and suddenly, I was alive again. It's not just my left arm that it recreated. I had a skull with a half-cooked brain inside, a torso, and about half of my inner organs remaining. Then, I was like this." I held up my six-fingered left hand and unfurled the too-long digits.

His eyes widened. I hadn't told them the full extent of my injuries before, because I knew they wouldn't take it well.

"So I *don't know* how to recreate what I did. Maybe we can go see Behelaino when it's safe. It's her power. She knows how to use it. If I try to fix your *spine*, when I'm not even confident I could fix a paper cut, I could kill you, Adam. If there's some chance you could be healed any other way, I'm not going to risk killing you. You're too important. And, you know," I took a deep breath, and lightened my tone, "Legs aren't everything."

He snorted, but when he spoke there was no anger in his voice. "Maybe you just need practice. Since legs aren't everything—incredible revelation, you know—I guess I can wait." He reached an arm up, hooking it around my shoulders so I could help lift him. "Carry me that way, servant." He pointed the way back down the hallway, voice completely deadpan.

———

THE WAY BLAINE, the kids, and Jacky were all staring at one of the screens on the console clued me in immediately that something was wrong. "Is it the wyrm?"

Gregor turned to me. "It's catching up. Unless something changes I estimate we've got less than an hour till then."

"Go get Torliam," I ordered, then helped Adam to one of the more comfortable chairs at the back of the room. I fiddled futilely with its controls till impatience won out, then used a quick burst of Chaos to eat through the rod keeping the back straight.

Adam raised an eyebrow, but didn't say anything as Blaine and I helped him to lay on his stomach on the now-flat surface.

When he was secure, I moved to the screen where the wyrm was displayed. It had changed. Some of its wings were bigger, toward the middle of its body. And it was closer to us. Much too close, and gaining quickly.

Torliam strode in and sat down in the captain's seat.

"How far out are we from this passage to the main level?" I said.

"A few hours at most."

I watched the wyrm open its maw slightly, as if it was grinning in anticipation of tearing us to pieces. It would overtake us in less than an hour, at this rate.

Gregor's bushy eyebrows looked even bigger over his wide eyes. "Being eaten sounds like a horrible way to die."

Kris wrapped her arms around herself and turned to me. "Is there anything we can do?"

I clenched my jaw, but before I was forced to respond that I didn't know, Jacky spoke. "Doesn't this ship have any weapons? Blast it out of the sky!"

Torliam touched the controls, and the ship began to rise higher, the sudden change of the floor's angle making the rest of us wobble till we regained our balance. "This is a passenger ship, meant for long, lazy travel through safe areas and the space between worlds. It is often escorted by smaller fighter ships. We have shields, but they draw power from the ship's speed when flying through atmosphere, and they are likely not strong enough to stand against the wyrm."

She tugged at her fingerless gloves. "Anything heavy we can drop off to lighten our load, then?"

"Why would the ship be carrying unimportant, heavy items that we could simply discard?" Torliam asked. "That makes no sense."

Jacky frowned. "In the films, they always do. You know, that 'ballast' stuff?"

Gregor shook his head. "Ballast was stuff like rocks or sand that ancient people used to steady their ships, because the construction was too poor for good balance otherwise."

"There is no need for this *'ballast'* on my world," Torliam said, his upper lip curling into a sneer. "Our ships can maintain balance without tying rocks to them."

I rolled my eyes. "You said the shields draw power when flying through *atmosphere*. You just started flying higher. Can this ship actually leave the atmosphere?"

He paused, then turned to me with a surprisingly straightforward smile. "Indeed." He returned to the controls, then ruined it with his next words. "I see your powers of deduction are not as stunted as I might have imagined." I could hear the self-satisfied smirk in his voice. "This ship does not require air to operate, but the wyrm does. And the wyrm has lived its life within the ground, a stranger to true cold. We will rise high, where there is not so much air to slow us down as we flee, and then we will dive like a hawk onto prey. If the cold of the upper air does not stop it, perhaps the friction of the fall will burn it up."

Gregor frowned, crossing his arms. "Isn't the outer atmosphere actually really hot? It wouldn't be cold unless we went all the way into space. Maybe we should do that."

"There is no sun on this level to heat the outer atmosphere," Torliam said. "Did you not notice that the light comes from the ground itself? If I thought there was much time to waste, I would agree. Even the wyrm might not adapt fast enough to survive the true emptiness of space, especially without any way to reliably propel itself. But the Sickness waits not for mortals. We must get to an array, and from there to Earth."

Sam frowned. "We're going to be diving from the upper atmosphere? Is that…safe?"

"I am a skilled pilot. However, you should most definitely take advantage of the safety straps on these seats."

Sam and I shared a look, and he sighed deeply. "Right."

Within the next half hour, we'd risen high enough that the wyrm struggled to keep up. Its wings were sluggish, and it now flew with its mouth fully open. I could see crystals form as the skin inside its maw froze. We began to draw ahead of it, as whatever propulsion method the ship had apparently didn't need oxygen or even air at all.

After another half hour, the wyrm was a small blip in our rearview screens. "Maybe we'll lose it entirely, if we get far enough ahead?" I said.

Torliam shook his head. "It is already adapting." He was right. With one more half hour, the wyrm was gaining on us. Its hide looked thicker, it had lost some of its massive size, and the obvious blood and membranes had completely disappeared from its wings, which had continued to grow and change shape.

Blaine peered intently at the creature, his excitement completely at odds with our impending doom. "This type of adaptation is utterly fascinating. The research implications are staggering. Do their alterations pass down to their offspring, I wonder?"

"How do you ever beat something like that?" My voice was tight, as I realized the true gravity of our situation for the first time.

"Kill it while it is small," Torliam said. "And kill it quickly."

"It's a bit too late for that."

He didn't reply verbally, instead pointing out the viewing window in front of us.

I peered out, but didn't see anything until I let my Spirit of the Huntress Skill sharpen my vision. We were flying far above an ocean now, instead of the blue grass plains. The surface of the planet was so far away I could see it curve away into the distance. Far out, there was a spot of water that looked different from the rest. A large circle of froth surrounded a dark mark. "That's the connection back to the main level?" I frowned. "I think I may have seen the other side of this, when we first broke you out of NIX. A whirlpool in the middle of the ocean, right? Are there many of those?"

"Not many."

When Torliam instructed, we once again warned all the passengers and helped to make sure they were secured fully as we prepared for extreme maneuvers. Then we strapped ourselves down into our own seats like we were wards of a mental asylum and any allowed movement might be dangerous.

The wyrm loomed large in the rear-view screen by the time Torliam angled the ship's nose down. I felt a second of strange calm, almost weightlessness, and then we were diving.

My stomach heaved up into my throat and I choked it back down, grinding my teeth together. Things only got worse from there.

Kris screamed, though I wasn't sure if it was out of fear or the same visceral sense of wrongness I felt, knowing that we were plummeting through the air, aided not only by gravity, but by the ship's propulsion.

We flew faster and faster, fast enough that I could see the air bending around the ship as we passed, lighting up with friction as it rubbed over the surface of our great clam. Behind us the wyrm suffered the same, but with less grace. The heat melted its flesh and the more tender part of its wings, and the pressure of the air threw it into a tumble instead of a controlled dive.

At the control console, Torliam laughed.

I felt like my body was about to be squeezed apart, and closed my eyes to keep them from popping out of my head. Wraith spread out within the room, but I didn't even attempt to sense outside the ship.

As we entered the whirlpool and flew up out of the ocean on the other side, the world flipped around me, so hard and so fast I thought I might be ripped apart, cut to pieces by the restraints I hoped would save me. I would have bruises where I'd strapped myself in, across my hips and legs, my forearms, my chest, and my forehead.

Gregor floated past me as the effects of gravity receded at the apex of our ascent, having slipped through his bindings in his Shadow form. It had probably been instinctual and unintentional, a reaction to the deep-seated fear of death.

I opened my eyes, looking out onto a dark sky with two moons.

We shot upward into the sky for a long while, as Torliam let our speed bleed off. Then, he leveled out the ship and guided us out across the ocean.

The wyrm didn't appear through the whirlpool behind us.

"Do you think we escaped it?" Sam said, his bruises and abraded skin healing as if being sped through a time-warp video.

No one answered, as we focused on that screen, the moonlight glinting off the water teasingly.

Then the water frothed, and the creature burst upward out of the whirlpool. It had gotten caught by the water, but even that hadn't been enough to stop it. I suppressed a groan. "This makes things more difficult."

Chapter 8

But the sea, the sea in the darkness calls.
— Henry Vaughan

"MAYBE WE SHOULD EVACUATE the ship, send it on along without us," Zed suggested. "Like we did with Torliam's little ship when we were trying to throw NIX off our trail."

"Can we do that without the wyrm noticing?" Sam said. "Plus, we'd have to get over land first. I can't keep a shipful of people alive if we're going to be swimming through monster-infested water for hours."

"What about getting to Earth?" Gregor said. "I don't have time to get stranded in the middle of the ocean for days. I have the Sickness."

Jacky opened her mouth, closed it, then opened it again. "Maybe this is another one of those things your people don't need," she said, "but humans usually put lifeboats on big ships, in case people have to escape, yeah?"

Torliam was silent, which drew even more attention his way. "Err." He coughed. "It appears that is an idea both our people have had. However, I doubt the wyrm would fail to notice an entire haul of emergency life-ships exiting the hull. It would be placing the civilians in danger, and the likelihood that some of them would die is high." He looked to me, eyebrows slightly raised.

I shook my head. "I don't want the media reporting about any civilian deaths. Anything Queen Mardinest can use against us, she will."

His shoulders relaxed a little. "I do have another idea, though some luck would be involved in the timing. There is a force of warriors that patrol the borders between the abandoned lands and the areas where the remainder of our civilization lives. Their ships are geared for battle, and I believe they may be able to damage the wyrm swiftly enough to kill it. We could also trust them to shepherd this ship and any civilians aboard to safety. The difficulty is merely in finding them before the wyrm catches us."

"No reason not to try it. We can use one of those life-ships to get to an array by ourselves, if we manage. We just have to make sure they don't try and take us back to Queen Mardinest, since she might have requested our capture," I said.

"We are already on our way. I felt no need to waste time when your decision was obvious."

I stared at the back of his head, unsure if he was being intentionally abrasive, till he twisted around and gave me a practiced, charming smile. I turned my back on him, and forced myself to ignore his mutter of, "Yes, that is right, I am too handsome to remain vexed with."

Zed overheard, and almost choked with the effort to suppress his laughter.

We did more planning while Torliam searched for the border patrol, but, to my delight, a group of faraway ships appeared quickly, their dark silhouettes crossing in front of the lower-hanging moon. The ships stilled for a moment, hanging in the air. Then, they shot toward us and the wyrm, much faster than our stolen ship could manage.

"They are the border patrol I spoke of," Torliam said.

"Somehow, that's not as reassuring as I was imagining," Sam said.

Gregor stared at the approaching ships, unblinking. "Don't we need to hurry up and get out of here before they notice us?"

His words sent the rest of us into a flurry of activity. We didn't bother to update any of the passengers, simply hurrying to the nearest life-ship and packing into it like sardines.

The life-ship had two cocoon-like contraptions we assumed were meant to hold the injured, so we put Chanelle in one and Adam in the other. It couldn't hurt, and maybe the cocoons had some sort of advanced Estreyan healing capabilities. The rest of us squeezed in together, with barely enough room for Torliam remaining at the controls.

When Torliam powered up the life-ship it started sending out a distress beacon, and he scrambled to turn it off. Then, the floor opened up beneath us, and the life-ship, mostly made of glass and wire, fell through a dark tunnel.

We steadied after a few seconds, and I looked up at the half-destroyed belly of the larger ship passing by above us.

Then the sky appeared. Our ship held still, floating right above the water, only rising to avoid the occasional wave that rose taller than the rest.

The wyrm passed overhead, pieces of burned and melted flesh still falling off it as it regenerated the damage the fall through the atmosphere and whatever getting stuck in the whirlpool separating the two ocean levels had done to it. Pus-like fluid leaked from the junctions of its earthworm-like segments. Some of its wings had broken and hung limply. Those were slowly reabsorbed into the body even as I watched. Even having lost a great deal of mass, it was a behemoth.

I could hear every sound, from the faint humming of the life-ship to the splashes as burnt worm pieces hit the water. I silently urged the wyrm to pass us over without notice.

When it continued on after the ship, its tail lashing back and forth as it propelled itself at high speeds through the air, we all let out careful sighs of relief.

Torliam turned the little pod of a ship, and we flew the other direction, staying low to the water.

We watched the border patrol as they zoomed past the passenger ship toward the wyrm. I let my claws slip out and my night vision sharpen, but when the ships caught the wyrm, I realized I needn't have bothered. Two of the fighter ships stretched out what looked like a long glowing thread between them. They flitted about the wyrm in circles, dodging like flies when it snapped at them. Once the glowing thread-thing was wrapped all around it, the two ships sped in opposite directions. The thread tightened, then sheared right through the wyrm. It fell in chunks to the ocean, and one of the other ships began targeting one of those chunks. It attacked with a beam that absolutely disintegrated the severed section of the wyrm, which had been sprouting a new mouth even as it fell. None of the other pieces tried to regenerate.

The remaining two patrol ships sped ahead toward the passenger ship.

"We're small enough they couldn't catch us in those ropes," Jacky said.

No one responded, but I'm pretty sure we were all thinking the same thing. They probably wouldn't need the laser ropes to defeat us if they caught us. They could just blast us out of the sky. Were those the type of ships Queen Mardinest had sent to Earth? I knew I would find out soon, since we were heading toward the nearest array at the maximum speed possible.

<hr>

WE STOOD outside the little life-ship, only a mile from the small array.

Adam had reawakened, and, while he was still sluggish, he wasn't pale or shaking any longer. He'd tried to use his Animus Skill again, but I'd ordered him to rest. Instead, he'd ripped apart some of the clear material protecting the wiring of the life-ship, and, with a little help from Blaine, cobbled together a receiver that allowed us to eavesdrop on the unsuspecting guards around the array.

Sam rubbed his jaw. "Are we seriously going to just walk right up to them?"

Jacky grinned, bouncing on the balls of her feet. "Hell yes. Like badasses."

"What if the soldiers attack us?" Gregor said. "It's stupid to think they'll be too star-struck to listen to the queen's orders."

"The soldiers aren't gonna attack," Jacky said. "Right, Eve? We're not *openly* wanted for treason."

I nodded. "According to the chatter, they have orders to escort us immediately to the queen, under heavy guard for our own safety. She hasn't declared us criminals."

"But that doesn't mean they're going to let us use the array," Sam said.

Zed shrugged. "Then we don't give them a choice."

Adam grimaced from atop the tree trunk he was sitting on to conserve his Skill. "Though walking right up to the queen's guardsmen, while currently wanted for treason, is stupid, the biggest problem here is that we don't actually have a real plan to find the god once we get to Earth."

Torliam stretched, reaching toward the sky. His back, which had been stuck in a hunched position for the entirety of our flight away from the passenger ship, cracked multiple times. "I will be able to find him, using the Tracker Skill. What is its purpose, if not that?"

"You don't *know* that," Adam muttered, glaring at Torliam. "Unlike the Skills the rest of us got, I've never even seen this supposed Tracker Skill of yours in action. Forgive me if I'm not optimistic that you can find him. I mean, last time you tried, you had a whole squad of spaceships looking! And you still failed, and got captured by some humans. We're supposed to go there without even the stupid little life-ship, into the middle of an interspecies war?"

"I failed, that is true. But I believe the Champion is on Earth, and if he is, that means we can find him somehow. In the meantime, I will be *useful* to the group, instead of a drain on our already limited resources, as you so aptly pointed out."

There was a beat of silence.

Adam turned white, his fingers digging into the tree bark as if it were a substitute for Torliam's neck.

"Staying on Estreyer isn't an option!" I snapped. "Yes, we're in a shitty situation. So quit whining and start coming up with solutions."

Torliam turned to me, meeting my gaze defiantly.

Adam took a couple deep breaths, and then released his death grip on the rotted wood beneath him.

The group was silent for a moment, awkward.

I took a deep breath, then followed my own advice. "I don't think trying to fight them is a good idea, not unless we could be sure to take them all out instantly, which is unlikely. But what if we make sure they're on our side? We have a common enemy, after all."

Zed grinned. "We give them something bigger to worry about than us."

"And a time limit, counting down so fast they don't have time to think it over," I said, already thinking through how it could work.

———

WE CRASHED through the forest without any heed for silence or secrecy, straight into the clearing surrounding the small array.

"Halt!" cried one of the guards, short-sword already pointed my way.

"Who's the leader here?" I snapped, gasping hard from my run and jumping a little to jostle Chanelle's body higher on my back.

"I am," someone else said, crouched and ready for attack. He kept talking, but I bulldozed right over his words.

"I am Eve-Redding," I said, moving toward him. "This is my team. We need to use the array to get to Earth, and quickly."

He straightened a little, frowning down at me. His eyes flickered over the rest of the bedraggled group trailing behind me.

Torliam didn't even bother to slow, carrying Gregor right to the array and setting him down inside it, despite the guard who moved ineffectually to stop him.

"The queen has given us orders to escort you and your team to her immediately, under guard," the leader said. "She said that your communications have been cut, or blocked. You are in danger, I believe."

"We just spoke to the queen," I said, walking past him and forcing him to turn to continue talking to me. "She must not have had time to send out the update yet. They caught us, and took out our ship and its comms, it's true. Queen Mardinest gave us this location and told us to escape, before it's too late."

"There are no experts in the doorways here," one of the other soldiers said. "You will not be able to use the array."

"That is not a problem," Torliam said. "As long as it is not blocked, I can activate it."

The leader hesitated, looking around at my team again, and then to me. Specifically, at the crystal symbol laid into the skin at the base of my throat. "Eve-Redding, I apologize, but I must verify these orders with the queen. We have direct instruction not to allow *anyone* through the array, and there were no exceptions given."

I let Chanelle down in the circle, where most of the others were already standing. "There's no time!"

He opened his mouth to protest again, reaching forward to grab my arm. "Protocol—"

I spun on him. "The allies of the Sickness are almost *here*!" I leaned in, almost hissing at him in my urgency. My eyes flicked around, as if looking for their forms amongst the darkness of the forest.

His eyes widened, and he looked around, too.

"Soldier," I said, clapping a hand on his shoulder. "I need you and your squad to protect our backs, just long enough for us to escape. No one will fault you for running, after that."

Torliam straightened and called out to me to hurry. "It is almost ready."

That was the cue. I spun and gasped, as a huge rent opened in the fabric of reality, near the edges of the trees. I pointed, then screamed, "There!"

Blackness bubbled out, a roiling mass that fell to the ground like heavy fog and built upon itself, coalescing into a giant, bipedal form as the rip behind it closed.

"Allies of the Sickness!" Kris shrieked. Really, it was just one of Adam's ink constructs exiting the Other Place.

Most of the soldiers, including the leader, attacked the dark form immediately. "Go!" he screamed. "We will hold them off, Eve-Redding! You must not fail!" A couple of the soldiers didn't bother to fight, instead turning and running away into the woods.

I stepped back into the circle of the array, just as another, much smaller rip opened right beside me, spilling Zed and Adam out of it. The plan had worked perfectly.

There was a *crack* of displaced air as someone appeared at the far edge of the clearing. I was spinning toward them, even as Torliam activated the array.

The armored figure lifted a hand. Something shot forward from it.

A wet sound like a watermelon bursting beside me accompanied a warm splatter over my face. I smelled iron. Sparks flew. My heart gave a single, painful thump of horrified denial, and, with a thrum in my bones, we were gone.

Chapter 9

I have harnessed the shadows that stride from world to world to sow death and madness.

— H. P. Lovecraft

WE ARRIVED in daylight on the other side, surrounded by tents, military pods and equipment, and a group of human soldiers that startled momentarily, but quickly trained their weapons on us.

I turned to the side, where the blood had come from, and looked down. Blaine's suit was sparking where whatever had killed him had damaged it, too. Most of his face was gone, and I could see little bits of scrambled gray goo mixed with the bloody remains. Blood pooled like dark syrup on the stone below him.

"Freeze! Get down on your knees and put your hands on your head!" one of the military men yelled.

Kris turned to me, following my gaze down to the ground. She screamed, stumbling a couple steps away from her uncle's corpse.

The soldiers yelled for us to surrender, first in English, and then in badly accented Estreyan, but my teammates' attention was drawn to Kris, and then to Blaine.

Gregor gasped, staring, wide-eyed and still, as if he'd been frozen.

Adam looked up at me. As if I had some answer for him.

I shook my head, silently.

Sam turned green and trembled.

The soldiers shifted nervously. They would attack soon. It was obvious from the tension in their hands and the sweat at their temples. Adam wasn't in any shape to shield us. "Torliam," I murmured, so low that an unaugmented human would never hear me. I lifted my empty hands toward the air in the human motion of surrender. My weapon wasn't so obvious as a gun. Could I take them all out, quickly enough that no more of us were hurt?

Maybe it was my movement that set off the soldier, or maybe they'd just grown impatient.

Torliam stopped the mini rocket with a wall of blue mist. It exploded, fire hot enough to fairly melt the air backlashing toward the soldiers.

There was a beat of silence, and then, beside me, Sam straightened. Darkness crept over his blue irises from the edges of his eyes, till it had taken over. His hands were steady, his breathing even. "Oh. That feels much better." He turned outward, toward the soldiers. "More." His voice lacked its usual awkward hesitation, its nuance, and I knew Black Sun had taken over.

I felt it, with that extra sense I had, when Black Sun grew even more powerful, like a cold miasma around him.

He made eye contact with that first soldier, and his Skill lashed out like a whip.

The soldier shuddered, his face going slack as he sank to his knees.

Sam had already moved on, attacking with his gaze till half our enemies had knelt or dropped their weapons, slow tears running from eyes that stared vacantly into the distance.

I couldn't hear anything but Kris' hysteric sobs.

Sam stepped around Torliam's shield, the brush of his arm against Torliam's making the much larger, more powerful Estreyan jerk back as if he'd been burned. Sam reached for the closest soldier. "Does that *hurt?*" His voice was almost wondering. He touched his hand to the man's neck, and the soldier's skin blackened, dark veins becoming visible as whatever Sam had done spread from that spot.

The man trembled, a whine like an injured animal hissing between his teeth, and then he fell forward, unmoving.

"Die, you alien bastard!" another man screamed, leaning through the window of the transport pod he'd been sitting in, unknown to everyone but me since we arrived. He aimed a gun big enough to worry me toward Sam, but before he could pull the trigger, his head jerked back, a red bloom on his forehead.

Zed lowered his gun and turned to me. "Are there any more, hiding?"

I pointed the last three men out with a mini-map Window, and Jacky and Zed left to deal with them.

Sam seemed completely unconcerned that he came close to being shot. He strolled leisurely to each of the men he'd incapacitated, and killed them. He turned to me, then, and I shuddered as my gaze met his. Whatever that blackness was, it wasn't quite *human*. He smiled, tilting his head a little to the side. "Would you like some apathy? I can give it to you. It might slow you down a little bit, but you won't hurt anymore."

I swallowed. When I spoke, my voice didn't crack. "No, thank you."

SAM SHRUGGED, then turned away.

I resisted the urge to let out a sigh of relief, and pulled up my Command Skill to take a look at his Game information.

PLAYER NAME: SAMUEL HAWES
TITLE: ONE OF NINE
CHARACTERISTIC SKILL: HARBINGER OF DEATH
SKILLS: BLACK SUN

STRENGTH: 19
LIFE: 59
AGILITY: 18
GRACE: 12
INTELLIGENCE: 17
FOCUS: 19
BEAUTY: 18
CHARISMA: 13
MANUAL DEXTERITY: 13
MENTAL ACUITY: 14

RESILIENCE: 96
STAMINA: 28
PERCEPTION: 8

I touched the Black Sun Skill, and the words "Ruination Class" popped up again. Wasn't that the same class as his Harbinger of Death Skill? I touched the other Skill, and found I was right. My Command Skill didn't allow me to access any more detailed Game information about him, and so I dismissed the Windows with a flick of my fingers.

I looked around. The military had known what the arrays were, it seems. Not so surprising, seeing as my team had used them twice, and Earth had been invaded through one. Still, I should have thought of that. If things had gone differently... I looked down to Blaine's body and shuddered. "We need to move. The people on the other side of this array know exactly where we are right now, and might decide to come after us." I walked out of the stone circle and dug my claws into the seam of the nearest fabric tent, slicing until the whole pseudo-wall came down.

Jacky and Zed returned from killing the other soldiers, which had been accompanied by a few gunshot sounds from him and some screams of rage from her. When had it become normal for me to send my brother out to kill? I shook my head to clear it. There would be time to think on things like that later. For now, I had to make sure the rest of us stayed alive.

Kris still hadn't stopped wailing. "His body is empty! Th—there's no soul in it. It's empty!"

Jacky hurried over, wrapping her arms around Kris and pulling the girl away.

I threw the canvas on top of Blaine's body. "Help me," I said to Torliam.

Together, we rolled him up in it, and carried his body to the back of one of the military cargo pods, stashing it inside an empty crate.

Gregor was entirely still, wide-eyed and silent as he stared at the pool of blood on the ground.

I moved to him and scooped him up, holding him close to my chest and tucking his face into the crook of my shoulder. I didn't know what to say, so I rubbed his back in little circular motions, instead. That was supposed to be soothing, right?

I met Jacky's eyes over the top of his head, then jerked my head toward the cargo pod. She clambered in with Kris, who was still crying but seemed to have exhausted herself. I tucked Gregor in next to her, squeezing his clammy hands. "I'll be right back."

Sam was rummaging around in one of the dead soldier's pockets. He stood, holding up a key fob. "I can't heal a dead person, but I can drive." With my approval, he moved to the driver's seat and started up the cargo pod.

"Adam, take a moment to disable the pod's GPS before we go," I said.

The bags under Adam's eyes looked heavy enough to drag his head down, but he nodded to me, ink construct's legs moving sluggishly toward the pod's cab.

The rest of us loaded up the most useful-looking of the military supplies, especially foodstuffs, and then climbed in ourselves. We didn't bother bringing the guns, since they were coded to the soldiers' DNA. It's not like we needed them, anyway.

Sam drove us away from the little clearing, following the shoddy dirt road the military personnel must have created to get to the array. We left their bodies where they'd fallen.

I wished, idly, that they were still alive to guard the array. Maybe they would have slowed down anyone else who tried to come through after us.

Jacky's voice was low. "Who did it?" She had wrapped a big blanket around herself and the kids, and they were huddled into her.

Chanelle looked to me, waiting for my response. Tear tracks streaked her cheeks. How long had she been lucid? I hadn't been paying attention. Sometimes, she faded into the background, so often lost in a fugue that I'd stopped expecting her to be normal, even as she was getting better.

"The person who attacked just popped into existence," I said. "I think Ichi may have teleported them there. Maybe it was even Ichi himself. I couldn't tell."

Torliam rubbed his hand over his face, his beard making scratchy sounds from the friction. "Was he aiming for you?"

I swallowed. Blaine had been right beside me. "He could have been." Or maybe he'd chosen Blaine on purpose, since he wasn't part of the Seal of Nine. I didn't say that out loud, conscious of the children.

"I…am sorry, Eve," Torliam said. He reached over and rubbed a spot of blood off my arm.

Adam let out a bitter laugh. "This is a complete shit-storm."

Self-consciously, I scraped at my face, where more of Blaine's splattered blood had dried. Adam was right. Blaine was the kids' only remaining family, and a huge asset to the team, with the combination of his stunning intellect and monetary resources. I'd considered him a friend. And now that was gone.

I looked over to Zed, who was meticulously cleaning one of his guns.

Blaine had been the only one of us who could make more nutrient paste for Zed's nanites.

There was only one other place to get them. "Sam," I said, raising my voice a little to be sure he'd hear me from the front of the pod. "Set a course for NIX."

I'D EXPECTED SOME SURPRISE, maybe even some disagreement from the others, but didn't get either. I didn't know if that was a product of their trust in me, or due to simple exhaustion. At that moment, I couldn't find it in myself to care.

I fell asleep in the back of the jostling military cargo pod and dreamt uneasily, till the feel of the pod slowing to a stop woke me up.

Sam's eyes were back to normal, but his hands were trembling and he looked almost as pale as Adam had. He stumbled into the back of the pod and laid down, passing out almost immediately. At least he hadn't fallen asleep while driving.

The rest of us piled out of the pod, unloading some dehydrated meals and scarfing them down despite the lack of flavor.

Chanelle sat beside me at the base of a large tree. Her tears for Blaine had dried, and now she kept a tremulous smile on her face.

Birch came over and sniffed at our meals, then flattened his ears in disgust and pranced away into the trees, presumably to catch something more appetizing.

She laughed at the twitch of short little tail, then smiled to herself as she popped the piece of hard candy that had come with one of the meals into her mouth. She offered another to me.

I took it, and thanked her. She looked so much like China, when she smiled. When she wasn't staring into space with empty eyes.

"I like being awake," she said in a soft voice. "Lucid, I mean." She ran her fingers through her shoulder-length hair, wincing at some tangles. "When I'm in the fugues, it's like life just passes me by. I wake up, and things have changed, and even though I struggle to stay aware, I can't, and the world goes on around me. At least it's getting better."

"Soon, it'll be back to normal all the time."

She sucked on her candy. "Maybe. But…even if it isn't, that's okay. I'm glad to be alive, to have this little moment of happiness. I'm not going to let any of these little joys slip away, while I still have the ability to enjoy them."

I frowned. "Chanelle, we *are* going to save you."

She smiled wryly. "I know you'll *try*. And yeah, I want you to succeed. But if you don't, I don't want to look back on any of the moments where I could have been fully alive and realize I wasted them."

I was trying to think of a response when she pointed into the forest and laughed.

Birch sauntered out from between the trees. In his mouth, he held a squirrel, which he proceeded to drop proudly into my lap.

My hand snapped forward and wrapped around its neck before it could move, and I lifted it. "Did you hunt this down for me?" I said.

Birch meowed out a scratchy sound I took for agreement.

Chanelle held her hands over her mouth to stifle her laughter.

The squirrel had a broken hind leg and a few puncture wounds from Birch's teeth, but was mostly intact. It hung from my hand limply, maybe playing dead, since I didn't think its spine was broken, and I could feel its heart beating a staccato against my palm.

My eyes caught on the honeycomb-scaling of my new skin, and I paused, thinking back to my conversation with Adam. Maybe, if I practiced enough, I could help him. I could get something *right* for once. "Thanks," I said. "You're a great hunter, providing for the team like this."

Birch let out a cross between a purr and a yowl, pleased at the praise, and stared at me eagerly.

I raised my eyebrow. Was he waiting to watch me eat it? I closed my eyes, pushing my awareness past the barrier of the squirrel's fur and skin, and into its body. I examined the broken leg carefully, and worked out how it might be fixed in my mind.

Then, I reached inside myself for just a smidgeon of Chaos, and coaxed it out. I turned it into black flames in my hand, imagining the bones of the leg shifting and fusing back together. How had I done it before?

Chaos flared, then rushed into the squirrel, which jerked and writhed against my grip. The black flames consumed and used the fuel to remake, but I could tell immediately something was wrong.

The creature began screaming, a high-pitched, half-choked sound. Its leg bones were fused together, but they were bare of any skin, muscle, or flesh, and they'd grown grotesquely thick in comparison to the rest of the creature's body—half of which was disintegrated—with lumps of bone growing out of its remaining flesh.

Its cries grew weaker, and I hurried to grab it in my hands again, twisting and neatly snapping its neck. Nothing deserved to die under that kind of torture, better to end its misery quickly.

Birch stared at the squirrel with wide eyes, then looked up to me, and then back to the squirrel.

He looked to Chanelle, and she shook her head mutely, as if denying any association to me.

"Err, sorry. I thought maybe I could practice using Chaos to heal its leg." I set the squirrel down. I wasn't sure if it was safe to eat any longer.

Birch backed away, then flattened his ears to his head and trotted away, yowling loudly. He jumped atop Adam's shoulder, digging his claws in and rustling his wings. He touched the side of my team-mate's face with his nose, and Adam's eyes widened as the growing tailos pushed images into his mind.

Adam looked over at me, then at the deformed once-was-a-squirrel lying at my feet. "Seriously, Eve?"

I groaned, tilting my head back. "It was an accident!"

Chanelle burst out laughing, doubled over and pounding her fists on the ground as she struggled to breathe past her mirth.

JACKY TOOK the wheel when we continued on, since Sam was still asleep. Beside her, Adam fiddled with the pod's media controls till he found news of the invasion.

Most of the AM and FM signals were looping the same automated message.

"The following message is transmitted at the request of the Department of Defense. At approximately 2:14 a.m. Eastern Time, numerous unidentified objects were detected in the skies over Antarctica, traveling north. These objects are presumed to be a form of controlled aircraft and have shown themselves to have hostile intent. Citizens are encouraged to monitor local media outlets, as more updates will follow as information becomes available. Please review your local emergency action plans and shelter locations, and stay inside your homes if possible. In the event evacuation of an area is necessary, you will be informed immediately. Please adhere to the orders of your local enforcers."

Adam nodded. "On Earth, it's only been a little over half a day since they arrived. I wonder if any of the other media outlets have updated information." The pod had access to some basic satellite broadcasts. Although Adam figured out how to access the satellite news channels, the only thing we could find was rampant—and sometimes panicked—speculation, and endless repetitions of what we already knew. A couple military planes had been shot down in Antarctica, but beyond that, no new intelligence.

I turned to ask Torliam if he knew anything about his mother's preferred style of invasion, what targets the Estreyans would go after first, and their policy on civilians and surrender, but he was asleep. The skin over his cheekbones seemed drawn, and he had deep shadows under his eyes, so I left him be. He needed rest, too.

Gregor and Kris had curled up in the corner in a pile of blankets. Her cheeks were wet with tears. Maybe that was a good thing. Gregor hadn't cried, and had barely spoken since earlier that morning. I didn't know what the normal response to seeing your uncle and guardian gruesomely murdered was, but I knew it would have damaged something important inside them. Their lives had changed, irrevocably.

My eyes burned, and I blinked to keep myself from crying. The world was a cruel place. NIX had power, and they used it to create Players and the Game. Queen Mardinest had power, and... I shook my head, swallowing hard. She hadn't needed to kill Blaine. She hadn't needed to do any of it. Could nothing good last, nothing pure and joyful flourish?

Forum Page 1

Welcome to the Earth Defense Force message boards.

You are currently logged in.

You are viewing thread: "Alien Invasion—This is not a Hoax!"

ORIGINAL POSTER "ANTIGONE" SAYS:

People, it's on the news, it's been acknowledged by the EDF, and we've got video documentation. This is real. Aliens have invaded Earth, and they are hostile. You can watch the videos _here_, and _here_. I'll add more as I'm made aware of them.

For those of us who've been saying the aliens were out there all along, we've finally got proof. Personally, I wish I'd been wrong. You can see an image of one of their ships _here_. If not for the windows cut into the side, it looks like a spiky stingray. It seems like the aliens are an aquatic species of some sort, judging by the construction of their ships.

We don't know what they want, and they seem to be ignoring attempts at communication. They've already shot down two human ships, but so far, I don't think we even know if they understand that we're trying to talk to them. I can only hope that there can be some peaceful resolution among our two races, because even if they are fish people, they're obviously more advanced than we are and highly dangerous.

Stay safe, people, and update this thread with more information as you receive it. I'll add any relevant information to the original post.

POSTER "SCI-FI JACK" SAYS:

I bet they're here to annex our oceans. Earth is over 70% water. It probably looks like a paradise to them.

POSTER "POOP HAPPENS" SAYS:

We'll blow those fish-freaks out of the sky. I've never much liked sushi, but I think I could grow a hankering for it if they don't realize what's good for them and go back where they came from.

POSTER "ALIEN77" SAYS:

You're just another one of the sheep, Antigone. They're not aliens. If you look past the surface lies, you'll find out that they didn't come from outer space at all. They've been here all along, in our oceans, probably somewhere in the Mariana Trench. The government has been lying to us all along.

POSTER "SCARED-IN-NEVADA" SAYS:

Why do you think they're attacking?

POSTER "ALIEN77" SAYS:

Scared-In-Nevada, obviously, they're attacking because we've been polluting and poisoning the oceans. They're fed up and they're going to wipe us out like the infestation of the Earth that humanity is.

POSTER "NOT-A-CONSPIRACY-THEORIST" SAYS:

Hahahahaha! Finally, I can say I told you so. I've been saying it all along, and everyone just kept saying I was crazy. The aliens are watching us. They're here! I was taken up in one of their ships back in '89, and they told me they'd be back once the microwave radiation in the atmosphere got heavy enough to support their needs. Now they're here, and they've brought their friends.

POSTER "PEPPER-POPPER" SAYS:

Oh my god. Is this real? I can't even think straight. Please, tell me this is some elaborate hoax.

POSTER "ENFORCER DAWSON" SAYS:

Not-A-Conspiracy-Theorist, didn't you tell people they sucked you up in a flying saucer and took you to their home planet, which is Mars? Kinda strange, seeing as someone probably would have noticed a whole race of people flying around inside ships shaped like giant sea creatures on a planet you can literally see through a telescope.

As for the real news, holy shit. I didn't realize those were ships at first. I thought we were being invaded by giant flying monsters.

They're calling us all in, and we've been approved to work unlimited overtime. If the world doesn't end, I'm finally going to have the money to take my wife on that vacation to the Bahamas.

I would advise people to stay in their homes if at all possible. There's going to be looters, and it might not be safe on the streets depending on where you live. If things get back, we will be opening up the emergency shelters for affected areas.

Having said that, please don't panic. We don't know

what's going to happen yet. We could still resolve this smoothly.

POSTER "POOP HAPPENS" SAYS:

Enforcer Dawson, there's no way we'll be resolving this peacefully. We're people. They're fish. They attacked us already.

Chapter 10

A shadow leaned over me, whispering, in the darkness,
   Thoughts without sound;
   Sorrowful thoughts that filled me with helpless wonder
   And held me bound.
— Alfred Noyes

I WOKE up curled into a fetal position on a stone floor. I instinctually reached for my claws, and the protection the natural weapon provided me. But nothing came. I flexed my fingers, then had to clench my jaw to stop myself from screaming at the pain the movement brought.

Startled insects scurried away into the corners and cracks of the stone walls.

I lifted my left arm slowly, staring in horror. A manacle surrounded my wrist, a chain connecting it to the wall. But the real problem, the cause of my pain, were the razor-like segments jutted from the inside of the manacle at regular intervals, slicing deep into my flesh. If I moved too much, or tugged too violently, I would probably end up freeing myself, at the expense of tearing off my own hands.

My stomach clenched, and I swallowed back bile. I stared at the torturous bindings. Thin-looking blood, as if maybe it had been diluted with saline, seeped out around the razor segments, dripping down my arm and onto the floor. At least I could still *feel* my hands, which meant I might be able to use them again with some help from Sam. That's when I realized there were only five fingers, and they were shorter, almost stubby compared to the modifications Chaos had made to me. I frowned. The skin of my arm was smooth and pale, not scaled. My chest felt tight. Was I dreaming? I'd never felt pain like this in a dream.

I looked around at the stone room I'd awoken in. There was no door, and the single small window was barred over to prevent escape. The dim light of the lone bulb in the cell showed dark brown words smeared onto the stones all around me, as if someone had been writing with their own blood. It said things like, "In the sea of change, even time and place are lost," "The flames of the abyss give no light, only darkness visible," and, "Where once was flesh, stone bloomed instead." They'd also drawn a bunch of watching eyes. It was creepy, to say the least.

I reached for the Wraith Skill, but found nothing.

I almost let out a whimper, but I choked it back. I looked around with my eyes instead. Seeing nothing else of note, I scrambled backward, pressing my back against the wall. Had I been drugged, maybe? It would have made sense, except for the reversion of all the changes my body had made after getting Seeds. Nothing anyone could have done to me should have taken away the new structure of my rebuilt hand and arm. Unless they'd used some exotic Skill?

I didn't bother to try Tumbling Feather. I could feel the lack of Grace, the leaden feeling in my feet that meant I could no longer flip and twist through the air like an elven dancer. I would have tried to consciously activate Voice, but I didn't want to draw attention to myself with the noise, and the symbol was no longer melded with the skin of my throat.

I tried to send a Window to the rest of the team.

UNABLE TO CONTACT SUBORDINATE VIRTUAL REALITY CHIPS.

I'd seen that message once before, when NIX had captured me and jailed me in that cell cut deep into the mountain. But there was no buzzing in the air, no indication of a signal scrambler like there had been that time.

I switched to the Attribute Window. Maybe there would be some sort of clue to why I couldn't access any of my Skills. The VR chip had been smart enough to update spontaneously before, especially since the Oracle had taken over from NIX.

PLAYER NAME: EVE REDDING
TITLE: BEARER OF TESTIMONY
CHARACTERISTIC SKILL: ~~SPIRIT OF THE HUNTRESS~~,
~~TUMBLING FEATHER~~
LEVEL: 38
SKILLS: ~~COMMAND~~, ~~WRAITH~~, CHAOS, ~~VOICE~~

STRENGTH: ~~23~~
LIFE: ~~76~~
AGILITY: ~~33~~
GRACE: ~~28~~
INTELLIGENCE: ~~32~~
FOCUS: ~~24~~
BEAUTY: ~~16~~
CHARISMA: ~~33~~
MANUAL DEXTERITY: ~~10~~
MENTAL ACUITY: ~~29~~
RESILIENCE: ~~70~~
STAMINA: ~~36~~
PERCEPTION: ~~33~~

The strike-through slashing most of my Skills and my Attribute levels confirmed something was wrong, but the fact that Chaos was still normal gave me hope. I reached for the Skill tentatively, just enough to feel if something was there. Whatever Perception boost I'd had that allowed me an awareness of myself on a meditative level was gone. But even so, I could feel the barest wisp of Chaos moving through my blood. I grasped at it, and it dissolved away from me like mist through open fingers. I tried again, this time pulling a little harder, and it came, spilling out of the cuts around my wrists along with my blood, as if the wounds were a tap, though the tendrils came out thin and wispy instead of their normal dark haze.

I let out a shaky breath. At least I wasn't completely helpless. But if I was going to escape, or be able to fight back against whatever had put me here, I would need my hands. Even if my claws *were* inaccessible.

I moved my fingers just a little, to help judge exactly how deep the razors went. I hissed at the renewed spike of pain. They were deep, and I wasn't sure, but I thought from the sensation that the tips of them might have been hooked, to make removal impossible without mutilation.

My breath started to come fast, and the room spun around me, so I tucked my head between my knees and focused on finding a *solution*. I had used Chaos once before to heal, through burning away the old and creating anew in its place, in the valley of the God of Knowledge. But while I still technically understood how to use the black flames, the fine control the initial rush of comprehension had given me was gone now, along with a lot of other things I'd understood at the time, but which had buried themselves away. I really didn't want to end up like the squirrel I'd tried to heal. Even so, if my hands were ruined either way, it couldn't hurt to try.

I would practice first, though.

I reached for Chaos again and it filtered out around the razors, flowing up to the outer manacle. I urged Chaos till it took on the characteristics of the black flame, and it ate away at the metal. "Flesh," I murmured to it, focusing hard on the image of the end product in my mind, the suppleness, the feel, the organic nature of what I needed it to become.

The flames devoured the metal and slowly receded, leaving a chunky ring of shimmery, pale skin behind. It detached from the razors and slid off onto the ground with a dull plop. My wrist was still impaled, but lighter without the weight of the surrounding manacle.

I poked at the ring of pseudo-flesh lying in front of me, careful not to hurt myself again with the movement. It was too stiff, and that metallic sheen definitely wasn't normal.

I tried again with the other hand, concentrating harder as I mentally went through every property of my skin that I could think of. The flesh-manacle slid off, this time glistening red in the places it had been attached to the razors. It was even *warm*. It was still too stiff, and off-color, but it would work.

This time, when Chaos filtered up through my wounds, I set it onto one of the embedded razors. Where it touched me, it hurt, and I jerked, biting down on my tongue to muffle a scream. I gathered myself and concentrated with everything I had, pushing at the boundaries where my flesh gave way to metal, trying to connect them. There was an instant where Chaos had burned and eaten away what had been there before, and I was able to reverse the destruction.

I changed the shape of the metal and my flesh both, connecting the foreign substance to my muscle and bones and skin. I smoothed away the part protruding out of me and created paths through the part inside me, connected to my veins to allow blood to flow. I tried to make it malleable, like flesh would be, but succeeded only in making it softer. It didn't have connecting tendons, wouldn't contract in bunches like my muscles, and wouldn't stretch like the flesh surrounding it.

It was quite a poor job, in fact. But it sealed off the wound, and left me with something I'd be able to move a little. After a minute of recovery, I examined the shimmery slivers on the back of my wrist, the only outward sign of what I'd done. "It'll be good enough for now."

I repeated the process for each of the remaining barbs jutting out of me, and, though Chaos weakened till its tendrils were almost transparent, I improved with practice. My fingers wouldn't do delicate work, and some sensation was dulled, but I could grasp things and attack with my fists without worrying my hand would fall off.

I stood gingerly and moved to the window, looking out through the barred opening.

A row of dim yellow bulbs lit the hall beyond, which stretched out a couple hundred feet before turning a corner. I listened for signs of anyone else. Were my teammates trapped in the surrounding cells? Was it safe for me to call out to them, to try and find out?

I could probably use Chaos to eat through the walls of this doorless cell, but, in my current state, it would exhaust me. If I needed to break multiple people out, my plan would need some more thought.

One of the bulbs at the end of the hall burst with a strange sound.

I jumped and, as I caught a glimpse of a form stepping around the corner, threw myself back from the little window.

I scrambled back to other the side of the room, keeping low to avoid being seen through the window, and curled up around the chains that had once been attached to my wrists. Maybe they wouldn't notice I'd freed myself.

I listened as the person approached, the light from the hallway dimming steadily, each time accompanied by a sharp crack and then a tinkle and splash. I pushed outward again instinctively, trying to activate Wraith. It didn't work. It grew warmer, though I couldn't tell if that was just my body heating up from the strength of my pounding heart pushing blood through my veins, or if the temperature was really increasing. I kept my eyes almost closed, watching the door out of a slit between my eyelids.

The last bit of light outside the room disappeared with that strange wet sound of breaking glass. The figure stopped in front of my cell, looking through at me. Dark hair, pale blue eyes, and a smirk.

Something inside me squeezed, shriveling in on itself with dread I couldn't quite comprehend. But I felt it. I began to whimper, despite my resolution to pretend to be unconscious. I couldn't control it.

I saw the shift of their shoulder as they lifted their arm, and I watched as a familiar dark power ate through the stone, following their hand as they drew a large doorway around the window. Black flames left behind sturdy hinges, and then, a door handle.

They pushed at the stone, and it swung open easily, revealing the silhouette standing in the darkened hallway. The figure stepped through the doorway and smiled down at me. I recognized it. How could I not? It wore my face, moved in my body. My familiar claws extended from its fingers, its left arm sported the honeycomb scale Chaos had rebuilt, and it was taller than any human female had a right to be. There was nothing off about it, nothing to say that something *else* was wearing my skin. That dark look in its eyes was all mine, that smirk was the one I wore, and that strange emptiness…

It chuckled with my voice. "Hello."

My voice cracked as I screamed. I clamped my hands over my mouth to try and hold back the involuntary reaction, my head shaking back and forth in desperate denial.

"I left some hints for you. Were they helpful?" She waved a hand towards the words written in blood, but before I turned my head to look at them again, Chaos burst forth, rushing toward me with familiar glee.

I brought my arms up, crossing them in front of my face and drawing my knees to my chest. My answering surge of Chaos butted up against the barrier of my skin, as if trapped inside.

But her attack didn't burrow into me and unmake me like I'd expected. It flowed around and underneath my body, seeping into the floor.

For half a moment, everything was still, and my eyes caught her gaze again.

"You're a slow learner," she said. "You'll come to hate that about yourself. I know I have."

Then dark blood bubbled out from the floor around me, warm and thick and rich.

The single remaining lightbulb in the ceiling above grew a drop of red inside it, and then welled with blood, dripping down the inside of the glass and filling up, till the bulb popped. The shards fell down, cushioned by the blood that gushed down with them and the softness of the floor. Impenetrable darkness pressed in around me.

I lurched upward, but my hands and feet sank into pulsing flesh. I screamed again.

The mass below me surged, and I sank, as if it had swallowed half my body in one massive convulsion.

I bit into my tongue, letting my blood flow out and Chaos with it, desperately trying to change the floor back into stone.

The other Eve sighed. "It will take more than that. Someone so useless doesn't deserve this power." The floor gulped me under.

Coppery, salty, hot blood poured into my nose and mouth, and the flesh squeezed at me, crushing and suffocating.

I struggled till I could struggle no more.

Chapter 11

Even after nights
    that lasted far too long,
    Morning presses on
    with new hopes, new songs.
    — Morgan Harper-Nichols

I SHOT UPWARD with a panicked gasp, my claws lashing out at the person holding onto my shoulders.

Torliam closed his eyes and turned his head away as my claws scratched the dark armor over his chest, but he didn't release me.

I reached desperately for Wraith, and it exploded out of me, checking for danger. It found none, only the military cargo pod, with everyone seemingly asleep but myself, Torliam, and Jacky, who was driving.

No stone cell walls, no torture devices or cryptic messages written in blood, and no horrific alternate version of me.

My pounding heart slowed, and I calmed. The stress of my panic and the subsequent relief made me weak. I slumped forward till my forehead hit Torliam's chest.

"You were having a nightmare," he said, his voice low enough not to wake the others. "I could feel it, and sense your panic, as if you were reaching out to me as you once did. I tried to wake you, but you were not responsive, though your terror only *grew*."

"It was a dream?" That was obvious now, but I still needed the reassurance. It had seemed so real.

"It was merely a dream. Yet it must have been impactful, for you to react strongly enough to reach out to me past the *warrior's-technique* that guards your mind." He'd slipped an Estreyan word into the English, and though I understood the word, I didn't know what he meant.

"The what? *Warrior's-technique?*" I pulled back to look up at him and caught Jacky's gaze in the rearview mirror. Chagrined, I settled back against the wall of the pod.

Torliam sat beside me, close enough I could feel the heat from his body. "It is a shield of the spirit that protects your mind from outside influence, like *skin-jackers*, or, to some degree, those Skills that might control your thoughts. Did you not know of this? You placed it around your mind while I was still trapped by NIX, in the long stretch of time where we were on different sides of the break between worlds. When you attacked them for the second time, it was there, blocking some of the *blood-covenant-bond*." His voice got even lower at the end, as if he were embarrassed to speak the words.

I frowned. "That doesn't make sense. We were on Estreyer during that time, and I got the Seed of Chaos, but—oh. Adam helped me make this mental construct thing to help control Chaos. I built this mansion-like house, and then…I put a wall with no gate all the way around."

Torliam huffed out sharply through his nose. "Of course. *Adam.*" He looked away, then back to me, staring silently.

I felt a brief moment of jealousy for the thickness of Torliam's eyelashes, as my mind struggled to settle back into normalcy. "What is it?" I whispered.

"I had thought you chose to ignore some of the other aspects of the bond. Truthfully, I do not mind. Sharing so much can be…intimate. However, if you do not even know how to reach out to me if danger makes it necessary, I cannot fulfill my duty as your *blood-covenant-champion*."

My eyes narrowed. "What other aspects of the bond? And what exactly are these 'duties?'"

He grimaced. "It is my duty as your champion to serve and protect you, in the simplest of terms."

"To *serve* and protect?"

His jaw clenched. "Do not expect me to bow and scrape at your feet, a slave to your every whim. I may be bound to you in *blood-covenant,* but my will is my own, tradition be damned."

I shook my head quickly. "That's not what I meant. I was just under the impression that we had some sort of 'allies-forever' type of pact, like…blood-brothers, or something."

He let out a sharp burst of air and pressed his lips together to conceal a smile. "You think of yourself as my *brother?*" His smile grew even wider as he saw my growing scowl, and he began talking again quickly. "As for the other aspects of the bond, they are varied, but you have taken advantage of them before. We have touched minds several times, before we met. Once, I fueled you with anger when you were falling to despair. We will always be able to find each other, or know where the other is in relation to ourselves. We share a portion of our *blood-borne* strength with each other. I am aware when you project a piece of yourself outward and send it to me. I believe you call this your Wraith Skill?"

I nodded slowly. "That makes sense. I recognized you, when I saw you for the first time, even though we'd never met. I didn't know what I was doing with the mental wall. Should I…take it down?" The idea of opening my mind up wasn't exactly pleasant, but I'd found the connection useful before.

He shifted, then looked away. "If you wish." It was obvious the suggestion made him uncomfortable, too. "Without it, our bond would connect us more freely, but if you prefer to maintain your shield, it does not mean the bond is completely severed. It simply requires more effort to breach, just as you did when you called for my help in your sleep."

I shifted my feet, and noticed a drop of fresh blood on the floor. Had I managed to nick Torliam in my panic?

Before I could ask him, the pod slowed to a bumpy stop, and we both looked toward the cab.

"We're here," Jacky said, her fingers gripping tight around the steering wheel as she stared out the front window. "Looks like someone got here before us, yeah?"

Stretching out before us was miles of smoking ruin and devastation.

———

THE TEAM LEFT the pod and walked on foot through the splintered remains of the forest around NIX.

Trees bigger around than the span of my arms lay in splinters. Smoking craters dotted the land. There had been multiple fires, though instead of turning into a raging inferno they seemed to have died out, or perhaps been *put* out.

Some of the ruined areas still held residue from whatever had created them. One crater chattered and buzzed with electricity, while another area deformed the passing light like a fun-house mirror. We avoided those.

We clambered past a downed military plane. I used Wraith to check for signs of life within, but found none.

One particularly gigantic crater in what had been the backside of NIX's mountain held the remains of an Estreyan ship, impaled by a giant metal rod that had collapsed and twisted around its target. Dust was *still* falling through the air. I frowned, and then followed Adam's gaze into the sky.

"They dropped that from orbit," he said.

Ah. "They've been preparing for this for a long time. I knew that, but…" I shook my head, looking around at the devastation surrounding us.

Torliam touched his hand to my elbow. "Are there any alive?"

We had to get a bit closer for me to tell, but the search was fruitless.

Torliam nodded when I told him, his jaw clenched. Perhaps the sight of the ship brought back memories of his own initial visit to Earth.

We came across the remains of quite a few more human planes and vehicles, a couple more downed Estreyan ships, many signs of Skill use, and widespread general destruction, but when we crested the last mountain ridge and looked down upon it in the evening sunlight, we were still shocked into silence.

Wispy tentacles of smoke writhed out from the wreckage like a living thing. A few pieces of equipment remained—a crushed ball of metal that had probably been a heli-pod at some point, some rubble that looked like collapsed tunnels leading away from the bowels of the compound. But mostly, where NIX had been was just a jagged scar in the side of the mountain. It reminded me of a large anthill that someone had taken a boot to.

Some of the inner border of what had once been the circular base remained—rooms and hallways torn open all the way down the mountainside, bared to the air. The rest of it was either burned away or lying in and across the river at the bottom of the mountain, creating a dam that forced the water to well up and spill over.

I looked around for the remains of the Shortcut, but didn't see it. Perhaps they'd had some plan in place, ready for the Estreyans to attack, and NIX had somehow managed to evacuate it. Or perhaps it was part of the thousands of tons of material that had been seemingly *vaporized*.

"What did they hit it with, a space laser?" Zed said. Everything was burnt, even the parts now covered with water.

"They were burning out the chance of further infection," Torliam said. "It is believed that strong fires can mitigate the further spread of the Sickness."

"But that isn't true, right?" Sam said, looking between Torliam and me.

Torliam let out a humorless laugh, short and sharp. "No one actually knows. It might work, it might not. We still do not understand the Sickness. Even Ifkana of the Panacean could only suss it out once it had physically affected the host. It may sit dormant for years, even decades, before symptoms begin. We *do not know*."

Zed turned to me. "Well, I'm guessing there's no way we're going to find any nanite paste left in there."

"Or any ships still capable of flying," Adam said.

"Or anyone who can reach out to the Estreyan ships, to ask them to stop all this so we can *talk*," Sam said. "We could have been in there, you know. There were plenty of Players, just like us, forced to play the Game and join NIX. People who were just trying to stay alive. They didn't deserve this."

"Ironically," Adam said. "NIX pretty much caused the very thing they were worried about. If they hadn't captured mister big-shot here," he gestured to Torliam, "and didn't start developing weapons to fight against the aliens, the aliens never would have attacked."

I closed my eyes and stretched out my awareness. Maybe there was some equipment that could be salvaged, or even someone still alive in there. Before Wraith even reached NIX, movement in the woods drew my attention. I turned my head to face that direction. "Someone's out here. A Player, I think. They're still alive."

I HURRIED TOWARD THEM, and the others followed. "They're pretty hurt," I said.

My words were confirmed when we drew near enough to see the Player. He was stumbling forward senselessly, badly burnt, with large swaths of his uniform melted into his blistered skin. "Hey, do you need help?" I called.

He didn't turn, almost as if he hadn't even heard me.

"Either he's in shock, or maybe his eardrums are burst," Sam said. "Maybe we can draw his attention visibly." He began to circle around, moving to get ahead of the wounded boy.

"Be careful," I said, walking with him. "He might attack out of fear, not realizing you're trying to help him. Whatever happened to him, I'm surprised he's still breathing, let alone conscious."

The Player turned his head a little toward us. His left eye was milky and bubbled, like an egg that had been fried in oil. The other eye was still intact, but whatever intelligence or comprehension he'd once had was absent from it. He opened his mouth, and saliva spilled out of it like a tiny waterfall.

My heart jumped.

He lunged forward clumsily, spluttering on his own indrawn breath.

I jerked back, tripped on a branch, and fell backward. I caught myself on one arm and spun away.

The infected Player lunged forward again, lips drawing back from his teeth in a feral grin. When Chanelle had been bitten in my first Trial, I'd seen that same look of mindless, inhuman hunger. "He's a wolf!" I called out.

He lunged at me once more, and I didn't even think, I just reacted.

I lashed out with my clawed left hand, all six digits ripping into his neck like it was play dough, tearing right through to the other side.

Blood fountained out toward me, and I instinctively closed my eyes as it sprayed my face, but a couple drops touched my tongue.

The boy dropped in front of me, throat hanging open.

I stumbled a couple steps away, shaking little bits of meat off my fingers and spitting frantically, my eyes still squeezed as tight as they would go. I fumbled at the water pouch by my waist, opening the cap and pouring the contents straight onto my face to remove the blood. "Meningolycanosis," I sputtered out, still spitting, making sure that I didn't swallow even once, just in case. "The blood could be infectious."

Torliam had already been moving my way, and without hesitation, he backhanded the air, a rush of misty blue power slamming me in the face and stripping away everything foreign, even bits of my skin.

I didn't care. I opened my mouth, pushing my tongue out, and he did it again.

The dryness was so extreme it hurt, and I was sure the skin of my mouth would crack and split. I could already feel beads of blood welling from my face.

Torliam poured his own water straight into my face, and I leaned into it, gasping with relief.

After a few moments, I dared to open my eyes.

THE OTHERS HAD SPREAD out in a defensive formation around me. Zed's guns were both trained on the body as he nudged it to make sure it wouldn't get up again, and Jacky's hair was floating around her face as she lightened her personal gravity in preparation for sudden movement. Sam's hands pressed onto my forehead, checking me for injury.

After a quick check with Wraith, I relaxed, swallowing gingerly a few times before I could speak. "There's no one else, and he's very dead."

Gregor walked past me and yanked one of his daggers out of a tree. He must have thrown it to try and stop the Player, but missed.

Zed scowled fiercely. "Are you okay?"

I moved over to the body, thinking of Blaine and what he'd said about the meningolycanosis. "I'm fine." I looked around, and almost jumped at the sight of another little body made of bugs and small animal bones.

It wouldn't even reach my knee when standing straight, but was crouched beside Kris protectively, head swiveling back and forth like it was watching for danger.

Kris noticed the direction of my gaze. "It won't hold together very long. If I concentrate hard enough, things that were once alive can hold a spirit again, but it's pretty weak, still, because the body isn't... real. Bugs and decayed squirrel pieces weren't meant to be in that shape, so my Skill is kind of forcefully holding them together."

Gregor walked back to stand beside me, staring down at the corpse at our feet. "Did he have the Sickness, too?" He looked up at me.

I'd been wondering the same thing. "I don't know. We can find out, but I think you and your sister should walk away a little, so you don't have to watch."

His bushy eyebrows drew down. "I can handle it."

He was eight. He shouldn't be able to handle it. "You don't need to be here, and there's no reason for us to provide you with any more nightmare fuel if we can help it."

Kris didn't have any objections and went willingly when Jacky took both kids' hands and settled down with them behind a big tree trunk about thirty meters away.

I pushed my awareness at the corpse, trying to work past its skin and into its body without touching it. "Adam, could you make me a couple knives?" He did, and I leaned over the Player, pausing for a moment to realize that I was about to dissect someone I'd killed. It's funny, the things that can become normal.

With Adam's help, I cut into the chest, breaking the sternum and peeling open the ribcage like some sort of grotesque flower.

Birch watched what we were doing with interest, and had to be shooed back a couple times when his curiosity brought him too close.

Wraith found no sign of Seeds, either their glow of power or their actual, microscopic bodies. "Looks like the meningolycanosis wiped out the Seeds. He must have had the same upgraded version Chanelle got." The same one we'd given the God of Knowledge to weaken him.

The rest of the dead boy's issues were obvious to the naked eye. Black veins ran through his flesh, spreading out from his heart.

Adam poked at the Player's lungs with a stick, and when he pulled back, they stretched out like freshly chewed gum. Pretty sure that wasn't normal for a still-cooling body. The tissue must have been decaying already, before death.

Torliam shuddered and looked away. "Do all humans defile each other's bodies upon death?"

Sam patted his arm. "I know, it's…unpleasant. But autopsies have contributed a lot to the human understanding of medicine."

After a moment to brace myself, I nudged the other organs away from the boy's stomach, then sliced into it. Finger bones spilled out, surrounded by a pink fleshy sludge. He had already begun eating someone. "The 'wolves' don't eat people," I said. "They just bite to spread the infection."

I stood and moved away from the body, dropping the ink knives Adam had created for me on the ground. "This isn't *conclusive* proof, but I think Blaine was right. The meningolycanosis is a vector for the Sickness. We're going to have to find a way to contact NIX's remaining branches."

CHANELLE'S NOSTRILS FLARED, as her eyes lost their wide vacant stare, narrowing as she focused on the remains. "Is that a dead body?"

We looked from it, to her. What was I supposed to say? Obviously, it *was* a dead body. Which we had cracked open like a nut and poked around inside. "Err…"

Sam shuffled sideways in front of the Player, as if hoping to block it off from her. "It escaped from NIX," he announced. "Which the Estreyans completely obliterated, by the way. It was infected with meningolycanosis, and it attacked Eve. It was completely rabid, even though its body was so injured already. She killed it."

"I noticed," Chanelle said dryly, staring at the Player's ravaged throat expressionlessly. "But it was a 'he,' not an 'it,' right? He was infected, so you just killed him?"

Sam's face scrunched into a cringe of guilt.

"She had to kill him," Adam said. "There's no way we could have taken him with us alive, and we don't even have any of the anti-meningolycanosis serum, which wouldn't have left him able to fend for himself, even if he wasn't rabid anymore."

"I guess I'm just lucky you didn't do the same to me," she spat. "But I'm not surprised. I remember when I was first infected, Eve. I was going to eat you alive." She almost grinned as she said the words. "And you were so terrified, scrabbling like a soft little pig as you tried to get away." The smile withered and disappeared, along with the lucidity in her eyes.

Sam put his hand on her arm and helped move her back onto the cot. "She's back in the fugue state, I think," he said, shooting me a look of dismay.

"She was probably just upset to see what could have happened to her," Zed said. "I mean, the body is pretty gruesome. If we hadn't rescued her from NIX… And, maybe not all that anger was natural."

I grimaced. Chanelle had the Sickness. It wasn't the same as the meningolycanosis, but we all knew that she'd lose herself just as surely as the corpse on the ground had, if we couldn't find the cure in time.

The quest Window popped up in front of my face, bright and completely incongruous with the ravaged earth around us.

WESTWARD BOUND
TRAVEL WEST AT TOP SPEED, MAINTAINING TREE
COVER FOR CONCEALMENT.
COMPLETION REWARD: ESCAPE IMMOLATION
NON-COMPLETION PENALTY: IMMOLATION, DEATH

I blinked. Then, I swiped the Window away and rushed over to the place where Jacky had stopped with the kids. "Just got a quest. Escape to the west with the trees as cover. Something's coming. Something that will burn us to death."

I crouched down, and Gregor slipped in between my backpack and my back so I could carry him. We all ran like deer for the next few minutes, being sure to follow what tree cover remained. I didn't trust the Oracle completely, or really much at all, but there was no way I would ignore the threat of *immolation*.

The Estreyan ships arrived behind us, flying in at top speed to hover above the shattered NIX compound. One was larger, like a huge stingray floating in the air. It was surrounded by ships that looked more like sharp-angled lobsters without the legs.

"Keep running!" I huffed, using Wraith to keep watch behind us.

Fire poured down from the stingray-like ship's belly. Our shadows stretched out in front of us from the harsh light, and even so far away I felt the heat on the back of my legs. The shockwave hit next, a storm of howling air and heat that blew outward from the impact with the force of a bomb. Below the attacking ship, the remains of NIX melted, vaporizing away or melting into slag.

Once NIX was nothing more than a bed of molten Earth, the ship took its plasma beam outward onto the surrounding battlefield, leaving nothing untouched as it scoured away every trace of the enemy in an ever-expanding circle.

We just kept running.

———

Chapter 12

———

Then leaf subsides to leaf.
   So Eden sank to grief,
   So dawn goes down to day.
   Nothing gold can stay.
— Robert Frost

AFTER A GRUELING AMOUNT OF RUNNING, the Oracle's quest announced it was completed, and we slowed, turning to head toward Blaine's house, our old base. I'd wanted to bring his body with us, maybe bury it and give the kids a funeral. But there was no way anything had survived the Estreyan ship's thermal attack. I could only be grateful the Oracle had kept the rest of the team alive. If we'd been in the military cargo pod when the attack started, I had no doubt they would have made extra sure we burned beyond crispy.

We'd traveled a good distance, and were setting up the simplest of camps as the sun went down. The need to stop was mainly for Adam's benefit, because he refused to be carried, and his Animus Skill was at its limit after a few hours of continuously renewing his leg construct.

Torliam had offered to pull him on a floating sled made of his own power several times. Adam's refusals grew increasingly clipped.

As I was settling in to try to play with Chaos again, the events of my nightmare rising up to the surface of my mind, Kris shuffled over to me.

"They burned him up, didn't they?" she said, her voice small.

I patted the ground next to me, an encouragement for her to sit down. "They did," I said. "But we can still hold a funeral for him when we get back to his house. I don't think he'd be the type to be too sentimental about exactly what was done with…his body." I held back a grimace, hoping that didn't seem insensitive of me.

To my relief, she let out a tiny snort that might have been taken for a laugh. "He told my mom, 'Donate my body to science!' but she said if he died she'd get revenge by burying him in the backyard." She sat down facing me, her legs crossed. "Of course, she ended up dying first."

I could tell she was leading up to something from the way she pressed her fingers together and kept shooting glances at me then looking away. "What is it?"

"Do you think… Do you think his spirit is still on the other side? On Estreyer, I mean? I could feel that it was gone, when we got here, but did it just disappear? I can feel the spirits all around us. Most of them are asleep, and I don't think they're all from dead people. It's not like ghosts. But back on that battlefield, where so many people got killed, there was a lot of energy. Anger, fear. And there were a lot of spirits who wanted a body. I could feel a few empty bodies, and dead things that could have been held together to make a body, but I was scared to try it."

"That was probably wise. We need to take time to explore your Skill, but we should be careful since it might be dangerous."

She leaned toward me. "I was thinking, what if his spirit is still around, on Estreyer? Maybe it would be kind of, like, an imprint of him? Maybe…I could feel it, if we went back there once all this is done."

I took a deep breath. "It wouldn't hurt to see. But don't get your hopes up too much. Like you just said, spirits and ghosts aren't the same thing. Maybe Torliam would have a better idea what you're likely to find."

Torliam's head turned at the sound of his name, and he rose as if to move toward us, but something caught his attention. His head snapped around to stare into a seemingly empty spot in the woods.

I'd searched out the surrounding area with Wraith when we stopped, but I pushed my awareness out again in alarm. Dead space encroached on our camp in a slowly shrinking circle, an area where Wraith pushed and got no feedback, like trying to sense through a feather pillow.

—INCOMING. USING A SKILL. LIKELY HOSTILE.—
-EVE-

I sent out the Window to the others even as I withdrew my awareness. I gritted my teeth and struck with a mental lance, all my energy focused on one point. This time, I pierced through into the dead space and caught a brief glow of power, shining so brightly I never would have missed it without the concealing effect. I'd never met a Player that strong.

—IT'S AN ESTREYAN.—
-EVE-

I used the same trick to puncture through the encroaching dead space in other directions, and found at least two more Estreyans walking within its protection. None of them seemed to be the source of the effect, so either it wasn't a Skill, or there was another of them I hadn't found yet.

—DID QUEEN MARDINEST SEND THEM TO CAPTURE US?—
-ZED-

—I DON'T KNOW. BUT IF THEY WERE FRIENDLY, THEY WOULDN'T
BE SNEAKING UP ON US.—
-EVE-

A vibration in the air ripped through the surrounding dead space and into our camp. The sound was like an explosion that just kept going. I dropped to my knees, my hands pressing into the sides of my head as I tried to protect my ears, and maybe my brain, from the noise attack.

It went on and on. I threw up. Wraith was useless. I couldn't get it more than a foot away from my body before getting so dizzy I couldn't hold my awareness together.

Still, our attackers were close enough by that point to see with my own eyes as they converged on our camp.

Torliam's power settled over the ground like a low-hanging mist and thrummed. For a moment, it brought relief from the sound. But one of the Estreyans lifted his arms, and the sound was back again, jumping around frantically, changing too often for Torliam to nullify it with opposing waves.

The blue mist thickened. This time, he didn't bother to try to nullify the sound. Torliam turned the air around us into a molasses-like barrier that I could feel against my skin, impeding the movement of the vibrations.

I drew my hands away from the side of my head, trying to ignore the blood on my palms from my burst eardrums.

—Zed, get us out of here!—
-Eve-

Zed managed to pull himself off the ground with the help of a tree trunk, then opened a rip in the world.

I took a single step toward him, and the world bent around me, like a lens coming into focus. He'd only been a few feet away, but suddenly those feet had *stretched*. I ran, but barely got anywhere.

I turned away from him, and without the effect of whatever Skill was playing with the physics between us as if it was warm toffee, I found myself all the way across our campsite in half a second.

Two four-legged creatures made of old bones, little pieces of shredded animal hide, and bug carcasses attacked one of the Estreyans.

The sound-creator was locked in his standoff with Torliam.

Zed was gone, probably in the Other Place.

Jacky was trapped by the physics-bender, running but barely inching forward. She stopped, crouched down, and then shot herself into the air before he could change the direction of the warp.

One of the Estreyans stepped into the camp across from me, wielding what looked like a literal whip of fire.

I tried to run toward him but couldn't. I jerked to the side instead, but only got a couple feet before space stretched again and trapped me. I raised my hand and Chaos shot forth, but the misty tendrils lost coherence before they got to him, instead nearly clipping Adam, who was busy shooting out flying ink constructs in all directions.

Fire-whip guy snapped his weapon toward Sam.

Sam caught the lash around his forearm and yanked back to disarm his opponent, screaming as his armor, and then his flesh, sizzled away. As soon as the whip left the Estreyan's hand, it disappeared, but Sam stumbled and almost fell, cradling his useless arm as steam and smoke rose from it. It had been nearly severed. A second or so more, and we'd have gotten to see if Sam could regrow his limbs.

Jacky shot out of the trees, landing atop the last Estreyan, who was distracted fending off Birch, but didn't seem to be doing anything Skill-wise. He'd probably been the source of the null-space.

Zed's torso appeared as he tore open reality to shoot his gun at the sound-creator from behind.

The fire-whip reformed in the hand of the one who'd attacked Sam.

I kept running at an angle, but raised my arm again, focusing harder on exactly what I wanted Chaos to do. The dark tendrils writhed out from my hand, this time staying closer and building up substance till they glistened like floating tar. It lunged for the fire-whip guy with an audible, almost sticky-sounding snap. It pulsed like blood vessels as it built upon itself like a spider web, keeping coherence as power rushed from within me outward through the whole structure. The movement from hand to enemy took less than a quarter of a second.

I grinned savagely.

Fire-whip guy lunged to the side, and Chaos followed, growing an offshoot to follow his movement.

I was just about to reach him when someone else yanked him away from my grasp, moving so fast my eyes could barely track them. Within a second, the four attacking Estreyans were gone, along with the noise attack and the space-bending effect.

I'd been running but barely covering any distance, and when things went back to normal, I almost ran into a tree before I could stop myself. I pushed Wraith out, looking for the fifth attacker who'd just saved his friends.

Instead, I found a group of eight more Estreyans. Our assailants were on the ground between them, unconscious. They had a human with them. I hadn't noticed her till she moved, because the glow of the others' power was too strong.

"Oh, shit," I said aloud, my voice sounding like I was speaking through water due to the damage to my eardrums. I turned toward the new group.

One of their number raised his hands high into the air and began to walk toward us slowly. "Do not attack," he called in barely accented English. "We mean you no harm."

The human woman walked beside him, stumbling a little, because, for some reason, she was wearing high heels.

They came into physical view between two trees, and my eyes narrowed.

Zed's muffled voice cut through the forest. "*Mom?*"

***

HER DARK HAIR was piled high in an uncharacteristically messy bun, and she wore only a little makeup. "You've gotten so big!" she said, smiling tearily at Zed.

Zed looked at me, the one who had literally grown a foot since I'd last seen her, and snorted.

"I'm so glad to see you," she said. "I've been so worried about you."

Torliam looked from the woman to us, then back again. "Is this surely your mother? Shape-shifting is not unheard of, among my people."

She had no glow of Seeds, and, as far as I could tell, none of the Estreyans were using a Skill. "It's her."

"Where have you been?" Zed asked, making no move to go towards our mother.

She shared a look with the man holding his hands in the air beside her. "I've been with your father."

My eyes darted over him again, moving jerkily. "Our…father?" I said, the words sounding strange on my lips.

"I am Eliahan, of the Remnants, once of the line of Matrix." He nodded to Zed and me. His slightly curly hair and the line of his jaw resembled Zed's a little.

I took a step backward and bit down on the inside of my lip, the pain of the bite a throbbing ache that quickened my thoughts.

Eliahan stepped forward, passing Zed with barely a second look. He stopped in front of me. "Hello, daughter." His gaze tracked over me, catching on the gifts from the Oracle, the crystal at my throat, and the extra finger on my left hand.

There were too many of them for us to hope to win in a fight, but I found myself almost hoping they were hostile, because at least I would know how to *deal* with that. "What do you want? If this is some sort of blackmail attempt—"

His laugh cut me off. "You are very untrusting. That will serve you well, in the path ahead of you. Cultivate your pessimism. But no, as I said before, we are not your enemy."

Torliam moved up beside me, taller than Eliahan by a few inches. "Please explain your presence and your intentions. I have not heard of the Remnants." Even Torliam's accent was more prominent than the other man's. How long had these Remnants had to learn English?

"That is because we have been trapped on Earth for millennia, after the doors of stone were locked and forbidden." Well, that answered my question.

Zed and our mother moved over to join us. "They've taken in the parents of the whole group, to keep them safe from NIX," she said.

Sam took a single step toward her. "My parents, too?"

She nodded. "Yes, both of them. Your father is there," she said to Adam.

He grimaced, turning to Eliahan without acknowledging her words further. "And those guys?" He gestured to our unconscious attackers. "Do you know them? It seems kind of coincidental that you show up to save us exactly as we're being attacked."

Eliahan looked Adam over, eyes lingering on his five-fingered hands. He raised his eyebrows in obvious dismissal, and turned back to me. "I regret to say they do call themselves part of the Remnant, but their actions do not represent our group as a whole, or even the majority of us."

I narrowed my eyes. "Why did they come after us?"

He shifted his weight slightly and paused before answering. "They believe you and your team will find the God of Shaping and Molding, and, with him, attempt to defeat the Sickness. They believe that if this is done, the world will…destabilize. They wish to keep what they consider to be the lesser of two evils."

Torliam's voice gained an edge of anger as he spoke. "Perhaps they feel the danger of upheaval or even war is greater than the Sickness because you have been sequestered on Earth, where you are *safe* from its spread. But it has found its way to this world as well, now. Let me assure you, there could be little *worse* than the total annihilation the Sickness promises if allowed to continue."

Eliahan nodded, "I agree. As do the majority of my comrades. We do not wish to continue on as we have been. We wish to return to Estreyer, and see the Sickness returned to the abyss from which it came."

This seemed to deflate Torliam's building ire.

Zed met my eyes, and then looked at the other Remnants standing somewhat awkwardly in guard around their murderous peers. "You didn't explain how you found us. Or how you discovered our parents were in danger from NIX. Were you…*aware* of everything NIX has been doing?"

Beside me, I felt Torliam stiffen again. Every eye was turned toward Eliahan, awaiting the response of this man who called himself my father.

"We do not interfere with the actions of the humans," he said. It was answer enough. Maybe he felt our hostility, because he continued quickly. "We have our own duties to fulfill, of great importance. We enter into the world of the humans only when it is necessary to replenish our numbers with children of new blood, or to ensure our own continued survival. As to how we found you, we have a *scryer* of some capability who took an interest in your return."

"Children of new blood?" I looked to my mother, whose lips were pressed tight together.

"Neither of you showed the signs of dominant Estreyan genes, so I got to keep you," she said. Her eyes flicked down to my left hand. "That's changed, now, I see."

Zed and I shared another look. I'd had six fingers and toes as a baby, and the faint scars to prove it after they'd been surgically removed.

Eliahan shifted again, clearing his throat uncomfortably. "As I mentioned, we have duties, and cannot be away from our home for long. Our strength is needed in these difficult times. We must return."

A muscle in Torliam's jaw pulsed. "Will you not aid our quest against the Sickness?"

"We have our own responsibilities. Perhaps one day, you will understand. We cannot spare the strength to aid you, but we offer hospitality, if you would visit us after your quest is done." He turned to my mother. "Let us go, woman."

She glared at him. "Give me a moment alone with my children. A few more minutes away from the safety of the compound isn't going to change anything."

He huffed. When she made a shooing motion with her hands, he nodded to me, his eyes lingering, before he walked back to the other Remnants.

She reached out and touched my arm, her hand seeming small against it. "Sweetie, you're in danger. Both of you are, if you keep trying to find this...*god*. I don't know the details, but I've heard them talking about some sort of prophecy. Which is apparently a real thing, with whatever alien powers they have. I'm worried something will happen to you. Why can't someone else deal with this disease? Someone more qualified? Live quietly, I always say. No need to go looking for trouble. Come back to the compound with us. There's a war going on out there. I'm sure I can convince Eliahan, if he knows *you* want to come, Eve."

Zed's lips pressed together, not so unlike our mother, but his expression indicated pain rather than disapproval.

I resisted the urge to glare over his shoulder at Eliahan, who'd barely acknowledged his son. They were far enough away that a human wouldn't be able to overhear us, but I knew if any of them were listening my mother's words would be clearly audible. "We know about the prophecy already, and we can't go back with you. It's not so simple as to leave it to someone more qualified. We *are* that 'someone.' I know you haven't seen us in a while," I ignored her derisive snort and continued on. "But we're much more capable than you imagine."

She opened her mouth, most likely to argue, but Eliahan called out for her again. "Come, woman!"

Torliam turned to glare at him. "Where is your respect, for the mother of your children? Have you been gone from Estreyer so long you have forgotten your sense of propriety?"

Eliahan raised his chin, somehow managing to look down on Torliam, though he was shorter. "I could ask a similar question of you, Torliam of the line of Aethezriel. I have seen more of you than you know. Is it not appropriate that one in *blood-covenant* to the line of Matrix treat their master with respect and deference?"

The line of my mother's lips thinned even more as she looked between Torliam and Eliahan. "I should go. *Be safe.*" She squeezed my arm and Zed's hand, as if to impress her words on us, then hurried over to him as quick as her impractical footwear allowed.

Eliahan lifted her in his arms, his touch more gentle than I expected from the glower on his face. "We will see her unharmed," he said to me. "As well as all the other members of your families. Farewell, daughter. Until we meet again."

My team stood and watched as the Remnants gathered up their unconscious members and disappeared into the forest with an inhuman blur. They were gone within seconds.

"Does this mean we're half alien?" Zed said. His mouth twitched halfheartedly, failing to smile properly. "When I was a kid, I would fantasize about our dad coming back and getting to meet him. I always imagined that meeting going differently, you know?"

I snorted. "I always figured he'd be an asshole."

Chapter 13

Time in hours, days, years,
  Driv'n by the spheres
  Like a vast shadow mov'd; in which the world
  And all her train were hurl'd.
— Henry Vaughan

ADAM DECIDED he'd rather rely on Torliam than spend the rest of the night in the woods where yet another thing might go wrong, so, after a break to eat, we continued on to our old base, dragging Adam on a low-floating, glowing stretcher. We walked with the light of the moon and stars filtering through the trees to guide our way, the smell of leaf mulch and moist dirt overcoming the residue of smoke we left behind.

"I'm glad to know my parents are alive," Sam said. "But…those Remnant guys really suck."

Chanelle grunted, jumping a little to get a better grip on Birch, who had demanded she carry him in her arms after he got tired. "Maybe, if they had tried, they might have stopped NIX before they became a problem. NIX would have never managed to bring the Sickness to Earth, and I would…actually, I'd be going to school with China. None of this would have happened at all."

Torliam hummed in agreement, and I heard him take a deep

breath and release it. He was probably thinking something similar about his own experience with NIX.

The sun hadn't yet risen when we arrived at Blaine's house. On the outside, it looked no different, except for a few plants that had become even more overgrown. We keyed in the entrance code and I let the security system scan me, since I'd been given access when we first allied with Blaine and began to use his extensive basement as a base.

As we moved through his house and down into the lab, we found that the concrete door had been blasted open. It was obvious that someone else had been there. Furniture was overturned and strewn about in the main house, and his lab and our basement training area looked like a tornado had hit it.

"NIX," I said aloud.

"Yes." Adam nodded. "They must have come searching for us, or any clues to our whereabouts, when we escaped."

Kris and Gregor were both dead on their feet, so Jacky and I took them back upstairs. "Did you live here, before?" I asked, carrying Gregor with his head on my shoulder. "Do you have a specific room that's yours?"

Gregor shook his head, so I chose a room at random. I set him down to go and try to find a blanket for the bare bed. He looked so small, standing alone and silent in a room that should have been decorated for a little boy by loving guardians.

I found a blanket that smelled only slightly musty, then heard a scream that sounded like Gregor's. I ran back to the room and opened the door to find the child throwing himself about in a frenzy of destruction, beating his limbs against the furniture and walls, his breath tearing out from his chest in desperate sobs.

Jacky ducked her head out from a nearby doorway, and I shook my head.

Gregor needed a release. Unlike his sister, he hadn't cried. The bruises he was no doubt accruing all over his body could be healed by Sam, if they were bad enough. I only wished we could heal emotional damage as easily.

I walked into the room and shut the door behind me, waiting for Gregor to tire himself out.

When he finally fell to the floor, still beating his fists ineffectually against it, I wrapped him in the blanket and picked him up, settling him on the mattress and sitting down beside him. Once his breathing had calmed a little, I said, "You know, Blaine did pretty much the same thing, when you were hurt in that mock battle with Squad Ridley."

Gregor squirmed to look at me from inside the blanket cocoon I'd created around him. "Really?"

"Yeah. You and he are very similar, you know. He even broke his glasses and didn't realize it, he was so upset. Then, he calmed down and started thinking really hard, and came up with a plan to help better protect you and the rest of us from NIX."

"But…there's nothing I can do to make it better. It's too late." His voice broke on the last word, and tears leaked down his cheeks.

I hugged him to my side, my hand combing through his hair. "I know. It's the most horrible feeling in the world." I was silent as he cried, and I tried desperately to think of something that would comfort him. "He loved you, though. More than anything, he wanted you and your sister to be safe and happy. He wanted you to live a good life."

Gregor's face ran with snot, and I looked around for something to wipe him off, finally settling on the far edge of the blanket. We could wash it later. He forced out words past choked sobs. "I can't be happy. I'm too *sad*."

"Well, you'll probably be sad for a while. That's normal, and it means you care. But if you find a chance to be happy, even if it's just a little one, you should take it." I was no good at this. I wished the boy had someone better suited for comforting and dispensing life advice, but I was the one there, so I had to try.

"Do you think he might have left some piece of himself behind? Kris said, maybe he did, even if it isn't exactly *him* anymore."

I squeezed him a little closer. "I don't know. It's not something I'd place too much hope in, but we'll definitely check, once all this is over."

He nodded, and the sniffling sounds of his breathing slowed, until I thought he was asleep. But when I shifted, his hands tightened around the edge of my armor at my waist. "You won't die, right Eve? Even if my Skill only protects me, you'll be strong enough to protect yourself, right?"

"I won't die. And I'll do my best to keep everyone else safe, too. I promise."

His fingers loosened, and he sank into sleep, dried tear tracks on his cheeks.

WE SPENT the better half of the next morning lazing about and eating all the nonperishable food from Blaine's pantries that we could fit in our stomachs. Sleep helped with the physical exhaustion, but the drain of the last few days, along with the months before that, had worn on us all.

Torliam had turned his Tracker Skill to finding the god soon after we got to Earth. The "pull" he'd described had started off too faint to follow, but had grown stronger with a bit of time. We would be heading north, when we were ready.

Halfway through the day, Adam got one of the smartglass screens on the wall working, and connected us to the news. This time, there was more than panicked speculation.

One in every seven alien ships was a different type, which the reporters had taken to calling "Destroyers." They were slower than the other, smaller, ships, but they created a beam so hot it could melt concrete and steel.

"Hot enough to burn out the Sickness," Torliam murmured, frowning at the images of panicked people running in the streets. It had been a destroyer that burned NIX as we escaped, and probably what decimated it so badly in the first place.

A slightly shaky film clip showed a distant cluster of Estreyan ships flying upward above the ocean, as what looked like a barrage of meteorites shot down from the atmosphere to meet them. "This is footage of a group of the alien invaders flying over the Atlantic Ocean," a reporter narrated. "The Earth Defense Force has commenced a series of kinetic bombardments above that area, apparently in the attempt to take out some of the invaders while they were far enough away from populated areas to avoid collateral damage." We watched as the things that looked like meteors, but were in fact a group of huge metal spikes with guiding thrusters attached, reentered the atmosphere and attempted to hit the Estreyans.

The Estreyan ships, so very different from our own airplanes, met the spikes with attacks of their own, disintegrating some of them before they could come into range, and evading others with that graceful speed that seemed more animal than machine. Still, a couple ships were clipped, and a couple more were caught unprepared for the spikes to *explode* in their midst.

"We are being told that the orbital spikes were seeded with small-payload nuclear weapons, which seem to be effective against the alien technology." More than half the ships still managed to escape, some showing signs of damage, but the reporter was grinning as if this was fantastic news. Maybe it was.

The clip cut to city scenes, where enforcers stood outside huge cement blast doors, keeping back a crowd of people. "Panicked citizens in many areas not under immediate threat of the invading aliens are still attempting to enter the emergency shelters, where enforcers have been stationed to keep them out. The leader of Nevada's Defense Force has made statements urging citizens to remain calm and return to their homes, as the emergency shelters will not be opened except in the case of imminent threat. Resources would be drained too quickly otherwise, and unavailable if future need arose."

Adam changed the channel when it devolved into more speculation between the newscasters.

"The aliens attacked a military research facility!" A man screamed into the camera. "It's obvious they're here to keep us from advancing technologically. They don't want us leaving the solar system. They want to keep faster than light travel to themselves!"

Another channel showed a woman in a lab coat talking about the effects of nuclear radiation spreading through the air and water after the orbital attacks on the Estreyans over the Atlantic.

Government officials gave statements, some calm and assured, and some—less proficient in the art of lying—sweating bullets and looking trapped by the reporters' harrying questions.

Once the news began to repeat itself, Sam turned to Torliam. "Is there any way we can contact the ships?" Sam said. "Torliam, you're the prince. Maybe, if we could just talk to them, tell them they're going about this all wrong, we could help. I mean, we could even *lie* to them. Tell them the queen called off the attack, or something."

"I know there is a communication system between ships, but I do not know how they function well enough to build one out of Earth components. Perhaps, if we had another ship to cannibalize…or, if we were able to gain access to one of their ships directly, but—" he shook his head. "I do not have military authority. By now, my mother has probably sent through updated orders to her warriors on this world. Even if she has not given the command to kill us on sight, she would have done her best to remove our ability to undermine her. She is not stupid. She plays the game better than any I have ever met. That is why she is queen."

I fiddled with my sixth finger nervously. There was a tiny chance that Earth might be able to stop the war from our end. If NIX could be made to understand the consequences of their actions, the reason why Queen Mardinest had ordered the invasion, maybe they'd agree to a peaceful disarmament. Plus, I needed to get nanite nutrient paste for Zed. "Adam. Can you find a way to contact NIX?"

He smirked at me. "I've got the system Blaine used to ask for a meetup ready to go already." When I raised my eyebrows, he said, "I've gotten familiar with your thought patterns. When things go wrong, inevitably the answer somehow involves *more danger.*"

WHILE WE WAITED for NIX to respond to our query, we trained, and we played with our new Skills. I was worried about what the Seal of Nine might mean for the individual members of the team. Whatever the "greater Trials" were, I had no doubt they would be dangerous. Each of us needed to be at the top of our game individually, in addition to working on our cohesion as a group.

At my request, Zed took me into the Other Place again. He'd bundled up till he looked like a three-hundred-pound homeless man. "I'll do whatever it takes to save my niblets from freezing off," he said, when I raised my eyebrows incredulously. He dumped a similarly huge pile of cloth in front of me, then snickered as I struggled to fit into the many layers.

Once we were ready, he lifted his hands to the air on one side of our base, away from the rest of the team. "There's a crack in the world, right here," he said. "Can you sense it, with your Perception Skill? Wraith, right?"

I nodded. "Yes, but I can't feel anything. It's just empty air."

He moved his hands, flexing his fingers, and Wraith slipped through the gap he'd created, rapidly extending to fill the room I was in…*again*.

I shook my head, disoriented by reality layering over itself like that. I pressed my awareness cautiously against the air around his fingers, focusing hard. "I can feel it," I said. "You've opened up a tiny hole, but the rip extends…" I traced it in the air, moving my hand along it, till I couldn't reach any longer.

"Yes, exactly. Do you feel any of the other rips?"

I searched the room, focusing my awareness in small areas and moving my attention slowly so that I wouldn't miss anything. "Only this one," I said, shaking my head. I reached toward the rip, gingerly touching the space. "I know it's there, but I can't touch it like you are."

"Hmm. Well, let's go. Prepare to be turned into an icicle." He dug his fingers in once again, grinning. Reality opened up between his arms, the void peeling back to reveal a cold grey shard of Other Place hanging in the air.

I walked around the rip. When I stood on the other side, I found myself still looking at the base in the Other Place. Zed wasn't there. I looked down and saw his legs extending from below the rip in the air, and when I walked back around, he was there, waiting for me with a raised eyebrow. The opening was like a multi-sided display screen. If I stood on one side of the rip and him on the other, would I see him if he stepped through from his side? Maybe not. Or maybe I'd be able to see a cross-section of his insides as he passed through.

"Pretty cool, right?"

I rolled my eyes. "Yes, yes, you're awesome. Can we go now?"

"Yes, but," he sobered, "just be aware of the effect it can have on you. It'll drain your warmth, your emotions, your energy… If you feel like it's getting bad, just let me know, and we'll come back to this side immediately, okay?"

"I remember." I braced myself, then stepped through after him. The cold hit me like a punch to the gut, and I exhaled swiftly, my breath instantly forming tiny ice crystals in the air.

I turned in a circle as I looked at the washed-out room. "You know, since this place is the same medium-gray with dim light all the time, you could probably use small rips as a flashlight in the dark, if you ever needed it." In contrast, the portal back to the normal world was painfully bright and colorful, and I could feel the heat emanating out of it. As I watched, tiny, ash-like pieces of fuzz coalesced in the air around the opening, as if drawn there by static electricity.

Zed let it close, the two edges melding back together again.

Abruptly, I felt vulnerable. Cut off from safety. The feeling didn't last long, though.

"No people here?" I said.

"No. None that I've ever seen, anyway. And I don't know how anyone could survive in this place."

"But the trappings of civilization are here. This building, people made it. We brought in those mats over there, when we were first setting up the base," I said, pointing. "Half the weights are missing, and it's like someone removed the door from the frame. In fact…it looks like anything we've *moved* recently hasn't transferred over to this side."

"Exactly!" He bounced up and down, though I thought it might be for warmth more than excitement. "So, I'm thinking this is some sort of other…dimension. One outside of the three we live in."

"Four," I said.

"What?"

"Four dimensions. Three spatial, one temporal."

"Okay, that makes sense. So what does that make this place?"

I chuckled, though the spark of humor was snuffed out as quickly as it had formed, as if it had died to the cold. "I don't know, I was just repeating something I'd heard. If you want an actual theory about this place, you'd be better off asking Bla—" I bit down on my lip. Blaine wasn't around to ask about these things anymore. I couldn't feel my fingers. I tucked them under my arms, shivering.

"Let's get moving," he said. "It helps a little, not to stay in one place."

We walked around the base and then moved outside. It was just as cold, but it wasn't any brighter, and the sky looked grey and uniform, like it was obscured by an ever-thickening fog.

At first, I thought it was snowing, and though that would have made sense along with the temperature, it wasn't frozen water falling from the sky. In fact, it didn't seem to be coming from the clouds at all. I caught one of the fluffy, light grey things floating gently down, and it crumbled in my hand. I didn't dare to smell the residue, in case it was poisonous, or a clump of infectious spores.

"I thought it was ash, at first," Zed said. "I'm still not quite sure. I think it might be some sort of condensation being formed out of the air. Like a snowflake made of something besides water. Hopefully, it's not toxic."

We walked around to the back of the huge house, where the lawn gave way to woods again. I coughed up phlegm as my lungs protested at the biting cold. "I'm…feeling very bland," I said.

"Do you need to go back? I can open up another rip."

I shook my head. "I'm alright. But a fire would be nice."

He dug in his pocket and held out his hands to mine.

I raised mine to match, and, with a little flick, the lighter in his hands flared to life. The flame was barely orange. It flickered weakly, then slowly shrank till it died out. "Did you run out of fuel?"

He shook his head, sticking the lighter back in his pocket. "No… I think this place just killed the flame. Maybe there's not enough oxygen?"

I breathed deep, and coughed again as my lungs protested the attempt to freeze them. "I don't feel winded or lightheaded," I said. "Maybe we just need a bigger fire." A thought sparked in my head, a faint curiosity. I turned to the trees behind us, spotting a couple branches that had fallen to the ground. "Maybe I could start a fire," I continued.

"With what?"

"With Chaos," I said. "That's all you need to burn something. The molecules rubbing against each other a little too quickly, and *whoosh.*"

"Wow. I didn't know you could do that. I thought it was just black tendrils of 'fear-me-because-I-can-disintegrate-your-face'. Have you lit a fire before? One that isn't black?"

I shook my head, shuffling over to one of the fallen branches. "No. Before, I couldn't use Chaos unless I had to, because it was killing me, and every time I used it I made it stronger. After we killed the God of Knowledge, I guess I could have tried, but it seems like we haven't really had a moment to stop and breathe, and there've been more important things than playing around with my Skill just for fun. And…because I've been afraid of Chaos for so long." I looked up to him. "Seems this place has frozen that out of me. I didn't even realize I was still resisting, till now that the feeling's gone."

He shuffled back and forth, hunching his shoulders. "Glad to help, you can thank me by starting a fire. If not, I'm opening it back up to find some warmth. Pretty sure the snot inside my nostrils is frozen solid."

I couldn't really find it in me to crack a smile at his joke. I stretched out my hand toward the branch on the ground, reaching inside myself for Chaos. Even as the intent formed, realized I knew how to do this. "Shiver," I murmured aloud, and Chaos roiled up.

The branch exploded, little chips and splinters shooting out in all directions. I jumped back, the sudden shock of surprise leaving so quickly that the adrenaline in my veins felt strange and foreign. "Oops."

Zed pulled a splinter the size of his finger out of the fabric of his chest, where it had pierced through both of his jackets. "*Oops?* You just made a bomb. Out of a tree branch."

"I agitated the molecules a little too hard." I moved to another branch, this one quite a bit larger, and held my hand out again. I coaxed Chaos out, asking it to *slowly* make the molecules of the wood shiver. The wood smoked, and I pushed it a little harder. The branch burst into flame, bright and hot and full of *color*. The light pulsed out like a bloom, bringing color to everything it touched. I felt a brief burst of joy, a surge of curiosity and wonder. Under the warmth, the feelings didn't fade right away. How long had it been since my curiosity wasn't ruled by necessity and fear?

"Wow…" Zed breathed.

I turned to grin at him, but the Other Place distracted me. Outside our little circle of light, the darkness had risen. The world was bending in on us, blackening and twisting. Something sucked at the flame, and it took a surge of Chaos to keep it going, a steady stream of power coming out of me. "What's happening?" I said, that old familiar fear searing through me.

"It's hungry," Zed choked out.

The Other Place warped, squeezing in on us. I could feel it, gathering, *actively watching* us. "Get us out of here!" I said.

Zed stumbled a few feet to the side and tore at the air.

I considered dropping the link to the flame, just letting it die out, but I didn't dare. What if the Other Place decided to take the warmth from us instead? We would die instantly.

Zed tossed himself through the rip, and I followed, stumbling onto the warm ground and scrambling away on my hands and feet.

He turned and closed up the rip, cutting off my connection with both Wraith and Chaos, then collapsed next to me in Blaine's backyard. "I wasn't expecting that," he said.

YOUR STAMINA HAS INCREASED!

———————————

Chapter 14

———————————

I have looked upon all the universe has to hold of horror, and even the skies of spring and flowers of summer must ever afterward be poison to me.

    — H. P. Lovecraft

SHAKEN BY OUR EXPERIENCE, Zed was reluctant to immediately open another rip, or let anyone else into the Other Place with him, until he was sure it was safe, and he better understood what had happened. Tentatively, he created a pinhole opening to the Other Place, and we found that it was no longer distorted or seemingly *aware*, but, even so, neither of us wanted to go back through.

While Zed was busy testing his Skill with small rips and sending small fires through, the system Adam had set up to contact NIX pinged loudly.

We all piled through into the lab, where one of the smartglass screens showed a retro-looking text interface, a short message, and a blinking cursor.

CONSOLE 1: DROP LOCATION REQUEST RECEIVED, CODE MENDELL-X90. PLEASE CONFIRM IDENTITY AND OBJECTIVE.
CONSOLE 2: _

Adam and I shared a look, and he scrambled to connect a hand-held pad to the console in front of us. "I'll try and track them. You handle the comms."

I reached forward to the screen, my fingers hesitating over it. What should I say?

CONSOLE 2: EVE REDDING HERE. REQUESTING TRADE OF NANITE BOOSTER FOR INFORMATION THAT MAY HELP END INVASION.

The response took a while to show up. Adam muttered with frustration at their encryption while the rest of us waited with bated breath.

CONSOLE 1: WE HAVE NANITE NUTRIENTS. PLEASE ELABORATE ON THE NATURE OF YOUR INFORMATION.

CONSOLE 2: EARTH HAS OFFENDED THE ESTREYANS IN A WAY THAT MAY BE REVERSIBLE. THE MENINGOLY-CANOSIS CULTIVATED BY NIX IS A VECTOR FOR A SECONDARY DISEASE WITH NO KNOWN CURE, WHICH IS ANATHEMA TO THE ESTREYANS. NO CONVENTIONAL METHODS OF CONTAINING ITS SPREAD HAVE PROVEN EFFECTIVE. EARTH IS IN DANGER OF A WORLDWIDE PANDEMIC, EVEN BEYOND THE INVASION THIS RESEARCH HAS TRIGGERED. I HAVE INFORMATION ABOUT A POSSIBLE SOLUTION TO THE PANDEMIC, AS WELL AS THE INVASION.

I didn't want to give away all my bargaining power, but, at the same time, the prospect of the Sickness was too dangerous to keep to myself. Even if NIX didn't agree to meet with me, they'd know the hazard posed by their infected research subjects.

CONSOLE 1: PLEASE ELABORATE FURTHER.

Adam glared at the screen, then shook his head. "I can't find them. No need to keep them talking just to draw out the conversation, and I wouldn't trust them with any more information than necessary."

I grimaced, but nodded.

CONSOLE 2: I WILL REVEAL MORE IN PERSON, WITH NANITE BOOSTER PRESENT. ATTEMPTS AT CAPTURE OR OBSTRUCTION WILL BE MET WITH LETHAL FORCE.

There was another long pause, but finally, they responded.

CONSOLE 1: PLEASE AWAIT COORDINATES.

As soon as I'd read the message, the connection cut off, leaving me staring at a black screen.

THE NEXT DAY, while we were still waiting for NIX to contact us with a meetup location, I took a walk in the backyard near the edge of the tree-line.

Jacky and Sam were sparring on one side of the clearing, and Kris sat by herself on the other, hunched over something in her lap.

As I walked past, Jacky muttered to herself, "Come on you idiot Skill, grow. Get bigger!"

Sam smirked. "Everybody watch out for Jacky the she-hulk. Jacky stomp, Jacky *crush*."

Her eyes narrowed, and she darted forward and punched him in the shoulder.

He clutched his arm, doubling over in pain. "Oh," he gasped, then straightened up again after only a couple seconds, the tension receding from his face. "Your cruel fear-mongering won't work on me, Jacky. I'm a super-healer, remember?"

She cracked her knuckles, one by one. "Oh? You mean I don't need to hold back?"

He paused, eyes widening a bit, then shuffled away.

"You know, your actions don't discredit his claims very well," I said.

"I *am* gonna cruelly fear-monger all over the place," she said. "But I'll do it like the stunningly beautiful woman that I am. Someone that no one would ever dare to call a she-hulk." She flicked her bangs back and grinned wickedly.

Sam ran to hide behind me, my taller body blocking him from Jacky's view. "Eve, let's band together against the forces of evil. No one person can stand against them alone."

Jacky snorted out a laugh. "The forces of evil welcome this challenge!"

I dodged out of the way as she shot toward us. "Sorry, Sam, you're on your own." I hadn't had a chance to talk to him about his most recent activation of Black Sun and the soldiers he'd killed, but, to my surprise, the signs of tension around his eyes and in the slope of his shoulders were almost nonexistent, though his eyes themselves looked slightly shadowed. He seemed…carefree. I guessed he was handling it better than I'd anticipated.

I left them to their sparring and walked up to Kris.

She turned away from a pile of wood shavings to greet me with a tired smile. "Hey, Eve. Are you here to practice your Skills? I can move, if you need the space." She looked over to Jacky and Sam, still sparring on the other side of the backyard.

I shook my head. "No, don't move. I just came over to see how you're doing."

"Oh." She smiled, her eyebrows rising just a little, as if she were pleasantly surprised. "I'm practicing," she said, pointing to a small pile of dead insects and animal bones in front of her. It moved, then, and I realized the pile was actually a four-legged form about the size of a cat. The little four-legged amalgamation picked up a stick about the thickness of Kris' finger and brought it to her, without any obvious input from the girl. She took it without even looking up, and began to carve at it with a laser tool she must have gotten from Blaine's lab.

"What are you making?"

"I'm building myself another marionette, since mine got eaten by that wyrm." She reached into the shavings beside her and lifted up a half-formed wooden puppet, with joints crafted to allow a range of movement greater than a human's. "I looked up the blueprints online, and I'm going to make it so it can unscrew its hands or legs and put on replacement parts that do different things. Modular." She said the word slowly, as if tasting it.

"And that should work better for your Skill than the…little pieces from things that were once alive?"

"Well, my marionettes before were a lot easier to use than the held-together bodies. But it's also weird…it feels like the spirits on Earth are pretty weak. At least the ones around here. On Estreyer, I could feel them in the air and the ground and the trees around us. Here, I have to reach really hard to call them. But already, this puppet feels like a good body. I just wish it wasn't going to be so small. There's no way it'll be able to carry me." She kept her eyes trained on the wood in her hand, using the laser to carve it with surprising deftness. "Oh!" She looked up into the air, a bright grin growing on her face. "I just leveled up my Manual Dexterity!"

I knew she must have been practicing a *lot*, to get a spontaneous Attribute level-up from the tiny amount of Seeds in her system. As far as I knew, the only Seed organisms she'd ever assimilated were the ones that gave her the Summon Skill. With a focused thought, I brought up Kris' information through my Command Skill.

PLAYER NAME: KRIS MENDELL
TITLE: ONE OF NINE
SKILLS: SUMMON

STRENGTH: 4
LIFE: 7
AGILITY: 4
GRACE: 4
INTELLIGENCE: 10
FOCUS: 8
BEAUTY: 9
CHARISMA: 3
MANUAL DEXTERITY: 13
MENTAL ACUITY: 10
RESILIENCE: 6
STAMINA: 10
PERCEPTION: 7

Her levels were actually quite impressive, for an eleven-year old girl who hadn't been augmented by stolen alien Seeds.

"Have you heard the term significance-based Skill before?" I said.

She frowned and shook her head, stopping carving to look up at me. "No. What does that mean?"

"Well, Adam has a significance-based Skill. He didn't realize till Torliam told him, actually. I don't know all the details." We'd been too busy fighting for our lives on a constant basis for me to take the time to delve into it. How many times had that kept me from learning, now, probably without me even realizing it? That was dangerous. Knowledge was power, and if I was too distracted to learn the important things, it would catch up to me. I realized I had stopped talking and Kris was staring at me expectantly, so I continued. "Basically, when Adam uses things that are valuable to him, or have some sort of *significance*, his Skill gets stronger. He once used the tattoos on his arms to hold back a goddess."

Kris' eyes widened a bit. "Is that why he adds blood to his ink sometimes?"

I smiled. "Exactly. So I wonder, what would happen if you treated that wood with your own blood? Or maybe wrote some sort of instructions or drew images on the inside with your blood? You'd want to be careful, of course. Make sure Sam is around to help you so there are no complications."

Her eyes grew even wider as I spoke. "Do you really think that will help? Why didn't anyone ever say anything about this before? I could have been making all my marionettes stronger, and maybe I could have actually helped out more." She didn't whine, but her words were accusing, all the same. "Did the others know about this, too?"

I grimaced. "Well, at least some of them did. They probably just didn't think to mention it."

"I know I'm still young," she said, "But I can make a difference to this team, too. You guys shouldn't count me out."

She was right. I said so, and she opened her mouth as if she'd planned to argue, blinked, and then closed it. "Yeah."

I called Torliam's name in a voice just a little louder than normal, knowing his Perception was high enough to hear me.

When he arrived, a greasy cloth in his hand that he'd been using to clean the joints of his armor, I asked him to tell us more about how Skills worked.

First, he explained significance and how some Skills seemed to adjust their power output based on it. "There is some argument among the learned ones of my people whether the Skill is somehow aware of the significance, or whether it simply allows your…lower consciousness? Is this the word?" He looked to me for confirmation.

"Do you mean subconscious?"

He nodded. "Yes. Some speculate that the subconscious affects the power of the Skill, and the use of significance is only a way to trick the deeper parts of our minds into believing more power must be channeled, and doing so. In any case, the method is effective for many, regardless of how it works. Others, like you and I," he said, turning to me, "may benefit by placing significance on our Skill use to some small degree, but are better served by conscious control and exploration of the different aspects of our greater powers. With mastery comes control and versatility."

He was right, I knew. As I gained control of Chaos, I'd moved beyond simple destruction. "What are the aspects of your Skill?"

Kris nodded eagerly, grinning in excitement. "Ooh, show us!"

Light blue mist blossomed out from Torliam's hands, but, before he could comply, Adam started shouting, the alarm in his voice drawing everyone's attention.

"Stop! She's down, leave her alone!" He was sitting in a lawn chair to give his Animus Skill a break, but had electricity crackling around both hands in obvious threat.

Sam stood over Jacky, who'd collapsed onto the ground and was moaning softly. His eyes had blackened again, and he looked up from Jacky to Adam, a discouraging smile on his face.

"SHE'S FINE," Sam said, staring Adam down without any hint of fear or regret. "I just gave her a little bit of weariness, maybe a smudge of depression, to counter her more lively emotions. It will wear off soon enough."

I stood and walked toward him slowly, checking Jacky to make sure she really was alright.

He turned to me, those black eyes meeting my own. I saw the sucking emptiness in them, felt an instinctive fear of it, but whatever power his gaze now carried, he didn't use it on me. "What's wrong? Don't you *trust* me, Eve?" He tilted his head to the side like a child.

I forced some of the tension to leave my body. "I do trust you. But we've also seen some of the things you can do with that new Skill, and you just used it on Jacky. You can imagine why we're a little worried."

He rolled his eyes. "She's already feeling better. I know, because I'm not getting as much charge off her."

Jacky did stir, sitting up and lifting trembling hands to hide her face, and taking ragged breaths that sounded like they might turn into sobs.

Adam spilled black liquid and grew ink legs from it, then moved to Jacky's side.

When he tried to wrap an arm around her, she flinched away from him like she hadn't done since they were strangers. Like she expected him to hurt her. "Sorry," she said. "I—I just…"

Adam scowled at Sam. "A charge?" he repeated. "The same type of charge you get when you hurt people?"

Sam looked down at Jacky, watching her struggle to her feet with detached interest. "This is much less permanent. I will admit, I am somewhat…desensitized at the moment, but I don't want to hurt Jacky. I've won the spar, and that's enough."

Gregor peeked out of the back door of the house, his eyes quickly taking in the situation, his hands moving to rest on his daggers.

When I reached for Jacky's hand, she took mine and allowed me to help her up. "I'm okay," she said, but her voice was small and shaky.

I positioned myself between her and Sam. "Why don't you tell us a little more about how your Skill works, Sam? It seems like you've got a better grasp on it than you did the first time."

He stared at Jacky, frowning a little as she refused to meet his eyes. "Black Sun works on a sliding scale. It dampens the things that make me weak. Fear, fatigue, guilt. The more I turn it up, the less I feel, and the stronger my ability to push those same debilitating feelings onto others. The psychological pain seems to count as damage for my Harbinger Skill, offsetting my ability to heal."

Jacky let out a shaky breath, finally meeting his eyes. "It just… caught me by surprise. I'm okay."

The faint frown marring his forehead smoothed. "I'm glad. Shall we go again?"

Her jaw tightened, and she shifted backward, away from him.

"Maybe you should turn it off for now, Sam," I said.

He turned, flicking his hand as if shooing away my words like a bug. "I don't feel like turning it off." The words came sharp and quick, and, after a pause, he continued in a more reasonable tone. "We don't have to spar any more, but this is a useful Skill for me, and it needs training. It's one of the nine Skills we got as part of the Seal." He walked away, moving to take Adam's empty seat without meeting any of our eyes again.

I shared a look with Adam and Torliam, but stayed silent. The uncharacteristic languor on Sam's face made me uncomfortable, but he was right. "Just don't use it on any of us without asking, alright?"

He waved his hand at me again, then closed his eyes. "Yes, yes."

ONCE SAM'S Black Sun Skill reached the limit of how long he could keep it active, and he was forced back to normal, he apologized more sincerely to Jacky, and once more promised he wouldn't use the Skill on any of his teammates again.

She accepted his apology, but her grins were a little weak for a while after that, and she spent a lot of time practicing her martial arts by herself. She also avoided physical contact with the men of the group, and would flinch if they got too close without her noticing.

I gained a couple more levels in Strength by trying to keep her company while she worked out, bringing that Attribute to a cool twenty-five. Compared to her, I might as well have been training with marshmallows on sticks instead of weights.

Zed kept experimenting with his Skill, and discovered a few things that had slipped past him. If a crack was directly touching a surface like a wall, he could distort space and travel through that surface by opening the crack. That was apparently how he'd used the Skill the very first time, when Ifkana's assassin was strangling him to death against the alley wall. He also didn't have to be actually *touching* a rip to open or close it, if he concentrated hard enough.

Despite his experiments, he didn't manage to recreate the strange phenomenon we'd experience when I'd used Chaos to create fire, and tentatively deduced that my Skill was the necessary ingredient.

A small test where I held a stick into a tiny opening to the Other Place and then lit it with my Chaos Skill proved this theory correct. It seemed to have something to do with the way flames created with Chaos were so much more *powerful* than normal fire, enough to bring real color and even emotion to the never-ending depression that seemed inherent to the mirror world of Zed's Skill.

We, very wisely, I thought, agreed that I would never use Chaos in the Other Place again.

Torliam grew antsy over the next couple days, as we waited for NIX to contact us again. At first, I thought it was just tension from watching the news and being stuck at the base, but when I said as much, he shook his head. "No. It is the Skill. Tracker wishes for me to move north, and is urging me onward with increasing strength as time passes. It is like…an itch, which I cannot reach to scratch. The longer we sit idle, the more trouble I have thinking of anything else but the desire to relieve its irritation."

To his great relief, NIX contacted us not long after, sending only a set of coordinates to the console. Luckily, the military base they wanted to meet at was also north, so we wouldn't have to backtrack to reach our eventual destination.

While we were making travel plans, Gregor Shadowed through a wall, and, when he came back, led us to Blaine's vehicle storage room.

I gaped, along with the rest of the team, as we looked at the row of bikes, lined up one after the other.

"Why don't we just ride these?" he said.

"He had these all along?" Adam said, scowling. "Why didn't he let us use them? These could have been—"

He cut off when the boy glared at him. "Uncle Blaine would have been caught if he let you guys use these, since he owned them legally and they're traceable back to him." He turned away, muttering something that sounded like, "ungrateful cretin," under his breath.

Birch ran forward and settled himself in a sidecar, ears perked up.

I stifled a chuckle. "They will be more maneuverable than a larger vehicle. That might come in handy."

"I'd prefer to take it safe in an armored van or something," Gregor said. "Too bad those didn't fulfill Uncle Blaine's 'need for speed.'"

Jacky picked Gregor up, setting him atop her shoulders. "You're basically *wearing* an armored van, kiddo." Gregor had been gleefully fascinated by the kinetic dispersal technology of the armor Blaine had created when he was still working for NIX, and had taken over the lab to create his own, making pieces to protect his entire body from harm with a zeal that bordered on obsessive.

Zed laughed. "So where exactly are we headed? All I've heard so far is 'north,'" he said, as we returned to the lab.

"All we *know* is 'north,'" Adam grumbled.

"The pull from my Skill has been growing stronger," Torliam said, pulling up a large map on one of the unbroken smartglass screens of the lab. "However, it is giving me direction only. I do not know how far away our destination is."

Zed frowned. "So we're just going to go north in a general way, and you'll know if we end up passing our destination?"

"The information my Skill gives me increases over time, if I stay continually focused on the same target. Perhaps there will be more, later."

Sam crossed one arm over his chest, gripping his opposite elbow. "The roads are filled with people," Sam said. "There's been a mass exodus from the cities, and you know there's a huge city directly north of us."

"We'll take the backroads," I said. "They should be less crowded. It might take a while longer because it's not a straight shot, but I think that's our best option. Besides, we need to meet NIX at their military base up north, so we'd have to go that direction, anyway."

We planned out our route more specifically and then started carefully loading our packs and the bikes.

We left the next day, early in the morning, before the sun had started to rise. I wore a shemagh to cover some of my facial features and the crystal at my throat. The chill air woke me up, but the scent of smoke from the fires all around put a damper on any cheer I might have felt. We were riding into mayhem.

Chapter 15

The only way to make sense out of change is to plunge into it, move with it, and join the dance.
— Alan Watts

WE DROVE through the smaller mountain paths and backroads, heading north as directly as we could. Adam rode lying down in a heavily cushioned sidecar attached to Sam's motorcycle. They drove at the front, and Adam navigated for us by sending instructions through Windows.

Despite the normally unused nature of the roads we traveled, we passed a lot of people going the opposite way, along with the occasional abandoned or wrecked vehicle.

People stared at us as we rode past. We were a mixed group of adults and children, heavily armored in a blend of medieval and military-looking gear, riding the wrong way—toward the city of Mordsmouth instead of away from it. Maybe we weren't as inconspicuous as I had hoped. The two-lane roads grew more and more crowded as the hours passed, and more than once we had to maneuver around vehicles using our lane to travel the wrong direction, in too much of a hurry to stick to their own side. Still, it was pretty smooth traveling till we came to a junction where several of the backroads crossed. There had been a bad wreck involving several pods and a couple large vehicles, and the roads were completely packed in all directions, unpassable. Smoke still rose from some of the pods, which meant the wreck was fresh enough the vehicles hadn't had time to suppress any chance of fire with retardant foam.

We slowed to a stop, and I lifted the visor of my helmet, examining the wreck and the woods to the sides of the road.

"The bikes will get stuck," Adam said, as if reading my mind. "We can't just go around. We're going to have to find a way through."

Jacky squinted. "Is there even a path through, Eve?"

I searched with Wraith, then shook my head. "No. I guess that means we're going to have to make one."

Torliam sighed, climbing off the biggest bike, which he still dwarfed. "Jacky, you may help as well," he said, as if doing her a favor.

We all dismounted, weaving slowly through the stopped pods, some of which had wrecked into others. When necessary, Jacky and Torliam would lift and move them, opening a path between vehicles for us and arranging them so people would be able to drive again, once there was somewhere to go.

People stared.

Near the center of the junction, the wreckage was particularly bad. Some pods wouldn't be drivable any longer, and a few were even crumpled together or stacked atop one another after apparently flipping through the air.

Adam let out a long, low whistle.

Sam nodded. "It's a good thing we're here," he said. "Otherwise these people would all be trapped, or have to abandon their vehicles."

A few pods away, a woman with blood running down her side tore at the passenger door of her tiny pod, somehow managing to pry the damaged thing open. She reached in and gently withdrew a smaller form. It was a child, a boy whose leg was obviously, and badly, broken, the bone jutting out of his skin.

He cried out when his mother moved him, clenching the front of her shirt as she laid him on the ground.

"Is anyone here a medic?" she called out. "I need a medic!"

People milled about, some watching in guilty concern, while others outright ignored her, more focused on their own situation, or already busy helping others. No one volunteered.

Zed looked around. "Is no one in this whole mess a medic? I'd help, but I really only have first aid training. I never had a chance to…" he trailed off, turning to stare at Sam.

Sam was already glancing between the child and me. "Err, I could…"

I let out a deep sigh. "Come on, Sam. Let me do the talking."

We stepped forward, and the woman looked up at us. "Is one of you a medic?" she asked, her hands trembling as they pushed the boy's hair away from his forehead, which was beading with sweat despite the chill in the air.

"We can help," I said loudly. "We'll need a place to take him. Somewhere we can work without disruption." Normally, I would never volunteer to reveal Sam's Skill, but the world as we knew it had all but ended, and I didn't see NIX managing to find out or come after us out in the middle of nowhere, even if they were inclined to piss us off by doing so.

"I've got a camper pod," an older man said. "It's not a sterile room or anythin', but we can clear off the table and put him on that. I've got some alcohol, too. For the infection, I mean. To make sure he doesn't get one." He shut his mouth very deliberately, and pointed to a large camper pod parked a few hundred feet down the road, a flush spreading across his cheeks. He was a bit overweight, and had dirt and traces of blood smeared on his hands and arms, probably from helping to get people out of the wrecked pods.

On Sam's advice, we found a chunk that looked like it might have once been a piece of roof from someone's pod, and laid the boy on it so he wouldn't be jostled. Then we followed the man to his camper pod, carrying the boy.

The man explained the situation to his wife, and she hastily cleared the small table and wiped it down with some antibacterial cleaner, shooting glances at Sam and me when she thought we weren't looking.

Once the boy was settled, I turned to his mother. "We can fix his leg, but there's a cost. A trade-off, of sorts."

Her mouth tightened, and she glared at me for a bit. "I have a few thousand credits." I shook my head, but she continued before I could speak. "You don't want credits? They might be useless soon, the way the world is going. How about gold, diamonds?" She held out her hand. "My wedding ring. You can have it. It's got to be worth the cost of an operation."

I shook my head again, holding a hand up to stop her from continuing. "It isn't that type of cost."

"Eve—" Sam said.

I raised an eyebrow, and he closed his mouth, frowning. "We don't have power to spare," I said. "If she wants the kid healed, we can help. But we have to get the same amount in return. We're going to need it, later."

Sam clenched his jaw rebelliously and sent me a Window.

—It's just a broken bone. I still have some charge left on Harbinger's healing side. It's a *KID*.—
-Sam-

—Don't bullshit me. I know you haven't regained a fraction of all the healing you've given out since you got that Skill. You're on the brink of not being able to absorb more injuries. You don't have to offset the damage on the kid, but this broken bone could be the difference between one of us being able to run away in the next Trial or dying, and we have no idea the next time you'll get a chance to recharge.—
-Eve-

"It's only fair," I said aloud.

Sam glared at me, but didn't respond.

The older man wiped at his hands with a rag. "What kind of price are you talkin'?"

I turned to the mother and the older couple. "Injury for injury. We can heal the boy, but the damage can't just disappear. It needs to go somewhere. We'll change the form it takes, so it won't be so debili-tating," I said, nodding to Sam, who nodded back reluctantly. "Someone needs to volunteer, or if you've got a live animal, we can use that."

"Is this some kind of magic juju?" The mother sighed, rubbing a hand across her forehead. "I thought he might be military, with the outfit and everything. And even you look kinda…" she trailed off, looking at my armor, which wouldn't exactly fit in with the military, unlike Sam's. "I need a *real* medic," she said, turning around.

"Stop," I said, and the crystal at my throat vibrated with the word. Everyone froze, even the little boy on the table who'd been whimpering quietly. I sighed. I hadn't meant to do that. "What we can do really will heal your son." I softened my voice a little, to make up for the earlier command. "I've experienced it myself."

The man and his wife were both staring at me, and the mother turned around slowly.

I held up my left arm. "His skin won't end up looking like mine," I said. "A broken bone is much easier to heal."

She stared at my hand, its six fingers, the honeycomb-scales that disappeared under my sleeve at the wrist. "I'll do it," she said after a long pause. "What are you going to do? Cut me? Chop off my fingers?"

I couldn't help the little chuckle that slipped out.

She glared at me in a way that said clearly she didn't appreciate being laughed at.

"The pinky toes," Sam said. "You don't need them for balance."

She paled a little, as if she hadn't expected the trade of injuries to be real. "Oh. Okay." She took off her shoes.

The man brought her a clean rag to bite down on, and turned to Sam and I. "You're not going to be cutting off her toes for nothin'. I haven't ever heard of a medic who needs to hurt people before she can heal someone else. But…I haven't ever met someone who can make me go still with a word like that. Or who has their skin made outta diamonds," he said, looking to the symbol at my throat, peeking out above my shemagh. "The world is a stranger place than I knew a couple weeks ago. I mean, there's aliens everywhere." He stepped back slowly, his gaze on mine.

Sam's head jerked around, his eyes widening as he processed the implications of the man's words. "We're not—I'm human. And so is she," he said. "We're not aliens."

The man nodded slowly. "Of course not. You're humans. And you can do healing magic that transfers wounds."

I rearranged my shemagh and rubbed the back of my neck, trying to release the rapidly building tension.

"We won't say anything," his wife said, speaking for the first time.

"I mean, you're helpin' that little boy." Her fingers twisted in the cloth she'd used to wipe down the table, white-knuckled.

"There's no need to be afraid," I said. "We really *are* humans, and we're not going to hurt you even if you say differently." I realized that I didn't know how true my words actually were. Was I still human enough to be considered one? But then again, Estreyans and humans weren't so different, except for the Seeds. Being born on Earth should be enough to qualify me as human. Probably. "And he's the healer, not me."

"Brace yourself," Sam said to the woman, lifting her right foot into his lap. He held her pinky toe between two fingers, and she started to scream.

She bit down on the cloth between her teeth, muffling her cries, and tried to jerk her leg away from Sam. It was probably an involuntary reaction to the pain.

Her son turned to her in alarm and began to cry, yelling for Sam to stop hurting his momma.

Sam lifted his hands from the woman's foot, and, where her toe had been, a lump of sharp red crystal remained, spiky enough to cut the adjacent toe. His face was pale, and he sent me another slightly resentful look.

She took a few shuddering breaths. "It's okay, baby," she said, laying a hand on her son's arm. "It hurts a bit, but it'll be over soon. And then your leg is going to be all better, too. It's like eating your vegetables. Sometimes you don't want to do it, but once you're finished, you realize it wasn't so bad after all. I just need you to be brave for a little while longer."

He continued to cry, but nodded, lower lip trembling. He whimpered again when Sam moved to her left foot, closing his eyes and covering his ears with his hands.

After both toes were crystallized, Sam returned to the first one, pinching the base of the digit, where the crystal met flesh. Her flesh melted under his fingers, and the crystal lump fell right off, hitting the floor with a sound like glass. When he took his hand away, the skin was healed over the stub, raw and tender looking. "It doesn't take much power to fuse the skin together, not much more than healing a cut. If I just left the toe like that, or the wound open, it could get infected," he explained, clenching his jaw as if daring me to reprimand him. "This is still a power gain."

I nodded acceptance. "Of course. It wouldn't make sense to leave her with an open wound, when there are no other medical facilities around."

He relaxed, and did the same to the other toe.

Everyone in the camper pod stared at the woman's four-toed feet for a moment.

Sam moved on to the child, first numbing his leg and then shifting and fusing the bone back into place, before finally healing the muscle and skin. Like his mother's missing toes, the boy's wound was left looking raw and tender. "He shouldn't walk on this for a while," Sam said. "The bone isn't completely healed. It will probably hurt for at least a couple weeks, while his body finishes up the rest of the healing."

The boy moved his leg, whimpering. "It feels funny. Bad."

"That's the numbing. It's quite unpleasant, but the pain would have been worse. It will wear off in an hour or so."

The woman stared at her son's leg, leaning close to it but carefully not touching the pink scar as she examined it. "You healed his leg," she said aloud.

I raised an eyebrow at her. "Yes. In exchange for your toes." I hoped she wouldn't get too excited about it.

She shook her head, her eyes filling with tears. "Thank you," she said. She took a few deep breaths and swallowed, the tears receding from her eyes. "Do you need anything? Food? I have some supplies in my pod, still. Some water, too."

Sam shook his head. "No, we don't need anything. Keep your supplies, you'll need them yourself."

"Just don't go yelling about it to everyone who will listen," I said. "We need to move on, as soon as the rest of my squad has cleared the road. We don't need people begging for help if they happen to believe you."

"Of course not," the man said, opening up a box of energy bars, and handing them out. He hesitated, with his arm outstretched to me. "Do you eat...protein bars?"

I took it from him and started to eat it. "Of course."

He nodded, seeming relieved. "Since you're human and all, and dressed like that, does that mean you're fightin' against the aliens? Is that where you're going?"

I didn't say anything, silently chewing my protein bar. The civilians shared a look.

"We don't like what they're doing," Sam finally said.

"And…hypothetically," the man shared a look with the other two again. "You might use your…*powers* to do something about it?"

I frowned. "We're not going to be getting ourselves killed by flashy heroics," I said. "Come on, let's go." I left the camper, going to help Torliam and Jacky finish rearranging the cars around the intersection.

Behind me, I heard Sam say softly to the people in the camper, "We might be able to do something. Don't lose hope."

I sighed, and strode off to get us back on the move.

IT TOOK us over an hour to clear the road enough to travel, and Adam had grown a constant scowl as he waited, eyes locked on the link he'd scrounged from Blaine's lab. "There's a map site where people are posting information and warnings about certain locations. The main road we were heading to is blocked off. There was some sort of train accident that spilled over onto it, and a fuel leak caused a fire. Which spread."

"Is there another way?" I said.

"Backroads, but they're all like this," he said. "Backed up, both lanes filled with pods trying to leave the cities, barely moving. The only clear roads are the larger ones heading *toward* the cities." He sighed. "Yes, I know what you're going to say, Eve. And yes, there's a large road heading to a city north of us."

"So…let's take it?" I said.

"We have no choice. We'll just have to travel along it as far as we can, then cut around Mordsmouth so we don't get trapped in the…" he waved a hand vaguely, "people."

Despite Adam's reluctance, we moved much faster once we'd left the side roads and made it to the expressway. He was right. Moving north toward the city, the road was almost completely free of traffic, though the other direction was a honking wave of pods inching forward like molasses. A few people with off-road vehicles or hover-pods had managed to get over the divider between the north and southbound lanes, and were driving the wrong way, speeding ahead of their counterparts.

Most of the vehicles on our side were military, which made sense since NIX wanted us to meet them at a military base. We kept out of their way while trying to look as inconspicuous as possible. They didn't stop us.

The expressway was blocked off in front of the city by a line of military-style humvees a few hundred yards before the road split and would allow us to travel around the sprawling metropolis. The blockade allowed the obvious military people through, but flagged us down and motioned for us to stop.

A soldier walked up to us, and I waved him over, flipping up the visor on my helmet.

"The emergency shelters are closed," he said with no preamble.

"We're not going to the shelters," I said. "In fact, we'd prefer to circle around, not even go through Mordsmouth. I hear it's a bit of a mess in there."

He grunted. "Been doing the best we can. But, *civilians*." He said it like a curse word. "Where you headed, then?"

"Going to the base."

He eyed my group, taking in the armor, the bikes, and the kids. "You military?"

I hesitated, and his gaze sharpened. "Not the same kind of military you are," I settled on. "In fact, officially we are a group of civilians." I didn't want to have to produce some nonexistent military ID if I lied.

"You got kids with you."

Was that a statement or a question? I nodded. "Between you and me, those kids are real valuable," I said, leaning in and trying to mimic his speech patterns. I'd heard that made you seem more trustworthy. "Niece and nephew of one of the best weapons engineers in the world."

"Ahh," he whistled, rocking back on his heels. "Special privileges, then? Damn, my family didn't get no offer of protection, and I'm out here risking my life, not up in some bunker safe and sound."

I shrugged. "Mine neither."

After a bit more eyeballing, he waved us through. "I'll let 'em know you're coming."

We'd barely even started rolling again before his radio burst out with a response. "Negative, soldier. I repeat, negative. We have report of incoming alien hostility. Send the group into Mordsmouth for rendezvous with our agents. I repeat—rendezvous will be inside Mordsmouth, at the central park."

His eyes widened, but by the time he opened his mouth, it was already too late to respond. One moment, everything was normal, and the next, there were alien ships in the sky. One destroyer, six smaller ships, each a bit scarred up but fully functional, as evidenced by their ability to blow up the expressway.

The military people had to have been as shocked as we were, but they immediately attacked. The blockade guard behind us shot at the ships with his gun, screaming at the top of his lungs. Missile launchers turned atop the humvees and started blasting at the ships. Many of the shots missed, as the smaller ships dodged, and those that hit the destroyer didn't do enough damage to matter.

I slammed the accelerator on my bike and we fled through the barricade. The Estreyans attacked behind us.

Chapter 16

Confront them with annihilation, and they will then survive; plunge them into a deadly situation, and they will then live. When people fall into danger, they are then able to strive for victory.

—Sun Tzu

WITHIN A FEW SECONDS, klaxons were blaring. As we reached the outskirts of the city, the flaw in our plan quickly became apparent. People were panicking. It was obvious that there had been rioting and mayhem even before this. There were broken windows, abandoned and looted shops, and wrecked pods that had been shoved over to the sides of the streets.

This was on a completely different level. Despite the number of people we'd seen on the roads heading outward, there were tons still left in the city, and all of them seemed to be scrambling like ants out of a kicked hive.

I swerved sideways, taking us down a side lane and away from the worst of the wreckage.

Next, we hit a riot forming outside what I thought might be a military surplus store. What could they possibly sell that would be effective against an Estreyan? Guns weren't something you could just *buy* as a civilian, after all. It forced us to adjust our route, again. Which in turn forced me to wonder *where* we were even going.

"We're never going to make it through like this!" Adam called out, even as Zed swerved around a man's body lying in the street.

If the change in plans for us to meet NIX's representatives in the park at the city center was spontaneous, due to the attack, then who knows when they would even show up? The park would probably be free of crazy people throwing themselves into traffic or deciding to bulldoze their way through smaller vehicles, but it was also exposed.

No, we couldn't go there. We needed a safe place to wait out the panic, someplace we could keep apprised of the situation as it unfolded, and which we could leave quickly if it became necessary. The emergency shelters were out of the question, too.

I pushed my extra-sensory awareness to its limits, hoping to chart a path for us, and noticed something else instead, high above.

—THE SKYRAIL ISN'T RUNNING.—
-EVE-

Zed's head swiveled to look at me, and he almost wrecked before regaining his balance.

—IF YOU SAY WE SHOULD DRIVE OUR BIKES ALONG THE RAILS,
I'M GOING TO MUTINY.—
-ZED-

—I'M AFRAID OF HEIGHTS.—
-SAM-

—NO, THAT WOULD BE CRAZY. BUT THERE'S A STATION NEAR
HERE, AND IT'S LOCKED DOWN. THOSE BUILDINGS ARE ALWAYS
REINFORCED IN CASE OF TERRORISM, AND THERE'LL BE A
CONCOURSE THERE WHERE WE CAN WATCH THE CITY FROM
ABOVE AND CATCH THE NEWS STATIONS.—
-EVE-

Adam threw out an angled shield, forcing an oncoming pod to careen out of our way.

—THIS WAY.—

-Eve-

I swerved sharply to the left, cutting into an alley barely wide enough for Sam's bike with Adam's sidecar.

We crossed a group of enforcers barreling down the road with no care for anything in their way, and narrowly avoided smashing into them.

Even at our breakneck pace, it took us another few minutes to reach the base of one of the skyrail lifts. I skidded to a stop in front of it, leaving enough room for the others to come in behind me. "They must have stopped running sometime after the invasion," I said, looking upward to the metal beams cutting through the air high above.

"Maybe the power cost was considered too great for nonessential use," Gregor said, hopping to the ground.

"Or people decided their jobs as skyrail operators weren't important anymore when the world was ending," Adam said, lifting himself out of the sidecar with a wave of ink that formed into the strange octopus-spider legs and carried him to the lift. He broke into the control panel beside the clear plastine door with a crackle of electricity, and, after only a few seconds of concentration, they slid open.

The lift wasn't big enough for all of us and our bikes, so I sent Jacky and Torliam along with the kids first, and then Adam brought the lift back down for the rest of us. I stepped out onto the empty concourse and moved to the clear wall of windows which surrounded three-quarters of the circular station.

Metal beams extended from our station in an array, reaching into the distance and connecting to other rails and lift stations. The skyrail was like a huge web, especially in the affluent portions of Mordsmouth. There, people could afford to travel above the smog, at a height where you could see the sunrise and sunset, and the grime of the streets was far enough away to seem unreal.

This close to the edge of the city, it was also high enough to catch a glimpse of the nearby military base, though the smog and other buildings obscured all but a hint of the conflict going on there.

We watched for what felt like days but was really only a couple hours, tense and quiet, as if making too much noise would attract danger. We could hear more of the battle than we could see—the boom of explosions, otherworldly screeches, and the sound of planes parting the air so fast it howled in their wake.

Eventually, the sounds of intense battle died down, leaving only the occasional distant rumble and the shrieking of the emergency klaxons. Between two buildings, gone in an instant, I caught a glimpse of an Estreyan ship skirting the edge of the city, like a shark circling prey.

Jacky's voice was loud within the relative silence of our group. "What's going on?"

I shook my head. "I don't know."

Within a quarter hour, it became apparent.

The air at the edge of the city shimmered like a heat mirage, then stretched upward at a rate that seemed slow, but managed to cover the entire city in a dome within half a minute.

I gaped. "Is it…" I turned to Torliam.

His face was pale under its tan. "Yes. A barrier. A ship with the necessary channeling stones can draw power from the warriors within to create a sphere. The sphere then draws power from the earth to sustain the half above, and from the air to sustain the half below, with minimal energy drawn from the warriors. It is not so dissimilar to the barrier we were trapped in at the palace, except that it is much stronger. Sometimes, they are used as a defensive tool, to protect against attack from outside. More often, it is a method of quarantine."

It was obvious which was more likely here.

Adam's link let out a crackle.

That same sound emanated from all the speakers in the concourse, and rose from the city below us, like a wave. Even the klaxons that had been blaring the emergency alarm crackled and began to speak.

"Your village is enclosed. You are not warriors. You need not to die, but those who are sickened must not remain hidden within you. Take them out to us, in the center of this village, and the sickened will be removed and the village released. If you do not take out to us those who are sickened, the village will not to be released and we will kill all your people. Our fires will cleanse all, the young and old, the animals and the bugs. Everything. You have three days."

The Estreyan-accented, grammar-mangling message played again, resounding from every piece of electronics with speakers across the entire city. When it was over, the klaxons fell silent.

———

ZED SHUFFLED a few feet forward and dug his fingers into the air, opening a small rip. "It's visible in the Other Place, too," he said. After a moment of hesitation, he closed the rip. "I don't want them searching for us trying to figure out what's costing them extra energy," he said. "Not until we know for sure what we're going to do."

"Get me the news if you can, Adam," I said, not taking my eyes off the shimmering barrier. Three days. It wasn't time yet to panic. "Do they think the Sickness has spread through our population?" I wondered aloud.

"What if they're after *us*?" Kris said.

Torliam shook his head, placing a large hand on the girl's shoulder. "They would call for Eve-Redding by name, if that were the case. More likely, they are either misinformed as to the spread of the Sickness, or this is merely an excuse to cow the rest of the world through a show of force."

I watched a spot of the barrier's base through a gap between buildings. A human, far enough away that they looked more like a bug, moved up to the barrier and attacked it with something that might have been a crowbar. They were blasted back, and lay on the ground smoking.

Adam managed to get the concourse's screens to access the news, some showing local channels, and some international. At first, very little about the attack on the military base or Mordsmouth showed up, with most of the local news channels completely down. But over the following hours, the national news stations caught on. Then, a couple of the local stations, whose people had either been turned away from the emergency shelters when capacity was met or had decided not to go to them in the first place, got their broadcast back up and running.

The military base had been overwhelmed, very much outclassed by the Estreyans. They'd only managed to *damage* a few of the ships, not a single attacker destroyed. Reinforcements weren't able to arrive in time due to other skirmishes around the world, so this base, relatively small and unimportant, had carried out a fighting retreat.

Mordsmouth's quarantine was the biggest news, though. People speculated about the technology the Estreyans had used to create the barrier, debated what they meant by "sickened," and wondered if the government would be able to save the city through either diplomacy or military action.

Despite the gravity of our situation, when no immediate danger threatened, we relaxed from the unsustainable tension. The kids fell asleep on one of the concourse's couches, while the rest of us discussed our options.

"We'll wait for the government to respond. I don't expect they'll actually succeed, but while they're working on it, we can take the time to study the situation and come up with a plan." I said.

"I don't like this." Adam ran a hand roughly through his curls.

I let out a huff that was almost a laugh. "No shit. So let's get to work figuring out how to fix it."

BY THE NEXT DAY, the citizens had already turned on each other.

Adam twisted away from the large window looking out on the city, his jaw clenched. "It's already happening. I just saw a guy drag a woman out of the house, along with her IV stand. People are panicking. They'll force anyone with the common cold to sacrifice themselves to the destroyer." It wasn't our first look at humanity's depravity, but it still managed to put a sick feeling in the bottom of my stomach.

Birch let out a low whine and curled up in a ball in the corner.

We'd gone out in the early morning to explore the barrier and the park at the city center, where the huge destroyer was hovering. It broadcast the request for "sickened" at intervals of about an hour and a half. The park had a high stone wall all around it to block out some of the city noise, but people had used this as a way to keep others trapped inside by barricading most of the entrances and guarding the others to make sure people could only enter and not escape. On the bright side, the Estreyans hadn't killed any of the people given up to them yet, and the broadcast hadn't changed.

Many of the people who'd been tossed to the mercy of the invaders fought back, trying to push through the gates or climb the wall, but some of them shuffled or lay on the ground listlessly, perhaps too sick to move. Too sick to be lying exposed in the park without medical care, if so.

I told myself it wasn't our fault, wasn't *my* fault, but when I used Wraith to inspect the nearby buildings and sensed two medics fighting in the doorway while a group of children huddled to the far side of the room, the doors to the rest of the hospital barricaded closed with the patients protected inside, I couldn't release the feeling of responsibility. If I didn't do something to stop it, maybe it would be my fault, and I didn't want to bear a burden any heavier than it already was.

Torliam tilted his head backward. "I have no love for humans, but what is happening now will only lead to shame."

"What are our objectives here?" I said, turning to the others. I had a good idea already, but, for something like what I wanted to do, it was best to draw the others into the decision making. I had unilaterally put them in danger many times, but I was realizing that might not keep working, if my plans kept backfiring. I thought I knew how they would respond, and this way, they could feel a sense of control while still doing what I needed.

"Save innocent people from being killed by the Estreyans," Sam said immediately.

"We'd have to stop the war to do that," Adam said, rolling his eyes. "How about we just help some of the people in this city."

Redness spread across Sam's cheeks. "That's what I meant."

Zed's antsy fingers played over the guns at his sides. "We have to find a way to get past the barrier."

Torliam nodded at him. "Yes. We must continue our quest for the god. But first, we must acquire this substance which will keep you from succumbing to the tiny bugs NIX put in your body."

Jacky snorted loudly. "Little bugs?" She completely ignored the irritated look Torliam shot her, and turned to me. "I don't think the Estreyans are just gonna let everyone go if we ask them. So either we do this sneaky, or we do this hard." She punctuated her last word by smacking her fist into her palm.

Zed pressed his lips together, a motion picked up from our

mother, but which looked so much different on him. "NIX isn't gonna be able to meet us in the park while the destroyer is hovering over there, either."

I settled down onto the cold tile floor, crossing my legs. "I think there might be a way for us to solve all our problems at once." I lifted my hand, ticking off fingers as I spoke. "Stop the civilians from being slaughtered, take down the barrier and escape the city, get the booster for Zed's nanites." I held up three raised fingers to the team.

Adam muttered sarcastically to himself, "Only three things? I'm sure it'll be so easy!"

I ignored him. "A lot of things could go wrong while we're trying to achieve any of those objectives, so I'd like to try and build redundancies into the plan. Hopefully, we can do this sneaky *and* 'hard.'"

Jacky grinned at me.

"The destroyer will hold the power-channeling stones," Torliam said. "If we remove or sufficiently damage them, the barrier will fall."

"Is that going to get rid of their death beam weapon, too?" Adam said. "My shields won't hold against one, and I don't think yours will either. How are we supposed to keep the people safe while evacuating them?"

Sam looked between the two of them, who were glaring at each other. "Are we so sure they'll attack? Why don't we just try to talk to them? They've been on Earth since before Eve's broadcast. Maybe we could convince them, or somehow…use Eve and Torliam's political capital to make them stop?"

"I want to try that, at least," I said. "But I'm less than confident it'll work. So we need to ensure we don't just make everything worse. Is there a quick way for us to evacuate the civilians? What about your Skill, Zed?"

He shook his head. "I don't think normal humans would survive in the Other Place for long enough to get them safely away from the destroyer."

Adam tapped away on his link. "What about underground tunnels?" He fell silent for a while, then seemed to find what he wanted. "Yeah. Mordsmouth has been expanding and building on itself for a long time, and the infrastructure to support this many people isn't all being held aboveground. I'm not just talking about sewers and stuff. We've made our own tunnels, before. We could get them to any nearby underground facility."

Torliam frowned. "How do we coordinate the rabble? We must also remember that there are many weakened among them. Some may not be able to escape with their own strength."

"I can help them," Kris piped up from the corner. "If we can find some bodies for me, I could probably control seven or eight at close range, and carry maybe twice that many people. Ooh!" She straightened with excitement. "What about if we hid my marionettes in the crowd and had them pass out messages to get ready ahead of time?"

Jacky ruffled her hair. "What about mannequins? From those fancy clothes stores?"

Kris frowned. "Yeah, maybe that would work, if their bodies don't just fall apart."

Adam leaned back and started playing with a coin, running it nervously through his fingers. "I wonder if this will actually work. You saw what was left of NIX, right? A few feet of earth and concrete isn't going to do anything to stop the destroyer."

Zed nodded. "But, if they don't just melt the city right away, it *might* keep them from being able to follow the civilians, if they get away quick enough, and we scatter them in different directions. I still think it's a good backup plan." He turned to Torliam. "I'm pretty sure I can get into the ship with Veil-Piercer. These power-channeling stones, do you have any idea where they'll be located? If they don't want to take down the barrier, maybe we just take that decision away from them."

Torliam's eyes widened. "If you damage the power-channeling stones, the destroyer will not be able to burn the city. Even though the smaller ships will not be hindered, this is a good idea."

"I'll infiltrate the ship with you, Zed," Gregor said, crossing his arms. Before anyone could protest, he continued, raising his voice. "Without a Skill, how is Zed supposed to damage rocks? With a *gun*, which will draw the attention of every Estreyan on board?"

Zed frowned. "I was thinking I could just pull the stones into the Other Place. That should stop them from working, right?"

Torliam snorted. "They will be built into the floor of the room. However, it is the runes drawn into them which allow them to channel power, similar to the arrays which we have used to travel between our worlds. You need not destroy the stones entirely. If you damage them enough in any particular spot, the runes will break their connection, and the device will fail."

"I'm still the best one for the job," Gregor said. "I can take a few chunks out of these stones with my swords, more stealthily than anyone else, except maybe Eve. But Eve is needed to distract the ships while the rest of you save the civilians, right? Just in case they don't listen to friendly reasoning?" He turned to me, bushy eyebrow raised.

I nodded reluctantly. "Yes. We can't count on them backing down. If they listen, great. If not, hopefully I'll have bought enough time for you guys to handle the rest. But you'll have to be able to deal with staying in the Other Place for pretty much the whole time."

"That…might be a problem," Zed said. "I've been noticing my tolerance to the cold seems to be building up, but I don't know if that's just because of my Skill getting stronger with use, or if anyone can acclimate to it."

Gregor rolled his eyes. "Just get me a thermal suit or something. I can probably make one myself, if we can find some wetsuits in my size and a couple other things, and some chemicals…" he trailed off, like how Blaine used to, his eyes looking into the middle distance as he thought too hard to concentrate on the rest of us. After a moment, he seemed to come back to himself, and gave a single, sharp nod. "And I'm not useful to this plan in any other way. So this is the obvious choice."

Torliam turned to me, blue-green eyes catching the light of the sun and shining almost like a cat's. "This may work for the warriors of my people, but what will we do about NIX?"

I bit the inside of my lip. "If talking to the Estreyans works, then I'll have time to get hold of NIX. In case it doesn't, I want to give them a signal for another place to meet after we do this."

We hashed out the rest of the planning as we prepared, digging connecting tunnels under the park, raiding abandoned stores and a not-abandoned broadcasting station, and preparing ourselves to confront an alien warship.

IT WAS the last moments of night before the morning of the third day by the time we were ready. I wanted to initiate the plan before the daylight came, hoping the confusion of the darkness might make things just a little easier for us.

I gave the signal, and the floodlights lit up my form, glaringly bright against the smoggy darkness, throwing my shadow out dramatically onto the building roof I stood at the edge of.

Birch stood at my side, thrusting his wings outward and fluffing his fur dramatically.

"Warriors," I called out in Estreyan, holding the modified sound-horn Adam had cobbled together up to my mouth. "I am Eve-Redding of the line of Matrix, the prophesied, known as the godkiller. I wish to speak with you. There has been a terrible mistake."

The sound-horn didn't amplify my voice, but I knew it was working when every device with a speaker throughout the entire city block echoed my words, a fraction of a second later. The Estreyans would get my message. NIX would, too, if Adam's modified copy of the Estreyan's hijacking technology was properly playing along military channels.

The destroyer turned in place, till it pointed directly and blatantly at me.

I gulped.

Nothing happened, for second after agonizing second, until I wondered what the hell was taking them so long. Wraith could reach the ship, but I had trouble penetrating the barrier of the hull far enough to spread through the interior. I had moved to focus my attention on the damaged part of the hull, hoping to find an easier way to push through at that spot, when they finally responded.

The link Adam had taken from Blaine's house crackled on my arm, then spoke back to me, along with all the devices in and around the city block. "This is Ravanan, leader of this squad. If you will, show us the three gifts and the mark of Testimony, to give witness to your identity." The voice also spoke in Estreyan, and I wondered what the humans close enough to hear this would make of it.

Down below, the crowds of people milled about with a little more energy, shuffling into more tightly bound groups around certain points.

I let out a breath, shifting the sound horn to my other hand so I could pull back my sleeve. I showed the ring, the armband, and the third, unsolved, puzzle, which I carried in my pack. Then I pushed away the leather jacket and shemagh I'd been wearing over my armor, to show both it and the crystal at my throat.

There was no response, so I raised my left hand and let a swirl of Chaos bubble up, dark tendrils distinct against the brightness of the spotlight.

"I thank you, Eve-Redding," the voice said. "Are you without your companions? Those who bear the other marks of Testimony?"

I lifted the sound-horn to my mouth again. "They are in the city. I have come to you this night to stop a needless slaughter. Please, heed my words. You wish to eradicate the Sickness and those who harbor it, but the humans do not understand what that means. The Sickness was cultivated in secret, and only the most highly trusted of warriors of that organization know of its existence. The humans fall to minor illnesses easily. These people," I gestured to those contained within the park fences below, "are no threat to you. Truly, none of the humans are a true threat to Estreyer, as you have proved with your attacks."

The commander's voice hardened. "The Sickness is a threat to everything living, as you should understand well, if you are to fulfill your role. We must remove it. But I have no desire to kill the innocent cattle of a people. Only those who have fallen to madness and hunger will be destroyed, if they are brought here."

My hands shook faintly. Would he let these people walk away, then, if I asked?

He continued, "They are here in the city, hiding. Let us bring you aboard to safety, Eve-Redding. Call your companions, and we will provide shelter to them, as well as help you to regain your way."

I heard something in his tone, like the faint sourness of milk just beginning to turn. Perhaps it meant I really was starting to absorb the cadence of the language, but it only made the hairs on the back of my neck rise.

—Start evacuating. I think he's trying to trap us.—
-Eve-

Below, the people milled a little more urgently, packing even more tightly into their groups. There was shouting, but I ignored it, and hoped the Estreyans would, too.

Birch growled, the rumble reverberating out from his throat and riding away on the winds.

"My path is on Earth," I replied aloud. "The path to the Champion is here."

There was silence again, for too long, and then the two smaller ships floated forward, their segmented-shelled, stingray-like bodies moving through the air with deceptively unthreatening slowness.

"Is that what you were told to believe?" Ravanan asked. "How is it that our god would be on this planet?"

What I was told to believe? Something had gone wrong, probably even before I'd revealed myself and started to talk. Queen Mardinest must have found a way to poison them against me already. I focused on the two smaller ships for any sign of attack.

—TIME TO GO, GUYS.—

-EVE-

I took a few slow steps backward, speaking again. "He has been here all along, hidden. That is why you have never found him, despite all your searching." I prepared to run to where my bike was stashed behind the air filtering unit sticking out of the roof.

A small wave of military vehicles burst around the corner of the two far streets, attacking the destroyer with a barrage of artillery and rocket launchers, all aimed with surprising accuracy at the damaged sections of its hull.

Chapter 17

The world is indeed comic, but the joke is on mankind.
  — H. P. Lovecraft

MY MOUTH DROPPED OPEN. I'd had Adam signal the military and, through them, NIX, to set up a new meeting point. I had *not* coordinated an attack on the Estreyans.

People screamed. Some of the angry mob of guards around the park gates scattered, while others seemed to be frozen in a kind of stupid shock.

The destroyer tilted to avoid the attack, surprisingly nimble for a ship of its size, but the projectiles twisted through the air like homing missiles to strike the damaged section of the hull at a single point.

That's when the Players burst out of a couple of the vehicles, wearing that familiar bodysuit and armor, and moving in a distinctly superhuman way.

Among the people trapped in the park, forms wearing heavy, concealing clothing scattered, each sprinting unerringly toward a specific person and swinging them into its arms like they weighed little more than a child. The marionettes then carried their cargo to another group of sick people.

One of the two smaller ships turned away from me, shooting a beam of concentrated fire toward the military vehicles. A tank exploded, and I felt the vibration and shockwave in the air, even from all the way across the park.

The civilians cowered, and a few of them ran away from their assigned groups. They'd likely just signed their own death certificate. Around each of the groups, blue light speared through the ground in a circle, as if they were at the center of some kind of mystical ritual. The people screamed again, even though we'd surreptitiously spread the news among them of what would happen if we needed to go ahead with the emergency evacuation. The ground beneath them collapsed in slow motion, and they disappeared into the holes in the earth. My teammates would help them escape, taking those in the most critical condition to a special location.

The destroyer lurched suddenly, and my heart jumped along with it. "Hurry," I murmured aloud, turning to run as the second smaller ship shot toward Birch and me. I let Wraith spread out over the battlefield. Being able to watch my own back was a great aid to avoid being killed. I sprinted around the corner of the air-filtering unit, but had to throw myself out of the way as the ship loosed a beam of fire and disintegrated any cover it would have provided. My bike was caught in the beam, and quickly turned into a heap of slag and melted rubber. I wasn't sure if the attack had intentionally missed me or not.

I rolled to my feet and sprinted away, Birch at my heels.

—Bike destroyed, might need a hand.—
-Eve-

I used mental commands to send the message to Adam.

The ship turned to follow, zooming around to cut me off.

True darkness appeared, spilling out of a tear on the side of the destroyer and coalescing into a huge winged shape. Three humanoid forms rushed out, the rip closed, and they rode away on the ink creature.

In the park, a group of vibrating, identical Players ran right through the tall wall, and it broke apart where they passed through, leaving rough holes. The humans who hadn't believed or listened to our instructions might be able to escape through them, if they didn't get caught in the crossfire and killed. I knew that Skill, but I didn't have time to wonder what Vaughn was doing here.

The ship attacking me blocked the far side of the roof.

I lashed out with a whip of Chaos, and it jerked backward to escape. I dug my claws into the roof and sprinted the other way, back toward the park.

A Player below shot dramatic-looking light beams at the destroyer, while another grabbed hold of the remains of the exploded tank by the end of its huge gun, swung it around, and launched it at the giant ship.

The tank didn't quite look like it would reach, but then it lurched in the air and rose the last few meters, crashing into the side of the destroyer at full speed.

A line of fire burst up in front of me, as the fighter ship that had come after me once again cut off my path to escape.

Adam's ink bird veered toward me, and Zed shot a few bullets at the small ship, drawing its attention for a second.

I picked up Birch with one arm and leapt through the wall of fire. Without the active attack from the fighter ship, the leftover flames barely singed my hair. I launched myself off the edge of the roof as Adam flew the ink bird past it. I hit the smooth black surface and started to slip off the side, the momentum too much, the ink feathers providing no grip.

Birch landed right beside me and bit at the seat of my pants ineffectually, too small to move my large body.

Zed grabbed me by the elbow just in time, yanking me to safety with enough force to bruise my arm. "What the hell is going on?" he screamed.

Behind us, the fighter ship was already giving chase. The air above it flickered with a burst of light and then darkness, and something landed atop it, expanding quickly and throwing the ship off balance.

I turned my head backward to confirm what Wraith was telling me.

Vaughn clung to the base of its wing like a barnacle, multiplying himself with ephemeral duplicates that sank right into the ship as it flew through them, disappearing somewhere inside it. Where the ship's hull touched them, silhouette marks formed on it, till it began to chip off and break apart. "It's NIX!" I screamed back.

At the front of the bird, Adam cursed, pushing it to fly even faster. Gregor's Shadow hand, even blacker than the ink beneath us, laid over my own with faint pressure, most of him too far in the Shadow state to affect the real world.

A section of the fighter ship's hull broke all the way open, and Vaughn slipped inside. The ship lurched and twisted, careening off toward the side in a spiral.

His limp form shot back out of the hull, speeding toward us like a rag doll launched out of a cannon. Vaughn hit the wing of our ink bird hard enough to send it careening through the air, too, along with the rest of us.

Adam cursed, and I wrapped my arms around Zed and Gregor and dug my claws into the ink feathers below us, heedless of the damage I caused the construct.

With a massive heave of wings, the bird almost righted itself, but it was too late. We plummeted toward the side of a building, the angle of the bird putting us between the building and itself. If it hit, we'd be crushed. I pushed Chaos out, forming it like a huge spike of darkness behind my back. I slammed it outward, and we crashed through the already bursting plastine windows of the building in a tumbling heap.

Adam screamed in pain, then caught himself and arrested his movement with a bubble of ink that squished around him like it was made of foam, absorbing the impact.

Wraith sensed it as the fighter ship that Vaughn had taken down smashed into the destroyer, impossibly finding that same section of ragged hull, already heavily damaged, and crunching right through it.

The destroyer lurched to the side like a drunken man, then crashed sideways into the ground at the edge of the park, throwing up a fountain of dirt and screeching as it crumpled and broke under the force of impact. The sounds of the battle seemed to die down, for a moment, as if the city held its breath. The destroyer shuddered, then stilled. Hopefully, the people heading through the tunnels we'd created beneath the park had already made it out.

I rolled to my hands and knees, then picked myself up carefully, looking around in horror. We'd landed in some sort of office building and smashed through half the cubicles before stopping.

Gregor's Shadow form stood, more easily than I had, and I let out a sigh of relief, able to focus on Zed instead. I put a hand on Zed's stomach, pushing Wraith into his body as I searched for injuries. I found extensive bruising and a fractured clavicle, but nothing serious enough to kill him.

Birch coughed, then poked his head out of the wall he'd smashed into. He hopped out and gave himself a good shake to get rid of the insulation covering him, then turned to growl at Vaughn, who'd smashed his own indentation into the wall at the corner of the room.

Adam released the bubble of ink, white-faced with pain as he lay twisted on the floor. He looked up to me and shook his head. "I'm okay," he grunted. "Just racked my back a bit. Nothing Sam can't help with."

I nodded, then turned to Vaughn.

The Player struggled to his feet, using the wall as support. He spat out a mouthful of blood. "This goddamn better be worth it," he muttered to himself, before looking up and meeting my gaze. "We've got the order you requested."

"WE'VE GOT A SECURE MEETUP LOCATION," Vaughn said. "The nanite booster is there. Follow me. It's not safe to stay here."

Behind us, the park and surrounding city center were in absolute shambles. The whole fracas had taken only a couple minutes. Despite the surprising destruction NIX had dealt the Estreyan ships, I was certain the backup ships from the border of Mordsmouth would arrive momentarily. Nevertheless, I shook my head. "Just tell me where it is. I'll link up with the rest of my team and we'll meet you there."

"I'll take you there," he insisted.

"Not without my team. Just tell me where to go."

An ugly look spread across his face. "There's no way I'm letting a traitor like you out of my sight. We're trying to save the world. And since that alien ship was trying to kill you, I'd think you'd be a little more grateful."

Zed grabbed Adam's arm and slung it across his shoulder, helping the older boy upright.

"We don't have time for this," I snapped. I sent Wraith to search for the fastest path out of the building. Luckily, we'd smashed in on one of the lower floors. "There's an elevator only a few doors down," I said. "The lights are still on inside, maybe it still has power."

I sent a Window to the members of the team who weren't with me.

—Is everyone out safe?—
-Eve-

—We're good. Almost to the sealed parking garage. Got a lot to heal.—
-Sam-

We started to move toward the elevator, and Vaughn pushed away from the wall, limping after us. "If you won't come with me, I'll come with you."

Adam's voice shook, and his ink legs shuddered, but held. "We can't trust him. What if he leads the rest of them right to us, and they decide they don't want a fair and square trade?"

"You owe me, Eve." Vaughn's voice was strained with urgency. "One small-to-medium favor, right? Or have you forgotten that you came to me when you needed help? Coming along to make sure you don't play one of your tricks shouldn't cost more than that. Besides," he said, as we rode downward in the claustrophobia-inducing elevator, "it didn't seem like those aliens were on your side. Maybe betraying the humans didn't work out so well for you?"

He was right, in part. Back when I'd first been forced into the Game, I'd asked him for information about it. I'd promised him a favor in return, and all but forgotten about it, with everything that had happened since. I didn't really feel like honor was worth risking my safety for, but we had to meet NIX anyway to get the nanite booster paste for Zed, so letting Vaughn come along didn't change much.

"Fine, you can come," I said. "But you do realize that everything NIX told us was a lie, right? The Estreyans aren't attacking just because they're *evil*."

We moved from the ground floor of the building out into the street, running through side alleys till we reached a manhole. At the park, other fighter ships had arrived, and it looked like the mixed group of civilians, military, and Players might be at a disadvantage.

"If any of them want to live," I said, "you better tell your people to get out of there, now. Players don't stand a chance against Estreyan warriors."

"We took out a destroyer," Vaughn said, following along. "I think we can—"

"No," I snapped, digging clawed fingers into the metal seal and heaving it upward. "My team deactivated the destroyer's power channeling system. You, along with a quarter of the city, would have been killed when you first burst out and drew attention to yourselves, otherwise." I dropped down into the tunnel beneath the street, then helped steady the others as they followed.

The four backup fighter ships unloaded beams of fire in every direction, preventing any follow-up attacks on the destroyer and protecting the single remaining original fighter, which was so damaged it barely managed to stay afloat.

He hesitated, but then started moving his hands about in mid-air, obviously using his VR chip to send a Window to someone. Had he not learned how to control the Windows with his mind?

I kept my voice low as we ran, despite the noise above. "They weren't even hostile to us, even after we kidnapped and tortured the son of their queen and farmed him for his blood. They had no intention of retaliating."

"And they *became* hostile after you broke it out and sent it home to tell its alien friends all our secrets. All this, for what?"

"Is escaping from an organization that has trapped you in a crazy death game against your will not enough reason?" Adam muttered, panting from exertion.

Vaughn sneered at him.

"The Estreyans would never have attacked if NIX hadn't started developing the super-plague to end all plagues," I said, and Vaughn's expression sharpened with interest. He knew about the Sickness, though what, exactly, I wasn't sure. "They're trying to protect themselves from us, because we made ourselves dangerous. They're not trying to kill sick people, Vaughn. They're trying to wipe out the plague which we brought over from their world and then started modifying to be even more deadly."

"Do you really believe that?"

"I've seen what the Sickness can do," I said. "It drives people just insane enough that they try to destroy everything they ever cared about, and that's before they turn into mindless cannibals. The Estreyans have reason to be afraid, and they don't understand us. They believe there are people with the Sickness hiding somewhere in the city."

He was silent as we splashed through the fetid tunnels. "But you evacuated the citizens. You know these 'Estreyans' are a danger to innocent people. They're destroying the world, and they obviously hold no loyalty to you. It doesn't matter who started things, we need to finish it. You could help us fight them."

I shook my head, peering out towards the park. "We stopped to help these people because we could, and because we were trapped in Mordsmouth along with them. But we've got bigger goals than taking down a few ships." I paused, then turned to examine him again. "I saw NIX's base. It was razed right out of the mountainside. How did you escape?"

His lip curled upward in a sneer. "I guess I'm just full of surprises, huh? It wouldn't be the first time I should have died because of you. At least being instantly incinerated is a better death than being *eaten alive* like the rest of my teammates."

I didn't respond. If I'd tried to save Vaughn from the God of Knowledge, I would be dead. He was there on a Trial, and must have been pulled back via the Shortcut before the god managed to kill him, but I hadn't had that insurance. Still, I figured leaving someone to die a horrible death wasn't something you could explain away and get them to just forgive.

I looked at him, taking in the Player uniform, letting it fan the spark of an idea I had ignored earlier. "You were at the military base they just attacked," I said.

"They've been attacking all the obvious targets. We've been busy evacuating the most sensitive and valuable people and materials."

I narrowed my eyes. "You were there because NIX had an interest in preserving something there. A weapon they'd been cultivating." My muscles tensed as the anger rose, urging me to snap forward and attack. "You evacuated subjects who had the Sickness, didn't you? And you brought them to hide, here in the city. That's why they put the barrier up and started threatening everyone's lives."

Vaughn's gaze didn't waver, but I knew I was right. I let out a scoffing laugh, the rage forcing itself out of my throat with nowhere else to go. "So once again, this is all because of fucking NIX."

"I WARNED THEM," I said. "They knew about the Sickness, and this is their reaction? They just endangered every—" Anger choked off my words.

"This is bad," Adam said. "The Estreyans have to think we were involved in the attack."

Zed let out a humorless laugh. "We were."

"But now we've made *enemies* of them," I said. "Before, I'm pretty sure they were just trying to capture us. Now?"

Adam cursed.

We arrived at the abandoned underground parking garage within a few minutes. The others were already there, and had lit a few glow-sticks to bring some relief to the absolute darkness. Birch immediately noticed the infestation of rats and ran to slaughter them. The civilians that had identified themselves as more severely ill or in need of a hospital were set up in one of the corners, with Sam doing triage to see who needed his help most urgently.

The rest of the team were spreading out what little food and water we could spare. They all turned to us as we exited the ragged tunnel we'd created earlier to connect the condemned and sealed off underground garage and the sewer line.

When they saw Vaughn, they bristled like angry cats.

Jacky squeezed her fists so hard the knuckles popped, and began to grow.

Kris stood beside Sam, her small wooden puppet in her arms, while her other marionettes moved into a protective formation around the civilians.

Sam's eyes darkened a little, but not so much that the shadows swallowed his irises.

None of that seemed to bother Vaughn, until Torliam moved away from the wall beside us, where he'd been guarding the tunnel.

He placed himself beside me, blocking Vaughn's line of sight to the civilians and throwing off heat and enough anger to lift the hairs on my arm.

"You're working with the *alien*?" Vaughn said, his lips curling back from his teeth in a snarl.

Blue mist wafted up from Torliam, and Vaughn started to vibrate, duplicating himself to create a defensive shield.

I snapped my hand out and grabbed Torliam's arm. "We need him to lead us to the others," I said. "They've got Zed's boosters."

Torliam didn't respond for multiple tense heartbeats.

Vaughn was similarly frozen, though, rather than self-restraint, he was doing it out of self-preservation. As soon as Vaughn had started to use his Skill, Gregor had slipped back into his Shadow state and pressed both of his daggers into Vaughn's stomach. With a thought from the boy, they would become corporeal again, and Vaughn would be impaled.

Torliam looked to Zed, to Gregor, and then to me. He let his Skill's power recede. "I find this abhorrent," he said.

I nodded, squeezing his arm. "I know. I'm sorry, but I don't have any other choice."

He turned his glare back on Vaughn, who very slowly raised his hands and dismissed his vibrating copies. "If you do not fulfill your end of the bargain," Torliam said, "I will remove your entrails while you still live. I know from experience, it is extremely unpleasant to look down and see your organs outside of your body, while someone pokes and prods at them."

Vaughn swallowed, his teeth clenched together so hard they creaked. He gave a single, sharp nod.

Gregor reluctantly withdrew his knives from Vaughn's stomach and moved a few feet away before releasing his Shadow state. "I'll be watching you," he said, the threat that much more disturbing coming from an eight-year-old.

The tension wasn't truly diffused, but without the risk of immediate violence, we all turned our attention toward the civilians. Vaughn surprised me, using a Skill that caused him to glow as he walked among them, spreading the glow to them for a few seconds when he touched them. Vaughn's wounds seemed to be healed, and the people he touched sighed in relief and wonder as the light suffused them. It was a healing Skill, and, judging by the way the sight of the light made the rage slip out of me, it might be some sort of Charisma-based mood influencer, as well.

Sam had taken a couple of the sick people aside, around a wall, but their muffled screams still echoed off the cement walls.

"It's okay," a man said. "It definitely does hurt. But we don't need our little toes anyway, and he said I'm cured. *Forever*. I feel better than I have in years. I think they're angels."

A woman snorted. "Are you kidding? Angels coming down from heaven while the world is ending?"

He looked pointedly at Vaughn, still letting off that healing glow.

The woman followed his gaze, and didn't say anything else.

ADAM RESTED and tried to recover his strength while Sam did what he could to help the injured and sick, offsetting a good portion of the damage back onto them in less debilitating ways.

The bruises and abrasions from our little tumble healed themselves quickly, and I even got rewarded for injuring myself.

YOUR LIFE HAS INCREASED!

When Sam was finished, we took the civilians to the edge of the city, where a rent-a-pod shop had half a parking lot full of abandoned vehicles. We advised them to leave Mordsmouth if they could, and Adam helped charge up all of their links so they could contact family and keep updated on the news.

Torliam surprised me, laughing with a couple of the humans and even letting a now-healthy little girl, whose parents had been forced into the park along with her by their neighbors, ride on his shoulders.

Some of the pods in the lot were empty, but others held peoples' belongings. Perhaps they'd been abandoned, or perhaps their owners just hadn't been able to return for them yet. A chemistry book in one of the pod's front seats caught my eye. Its cover showed a rock dissolving in acid. I stared at it for a moment, then used my right arm, which was armored, to smash through the window and grab it.

Jacky snickered at my "first step down the life of crime" as I tucked the book away in my pack.

Some of the people we'd helped thanked us, while others were still angry and wary.

We left, following a very impatient Vaughn to the place where his boss and, supposedly, the nanite booster were waiting. It seems they'd had the same idea as us about staying hidden underground, but instead of hastily created tunnels and a condemned parking garage, they had a nice bunker. In fact, it looked like a more refined version of the emergency shelters they'd built after the government first learned about the Estreyans, with actual rooms in lieu of big open levels for people to pack themselves into.

Walking down into the ground gave me flashbacks to NIX, the feeling of dirt pressing down above me making me tense. We passed a few Players along the way. Some of them recognized me, and some of them seemed to recognize Torliam, or at least understand that he was an alien. All of them were hostile.

Vaughn waved them off. "They're here for a meeting with the boss. Play nice, now."

When we walked into the room where most of the Players were gathered, I stiffened. The reaction rippled out to the rest of my team, as they realized who it was. "Of course it's you," I said to Kilburn.

He sat perched on a chair atop a raised platform in the corner of the room, like it was a throne.

Despite the weight of all the hostile stares, my fingertips tingled, and my claws slowly slid out, the structure of my hands and feet shifting to accommodate them.

Kilburn rose to his feet without trouble and smiled, whatever damage I'd done to him when we last fought seemingly healed without issue. "I'm glad to see you again."

I shuddered.

His eyes swept over my teammates, lingering on Torliam a little longer than most. "Please, be at ease. I wasn't originally slated to negotiate with you, but, when the aliens attacked the base, necessity dictated a change of plans. Whatever our past differences, we have a mutually beneficial goal now, and I have what you requested."

I threw Vaughn a glare.

Vaughn shrugged, leaning casually against a steel and cement support beam. "I thought you would have guessed."

Chapter 18

Never can true reconcilement grow where wounds of deadly hate have pierced so deep.
— John Milton

"PLEASE, SIT WITH ME," Kilburn offered, waving his arm flamboyantly and causing a second chair to flip off the ground and onto the platform next to him. "Let's talk."

I didn't move right away. We were in a room full of Players, fairly deep underground. Adam was almost out of energy and wouldn't be able to help in a fight. Quite a few of the Players were also injured or obviously exhausted, but they had military equipment that could make up for that. We didn't have the advantage of surprise. And most importantly, I still needed the nanite booster for Zed.

I looked to Chanelle. She had asked us to leave her sister's murderer alive until she was well enough to kill him herself. But she didn't even acknowledge his presence, staring off into the distance and nibbling at her raw fingertips.

"Show me the nanite booster," I said.

Kilburn clicked his tongue mockingly and shook his head with fake sadness. "So distrusting." Still, he walked to the edge of the platform and opened a door to a small room. He grabbed a compact metal briefcase and brought it out, sitting it on the second chair and then opening it.

I was somewhat familiar with the nanite booster, and though I wasn't an expert, a focused examination with Wraith didn't show any differences between the vials within and the ones we'd originally stolen from NIX.

I moved to take a step forward, but Torliam grabbed my arm. "If any harm befalls you, I will take retribution in blood a thousand fold." He looked at Kilburn while he said it, his voice reverberating off the walls and making the hair on the back of my arms raise. "None here will leave this room alive."

"You can *try*," one of the Players yelled.

Kilburn waved his hand in a sharp motion, and the Player jerked back like a puppet on a string, but clamped their mouth shut and only glared silently.

"All my people are here as hostages, just as yours are," Kilburn said. "Relax. I need them to save the world, so I won't do anything that would cause the rest of you to try to kill them."

I turned to Torliam, making eye contact with the other members of my team as well. "Don't worry. I've grown so much stronger, since the last time we met. He can *try* to hurt me." I threw a grin at the Players and made my way forward to join Kilburn on the platform.

—THINGS MIGHT GET A LITTLE HEATED. DON'T ESCALATE IF YOU
DON'T HAVE TO.—
-EVE-

I set the briefcase beside my chair and sat down. "Let's talk," I agreed. I looked at his gaunt face and remembered China's eyes, staring at me after he broke her. I still wondered, sometimes, if she'd been alive when her eyes met mine, or if he'd already killed her.

I realized my claws were out only when they scraped against my palms, digging little furrows and leaving faint lines of blood behind. With effort, I relaxed again, forcing my claws back into hiding.

His eyes tracked my fingers, lingering on the sixth finger on my left hand. "I've thought about you a lot, since the last time we met," he said unexpectedly. "I had plenty of time for reflection, while NIX was healing me. Not all regenerative Skills are as instantaneous as your healer's. I don't think I've ever been closer to death than when you turned that power on me." He shuddered, but his eyes were bright and the ends of his lips were curled up in a weird smile. Seeing the expression that must have leaked onto my face, his smile got bigger. "I'm not a masochist. I don't *enjoy* pain, but in a way, that cusp between life and death was thrilling. I was angry with you at first. All I could think about was killing you. When I was able, I studied you, your past, your psychological profile, stored video imagery of you, anything I could get my hands on. I realized that you and I aren't so different, but somehow, you're so much more *effective* than I was. So then I learned from you."

"Why don't you get to the point?" I said, wishing I could just take the briefcase and run. I'd expected him to ask me about the hints I'd tossed them about ending the war, not go on a creepy monologue.

He ignored me. "I admit that I am cruel and violent. People have diagnosed me as a sociopath, though take of that what you will. I have a need for conflict and excitement. I am a narcissist. I think you're not so dissimilar." He paused then, as if waiting for me to agree.

I raised an eyebrow at him.

He chuckled. "In the past, I was aimless. I wanted power, and I needed an outlet for my urges, but in indulging myself, I unwittingly stymied my own ability to grow more powerful. This was…unavoidable, I think. There was nothing to attract all the attention and energy of a man of my particular talents. No goal. That's changed now. I think saving the world is a glorious enough ambition for anyone, don't you?"

He was serious about that?

"After all…you have a similar goal, right?" His smile was conspiratorial, as if we were best friends who shared a secret. "I think we can help each other. I have the manpower, you have the information."

The room filled with a susurrus of whispers from those listening.

—IF THIS GOES DOWNHILL, BACK UP TO THE NEAREST WALL AND BUY SOME TIME. I'LL TAKE OUR PEOPLE INTO THE OTHER PLACE AND THEN GRAB YOU.—

-ZED-

I sent back a Window acknowledging him, making sure not to reveal our communication outwardly, since everyone in the room was familiar with that gaze into the middle ground that signified use of a VR chip.

Kilburn continued. "NIX hasn't contacted me since the attempts to break through that forcefield failed. They probably expected us all to die in here, and have allocated their resources toward more profitable assets. It's not unreasonable, but still… That was a mistake. Now they've left me with all these assets and no one to tell me what I can and can't do with them."

"You want to join me?" I had to say the words aloud for confirmation, since they seemed so incredibly unlikely.

"If you have a plan that's better than mine." He raised his eyebrows and steepled his fingers together, like a kid with a secret they were bursting to tell.

I sighed, and acquiesced to his obvious desire. "What's your plan?"

"The aliens didn't get here through space. Not this time. They didn't use a Shortcut, either. They used a stone circle that was buried under a few tons of water and ice at the South Pole, the same way *you* did. So." He stopped, tendons straining against his skin. "I need to know how you did it, and how I can stop them from sending more reinforcements. If I can do that, it gives Earth the next few years to prepare. They'd have to physically fly all the way here to attack, and NIX's Thinkers already deduced that should take years. We could use that time to rebuild, and to strengthen our military."

I thought of Torliam, because I knew Kilburn didn't just mean inventing better weapons. NIX would want more Seeds. With so many Estreyans effectively trapped here on Earth if the arrays were destroyed, they could capture and farm them for Seed organisms on a much larger scale. Hypothetically, the Estreyan warriors could just leave and fly back the long way, but I doubted they had the resources to survive a multi-year journey through space. I also knew I couldn't trust Kilburn or NIX not to keep an array to study, trying to reverse-engineer or figure out how to work it. I could imagine them traveling to Estreyer only to perpetuate the war with a crop-dusting of nuclear bombs. "What is left of NIX?" I said.

"You didn't manage to cause our destruction," he said with another razor-blade smile.

I suppressed a shudder. "Is their leadership in place? An intact chain of command?"

"Some have died, but most of the leadership is still alive. Enough to keep operations running."

"Do they know about your plan?"

He stared at me for a moment too long, like a snake before it struck. "They are human, without an ounce of real power. They see us as tools and weapons. Which we are."

"But you don't discuss your battle plan with your sword, or take suggestions from it," I said, feeling like I understood a little more of Kilburn's motivation. "Do they still have Thinkers?"

"A few that had the right Skills and enough power to escape, or to not be where the attacks happened in the first place. Many of them died. Are you convinced, yet? I think it's time for me to hear *your* plans."

Kilburn might not be completely loyal to NIX, but that didn't mean I could trust him. And even if I did, I doubted the rest of the team could ever agree to work with him. He had resources, true, but I couldn't control them, and I didn't even know how useful they would be in finding the Champion. "What do you know about the Sickness?" I asked.

"Only what you told Vaughn on the way here," Kilburn replied promptly.

I wasn't truly surprised he'd been listening in. "The meningolycanosis NIX has been developing is a vector for it. But it's not the only vector. The problem is, no one really understands what the other vectors are, or how to stop them. It's the most virulent pandemic introduced to Earth in the history of the human race, and it's also the reason the Estreyans have used to justify the attack on Earth. They call it *the* Sickness, because it's the only disease important enough to matter."

"You want to weaponize it?" He frowned, tapping his fingers together.

My insides went cold. No, I couldn't work with him.

He continued, oblivious to my thoughts. "But without any way to control its spread, we won't be able to prevent mutual destruction. That's one way to win a war, but definitely not the *preferred* method."

"I want you to work on a cure," I said, making sure my voice didn't waver. I had to redirect his train of thought immediately. "If not, humanity is doomed. The pandemic is much bigger than the alien invasion. Additionally, if you're able to develop a cure, it would be the biggest bargaining chip with the Estreyans that you could imagine. Two birds, one stone." That wasn't a lie, but there was no way I was going to tell him about the God of Shaping and Molding or my real plan now.

"I can do that…but I'll want information about the stone circles in return. Your pet alien knows where they are and how they work, doesn't he?"

Yeah, not gonna happen. But I nodded slowly. "I will need time to consider."

He stood up and took a single step toward me, head tilted to the side and skin stretched tight around a smirk. "The fate of the world is at stake, and more of us are dying every day. You will tell me, and you will do it now." I could sense his power gathering, a brightness that coiled up inside him, ready to lash out.

I stood to match him, a little surprised to note that, despite his lanky, stretched frame, I was taller. I showed my teeth, the expression not nearly friendly enough to be mistaken for a smile. "You brought this fate on yourselves, and, with your track record, I can't trust you not to make it even worse. So, no. I will take time to consider, and *you…*" The crystal at my throat hummed, lending gravitas and an echo to my words. "You will await my decision patiently."

Wraith could sense his heartbeat in the air, pounding faster as his eyes dilated and his nostrils flared. "I am not uncontrolled," he whispered. "I have priorities. But when this is over, we will fight again, arrogant child. I will introduce movement into your flesh where there should be none, and you will die, unrecognizable even to those who know you best."

Chaos bubbled out from my skin like a thin mist, taking advantage of my rage to assert itself.

He jumped back, clearing almost the whole room in a move that reminded me of Jacky.

My teammates and Kilburn's people bristled immediately, likely to break out fighting within seconds.

But I didn't pursue him, instead waving to my team to calm them down. "As long as you wait till this is over, you're welcome to try," I called back to him.

YOUR CHARISMA HAS INCREASED!

AFTER OUR LITTLE DISPLAY, Kilburn's people were even more hostile, but, though they watched us like we were rabid dogs ready to attack at any moment, none of them tried to start anything.

Kilburn assigned us a room and most of the team piled in to rest. We kept a rotating schedule, so someone would always be awake to alert the others of trouble.

I was tired too, but my Resilience was high enough that I didn't need the same amount of sleep as before, and I was too tense to nap. I used Wraith to find a door one hallway down from the common area. Guards stood in front of it. I had an idea what was behind it, but instead of using my Skill to find out for sure, I went there in person. It seemed fitting.

The guards stopped me from going through at first, but Vaughn came down the opposite hallway and waved them away. "I thought you might come down here. Is it safe for you to be in the same room with them?"

I shrugged. "As long as I don't get bitten. That's the surest way to transfer the disease, but you can still get it even if you've been living as a hermit in the wilderness for the last twenty years, so who even knows?"

"Still…" he handed me a face mask. "Don't think I'm doing this because I like you, traitor. It would be inconvenient if you went crazy and died right now."

I accepted the mask without response and followed him into the room. My eyes took a couple seconds to adjust to the dim light, but my ears caught the sounds of torment right away, and the smell of decay and infection spread itself over my nose and throat like a film. I swallowed back a gag.

Vaughn walked to the corner of the room and sat on a chair, staring at the wall with an expression of grey exhaustion.

The room was filled with smaller quarantine cells made of reinforced plastine walls. In each cell, a couple people were locked up. Some were free to wander with blank, drooling faces, while others were restrained. Those infected with meningolycanosis wouldn't attack others who were also infected, so, as long as they were locked up, they didn't also need to be physically restrained. Which meant that the ones in shackles or straight-jackets were either a danger to themselves, or had the Sickness without meningolycanosis. Some showed no signs of the Sickness. But many had distended bellies, blackened veins, or were thrashing against their restraints with obvious insanity.

I stopped before one cell, where a red-headed girl with her hands bound together was gnawing on her own arm till it bled. When she saw me, she rushed forward and slammed herself against the plastine in an attempt to get at me. She drooled, alternating between snarls and shrieks. She tried to bite at the glass, and one of her teeth broke away easily, like it had been barely rooted in her blackened gums.

I swallowed, but didn't step back. Instead, I watched her, and I thought.

Her fate would be shared by Chanelle, Kris, and Gregor if we couldn't find the lost god. But countless others before them had succumbed to this disease, and the Estreyans had threatened the lives of an entire city because of them. NIX had weighed power over the lives of everyone in Mordsmouth, and found power more compelling. Either that, or they just didn't believe my warning.

But…what should they have done differently? Should they have abandoned the infected to be immolated by the Estreyans? The lives of a few over the lives of many? If this girl were one of my team, I knew I'd choose her over a hundred cities like this one. But she was a stranger, and, for some reason, that made it so much easier to see her as just a number. Unfortunately, even giving up all the infected probably wouldn't stop the war at this point. Things were too far gone. Even so, the people turned into mindless attack beasts by the meningolycanosis were a real threat, and the easiest way for the Sickness to spread. Had Blaine given NIX the updated version of the anti-meningolycanosis serum, the one we'd used on Chanelle? If so, they definitely should have used it to mitigate the risk, even if they *did* plan on keeping these test subjects to search for a cure.

Vaughn rose from his spot in the corner and moved to stand beside me. "You lied to Kilburn."

I raised my eyebrows and turned to him.

"Or at least, you omitted something. Doing research on these people to find a cure isn't your real plan. The alien technology is so much more advanced than ours. If the cure was that simple, we wouldn't even be having this conversation. You don't trust Kilburn not to turn on you, so you kept it a secret, but there's another way to end this war, isn't there?"

The door to the hallway opened again, and Torliam walked in, silhouetted against the light. He brought a wave of stale air with him that still smelled heavenly compared to the caged Players around me. He sneered at Vaughn, and then moved to my side. "I felt a hint of your distress and came to find you. I hope you were not planning to answer this boy's question. We must not give them information about our plans," he said in Estreyan, his voice low and rumbling. "NIX cannot be trusted. You have seen how they respond when given a chance at power."

I bit the inside of my lip and responded in Estreyan, ignoring Vaughn's grumble of displeasure. "As for the lost god, no, I definitely won't be telling them about that. But…what about the arrays? We have no idea what's going on over on Estreyer. What if my news messages don't work, and *she* keeps sending more warriors? These people, they're innocent. Your warriors are fighting a shadow enemy, causing bloodshed without an endgame. They made the choice to follow her into a war. Doesn't Earth have a right to fight back?"

Torliam leaned forward, his voice urgent. "There is no shame in fighting back. But these warriors do not have evil in their hearts. They believe themselves to be saving your world from the Sickness as much as Estreyer, don't you see?"

I nodded, wishing I had a solution. If I could cut off the arrays myself, I might do it, but I didn't have the resources and I wouldn't give NIX any information they could use to make things worse, because, based on their past decisions, they definitely would. "It doesn't really matter anyway," I said belatedly. "They know where two of the arrays are already. Some of the stone circles might just be imitations made by ignorant humans, but there are hundreds of them all over the world. Even if we don't tell them anything, they'll have plenty of research material. And they probably have someone who's already translating my talk with that ship, so they'll know the broad strokes of our ultimate plan, as well."

"You two are being incredibly rude," Vaughn said, obviously in English. "If this continues, I might take offense."

I shrugged. "Maybe *I* should take offense that you reported everything I said to you about the Estreyans and the Sickness directly to Kilburn? I'm sure you'd do the same right now."

Torliam straightened, looming over Vaughn, who had to look up at both of us. He spoke in English. "Your presence irritates me, two-legged-maggot. Remove yourself from the presence of Eve Redding."

Vaughn paled with anger.

"Do you wish to fight, human? I wonder, do you know where those 'Seeds' you are so proud of came from? Do you understand the magnitude of my power?" As he spoke, Torliam's voice grew deeper with anger, and his Skill seeped out to form a glowing nimbus around him.

Vaughn clenched his fists and flickered away, reappearing at the door before opening it and slamming it again behind himself.

Torliam smiled, crossing his arms over his chest proudly, then looked to me like a kid hoping for praise. "It is obvious to anyone who looks that I am a mighty warrior. If he bothers you again, I will send him scurrying away."

Despite the scenes of horror surrounding us and the heavy mood, I let out a small laugh. Even Torliam could be childish sometimes.

WITH ONE LAST look at the crazed red-headed girl, Torliam and I went back to the common area. I wondered if Kilburn would try to stop us from taking the briefcase of Zed's nanite booster when he learned I had no plans to cooperate with information about how to use the arrays, or any of my further plans. The briefcase had been taken back to the little room he'd gotten it from, which was apparently Kilburn's personal "office," so the answer to my musing was pretty obvious.

One of the Players, I thought maybe the one who'd shot lasers, was using a Skill to project the image from a link onto the wall. It was displaying a news channel. *I* was on the news.

I watched in stunned horror. They had footage of the night before, starting shortly after I confronted the Estreyans, and ending when some Skill had wiped out all the electronics in three city blocks, like a miniature EMP. The government-placed cameras had caught some of it, but the majority of the footage came from civilians who had been filming with their links. With multiple films from different people, they had managed to catch almost the entire altercation, from my appearance to the crash of the downed destroyer.

"In breaking news, the military and a group of the superhuman troops that have caused such controversy attacked the squad of alien ships holding the city of Mordsmouth hostage, shortly before dawn. They managed to take out several ships, including one of the destroyer-class ships, and dispersed the forcefield which held the city hostage. The remaining ships seem to have retreated, though their location is currently unknown. The scene of the battle has been closed off, while the military inspects the area. Officials have no news on whether alien reinforcements may be coming to retaliate for this loss, but enforcers are aiding in the mass evacuation of all civilians who have not been able to enter one of the emergency shelters. Due to the shortage of resources, many question where these people will go, and how they will survive."

The link switched to another station, where the reporter was already speaking. "An unidentified woman seemed to be conversing with the alien ship in their language. Experts are examining the footage, but as of yet we still do not have enough information for them to reliably attempt to translate the conversation. Body language experts tell us she may have been negotiating with the aliens or attempting to convince them to let the hostages go.

"Others wonder about the significance of the creature she had with her." Film clips of Birch, yowling at the destroyer, and then running with me as the fighter ship came after us, played on the wall. "By all appearances, it is a cat with wings, though there is controversy over its origins. Is it a result of genetic manipulation, or is it somehow related to the aliens themselves, perhaps? The creature isn't the only strange ally that appeared last night. Seemingly cued by the alien ships' move to attack the woman, the civilians in the park were evacuated through tunnels dug underneath it, while the military attacked, with more young soldiers displaying distinctly superhuman abilities. Effects that seem like something out of a film were on open display last night, as caught in these clips."

The channel played through films of Chaos rising from my hand, then showed Torliam's signature light lowering the civilians, along with the dirt they stood on, into the tunnels dug beneath the park. "These people seem to have kidnapped a number of sick and injured people that the aliens were holding hostage. If you have any news of their whereabouts, please contact your local enforcers."

It showed an indistinct black form flying through the sky, its form resolving when it passed in front of the flame the fighter ship had been shooting at me. "This appears to be a bird, which carried some of the woman's allies, and helped her to escape from the alien ship's attacks."

A Player picked up the burning tank and hurled it at the destroyer. Another shot beams of light at it. The clips went on. "In a feat that has caused rejoicing across the world, these people were able to, along with the help of military survivors from the nearby base, take down a destroyer." The reporter blinked a few times, clearing tears from her eyes as the footage played beside her. "This is the second destroyer we have managed to eliminate. An escort ship was also downed last night. Footage was taken that confirms some of the rumors we had been hearing from the Republic of China. The aliens are bipedal, and humanoid. What does this mean? We have a guest on next, a renowned geobiologist and archaeologist, who will talk with us about the implications of this discovery. In the meantime, if you have any knowledge related to the identity or the whereabouts of this woman," my brightly lit form, standing on the edge of the roof, appeared again, "or any of her companions, please contact the Department of Defense. There is a reward of one million credits for any information leading to her location." Their contact information came on the screen and stayed there for a while, presumably to give everyone time to save it.

I took a few deep breaths. We would have to be more careful, but the coverage didn't really change anything, and I didn't have time to worry about it at the moment. I needed Zed's nanite booster. I turned to the small room, where Kilburn had set himself up, and opened the door.

I heard the sounds first, something wet ripping and tearing. Then I saw red, and smelled the blood.

Chanelle looked up at me from atop Kilburn's body, her mouth and face bloody, a chunk of meat visible between her teeth.

Forum Page 2

———————————

Welcome to the Earth Defense Force message boards.

You are currently logged in.

You are viewing thread: "Mordsmouth strikes back."

ORIGINAL POSTER "MORDSMOUTH-CITIZEN" SAYS:

As you can see by my username, I live in Mordsmouth. I was there by the park when it all went down. I've uploaded video, *here*. The news has gotten half the information wrong, as usual. My aunt has polycystic liver disease, and her doctor shoved her and a half-dozen other patients on a transport pod and gave them up to the aliens. She was sitting in the park waiting to die.

That group of people used their superhuman powers to help the sick and injured people escape. They didn't kidnap them. The whole thing with talking to the alien ship was just a distraction so they could get the civilians out of there. They took them to some abandoned underground warehouse or something, and they healed them.

I'm serious. My aunt no longer has PLD. Her liver is free of cysts and working normally again.

Now, it's obvious that these people with powers have some connection to the aliens. Why else would they show up at the same time? But as you'll see in my video, the military has their *own* group of superhumans, too. I couldn't catch everything before the fight got too crazy and I had to leave, but trust me, the stuff they were doing looked like it was out of a comic book. Gamma rays, anyone?

I can only wonder why the military is so desperate to get their hand on that woman and the others. Maybe they're deserters?

POSTER "ANTIGONE" SAYS:

Maybe the military wants her because she can speak the alien language. So far, no one has been able to negotiate with them without getting blown up. This proves, at least, that they understand the concept of language and speech. Even if it did backfire, it means there's a *chance*.

POSTER "JABRONEY" SAYS:

I'm not so sure. It's very suspicious that she speaks their language. Is it possible she's actually an alien, just somehow disguised as a human?

POSTER "NINJA PIRATE WARRIOR" SAYS:

Jabroney, are you listening to yourself? An alien disguised as a human?

POSTER "JABRONEY" SAYS:

Ninja Pirate Warrior, have you watched any of these films? There are giant alien sea creatures flying through our skies, and there are real people running around fighting them with *superpowers*. Let me repeat that. Superpowers. And not just stuff like fireballs and shooting lasers out of their eyes. If you watch closely, those people that walked through the side of the destroyer summoned a giant bird of darkness into mid-air and flew away on it. Why is it so crazy to think the aliens might be able to disguise themselves as humans?

I think the more interesting question is, if this woman is an alien, why was it trying to save the humans? Maybe, it's lived disguised among us for so long that it's grown sympathetic and actually wants to live in harmony as one of us.

POSTER "JANET MASON" SAYS:

I can confirm the benevolent nature of that woman, and the one who can heal. My son and I met her on the road half a day south of Mordsmouth. We'd been in an accident and his leg had been broken. I was devastated. I had no idea how I was going to get him to a hospital or what it would mean for him to be unable to walk with all this panic and fighting going on around us.

The woman and a blonde man who doesn't appear in the films took my son into a camper so no one would see what they could do, and traded my little toes for my son's broken leg. I have eight toes now, and my son could walk within an hour of whatever they did.

I and the people who owned the camper talked to them a little bit. It was clear that they are aliens, though they tried to deny it. I am not sure they are the same race as the ones who are attacking us, though.

I think it is most likely the woman and the others are some sort of third alien race, perhaps even interstellar guardians who've come to save us from the fish-people.

POSTER "NINJA PIRATE WARRIOR" SAYS:

Pics or it didn't happen.

POSTER "JANET MASON" SAYS:

Here's a picture of _my feet_, and one of _my son's leg_.

That's the best I can do, since I didn't dare to try and film them when they might notice. Notice the lack of stitching on my son's scar.

POSTER "POP-TARTS LOVER" SAYS:

That…is surprisingly convincing, Janet Mason.

POSTER "HAIRY-POPPINS" SAYS:

Everyone is missing the most important thing! Did you guys see that _winged cat_?!?

Chapter 19

These violent delights have violent ends.
— Shakespeare

CHANELLE CHEWED FOR A MOMENT, her expression wild, desperate. She snarled at me, a sound that would better suit Birch.

Kilburn was dead, I knew. His bowels had released, and I could smell it on the air. Wraith picked up no heartbeat from the gaping hole where his throat had been. I stepped into the room and carefully closed the door behind myself.

Chanelle snarled and lunged at me, moving too fast, even for someone with a few handfuls of Seeds in their system.

I thrust my hand forward, claws extending against my will. My palm slammed into Chanelle's forehead and kept going, taking her off her feet. I pushed her head against the wall and pinned her much smaller body with one of my legs. "Chanelle!"

Her eyes rolled crazily and she writhed against me, unable to move.

I let out a shuddering breath, and placed my other hand against her throat, forcing my claws to retract so they wouldn't cut her. I pressed on her carotid artery, squeezing hard enough that she could still breathe, but blood flow to her brain would be reduced. I watched carefully as she struggled, harder at first, then calmed, sinking into unconsciousness. Then I let go of her throat and waited for her to wake again, counting the seconds in my mind.

Her eyes blinked open blearily and met my own.

"Be still," I said, my voice vibrating uncannily. I kept her head pressed to the wall firmly. "Do you know who I am?"

She let out something between a cough and a laugh. "Eve."

"Do you know who you are?"

She didn't answer me, her eyes turning toward the ravaged body on the floor. She took a shuddering breath. "I… I did that."

"It wasn't you, Chanelle—"

I felt her try to shake her head, though my hand held her still. "No! It was. It really was." She squeezed her eyes shut, tears running down her face. Her breath quickened and deepened, till she was gasping for air as if she were drowning.

I slowly released her, stepping back.

"Don't let me free!" she gasped out, covering her head with her arms as she slid to the floor. "You have to stop me, Eve."

I watched her fall apart for a moment, then took two steps forward, settling on the floor beside her and pulling her into a hug. I kept Wraith focused on her, a little part of me telling me I couldn't trust her not to lose herself again. "Take a breath and hold it. I think you're having a panic attack."

She collapsed in my lap like a little child hiding from the world. After a few minutes, she was able to calm her breathing.

"It's going to be okay," I said, though I was already running through the ramifications of Kilburn's death. This was bad. It probably wasn't going to be okay.

"No." She shook her head and sat up, pressing her back against the wall. "I remember what happened," she said simply.

I didn't say anything, waiting for her to continue. I knew that when she went into her fugue states, she didn't remember the time that passed until she regained lucidity. She'd been getting better, staying "awake" longer and longer.

"I wasn't sleepwalking. It's warping my brain."

She was talking about the Sickness. I resisted the urge to gag on the smell of feces and bloody meat mixed in the air.

"Things don't make sense, sometimes. I'm so hungry all the time, and I can feel myself dying. I look around and it's like I'm wearing funhouse glasses and everything's distorted and this world, and you guys, and everything needs to be destroyed. Utterly ripped apart, not just your bodies but your lives, everything in my old life needs to turn to ash. And then the glasses are gone and I remember who I really am and *I* don't hate you, but I'm still so *hungry*. It was happening. I couldn't totally remember who I really was, and Sam was there and I wanted to hurt him but *I* was holding that other, hateful thing back, but there's less and less of me as that other thing spreads. But then I saw Kilburn, and it was *okay* to hate Kilburn, and then I was going after him and acting normal. I came in here and pretended I wasn't going crazy and then that thing inside me was attacking, moving my body so fast I could feel my muscles tearing. He was surprised. He started to fight back. But then I bit down…and I was so hungry."

She stared at the body and the puddle of blood that was still spreading outward. She scrambled a few feet to the side and heaved, her back arching as she threw up. Chunks of meat and bloody stomach juices splashed over her hands. She sobbed, then stuck her hand into her mouth, forcing herself to throw up again.

I shuffled over to her, rubbing her back. The smell burned my nostrils. I tucked a few locks of soft blond hair behind her ears as best I could, and closed my eyes.

I hated the Sickness. I had thought I understood what it was, before, but I hadn't, not really. I *hated* it. I swallowed past the lump in my throat and let out a shuddering breath. "I'm so sorry, Chanelle," I whispered. "You don't deserve this. But I promise. I *promise* I'm going to make it better. We're going to find a way to heal you. Just hold on a little longer."

Under my hand, she convulsed again, throwing up till green bile spilled out.

I TURNED BACK to Kilburn's mutilated body, jaw clenched. I used mental commands to send a Window to the rest of the team.

—GET READY TO LEAVE, QUICKLY AND WITHOUT DRAWING ATTENTION TO YOURSELVES.—

-EVE-

One of them would have to make sure Torliam received the message, as well.

I helped Chanelle up and away from the bloody mess she'd vomited.

"I said I wanted to kill him," she mumbled. "But I didn't want it like this."

"Stay calm." I helped her out of her filthy jacket, poured water on it from the flask at my hip and handed it back to her. "Wipe off the blood, as best you can. We're not going to leave any evidence behind."

She took the jacket. "Crap. I didn't even think about that. His whole team is out there… What are we going to do?"

"We're leaving." I took a deep breath, moved to the edge of the spreading blood and drew Chaos outward.

It responded eagerly, flowing out and flickering into black flames that splashed down onto the puddle, eating away at it. I pushed the flames closer to the body as the blood was consumed, and then poured out more atop it, feeling the drain on my strength as Chaos ate the flesh and bone from the top down, leaving nothing behind but a few wisps of powdery dust I didn't have the fine control to stop.

The door opened.

My head snapped toward it, and Chanelle froze, the jacket held against her still half-bloody face.

Vaughn took a step in. I watched as if in slow motion as his eyes tracked over her, then to the body on the floor, and me, standing over it, power still spilling out of me. He blinked. He looked at the puddle of vomit, the half-digested contents.

I sent a Window to Sam, then opened my mouth and started to babble. "It's not what it looks like." I kept my voice low and urgent, hoping none of his other team members would hear and come to investigate. "Come in and close the door."

He stepped forward again, but didn't close the door behind himself. "What is this?" His words were calm, over-enunciated, and held an undercurrent of danger.

"Chanelle has the Sickness. NIX gave it to her. I know this looks bad, but Sam can fix it. I already called him."

"He's dead. Very dead. And you're halfway through burning his body. How is Sam supposed to fix—"

Sam laid his hand on the back of Vaughn's neck.

Vaughn's eyes widened. He got halfway through a deep breath, and started to turn, trying to twist away. Then he collapsed to the floor, falling almost gracefully as his eyes rolled back in his head.

Sam closed the door.

"Like that," I said, answering the question Vaughn hadn't been able to finish. I returned my attention to the body, redoubling the power I fed to Chaos.

"He'll sleep for a half hour at most," Sam said. "That particular poison is fast-acting, but a Player can burn through it quickly. Even faster if that healing Skill of his increases passive regeneration."

I nodded.

Chanelle scrubbed frantically at her face and hands, and Sam moved to help her get the rest of the evidence off her person. He didn't ask what had happened, but I heard him almost whisper to Chanelle, "It will be alright."

I finished with Kilburn's body and moved on to disintegrating the vomit. "Are the others ready?" I asked without turning.

"I think so."

I dragged Vaughn into the corner. I stared at him for a couple seconds, then let out a shuddering sigh and released Chaos. I killed him and disintegrated the body as quickly as I could, jaw clenched tight.

I turned around to find both Sam and Chanelle staring at me. "I had to do it. He'd never forgive us, and we can't afford that kind of enemy." The words felt hollow in my mouth. I swallowed. I hadn't liked Vaughn, but something about the way he'd just died for nothing made my stomach burn.

The metal briefcase caught my eye, and I quickly checked to make sure it was still full of the nanite booster, then picked it up. "Let's go."

WE EXITED the room close together and closed the door behind ourselves, hoping that none of the other Players would see in. I held Chanelle's arm as we walked, staying between her and the others. The briefcase was too big to fit in any of our packs without emptying them of all our essential supplies, so I had no choice but to hope no one inspected us too closely.

Torliam looked to me, and I gave him a subtle nod, then flicked my eyes toward the exit.

I sat down at the chair Kilburn had placed for me before, and pretended to be engrossed in the news still playing on the wall.

Kris' mannequins stayed in place, but she held her little wooden puppet in her arms and walked out of the room inconspicuously.

One by one, the rest of my team members left the room, until only Torliam and I remained.

Just as I was getting up to leave, someone down one of the far hallways screamed and the *ra-ta-tat* of gunfire echoed off the concrete walls. It came from the opposite direction of the entrance we'd come through. Maybe one of my teammates had somehow set up a distraction?

I didn't wait to find out, slipping out the doorway with Torliam on my heels while everyone else was distracted. We passed a few Players and military people along the way, but they didn't try to stop us, despite their suspicious stares. Behind us, the commotion increased, and I heard the crackle of a radio, as someone asked if we were supposed to be wandering around.

Our teammates were waiting in the open space off the main doorway, where we'd stored our bikes.

I swung my leg over the bike that had been Zed's, since my own had been melted into a roof. He got on behind me and gripped the sides of my jacket tightly. I re-wrapped my shemagh around my face to disguise my features from the surveillance cameras outside, for what little good it would do.

"Where are you going?" one of the Players asked, taking a step forward as if to cut our escape route off.

"Kilburn will tell you about it once he's done with Ridley," I said, flipping the visor on my helmet down. "Move."

The Player hesitated for a moment, looking between us and his teammates.

Chanelle was staring blankly already, whatever horror and fear she'd been feeling lost to the haze again.

Jacky helped her onto the bike behind herself, and secured the other girl's arms around her waist.

"One of our teammates is out there," Adam snapped. "We need to go get them. If you don't move out of the way right now, we're going to go through you."

Unfortunately, his deceit didn't work.

"Stop them!" Someone near the common room shouted.

I sighed, and lashed out with Chaos in the shape of a black whip, spearing through half the boy's neck. We slammed down the accelerators before he even hit the ground, a group of people rushing up on our tail.

Adam dropped an ink shield to plug up the hallway behind us, but I knew he hadn't had time to recover fully, and was still close to exhaustion. If he pushed himself too hard, he might pass out again.

When we reached the door to the outside, Zed shot both of the guards, while I used Chaos to rip a hole for us.

The smoke and acrid stench of the city burned my nostrils as I inhaled the unfiltered air, but I barely noticed it as I weaved through the large open lot and knocked down the solid gate of the wall separating the bunker facilities from the rest of the city. I bumped over the sidewalk and into the road, ignoring the shocked cries of pedestrians and the angry honking of what few pods were still brave enough to try and traverse the roads.

Those cries of shock grew even louder, as Players and soldiers alike burst out of the bunker behind us, one of them *flying*.

I barely managed to duck as a hard-light beam swept over where my head had been, disintegrating a wall in front of me in a thin line.

Birch roared, and a gust of wind slammed out of the sky like the hammer of a god.

The flying Player was smashed into the ground, only to be run over by a pod.

Zed aimed some shots over his shoulder and, astoundingly, managed to hit one of the Players in the shoulder, though most of his bullets missed badly and only served to terrify the civilians even more.

Another Player breathed out a huge fireball, then grabbed it in their hands, spun around, and lobbed it toward us.

Torliam responded with a lance of power that exploded the fireball before it managed to reach us. It blackened the street below it.

We got a few moments of relief when we turned a corner and their line of sight was cut off, but they caught up quickly afterward, and the next street's travelers found themselves similarly surprised and terrified as the attacks continued. NIX's people weren't as strong as us, but there were a lot more of them, and with the crowded and blocked streets, we couldn't accelerate fully and get away from them. If it continued on, with more and more of them after us, things might get tricky.

"This isn't working!" Adam shouted. "We either need to stop and fight them, or find a way to escape."

I pushed out my awareness to its limits, hoping to chart a path for us, but remembered something else instead. I turned my head a little to the side and yelled at Zed, who was still shooting at our followers. "Remember how you said you'd mutiny if I said we were going to drive our bikes on the skyrail?"

He turned back around to me, expression drenched in horror. "*No!*"

I grinned.

Adam shot out a bolt of electricity, the lightning arcing through the air like a tree branch and cracking into the chest of a lizard-skinned Player. "Where's the nearest lift?"

He could have looked it up on his link, but Wraith would be faster.

"This way." I swerved sharply, cutting a dangerous path through an intersection completely filled with crashed and abandoned pods.

When we got to the skyrail lift, we coordinated to carry our bikes over our heads so we could all fit into it, and it went shooting up just as the Players reached its base. Both Sam and I struggled under the weight, and Jacky and Torliam helped to support our bikes along with their own.

The ones with long-ranged attacks tried to break into the little cubicle protecting us, but Torliam's Skill and the reinforced plastine held up long enough to get out of their range.

I let out a sigh of relief, but my breath caught in my throat before my lungs had a chance to fully empty themselves.

Estreyan ships flew in the sky, battered and bruised and heading our way, likely drawn by the commotion. "They didn't leave?" I said aloud.

The others followed my gaze.

Jacky cursed.

"Maybe they were hiding, waiting for NIX or us to show ourselves," Adam said.

Sam groaned, grimacing under the weight of his bike, which had the sidecar attached to it. "Uh, so we walked right into their trap?"

The ships spread out. A few hovered over nearby buildings, while one closed in on us. A side door on the other ships opened up and groups of Estreyans dropped out, landing on the roofs.

Adam's link crackled, and, once again, every speaker in a city block started speaking to us.

"Eve-Redding, you have been accused of treason against the Estreyan people and conspiracy to shelter those with the Sickness. Surrender, and you and your companions will be returned to Estreyer and tried before the throne for your crimes."

I let out a sobbing laugh as the lift opened up onto the concourse. "Guys, let's run."

Chapter 20

I have seen beyond the bounds of infinity and drawn down daemons from the stars...
— H. P. Lovecraft

ADAM TURNED TO SAM. "You better drive real carefully." He let the ink legs settle him back down into the sidecar, and flipped down the visor of his helmet.

"This. Is. Awesome." Jacky said.

"Did I ever mention that I'm afraid of heights?" Sam said, wiping his palms on his pants before mounting his bike.

I wasn't optimistic about outrunning an Estreyan fighter, but I also wasn't going to surrender, so our options were limited. I leaned forward and rode out of the concourse and onto the smooth metal track. The wind made my heartbeat spike with every gust, but it was even easier than I'd thought to control the bike. The ten-foot-wide rail left me plenty of space for error.

The others followed after me, and, after we'd become accustomed to the novel experience, we rode faster, shooting straight forward on a path out of the city.

To my surprise and cold dread, the Estreyans didn't follow at first, and when they did, it was languid and unconcerned. The ships flew slow enough so as not to outpace the warriors following on foot, who were using their superhuman strength to leap the gaps between rooftops.

—TURN LEFT UP AHEAD.—
-EVE-

When we got to the junction where the skyrail line we were on crossed another line in the great web, we swung left, still going almost full speed.

Torliam threw up a rounded blue barrier attached to the side of the rail.

My bike rode up it for a moment and Zed screamed in my ear, before we settled back down on the rail, now going west.

I reached out with my Wraith Skill to see if the Estreyans behind us made any move to follow.

They didn't. But when I centered my awareness again, I caught a faint hint of power ahead of us. It was too far to make out details beyond a vague sense of placement. My focus snapped forward, and I let out a hiss of air. "Someone's ahead of us," I yelled out, loud enough to be heard over the rush of wind. The glow of their power was stronger than any Player I'd ever seen. Maybe even stronger than Torliam himself. "An Estreyan," I concluded.

"Shit," Adam cursed as we rocketed forward. "Just the one?"

As we grew closer, I sensed another glow, and another. "No. A couple on the skyrail, a couple on the roofs of surrounding buildings." I sent out a Window with icons marking the Estreyans ahead.

"They are likely attempting to ambush us," Torliam called.

"No shit," Adam snapped. "Any other obvious statements to make?"

"We've got another cross-joint coming up," I said, raising my voice as Torliam scowled. "Turn right. If they don't have someone with high Perception levels, we might be able to lose them." I wasn't optimistic about our chances. Being limited to the path of the skyrail, we didn't have many escape routes, and, if they really were after us, they would know that. "Faster," I urged, pushing my own bike even harder as I crouched down over the handlebars.

Zed's grip on my jacket was white-knuckled, but he didn't protest.

When we took the right turn, Torliam once again threw out a

curved barrier for our vehicles to ride up onto before rocketing down onto the north-running rail.

I strained to keep the Estreyans within the range of my awareness. My heart sank as the spots of power began to move, turning north and keeping pace with us. We were quickly being encircled. I could sense the potential ambushers moving on our left and waiting not far ahead, and behind us were those from the lift, herding us to our doom.

I had an idea, but we needed to be concealed for it to work. I snapped my awareness outward till my physical vision wavered, almost growing dizzy with the effort. There were no lifts anywhere nearby. No way to get down to the ground and the cover of the surrounding buildings. The Estreyans would be on us before we could find one and double back.

I pulled Wraith back. It would be monumentally stupid to crash because I wasn't paying enough attention to driving the bike. "We need to get inside a building, but there's no way down," I yelled.

"Can we fight them?" Jacky said, one hand firmly clasping Chanelle's hands around her waist.

"They're as strong as Torliam," I said. It was answer enough.

"Damnit!" Jacky's voice was tight, and the tendons in her throat stood out in sharp relief as she clenched her jaw.

"Maybe if we don't fight back, they'll capture us without a fight," Sam yelled. "We could try to talk to them, or maybe escape when their guard is down."

I thought of Chanelle and the kids, all infected with the Sickness. We didn't have *time* to waste, and we couldn't risk the Estreyans finding out and executing them. We also couldn't risk being trapped on Estreyer till they died, if Queen Mardinest didn't see to that first. "We're not getting captured," I said, trying to think of a way out of the rapidly tightening noose. I needed a way for the team to get down from the skyrail. A way for us to escape the Estreyans tracking us.

The glint of rushing water caught my eye, as we drew alongside a huge building, only a couple stories lower than the skyrail. It was the city's high-class shopping mall, and was made of alternating strips of reflective mirrors and fancy glass. Decorative waterfalls rushed down the side of the building. Whatever power source was circulating the water was still going. Half the walls on the lower level were broken, either from looters or accidents. But the roof was intact, and it was only a couple hundred meters away from us.

"Adam!" I screamed. "Do you remember the broken bridge of the North?"

He cursed, but turned to Sam and snapped, "Get in front."

Sam sped up and maneuvered to the forefront of the group while the rest of us slowed down a bit.

"There's no architectural support for me to build on," Adam yelled.

The Estreyans following us had moved up on our left, while the others moved in front of us, cutting off any remaining hope of escaping them via the skyrail.

"There's no time!" Zed said, obviously paying attention to the movements on the Window I was sharing.

"I will help," Torliam called. "One *furdak* for each of us, alternating till we arrive."

"I have no idea how long a *furdak* is!" Adam screamed, slashing the canister of ink before him so that the black liquid flew forward. It formed into huge clamps around the skyrail, attaching in several spots like a spider's web.

Then it spread into a narrow bridge in front of us, and Sam swerved off onto it, with the rest of us following right behind, turning hard.

While Adam's left hand threw out ink, his right stayed outstretched, muscles strained to the point of trembling as he formed a pathway under us, the ink coalescing as fast as I'd ever seen it form.

There was a snapping sound behind us, and Adam's face whitened as the ink hastily connected to the skyrail broke, crumbling to nothingness. "Too heavy!" he squeezed out, still forming the path ahead.

The ink-road lurched as Torliam threw out a wave of power to push upward against the bridge below us.

The front tire of my bike bounced upward, and, when it met the ink again, it slipped, the handlebars wrenching against my hand as the tire tread failed to gain purchase.

I pulled hard, and the tire bounced again as it twisted under my strength, then Zed and I were sideways, sliding with the bike half on top of us, spinning out of control.

Jacky yanked upward, trying to avoid smashing into us, but her

Skill wasn't strong enough to lift herself and Chanelle along with the bike. She crashed into us, and then we were all tumbling and sliding.

Torliam's power spread out into a bowl underneath us, keeping anyone from falling to their deaths as we slid, rolled, and tumbled off the ink bridge.

Sam crashed into me in mid-air, the side of his bike slamming into my outstretched arm and forcing it to bend a little too far in the wrong direction.

A powerful gust of wind rushed up from below, as Birch unleashed his Gale Skill with a yowl that seemed impossibly loud for the size of his lungs. It went on and on, rising in pitch as the strength of the wind increased.

I caught a glimpse of crimson amongst the mayhem as I spun. Adam had drawn his twin butterfly knives across both forearms at once, cutting deep. He flung out his arms, and the blood flew outward, spinning around the group.

A crimson wedge formed below us, a kind of simple glider stabilizing our descent.

Torliam's Skill rushed around below it, pushing upward to give us lift again, and Birch's yowl continued on, the wind turned to our aid.

We weren't going to fall to our deaths.

I wrenched my arm out from under Sam's bike, hoping the bone wasn't broken, and threw myself toward the front of the glider, which was now rushing toward the faceted, glasslike wall instead of the roof. We were about to career uncontrollably into the side of a building for the second time in two days.

Like before, I lashed out with Chaos, drilling into the wall. Chunks of clear material blasted outward at the force, but we were moving too fast for me to drill all the way through.

The nose of the glider slammed into the jagged remains of the wall and crumpled like aluminum, dissolving from the tip backward.

The force of Torliam's protective power and the impact from the glider, along with another desperate surge of Chaos, finally broke through.

We hurtled forward, stabilized only by the remainder of Torliam's Skill and a few wisps of red blood. Globules of water from the decorative waterfall outside and chunks of broken glass flew with us, fracturing the sunlight. I watched as if in slow motion as the sunlight played through the glass shards and across the surface of the pool that fed the waterfalls below us. It sparkled like a living diamond.

We slammed into the water with enough force to knock half the air out of me and whip me around like a tossed stone. Water crashed up and outward from the impact of both our bikes and us, then swept back in on us, pushing us further down. We sank, buffeted by the currents as the motors fed water up from below and the vacuum pulled it down from above.

I regained my bearings with the help of Wraith, pushing it sluggishly through the water, hoping against all odds that Torliam had managed to protect everyone with his wonderful Skill, and that the rest of the team was alright.

Zed's helmet had cracked, and blood mixed with the water near his head. His limbs moved weakly.

Jacky had Chanelle tucked under one arm and was shooting through the water like a superhero, the buoyancy combining with her Gravitational Autonomy Skill's effect.

Sam had ahold of the back of Adam's shirt, and was dragging him upward.

Adam trailed along limply, blood from his arms creating a cloudy stream behind him.

Gregor had transformed with his Shadow Skill and was floating like a slow-moving ghost, catching one of the currents to push his ephemeral body upward.

Torliam pushed out the glowing blue mist of his Skill yet again, reaching out to Kris and Gregor and helping to force them upward as he swam in my direction.

I swam to Zed and grabbed him by the shirt with my good arm, then thrust him upward, hoping to help him get his head above water till we could drag him out of the pool.

I GRABBED the edge of the pool with my aching left arm and heaved Zed upward with the other, then dragged myself out of the water, my claws scrabbling at the tile floor for purchase.

Zed fumbled with his helmet and ripped it off, coughing out liquid.

I placed my hand on the back of his neck and forced my awareness through the barrier of his skin, searching for injuries. He was a little bruised, had breathed in some water, and had a slice on his forehead that had probably happened when the visor broke off from his helmet, but seemed otherwise unharmed.

I let out a sigh of relief, blinking my burning eyes against the chlorine in the water as I climbed to my hands and knees.

Birch bounded over to me, only his paws wet, as he had somehow escaped being plunged into the pool.

I ripped off my helmet and pushed my hair away from my face, stilling as I looked up into the shocked face of a stranger.

My eyes traveled up from the woman's impractical heeled shoes, to the microphone held in her hand, to the auto-recording orb floating over her shoulder, sporting the logo of a local news team. "You've got to be kidding," I said aloud.

She'd been staring at us, her eyes trailing over the odd group as we struggled out of the water. At my words, her gaze turned to me. "It's you," she said.

I threw a glance toward the skyrail and the buildings beyond it before speaking. "We are being chased by aliens," I said. "I doubt they're friendly, and I doubt they're going to care if you get squished as collateral damage. We can't protect you. Run away if you want to live."

She stood still, her arm slowly stretching out to hold the microphone in my direction. Was she in shock?

I turned to the hole in the wall we'd created, pushing Wraith out through the open air.

Zed stepped forward and slapped her lightly across the face. "Run away!" he snapped. "They're coming!"

She lifted a hand to her cheek, looked at the remains of the wall, and turned, clattering away on her high heels with surprising speed.

I watched as a couple of the Estreyans came into view, one moving along the skyrail, and one atop the roof of a building.

Torliam streamed water as he climbed up beside me, looking like Poseidon. "Some of them may be warriors from the downed ships. I doubt they all perished due to a small crash like that, and it's equally doubtful that NIX's warriors were able to kill them off before the reinforcements arrived."

"Did they come to get revenge on us for crashing their ship?" Gregor muttered, sidling closer to me and squinting out into the distance.

"We've got to go," I said.

Jacky coughed hard, clearing water from her lungs. "The bikes aren't gonna run now that we drowned them. How are we gonna get away?"

I hesitated. "It's better without them, anyway. The Estreyans won't be able to use Perception to follow us by sound later. I'm hoping, if we can just erase any sign of a trail, we can lose them. Can everyone still run?"

Adam was panting on the ground, but the wounds on his arms were healing under Sam's touch. He reached into his belt and pulled out one of the few remaining ink cartridges to form the familiar harness and octopus-spider legs, lifting himself up. "I can't do much more," he said. "I've got maybe fifteen minutes of simple use of my Animus Skill left, and then I'm going to pass out."

"If that," Sam said, shaking his head. "He lost a good amount of blood with that stunt."

"You're *welcome*," Adam grunted. "Since that *stunt* just saved everyone's lives."

I clenched my jaw. He was right. If not for him, it's likely everyone except for maybe Torliam and Birch would have just died, splattered like little bugs on the ground. "You did great," I said. "My plan doesn't need you to do anything else. Just stay with us a little while longer." I started running, and the others followed.

Another sweep of Torliam's Skill stripped the moisture from us and our clothes. "The water would leave a trail," he said.

I nodded gratefully, too preoccupied to respond verbally.

My Wraith Skill quickly searched the mall for what we needed, then I returned it to trying to keep track of our pursuers.

The Estreyans that had come into view of the building had moved, one climbing down the outside with frightening speed, the other moving into the distance, probably to the nearest skylift. I couldn't sense the others yet, but I knew they must still be after us. Maybe circling around to enclose the mall.

The shop I wanted, a winter sports store, was closed, the glass doors reinforced by a metal grate. A surge of twisting Chaos drilled forward, dark tendrils breaking right through with a crash of glass and screaming metal and leaving a hole for us to duck through.

"Get into the warmest clothes you can find," I said, tearing a pair of thick snow pants off one of the racks.

Zed looked to me, his eyebrows raised in a silent question.

I nodded.

"Make sure you get gloves and hats, too," he said. "However cold you think we're about to be, multiply that by three and then add a weird depression that makes you just want to lie down and die."

"We're going through the Veil?" Gregor said, pulling a furred cap down over his ears.

"Yes," I said, words rushing out as I stuffed gloves into my pockets and ran to grab some glow sticks and heavy duty hand-warmers. "But we have to hurry. They're almost here, right outside the building." Even as I spoke, I heard the faint sounds of destruction down below, as our pursuers broke through one of the windows on the ground floor, moving *fast*.

Torliam ripped a pack of thermal blankets out of a box from the back of the store. Kris' little wooden puppet helped her to lace snow boots on over her own shoes.

Torliam was too big to fit into any of the clothing, but he'd slipped a heavy sleeping bag over himself and tore arm and head holes through the sides and bottom.

Zed dug his hands into the air and opened a rip. He waved us through. "Go, go, go!"

Sam jumped through with Chanelle, followed by Jacky and the kids.

"Hurry!" I urged, as an Estreyan rushed up the stairs, floor after floor, while other points of power converged around the building down below, cutting off any normal escape routes.

I watched as the others went through, then leapt through myself as the closest Estreyan burst out of the stairwell less than fifty feet away.

Just as they blurred into view through the hole in the shop's front door, Zed closed the portal, cutting us off from the normal world and our pursuers.

AS BEFORE, the cold was aggressively biting, and despite the lack of sun or manmade light source in the room, a tepid grey glow washed everything out. The glass doors and metal grate at the front of the shop were both gone, and half the inventory had disappeared. "If we can get far enough away, we should be able to lose them," I said, already moving.

I picked Gregor up, setting him atop my shoulders so his little legs wouldn't slow us down, and Jacky did the same for Kris.

"Urgh," Chanelle said, sidling closer to Torliam. "Why is it so cold?"

"We're in my Skill," Zed explained to the newly lucid girl. He was the least affected by the Other Place out of all of us.

Torliam stooped down and picked Chanelle up, carrying her like a princess.

Birch whined and jumped into Sam's arms, wriggling frantically to get inside the boy's thermal suit.

"So what happened?" Jacky said, at the same time as Zed asked, "Why did we suddenly need to escape?"

Sam ducked his head till half his face disappeared in Birch's fur. "Kilburn's dead."

Adam looked at me. Then he looked at Chanelle. "You didn't kill him," he said, looking back at me.

I grimaced. In some ways, it would have been better if it were me. "No. Chanelle attacked him."

Sam let out a deep sigh, the air hissing between his clenched teeth as we ran down the emergency stairs. "I know we all hated him, but he may have been a spark of hope for humanity, and a way for us to buy time for ourselves."

Gregor scoffed. "So she should have kept him alive for the greater good? You can't trust someone like him to do the right thing. Chanelle may have just saved the world."

"She didn't kill him on purpose. At least not..." I trailed off as we came to the bottom of the staircase and found the emergency exit door. It was one of the few still in place on this side of reality. I slammed it open, and we spilled into the street, where the ash-like flakes of the Other Place floated down, dissolving as soon as they touched anything.

Chanelle's face was full of despair, and her usually rosy cheeks had gone pale. "The Sickness pushed me to it. I'm losing my sense of self, and it wants things to destroy."

Sam reached over and grabbed Chanelle's hand as we ran, squeezing for a moment before letting go. "Just hold on a little longer," he said.

"We need to hurry," Jacky said. "Look at them."

Gregor's eyelids drooped, and Kris's lips were blue, frost crusting in her eyelashes. "I'm fine," she murmured, but her eyes were vacant, and she sounded half drunk.

Chanelle took short, rapid breaths and her teeth chattered, even as her eyes rolled back in her head, the Other Place draining her fragile body of heat and energy.

Torliam jostled her and smacked lightly at her face, but though her eyelids fluttered, they didn't open.

I pinched Gregor's thigh, and he gasped. His fists dug into my hair, grabbing to stabilize himself.

Jacky imitated me, and though Kris protested, she was able to enunciate her words this time around.

We made it quite a few blocks away before it got too dangerous to continue, then managed to stumble into an old office building. We moved to one of the interior offices on the ground floor, adjacent to both a room with a large window and the stairwell in case we needed to escape. We tumbled back out into the normal world, shockingly bright and warm.

YOUR RESILIENCE HAS INCREASED!
YOUR CHARISMA HAS INCREASED!

Chanelle's cheeks quickly regained their rosy hue and her breathing returned to normal, but even as she opened her eyes they lost their lucidity, and she stared vacantly around, then started nibbling at her knuckles.

After a minute, I went out to the hallway and leaned against the wall, hoping the others wouldn't notice the tremors in my fingers and the flutter of my eyelids. I tilted my head back and bit the inside of my lip, letting the pain increase till it distracted my brain from how tired and fragile I felt.

Once my hands had stopped shaking, I reentered the large room, swinging off my pack and setting it in the corner.

Torliam crouched next to Chanelle, holding her hands within his own. Her eyes had gone vacant once again. Blue mist wafted out between his fingers, spreading into the lines in her palms and digging underneath her nails. It spread to her shirt, then her face and hair, and where it went, the remnants of blood disappeared.

He took the flask of water from her hip and uncapped it so she could drink, and then settled down beside her, back against the wall.

I walked over and slid down next to him. "How long do we have?" Despite the fact she was right beside me, I knew she wasn't aware of our conversation and wouldn't remember it when she became lucid again.

He understood what I meant. "It progresses faster, once the symptoms begin to show like this. However, every person is different, and even the symptoms will vary slightly. Perhaps two or three Earth moons remain for Chanelle. In the case of the children, I do not know. Longer than that."

I nodded. "Any other information out of your Tracker Skill yet?"

He looked down at his hands. "North. That is all I know." We were silent for a moment, and I watched as our other teammates shot the three of us worried looks from across the room.

"This is different from the Sickness of my sister," he said.

I tilted my head slightly to look at him.

"There was nothing we could do. My mother called healers from all across the land, pushed even more funding into research than she had before. She called in favors, indebted herself to other bloodlines. We tried everything. Even so, even though I refused to give up hope until the end, I knew. We all knew that Tonila would die, and that along the way she would turn into something monstrous. She would not be any different from the myriad of others who had gone before her. We knew that, one day, it would very likely be us following her to her fate. I kept searching, even after she was gone, because I hated the Sickness enough to burn my life away fighting against it." He touched the crystal mark on the back of his hand almost wonderingly, and then looked up at me. "This is different. There is hope. There is hope for all of us."

I swallowed against the lump in my throat and leaned my head backward.

After a few minutes, Jacky and I used plastine rope to tie Chanelle loosely to one of the desks that was bolted into the floor. Like an animal on a leash. Guilt burned in my throat, but I swallowed that down, too.

"What are the chances that this is actually gonna work?" Jacky said.

I examined the loose harness around Chanelle's torso and the bolts securing the table to the floor. "She could probably get free, if she was willing to hurt herself to do so," I said. "But it'll slow her down, give us time to respond. Honestly, I almost hope she just sleeps or stays in the fugue state. If she becomes lucid and sees herself like this, realizes what we had to do… It'll hurt her."

Jacky shook her head. "No. I mean… Are we actually gonna be able to fix her? Save her, and the kiddos?" She secured the last knot and tugged on it, then stood and looked up at me. "Are you just trying to give us hope?"

I looked down into her dark eyes. "I need hope just as much as anyone. I don't know what we're going to find. But I think Torliam's Skill is real. And even if I have to crush this Champion into the ground to get him to help us, or pull him up from the depths of hell, I will. Because I have to. I can't let the Sickness win."

"And you don't lose, right?" she frowned at me, hands clenched into fists.

"I won't lose. But I'm probably going to need some help." I quirked one side of my mouth up wryly.

Her lips slowly stretched into a grin. "Good thing I'm here to protect you, then." She punched me in the arm, and I didn't even regret the bruise that would surely form there. My Resilience levels could deal with it in a few hours, anyway.

Chapter 21

I looked up and saw Night, this world's defeat.
   — Ilium Troia

WE DECIDED to stay hidden until night and escape from the city under cover of darkness. Sam tended to our wounds, partially healing the arm that had been injured by his bike. When he was finished, it was still tender, but it didn't throb and ache every time I moved it, and leaving some recovery for our own bodies to do helped increase our Resilience and conserve his limited healing ability.

I went to lie down in the corner of an adjacent office, my head resting on my pack and a thin blanket wrapped around myself for warmth. Jacky was keeping guard, and the soft sounds of the others slipping into sleep lulled me on my own way.

I woke in complete darkness, the sound of my breath echoing strangely back to me. I reached for Wraith but found nothing. No Skill responded to me. I stiffened as my brain released chemicals in a spasm of fear, speeding my heart and quickening my muscles.

I lifted a hand and met a solid surface about a foot in front of my face. Careful exploration revealed that I was within a rectangular object. A coffin, my subconscious offered. I took a deep breath of the quickly warming air within. I flexed my fingers and hoped for claws, only to be disappointed again. "It's okay," I murmured aloud to myself as I ran a finger across the too-smooth skin of my left hand and forearm. "It's just a dream."

It didn't feel like a dream. I pinched my nose shut and tried to breathe through it anyway. In a dream, that always worked. But no air entered my lungs.

I lay back, pressing my hands against what felt like smooth stone beneath me. "Calm down," I told myself again. Last time, when I had died, I'd woken up. I gritted my teeth. There was no way I was going to let myself die. What if it *wasn't* a dream? I was already forced to take deeper than normal breaths as the oxygen ran out. My fingers scrabbled at the stone, first searching for a seam or a latch, then scraping ineffectually as if I could dig my way out. I kicked at the stone, knees bashing and bruising, fists still pounding. I strained, pushing upward with all my might.

It absorbed my blows, unconcerned, and I didn't even hear the hint of hollow echo that would mean my coffin was thin, or the grave shallow.

I reached for Chaos and let out a sigh as I felt it stir weakly within me. Not enough to bring my power to bear on the world, but at least it was *there*. I forced my limbs to obey me, to stop fighting something they were of no use against. I brought my left forearm up to my face and pinched at a small section of skin on the back of it, then bit down as hard as I could, till my teeth sank through.

Blood trickled out, and Chaos came with it. Tears slipped down my temples, running into my hair. "Oh, thank you, thank you," I gasped.

With careful concentration, I focused on the stone above me, urging Chaos to morph into the black flames and re-make it into oxygen. "It's just a dream. You control it, you can make air if you want to," I mumbled to myself. I couldn't tell if it was working at first, so I concentrated even harder, pushing my desperation and fear into the Skill. "Eat, and turn stone into air," I said aloud. "Air. Make air."

I breathed easier as the fresh air fell away from where the stone above me had once been. I let out a sob of relief, and kept going.

Eventually, Chaos had eaten enough that I could sit up, and then, finally… finally, it broke through to natural air above.

I stopped and took a moment to rest while my ears popped as the pressure equalized again, wiping sweat from my face. Then, very carefully, I used the normal misty tendrils of Chaos to disintegrate a thin line through to the surface of the stone, drawing a circle not so unlike the manhole the team and I had descended through that morning.

I waited, listening for any sounds of movement up above. When nothing happened, I stood, lifting the lid I'd created in my stone burial ground. Cold air rushed into my little hole, chilling my sweat and making me shiver. I poked my head out, only far enough so that I could see, and looked around.

I was inside a room, my head poking out of a hole in the polished marble floor. The ceiling was half transparent, letting grey light into the room. Around me were pillars and angled walls that served no discernible purpose except to create multiple different paths. They seemed to be made out of silver, or maybe mirrors, but were covered in cobwebs and grime and strewn with little bug carcasses, as if the place had been untended for a hundred years.

I waited, again, for any response, any indication that I was not alone. When nothing happened, I climbed out of the ground, settling the lid I'd created back into the floor carefully.

My reflection did the same, copied several times onto the grimy surfaces surrounding me, so blurred that I was little more than a grey humanoid shape.

I shuddered, the cold biting at my exposed flesh, and crept forward. The room was maze-like, paths twisting and turning and crossing each other. Without Wraith, I had no way to tell what was around every reflective corner or column, and no idea where the exit might be. I had grown used to that constant feed of information, and without it, I felt like someone had placed a bag over my head to keep me blinded.

My footsteps and breath sounded loud to my ears, and bounced off the surrounding surfaces. It was consoling, in a way, because I thought I would probably hear if anything else moved, though I probably wouldn't be able to tell which direction it came from.

I turned to the wall next to me, my eyes drawn almost involuntarily to my featureless, blurry reflection. I shuddered and stepped away, then hurried on, a bit faster than before.

I pulled up my VR chip Window, to see if there was any difference from what it had shown the last time.

PLAYER NAME: EVE REDDING
TITLE: BEARER OF TESTIMONY
CHARACTERISTIC SKILL: ~~SPIRIT OF THE HUNTRESS~~,
~~TUMBLING FEATHER~~
LEVEL: 38
SKILLS: ~~COMMAND~~, ~~WRAITH~~, CHAOS, ~~VOICE~~

STRENGTH: ~~25~~
LIFE: ~~77~~
AGILITY: ~~33~~
GRACE: ~~28~~
INTELLIGENCE: ~~32~~
FOCUS: ~~25~~
BEAUTY: ~~16~~
CHARISMA: ~~35~~
MANUAL DEXTERITY: ~~10~~
MENTAL ACUITY: ~~29~~
RESILIENCE: ~~71~~
STAMINA: ~~37~~
PERCEPTION: ~~35~~

Other than the handful of Attribute levels I'd gained through training, it hadn't changed. I closed the Window and looked around carefully, feeling exposed without Wraith to watch my surroundings in all directions. I couldn't help but feel that something was watching me. I had been walking for a long time, and still had not found anything resembling a way out of the maze.

I turned in a circle, within a group of walls that created a room-like opening with four paths converging on it. My eyes caught on my reflection again, and I shuddered as I realized what was wrong with it. When two mirrors face each other, each reflects the other's reflection, creating an infinite, repeating tunnel of sorts. That wasn't the case, here. Each reflective surface showed only one blurry form. In fact, they didn't seem to show the other walls or columns at all.

I fought down the urge to run, as the hairs on my arms and the back of my neck rose up in alarm. I stepped forward, questioning my own idiocy as I did so. But I knew I couldn't keep wandering help-lessly, searching for an exit I was beginning to suspect didn't actually exist. I lifted my hand and rubbed at the wall, clearing away the obscuring grime in a little patch.

I brought my hand away, revealing my face. I jerked backward with a gasp, stumbled, and fell to the floor, scrabbling backward as a moan of horror escape my lips unbidden.

My reflection did not copy me. Instead, it remained standing. Its smooth, featureless face seemed to stare down at me, despite the lack of eyes, nose, or mouth.

My back hit the wall behind me, and I turned to look up, then screamed.

The wall behind me had a clear spot, identical to the first. The thing I had thought was my reflection stared down at me through it. It, too, had no face.

I fell away from it, then brought my hands to my own face frantically, searching to ensure I had a nose, a mouth, two eyeballs. My features were there, intact. I let out a sob of relief and pushed myself to my feet, moving to the center of the clearing, as far away as each wall as I could get. I spun around, watching as all four forms looked out at me from the clear patch at my head-level, even though I'd only cleaned one wall.

One of them lifted its arm and knocked silently on the surface, twice.

I froze.

It rubbed two little dots into the surface and drew an upside-down arch below them. A smiley face.

My legs were shaking. I whipped my head around to look behind me, half-certain that the wall would be stretching as the thing reached out to attack me unawares. It wasn't. In fact, the faceless creature stood still and inscrutable. No smiley face.

I looked forward again.

The thing stared back at me. My brain wondered inanely if it even counted as staring if it didn't have any eyes. How did I even know it could see me?

It reached forward and the metallic mirror rippled like the surface of a pond, and then began to distort, stretching outward as it kept pushing, forcing its body forward. The mirror hugged its form like a film of shiny plastic just about to break.

My breath came faster. A bead of sweat dripped into my eye,

burning. I dared not blink. I thought of running, but knew it wouldn't improve my situation. Panic would only make things even more helpless, in a room like this, against a creature like that.

Then, with a soundless pop, the mirror broke into a thousand little shiny granules, and the thing that had been my reflection stepped forward, metal rippling around her till she once again resembled me in every way. Except she was changed by the Seeds, while I was reverted to my original, normal human form. Her footsteps left behind bloody prints. My features coalesced on her face, smiling like a wolf, all teeth. "Welcome back," she said.

I swallowed, skin tingling, hair raised up, heart racing. There was something *wrong* about this. It wasn't that something else was wearing my body. It was that something else *wasn't*. She was me, in every way that I could tell.

Around me, the mirrors reflected neither of us, as if they weren't really mirrors at all.

I lunged forward and slashed at the air with the arm I'd let bleed, attacking with a vaguely sword-like line of Chaos.

She laughed, even as the skin crumbled off her bones. The black flames of Chaos surged up from her fingers, sweeping my own efforts aside like one might bat away a fly. Her skin reformed under her flame, and then the air rushed toward her like she'd created a vacuum.

Loose strands of my hair whipped at my face in the artificial wind, and I had to brace myself against the sucking pressure. My mouth opened like a fish as I gasped for air and found nothing. Was this how she meant to kill me this time?

The pull stopped suddenly, and I stumbled back and had to regain my balance. Another surge of power left a long black sword in her hand where once there had been only air. My eyes widened. "Who are you?" I said, my voice cracking a little.

She scowled, lips pulling away from her teeth. "You're asking the wrong question. I know a better one. Who are *you*?" She swung the sword forward.

I dodged, but she was much faster than me. The black sword scored a line across my arm, cutting through my skin but just barely ripping into the muscle below.

Instead of pressing the attack, she stepped forward languidly, flicking my blood off her sword. It splattered against the ground, washed-out red against the dirty stone. "*What* are you?" the other Eve's voice whispered in my ear, even as she stood across from me.

I urged Chaos up through the fresh cut, and shot it toward her with the new technique I'd learned when the Remnants ambushed us. It built on itself like a muscle, fibers attaching and interweaving as it shot forward, the pieces behind feeding power and speed to the ones in front.

This time, she was the one who tried to dodge and failed, losing a chunk of her sword hand to my attack.

She laughed. "You're half-clever. But, even when you're dying, I still want this more than you do. Where you're going, there's no space for weakness. If you can't even beat me, then what use do I have for you? I'd be better served taking your place." She waited a moment, for the full understanding of her threat to settle in my mind. Then a lunge brought her in range of me again, so fast I could barely respond.

I leaned back, pushing Chaos at her sword, trying to force it to crumble away in the easiest use of the power I could manage. I wasn't fast or powerful enough.

The black metal pierced through my chest, cutting through skin, then muscle, then bone and organ.

My chest heaved as I gasped, and my impaled lung filled with blood. For an instant, the world stilled. I looked into her ice-blue eyes, reached up, and gripped the blade of the sword with both hands. If the little wound on my arm was a tap, the sword had created a spigot. I let Chaos spill out into the wound, urging it to become the black flames of re-making. I could heal this wound just like I'd healed my injuries down in the dungeon cell. I felt it start to work, skin melding with metal, metal turning malleable and mimicking the flesh around it even as Chaos ate it away, leaving behind something I could work with.

She smiled. "*Good girl.*"

I spat in her face, the metallic taste in my mouth showing as pink-tinged saliva on her skin.

She didn't even seem to notice. "You died last time. You will die again here. If you continue to die, I will make it permanent. You will stay here, trapped inside the palace you built in your mind. *I* will wake up to the real world, to a body made of blood and bone, and do your job properly." Before I could respond, she brought up her free hand in a swipe. Long, razor-sharp claws whistled as they parted the air, and then my throat.

My head tilted back unnaturally, as the muscles keeping it upright were no longer connected to each other. Blood fountained out like a pulsing geyser. My world went red as the blood coated my eyes, and then black.

I WOKE, gasping. I shot to my feet, claws out and scrabbling at my own throat. They slid off the crystal symbol and cut shallow lines into my skin. But I was alive.

Large hands grabbed my wrists and forced my claws away from my throat. They held me still till my breath stopped heaving and my eyes were able to focus.

"You dreamt," Torliam said, looking down at me in the darkness. "I could feel your distress, but I could not wake you."

Flashes of the other Eve attacking me played in my head, and I closed my eyes against them. I reached for Wraith, and my awareness rushed outward in an eager pulse, comforting me with knowledge of my surroundings and a sense of control.

He pulled my head forward till my forehead rested against his chest. "Be calm. You are safe. I would not allow you to be harmed." When my breathing slowed, he said, "You often have nightmares, but they have been growing stronger, lately."

I pulled away from him, willing my fingers to stop trembling. I hadn't known my troubled sleep would be so obvious to him, and the normal nightmares had become so commonplace I hardly noticed them anymore. "Yeah. Maybe it's just the stress. I'm fine now. Er, thanks."

He stared at me in silence for a moment. "Are you sure you are alright? I know dreams can be impactful, even if they are not real. If you wish, I will stay with you, till it has faded from your mind and you can rest easily again."

"I'm fine," I said again.

"It is no trouble," he insisted, sitting down on the thin bed mat beside me despite my protest. "Let us talk about brighter things."

I sat back down too, but couldn't think of anything to say. When the silence dragged on awkwardly, I cleared my throat. "Why do you think the humans never found the lost god, if he's been on Earth all this time?"

He shrugged, a human gesture he'd probably picked up from us. "Perhaps they have, but have forgotten it. Human lives are so short and your people so technologically stunted, stories of the god could have faded into myth long ago."

I frowned. I wasn't very knowledgeable about various cultures' mythologies, so couldn't say if his theory was likely or not.

"It is even possible that your government is aware of his existence and has chosen to keep it a secret. However, if a god truly does not wish to be found, there are few mortal means which could succeed in revealing them."

"Is your Skill one of those methods?"

He cleared his throat. "I believe so. There is no point in doubting ourselves now."

I leaned my head against the wall and sighed, some of the residual tension flowing out of me. "Right."

I caught a hint of his smile in the darkness, and, after a few more minutes of talking, he left me to go back to sleep.

I sat in the dark for a while till I felt tired again, then lifted the cover to slip back under it. I stopped at the sound of small pebbles or maybe sand shedding onto the floor. My heart started beating a little harder, and I took a deep breath to calm it. I reached into my pack, which lay under the head of my mat like a lumpy pillow, and took out a small flashlight from one of the pockets.

With the flick of a switch, light beamed out of it, reflecting off the shiny metallic granules spread over my bed mat and the surrounding floor. "Oh, shit," I said aloud.

Chapter 22

Now there's a look in your eyes, like black holes in the sky.
— Pink Floyd

I COULD THINK of two obvious explanations for the metallic granules, which were the same as those created in the dream when the mirror image of me burst free. The first was that the granules had been there before and my subconscious noticed what my higher mental functions didn't and inserted them into the dream. The other option was that somehow they'd been placed there while I slept, either by someone else as a subtle threat to me, or by the dream itself.

I scrambled up from the bed and moved to go after Torliam, but, as I was walking past the room where Chanelle slept tied up to the table, a dark form caught the corner of my eye. My first thought was that someone had intruded into the building and was sneaking around without anyone noticing. Maybe the same person who'd left the metallic granules on me.

Then I recognized Sam. He looked up at me from where he was crouched over Chanelle's prone form. His eyes were empty, black. He blinked, lids closing over the darkness of the abyss for just an instant, then stood. When his gaze met mine again, something in them ate at my insides, taking away my fear and leaving me with a weariness so deep I couldn't even cry about it.

I blinked rapidly and looked away. I then turned my extra-sensory awareness to Chanelle, dreading what I would discover.

Chanelle was still alive, and had no injuries that I could sense.

"It would be idiotic of me to kill her," Sam said calmly. "Even if it would be safer for all of us, it would be a blow to the other members' sentiment, and I might be the one who ends up being tied up because the others can't trust me not to go 'crazy' and attack."

I watched him for a moment, noting how much more assertively he held himself while under the influence of this Skill. Dredged up by my fear, flashes of the dream were again grabbing at my attention, but I pushed them back. I couldn't deal with that right now. I just… couldn't. I would think about it later, when my hands had stopped their tremors, and the sun had risen again. Humans are not creatures of the dark. "I've been wanting to have a conversation with you for a while," I said. I nodded toward the adjacent room, the one with a window looking out onto the city, and we quietly made our way there.

I leaned against the wall to one side of the window, and he did the same on the other side.

"She's dangerous," he said. "And in protecting her, the group is weakened. She may have the Sickness, but, as far as I can tell, she's not going to be any help in finding the cure. The smartest thing for us to do would be to stash her in a safe place somewhere and come back for her once we've found the Champion. If we take her with us, we might even end up putting her in danger, since she can't be trusted to look after herself." His voice was still expressionless, but he tilted his head to the side as he said the last bit, as if curious whether his argument was persuading me.

I looked out into the street. Most of the lights were out, either from loss of power, or people being too afraid to make themselves a beacon in the dark. I heard faint screams in the distance, far enough away that the wind carrying them gave them an unreal quality. "All of those are logical arguments. But where is this 'safe space' we're supposed to leave her in? And what about the morale of the team? We're already struggling to deal with everything that's happened. Spirits are low, tempers are high. She's still capable of traveling with us for now. And truly, I just don't want to imagine her when she wakes up lucid, abandoned and imprisoned somewhere, hoping we'll come back for her before the Sickness completely eats her up from the inside. I don't *want* to leave her behind."

"At least you're honest about your irrational decision. With this form of me, anyway. Would you have said the same to…" he trailed off and gestured vaguely to himself.

"The version of you not under the influence of Black Sun? I don't know. Would you have suggested we leave her behind?"

"When I'm filled with those illogical, hobbling emotions, I think differently." He tilted his head to the side, staring at me with those black orbs without blinking. "I don't believe Kilburn was right. You're not a sociopath."

It didn't take much to follow that line of thought to its obvious conclusion. "But *you* are, when you turn the Skill up too high, right?"

The sides of his mouth quirked up in a startled smile. "Right. Does that bother you?" He leaned in, and would have come off as flirtatious if there were any real warmth in him.

"Are you planning to harm the team or yourself?"

He leaned back again, nodding as if satisfied. "No. Though to be honest, I might end up slipping. Like this, my restraints are all theoretical understanding of the consequences I'll face, once the Skill reaches its limits and I go back to being normal. I'm not stupid or masochistic. That is what you want to ask me, right? You want to know if I can be controlled."

Sam was so different like this. It was hard to think of him as the same person. But he was insightful in a way I couldn't deny. "And if you could keep the Skill active forever?"

"It's addictive," he said simply, staring out into the night.

At least he was being honest. I could understand the lure of removing all the negative emotions, even if it meant not feeling much at all. "Why do you think Testimony and Lore gave you that Skill? This isn't the first time they've tried the Seal of Nine. What's the end goal, the 'greater Trial' we need to overcome that requires you to be able to manipulate and feed off emotions?"

He tilted his head to the side, turning those soul-sucking orbs in his face on me for a few endless seconds. "You've got everyone convinced that these Skills mean we're going to stop the Sickness, but I'm not so sure. Not when I'm like this, at least." He blinked, releasing me from the gravity of his gaze. "I don't know anything normal Sam doesn't. But I do *understand* things when I'm like this that I usually can't bring myself to contemplate. I might say my reason for existence is to do the things I normally cannot or refuse to, but, in reality, what reason is there for existence at all? Perhaps this Skill exists to drag me down into ruin." A small smile, the first *real* expression I'd seen on his face that evening, tilted up the edges of his lips.

I held back a shudder as emotional darkness rolled off him, tinged with black amusement. I looked away from Sam and out into the street, but kept Wraith focused and alert. There was ash on the air. I could taste it. In the distance, the screams grew louder. "Do you want to die?"

He stared at me, but didn't respond.

"I don't think you do." My voice was smooth, calm, and unthreatening.

He stepped closer to me, and would have been looming if he weren't shorter than me. "Then what do I want, Eve? Tell me. Entice me to your service and bend me to your will with words and the allure of power." His voice was a murmur, and, despite the hostility of his words, I heard the faint hint of amused camaraderie in his tone instead of a threat.

I turned to look into his eyes again, despite the effect I knew it would have, to search for meaning within them. Movement on the horizon drew my attention instead. I let my claws slip out and my vision sharpen predatorily, distance and darkness losing some of their obscuring power.

People were spilling over the rise of the street, a few outliers in front, and then the crowd behind them. They were screaming. The crowd surged forward, those in front desperate to get away, while those behind strove to overtake them. I watched as someone stiff-armed their way in front of someone else, shoving the other person back and making them trip and fall, only to be stomped under the careless feet of the crowd. The yells grew louder as they rushed closer.

Faint rustling came from the rooms where the others were sleeping as the sound woke them.

At the edge of the hill, a person sprang atop one of the pods parked alongside the road, then leapt forward like an animal. They landed on someone else's shoulders and leaned down to bite, even as they fell down together. The two disappeared between the stomping limbs of other panicked, stumbling, screaming people.

I turned to share a glance with Sam as the others hurried into the room.

Jacky's hair formed a halo of tangles around her head, but sleep hadn't slowed her reactions any, and she was by my side in an instant.

Torliam moved to tower beside us.

Jacky's eyes widened, and she gripped my elbow. "Wolves—the meningolycanosis," she said simply. "It's spreading."

<hr>

I WATCHED AS MORE people in the back of the crowd went down. "Do you think...? That commotion when we were escaping... I heard gunfire and screams down the hallway where they were keeping the infected. Maybe not all the panic was because of us."

Jacky shrugged. "An infected person got out *somehow*." She jerked her chin to the panicked horde. "And it found some people to attack. With that many, I hope it didn't get into one of the emergency shelters."

Zed's voice was scratchy from sleep. "As an expert on horror films, I can tell you now that shit has hit the fan, and is going to spray everywhere."

Torliam stared out at the panicking mass of people, probably picking out the military uniforms among the crowd. "If these 'wolves' have not only the meningolycanosis, but also the Sickness..."

Smoke and fog filled the night sky, almost obscuring the dark silhouette darting toward the mob of humans. Nothing could have disguised the beam of cleansing fire that poured down from the Estreyan ship, though. It wasn't a destroyer, with the mountain-melting beam, but that just meant it would have to keep attacking for longer. The heat cut through the crowd like a scythe, razing a line three meters squared through the humans and cutting through a building beside the street where a few of the forerunners had escaped from the stampede. The building let out several rapid explosions as the fire swept back and forth. Instead of a building, there was now only a few feet of glowing slag.

I stepped back from the window. "Staying hidden here has just become counterproductive to our survival. Time to move."

We were ready to go within moments, since most of our stuff was still packed from the night before. Luckily, Jacky and Torliam had already procured a few new rides for us from the building's parking garage and Adam had gotten them running. We rushed back down to the ground level where the new bikes were stashed, loaded up our stuff, and rode off into the streets. Behind us surged the now even more terrified mob, pursued by the Estreyan death-beams.

We weren't the only ones who'd noticed what was happening, and people who had been hiding out in the surrounding buildings rushed into the streets to avoid being killed when their cover was turned to rubble. Warning klaxons began blaring again.

We'd taken care to cover our faces in case NIX had the resources to spare looking for us in camera or satellite footage, but I knew it wouldn't do much good.

Adam screamed to be heard over the wind, frantically manipulating the screen of his link. "There's a subway, up ahead. We'd need to go east a few blocks, but if we could make it into the tunnel, we might be able to hide all the way out of the city."

Thank god for Adam. "Lead the way," I screamed back.

With a deep frown of concentration, he used my little mini-map trick, sending us the route through a shared Window.

It only took a few minutes to arrive, and we drove recklessly down the stairs and then jumped our bikes down onto the tracks. The first couple miles, we encountered a surprising number of people, either homeless or just seeking the protection of concrete and earth above their heads, but after that, the tunnel was mostly empty of humans, even if the same couldn't be said for rats. I kept circulating my awareness both behind us and in front of us through the long tunnel, but caught no signs of pursuit. It seemed none of the trains along this inter-city line were running anymore. I couldn't keep my mind from turning to all the sick people we had saved from the park. Had we even saved as many as we had watched die?

We kept going till we passed the next two cities, then stopped to sate our boosted appetites in one of the small alcoves cut along the subway tunnel.

Kris' puppet came and crawled into her lap, and she started to fiddle with it, using her free hand and both of its own hands to take apart its chest plate.

Jacky tended to both children, making sure they had enough to eat, someplace comfortable to rest, and then joking around with them to keep their spirits up.

Zed took the suitcase of nanite boosters out of his pack and removed one of the little tubes. "I guess the only way to know for sure that it's going to work it to take it, right?"

"I'm not a scientist, but I couldn't find anything wrong with it." I didn't say that he had no choice, since, without the nutrients for the nanites to repair themselves, they'd start to die off and eventually kill him. We all knew that already.

He used one of the vials, and after a few minutes with no reaction, we all relaxed.

Chanelle smiled when I handed her some food, despite the fact that we'd bound her hands.

I sat down next to her, heedless of the grime on the concrete floor. "This…is only temporary," I said, motioning to her restraints.

"It's okay," she said, her lips trembling faintly as she widened her smile. "I know why you have to do this. I want you to. I couldn't bear it if I did something I couldn't take back during one of my episodes."

I could tell she was trying not to cry, so, instead of forcing her to keep talking about it, I ran my fingers through her growing hair while she ate, slowly combing out the tangles and then braiding it into two short pigtails. "You look cute," I said.

She grinned, and then frowned. "Wait. You meant cute like a little kid, didn't you?"

I snorted. "If we were in an animated movie, you'd be the princess' kid sister."

Her eyes widened in outrage, and she puffed out her cheeks, then couldn't hold it in and burst out laughing, spraying chewed-up food all over Adam.

Birch let out an almost human-like chortle of laughter at Adam's look of astonished disgust, which set the rest of us off as well.

Chanelle laughed and played around with us for a while, for once fully a part of the team. She fell asleep still lucid, with a small smile on her face.

SAM NEEDED the least sleep of anyone in the group, except for Torliam and me, because of his high Resilience and Life levels. So when everyone else fell asleep, he acted as the lookout while I took a walk down the tunnel with Torliam.

I wanted to talk with him without waking or worrying the others.

Sam's Perception wasn't high, so once we were far enough away that our conversation wouldn't carry back to him, I spoke, soft echoes of my words spreading through the tunnel. "I don't think the dream earlier was just a dream." I explained the metallic granules and my speculation on the ways they could have appeared in both reality and my sleeping mind.

A furrow grew between his eyebrows. "Tell me about these dreams, from the beginning."

"This is only the second one. They feel…incredibly realistic. If not for the fact that Chaos was so much easier to use and I don't have any other Seed augmentations or any of the Skills I've gained, I might not be able to tell the difference between them and real life. The first time, I woke up in a stone room with no door. A cell, really…" I explained the dreams in detail.

As I spoke, his frown grew even deeper. "I see little likelihood of this being anything other than an attack," he said. "Did you not mention this mental house to me previously? You created it with the help of Adam, using a *warrior's-technique*. Though I do not know how they broke through the guardian wall, perhaps they are using a Skill to access it, and somehow affecting you in this way. In any case, we must not take the threat lightly."

Torliam acknowledging the danger wasn't unexpected, but I still sighed. Why couldn't things ever be easy? I just wanted to find the lost god so he'd start helping the mortals again. A thought occurred to me. "Torliam, what if this person is actually trying to help?"

He stopped walking and turned to look at me, eyebrows raised as if I was crazy.

I waved my hand at him dismissively. "Obviously, they're dangerous. But this person imitating me seems to want me to get stronger. Strong enough to beat them with Chaos specifically, seeing as it's the only Skill I'm able to use. What if it's one of the Remnants, and they have some clue about what I'll need to get through the greater Trials? Well, who knows who they are, but what if they're not attacking me just for kicks?"

Torliam rubbed at his beard. "This is a good point, though it does not explain how this person knows how to manipulate Chaos better than you yourself. In any case, I am not willing to take any risks with your life. You must grow strong enough to defeat them, or find a way to shield yourself from further attack. Are you able to enter your *warrior's-technique* and examine this mansion and its defenses for weaknesses?"

I'd done so nearly every day, when I didn't know how to bear Chaos safely, and it was still eating away at me. "Sure." I stopped moving and closed my eyes, taking deep breaths of the musty air as I turned my focus inward. It took a little longer than it once had, because I was rusty, but before long I'd fallen into myself. The mental construct of the mansion, the grounds, and the stone wall with no gate bloomed in my mind. I looked around. The place felt more ephemeral than it did within the dream world, and it also lacked that vague sense of dread I got when in one of the horror-dreams. I had six fingers on my left hand, and looked like an Estreyan warrior, not a squishy human.

With a sigh of relief, I set to exploring. I didn't remember creating the dungeon cells or that room of mirrors, but, after a couple hours, I found both of them. They were innocuous, without any traces of what had happened in the dream or any residual sense of danger. The stone wall all around was intact and as imposing as ever.

Still, the most clearly defined place in my mental world was the room of serenity. The box of silence sat in the middle of it, and within that, the chest of stillness. I opened them, but Chaos had long been freed, and there was nothing within.

Frustrated by my lack of progress, I returned to the outer wall and planted a row of massive ash trees formed with the abstract memory of human forms all around, like what had grown after I burned the warriors who'd died fighting the God of Knowledge and reformed them into a small, glittering woodland. I pushed them to grow upward and outward with my mind, and set them the task of capturing any intruders.

AFTER THE OTHERS woke up from their nap, we exited the subway tunnel into a small town a few hundred miles north of the meningolycanosis outbreak. It was early morning, and we were almost alone on the roads. At the edge of town was a diner with lit signs, surprisingly still open for business despite current world events.

Jacky reached over and grabbed my arm. "We should stop and have breakfast," she said.

I stared at her blankly.

"Having breakfast with your family is normal, no?" She looked at the kids. "They haven't gotten to try out normal stuff in a long time."

"Ah." I looked over to them, the two little faces serious and stoic behind their helmets as they rode behind Torliam and Zed. "That's… actually a good idea."

She scowled at me. "What do you mean, 'actually?' I have good ideas all the time!"

I grinned at her. "You realize we'll have to take off all our armor before we go in there, right? We might be recognized otherwise."

Her eyes widened. "Err… Breakfast is overrated anyway—"

"We're stopping for breakfast, everyone!" I called out, overriding her mumbled objections.

In an alley behind the restaurant, hidden beyond a huge trash bin, we stashed our bikes and armor and made sure we were bundled up in enough cold-weather gear to hide as many of our distinguishing characteristics as possible.

We thought Adam might be a problem, but he used ink to coat his actual legs and controlled the ink to make it look like he was walking normally. Still, his eyes narrowed as he examined the diner's entrance. "Are you sure this is a good idea?"

Jacky seemed to have regained all her enthusiasm when she smelled the scent of hot food wafting from the inside of the restaurant. "Yes! All my ideas are good, Adam. You agree with me, no?" She cracked her knuckles threateningly.

He just groaned in a put-upon manner and grumbled to himself.

Birch hid inside Kris' pack, and though a few patrons glanced our way as we entered, no one paid us much attention.

Our group took up two whole booths, and when the tired-looking waitress took our order, her eyes grew wider and wider along with the size of our meal. She hesitated before going back to the kitchen. "Um, will you be wanting any of this to go? We can wait to cook it till you're finished eating."

"No," I said, speaking through the shemagh still covering my lower face. "We've been on the road for a while, so we're pretty hungry. I doubt there will be any left over."

We were so excited to eat something besides preserved rations that, when the food arrived, we dug in like animals, practically inhaling it off our plates. That drew a few more looks, as did Kris feeding sausages into her pack, where Birch was hidden, but, in general, the other people in the restaurant continued to ignore us.

Most of the patrons were focused on a smartglass screen hung at one corner, which was displaying a fluffy pseudo-news station.

When my face popped up on the screen with a reminder to contact the Department of Defense with any information about me, I choked on my eggs. They had my name as well as a general description of me now, probably obtained from NIX.

Jacky pounded on my back, doing more harm than good as she tried to help me breathe again. The image changed away from my face to a film clip of a group of people crashing their motorcycles through what looked like a glass wall in slow motion, shards and water flying everywhere.

The people landed in a pool and there were some glowing blue light waves under the water, one person who shot through the water like a fish, and another small form that had turned completely black. Then the camera focused on the nearby edge, where Zed popped out of the water, followed by me again.

In the film, I crawled out of the water, hair plastered to my face, my eyes glowing in the light of the sun. I slowly looked the person behind the camera over, from their feet to their head. "You've got to be kidding," I said, my voice rough and a little deep, like black coffee. When I stood, I towered above the eye-line of the camera. I gazed into the distance like a character shooting a dramatic commercial for shampoo or something. Or maybe a trailer for an action film.

Watching this in the diner, I gaped stupidly at the screen as the reporter responded to me in shock. Was that what I looked like to other people?

"We are being chased by aliens," the Eve on the screen said. "I doubt they're friendly, and I doubt they're going to care if you get squished as collateral damage. We can't protect you. Run away if you want to live."

The reporter and her camera stayed for a few more seconds before Zed snapped at her and she ran off, taking her camera with her.

The clip ended there, and the screen cut to a man and woman, the show's hosts, both leaning forward in excitement. "If you've had access to the news channels or the net, you've probably seen this clip. We have with us Maria Vanderhurst, the reporter who managed to film the mysterious woman, now revealed to be Eve Redding, and her group of fellow superhumans who have been fighting against the alien invaders," the female host said.

I turned to Jacky and elbowed her in the side surreptitiously. "I look so cool!" I gloated, low enough none of the other patrons would hear.

The camera cut to the reporter who'd happened to be standing next to the mall pool when we crash-landed into it. She smiled brightly and thanked the two hosts.

The man flashed a too-white smile at her. "So, Maria. How did it feel to meet Eve Redding? What did you think when the wall behind you exploded into pieces?"

Maria grinned proudly and leaned toward the camera as if sharing a secret. "Well, Brad, I'll be honest, I was shocked. There's something the camera didn't catch. I saw them coming, and I thought they would smash into the side of the building and then fall to the ground. I don't know if you're aware, but the reinforced plastine that wall was made of isn't some window glass you can break so easily. They flew over using some of their powers, and then, just as they were about to smash into the side of the building, a black spear formed and blasted right through the wall! Everything blew up, and they landed safely in the pool."

The questioning went on from there, and Maria answered confidently, making things up about our powers and personalities like an expert, despite the fact she'd met us for less than a minute. On the bright side, she was adamant that we were the good guys, and hadn't *kidnapped* anyone.

One of the other restaurant customers turned to another table and asked loudly, "Look at what they were wearing! No way that's military, I tell you. They don't even match each other, not to mention they're completely different than those bodysuits the other guys were wearing."

"But they have powers," a man at the other table insisted. "You ever met a normal person with powers? How else did they get them if they're not part of that secret military division?"

A younger man at a booth scoffed loudly, turning around to face the rest of the room fully. "I'll tell you what's going on! Obviously, they escaped from some government research facility. You want proof? Look at the rest of the group. Some of them are *kids*! How else does the military suddenly pop up with superhumans perfectly suited to fighting these aliens and their powers? They've been planning for this! Experimenting on people in secret! They must have known about the aliens before they said anything, and this Redding chick and the kids were some of their experiments."

The man who'd insisted we were military rolled his eyes, but the first speaker smoothed his mustache thoughtfully. "That would explain why they're offering a reward for her."

A woman with a smoker's hoarse voice said, "How the hell would they get away with experimenting on children? No, if you ask me, this girl was experimented on by the *aliens*. Did you notice that skin on her arm and that weird thing stuck in her throat? Hell, she had *six fingers*, and she *spoke their language*. She had to have escaped from one of their ships and now she has a grudge against them. That's why the aliens were coming after her and they crashed into the mall to escape."

Our whole group stared at the other patrons in astonishment.

—ACT NORMAL, GUYS. AND MAYBE WE SHOULD HURRY UP AND GET OUT OF HERE. WE'RE JUST ASKING TO BE RECOGNIZED.—
-EVE-

We called for the check and had the second half of our food boxed up to go. Adam paid with some random person's hacked account information, and we tried to look as normal as possible, despite still being all bundled up inside the warm restaurant.

The waitress gave us an amused look, no doubt thinking we'd

gotten full earlier than expected. When we pushed back into the cold of the outdoors, however, she opened the door behind us, holding a couple more bags of boxed up food. "Here," she said simply, thrusting them out toward me.

I reached forward slowly, and took the bags from her.

Before I could ask what she was doing, she said, "Thank you. My sister was in that city." Then she turned back around and hurried into the restaurant, leaving me standing there, speechless, with two full bags of food in my arms.

Adam groaned and rolled his eyes. "Is this the time for an 'I told you so?' Because I did."

Sam, surprisingly, smiled. "I don't think she's going to report us."

I grimaced. "We'd still better get out of here. She might not be the only one who recognized us. Besides, we got what we came for."

Jacky grinned, completely unconcerned, and grabbed one of the kids under each of her arms, sprinting to the hidden bikes and armor while they shrieked in delight and struggled to escape her grip. "If NIX comes after us, we'll just beat 'em up again!"

———————————————

Chapter 23

———————————————

On the coldest nights
  I'll look for your glow
  among the burning embers
  of your fiery soul.
  — Christy Ann Martine

WHETHER OR NOT ANYONE ELSE RECOGNIZED US or reported us, we didn't see any signs of pursuit.

At another small town we passed, Adam stopped at a local tattoo parlor and purchased a whole box of ink. He used some of it to refill his stash of cartridges, but, to my surprise, he had something else in mind for the rest.

When we stopped again at a roadside rest stop to stretch our legs, he came over to me with one of the bottles. "You need some shields," he said, no room in his tone for argument. "Permanent ones, that you can use at any time, even if I'm not able to protect you."

"You want to give me a tattoo?"

"I want to give the whole group a series of tattoos," he corrected. "But you're first, because, in my experience, you're the most likely to get yourself killed doing something stupid. And," his voice softened a bit, "whatever's coming isn't going to be easy. We need every edge we can get."

I nodded. "It's a good idea. Let's do it."

Gregor and Birch both trotted over with almost identical looks of curiosity. "Us, too? Even though I'm still eight?" Gregor said.

"Err," Adam looked to me. "The tattoos won't actually be permanent, they'll go away as soon as they're used—"

I waved my hand at his hesitation. "It's fine. After everything else that's happened, a tattoo isn't something to be worried about."

Adam agreed, then settled down and started shoving ink into my skin. He didn't need any sort of equipment, he simply let a drop fall onto me, then used his Skill to shape it and force it past the surface of my skin. It hurt, but, compared to the injuries from the things we'd been through, the pain was negligible. "These are normal shields," he said, pressing the ink spot on the back of my wrist into a dark grey oval shape and then covering it with a fractal web that stood out from the background. "I've been experimenting whenever I've got energy to spare, and my Skill seems to like the design aspect. It might look weaker because the base layer is so thin and it's covered in raised lines, but it'll do a better job of defending you than a plain black circle." When blood welled up around the tattoo, he gently wiped it away with a sterilizing pad and then covered the area with a strip of liquid skin bandage.

"I'll heal in a couple hours. I probably don't need a bandage."

"I know," he said, but he still pressed it onto my skin and rubbed it softly to make sure it was fully attached.

Next, he sank an image of a three-dimensional sphere beside the oval shield. "This is a spherical shield. It won't move with you once you've activated it, though." Once again, he covered it with abstract designs. "Since these are actual tattoos, using blood and flesh, and significant as I can make them, they should be fairly strong. At my current Skill level, each one should last for about five minutes once you activate it, unless whatever you're defending against puts undue stress on it." He continued that way till I had a bracelet of seven complex little shields lined up all the way around my wrist, his cold fingers pressing into my skin as he worked.

It only took a few minutes, but he was tired by the time he'd finished. "My Bestow Skill isn't very strong yet. I'll do more later, for everyone."

Torliam, who'd been sitting nearby and glaring at Adam as he worked, crossed his arms. "Hmph," he scoffed. "Save your strength. I will not need such a limited method of defense."

Adam's hand, still holding my wrist, tightened in anger.

"Adam can do more than just shields," I said. "He gave me *wings* last time."

"My Skill is of the upper air. When I am at full strength, I can fly on my own. I struggle to see what his weak Skill might do for me that I cannot do better myself. With me by her side, Eve will not have any need of your little scribbles." Torliam sneered at Adam, obviously trying to provoke him.

"But you're not at full strength, are you?" Adam snapped. "I certainly haven't seen you flying around like it's nothing. And if you don't want it, that's fine with me. I'll save my energy for doing something *worthwhile*." He used an ink construct to help him stand, the multi-legged form raising him even higher than Torliam. He opened his mouth to continue, but, instead of speaking, he looked to the side and frowned.

I followed his gaze to Zed, who was sitting at one of the picnic tables. My brothers' eyes rolled around spastically as his eyelids fluttered.

My Wraith Skill had exploded out of my skin before I realized it, searching for an enemy or signs of a hostile Skill, even as I hurried toward him. I found no evidence of an attack, and pressed my hands against his shoulders, both to help steady him and to make it easier to push Wraith into his body and search for signs of injury.

"'M not hurt," he mumbled. "It's my VR chip. Windows are going crazy with gibberish, and I'm tasting and feeling things that aren't there."

I forced my mind to calm and focus, then pushed my awareness gingerly into Zed's brain. When I found the VR chip, which was one of a few chips in his brain, I focused Wraith on it, forcing my awareness to deepen, till details too small for even my augmented eyes became clear to my senses.

His VR chip was…teeming with little artificial bodies. I frowned. It was made of nanites, but the way they were swarming around it seemed abnormal. I couldn't be sure, though, because none of us had the same concentration of nanites he did, or any bodily augmentations which depended on them. I caught a hint of a few scattered

Seed organisms, too, but nothing that seemed dangerous. In fact, the nanites appeared to be repairing or replacing sections of the chip.

I withdrew my awareness and motioned for Sam to do his own check. "It looks like maybe there was damage to the VR chip, and the nanites are repairing it," I said.

Adam scowled. "Do you think NIX gave us defective booster?"

Zed's disorientation seemed to settle. He shook his head and rubbed at his eyes. "I don't think so. I can feel when a lot of the nanites start to degrade. I get tired and sick and my body starts to ache. After I took the booster, that went away, so unless they hid something else in it, I don't think the ingredients were off. My nanites repaired themselves just fine."

Sam drew his hands off Zed's forehead. "He's not injured, for what it's worth."

Zed shrugged, his smile a little lopsided. "Maybe this is just what happens, when your whole body is full of nanites and you starve them of the elements they need to repair themselves. Besides, I feel better already."

Adam and I shared a doubtful look. "Let us know if it happens again," I said. Though what we could do to help him, I didn't know. I hoped Zed was right, but I couldn't quite bring myself to believe it. Nothing was ever so easy.

WE CONTINUED NORTH, meticulously avoiding any large cities despite the crowding of even the backroads. It grew colder and colder as we went. Keeping a group of irritable, frustrated, cold, and wind-bitten people and children driving all day, every day, was a recipe for hot tempers and bickering.

I spent some time looking through the chemistry book I'd taken from the abandoned pod and trying to refine my control of Chaos with simple things like wood carving, turning water into mist both by boiling it and by instantly subliming it, and a couple other tricks that weren't as cool as what I could do in the dream, but were more appropriate training for my actual ability. I was beginning to understand why Behelaino had thought I was so stupid when I was barely able to grasp the simplest use of Chaos.

We made it all the way to northern Canada before we had to rent a plane. Adam paid way too many credits for us to ride along with the cargo. Of course, we didn't care, because they weren't our credits.

We flew north to a land of semi-eternal darkness, Ellesmere Island. Weak lights glimmered from the few buildings that housed the people who stayed there even during winter.

"This close to the north pole," Gregor said, "it will be dark all day long."

I was glad that we had kept the winter gear from our trip through the Other Place, because the temperatures were miserably frigid. Just standing there on the landing pad of the tiny little airport nearly froze me solid.

"We must still go further north," Torliam said. "However, I have the sense that we are drawing close."

Gregor huddled further into the hood of his jacket, like a turtle. "This is the northernmost island in the Arctic Archipelago. This god better be close, or we'll have to cross the Arctic Ocean. If we keep going, we'll be in Russia, on the other side of the planet."

Jacky reached out to pinch his cheek, but was rebuffed by a slap of his hand. "Aww, you're so smart, bambino," she cooed.

He glared at her and stomped away to hide behind Torliam.

Our bikes weren't really meant for off-road travel, so we decided to find a sturdier ride before beginning our exploration.

Since Sam was the most harmless-looking and simultaneously forgettable adult in our group, we sent him to one of the few local businesses to get supplies and information, while the rest of us hunkered down in an unlit, unheated waiting complex near the airfield.

I kept an eye on him with Wraith so we could respond instantly if anything went wrong.

The shopkeeper didn't seem particularly excited to see him, and, after gathering some of the supplies, Sam stood awkwardly at the counter for several moments, shifting from foot to foot as he waited for the other man to ring up his purchases. "You got everything?" the man asked, finally.

"Err, actually, I was hoping to rent a couple snow pods, too, and maybe find a hotel to stay at, if you could point me in the right direction."

"Got one snow pod, but the inn's closed this time o' year," the man said, shaking his head.

Sam didn't seem to know what to say. He settled for "Oh."

"What you need a snow pod for, anyway? Ain't nothing out there 'cept tundra."

"I'm…with a research group. We want to study the fungi at the north of the island." Sam only hesitated a little, and I was proud of him for coming up with an excuse boring enough to stop anyone from asking further questions.

The man snorted. "Ain't nothing alive at the north of the island. Even funguses are too smart to try and grow in that dead zone." But despite his derision, he grabbed a key off the wall and tossed it to Sam. "Snow pod's out back. Ten thousand credits and you return it before we get sunlight again." When Sam nodded, the shopkeeper stared at him for a second, and then spoke again. "My sister's got a cabin, empty this time o' year. It's a little isolated, but it'll keep you cozy. Thirty thousand credits."

Sam accepted all of it, carefully paying with the link Adam had given him, which was pulling the credits from random accounts all over the world, as well as corrupting the data from the payment console so that nothing could lead back to us. If I were more morally upright, I might have felt bad about using unknowing and innocent peoples' credits like this. But I knew their links had insurance against fraud, and since I had not one, but two worlds to save, I figured they could deal with the hassle of getting a refund on my behalf.

I drove the cross-terrain snow pod to the cabin, letting Zed drive his own bike for once. The cabin was small, but well insulated, and the wood-burning stove's exhaust pipe wove through the walls, keeping the place warm enough to sleep through the night without shivering.

The snow pod was too small to carry everyone, so Torliam, Adam, and I rode out alone to search, while the others stayed behind to rest.

WHEN WE REACHED the northern sea, Torliam frowned, looking down as if he could peer into his own heart. He lifted his head and turned to me. "I believe we have passed it," he said.

Adam rolled his eyes, legs twitching as he fed little motes of electricity directly into his muscles, a way to keep them from completely atrophying. "No, *really*? Does that observation have anything to do with the fact that we just ran into the Arctic Ocean? There's nowhere for us to go forward."

Torliam's jaw clenched. "My Skill's bidding is still vague. However, the 'tug' inside me is pulling the other direction, now. We have passed it."

"I didn't sense anything," I said, checking our location against the map. "Maybe we were too far away. My Skill only extends a couple miles at the farthest. Maybe searching in a grid pattern would be best," I said. "We can use both Torliam's Skill and my own to narrow down the location."

Having found no hint of the lost god, we returned weary and discouraged to the cabin. "We cannot expect it to be easy," Torliam said. "If it were, he would have been discovered long ago."

When we entered the cabin, Zed was laying in the corner with a wet cloth over his face.

"He had some more VR chip glitches," Sam said. "It gave him a headache. I checked, and he's technically fine, he's just resting."

Adam pulled up the news on his link, and we sat down at the crowded wooden dining table to watch.

This time, instead of some fluff story, we saw a real update on the state of the world. My throat tightened as I watched distant views of the city we'd escaped from, ships flying overhead and smoke rising up from the decimated streets.

The meningolycanosis had spread, despite the Estreyans' efforts to kill all the infected. They couldn't catch everyone, and it seemed like the virus had already been loose at multiple points before the screaming crowds had drawn attention to it.

A ton of people had made it out in the meantime, despite attacks on the roads and the invaders' attempts to keep the city's residents from leaving, but the escapees had nowhere to go. Many of the nearby cities were refusing to house refugees, either because of overcrowding, lack of resources, or because they were afraid of the new plague spreading through their own cities. People were divided. While some believed the diseased people would cause another quarantine if brought to a new city, others thought that it was actually biological warfare from the Estreyans, meant to wipe us out. Either way, they were afraid to help.

So the Estreyans brought in another destroyer and quarantined the city again, except this time the barrier extended way past the city limits. It caught almost all the displaced refugees that had managed to escape but didn't have anywhere to go or a way to get there.

This time, they didn't ask for the sick. Their warships just kept burning things to the ground, while ensuring no one else could escape.

———

THE REST of the team took turns going out with Torliam and me to search for signs of the god as we meticulously covered the entire island with a grid strategy. Travel across the wilderness was slow. We found nothing. When we weren't searching, Torliam and I were speculating, trying to come up with some idea to help us solve the seemingly unsolvable.

Both his Tracker and my Wraith Skill grew stronger with constant use, but we were obviously missing something. The vague 'tug' of Torliam's Skill would often change direction after hours of searching, sending us back over terrain we'd already scoured. I even tried to spread my awareness over the entire island one day, thinking that perhaps the god's presence was just so dispersed I was missing it. That earned me a migraine so bad Torliam had to take me back to the cabin for Sam to look at, and a scolding from everyone when they learned the reason for my condition.

We even sent Sam out to ask the locals about any rumors of magical beings or deities native to the area, but he didn't learn anything, and had to dodge a few awkward questions about why a biologist was so interested in the local myths.

Torliam's Skill grew slightly more specific as it strengthened, but he still couldn't pinpoint what it was trying to lead us to, only alert us a little more promptly once we'd passed it.

We returned to the little cabin long enough to sleep, and then headed out again into the endless night, crossing the island in long lines of boredom and frustration.

Jacky kept trying to activate Struggle in the absence of real danger, but only managed to do so a couple times out of hundreds of attempts, one of those times being while she was having a nightmare.

Adam took the time to give everyone—except Torliam—a bracelet of shield tattoos. Then, he gave the kids a couple small symbols which would create a harness-type construct that would enclose them in a bubble, and then use spider-like legs to skitter away at top speed with them safe inside. When he was finished with that, he threw himself into working on a secretive tattoo project for himself. "I'll do more shields and some custom ink for everyone when I get the chance," he promised.

For the first few days, Zed's VR chip kept acting up, giving him synesthesia and bombarding him with Windows full of gibberish until he grew nauseous. There was nothing we could do about it, since none of us had the confidence to try to remove the chip via brain surgery. One night, he woke the rest of us up with a shout.

I rushed into the room, to find him staring into mid-air with amazement while waving his arms about and wriggling his fingers with fascination, like they were brand new. "What happened?" I snapped.

He turned to me with a huge smile. "It wasn't glitching out."

"Did you have a nightmare?" Jacky asked from behind me, rubbing her eyes sleepily.

"My VR chip!" He explained, waving his hands around in excitement and stumbling over his tongue as he rushed out an explanation. "It wasn't glitching. It was updating! The nanites are all programmed to follow the orders of the principal guide, except that was NIX, so they haven't been receiving any new orders since we escaped. But they're not completely mindless. They were made to emulate the Seeds, right? I think they've been doing more than that. I think they've been learning from my Seed organisms, and since the Seeds are monitored by the VR chip, the nanites decided they should be, too!" He took a deep breath. "I have access to all my nanites now."

My heartbeat slowed in the absence of immediate danger. "What does that mean, exactly? What can you do with access to the nanites?"

Some of the excitement slipped away, and he rubbed the back of his head awkwardly. "Ah, well, actually I'm not too sure. I know what they're doing. Maybe I'll be able to give them orders, or…something?"

Jacky snorted at him and moved aside so Sam could get into the room to examine Zed.

Sam, who apparently hadn't been asleep, again found nothing wrong.

We stayed up for a little while longer while Zed played around with the new function of his VR chip to make sure nothing went wrong. He was fascinated at being able to see a "galaxy" of nanites circulating around and augmenting his body, but nothing actually happened.

IN THE MORNING, Jacky and I sat blearily eating breakfast at the dining table.

Kris walked in, her little wooden puppet following along behind her. She grabbed a bowl of sloppy oatmeal and sat at the table to shovel it into her mouth, eyes half closed. She was hungry all the time now, a subtle sign that the Sickness was growing stronger within her.

Beside her, the puppet hopped onto its own chair. It looked at her, seemingly curious, and then turned to the table. It was so short it had to stand rather than sit on the chair, but it reached out into the air and pretended to grab something, then began to imitate her, shoveling invisible oatmeal into its mouth.

I pinched my nose and tried to breathe through it to make sure I wasn't dreaming. I elbowed Jacky till she looked up through the tangled halo of her short hair to see what was going on. "Kris," I said. "Are you making your puppet do that?"

Kris stared at me, and then looked over at it.

It stopped pretending to eat and looked back at her.

"Nah," she said. "It's just imitating me."

Jacky and I shared a look. "It decided to imitate you on its own?" I said, keeping my voice neutral.

"Yeah. My Skill's getting stronger, I think, giving it more power to work with. I've kept the same spirit in that body since I first made it, so it's learning some things." She returned to eating, as if this was no big deal. "Didn't you notice by now? It's always following me around."

I looked at Jacky. "I've been gone most of the time. Did you notice?"

She pursed her lips, avoiding my eyes. "Well, I wasn't really paying attention. I thought she was just playing with it. An imaginary friend type deal, yeah?"

Kris frowned at her. "I'm not a little kid! I don't have imaginary friends anymore."

"Does your puppet...have a personality?" I said. "Its own thoughts?"

Kris' eyes widened as she understood my thought process. She turned to the puppet as if seeing it for the first time. "Well, maybe a little? Its original spirit was kind of...playful? In a nice way. Spirits aren't the same as humans, so it's hard to explain. But lately, it's been acting kind of like a person. It could just be because it's imitating me, though."

Jacky smiled at the puppet and waved her hand. "Hi, little one."

It waved back at her, then turned away and jumped off the chair, running to the corner where a pile of wood shavings and some spare puppet parts lay. It sat down and fiddled with a piece of wood, seemingly having forgotten about us.

"Wow," I said.

Kris nodded at the sentiment. "Yeah. I think I'm going to name him Pinocchio."

ONE DAY, during one of the rare times I was actually at the cabin—because the migraine from overusing Wraith put me out of commission—I struggled blearily with the Oracle's third gift while listening to the news in the background.

People were panicking, and the government had officially blamed the meningolycanosis outbreak on the Estreyans. The invasion itself was enough to disrupt the lives of the entire planet, but the plague brought out whole new levels of fear and despair in people. People wore a face mask to go outside, industry had pretty much shut down with employees refusing to go to work, and society was crumbling.

On the other hand, recruitment numbers for the military had never been higher.

I threw the puzzle ring into my lap, squeezing my eyes shut in frustration. I had searched the whole island, and I still couldn't find even a *trace* of the Champion who could fix all this. I'd gotten out of the snow pod and screamed out to the dark for him, demanding and pleading that he answer us, but still nothing. That's when I'd pushed Wraith too hard again and ended up back at the cabin with what felt like an icepick jammed into my brain.

Sam, eyes shadowed with the evidence of Black Sun's partial activation, turned off the link playing the news. "It's nothing new. Don't you think it's time we do something different? It's not working, Eve. You have no idea where this god is. You've gridded out basically the entire island by now, and you're no closer to finding him than when we arrived."

My head swirled dizzily. "We'll find him."

Sam rolled his darkened eyes and walked out the door, ducking past Torliam, who was entering.

I knew that Sam wasn't completely correct. We had a broad idea of where Torliam's Skill was leading us—a large, vague circle drawn on the map. But we had indeed passed over the whole island, specifically that circle, multiple times, and I hadn't felt even the glowing outer penumbra of a god's power.

Torliam stepped more softly than a man of his size should be able to, the swirl of cold air from outside following him and making me shiver. He moved to my side and handed me a steaming thermos of the local tea.

I sat up gingerly and accepted it with a nod.

"Sam is skeptical," he said in a low voice.

"They all are." I let out a long sigh, closing my eyes and leaning against the wall.

"I am sorry," he said, then paused for a long moment. "My people have searched for the Champion for thousands of years now. Though I will admit I thought for some reason that I would be different, I did still feel some trepidation that even this Skill bestowed on me by the Goddess of Testimony and Lore would not be enough. It seems that may indeed be the case."

"I don't think your Skill has just failed," I said.

He let out a humorless huff. "And what if it is impossible to lead us to the God of Shaping and Molding? Perhaps my Skill is in fact directing us to some ancient relic that is just another cryptic clue toward finding him, and is buried out there under tons of rock and ice?"

I took another sip of bitter tea as I tried to think of what to say, and then my eyes snapped open. I closed them again quickly, wincing against the spike of pain that caused. "Torliam!" I said, my voice tight with excitement. "What if that's it?"

"My Skill leads us to a clue, rather than the object I seek?"

"No!" I refrained from shaking my head. "What if this god is buried under the ground? My Wraith Skill travels best through the air. I've been looking for caves and things, but I haven't been pushing *deep* into the ground. What if the god is *buried*? How much dirt could accumulate on top of something over the last few thousand years? That would explain why we keep passing him over and over again, and I can't seem to sense anything!"

"We must go out again!" Torliam said, standing up quickly enough to knock over his chair. "Perhaps with this new revelation, one of us will be able to find him."

I nodded, but the motion made me dizzy and nauseous again.

"After you have rested," he amended, putting a hand on my forehead to keep me still. "If he has been hidden for so long, he can stay hidden a while longer. Sleep."

I lay down again, though I didn't think I would be able to sleep past my excitement. Despite my skepticism, I drifted off within minutes, and didn't even wake to my VR chip notifying me of my increased levels of Perception and Stamina. Those had become a common occurrence throughout our futile trips across the barren tundra.

Chapter 24

I'll sift through the ashes
    in search of the spark
    that ignited my mind
    and lit up my heart.
    — Christy Ann Martine

AFTER OUR MINI-REVELATION, spirits rose again amongst the group, and we returned to our search with renewed energy. Once again, however, neither Torliam nor I found anything of significance.

I pushed myself to delirious migraine day after day, forcing my awareness down through the frozen dirt, ice, and rock, deeper and deeper in hopes that if I stretched far enough, we would find what we searched for. My efforts remained unrewarded.

The others began to train with a certain level of desperation, as if trying to reach levels of exhaustion similar to my own. The complete lack of sunlight only made things worse.

Jacky's Struggle Skill came easier, but, from the dark circles under her eyes, I wondered whether it was because she was getting control of it or if she was just closer to the edge of helpless desperation than she had been.

Zed started meditating, trying to increase his Perception from the tiny base of Seed material he had to work with, because his Veil-

Piercers Skill required him to be able to sense the rips in the fabric of the world to use it, and some of them were too subtle.

Sam used his Black Sun Skill more often, its effects allowing him to escape from the boredom and a growing sense of defeat we all felt. He'd started helping Kris upgrade Pinocchio by healing her wounds when she cut herself for blood to use on her puppet's wooden body.

Gregor kept having nightmares and falling through the floor due to activating his Shadow Skill while asleep. He could control his level of corporeality to some degree while awake, which allowed him to walk across the floor without sinking into the floorboards, and even keep his clothes or small objects with him when he shifted, but while sleeping and panicked, that control abandoned him.

I wondered if there was some prerequisite we had to meet or some requirement we hadn't fulfilled that kept the god hidden. If so, I had no idea what it might be, and I was losing hope of that changing. I even wondered if we might never find him. Maybe we weren't meant to. I'd lied about the quest reward for killing the God of Knowledge, and, as soon as I did that, it seemed like circumstances kept bending to make my words the truth. But maybe I'd just deceived myself as much as everyone else. There was a saying, after all. "If you repeat a lie often enough, people will believe it, and you will even come to believe it yourself."

Weeks of darkness and futile exploration had passed, and Chanelle's condition was worsening. She was lucid more often than ever, but she also often grew nasty and violent. "You'll never find him," she snarled at me one day after I came back from fruitless hours spent searching. "You're going to fail, and keep failing till everyone in the world is like *me*!" She clawed at her own chest, yanking at her clothes as if to punctuate the last word. "You *liar*!" Then her expression crumpled, and she collapsed to the floor, sobbing miserably.

Torliam stepped forward and picked her up gently, and we carried her back to bed.

"I'm sorry, I'm sorry," she mumbled. "I didn't mean it."

I shared a grim look with Torliam, because I doubted that was completely true. Without the Sickness, Chanelle wouldn't have lost her composure like that, but, deep down, I knew she must be scared and full of doubt, maybe even rage at her own helplessness. "It's okay," I said softly. "Keep fighting it, okay? I'm not giving up, so you can't either."

We stayed with Chanelle for a while, till she fell asleep, tear tracks staining her cheeks.

We returned downstairs. As soon as I saw everyone standing around the dining table, staring at the wall where the link was projecting the news, I knew something was wrong.

Then I saw the smoke, the molten earth, the charred hole of a scar stretching as far as the eye could see. The camera drone flew above what had once been the quarantined city. Occasionally, part of a building that had survived the attack poked out, the only evidence of what the land had once been.

The station cut back to a reporter, ash and hot wind blowing around him as he stood with the razed remains in the far distance behind him. His hands shook on the microphone, and a mix of ash and tears had dried on his face. "As our viewers know, the aliens have had the city and surrounding areas behind me quarantined for the past two weeks. This was the second time they had done so, after their forces were attacked from within the city and the barrier was destroyed along with some of their ships. After renewing the quarantine, their smaller ships went on periodic raids, destroying buildings and killing thousands of those trapped within who had not joined one of the emergency shelters. There is speculation that this was in retaliation for our earlier defiance, or as blackmail to dishearten our soldiers fighting against them elsewhere. Others believe they were attempting to cleanse the city of the new disease, though most experts believe the disease, which is similar to rabies and highly contagious, was originally introduced by the aliens themselves. Despite numerous attempts, the military was not able to break through the barrier from the outside. However," his voice broke, and he paused to swallow a few times, clearly forcing down tears, "this morning those periodic raids on the city and surrounding areas stopped. The destroyer lived up to its namesake. When it was finished with the annihilation of the city, it lifted the barrier. The ships were last tracked into Earth's outer atmosphere."

The camera panned past him to the smoking ruins as he continued speaking. "No survivors have been found thus far. The emergency shelters did not stand up to the destroyer's heat attack. The death toll has not been confirmed, but estimates put the loss of life to be around four million people." The reporter choked again, and this time couldn't hold back the tears. "Damn you," he said. "To the aliens, I say, damn you. We will never forget, and we will never forgive."

DENIAL LURCHED WITHIN ME. I bolted up from the table, slammed the door open and stumbled outside without my winter gear. I fell to my knees in front of the cabin and shook with suppressed rage, fear, and guilt.

My fingers curled, clawing uselessly against the ground, and I let out a low moan as tears ran freely down my cheeks. They turned cold and began to freeze, but I didn't care.

Inside, the others were shouting. I heard something break. Someone was crying, sobbing.

Footsteps crunched behind me, and then Torliam was sinking onto the hard-packed snow beside me. He wrapped an arm around my shoulders and pulled me toward him.

I shuddered, gasping past the pain in my heart and the tears soaking into his shirt. "My fault," I managed, the words half-mangled.

"No," he said, and I was surprised at the thickness of tears in his own voice, the feel of his breath hitching in his chest. "No, not your fault."

But I knew the queen wouldn't have ordered the attack on Earth if not for me.

"My mother, she caused this. Not you. And before her, NIX is responsible. They did this, all of them, playing with the lives of others without regard."

I knew that wasn't the whole truth of it. I was at fault, in my own way, because I'd been so afraid to die that I'd pushed for people to believe I was the chosen one who could find their lost god. I'd given Queen Mardinest the reason and the justification to attack Earth.

I was the reason China was dead. I was the reason Chanelle had the Sickness, and the kids, too. I was the reason Adam's back was broken. Blaine was assassinated because of me. It was all me. All my fault.

If I'd just been willing to die from the beginning, maybe none of it would have happened. Maybe that city would still be standing. I couldn't even find the Champion. Maybe because I was never going to be the one to find him.

"No," I rasped. "My fault. I…I lied." The confession almost made me dizzy.

Torliam didn't respond.

"I lied from the beginning," I continued. "My quest to defeat the God of Knowledge, the reward didn't have anything to do with the Sickness. It was information about the Seed of Chaos, and it was killing me. You weren't going to help, so I lied, and then everything seemed to work out with the Seal of Nine and the prophecy, but what if I can't find the Champion? That means it's my fault—" I stopped rambling as I ran out of air. I looked up slowly, afraid to see the look on Torliam's face.

When I did, it was like a punch in the gut.

Pain, anger, and disgust. He drew back from me and stood up. He took another step backward and paused for a moment, as if he wanted to say something. Then he shook his head and walked away, moving into the darkness instead of back toward the cabin.

I didn't watch him go, but after a few minutes I heard his ragged shout echo back to me, full of all the same emotions his expression had held.

I stayed in the dark for a while. The air felt brittle with frustrated hope and despair, as if the wrong word would shatter it like glass, and me with it.

Footsteps crunched from behind me again, but this time it was Zed, wrapping a blanket around me and helping me to my feet.

I told him what I'd done, and waited for judgment.

He was silent for a moment, then shrugged. "I don't care. I'm still on your side, you know. And even if you were lying to start off with, it doesn't mean you weren't accidentally telling the truth. We have the Seal of Nine, after all. Do you think that's something the gods give out so easily?"

I turned my head to look at him dubiously. "*You don't care?* A whole city just burned to the ground."

The arm around me squeezed a little tighter. "I do care about that. But I don't agree that it's your fault. And even if it was… Let me ask you this. If you found out that I was a murderer, but it was an accident, would you turn me into the police?"

"No." I replied without even thinking about it.

He grinned. "You'd help me hide the body, right?"

I let out a startled, half-sobbing laugh. "And you're going to do the same for me?"

"Well, we've still got a god to find. Once that's done, I'll disown you like a red-headed step-child."

He grinned widely, watching for my reaction from the corner of his eye.

My mouth fell open, and I shoved him away.

He laughed, then shoved me back.

I HAD a hard time falling asleep at first. I couldn't help but think of Torliam, still out there in the dark, coming to accept the fact that he'd been betrayed by me.

Adam, grim-faced, called for Sam to force me to sleep with his Harbinger Skill.

When I woke, both Adam and Zed were sitting in the corner of the room talking to each other in murmurs.

When Adam saw my eyes were open, he stood up and walked over to me. He put his hand on my head, as if to check for fever, and then nodded in satisfaction. "You got a little warm last night, while you were sleeping. Sam said you were showing the effects of long-term stress, and you need to rest more, or even a Resilience as high as yours won't be able to keep you healthy forever."

I blinked up at him, then wiped the crust from my eyes. "Am I dreaming?"

He snorted and ran a hand dramatically through his hair. "I know I'm handsome, but this isn't a fantasy." He shot a smug look toward Zed. "I told you my good looks make the ladies lose their wits."

I snorted. "Okay, now I know I'm definitely awake. I'd never think up dialogue that ridiculous by myself. But how are you walking?"

Zed covered his mouth and laughed, pointing a finger at Adam, who huffed and rolled his eyes.

Adam turned his back to me and lifted up the bottom of his shirt, baring part of his back. Thousands of little ink strands intertwined, running along his spine and branching out from there, disappearing below the waistband of his pants. "I found a more efficient way to replace my legs. I'm still experimenting, but I think I'm on the right track."

My smile almost split my face in two. "Adam, that's wonderful! Is this the secret project you've been working on?"

"I didn't want to tell everyone and make a big deal out of it in case it didn't work. It's still not perfect, but it's useable at least."

I indulged him by making impressed sounds as he walked back and forth a few times, but then he turned back to me with a serious expression. "After what happened last night, the rest of us have been talking," he said.

I sat a little straighter, hoping I wasn't about to get more bad news. "Talking about what?"

"We've been shirking our responsibilities, and placing them on you," he said.

I frowned. "What?"

Zed grimaced. "It's true. Every day, you and Torliam have been going out there to search, and most of the time the rest of us stay here and train or laze about. It started because there isn't enough room in the snow pod for everyone, but we shouldn't have let it continue, especially when you couldn't find anything yourself. Just because you have that Perception Skill doesn't mean the rest of us can't be useful. And maybe that's why you haven't had success. What if he's going to keep hiding until the whole Seal of Nine appears? I mean, can you imagine the danger you could be in, suddenly revealing a god who had been trying to hide, with only two people? Maybe it's a good thing you haven't found him."

"I...hadn't considered that," I said. "I assumed I'd find some clue to his location and then come back and tell everyone."

Adam waved his hand impatiently. "It makes sense that you wouldn't be able to find him alone. So we're all coming out with you today. Except Torliam, I guess. That selfish asshole is still somewhere outside moping."

I knew Torliam was still alive because I could vaguely sense his location through the blood-covenant bond. The fact that he was so angry he'd stayed out this long made me cringe, but I wasn't worried for him. Besides, very few things could actually pose a threat to him on Earth.

After breakfast, everyone bundled up, and we headed out. Before I'd woken, Sam had gone into town and rented a trailer for the snow pod so that it could carry the whole team, some in the cab up front, and some being towed behind. The extra weight increased the vehicle's energy consumption a lot, but with Adam coming along we were able to recharge the cartridge whenever we needed.

Since the kids and were more delicate, they rode with Adam and me inside the pod.

Everyone who could do so while moving kept their senses peeled and their Skills active in the hopes that maybe they would be able to find the clue I'd missed, and we stopped periodically for Zed to peek into the Other Place. I called out for the god to show himself, using Voice to lend weight to my words. When I managed to activate the stubborn Skill, that is.

Gregor stayed in his Shadow state, just corporeal enough that he didn't shift through the pod and get left behind, looking around like a silent statue made of obsidian. His Skill gave him better night vision than the rest of us put together.

Kris kept her eyes closed in a kind of meditation as she practiced with her Summon Skill. Every once in a while, the lights of our snow pod would catch an animal form darting along with us, as she lifted the spirits of the land and guided them into a long-frozen carcass which had been preserved by the cold. We were passing through the vague circle where Torliam's Skill insisted our answer lay when she leaned close to me and, shivering, whispered, "This place is *creepy*."

I opened my own eyes, the world spinning dizzily as I drew my awareness back into my body. I could reach miles into the air and about a third that distance into the ground now, without even touching it directly, where before that would have been unthinkable in anything but the clearest of air. "The sun will rise in summer, and stay up all day and all night," I said.

She shook her head. "No, that's not it. I mean, yeah, the total darkness all the time *is* driving me crazy. Sometimes, when it's cloudy outside, I look up at the sky and blink over and over again because I can't figure out if my eyes are actually open. I'm tired all the time, but I've stopped getting *sleepy* properly. But, that's not what I mean. This place we're at right now is creepy."

"How so?"

"It's dead. There aren't any living things."

"It's winter."

"And we're near the geomagnetic north pole. I know." She grimaced. "The other parts of the island have things that are hibernating. Or old frozen skeletons and dead things. This place hasn't had anything living here for a really long time. They would have left pieces of their bodies behind, and I would have been able to feel them with my power. There are no souls here, and our team, plus Pinocchio, are the only bodies recognizable as containers to my power."

I shared a look with Adam. "That may be significant, Kris. Does your Skill tell you anything else? When did this feeling start?"

"It started a few minutes back. And I don't really feel anything at all. I'll let you know if I sense any other bodies or anything strange." She straightened and looked up at me, eyes wide and excited. "Do you think this means the god is somewhere in the dead zone?"

"I hope so," I admitted. It would be a clue, where we hadn't had one for so long.

We stopped to let Zed open a rip into the Other Place, where once again there was *more* light than existed in reality. The hole hanging in the air shone like a kind of grey, washed-out flashlight. He frowned, then widened the rip with a grin. "There's no ash-stuff. I didn't realize before, but everywhere else I've been there's always that ash-stuff falling from the sky."

I gave him a huge grin. "That's great!"

Adam nodded, but sighed. "But what does it mean?"

"It means we're probably looking in the right place, at least," Zed said. "Maybe we just haven't been looking for the right type of signs."

Using Kris and Zed, we mapped out the space where the Other Place's strange sediment ceased to fall, which coincided pretty cleanly with Kris' sense of where the dead things disappeared.

We went to the middle of the vague circle and looked around, but we still didn't find anything. I closed my eyes and swirled my awareness outward one last time, hoping that I would miraculously notice something I hadn't before. We had been out for a while, and everyone was ready to head back to the cabin.

"Maybe we need the jerk here with us," Adam muttered. "It's his Skill that's supposed to be doing this in the first place, right?"

I opened my eyes and said, "Stop."

"Did you discover something?" Kris' voice was almost heartbreakingly eager.

I grinned. "No. But I have an idea."

Chapter 25

Three things cannot be long hidden: the sun, the moon, and the truth.

— Buddha

"GET OUT, ZED," I said, scrambling out into the cold of the sunless wilderness.

"You want me to open the Veil again?"

I nodded eagerly.

"What's the plan, Eve?" Adam said, joining us.

"You were right, about needing the rest of the team. We were able to discover a serious clue because of Kris and Zed, but now we're stuck again, in pretty much the same situation as before. So, maybe what the search needs is another change of perspective. If the Other Place can show us where we should be looking because the ash doesn't fall, maybe it will have some other indicators as well. Something Zed can't know, because he can't do what I can."

Adam's gloved fingers played restlessly with the air, as if wishing he had something to twiddle. "Is that safe?"

Zed turned to the others. "I'll go with her. We have to do this. If it gives us any chance of making some headway, it'll be worth it. We'll stay right by the opening, so be alert, and be ready to pull us out if anything happens."

He stepped through first, and I followed him. "Ack," I said, almost choking. "I don't know *how* this place somehow manages to be even colder."

"It's because the cold isn't just temperature-based," Zed said.

First, I sent my awareness up and out. There was no hint of Seed glow, but I'd given up on that long ago and didn't let it discourage me.

I knelt on the ground, and very carefully stretched my senses out. Nothing responded. No watchful eye turned to us. No sucking hunger pulled at us. I let out a sigh of relief, then delved down, pushing my senses outward, deeper and deeper, spreading out through the earth like a weighted net. I searched for anything strange, anything different from the ice and rock and dirt I knew so well by now.

Minutes passed. The Other Place eased away the tension in my shoulders, the little frown between my eyebrows that I didn't realize was there. I slumped forward onto the ground, relaxing as I pushed farther. We were only a few miles out from the ocean, and the sea-spray tasted metallic at the back of my throat. The water flowed beneath the ice, cutting into the rock and dirt. Over time, it had carved out caves, tunnels, and trenches far below, hidden to man and eschewed by the animals and even the little pieces of vegetation that could survive such conditions.

My awareness rode the currents, drawn into the water as if it were a gently rocking cradle. I blinked slowly, lazily. I had been cold, but I didn't feel it anymore. I knew that was probably bad, but I would deal with it…in a moment. After. My eyes closed again.

Deep below, I brushed against something. My eyes flew open.

Something grabbed me roughly, yanking me upward painfully and holding my limp form.

Suddenly, the air burned my face. I leaned over the shoulder of whoever was carrying me and threw up, my throat burning not only at the feel of acid, but from cracks and burst blood vessels in the flesh.

Adam cursed. "Did you not notice the blood?" he snarled.

"Her face was hidden!" Zed's voice said. "It's only been ten minutes. I was doing okay, and she's kept up with me before when she came into the Other Place. How was I supposed to know she was turning into a popsicle and not just meditating?"

Hands wiped the vomit away from my face. "Get her into the pod. It's warm in there. Sam!"

I was jostled roughly as they packed me in between them, and then hot hands pressed against my forehead. "You'll be fine," Sam's voice said, a little too stressed to be reassuring.

I coughed again, swallowing bloody saliva. "I found it," I croaked.

There was a long beat of silence.

"What? You found the god?!" "Tell me I'm not hallucinating." Adam and Zed spoke at the same time.

I fumbled for the water thermos at my waist, and Zed helped me, lifting it to my mouth so I could drink, then clasping my cold-burning fingers between his hands and rubbing the warmth back into them. I could feel the weight of everyone's attention on me, waiting for me to speak.

"I found a spot, deep under the ground, where the ocean has eaten away at the coast. There is a place where the water is warm."

Adam and Zed were silent as I swallowed painfully again.

"The Other Place doesn't have any places with warmth," I croaked. "I think it might be an opening to somewhere else. Just like what Zed does." My lips cracked as I smiled, but I ignored it. The wilderness burst to life with cheers of elation.

WE MARKED the spot where I'd found the anomaly on the map with as much accuracy as possible, and I added notes about the structure of the underground caverns and rivers, as well as the approximate depth. I wanted to be able to find it again more quickly when we returned.

A couple hours later, the snow pod arrived at the cabin. I could sense Torliam inside.

I burst through the door, and, before he could say anything, started talking. "We found it."

He was sitting at the dining table, and turned his head toward me slowly.

"We found the thing we've been searching for," I said. "It's not the god, but I think it might be a portal to him."

Whatever expression had been on his face was washed away by excitement. "Tell me more," he ordered.

I explained what I'd sensed, and the energy he'd been lacking suffused him as I spoke.

"This is most promising," Torliam said, examining the spot on the map. He looked at me, and his voice cooled a little. "However, we should be wary of throwing ourselves blindly into what could be a dangerous situation. We have no idea what this anomaly might do. It could be harmful."

"No," I agreed. "But we don't have time to waste. We need to research and prepare as quickly as possible."

"I'm hungry all the time, now," Gregor said, coming up behind me. "It's not *normal*. I'm not waiting any longer than I have to. I want to find this stupid god and get him to heal us."

We were silent for a pained moment before Torliam said, "I have no intentions of hindering our mission. However, we cannot allow haste to ruin us if there is danger to be avoided."

Zed pressed his lips together. "So what do we need to do?"

Torliam turned back to the map. "We must examine this 'warm space' and do our best to determine its purpose and what effect it might have on us. The fact that the animals and even the plants avoid it for miles around could be a bad sign."

"Maybe radiation, or some other undetectable emission," I said. "Or maybe it's some sort of Seed-created barrier set up by the god for anyone who's not part of the Seal of Nine."

Gregor clenched the edges of his seat with his hands, turning to me instead. "Chanelle's dying. When she's lucid, she's either being venomous and hateful, or crying. She's like a starving animal, and I can *see* her veins, all dark and sick-looking. We have to hurry."

I laid my hand on Gregor's shoulder and squeezed. "Trust me, we're not going to procrastinate on this. We'll need a way to get down there, to start," I said. "Maybe a boat, and some heavy duty diving gear?"

Adam nodded, already tapping on his link. "I'll order some detection equipment for radiation and poison. We should be able to get it flown up here in a rush order, if we pay enough. And I'm getting some cameras. If the portal is like Zed's, we should be able to send one through and see what's on the other side."

"Electronics lose their charge quickly in the Other Place," Zed warned.

"I'll see if an EMP shielding case helps with that at all. Not much else we can do, I think."

Torliam rubbed at his jaw. "We must be ready for the possibility that things will go wrong. We should not approach the area unless we are as prepared as possible for what might be on the other side, whether we *plan* to encounter it or not."

"We should all go together," Jacky said. "We can tie ropes to connect us all, like we did in that ratman Trial, or when we crossed the broken bridge of the North."

"And extra supplies," Sam said. "What if it sucks us through? What if what's on the other side is an underwater realm or something? We have to make sure we won't run out of oxygen. And I'll make sure my healing is well-charged." Sam turned to Adam. "Maybe we could go fishing?"

Adam nodded. "And I'll get some more standard ink constructs ready to be Animated. As strong as I can make them. It'll save time if we're in an emergency. If only I could get my legs working again, I wouldn't need to use Animus so much just to get around."

We continued talking and planning for a few more hours till I nodded off in my chair.

I woke the next day to darkness, but the mood in the cabin was enough to brighten the air, everyone rushing about with barely contained excitement.

CHANELLE WORE A MUZZLE. When she turned to me, she smiled widely behind the metal cage covering the lower half of her face and strapped securely onto her head with strips of leather. "I got Gregor to make it for me, when I heard," she said. Her fingers twitched, and she pressed them to the table in front of her with a frown. "I know I'm not in very good shape. But I want to come with you. And this way, you'll be safe from my teeth."

I moved to sit beside her, wrapping an arm around her shoulders and pulling her closer. "You realize all this will be over soon, right? I know it's been hard. But you're going to feel like yourself again. You are going to be able to walk around and be part of the team like normal. Like it *should* be."

A warm drop of clear liquid splashed onto the table in front of us. My Perception was high enough that I smelled the salt in it, but I didn't need that to know it was a tear.

I reached up with my other hand and stroked Chanelle's short hair like I would Birch's, hoping that the motion was comforting. I tried to think of something else to say, but I just felt awkward and helpless, the emotions battling against the anxious hope I was also feeling. What if I were wrong, and the place I'd found wasn't our answer?

We spent the next few days preparing, and Zed and I returned with Torliam to the spot at the north end of the island. I went into the Other Place again and, under careful supervision from both of them, pushed Wraith down to the spot of warmth, finding it much more quickly the second time around. I wrote detailed instructions for how we would navigate the underwater caverns to reach it, exiting the Other Place several times to warm up within the snow pod before returning to mapping our way.

I found the same spot in the normal world. While the terrain was the same, there was no indication that anything about that spot of water was different from the rest. I wondered if Testimony and Lore had known this would happen, when she gave us each our Skills. "One for each of the greater Trials," she had said. The thought made me shudder, hoping that whatever was on the other side, we would be ready for it. Why couldn't one of the gods have given us clearer information about what we would be dealing with?

I pulled up my Attribute Window, running my eyes over my levels.

PLAYER NAME: EVE REDDING
TITLE: BEARER OF TESTIMONY
CHARACTERISTIC SKILL: SPIRIT OF THE HUNTRESS,
TUMBLING FEATHER
LEVEL: 38
SKILLS: COMMAND, WRAITH, CHAOS, VOICE

STRENGTH: 25

LIFE: 77
AGILITY: 33
GRACE: 28
INTELLIGENCE: 32
FOCUS: 26
BEAUTY: 16
CHARISMA: 35
MANUAL DEXTERITY: 10
MENTAL ACUITY: 29
RESILIENCE: 71
STAMINA: 41
PERCEPTION: 42

The harsh conditions had toughened me up a little more, and all the searching had increased my Perception. Even though I'd never put many Seeds into that Attribute, I had meditated exhaustively before I got control of Chaos, and I used Wraith all the time, so Perception had leveled up spontaneously.

With my Life and Resilience so high, my healing factor was inferior only to Torliam and Sam. Nevertheless, from my collapse shortly before, it was obvious that I still had limits. I thought back to the time when I'd received my first Seed. My levels had been so much lower, then, but even with all the improvement I'd done, it never seemed to be enough.

When we were as ready as we could be, with equipment to get us to the spot and keep us alive while doing so, we headed out for the coast. Adam had found a man with a boat that should be able to get us closer, and, since none of us knew how to operate a water vessel larger than a rowboat, we needed the owner along with his boat.

"Let me handle this," Torliam said, before knocking on the door.

A grizzled man with a weathered, sagging face opened the door suspiciously, glaring out at the group illuminated in the glow of his porch light. "Watch'a want?" he asked, his accent turning the words in a way that sounded strange to my ears.

"We wish to rent your boat, and your services as a captain," Torliam said. "We are doing some research about a section of the reef to the north of the island."

"Come back in th' summer," the man said, moving to shut his door.

"Wait!" Torliam thrust a hand forward to stop him, removing it awkwardly when the man glared at the offending appendage. "We can pay well. Thirty thousand credits, for a few hours of your time."

The man grunted. "Where exactly, north o' th' island?"

"Just off Somer's Rock," Torliam said.

The man drew in a breath, as if Torliam had just called his mother a whore. "Don't matter how many credits you're payin', I'm not takin' my ship into no cursed waters." He slammed the door before Torliam could stop him this time, and the resounding click of a lock sliding into place sounded through the wood. Then the porch light turned off, leaving us in darkness.

"Well, that's just rude," Zed muttered.

Torliam turned to Jacky. "Do you wish to break down the door, or shall I?"

Her eyebrows rose, but she grinned, then hopped forward. She slammed a foot through the wall next to the door handle, then shouldered the door open, banging it into the inside wall.

"What th' hell?" the man screamed.

Torliam reached into his jacket pocket and calmly drew out a handgun, an old model that was probably around before guns were made illegal to civilians.

I gaped stupidly.

He grinned like a little boy. "I saw one of these 'guns' in one of your human films about the 'old west.' Very entertaining. I bought it from one of the townspeople. It is much less conspicuous and atten-tion-drawing than threatening this man with our Skills or physical power."

"Whoa, mister, I don't want no trouble," the old man said, arms raised as he backed away.

"That is why you are going to take us out in your boat," Torliam said. Then he twirled the gun around his finger dramatically, like he really was in a film.

I resisted the urge to roll my eyes.

The man tried to talk his way out of it, but Torliam was very convincing, and didn't even need to threaten or torture him with any superhuman abilities.

Jacky pouted. "At least I got to kick in the door," she muttered.

Under Torliam's watchful eye, the grizzled boat owner got dressed for the task at hand and readied his vessel, watching suspiciously as we loaded our gear, and ourselves, onto the deck.

Birch wore little booties and a thermal sweater, both for warmth and to cover up his wings. Still, he was obviously not a domesticated animal, and he snapped his teeth at the man as he passed, letting out a cat-chortle when the man jumped back in fright.

After the process of undocking, we slid out into the icy dark waters, our captain muttering complaints and cursing us under his breath the whole way. A couple hours later, he brought us as close to the edge of the reef as possible, and we suited up, doing one last check of both the waterproofed packs on our backs and the wrapped pallets of supplies we would be dragging with us.

Chanelle was lucid, for the moment, and filled with such a combination of excitement and trepidation that her hands shook while she fumbled with her suit. She'd kept the muzzle on despite the boat owner's strange looks, worried that she'd go crazy at a crucial moment and harm our chances of successfully finding the Champion.

I hoped, not for the first time, that I was making the right choice in bringing her. She had a good number of Seeds in Life and Resilience, so she was much harder to kill than a normal human, but she was also struggling with the later stages of a terminal illness.

Since we hadn't been able to buy any diving equipment to fit him, Birch instead climbed into a little bubble with a small oxygen tank. We tied ourselves and the supplies all together with a long length of plastine rope and stood on the edge of the boat with our backs toward the water.

DEAD WEIGHT
LEAVE CHANELLE BEHIND.
COMPLETION REWARD: NO CHANCE FOR THE SICKNESS
TO AFFECT YOUR SEARCH
NON-COMPLETION PENALTY: BRING THE SICKNESS
WITH YOU

I did a double-take when the quest popped up in front of my face. What kind of mission was this? Was the Oracle just responding to my doubt? Or maybe she had some sort of prejudice against Chanelle, since she didn't have one of the Nine Skills.

I looked to Chanelle, and she met my gaze, grinning. She checked her oxygen supply one last time, then threw herself backward over the edge of the boat, disappearing into the water.

The rest of us followed, one after the other.

Chanelle would be heartbroken if we left her behind. I couldn't do that to her, even if she *would* be dead weight. Truthfully, I had no idea what we would find on the other side. What if we weren't able to return for her in time, and she died waiting for us? I'd already made my decision about this. I waved my hand in front of my face, and the quest disappeared.

The supplies wanted to float, but we'd sucked all the air possible out of them and sealed them, so, with a bit of tugging, they sank down through the water with our flippered forms. Only the bubbles we released with every breath marked our path, shimmering slightly in the light of our headlamps.

I led the way into the water-eroded caverns, which loomed around us like the gullet of an enormous sea-whale—ominous and utterly silent.

Chapter 26

And so, all the night-tide, I lie down by the side
    Of my darling—my darling—my life and my bride,
    In her sepulchre there by the sea—
    In her tomb by the sounding sea.
— Edgar Allan Poe

SWIMMING into the dark with only the light of our headlamps was somewhat nerve-wracking, especially since our mobility was limited by the rope tying us all together and towing our supplies. Despite knowing there was nothing alive in this section of the island, I kept expecting a monster to swim out of some shadowed corner and attack us.

At one point, Sam got his section of the rope caught on a jagged rock, and we had to carefully untangle it before continuing.

One of the tunnels we needed to travel through was narrow enough that the supply pallets barely fit through, and it took a lot of gentle maneuvering and tugging before we made it to the next cavern.

From there, we moved onto a larger tunnel, but, as if something had realized we were there and wanted to expel us, the water started moving against us, pulling us in the opposite direction of the anomaly. The extra drag of the supplies and Birch's bubble made it impossible to win against the current, and we lost a few hundred meters of progress before Adam used one of the ink cartridges he'd strapped to the outside of his wetsuit.

He created a pair of huge dolphins, and they grabbed the plastine rope with their mouths and pulled us forward, dragging our helpless forms after them until we burst out into the cavern with the anomaly. Adam dismissed them while the rest of the group looked around curiously.

The current had disappeared, leaving us in a dark hole of still water. There weren't even any little pieces of biological sediment floating through the water, so it was crystal-clear. We hung back at the entrance while I felt around with Wraith and Adam scanned the area with the waterproof monitoring devices he'd brought.

I shivered from the cold, despite the thermal wetsuit and the hours of exertion. No wonder no other human had ever found this spot.

When Adam detected nothing out of the ordinary, Zed opened up a rip into the Other Place, big enough for us to see the undulating globule of the anomaly hanging in the center. It looked like some huge amoeba, or maybe a distant mirage.

Adam and I examined the alternate version of the cavern.

I didn't find anything except the same warmth and a buzzing sensation from the anomaly.

Adam took a bit longer to poke at the instruments and frown, then sent out a Window.

—I AM GETTING SOME STRANGE READINGS, BUT IT IS POSSIBLE THEY ARE BEING THROWN OFF BY WHATEVER ZED'S SKILL JUST DID TO THE FABRIC OF REALITY, OR THE OTHER PLACE ITSELF.—
-ADAM-

He swam through the rip without another word, scanning the distortion again on the other side. He returned after only a couple minutes, when his devices started to fail. He shook them in irritation, and, after a little while back in the normal world, they recovered.

—LOOKS LIKE THE EMP SHIELDING DIDN'T WORK. I WASN'T ABLE TO GET DETAILED READINGS, BUT THERE DON'T SEEM TO BE

ANY DANGEROUS EMISSIONS. THAT DOESN'T MEAN THERE ISN'T
ANYTHING, THOUGH.—
-ADAM-

I nodded.

—NOW FOR THE REST OF THE TESTS.—
-EVE-

To be honest, I wasn't optimistic that tests beyond what had already been done would discover anything useful. But it was better to be as safe as possible, just in case.

Adam sent out an ink fish, which he had ingrained with instructions to swim out one hundred feet toward the distortion and then return. As soon as it entered the spot of warmth, it visibly disintegrated.

Adam shook his head silently, all the answer I needed.

Kris went next, bringing out a fish she'd brought with her. I knew from its lack of vital signs that it was dead, but it swam around her like an affectionate pet before following her pointing finger out into the cavern. It hesitated, first at the edge of the rip in the Veil, and then again at the edge of the distortion in the Other Place. It swam around a few times and even turned back, as if to return to Kris, before she jabbed her finger at it again in a commanding motion. It moved nearer the anomaly and, after a few seconds, disappeared.

A shock-wave spread out from the distortion, rolling through the water and over us a few seconds later.

—I LOST THE CONNECTION. IT'S PROBABLY JUST A DEAD FISH ON
THE OTHER SIDE, WITHOUT MY SKILL TO BIND THE SPIRIT TO
THE FLESH.—
-KRIS-

—THAT'S OKAY. I THINK WHAT WE JUST GOT FAIRLY GOOD
EVIDENCE THAT WE'RE LOOKING AT A PORTAL TO SOMEWHERE
ELSE. ADAM'S INK FISH WAS APPARENTLY UNABLE TO WITHSTAND
THE VIBRATION, THOUGH, SO WE'D BETTER BRACE OURSELVES.—
-EVE-

Adam released a couple small devices into the water, compact propellers pushing them forward.

—These are programmed to turn around, and if the portal is the same on the other side, may be able to return to us with more information.—
-Adam-

The shockwave rolled out again, but the devices didn't return. It was no surprise, taking into account the electronic-killing properties of both the Other Place and the damage an uncalibrated Shortcut could do.

I looked around at the others, who were, by now, starting to shiver noticeably.

—Any more tests?—
-Eve-

Torliam, the only one of us besides Birch without a VR chip, pointed silently to the distortion, walked his fingers forward in the water, and then nodded emphatically. I took it to mean that he felt we needed to enter the distortion.

I nodded decisively.

—Then it's time.—
-Eve-

We all swam forward, bracing ourselves against the unknown. Zed allowed the rip behind us to close. We gathered around the rippling spot of water, and then closed in on it together, grabbing onto each other and our supplies for extra security.

THE VIBRATION BUILT up in a familiar manner, running through me till it felt like my bones were shivering. Then things snapped, but, unlike the Shortcut or one of the arrays, I did not find myself suddenly somewhere else. My senses abandoned me at first as my existence kept snapping, again and again, but then I saw flashes of color and light in the darkness, as if a god had been playing with sprinkles of light to fill the void, though I felt only emptiness beyond my teammates, and I wasn't sure if my eyes were in fact open or closed.

Then it was over. I fell, collapsing forward onto hard, jagged stone. The world spun, my stomach heaved. I scrabbled at my helmet, barely removing it before spewing up vomit onto the stone in front of me.

I heard the others doing the same, and hoped that the nausea was the worst of whatever the teleportation had done to us. At least we weren't still underwater. I mentally cursed the gods for my weak stomach. Why couldn't I just get nosebleeds or something?

Gregor threw up inside his mask, and then used his Shadow Skill to turn incorporeal, excluding the mask from his transition, thus slipping it off his face without ever actually opening it. Some of the vomit had still gotten in his nose and eyes, and he screamed, wiping desperately at his face. "I'm blinded! I'm blinded!" Then he threw himself to the ground in panic, flailing about.

Torliam held him down and used his Skill to remove the vomit while Sam healed the minor damage that had occurred to the boy's sensitive tissue.

When it was done, Sam just blinked rapidly for the few seconds it took his eyes to heal, and Gregor climbed back to his feet, simultaneously scowling and blushing while he refused to meet anyone's eyes.

After my stomach was empty and the world had stopped doing ballerina-twirls around my pitiful, prostrated form, I stood. "This is not what I expected," I said, wrinkling my nose at the sulfuric, acrid smell on the air.

For some reason, I'd imagined that whatever was beyond the portal would be like Estreyer. Probably dangerous and maybe deadly. But heartbreakingly beautiful.

Instead, barren land stretched out before us, where we stood atop a hill made of dirt and jagged shale. A red sun shone in the mottled sky, pouring down heat that made me dizzy from system-shock as my body attempted to acclimate from the harsh cold of the Other Place.

There were no animals or vegetation in sight, and the clouds in the distance were a sickly, poisonous mixture of grey and purple. It was a barren wasteland, a hellscape from a nightmare.

I was prepared for something to attack, or some sort of Trial to start immediately, but instead, things were somewhat anticlimactic.

Sam checked the rest of us for decompression sickness, since we'd transition from diving with the pressure of millions of pounds of water to suddenly arriving somewhere…*else* without any time for our bodies to adjust. He found a few bubbles, and instructed Torliam on how to remove them, since his own Skill wasn't the best at dealing with such things. Torliam found it relatively simple to fix the issue with Sam's aid.

My eyes soon began to sting and water from the toxic air, and I started to cough as my lungs and throat grew irritated.

Torliam waved an arm, blue mist trailing behind his hand. "The air in this place is acrid and low on oxygen. It will slowly degrade your mucous membranes if you are not strong enough to resist it. Perhaps, for the weaker members of our group, this will be dangerous."

Sam raised a hand, one finger pointed upward like an exclamation mark. "I prepared for this," he said, hurrying over to one of the pallets holding our sealed supplies. "Well, not this *specifically*, but an environment where the air would be hazardous." He rummaged around for a while, then pulled out a set of gas masks. His eyes flickered over them and the oxygen tanks as he muttered silently to himself. "If we hook the oxygen up to the gas masks to combat the lack of sufficient oxygen in the air, we have enough to support a low feed for a couple weeks. The only problem is, we won't have any left to swim back the same way we entered, which we may need to do."

I turned to look at the spot on the ground that had spat us out— a circular mound that reminded me of a burst pustule, and which was sporadically spitting up a spray of salt water behind us. A dead fish lay beside it, but Pinocchio, who had come through with us, was very much still animated and was actually poking the fish with a stick.

Birch shouldered the little wooden puppet out of the way, grabbed the fish, and ran away to eat it while giving Pinocchio nasty looks.

Torliam frowned and turned to me. "Perhaps Zed, Chanelle, and the children would make best use of the oxygen."

"Let's try it, at least," I said. "I don't want to run out of oxygen if there's any other way."

"I don't need any," Zed said, releasing the wheels built into the bottom of the supply pallets so that they would travel easier. "The nanites are augmenting my body, just like your Seeds do for you, remember? I can hike just fine with a gas mask alone."

Sam had even ordered a gas mask sized to fit a bomb squad dog, for Birch. The muzzle was much too long, but it sealed just fine to his face, and Birch ruffled his wings with a pleased chortle, breathing deeply to exacerbate the eerie sound of air passing through the filter.

Adam scowled at the barren landscape stretching out in front of the range of hills where we stood, then turned to Torliam. "Do you have any idea where we are? Does this place look like anywhere you've been before?"

"No," Torliam said. "I do not recognize this place. It is not one of the layers of my world. A god powerful enough would not be restricted by such things, however. Estreyer was made by and of the gods, after all."

"Do you at least know where we're supposed to go from here to find him? I don't see any gigantic humanoids—except yourself and Eve—ambling around."

Torliam stretched out an arm and pointed forward.

"The compass isn't working," Adam muttered. "So I hope your Skill can handle the navigation all on its own."

Torliam threw him a derisive look. "It has been accurate thus far."

"Yet *you* didn't manage to find this place," Adam muttered back, looking away and pretending he wasn't talking to Torliam, even though it was obvious and we could all hear him.

"Let's just get going," I said, hoping to forestall yet another argument between the two.

As we removed our thermal wetsuits, so we didn't sweat to death in the heat, I sent out my awareness. There was power all around, infused into this place, similar to the lands I'd felt on Estreyer when drawing near a god. It lifted my spirits a little, despite that fact that I sensed no single brighter spot of power to indicate our search was at an end.

Kris frowned, turning in a circle atop the hillside. "There's nothing alive here. No spirits or any dead bodies, either." She shuddered. "It's creepy. And it means none of my mannequins are going to be useful." We'd ordered a couple and put them in the supply pallets. They were just high-quality clothing mannequins, but we'd thought they were better than nothing, and had no way to get weaponized bodies like she'd had on Estreyer. She hadn't put spirits into them yet, because the ones on Ellesmere Island were quite weak and she'd hoped to find something stronger on the other side. Now, however, it looked like that had been a mistake.

We made our way down the side of the large hill gingerly, slipping and sliding often when the shale beneath our feet crumbled away. Once, after one of the supply packets took a particularly nasty tumble, a few larger rocks broke off and pelted down toward us.

Torliam batted them away with a casual display of his Skill's strength, swatting them to the side like one might shoo a fly.

After we'd been walking across the rocky, barren plain for a couple hours, the clouds in the distance rolled in thickly, bulbous and threatening as they blocked out the mottled sky and angry sun.

Lightning struck down, coming more and more frequently as the wind picked up. There was no shelter for us to run to, nowhere for us to hide. I was considering taking one of the plastine blowup tents from the supplies for us to huddle inside when the hair on my arms suddenly rose up as if trying to escape my skin.

My eyes widened in alarm.

Adam raised his arms and screamed, "Get down!"

I let my knees buckle under me, and then the world exploded.

THE LIGHT SEEMED to rise up from the ground and strike down from the heavens at the same time, meeting where Adam stood. It coursed through him, branching off and reaching for us with arms of electricity.

The blast knocked me off my feet. I blinked, eyes wide open but seeing only the dark shifting almost-colors that came when something too bright burns its memory into your retinas. My ears rang tinnily.

With some effort, as tingling sparks jumped along my skin and my muscles twitched, I rolled over and threw up for the second time that day, this time only expelling the small amount of bile still remaining in my stomach.

After taking a moment to collect myself, I accessed Wraith to take the place of my useless sight and hearing.

Jacky rose from her fetal position, grinning widely and saying something that I thought was, "I didn't get caught this time!" until she spotted Adam's prone form. She turned to look for Sam, but Torliam was already there, dragging our healer over to Adam's body.

Adam was literally steaming like a roast turkey, still twitching sporadically.

As Sam set to work, little bits of blackened flesh fell off Adam, leaving fresh, tender skin behind, and Sam's mouth set into a grim line as his own body assumed the wounds. His Resilience was over level ninety by now from all the Seeds and training that had gone into that Attribute and the Harbinger of Death Skill.

I almost heaved again, but managed to regain control of myself. I remembered, with a sort of frantic delirium, that lightning actually did often strike the same spot twice. And as the only standing things in this barren stretch of desert, we were basically walking lightning rods. When one person was struck by lightning, the current would often jump to someone nearby. Adam had protected us from all being electrocuted, at a cost to himself.

I stumbled a few feet away and let out a wave of Chaos, crumbling the earth beneath me in a long sweep. I looked for Torliam, but he was busy, so I motioned to Birch to clear the dirt with his Skill.

The monster-cat bounded over, slamming a gust of wind borrowed from the storm into the ground in front of us. It easily swept away the mass of pebbles that had once been hard ground.

I judged the trench we'd created, and shook my head. "Not deep enough," I muttered, barely able to hear my own voice past the ringing in my ears and the howl of the wind.

I reached for Chaos again, but Birch distracted me. He crouched down and the familiar dark tendrils of my power spilled out from his mouth, breaking up more earth for him to blow away. He turned to look at me expectantly, like a child showing off for their parent.

"Good job," I told him, ruffling his fur while sending a Window to call the others into the protection of the trench.

Sam moved Adam, who was still breathing, thank goodness, into my makeshift shelter.

—CROUCH DOWN WITH YOUR FEET TOGETHER. NOBODY TOO CLOSE TO EACH OTHER.—
-ADAM-

We followed his instruction and huddled down. The storm went on for hours, till we were all half-deaf from the booming of thunder. Though the lightning often struck uncomfortably close, it didn't hit any of us or do more than lift our hair with the residual charge in the air. Slowly, the lightning petered off, and, though we stayed in the trench just in case, I allowed myself to hope the worst was over.

Then, it started to rain. After a few minutes, the dirt grew muddy, and we all began to shift around uncomfortably. The rain burned my skin.

I closed my eyes to keep the liquid out, which seemed to be concentrated with whatever made the air so acrid. A few strands of my hair broke off and slipped away from my head, leaving me with a mental image of what I might look like bald, if the rain continued to fall. I was about to dig out a scoop from the side of the trench to create a barrier of dirt above us when the clouds cracked like an egg, sending torrential sheets of water to smash down on us. The trench would be flooded within minutes.

I wondered if we might use some plastine sheeting to shelter from the rain. With Wraith active, my awareness focused on the pallets instinctively.

To my horror, I discovered the fibers in the reinforced plastine sheet covering our supplies weren't immune to the corrosion of whatever the rain was filled with. Which meant that we couldn't use it as a protection, but also that our supplies were in danger.

A blue, transparent shield swept over the top of the trench, forcing the rain to the sides.

I looked to Torliam and screamed to be heard over my gas mask, the torrential rain, and the howling wind. "It'll destroy the supplies!"

He raised himself to look over the edge of the trench, and then turned back to me. "We must go to them," he roared. "I cannot hold off the rain from both ourselves and the supplies!"

Nothing more needed to be said, so we all scrambled out of the rapidly submersing trench and huddled around the supply pallets, crouched low to the ground. The rain continued to crash down, seemingly endless. At least the lightning had stopped. Torliam's shield flickered more than a few times under the force of the storm, and he grew pale, but Adam wasn't in any shape to take over for him, and I couldn't consume more than a minute of rain with Chaos.

Zed looked around, squinting to see past the obscuring sheets of acid precipitation. "There aren't many cracks in this place. I think I see one about a hundred meters that way," he pointed. "But I'm not sure escaping into the Other Place is a good idea, with how wet we are. Still, maybe we could shelter the supplies in there. Anything with a charge will get drained, but it's better than all our supplies getting melted or contaminated."

I knew Torliam was weakening, so, unless the rain stopped soon, Zed's ability was our only option. Each of us grabbed part of the pallet and hauled it forward together, and when we reached the crack, Zed tore it open. There was no rain in the Other Place. We shoved the supplies through.

I leaned away from the rip as the bitter smell wafting through it somehow filtered through my gas mask and burned the hairs off the inside of my nostrils, while the cold turned the rain falling through the opening into sleet almost immediately. "That's not a solution for living beings," I agreed, coughing.

Without the supplies, we huddled much closer together, and Torliam was able to conserve his power. The downpour continued till the stone and once-cracked earth beneath our feet turned to shallow, fast-moving rivers and mud. Then it stopped, as abruptly as it had started.

We waited a moment, too wary to fully trust in our reprieve.

When the light of the red sun shone down on us again, we retrieved our supplies from the Other Place and Gregor returned to normal from his Shadow state. He weaved a bit from the fatigue of holding his Skill active through the whole ordeal. "I *hate* camping," he said, the words even more vehement for having to be forced out through a gas mask.

I sighed, refraining from voicing my own agreement. Maybe I'd like it more if nature didn't always try to kill me. "Torliam, is your Skill giving you any idea how far we might need to go, till we reach the god?"

He nodded, smoothing down his short blonde beard while studiously avoiding looking at me. "*Far.*"

THE DAYS in this strange new land were scorching, while the nights grew frigid, like a never-ending temperature see-saw designed to kill everything. Or, according to Kris' Skill, designed to make sure nothing ever had a chance to live in the first place. In fact, though the landscape held none of the Estreyan beauty, it was similar to Estreyer in that it did its utmost to kill us.

One day, an earthquake opened up gaping chasms in the ground that seemed to reach after us as we ran desperately away, forced to outrace the earth as it fell apart behind us.

Another day, we came upon our first sign of real vegetation—desert cacti with bulbous red fruit sprouting from their green pads.

Chanelle reached for one, ignoring the tiny spines that dug themselves into her flesh.

Jacky slapped it from her hand before the other girl could bite down on it.

Chanelle looked down at the red fruit, now covered in dirt and sand, as if she would cry.

Jacky grabbed her hands and started pulling out the spines. "Don't be stupid," she said. "You can't eat anything till Sam tries it first and makes sure it won't kill you."

Sam obligingly plucked another of the fruits, burning the spines off carefully with a lighter from his pack before ripping it open and biting into the juicy middle. He moaned aloud as juice dribbled down his chin. He swallowed and moved to take another bite, but suddenly froze.

"Poisonous?" I asked.

"I think…it's a hallucinogenic. My Skill should be able to handle —" his words cut off as a violent heave wracked through his body. Vomit burst from his mouth, streaming out like a repulsive geyser.

Jacky quick-stepped backward to avoid being splashed, and we watched in morbid fascination as Sam emptied his stomach, down to the last drop.

He wiped his mouth, color returning to his face surprisingly quickly. "Yeah. Don't eat those."

I gave him an emphatic nod. "I have absolutely no desire to eat them, I promise."

Gregor scowled at the ground, which was already soaking up the vomit. "Can we move on, please? The smell of Sam's stomach juices is not my fragrance of choice."

Kris frowned at the ground around the cacti. "There aren't any dead plants around here. Either these things are like…immortal plants, or they just popped out of nowhere."

After that, we avoided them even more warily.

When we'd passed them by a few hundred meters, Sam groaned. His face was still pale and beaded with sweat, despite having already expelled everything from his stomach. Then, he wandered off, mumbling incoherently to himself.

"Crap," I said. "It must be that fruit. Jacky, grab him."

Jacky went over to do just that, but as soon as she grabbed his arm, her skin started smoking. She jerked her hand back with a scream.

As if startled by the sound, Sam stumbled away from her and started screaming, too.

I stepped forward, ready to act if Sam started attacking with Black Sun's power.

Instead, he dry heaved a few times and then violently flailed at the air, as if he could see something we couldn't.

I checked with Wraith but found no sign of an attack. "I think he's hallucinating," I said. "Let's just let him wear himself out. He's too dangerous like this."

Sam fought invisible enemies with surprisingly realistic motions, even tossing himself to the ground when he was "hit." His hands sprouted a variety of damage effects, some of them that I'd never seen before, like glowing green spores that floated on the air like tiny dandelions. I completely disintegrated those with a wave of Chaos, to be safe.

Finally, after a good hour of fighting and dry heaving till he dribbled out green bile, he fell to his knees in exhaustion. I wished belatedly that I'd had something to record him with, so that we could tease him once he came back to his senses.

Without any more resistance from Sam, Torliam made a sled out of his power and pulled the exhausted boy along behind us.

A couple weeks into our travel, we hadn't found a hint of the god's presence yet, and were nearly out of water. It had rained several times, and we'd even been forced to cross a fast-moving river. The problem was, all the water in this place was dangerously acidic.

At night, when I wasn't one of the two people on rotation for the watch, I tried and failed to solve the Oracle's puzzle or practiced using the black flames when no one was around to see me screw up. The chemistry book had given me a lot of ideas, but a theoretical understanding of molecules didn't seem to allow me to actually control them with Chaos in the real world. My numerous attempts to extract oxygen from water were evidence of this. Finally, I had an idea, and I set Wraith to work on a drop of water, focusing all my awareness on it. If I could go deep enough, maybe I'd be able to *see* what it was I was doing wrong. That didn't work out so well, either. My Perception was mostly trained for wide-area searches. Distinguishing individual molecules was about as opposite of that as one could get. Still, thoughts of those horrifying dreams kept me practicing till I fell into an exhausted sleep for the few hours my Resilience needed to replenish my energy every night.

Kris had taken to letting Pinocchio ride on Birch's back. The two of them would bound about, Pinocchio directing Birch or drawing the monster cat's attention to whatever happened to interest the spirit. Torliam, who had not known of Pinocchio's autonomy, watched with wide eyes as Pinocchio grew excited and hopped off Birch's back to pick up a slab of rock shaped vaguely like a horseshoe and hang it around his neck, all while Kris was busy having an argument with Gregor about the best way to assassinate an enemy.

Pinocchio proved his worth when Kris and Birch were playing

with him a short distance away from the main group, and Kris was swallowed by quicksand.

Birch had been able to blow himself and his tiny rider into the air with his Gale Skill, gliding over to the rest of us while wailing loudly.

Pinocchio jumped off Birch's back onto the nearest person, Zed, and tugged desperately at his ear while pointing to the spot Kris had disappeared.

We rescued her without much trouble, and were able to filter the quicksand for its water content to replenish our own supplies, since the sand had already removed most of the other impurities from the water.

Torliam had praised Birch, "the magnificent creature," and gave him a strip of jerky. "It is a tragedy, that he is the last of his kind." He looked into the distance, in the direction we'd been traveling. "Perhaps, when we find the God of Shaping and Molding, he will be able to make another, for Birch to have a companion."

I followed Torliam's gaze. "He can do that?"

Torliam's expression closed off, but he nodded. "The histories going back that far do contradict one another sometimes, but it is said that he molded the gods to make Estreyer itself."

Internally, I sighed. I hadn't realized how much Torliam's attitude toward me had changed since we first met, till he reverted to coldness and anger. "Do those histories say why he disappeared in the first place?"

"There is only speculation. Some believe he never truly existed. I believe that is obviously false. Some say that he may have been wounded in his struggle against the Sickness, and retreated to recover. Some postulate that the Sickness actually killed him, or that he was exiled against his will. Others believe he removed himself from the realm of mortals because we proved ourselves unworthy of his aid."

I stretched my awareness into the distance, as I had done so many times before, and found nothing except the power that infused this whole land. "Do you think he made this place, too, perhaps? I can feel power everywhere, just no actual god."

"I believe it is quite possible this realm is entirely his creation. When we find him, our questions will be answered."

"How much farther?"

"Far."

"That's what you always say." I turned to scowl at him.

He raised an eyebrow, looking down his nose at me. "And yet, you all continue to ask me the same question, like children, though there are only two true children here."

My nostrils flared in irritation, and I stomped away to go blow up rocks with Chaos.

Chapter 27

And yonder all before us lie Deserts of vast eternity.
—Andrew Marvell

JACKY HAD TAKEN to training the kids whenever we weren't fighting for our lives against the volatile wilderness. "This is dangerous. The best defense is an overwhelmingly powerful offense, remember? I gotta make sure nothing happens to them," she'd said to me.

Adam sat on a large rock at the edge of the campsite where they were practicing, bottles of ink laid out beside him.

Chanelle lounged on the ground next to him, cheering for the children. To our surprise, she'd been dealing pretty well with all the travel. She was more lucid than ever, and hadn't had much trouble with the Sickness making her act crazy, though her body still showed signs of serious illness and she had a burning hunger that no amount of food would sate.

I perched beside them in an empty spot atop the rock, watching curiously as drop after drop of ink disappeared into his skin. "What are you doing?" This wasn't a tattoo. Instead, it looked like he was actually absorbing the ink.

"I'm experimenting," he said simply. "I think weaving the lattice through my muscles and onto my bones might be more efficient than trying to control something woven over my skin. I didn't realize at first that I could actually do this, but I was watching you work with Chaos, and I realized maybe I'd been limiting myself because of a lack of imagination."

"It's really amazing," Chanelle murmured. "I wish I still had a Skill and could do useful things like that."

I was about to ask for more detail, but in front of us, Jacky kicked the daggers out of Gregor's hands just as he brought them back to corporeality. "Too slow!" she yelled at him, even as she dodged Pinocchio's stab from behind and flipped Kris over her shoulder in a full-body throw.

Gregor hopped back from her, his little Shadow body panting obviously, even though no sound came from him, and he technically didn't have much of a physical form while the Skill was active.

Kris hit the ground and tried to regain her feet, mouth gaping and eyes bulging as she struggled to draw air back into her lungs.

Pinocchio attacked viciously with all six of its appendages, using the second pair of modular knife-arms Kris had screwed into its sides to the best of its ability.

Jacky's foot wove in between its attacks like a blur and tossed the wooden body away.

Gregor switched back into a flesh and blood boy for half a second, shouting "Animus!" Two large ink crows burst from the skin on the backs of his hands, one flapping up and then diving right towards Jacky's face, while the other swooped away and grabbed Pinocchio, carrying him right back to Jacky.

Kris kept her distance, but grabbed a few rocks from the ground and threw them at Jacky as a distraction.

Jacky caught them in mid-air with a wicked grin.

Chanelle let out a low groan of disappointment.

The kids and Pinocchio all froze in horror, since by now they'd learned what that grin from her meant. Only the ink birds were stupid enough to close in on her, and were disintegrated by two of those rocks in exchange.

Pinocchio raised both sets of arms in surrender, and with a frustrated glare at it, Kris followed suit.

Gregor stayed stubbornly in his Shadow form, but his whole body cringed when Jacky turned fully toward him.

"You wanna keep going?" she said, still grinning. "Without backup, is that the smartest idea?"

Gregor's fists clenched for a moment, but eventually, he released his Skill and raised his hands in the air. His bushy little eyebrows drew down in a ferocious scowl.

Jacky grinned at him and walked over to ruffle his hair, laughing when he batted her hand away and smoothed it back down. She'd discovered that, while Gregor's Skill made him extremely hard to hurt, it wasn't invincible. If his Shadow form was disrupted *enough*, especially within a short period of time, his Skill would run out of power and the attacks would start to injure him, leaving deep tissue bruises or tears that were difficult to fix without Sam's help. If the Shadow form was disrupted beyond that, his Skill would give out, leaving him completely vulnerable.

Gregor rounded on Adam. "Why were the birds so weak and stupid?" he yelled.

Adam rolled his eyes. "They're birds. You're the one who asked me for something that could fly."

Gregor stomped over, holding out his hands. His knuckles were a little red and swollen, like those of an old man with arthritis. "I need replacements. Make these ones eagles or something. A real predator. Why not give me a couple wolves while you're at it, too?"

I caught movement behind Adam out of the corner of my eye and suppressed a smile when Chanelle quickly pressed her finger over her lips to signal me to silence. I cleared my throat loudly, drawing Adam's attention. "Gregor, I wonder if you can take an ink construct with you into your Shadow form? If so, maybe Adam could make you some longer-distance weapons, like a spear or something. That way you wouldn't have to allow yourself to be so vulnerable getting in close for an attack."

Kris, red-faced and also frustrated, shuffled over to me. "I was too slow to activate my shield when Jacky threw the rock at me," she admitted, looking at me as if confessing a horrible sin.

"You'll get better with practice," I said, smiling. "Besides, you're at a disadvantage because you can't use your Skill to its full ability here. Pinocchio's great, but he's only one more body, and Jacky's fighting experience and Attribute levels both make her a really difficult opponent."

Jacky was always dedicated to her training, and it showed in her levels.

PLAYER NAME: JACQUELINE SANTIAGO
TITLE: ONE OF NINE
CHARACTERISTIC SKILL: GRAVITATIONAL AUTONOMY
SKILLS: STRUGGLE

STRENGTH: 82
LIFE: 32
AGILITY: 54
GRACE: 24
INTELLIGENCE: 12
FOCUS: 20
BEAUTY: 29
CHARISMA: 15
MANUAL DEXTERITY: 15
MENTAL ACUITY: 15
RESILIENCE: 26
STAMINA: 37
PERCEPTION: 19

Gregor, noticing the same thing behind Adam that I had, covered his mouth with his hand to suppress a smile, then settled his face back into its frown. "Who's better in a fight, Adam? You or Jacky?"

Before Adam could answer, Birch, who had been sneaking around behind Adam, pounced forward and batted Adam in the side of the head with a paw, his claws retracted so that it wouldn't do any real damage.

Adam's head whipped around, his eyes and mouth both wide open. He turned back to me and the kids accusingly. "You knew! You distracted me for him!"

I grinned nonchalantly and buffed my claws on my armored chest plate, while Birch let out a triumphant chortle and Chanelle and the kids burst out in giggles.

———

THE DEADLY, endless trek continued on. We traded one barren landscape for another, and then another, and another. We grew leaner. Though none of us had been overweight before, now our muscles grew tight and defined under our skin. We all leveled up our Resilience and Stamina, and my Perception continued to strengthen. Our food supplies dwindled, and I knew that we could not make it back to the salt-water portal on what remained. I only hoped that we could reach the god in time, and that he would be able and willing to provide for us.

While we were crossing a rolling desert filled with dunes of sand that reminded me of a gigantic ocean, the winds died down till the sand settled into eerie stillness. In the distance, dark, low-hanging clouds lifted up the sand and flung it toward us like a wall of death.

"Sandstorm!" I called out, my voice lacking the alarm it would once have carried. This was only one new way from the myriad attempts the world had already made to kill us.

"There is no shelter," Sam said, his voice slow and heavy with fatigue.

"I cannot hold this off," Torliam said. "My power's barriers will not stand against the force of a sandstorm."

Adam lifted his head from where he'd been taking a nap across the pallet Torliam was pulling and ground his teeth. "If his shields won't hold, mine definitely won't. Animus still isn't strong enough to handle everything I need it to do during the course of a day," he said, fists clenched till his knuckles whitened.

"What are we going to do?" Sam squeezed his eyes shut, and when he opened them again, they were darkly shadowed all the way across, clearing the weight of emotion from his body. He straightened, rolling his shoulders to release tension, and turned to me. "I've noticed you playing around with those black flames. Why don't you build a shelter? There's no chance to kill or maim anyone when the subject of your experiment is sand." His lips quirked in a small smile.

I grimaced.

"You are not as careful as you think you are. Yes, I noticed," he said. Sam was activating Black Sun more and more often, sometimes so surreptitiously that we didn't notice till our eyes caught his nihilism-inducing gaze. I worried that it meant Sam wasn't handling the stress of ever-constant death mixed with the mind-numbing boredom of our hikes very well.

"That may, in fact, be our only option, unless we can rig something up with the supply pallets and some tent material," I said. "Let me try it, at least."

I knelt to the ground and closed my eyes, sending my awareness inward, where Chaos swirled through my flesh and blood in twists and eddies, playfully restless. It responded eagerly to my call, slowing only reluctantly as I insisted on caution and finesse. Black tendrils spilled out and turned to black flames, eating into the sand and forcing a very simple transformation. Sand to glass. I built it into blocks, letting them cool before removing them from the sand. With the others' help, I stacked them in a circle, fusing them together with another quick application of Chaos. Around and around we went, building layer atop layer, each one a little narrower than the rest, till we had an igloo made of mottled glass and sand, the front opening protected by a wide overhanging lip. I hurried to create a chimney-like tube extending from the ceiling, since I didn't know how long the storm would last, and I didn't want to run out of air if we were trapped inside the igloo for a long time.

We crawled inside, leaving the supply pallets to the anger of the oncoming storm, since they were too big to fit through the opening.

Inside, it was oppressively hot, the cooling glass blocks adding their own radiation to the ambient temperature, and our bodies heated the mostly enclosed space even further.

The towering wall of sand, tinged with swirling bands of purple and plumes of pale dust, hit us all at once, with a *shahh* sound that quickly deepened with rolling drum sounds, like thunder. It passed over us like a tsunami of darkness, but we were safe inside.

SILENCE SETTLED IN AT FIRST, but then Adam's voice came out of the darkness, although he had to speak up to be heard over the sounds of the sandstorm. "So why hasn't some other Estreyan thought to go to Earth to find this god? Or even if they didn't deduce the way to reach him from history, like Torliam did at first, you'd think someone in the last few thousand years would have some Skill that allowed them to find him."

"People have tried," Torliam said. "But it was prophesied that one of my line would be the one to find the 'spark.' It appears that the previous members of the Seal of Nine were meant to attempt this, but either their Skills were not properly suited for the task, or they failed for some other reason." He looked toward me in the darkness. "It was also prophesied that the spark, descendant of the god himself, would be the one to bring him back. People have scried for him and scanned the stars and all the places in between with what technology we have left to us. None were able to find him. He was well hidden."

"Or maybe," Sam said, "they didn't try hard enough, because they knew they didn't meet the requirements of this prophecy. The prophecy may have sealed fate as it was spoken, when the future was not so certain beforehand."

Torliam raised an eyebrow. "Indeed. You are wise, Sam, and most so when you are not afraid to speak."

Sam tilted his head and opened his mouth as if to reply, unseen to the others in the darkness, but then he closed his mouth, and the silence stretched on for a while longer.

With the darkness as a kind of blanket around me, I said something I'd been thinking about for a while but hadn't had the courage to say aloud. "What if the god really doesn't want to be found? Why else do you think he's disappeared for so long, and none of the other gods have brought him back, even though it's pretty obvious they want him to cure the Sickness? I mean, hell, we've gone through all this and we even found his little secret planet, but he still won't show himself."

Chanelle, who'd become lucid without me realizing it, ducked her head like my words were a blow.

The others shifted awkwardly for a bit, but Jacky reached out her foot and nudged it into me. "It doesn't matter if he wants to stay hidden or not. We're gonna find him, and if he doesn't volunteer to help, we'll just drag him back kicking and screaming."

Adam sighed. "Is that really realistic?"

Jacky popped her knuckles. "We killed a god last time, and we're stronger now. Why not?"

He rubbed his temples and frowned like she was giving him a

headache. "Because we don't have a whole ton of elite Estreyan warriors to boost our Attribute levels or wear him down for us ahead of time?"

She humphed. "And how much damage did they really do?"

"A *lot*," he deadpanned.

"But in the end, Goldilocks was still fine, and it wasn't till Eve ate him up with Chaos that anything changed, right? So who needs them?" she said, crossing her arms and nodding as if the argument had been won and the case was closed.

Adam leaned his head back and shook it silently, apparently giving up on convincing her.

"So, I've been wondering, why didn't I have the Estreyan gene?" Zed suddenly said. "Eve has it, and as far as I know this Eliahan guy is my father, too."

Torliam shrugged, though I doubted anyone but I would notice, since Gregor wasn't in his Shadow state. "He is likely far from pure-blooded, himself. It is purely a roll of the dice, with the odds stacked high against you."

Jacky pursed her lips. "Still, doesn't that mean that technically Zed could be the one to find the god? Since he's got the same blood-line as Eve?"

"He kinda did," I said. "He's the Veil-Piercer. There's no way we could have found this place without him."

"I wonder if there are any more places like this out there, just… hidden," Zed said. "Maybe there are a ton of inhabitable planets besides Earth and Estreyer."

"There are many," Torliam said. "Some of them bear life and even host other people, while some are barren but could be made lush with cultivation."

We all took a moment to think about that. "After this is over, I think I'd like to see some of those planets," Zed said. "Interplanetary travel might be expensive, but since we're pretty much saving Earth and Estreyer right now, I bet we can wheedle a pretty big reward out of their governments. What do you guys think?"

Chanelle smiled brightly. "I'll come with you. That sounds amazing. Tell us more about the other planets and the people on them," she urged, tugging at Torliam's arm.

Torliam grumbled, but cleared his throat and began to tell us what he knew, though apparently travel had been restricted for a long time due to the Sickness, so he had no first-hand accounts, only what he'd read.

Despite the inherently interesting nature of the topic, I found myself tuning out, my thoughts occupied by Zed's earlier words. When this was all over, what did I want to do? The question brought no immediate answer to mind. I couldn't imagine an Eve who lived a normal life, who wasn't constantly desperate to grow stronger and fighting to keep herself and those around her alive. What once had been my accepted, mundane future now seemed alien to me. I tried to put the thought out of my mind, but it lingered, irritating me like a phantom itch I couldn't scratch.

Chapter 28

I walked a mile with Sorrow.
    And ne'er a word said she;
    But, oh! The things I learned from her,
    When Sorrow walked with me.
    — Robert Browning Hamilton

WEEKS HAD PASSED, and we had grown able to casually bat away dangers that would have once caused us to scramble. Even the weakest of us had long since grown accustomed to the low oxygen in the air and tossed away our gas masks when their filters deteriorated and we ran out of new cartridges. We had all leveled up both Stamina and Resilience several times, with a smattering of Strength and Agility thrown in as well. Finally, we came to a group of hills made of rock and shale, and entered a small cave to avoid yet another storm.

The roof nearly collapsed on top of us, so the others stood back while I used Chaos to heat the rocks inside until they melted together, cooling into a safe space incapable of collapse without significant assault. In any case, it was much safer than the watermelon-sized hail heading our way. I went to sleep on the ground, not bothering to unpack my slowly disintegrating tent. When I woke, I found myself once again inhabiting a smaller body, an entirely *human* body.

I gasped, and wished I hadn't, as the black sword in my chest tugged at my insides. I looked around frantically, cursing my inefficient human eyeballs, so much less robust than Wraith's sensory abilities. My arms and legs were stretched out and spread wide by huge pins piercing through them. I was impaled onto the wall in five places, and glass enclosed me.

Butterflies and moths were pinned similarly all around me, each with a little card underneath them. It was that, more than anything, which helped me understand where I was—in a display case, pinned like an insect.

I tried to calm my breathing, as the pain flared with every tiny movement, making the agony of hanging from the wall by spikes even more unbearable.

I couldn't really move anything but my head. But I didn't need to, because blood was trickling out of my wounds. I reached for Chaos, dissolving the part of the sword sticking out through my chest, then the part exiting my back and into the wall.

My weight hung more heavily on my wrists and ankles, the pain forcing an involuntary whimper through my gritted teeth. Seriously, what could I have possibly done to deserve this?

My wrists were next, and when I fell forward, the glass broke under the weight of my body. The pins through my ankles ripped out of the wall as I collapsed forward onto the wooden floor, tearing open gaping holes in my flesh.

I held back a keening sob and took a few deep breaths while I waited for the pain to recede to manageable levels.

Around me, some of the butterflies and moths had fallen, too, and they flapped their wings feebly, somehow still alive.

Chaos, always so much more malleable in this dream world, perhaps *because* of its relative weakness, obeyed my instructions and worked at the metal still in my chest from the last dream, finishing the work of melding it into flesh and healing the wound that pretend-Eve had dealt me.

My wrists and ankles came next. I left a wound on the skin of both hands so that I could access Chaos. Finally, I stood, wincing at the not-quite-right sensation. I felt insect legs latch on and prickle against my scalp, and ripped a large moth out of my hair. I shuddered, watching it flop around on the floor with its brethren. Then I limped down the dreary hallway. Display cases, filled with more moths, covered almost every inch of the walls.

I knew this place was in my mind, not just as a dream, but occurring inside a construct that I had created to contain the power of a god's Seed. But I had never created this hallway, just like I'd never created the previous two rooms from the other dreams.

Frequently, as I walked down the abnormally long hallway, one of the displayed insects would flutter its wings futilely, as if startled by my passing and trying to get away.

The hallway ended on a pair of double doors, large and ominous.

I straightened my shoulders and steeled my resolve, then pushed them open. On the other side was a huge ballroom with a blood-red marble floor. Alcoves and balconies were spaced all around between floor-to-ceiling windows.

In the center of the circular ballroom stood the other Eve, fully armored and facing away from me. She turned around when the door opened, looking me up and down with a faint smile that didn't hide the judgment in her eyes. "You didn't run away, at least," she said with a grudging nod.

Seeing someone else wear my face, my body, and my mannerisms still sent a visceral shudder through me, but I reminded myself of the importance of this meeting. I needed to get information from her, and if her previous threat of taking over my body was true, I needed to impress her.

"Did you think about my question?" she said.

I repressed my instinctive frown of confusion, quickly running the last dream through my mind. "Who am I? What am I?" I asked uncertainly. It had been so long my memory had faded, but they were the only questions I could remember her asking. "I'm Eve Redding," I said, trying for confidence I didn't really feel.

Her face crumpled into a scowl. "You did *not* think about my question. Are you *stupid*? I warned you very clearly what would happen if your performance continued to be so abysmal."

I returned her scowl. "So how about this? I'll kill you, and you stop sneaking into my head. How are you doing this, anyway? Some kind of Skill? Are you one of the Remnants? One of Queen Mardinest's people?"

She laughed, then narrowed her icy eyes and grinned like a wolf.

"Your brain really must be made out of mashed potatoes. Come, then, and *try* to kill me." In other words, she wasn't going to answer any of my questions.

I crouched down, making sure to remember that this was not reality. I had control over my dream world. Chaos spilled out of my fingers as they sank into the crimson marble. I gripped the stone in my hand, then pulled upward, drawing a crimson sword from the floor. I didn't want to waste energy trying to create a solid from air, even if that might have looked more impressive.

"It's much cooler if you do it this way," she said, holding out one hand and letting out a devouring burst of Chaos. Wind rushed toward her and once again coalesced into a black sword. I would have made some snarky comment, but she shot forward immediately, toe claws digging into the marble for traction and leaving scars behind.

I barely managed to block her swing with my own sword, and it still pushed me back several feet. My hand and arm were numbed from the impact of that single strike.

"Do you know what Chaos is?" she said, letting misty tendrils rise out of her free hand and dance through the air. "It's not just some Skill."

I pointed my sword at her with one hand, and then pushed Chaos through it. The sword tip shot forward, elongating into a razor-thin spike as it stretched toward her gut. I was taking careful note of everything she said, but I wouldn't let her distract me with her words. I took her threat of body-jacking me very seriously, and had no intention of being trapped and helpless within my own mind.

She leapt backward lightly, knocking away my sword with her own, but my other hand was already making its own attack, shooting out those fleshy, tendon-like branches of condensed Chaos. This method of attack was so quick it was difficult to follow its growth with the naked eye, so much faster than throwing out unformed misty tendrils, but also requiring much more concentration and power.

The black filaments built upon each other in an instant, then frayed like the end of a rope, reaching toward her from a hundred different directions at once.

She grinned, and then pulsed with darkness, like shedding an explosive skin. It expanded in every direction, smashing into the piercing tendrils of my attack and forcing them back. "Chaos is the power of a god. In fact, it is a tiny piece of the goddess of Khaos herself, living inside you."

I clenched my jaw and fed the fibrous construct more power, and the tips pressed in toward her.

She raised an eyebrow, and the shell of Chaos expanded even further, as if it didn't even strain her to completely overpower me. "Do you know how gods fight with each other?"

I'd wanted to be closer before I tried my next trick, but she didn't give me much choice. I closed my eyes and fed one last surge of power into the pulsing strands of blackness extending from my left arm. Instantly, the air around my counterpart exploded with light and heat.

I opened my eyes as soon as the blast had passed, the warm wind I'd created blowing back my loose strands of hair and rippling the softer skin of my cheeks.

Her shield was gone and some of her hair had been singed away. "Superheating the air to create an explosion?" she said. "Do you think you're being clever?" Until that point, she'd seemed dangerous, but still jaunty, as if she wasn't taking me too seriously. Now, her mood darkened.

She never gave me a chance to respond. She shot forward once again, this time too fast for me to even see her. She ripped my sword away with her bare hand, her claws digging into and through it as if I'd formed it from butter.

I scrambled backward, but she said, "Stop," and the crystal at her throat pulsed. My back arched, like I'd been hit with a defibrillator, and I found myself unable to move.

She paused for a moment, as if waiting for me to respond somehow, but I *couldn't*.

She shook her head with exaggerated disappointment. "Eve," she said, her voice low and kind and full of the promise of my death as she walked around and then behind me. She whispered in my ear. "Do you know why you can't beat me? It's not because I've stolen your stronger, better body." Her voice moved to my other ear, her warm breath blowing against my neck and the sweat on my skin. "It's not because I have access to all the other Skills you've grown to rely on like a crutch."

I fought against whatever she'd done to me the same way I'd fought against Reglium's control, and finally managed to break free, stumbling forward with a panicked gasp.

She sneered down at me in derision, then walked past as if I wasn't a threat at all.

I lashed out with another branching cord of solidified Chaos, but she knocked it aside with her bare hand, without even looking. I screamed in denial and tried to attack again, but Chaos didn't come. I looked at my wrists and saw that they had been healed. Without a thought, I bit down on my skin, grinding my teeth and ripping at the back of my forearm till I broke through and the blood flowed again.

She'd returned to her spot in the middle of the crimson ballroom and turned to face me again. "You can't beat me, because, even when your life is at stake…" The sky darkened outside as if in response to her anger, and the wind began to howl. The sound of glass breaking in the hallway behind me made the hair on the back of my neck rise.

"Even when you're terrified of what I will do to you if you lose…"

The moths and butterflies flew into the room and swirled around me, only a few at first, and then more and more.

I tried to run, but there was nowhere to escape to.

They swarmed in numbers beyond belief, more than had been in the hallway, more than I could count in a month. They amassed around me until I couldn't see past them, cutting off my view of whatever the other Eve might be doing, clogging up the air.

"Even then, I still want this *more* than you." The last statement echoed with the gravity of the Voice Skill, but beyond that, her words seemed to come from everywhere at once, as if each of the moths were an amplifier. The sound rippled at my skin and mirrored my heartbeat.

I let out as strong a wave of Chaos into the air as I could manage, a multi-directional explosion similar to the one she'd created earlier.

That only set the moths off, and they converged on me like a wave, the weight of all their bodies lending their attack a crushing force I never would have imagined possible. They smacked into me and beat at my face with their wings, tried to crawl inside my nostrils and ears, shoved themselves at my mouth and pried at my eyelids. I let out another wave of Chaos, and they died and fell away by the thousands, but more remained to take their place.

They swarmed up beneath me, lifting me off my feet and turning me around till I lost all sense of direction. The heat of their bodies felt like an oven. I couldn't breathe, but I clawed at myself desperately, breaking the skin and releasing wave after wave of Chaos, pulses as quick and desperate as my heartbeat.

I caught the faint sound of glass breaking once again. Then the howl of wind and the sensation of violent movement. My body smashed into something and splattered apart, as if I were one of the bugs and had just had an unfortunate encounter with a windshield.

It hurt.

I WOKE up immediately and jerked upright, gagging and coughing up a huge atlas moth onto my lap. Other insects lay strewn about me, flapping feebly as they died. I thought for a moment that I was still dreaming, but my teammates had crowded around me, and I sat in a small cave with acrid air. My left arm was scaled, my claws were out, and Wraith moved through the cave with an instinct that had become as automatic as breathing to me.

"She's awake," Sam screamed, and those who had been facing outward, guarding against an attacker that did not exist, spun to face me.

"What happened? Another dream?" Torliam said. "Are you well?"

"The bugs just started crawling out of you," Zed said, breathing heavily from panic. "You couldn't breathe, and we didn't know where they were coming from, and they kept appearing. Torliam and Birch kept clearing your airways and trying to get oxygen into you, but you were choking, and you *wouldn't wake up.*"

I took heaving breaths, trembling and unable to reply.

"It was *him,*" Adam snarled. "What else do you think could have done something like that? This god's been trying to kill us since we arrived here!"

"This is not the first time she has had a dream that left residue in reality," Torliam said. "We cannot discount the god, but it is not necessarily him. I have suspected a particularly powerful warrior from among my own people, but I did not imagine they would be able to reach her even here."

Zed stood, and started stomping insects viciously under his feet, as if to get back at them for hurting me. "You mentioned you had some weird nightmares, but nothing like *this!*"

I coughed, spitting out wing powder and a little blood. The insects must have damaged something in my throat, though I didn't think it was a serious injury. "It wasn't this bad, before." My voice was hoarse, and I fell into a coughing fit again as I finished speaking. Tears built in my eyes, first from irritation, but, as soon as the first drop spilled over onto my cheeks, more came behind them. I'd experienced a lot of difficult and painful things before, but that dream, my *death*, had been on a completely different level. I couldn't think of it as a simple nightmare.

I'd died, terrified, alone, and completely helpless.

One of the moths on the ground flapped feebly, dying from the tainted air.

I flinched back from it, then shuddered, feeling cold despite the sheen of sweat covering my body and the heat in the air.

Torliam followed my gaze, then swept the area around me clean of insect carcasses with a sweep of his Skill. "Were you able to gain any other clues about your attacker's identity?" His tone was kinder than it had been since I revealed my duplicity.

I tried to talk, but it irritated my throat and I descended into another ragged coughing fit.

Adam turned on Torliam. "You knew more about this than the rest of us, it's pretty obvious now. But what have *you* been doing to figure out who's hurting her? Or have you been too busy acting like a hypocrite and being angry at her for saving her own life!?" His voice rose as he spoke, the words spilling out of him like he'd been holding them in for a long time. "If you weren't so hung up on yourself, you might remember that she's not the *only* one who lied. *You* decided to tell everyone that the God of Knowledge would give us a Bestowal if the mortals could prove themselves in battle against him! You knew it would be a fight to the death, that we actually needed to kill him, and you helped convince all those Estreyan warriors who died to sacrifice themselves. I'm sick of you acting like you're better than the rest of us. Eve may have lied about the exact nature of the reward, but you knew full well the danger of what you were getting into." Adam was panting by the time he finished, and the others stared at him in shocked, awkward silence.

I'd managed to stop coughing, but I didn't know what to say in this situation, and even if I did, I might not be able to choke the words out.

Gregor scowled, unnoticed, at the two older men, his abnormally cold fingers patting at the back of my neck as if to soothe me.

Torliam had clenched his fists, staring at the far wall of the little cave. He turned to face Adam, slowing unfurling himself to his full height.

Adam had to look up at him, but his glare didn't falter.

Then, Torliam bowed to Adam. "Your words hold truth," he said. "I have also been at fault in this matter."

Adam's eyebrows rose and his eyes widened, but after a moment, he regained his composure. He coughed gruffly and folded his arms. "Well, as long as you realize."

Torliam turned to me and bowed even deeper. "Please accept my apologies—"

Before he could finish, Chanelle wailed. The sound raised in pitch and ferocity till she was shrieking. She stood up, fingers wound through the muzzle over her face, yanking so fiercely she jerked her entire body around. The screaming kept going, even as her voice began to crack under the strain.

CHANELLE HAD GONE PHYSICALLY crazy a few times already, each time much more disturbing than the verbal vitriol the Sickness pushed her to more often. It drove her to feats of strength and athleticism that her body wasn't meant for, and though she was dangerous, she was just as likely to hurt herself as one of us.

When it was over, she always cried till she was too exhausted to move, apologizing over and over. We'd grown somewhat complacent as we traveled through this strange world, because she'd been doing well. Now, that changed.

She scored lines in her cheek as she clawed at the leather straps of the muzzle, then wove her thin, emaciated fingers into the wire. The sound of her fingers breaking was distinct.

Torliam shot to her side in an instant, pulling her hands away from the metal and forcing them down against her sides.

Adam threw ink onto her, and it spread into straightjacket-like bands.

Jacky and I wrapped her in some cloth bindings we'd rigged up, then laid her onto the bedroll she'd been sitting on before.

I stroked her head as she screamed soundlessly, her voice gone.

She bit at nothing.

Sam crouched down beside us and laid a hand on the back of her neck as she struggled in her bindings like an angry caterpillar. He would ensure that she did no more real damage to herself, like the time she'd bitten through her tongue and almost drowned in her own blood before one of us noticed.

I leaned back on my haunches and spit to the side to get the taste of moth dust out of my mouth. I rested my head on my knees, still stroking Chanelle's hair. I could only hope that it helped, somehow, because there was nothing else I could do for her. I was so tired.

The ground trembled. That was likely the sign of an impending earthquake. We'd been through many of them, though the effects varied from chasms ripping open in the earth beneath our feet to geysers of scalding water erupting to try to cook us alive.

This time, however, the shaking built up faster than I had expected. The pebbles on the floor of the cave bounced, and the earth roared as it cracked apart right in front of us.

Sam and I grabbed Chanelle and hauled her with us as we all scurried out of the cave. I may have reinforced its structure, but I didn't trust that to hold up under an earthquake.

Outside, the storm had stopped, so it was now safer to be under the open air, as long as the shards of ice didn't start letting off invisible, poisonous gasses as they melted, or something equally ridiculous and deadly.

Instead, the hair stood up on my arms, and then the hair on my head lifted as my skin started to tingle. "Adam!" I screamed, pulling Chanelle down to the ground with me as I crouched.

Adam had rigged a lightning rod after the second time he had to redirect a strike and almost got fried to death doing so. It was a metal pole with a rubber hand grip, and he used it as a walking stick. Now, he slammed it into the ground, redirecting the lightning strike through the combination of metal and Skill, keeping more than a few stinging sparks from reaching the rest of us. The dirt exploded upward, and the crack was loud enough to set my ears ringing.

I'd remembered to close my eyes, but I could see the branching afterimage of the electricity anyway.

Adam fell forward onto one knee, gasping, but at least not steaming. His skin wasn't sloughing off him, so I figured he was okay.

We all stilled with awe, the only sound the ringing in my ears.

Then an ice boulder plummeted out of the sky.

I screamed, tackling Chanelle out of the way with only moments to spare.

The boulder smashed down right where we'd been standing and shattered, spike-like chunks shooting out toward us.

Chaos exploded out of me without my conscious direction, disintegrating the deadly projectiles about a foot before they reached me.

I rolled to my feet, dragging Chanelle with me by pure force.

The ground, which had never quite stopped rumbling, gave a forceful heave underneath us.

A wave of blue slammed forward into Chanelle and me, knocking us off our feet, safely away from the tiny sink-hole that had just opened up into a chasm where we'd been standing.

"It's targeting Chanelle!" I screamed, sending Wraith lashing out in every direction. I felt the glow of foreign power coalescing around us, like a ghostly storm. "Show yourself, you coward!" I yelled, struggling back to my feet. "If I wanted to get rid of the Sickness by killing people, I could do that myself!" My voice cracked. "We came to you for a *cure*." My words echoed off the hills around us and faded into the distance.

The rumbling of the earth stilled.

A small person walked over the top of the highest hill and looked down on us.

Chapter 29

He who destroys a god kills reason itself.
— Kaiser Fell

THE GOD, for surely that's what he was, judging by the power shining from his body, was smaller than I had expected. In fact, he was smaller than *me*, more of a height with *Jacky* than Behelaino or the God of Knowledge. It was a little underwhelming. His features shifted constantly. Even as I watched, his ears grew tufted, then shrank down while his skin instead took on a bark-like roughness.

Torliam bowed deeply, and the rest of us, except for Chanelle, followed suit afterward, with a kind of embarrassed awkwardness.

I bowed, but remained on edge, wary in case he used our distraction to continue his attacks.

When we straightened, the god's eyes met my own for a moment, their pupils horizontal and almost rectangular, like that of a goat's. They shifted again soon after. He waved his hand and power flowed out from the ground instead of the body he was using. It welled up beneath me before I could even react, wrapping around Chanelle.

I tensed, but Chanelle didn't seem to be harmed. She slumped forward, her breathing slowed and muscles relaxed, ceasing her struggles and broken attempts at screams, apparently falling into a peaceful sleep.

Still, I couldn't quite hold back my glare when I looked up at the god, and my claws stayed out. I needed the boost to my Attributes that having the Skill active provided.

The god's gaze traveled over us, and with it came the weight of his judgment. I could see from his expression that we had been found lacking.

Torliam cleared his throat. "I am Torliam, of the line of Aethezriel, and this is Eve, of the line of Matrix," he placed emphasis on the last words, gesturing to me. "The Goddess of Testimony and Lore has bestowed upon us the Seal of Nine, and the Oracle has helped us on the path to find you. We come before you to petition you for aid against the Sickness once more, if you will return with us to the realm of mortals."

The god waved his hand and half the hill in front of us seemed to suffer from a mini-collapse. The detritus and shale tumbled away, revealing semi-familiar symbols cut into the smooth stone.

"This is an old written dialect of my people, from before the exodus," Torliam explained, turning his head toward us. "It is more complex, with each symbol indicating a word or concept rather than being a phonetic representation of the language."

"Like Chinese," Zed said.

Torliam nodded absently, though I wasn't sure he actually knew what Chinese was. He was busy reading the message cut into the stone, over and over. He frowned, muttering to himself.

After a few minutes of this, Jacky shoved her way to the front of the group. "Are you gonna keep making faces to yourself? Read out loud! The rest of us wanna know what's going on, too."

He grimaced. "I am a bit…rusty? Is that how you say it?"

"Well, I don't see him talking," she pointed to the god, "So you're the best we've got. Don't worry, none of us are gonna be able to tell if you get it wrong, anyway."

He sighed, shooing her away from the symbols beneath her feet. He spoke slowly, often seeming unsure or clarifying a word. "*You mortals have invaded the domain of me, the Shaper and Molder, after peace of an aeon, and must prove yourselves worthy through my…Trial—*that's the word for Trial—*and show that you are capable of creation as well as destruction. You may admit…at any dot,* any *time,* maybe, *that you are unable to fulfill my requirements, and the wonderful me will* *return you alive to the realm of mortals with your...Sickened,* or maybe *'infected' people, still alive."*

"The wonderful me?" Jacky mumbled with a large grin. "Maybe I should start using that."

Torliam shot her a repressive look, then continued reading. "*If you fail, all will die. If you...* it's a mixed word. Maybe *unlikely-succeed.* It seems to mean he doubts the likelihood of our success. *If you doubtfully succeed, the wonderful me will remove the taint from yourselves and return to the realm of mortals to continue fighting, but your mortal selves must remain in this realm forever, until death."*

"What the hell?" Adam snarled. "If we lose, we die, if we win, he traps us here *forever?*"

Torliam stared at the words for a moment longer. "We must accept. Our remaining in this realm is nothing compared to the lives of all the mortals across both worlds."

Sam, whose eyes for once seemed quite clear and bright, despite the tension of our situation, nodded. "He's right. Plus, it's the only way to save the kids and Chanelle. It's the right thing to do."

I was careful not to grimace. I had no intention of being trapped on this little hell-planet for the rest of my life, regardless of whether we could live here cured from the Sickness. I wanted to be cured, *and* I wanted to go back to Earth with the whole team. But for now, I only nodded.

—We'll...negotiate further...after we've proved ourselves through the Trial. We don't have any bargaining power, in the current situation.—
-Eve-

No one was happy about it, but we all agreed.

The God of Shaping and Molding waved his hand again, and more of the hill fell away, revealing nine shiny little marbles settled into its side.

WE DIDN'T MOVE, just looked at each other and the god in semi-consternation. Zed leaned a little closer to me. "Are those Seeds?"

I frowned. "I don't know. They look similar, but I don't think they're the same as the Seeds NIX gave us." These were glossier, without the maze of metallic lines around the outside, and each of them seemed to be a different color, instead of a sparkly cream.

A new section of the hill crumbled away, again leaving words behind.

Torliam examined it for a moment, then began to read. "*You must cultivate these seedlings with the blood-borne powers bestowed on you by the Goddess of Testimony and Lore. Each seedling will grow around the others, creating the nine-part...*I don't know the last word. *No part of it may die. If it grows strong enough to sustain itself, you have succeeded. Begin now.*"

I stepped forward, crouching over the "seedling" placed in front of me. It looked like a clear marble, unlike the others, which had colors or even texture on the inside. "Do you understand what he means?"

Torliam reached down slowly and picked his up. It had green threads and little sparkles of color like the stars seen through the atmosphere on the level of the Spire of Prophecy.

Seeing that it didn't hurt him, the rest of us followed suit.

"I believe we must push power into these to feed them, similar to how my people push power into runic arrays or other devices to power their effects. I have some experience with this." We all jerked in surprise as the seedlings pricked us, just like a normal Seed did when injecting its contents into you.

I focused my awareness on the spot of pain, wondering if some invisible Seed material was filtering into my bloodstream even now. I found nothing, but a couple seconds later, a Window popped up in front of my face.

ACCESS TO THE FOLLOWING SKILLS RESTRICTED: SPIRIT OF THE HUNTRESS, TUMBLING FEATHER, WRAITH, CHAOS

Adam, Jacky, and Sam's eyes all flickered over something invisible in front of their own faces, which I assumed to be similar messages to the one I'd just received.

Torliam rubbed at the already-healed spot on his palm where the seedling had cut him, then at his chest. "Something has happened. I feel strange."

He didn't have a VR chip like us, I remembered. "It just cut off my access to all the Seed-based Skills except for Voice. I'm going to assume it did the same to the rest of us." I forcefully kept myself from hyperventilating, wondering if, somehow, this was another dream. I looked down at my left hand and managed to partially reassure myself with the honeycomb scales on my skin and the sixth finger. I never had those in the dreams.

At that point, Adam's legs collapsed underneath him. He barely kept his head from banging into the rocky ground. He let out a string of curses, struggling to maneuver and lift his torso up with his arms while keeping one hand clenched around the seedling that had just caused his misfortune.

The kids and Zed only had the one Skill, so nothing had changed for them. But for Adam, Torliam, and myself, our Seal of Nine Skills weren't exactly combat related.

"This is ridiculous," Adam snapped. "How the hell am I supposed to get through a Trial without any of my useful Skills?"

Torliam was pale and kept rubbing his chest. "While I also find this disturbing, it seems that we do not need the other Skills. Perhaps this is a test to see if we have properly strengthened the powers of the Seal of Nine. Nine Skills, for each greater Trial." He frowned with concentration, and the shiny ball in his hand changed shape, sprouting a tiny little stalk, a couple leaves, and roots. "See?"

As soon as he looked away from the sprout, it started to wither. He turned his focus back to it, and it regained its health.

"You're supposed to plant things in the ground," Zed said. "Maybe it needs soil and water."

Torliam immediately crouched down and dug a little hole in the arid ground, then placed the sprout in it and covered its roots. Nothing happened, and when he pulled away, it started to wilt again. He pushed more power into it, and it perked up, growing a couple more inches. This time, it took longer to start wilting when he withdrew. "You must join me. 'Each seedling must grow around the others,'" he quoted.

We grabbed some empty plastine containers from our supplies and crushed them together into a makeshift chair for Adam through sheer physical strength. At least our Attributes hadn't been decimated, too.

I knelt down next to him and dug my own hole into the ground. I placed the clear seedling in it, covered it mostly with dirt, then touched the top of it with my finger. Feeding power into it wasn't difficult. I reached for Voice, as if I were going to try and say something cool, and the seedling greedily sucked at the power. I fed it a little more, pushing along that same channel, and it sprouted. I could feel its roots digging into the hard ground as its stem and leaves stretched upward toward me.

Zed grabbed some of our precious water from his pack and moistened his patch of dirt before doing the same, and then the others all followed suit. We pushed power into the little sprouts till they grew about a foot high. Each crystalline sapling was distinct in appearance, and each of them reached for the others like they were reaching for sunlight, intertwining their branches and then, when they grew taller, weaving a single large tree from their trunks.

We stepped back to look at the admittedly beautiful sight, which stood out even more in this wasteland.

Gregor said, "How big does it need to get before it can sustain itself? Normally, I'd think that the root system needed to reach a source of water and nutrients abundant enough to support future growth, but I'm not entirely sure what this thing is made of and this dirt doesn't seem exactly rich."

Sam, who had activated Black Sun to feed his portion of the tree, shrugged. "Maybe it doesn't eat anything but Skill power. Maybe that's why the little guy wants us to stay here for the rest of our lives."

I didn't say it aloud, but internally I waited for things to take a turn for the worse. The Trial couldn't be as simple as feeding power to a tree. If it was, there wouldn't have been the clause about giving up at any time, and there's no way it would have counted as a "greater Trial" for each of us.

Sure enough, after we'd each been feeding our part of the nine-part tree for about an hour, taking short breaks to make sure we didn't exhaust ourselves, little motes of light floated toward us. I didn't know where they'd come from and hadn't noticed their arrival, but they coalesced around and landed on the tree despite our efforts to shoo them away.

The tree immediately started to wither where they touched it. Without Chaos or any of my combat Skills, all I could do was reach out with my bare hands and try to crush the little light motes.

Luckily, despite the glow coming from them, they didn't seem to be made of actual light, and succumbed to my squeezes like any other bug.

Still, there were too many of them to crush one by one and still keep the tree alive.

Birch let out a low yowl and the wind picked up, blowing the light bugs away from the tree and out into the wilderness. This helped a lot, but many of the ones who'd already reached the tree clung onto it and continued to drain its vitality.

My section, a crystal-clear sapling, was drooping limply and losing some of its leaves, and many of the other sections were doing even worse, like Birch's and the kids'. "Damnit! Get the hell off my tree!" I snapped. Voice kicked in, sending my words vibrating out through the air.

The motes lifted up and flew away, all at once, like they'd been frightened off.

I watched at their retreating formation. "Oh. So that's what the Trial's about."

ZED HAD STARTED CALLING the tree Yggdrasil after the mythical world tree that connected the nine realms. It came as no surprise that the light bugs weren't the Yggdrasil's last attackers. They attacked in waves, their forms different each time, but always a little larger and a little stronger than the wave before. Their bodies grew more typically monstrous, and some of them even had non-physical abilities not so dissimilar from Skills.

When we killed them, their carcasses melted into the ground after a few hours. We speculated this may have been a form of nourishment for the tree, but without access to most of our Skills, we had no way to be sure. Yggdrasil took longer to start wilting as it grew larger, but still required us to feed it our power to stay alive and grow.

This continued over the course of *days*, the longest Trial we'd ever participated in, and in many ways, the most grueling. Those on the team without high Resilience and a heavy concentration of Seeds augmenting their bodies simply couldn't keep up. The kids had been mostly removed from the fighting, their time divided between fueling their sections of the tree and sleeping. Gregor continued to have nightmares, and had a sporadic fever that made him irritable and lethargic. Kris didn't say anything, but, from the paleness of her cheeks and the dark circles under her eyes, I knew she wasn't doing much better, and we were all worried about the signs of the Sickness' progression. Zed had slightly more stamina than the kids because of the nanite augmentation, and his guns actually allowed him to be one of the more effective members of the team in a fight, but he was wearing down, too.

Chanelle was still asleep from whatever the god had done to her. Or, more accurately, she was in a coma. I would have been more worried about her, but she showed no external signs of dehydration or any of the other dangers a normal coma patient dealt with.

Without the ability to move on his own, Adam was pretty much permanently stationed at the base of the tree. We took turns going to him for tattoos. Despite his inability to use his Animus Skill himself, he could still give tattoos to others through his Bestow Skill.

We'd used large rocks to create a kind of wall around our camp and the Yggdrasil as a way to slow down the ground-bound enemies, and we kept a lookout in the upper branches of the tree to give us early warning of each wave. We'd also dug quite a few pits into the ground, but as the monsters grew smarter, they served more as a means to funnel our attackers toward a few specific points rather than effective traps. When we fought, we used our Seal of Nine Skills or physical combat, aided by ink weapons and shields Bestowed by Adam.

Our problem was a lack of both stamina and supplies. The enemies were getting stronger, and we were growing more exhausted. Whether or not we could otherwise keep fighting forever, our food would soon run out. In desperation, we pushed the Yggdrasil to grow faster. Even so, no matter how much power we gave it and how large its crystalline branches with the little veins of color and motes of light threaded through them grew, it could not survive on its own. At the top of the main twist of trunks, where they separated and spread their own directions, what looked like a fruit of some sort had started to grow. We hoped this meant it was getting close to self-sufficiency, but we didn't know how much longer it would take, or even if the fruit actually had any significance.

The god still sat unmoving at the top of his hill, his eyes closed and his legs crossed. We'd tried to get him to talk, but he ignored us completely until we gave up and returned our hopes to winning the Trial.

Early one morning, a few hours before the red sun rose, I tossed myself down beside Adam, who was giving Jacky a series of tattoos across her hands. Without her Gravitational Autonomy Skill, she couldn't toss her body around like a superhero, but she still had her fighting Skills, and adding ink blades or spikes to her attacks made her impressively lethal.

Torliam was still the strongest of us by far. The number of Seed organisms strengthening his body meant he barely needed to sleep in times of pressure, and he could blur across the battlefield like time had slowed around him, each step cratering into the ground and each blow killing an enemy. As if to rub salt in the rest of our wounds, he lamented about how weak he was still, after NIX's extended torture and siphoning off his Seeds.

"I wonder if we can eat the monsters, if we get to them before they melt into the ground," I said.

Adam stared at me like I was an idiot. "They *glow*, Eve. And I'm pretty sure they're not made of real flesh and blood, or Kris would be able to sense their corpses as possible containers with Summon. I'm not eating that."

Jacky looked over her shoulder to the side of the hill, which still displayed the requirements of the Trial, specifically, the clause that said we could give up at any time and go back to Earth. "Think he's trying to starve us out?"

Adam finished with her and moved on to me.

I didn't shrug, since he was sinking ink into my neck and shoulders. "He's definitely trying to get us to *give up*. I mean, even the 'win scenario' is unappealing. But if I was going to just give up, I wouldn't have made it here in the first place."

"None of us would have," Adam said softly, frowning as he worked on the details of an ink image.

Jacky glared up at the god. "Why doesn't he talk? Even if he doesn't know English, all the other gods were able to learn it just from having us in their Trials, no?"

Adam rolled his eyes. "Torliam says the god gave up his voice for power, or something. It's bullshit, if you ask me. He's just addicted to control and wants to make things as difficult as possible for us."

I grunted. Unfortunately, that sounded much more plausible, from what I'd seen of the god so far.

Despite my exhaustion, I had nightmares and a difficult time falling asleep, because I was afraid those nightmares would turn into another too-real dream with the person who wore my body. When I was awake, I found myself thinking of her words. "I want this," I murmured. "I won't give up."

As if in response to my words, Zed yelled from his spot in the transparent branches at the top of the tree, "Wave incoming!"

Chapter 30

Time flies over us, but leaves its shadow behind.
    — Nathaniel Hawthorne

I ONLY WAITED LONG ENOUGH for Adam to complete the little tattoo he was working on before hopping up and running to the stone wall.

Skittering toward us from the plains were hundreds of monsters that looked like human women whose legs had been replaced by the latter end of a giant centipede. The segmented bug shell extended onto their human parts, and two pairs of glowing red eyes sat above their sideways-opening mandibles. They had one set of human arms that held weapons, and two more sets of bug arms tipped with serrated claws that dripped goo that, I assumed from Murphy's Law, was poisonous.

They screamed as they skittered toward us, a sound that rang in my ears like nails on a chalkboard and didn't seem to require them to stop for air.

Zed took out his guns, said, "Animus," and loaded up. He had long ago run out of bullets, but Adam had created ink replacements and anchored them in Zed's skin. They didn't fly with the force of real gunpowder since Adam had used some sort of pressurized air mechanism from a sea creature for propulsion instead, but they exploded on impact and could still do a fair amount of damage. He started shooting long before the monsters reached us, but they scattered and dodged like the bugs they resembled, and he only managed to kill a few of the incoming swarm.

As they grew closer, their screams grew louder. I pressed my palm to the side of my head and winced. The scream wasn't just an intimidation tactic. It was some sort of attack.

Torliam Animated one of his own sets of tattoos, having set aside his pride and admitted that Adam's Skill was indeed useful. A dozen ink spears burst out of the Estreyan's chest. He aimed carefully and shot one off.

A couple hundred meters away, one of the centipede women went quiet as chunks of flesh sprayed outward from the force of the spear ripping through her body.

With a scream of defiance, Jacky's body grew, and when she reached Torliam's size, she released her own set of ink spears and started to attack. Unlike Torliam, her aim wasn't unerring, and when she did hit, the monsters didn't always die, but she was the only other one of us who could hope to be effective with a spear at that range.

I stood up on top of the wall and spread my arms out, trying to look as imposing as possible, because that seemed to help. "You run toward your *doom!*" I yelled dramatically. Voice propelled my words and gave them a weight that my cartoon-villain dialogue shouldn't have carried. I could feel the power of my voice in the surrounding air, a kind of buzz that I'd experienced in front of the more powerful Estreyans, and which I believed was associated with high Charisma levels. "*Fear* us, for we are the demons that dwell in the night, the whisper behind your back, and the emptiness in Death's eyes."

The monsters faltered, some of them slowing, a few even retreating, but, despite Voice's improvement after constant use, it still wasn't enough to stop their attack entirely. The creatures regained their momentum quickly, and their incessant scream only grew louder.

"We're gonna need everybody for this one!" I yelled over my shoulder.

Kris and Gregor, who'd run to stand by Adam at the sound of the alarm, acknowledged me with quick hand motions and started climbing the tree.

When the centipede-women arrived at the wall, some of them rushed forward, scrambling over the deliberately lower points in the ramshackle defense. Others stayed back. Those ones were the screamers, or the ones with long-range abilities. More of them were still coming, as if appearing out of nowhere, and sprinting in from the horizon.

"Animus," I whispered. A sword popped out of the palm of my right hand, and a small shield grew around my left forearm. I threw myself directly into the fray, the incredibly thin ink of my weapon cutting through carapace and flesh like I was hacking at a summer-ripe melon. It put a lot of strain on the sword, but I had twenty more like it waiting right under the surface of my skin.

I took a blow with my shield, then pirouetted to avoid an attack from my flank. When I meant to steady myself, the scream grating against the walls of my skull intensified, and I stumbled.

Three of the nearest monster-women hurled themselves at me, but I dropped to one knee and activated one of the shields around my wrist.

Ink sprang outward quicker than my eyes could follow, and a spherical shield with jagged spikes jutting out on the other end snapped into place.

The monsters weren't able to pull themselves back in time, and one of them impaled herself on a particularly large spike and died, while the other two took only glancing wounds.

By now, everyone was fighting in melee range except for Adam, who could barely fight at all, and Zed and the kids, who were up in the tree. I sent the three of them a quick message from within the safety of the spherical shield.

—THE SCREAMERS HAVE PRIORITY. TAKE THEM OUT.—
-EVE-

—ALREADY ON IT.—
-ZED-

While Birch supported the team by sending strategic gales of wind to buffet our enemies and blind them with picked up dirt and pebbles, Pinocchio was too small to do much direct damage against the enemies and instead guarded Adam.

Above, Gregor went into his Shadow state and used a small arm-anchored slingshot made of rubber tubes and some carved up, reinforced plastine to shoot rocks toward our attackers. Normally, this wouldn't have done much, but since the rocks started out incorporeal and thus had no wind and very little gravitational resistance, they picked up serious speed before turning back to normal and hitting their target. He fumbled uncharacteristically a few times, but after that his aim improved.

Some of the monsters had reached the tree and were hacking into it, their weapons injuring it while their proximity drained its vitality. Faintly colored crystal leaves withered and fell to the ground.

Kris Animated an entire sleeve of tattoos, and ink-black scorpions spilled out from her flesh, scurrying down the side of Yggdrasil to jump at the monsters.

A group of the monsters who'd stayed back from the wall cooperated to launch what looked like a blue fireball.

Torliam blurred to a stop in front of it and Animated a truly gargantuan forearm shield. He slammed it into the ground and braced against it. The fireball hit.

It exploded with burning goo, disintegrated the shield, and blew him backward. If that had hit us directly, we might have died, and judging by the way the fallout continued to burn, it would have been devastating for Yggdrasil.

The ones who'd created the fireball had made themselves the priority target. Torliam and Jacky both headed straight toward them, while Sam and I hung back with the others to protect the tree and Adam. If anything happened to him, we wouldn't be able to hold out against the monsters for another day.

I went through dozens of ink constructs as we fought. Swords, various types of shields, a couple flocks of razor-beak birds and a swarm of bees, a set of throwing knives, and a few of some weird shelled creature that was based on a pistol shrimp, which basically acted as a flashbang. When the numbers got a little too overwhelming, I used Voice to make them falter.

Torliam blocked against a few more of those huge blue-burning jelly attacks before he ran out of the giant shields.

While he returned to Adam to get a couple of them replaced, Zed took his place in defending against them. With higher Perception, my brother was able to open cracks that he couldn't before, which was especially important because there were so few of them in this realm. Still, even if there weren't a lot of them, he could stretch the openings much wider as his Skill grew. When the fireball jelly came again, he tore open a towering portal in the air and swallowed it right up. The cold of the Other Place washed over the enemy like a burst of frigid polar wind before he closed it up again and had to retreat, having just made himself the focus for their attacks.

While fighting two monsters at the base of the tree, holding off strikes from their multiple arms while retaliating with both sword and shield, the scream that had been clawing against our brains the whole time twisted like a knife in my mind, and I faltered. Then, something inside me *wrenched*. My body lunged to the side in completely instinctive reaction to the pain, trying to follow the pull of whatever was hurting me.

A dripping claw stabbed into the air where I'd just been, from the centipede woman that had apparently been sneaking up on me. I hadn't even noticed her, and would definitely have been injured.

Whatever the thing inside me was moved again, and my body followed, springing back to my feet and into a guard stance as all three of them attacked at once.

Three ink bullets and a rock smashed into them, and they collapsed.

"Are you okay?" Kris screamed down to me. "I saw you were about to get stabbed, and I reacted without thinking. I didn't think it would actually *work*!"

I trembled against the memory of that feeling, phantom pain twitching through my back and out toward my limbs. "Did you just…use your Skill on me?" I called to her, my voice weak.

"I did," she said, her pitch rising as she noticed my condition. "Did I hurt you?"

"Thanks for saving me, but don't ever…do that again," I panted. After less time than I'd have liked to gather myself, I returned to the fight.

Sam and I each took one side of the base of the tree. He attacked with the debilitating effects of Black Sun, driving them crazy until they collapsed to the ground without their minds or committed suicide to escape.

The battle went on till I was moving on autopilot, too tired to really analyze what I was doing any longer. I collected a few wounds, and Pinocchio came over to me and bandaged them up with what little first aid supplies we had, climbing on and around my body as I continued to fight. We took turns returning to Yggdrasil and revitalizing it while Adam replaced as many tattoos as he could. Adam used the last of his ink halfway through, and had to resort to drawing his own blood to continue using his Skill.

Finally, when the heat of the red sun had started to bake us, the last of the centipede women died, and no more rushed in from the distance.

I crawled to the base of Yggdrasil and closed my eyes. "Just a little rest," I mumbled, patting its trunk.

When I woke up, the carcasses had dissolved, and something cool was running down the back of my neck. I leaned forward and touched it with my fingers, then looked at them. It was clear. Water?

I stood and turned to the tree. More water spilled down its sides in little rivulets, sinking into the thirsty ground below.

"You're up," Zed said tiredly, looking up from where he was crouched over Sam. "He's okay," Zed said quickly. "Just Skill exhaustion. You've been out for an hour or so. His Resilience is high. He should wake up soon."

"Who's on lookout?" I said.

"Kris and Gregor."

"Did they mention this water?"

He frowned, following my hand to the tree. "No. Maybe one of them spilled their canteen?" He called up to them, but neither responded.

The gnarled, twisty trunk was easy to climb.

At the top, Kris and Gregor were curled up together, asleep. They must have also been too exhausted to keep going after the fight.

Next to them, that fruit that had been slowly growing seemed to have burst. From its base, water flowed out, gently spilling over the sides of the tree and down to the ground. It was much more water than the fruit itself could have held.

"Guys," I called to the others, though only Zed and Torliam were awake to hear me. "I think maybe the tree is creating its own water."

AT THE TOP of the tallest hill, the god opened his eyes for the first time in days.

Something that had been constricted in my chest opened up, and I took a deep breath. With an eager grin, I pushed Wraith out into the world, once again able to see without my eyes. I hadn't realized how much I missed it.

I whooped, and the kids woke up with a jerk.

Chanelle, who we'd hidden away with the supplies, crawled out yawning and rubbing her eyes, surprised by the change in scenery and the passage of time. Still, this was nothing new for her, since she lost lucidity and woke up to changed surroundings all the time. She gathered with us and ate without taking off her muzzle, awkwardly feeding food through the metal bars.

Behind us, a weaving path appeared up the side of the hill. Intricate designs emerged on the stone surface and statues rose beside it, like they had been there all along.

We didn't follow the path immediately, instead taking some time for everyone to wake up, recover, and eat a big meal first. Sam used some of the extensive charge his healing Skill had built up fighting the monsters to fix the myriad little wounds and injuries we'd accrued.

Then we packed up the camp and our supplies and stepped onto the path. No matter what the god had said, we intended to go back to Earth, even if we had to fight him to do it.

The path and the scenes depicted in the little statues around it were all exquisitely carved, fitting for the God of Shaping and Molding.

I noticed a familiar pustule formed of rock, feeding up from the ground and spraying salt water intermittently. My eyes widened. I was pretty sure that was the same portal we'd entered this place through, which meant these were the same shale hills, which meant that we had somehow circumnavigated the entire realm searching for the god, when he was right there all along, hiding from us.

I knew it was stupid to be angry, but I couldn't help it. What an asshole.

That wasn't the only pustule peeking out of the surrounding hills, and though not all of them spewed water, I was pretty sure they were all portals to somewhere else.

The god sat in a valley at the base of the highest hill. He held some tools, and was slowly chipping away at a small rock in front of him. Had he made all those sculptures before by hand? Maybe he'd been bored, stuck here alone for the last few millennia.

Once again, Torliam took the initiative to speak. "Have we proved our worth to you?"

The god nodded his head, which sat atop a neck that had elongated to look like a swan's.

"We wish to return with you to the realm of mortals and aid you in your fight against the Sickness. We are willing to undergo whatever tests you wish, that we may prove ourselves worthy of your aid. Estreyer is dying, and the Sickness has spread to the world of humans, as well. We are in desperate need of the cure you hold. Please, let us return to the realm of mortals together."

The god turned to look at us, and shook his head "no" quite deliberately. He waved a webbed hand, and the stone at our feet shifted into words.

Torliam's breath huffed out of him like he'd been punched. "It says, *'The wonderful me…lied.'*"

<hr>

A COUPLE BEATS of silence passed.

If the god wasn't going to help us with the Sickness, I was going to lose my temper. Perhaps we could indeed defeat him. Would consuming a portion of his Seed core like I'd done to Behelaino give me the power to heal people?

"*Mierda.*" Jacky's fingers curled into fists, and she took a step forward.

I lifted my arm and held it in front of her, pressing her back. "What do you mean?" I asked the god.

The rock shifted into new words, and we turned impatiently to Torliam, while the god went back to chipping at his rock.

Torliam's eyes skimmed over the symbols quickly, and then he began to translate. *"You will leave this realm and return to your own, after you have been healed."*

Well, that was good, I thought.

"I, the Shaper and Molder, who remembers the time before and fought against that which is abhorrent…in its many aspects, healing the insidious, or that symbol could also mean *'parasite' of…pestilence."* Torliam looked up. "He means he fought against the Sickness."

He turned back to the symbols. *"The Sickness' strength is great and…never-tiring,* or maybe *relentless? It advanced,* or *spread,* or *overtook, and desired to destroy the wonderful me. I, the Shaper and Molder, created a…"* He pointed to a complicated symbol. "This is a mixed word. It looks like a combination of *place* and *shield. I created a place that is also a shield, and stand behind it,* and this last word means *always,* or *till the end.* I believe he means that he does not intend to leave this place, as he said he would before."

"So," Jacky said, "He was fighting the Sickness, but it was too strong for him, so he ran away and hid here?"

Torliam's eyes widened, and he turned toward her in a sort of horrified slow motion, as if doubting the lack of self-preservation that would allow such words to come out of her mouth in the presence of the only god who could defeat the Sickness.

The god swiveled around, now-pebbled face pulled into a deep scowl made even more disturbing by the force of his anger and outrage pressing on us through his ambient power. He flicked his hand at us, and the earth *cracked,* revealing another message.

Black Sun came out, snapping into place like a shield over all the things that made Sam soft. "If you open your mouth again, you will be asleep for the remainder of this conversation," he said matter-of-factly, staring at Jacky with such a calm expression that she could only gape at him in stunned silence.

Torliam bowed deeply to the god, and the rest of us copied him, though Sam had to grab Jacky by the back of the head and force her down. "I apologize for the foolish words of this mortal," Torliam said. "She is young, and has not yet learned patience or tact."

When the god went back to sculpting, though the frown didn't quite leave his face, we straightened and let out a cautious sigh of relief.

"The place-shield stands against the Sickness," Torliam read.

"Stands against means something like opposes or fights?" I said. "He's fighting the Sickness always?"

The anger wafting off the Champion receded, and we all let out a relieved breath, even Jacky.

I turned toward the god, who was at least facing us this time. "There was a prophecy, that the spark would be able to find you. And it said the Sickness *can* be defeated. You know how to do that. We want to fight against it, too, but we need your help. We need healing for more than just ourselves. The mortals of multiple worlds are in danger."

When I stopped, and the god didn't respond, Torliam spoke again. "We may be mortals, but if you will lend us your power once more, we will do whatever we can to help you in return. Is there a way to increase your strength? Is there aught you need or desire?"

"Or maybe we could get some of the other gods to actually help you in this fight against the Sickness?" I said. "If you could even just explain how the cure works or what you need, we can find a way to fix things together."

A second eyelid like Birch's flickered sideways across the god's eyes before melting back into his features, which turned shiny and slippery-looking, like an oil-slick. He seemed very sad as he looked up at the sky, then down to the portals in the surrounding, lower hills. Then he looked at each of us in turn. The tension built. Finally, he nodded. He stood up, holding his hands behind his back like an old monk. A few feet in front of him, delicate-looking petals made of some sort of metal glowed into being from the air, then coalesced into a small, pointed rod. It toppled over, clanking against the stone with a deep sound. It looked like a chopstick, or maybe a decorative hairpin.

The god pointed at me, then waved me forward. The ground behind me buckled, and Chanelle was carried forward on a rolling wave of stone, as if she were a paper boat in the ocean.

She let out a high-pitched squeak of alarm.

He let the stone fell flat again, depositing her just in front of the hairpin-thing.

He pointed to the hairpin, and then to Chanelle, making a motion as if popping a balloon with a needle.

I picked it up, but hesitated.

"Do it," she urged, her eyes trained on the hairpin in my hand like a starving child might stare at a plate heaped with food.

I focused on it with Wraith, but I didn't really know what I was looking for, and didn't notice anything blatantly dangerous. I gently pressed the pointy end into the side of Chanelle's arm, pressing until it broke the skin.

As soon as the hairpin touched the first tiny speck of blood, Chanelle lit up from the spot of contact with a rushing brightness that filled my mind's eye as if I were examining her with Wraith. But this was so much more, as if something had lit her cells up from the inside, the light showing the impurities, the *errors*, clearly. It was like there was a blueprint for what made Chanelle who she was, and it was made of millions of words, and huge sections were distorted or scrambled. Where that distortion touched, it spread to the surrounding words.

I opened my eyes, though I didn't remember closing them, and the god, who called himself the Shaper and Molder, nodded down at me, flicking his fingers in a "get on with it" motion.

I closed my eyes again, focusing on the errors, and willed them away. Chanelle should be only Chanelle. The hairpin pulled at me like the Yggdrasil seedling had, sucking something from inside me that wasn't any of my Skills, but felt similar to the flow of power when I used one. I froze in alarm, then calmed myself as the god sent a wave of reassurance my way. I let the hairpin keep pulling, feeding it power without restraint, like I was a bucket with no bottom.

The errors were unscrambled, the warped sections returned to the clarity of the language that made Chanelle what she was. I noticed, once the glaring impurities were gone, that there were other sections where things were wrong. A scar here and there, and some damage spreading throughout her brain. I focused on them and pushed more power into the hairpin, but, though it accepted the power, it did not continue to heal.

I opened my eyes.

Below me, Chanelle opened hers as well. She sucked in a huge gasp of air, back arching as if she'd been held underwater for a long time. Tears welled up in her eyes, and as she breathed out, she began to laugh. Her laughter melded into sobs, but her mouth was stretched wide open in an awed smile, and she threw her arms around me in a crushing hug.

She withdrew and began to paw at herself, pulling up her sleeves to look at her arms, where the veins weren't dark. She rubbed at her stomach, which was no longer distended. Her fingers were still raw at the tips from all the biting she'd done, but her joints weren't swollen or red. She scrabbled at her muzzle, and I rushed to help her take it off, using a delicate scalpel of Chaos to cut through the straps.

She stuck her fingers into her mouth and pressed at her gums. They weren't blackened or bleeding, and her teeth held firm. "I'm hungry," she said. "But I'm not *starving*." She laughed aloud again, gleeful and full of life.

———

WE WERE all laughing and grinning till we gasped for breath and our faces hurt. I felt joy rise up in me as my eyes welled with emotion. Even though I had been so determined to find the cure, somehow I was still amazed this moment was actually happening.

Torliam reached out and clasped his hands around my hand that held the hairpin, tears running unashamedly down his face. "I thank the gods that I was able to meet you, Eve-Redding. Everything—NIX, my mother—*everything* was worth it."

Jacky had Gregor and Kris wrapped into a hug tight enough to lift them off the ground, beaming wide and snorting through her laughter.

Gregor pretended to try to get away, but he was laughing, too. "Kris can go next," he said. "Heal her, and then I'll go."

Sam stepped forward and touched the hairpin almost reverently. "With this, we can save everyone." He'd let go of Black Sun completely, his eyes sparkling bright blue through his own tears.

Birch pounced on Chanelle and licked her tears away, his tongue turning her cheek bright red as it abraded her skin.

I felt the crushing weight of everything lift off my shoulders. It had been so long since I felt so light... I knew we had accomplished something unequivocally *good*, and I turned to the god. I didn't know if I meant to try and share the wonder of the moment with him, or thank him, or promise him we wouldn't let him down, but he was looking to the sky in the distance.

I followed his gaze, eyesight sharpening as I let Spirit of the Huntress sharpen my claws and enhance my senses. A sour note spread up from the pit inside me, spoiling the first portion of my pure elation. "Is something wrong?"

He turned to me, and his expression held so many different things that I couldn't decipher what it meant. He looked to Chanelle, and the words carved into the ground changed once again.

I grabbed Torliam's arm and gestured to the symbols urgently. "Hurry, I think something's up."

He looked away from Chanelle, sobering when he saw the worry on my face. *"Pestilence has ridden with you, he of the secret steed. Now, the wonderful me continues to battle against the abhorrent. My realm is the place-shield of protection."*

A tremor ripped through the world, and I whipped around. Where the god looked, clouds gathered in the distance, unnaturally thick and flat, as if pressing against the edge of the sky.

The tremor rippled through us all again, and the sky seemed to shatter. Literally, chunks of mottled heaven fell down, leaving something else behind. I had averted my eyes from it before the decision to do so even registered, like jerking back from a burn before you even feel the heat. I knew that I couldn't look back if I didn't want to be hurt.

The God of Shaping and Molding stood before us, smaller than me and lacking the intimidation factor of some of the other gods I'd met. But his face was grim, and his eyes held no hesitation. He lifted his hands, and the remaining sky darkened unnaturally as the winds rose in a shrieking howl of speed.

He turned away, and I thought I caught a glimpse of resignation, maybe a hint of fear.

Then, with a horrible *wrenching*, we had moved, and the vibration of teleportation ground through my bones, wave after wave of it as galaxies burst apart in front of my eyes, and then I was plunged, tumbling, into darkness and a cold so intense it burned, shocking the air from my lungs as I convulsed against it.

The blue mist of Torliam's power bloomed, illuminating the bubbles floating away in front of my face, the rest of the team, and the familiar underwater cave around us. We'd shot out of the anomaly at speed, each in different directions.

The distortion marking the portal that had led us to the god's realm, and had just spit us out again, wavered, and then disappeared like a popped soap bubble.

Chapter 31

Death is the golden key that opens the palace of eternity.
— John Milton

I LOOKED DOWN IN FRIGHT, but the hairpin was still in my fist. I couldn't tighten my fingers, because they were already unresponsive with cold.

I knew we were in the Other Place again because it was sucking up my panic, along with any warmth that wouldn't have been torn away by the freezing seawater. It may have been the only thing that kept me alive, because without the panic and the focus on the horrible burning of the cold, I was able to think. Time seemed to slow as my mental augmentations kicked into overdrive.

Our supplies had been shoved through from the god's realm along with us, so we had thermal wetsuits and a little oxygen left, but by the time we would be able to get them out of the supply pallets and struggle into them, we would be dead. Even if we could get out of the Other Place, the normal world's water was only slightly less freezing. It might buy us a couple seconds at most, but it would take us longer than that to have Zed open a rip and then swim through it. There were no pockets of air or warmth in these underwater caves, and obviously, a multi-hour swim to get back to shore was impossible.

Gregor might survive if he could stay in his Shadow form, and

Torliam, *maybe*, since his Skill might be able to filter oxygen from the water, but I doubted it. The rest of us needed air and warmth immediately.

I looked upward to the roof of the cave, a desperate idea forming. I refused to die, not after we'd come so far and were so close to fixing everything.

Torliam was ripping at one of the supply pallets. As I swam clumsily upward, he managed to get one of the remaining oxygen tanks and a mask free, and followed me.

When I reached the top of the cavern, I let out a coarse drill of Chaos, straight upward. Rocks fell out, sinking down through the water. I sent a Window to the rest of the team.

—GET UP HERE. TOP OF THE CAVERN.—
-EVE-

Torliam batted a few of the falling rocks away from me, then reached around and fit the oxygen mask to my face, a quick swipe of his Skill pushing the water out of the inside of the mask so that it could fill with air.

I took a deep, gasping breath, then turned and gestured to the others.

He shook his head, pressing the mask more firmly to my face.

I scowled at him, even as I took another breath, then ripped the mask away from my face and shoved at him.

He turned away reluctantly, and I lashed out at the roof of the cave with Chaos again, this time with more finesse, creating a wider hollow beyond the initial opening in the rock, so that there would be only a small hole in the floor of the secondary cave I was creating.

Below me, Jacky convulsed against Sam's arm, making it difficult for him to drag her through the water.

Gregor wasn't in his Shadow form. He and Pinocchio were both tugging at Kris, who was flailing upward but didn't seem to know how to swim.

Zed used one arm to hold Birch, who had managed to use his wings to swim to the boy before his small body succumbed to the cold.

Chanelle, unable to resist the depressive cold, had already passed out, and was floating serenely.

Torliam's power brightened the cave even further as swaths of it reached for the others, pushing slowly through the liquid and wrapping around them. He pulled them toward us.

When they arrived, he gave them each a little oxygen from the mask he'd freed. It wouldn't be enough, I knew. Not when shared between ten people. If we didn't get out of the Other Place water *soon* it wouldn't matter, though, because we would all pass out. And then we would die.

I sent black tendrils of Chaos out, urging them to turn into devouring flame, and re-make the water within the mini cave into air. I knew the composition of nitrogen and oxygen that made breathable gas. I knew what the molecules looked like in the chemistry book. Unfortunately, I hadn't yet managed to properly transmute one substance into another in real life, not since the fight with the God of Knowledge. I didn't want to take a chance with our lives by trying to forcefully create nitrogen and oxygen. However, I'd also read about something called electrolysis, which used electricity to separate the hydrogen and oxygen particles that made up water. Why couldn't I do something similar? I focused Wraith on the water above me, forcing myself into a meditative calm despite the burning in my lungs, and pushed until I could vaguely feel the molecules. I imagined the water separating into the two different types of gas, pushing my burning desperation through Chaos as fuel.

Huge bubbles blossomed out of the water, much larger than the amount of liquid Chaos had devoured. The air rose, pushing suddenly warm water back down. I felt a moment of trepidation when I remembered the last time I'd used Chaos to create warmth in the Other Place, but nothing happened. I kept going till the little cave was filled, then grabbed Zed and forced him through, more of a pummeling motion than a grabbing one, because my arms were barely responding to my commands anymore.

—OPEN THE VEIL.—

-EVE-

Torliam pushed me through next, fairly tossing me through the hole and out of the water.

I flopped onto the stone ground and took great, heaving gasps of the air, spewing out a little of the briny water that had somehow made its way into my mouth and down my throat. I was dizzy, but a few more breaths brought my spinning senses under control and soothed the burning in my lungs, so I knew I'd managed to create some oxygen. Hopefully, not too much, or it would burn our lungs and we would all die of oxygen poisoning.

The kids were pale and shivering violently, but Jacky and Chanelle were still, their lips blue, their chests not rising and falling.

"Open the Veil!" I shouted weakly at Zed, who was coughing loudly and twitching his arms, which didn't seem to be working properly. "They're d-dying." My voice was strangely high-pitched, probably because of the hydrogen concentration in the air.

I scrabbled for Jacky as Torliam helped Sam and Adam to the slightly-more-safe cave I'd created. My hands weren't working, and my arms responded with less force than I pleaded with them for, but with her small size, it was enough to turn her over. I pressed on her back, forcing water out of her lungs. I flipped her back over again and began to breathe air into her mouth, pinching her nose shut so it couldn't escape. Her heart was still beating on its own, though weakly.

Birch spewed out water on his own, lying still except for the rapid heaving of his sides as he struggled for air.

Zed let out a weak shout of frustration, and suddenly, a rip opened in the air in front of him, without his hands ever having made it to that spot.

Torliam shouldered me out of the way and pressed his hands to Jacky's chest. Blue mist seeped through her skin. It returned out through her nose and mouth, pushing the water she'd inhaled with it. Then, he shoved the oxygen mask to her face, using his Skill to push air from it into her.

With his other hand, he forced the water out of Chanelle's chest, and I moved to her instead, forcing a few lungfuls of air down her throat.

Then, I shuffled toward the rip in the world. It had opened up onto a flat plane of rock, since this little cave only existed in the

Other Place. I sent Chaos through and turned the normal world rock to chunks and pebbles at an upward angle, so that gravity forced them to slide downward through the opening, falling past us and down into the water of the cavern in the Other Place. They left a new cave-like room in the normal world.

I used the pseudo-electrolysis trick again as that room sucked away the air in our current cave, flinching at the burst of warmth it created.

Jacky was breathing, but her eyes hadn't opened, and her lips were still an alarming shade of blue.

"Help me g-get her through," I said.

Torliam and I lifted her, placing her on the other side, and then waving the others through. The team scrabbled back into the normal world with jerky movements and violent shivering, and Torliam and I followed.

Once the whole team was through, Zed closed the rip to the Other Place, leaving us in a pocket of hydrogen-filled air, surrounded by rock on every side, deep below the surface of the earth.

"The healing stick. D-do you have it?" Sam asked, his voice jerky with chattering teeth and shivers so strong they wracked his body.

"I've g-got it," I said. Now that we were out of the Other Place, I was still ridiculously cold, but I felt a surge of energy return along with the emotions and richness of the real world. I was trembling as much from exhaustion as from cold, but that didn't stop me pushing Chaos out once more, asking it for the simple task of giving energy and movement to the molecules in the air. *Not too much*. I didn't want to set it on fire, since hydrogen was extremely flammable and would explode, turning us all into charred meat. Warmth blossomed out from me, making my skin feel as if it was burning. Still, it was better than the hypothermia that was no doubt already setting in.

"D-don't use electricity or anything that c-could cause a spark," I warned.

Torliam's Skill swept through the cramped space, stripping most of the water off us to pool on the floor. He adjusted the oxygen tank's release valve so that it let out a steady hiss as its contents slowly mixed with the air. It would help ensure we didn't succumb to oxygen deprivation, and hopefully give the little cave a more normal mix of gases, with some nitrogen mixed in. He let a little of his Skill mist linger, giving enough light for us to see in the otherwise pitch-black darkness.

We were content to shiver miserably for a while, till the warmth in the air seeped back into our bodies and some of our strength was replenished. I warmed the rock beneath Jacky and Chanelle, and Sam checked them over.

"They're okay, I think," he said. "Being cold isn't exactly an injury, except for some of their cells that have died due to it."

I saw a couple of the others looking into mid-air and then waving away a Window that I couldn't see, though I assumed it was a level-up notification due to the ordeal we'd just barely escaped from. A couple minutes later, I got my own Window, probably based on the mental strain using Chaos in such a way had caused me.

YOUR FOCUS HAS INCREASED!

Jacky woke up not long after, coughed a little, and leaned back woozily against the rock. "Did you save me?" she said, looking to me.

"It was Torliam," I said. "You'd inhaled a lot of water."

She nodded, blinking sleepily. "I didn't mean to. When the cold hit me, my body just…reacted. I'd breathed in the water before I even realized what was happening, yeah?"

Zed rested his head on his knees. "It's an automatic response to super-cold water. It's called the cold-shock response. We're just lucky more of us didn't start hyperventilating uncontrollably, or we might not have made it out."

"How do you know that?" Sam said.

"He wanted to be a medic for the Peace-Corps, before all of this," I waved my hand around vaguely, "happened."

"Now I'm struggling to save the world in a whole different way," Zed said, something bitter seeping through in his tone.

"But we've got the cure now," Jacky said. "Everything is gonna be okay. We can fix it all."

Adam coughed wetly. "Except we're trapped hundreds of meters underground and surrounded by an ocean of literally freezing water. We have to survive before the cure does anyone any good."

TORLIAM INCREASED the glow of his power. "We must find a way back to the surface of the island above."

I trembled as a residual shiver slid through me. "I don't have the strength left to tunnel all the way up through the ground. Not after the Trial, healing Chanelle, and making this." I gestured to the small cave around us.

"We can't swim out," Adam said, his voice a tired murmur. "All our gear is still in the water, in the Other Place."

"I could send Pinnochio back for it," Kris said. "He's not very strong in the water, since he doesn't have any fins or flippers, but he could probably bring things to us out of the supply pallets, one at a time."

Adam nodded, the motion slow. "I don't have much energy left either, but it wouldn't take a lot to make a couple flippers in his size to help him swim."

Chanelle leaned forward. "You're out of ink, right? Use my blood, instead." Adam frowned and was obviously about to deny her, so she continued quickly. "I'm the least useful out of any of us. I don't have any Skills anymore, but all the Seeds you guys gave me are in Resilience and Life, so I'll be fine, and Sam can heal me. I want to help."

Soon, we'd gathered a small amount of Chanelle's blood in one of Adam's empty ink cartridges and re-opened the crack below us. Pinocchio slipped out into the mini cave in the Other Place. He dropped into the water with a little *plop*, crimson-flippered feet wriggling behind him. He had to make quite a few trips, but under Kris' guidance, he retrieved our thermal wetsuits, the remaining oxygen tanks, and a few other useful supplies that we weren't already carrying in our packs, like glow-sticks.

We left the rest of the supplies in the water, since we didn't need them anymore, and our limited oxygen meant we needed to return to the surface as quickly as possible and couldn't waste any time or energy dragging pallets behind us. We suited up awkwardly in the increasingly crowded space.

Gregor's fingers were stiff and more swollen than normal, and Jacky had to help him maneuver into his suit. He kept clenching his jaw, and I knew the movement caused him pain, even if he was impressively stoic for a child.

Once we were all kitted out with the thermal wetsuits and oxygen supplies, with Birch once again in a sealed plastine bubble, Zed closed the rip to the Other Place, and the rest of the team pressed against the wall, out of my way.

I drilled downward with Chaos, the sound of breaking rock almost deafening in the small space. I kept going till we hit water, and then we waited for the rock to fall and float down. Then we jumped down, too, one by one, into the familiar cavern. With the wetsuits, and without the Other Place to suck at our strength, we were fine.

We swam out, moving as quickly as we could manage. Adam used a little more of his almost-expended power to give us all flippers, which helped a lot, though the drag of our packs in the water still slowed us down. Without the extra supplies and the caution we'd shown when coming the other direction, we made much faster time. We broke the surface of the ocean with barely any oxygen remaining, then swam toward shore.

We pulled ourselves onto the rocks and collapsed. After a few moments of exhaustion, we dragged off our masks.

Jacky let out a small "whoop!" as she cracked a fresh glow-stick and tossed it to the ground between us.

I shrugged off my pack and retrieved the hairpin from where I'd stashed it safely inside. I held it up in the air like some sort of trophy, flopping back against the cold, wet pebbles that made up the beach. "We did it!" I crowed, elation suppressing my fatigue.

"We," Torliam announced, "are remarkable."

Chapter 32

There are horrors beyond life's edge that we do not suspect, and once in a while man's evil prying calls them just within our range.
— H. P. Lovecraft

AFTER A FEW MORE MINUTES OF flopping about like fish, we got up and huddled around Kris and Gregor. Despite our exhaustion, none of us wanted to put off the most important thing any longer than we had to. "We'll heal you two now, and once we get back to the cabin, we'll use the hairpin on everyone else to try and see if any of us need the cure, too."

"Hairpin?" Sam said. "Oh. The metal thing. I was thinking of it more like a lance for infected wounds, myself."

I opened my mouth, then closed it. "That makes way more sense, actually," I said belatedly. "I wanted to name it," I muttered childishly under my breath.

Gregor rolled his eyes at me, but totally lacked the nonchalance of his normal attitude. "Yes, well I certainly hope you weren't intending to dawdle around about healing people." His cheeks were fever-bright, and he fidgeted as if he wanted to grab the lance out of my hands and jab himself with it.

I pretended not to notice his extreme impatience, but couldn't help my expression of surprise when he nudged Kris and said, "Heal her first."

She shook her head vehemently. "No. You've been getting really sick lately. I'm still feeling okay." She turned to me, deadly serious. "Heal Gregor first."

He scowled and moved away from me. "Kris has been biting herself when she sleeps," he said, ignoring her look of betrayal. "The inside of her cheeks are all cut up. I'm not going first, and I'll go Shadow if you try to make me. Let's just save us all some time and heal her first."

Jacky glared at the both of them. "Have you guys been keeping this a secret?"

Kris rubbed her foot against the ground, shuffling some pebbles. "There was nothing you could do. The whole team was already trying so hard. We didn't want to worry you for no good reason."

Jacky scowled and gave Kris a feather-light smack on the side of her head. "Next time, tell me."

Kris nodded, looking down.

I hoped there would never be a 'next time.' I knelt beside Kris and held her hand as she settled down next to me. I pushed my non-sensory awareness through the barrier of her skin, searching for any signs of the Sickness. I found faint traces, sections of her body where the connecting tissue was a little weaker than it should have been. They hadn't been there before, but I wasn't exactly sure it was the Sickness, and not simply damage that the God of Shaping and Molding's realm had done to her via prolonged exposure.

When I pricked her hand with the lance, it became clear. She lit up in my mind like a lightbulb was shining inside each and every one of her cells, and the paths of corruption were obvious, tar-like pollution seeping through her.

I frowned and opened my eyes. "Sam, before I heal this, you should come take a look, too. It might help us figure out how this thing works."

He nodded and took Kris' other hand.

She swallowed. "You can fix it, right? Whatever it's doing to me?"

I smiled. "Yes, don't worry." I turned back to Sam. "Do you feel the damage around her lungs, and in the lining of her stomach?"

"Yes." He paused, and then frowned. "But I can't heal it. Something's blocking me from transferring the damage to myself."

Gregor had crept closer and closer, his eyes locked onto the point where the lance pierced his sister's skin. He laid one tiny hand on her shoulder.

"That's the Sickness," I said. "Keep an eye on it while I set Kris back to normal." I then explained how the lance had worked so far, the sense of pristine blueprint and the corruption of the blueprint's language that was the Sickness. I pushed my power through the warm metal under my hand, and it began to heal her.

The process was much easier than it had been with Chanelle, probably because the corruption was much less extensive. Still, by the time the lance had pulled enough energy from me to untwist and rewrite the language of Kris, my fingers trembled from exhaustion.

"I…feel way better," she said, her voice rising in excitement. "I didn't even realize how crappy I was feeling till it went away. Does this mean I'm cured?" She turned to me, her body fairly vibrating in a way that would have had her tail wagging frantically if she were a dog.

I nodded, smiling but too worn to talk for a while.

Gregor blinked away tears, and, in a rare display of open affection, hugged Kris around the neck.

"It's your turn now," she said to him, urging him down onto the cold beach beside me.

"Your strength is depleted," Torliam said, wrapping his hand around my own and gently removing the lance from my grasp. "Rest. I still have energy to feed through the healing artifact. If it will accept me, there is no need for the burden to lie upon you. Indeed, we should *all* attempt to use the lance."

Adam grunted in what was probably agreement. "Did you get anything useful out of that, Sam?"

Sam looked up from Kris' much smaller hand, which he was still holding. "It is very strange." He didn't continue, until Adam urged him on with an exasperated roll of his hand. "It didn't feel quite like healing. It felt more like…transformation. Like a motion-capture video, in reverse. When I heal something, I take the wound onto myself, and my body knits together and rearranges or regrows something. This…felt different. It's hard to explain. Hard for me to quite understand, to be honest. I don't think I'll ever be able to replicate it."

That didn't lower anyone's mood. Torliam clapped a hand on Sam's shoulder like he was encouraging a child, or a pet. "That is to be expected, I suppose. If it were normal healing, it would have been accomplished by an Estreyan long ago. And if it were easy to understand, we would have been able to thwart the Sickness another way, by creating countermeasures against it. Continue to analyze. You might still learn something useful." He pricked Gregor's hand with the metal artifact. Torliam's eyes widened, and he looked to me. "This is quite astounding."

"Think about healing the places that feel wrong. It will pull on your power. Let it. Keep feeding it till everything is back to the way it should be."

Torliam returned his attention to Gregor. A short time later, he drew away the lance piercing the boy's skin, and Gregor released a great sigh of relief, slumping forward till his forehead rested on his knees.

"The pain must have been great," Torliam said. "It is gone, now?"

Gregor nodded and sniffled with tears, though he kept his face hidden.

Torliam was grim-faced. "The Sickness had been concentrated around the nerves of his spine and in his joints, probably causing deterioration of his motor control, and an increasing amount of pain."

Jacky scowled. "You shoulda said something," she repeated.

The boy swallowed, then took a deep, sniffling breath before answering. "What could you have done, anyway? We all knew I was sick. You didn't need to worry any more about it. Plus, if it got really bad, I just had Sam put a little of his numbing juice on my back. It was uncomfortable, but it helped a little."

Jacky turned her glare on Sam.

"He asked me not to say anything," Sam said quickly. "Black Sun was active the first time he came to me, and…his reasoning made sense. Stress is detrimental to performance. Adding more of it wouldn't have helped us find the god or the cure any sooner. Chanelle was enough motivation for all of us, don't you think?"

Chanelle flinched. "That's over now, though. We don't have to worry anymore. I'm normal again…and everything is going to be okay." Her words were forceful, as if they were as much for her as the rest of us, but she met my gaze with a small nod. Her eyes held a measure of loyalty heavy enough to make me uncomfortable, so thick that it looked like adoration.

I straightened, reinforcing my spine with a bit of mental steel, and nodded back.

Chanelle's gaze grew vague, her posture loosening as she lost lucidity, staring into the air with a slack face.

"There was still some damage to her brain that the lance couldn't heal. I was hoping whatever's wrong with her could be fixed, now that the Sickness isn't there to stop us. Sam?" I turned to him, and he nodded.

He laid his hand on her forehead, then smiled. "Yes. I can…" he trailed off, paling. He was silent for a couple minutes as we stared at the both of them intently. Finally, he took a deep breath, then let out a sigh that shuddered as it left his lungs.

Chanelle's gaze cleared, and when Sam told her she was healed completely now, she started crying again through her face-splitting smile.

WEARILY, but in good spirits, we got up and began trudging toward the closest bit of civilization on the island. We'd stashed our snow pod not too far from the boat owner's house, and were hoping it would still be there waiting for us. None of us wanted to walk all the way back to the cabin in flippered wetsuits.

"I can't wait to get a fire going," I said. "And sleep with walls around me."

Zed leaned his head onto my shoulder as we walked side by side. "I can't wait to sleep without worrying that something is going to try to kill me."

Torliam snorted. "Humans. Where is your sense of adventure?"

We all turned to stare at him.

He scratched the back of his head. "Err, I can admit, the god's realm was not pleasant. Despite the necessity of our travel, I, too, am glad to be back on your planet."

"At least my Struggle Skill got plenty of workouts," Jacky said.

"And we've gained the means to save the world," I said.

She grinned. "Yeah, that too."

We found the snow pod right where we'd left it and unceremoniously piled in, only removing whatever pieces of our under-water gear was absolutely necessary for us to fit. Torliam, Jacky and Sam rode in the trailer with what was left of our equipment.

When we arrived at the cabin, we immediately started a fire in the wood-burning stove, then gathered in the main room, shoving the nonperishable food rations we'd left behind down our gullets.

Adam picked up his link, which he'd left behind to keep it from being damaged or broken by the passage to the god's realm, and laid it out flat on the table. Its surface flickered to life, and he frowned. "It's only been a week."

I raised my eyebrows. "Are you sure? Is it properly connecting to the data signal?"

Adam was indignant. "Of course I'm sure!"

After a second, I nodded. "Time passes differently on Estreyer than on Earth. I guess it's not so surprising to know that the god's realm was the same."

At first, we chattered happily to each other, but after a while, that petered off. In the quiet, Zed spoke up again. "So…what happened, at the end there? When he shoved us back here, into the water?"

We shared a grim look. When I spoke, my voice was halting, hesitant. "I saw something behind the sky, for half an instant. Whatever it was, it wasn't…I feel like I would have gone insane if I looked at it for much longer." It had been a break in the world, and it reminded me of Torliam's explanation of what was in the emptiness between worlds, what we risked when we used the arrays to travel between Estreyer and Earth.

Torliam frowned. "If I am correct, that place was an enclosed realm made by the god. It was completely under his control, you might even say, a part of his body. For it to be damaged, either something was attacking him, or his own power has weakened to the point that he cannot even maintain the solidity of the realm."

Jacky pursed her lips. "Neither of those sound good."

I remembered the Remnants had said something about the world destabilizing if we succeeded. Was this what they meant? "What could have been attacking him?" I said.

"Another god is the only thing I can imagine, but that seems unlikely. I fear that he has simply grown weak, expending more energy against the Sickness than he is able to replenish. I believe we may have made this more difficult, as we brought the Sickness behind his barriers. He mentioned that it had ridden with us, as if this was significant. Perhaps, his realm, being clean of it, gave him some sort of advantage in holding it back. Then, when he used his energy to create the tool…"

I looked down to the lance, tucked between the Oracle's armband and the skin of my left forearm. "You think giving us the lance made him weak enough that he couldn't even keep his pocket realm from crumbling apart?"

Torliam grimaced and gave a very human gesture that wasn't quite a nod and wasn't quite a shrug. "He may have also expended a significant amount of energy in the Trial. Nevertheless, I am only speculating."

"I know that place was pretty big, but he went there to conserve his strength when it wasn't enough against the Sickness. If he can't even keep it stable, what exactly does that mean?"

Torliam shook his head. "I do not know. However, there are ancient stories of some of the lesser gods dying. It is not quite clear whether this is simply one of their manifestations being dispersed, or not. In any case, I fear for what it may mean, if he is weak enough for that manifestation to be dispersed. If he has been holding back the Sickness for so long, what might it do, free from his influence?"

We sat in grim silence for several long moments.

Adam leaned forward, his fingers twiddling restlessly. "On the off chance that this lance thing stops working when something happens to its creator, we really should check the rest of the team for the Sickness immediately. It spreads, if you haven't noticed."

Torliam gave him an unamused look but did as he suggested.

Sam volunteered to be checked first, followed by Birch, and then Jacky.

Jacky had traces of the Sickness.

Before healing her, Torliam allowed the others to use the lance so they could sense what it revealed. All of us, even Chanelle and Birch, were able to sense the Sickness using the lance, though Birch had to hold the metal in his mouth when he poked Jacky.

Torliam healed Jacky, and then found the Sickness in Adam.

When it was my turn and the lance broke the skin, Torliam's jaw clenched, and the muscles around his eyes tightened.

I knew before he said anything. I had it, too. "We can fix it, now," I said, swallowing down the hot rush of fear that had bubbled up.

His jaw clenched, and his eyes squeezed shut. Seconds passed. Then he nodded.

I let out a slow breath as his power, filtered through the lance, healed me.

WE WENT TO SLEEP, and in the morning, Jacky dragged me back down to the dining table and made me explain my dreams in more detail to the rest of the team. Torliam set his Tracker Skill to looking for the enemy that was attacking me with the dreams, but we knew it would take time for him to get any definite direction.

In the meantime, they set a watch so someone would always be awake and keeping an eye on me while I slept. Luckily, I now only needed four hours or so of sleep per night, so it was less of a hassle than it could have been. They grumbled, as that wasn't quite enough to mollify their worry, but there really wasn't much more we could do, except for me to train so that I didn't lose and die again the next time my dreams were invaded.

We turned to the news to see what had changed over the last week. Our faces were being displayed less frequently, now that so much time had passed since the last time we'd been sighted. The Estreyans had continued their destruction, and NIX and the military had in turn continued to fight back against them, losing twice for every small victory they gained. The Earth Defense Force, the EDF, was a conglomerate of what remained of the mundane military, NIX, and a couple of NIX's counterparts in other countries. Apparently, the EDF had taken down a couple more Estreyan ships, and driven off, but not downed, another destroyer.

People were starving to death, dying of disease due to the lack of clean water and medical facilities in some areas, and being killed by other civilians. A group of enforcers had commandeered a supply cache in one city, hoarding the resources and refusing to distribute them to the helpless civilians. A kind of desperate, despairing selfishness seemed to have bred in everyone. Earth, with all our armies and years of preparation, was still losing.

There were more outbreaks of the meningolycanosis. The most critical area was another large city, a few hundred miles from the city we'd been in when the initial outbreak had happened.

According to the news reports, an investigation had discovered what they thought was the first infected person to enter the new city, San Mateo, after escaping Mordsmouth. A family had escaped when the barrier came down. They'd found a wrecked military vehicle on the side of the road. They stopped, hoping to help anyone who was still alive. Their daughter had been infected by one of the rabid soldiers, and they had escaped with her, tied her up in the back of their pod, and rushed to the next city in hopes of getting her medical care. It didn't work out like that.

San Mateo's local military had taken to killing the infected to keep the disease from spreading enough that the Estreyans would be drawn to the city. If that happened, they knew they were all doomed, so sacrifices had to be made, despite the opposing outcry from one faction of the country, who believed these people needed medical care, not summary execution.

I looked at the lance tucked against my skin. I felt disconnected from the lives on the other side of the screen, in a way. My team was safe, now. I was safe, too. If we tried to help the rest of the world, we'd be putting that safety at risk. But even so, I knew the guilt would crush me, if I let all those innocent people continue to die. If I let the multifaceted plague wipe out the rest of humanity. I may not have been connected to all those people directly, and none of them were as important to me as myself and the members of my team, but still… I stood up from the table, put on my winter clothing, and left the cabin for a walk in the dark.

I remembered Kilburn and his assertion that we weren't so dissimilar. If he was a sociopath, what did that make me? I wanted to try and save the world, not because I was good, not because I truly had some moral core, but because I was afraid of the guilt. Besides, even if we continued living safely, our quality of life would deteriorate during a full-blown apocalypse. I nodded to myself. That was a good reason to interfere, right? Anyway, unlike most of the things I'd dragged them into before, I could give the other members of the team a chance to make their own decision about this. It would be politics, probably, instead of the life-and-death battles we were accustomed to. I didn't need them to come with me just to ensure my own survival.

Feeling lighter, I returned to the cabin. I had no delusions that I was actually a good person, but I could still do good things.

WHEN I ASKED the rest of the team if they wanted to help me stop the Sickness and end the war, or if they'd rather retire to some safe place in the country, they all stared at me like I was an idiot.

Adam shook his head and sighed, looking to the ceiling as if praying for patience. "Eve, we're a team. Even if we weren't, we *all* want to stop the Sickness and this idiotic alien invasion. We've even discussed this before, so I don't know why you're bringing it up now. Why don't we spend our conversational energy on something more important, like…planning our course of action? That seems like a much smarter idea."

I wanted to scowl at him, but I couldn't help the small smile that ruined my expression. Adam could be amazingly rude, but a lot of it was a cover for his soft innards. I pressed my hands flat to the table. "The lance is our greatest resource right now. We need to make sure we employ its influence correctly."

Adam nodded. "It's not so simple as going out and announcing to the world that we have it, or healing every affected person we happen to come across."

"We have to use this power to actually fix things," I agreed. "And that goes beyond stopping the Sickness. We have to stop the war, heal both the Earthlings and the Estreyans, and help Earth to rebuild." The words felt strange coming out of my mouth. I reminded myself that I wasn't an altruistic do-gooder. I just wanted to be able to live without crushing guilt.

"We must have diplomacy," Torliam said. "It cannot only be a ceasefire between our two peoples, or war may start again because of resentment. You humans may not have the technological or personal power of my people, but you excel at putting your energies together to advance, and it seems vindictiveness is in your nature."

I fingered the lance, holding it up so the light glinted off its pale metal surface. "Since we're the ones with the bargaining chip, we'll have to handle the negotiations, at least to start."

Sam shifted in his seat. "But we are going to heal people, right? As many as possible, as quickly as possible, before it's too late? If we see someone who needs it, we heal them."

Torliam frowned at him. "That is a certainty. If not, what was our purpose in this entire quest?"

Adam shook his head, ignoring the astonishment which preceded Torliam's glare. "We'll be most effective if we get infrastructure and allies set up first, and *then* start healing. This isn't about making ourselves feel good. It's about helping as many as possible, as quickly as possible," he repeated Sam's words with a glance to the blonde boy. "And that means being smart about it. We can't go around searching out and healing people one by one."

Before Torliam or Sam could retort, I said, "Adam's right. We need to be doing mass healing. That means we need other people bringing the infected to us, and extensive organization and infrastructure to make it as efficient as possible. We've only got one lance. Plus, it's not just the Sickness we're dealing with here. The meningolycanosis is a huge problem even without the Sickness using it as a vector, and people are going without basic necessities like clean water and food."

Sam leaned forward, his outrage gone. "Okay. But where do we even start? And how?"

I wasn't quite sure. Instead of saying that, I talked through my thought process aloud. What did I have, what did I need, and how was I going to get it? "The two most critical issues, as far as I see it, are the rapid spread of the Sickness through the meningolycanosis, and the Estreyan attacks. Either one is going to cripple Earth. We have to stop them both, immediately. Preferably at the same time. Both Earth and Estreyer desperately need something, and we have to offer them that. We hold all the leverage, so there's no way they won't agree to any demands we make, as long as they feel they have no other option."

"Like kidnapping and torturing us, or something," Gregor muttered.

My mouth twitched upward at one edge. "Yes. That would be a supremely bad idea on their part. We'll just have to make sure they fully comprehend their current position."

Sam nodded, but the frown had returned to his face. "So now we can cure the Sickness, but what about the meningolycanosis itself?"

Jacky turned to him. "Can't you heal that?"

"No. Not without stripping the virus of its camouflage, anyway. I can heal the *damage* it does to the brain, but that doesn't help if it's still active inside their bodies. It doesn't register as a wound directly. But even so, the bigger problem is that I can't heal thousands of people." He held up a hand when Jacky opened her mouth again. "It's not about offsetting the damage. It's about the logistics of trying to heal people infected with an extremely contagious virus, one at a time."

Torliam nodded slowly, crossing his arms over his chest. "We could bring healers in from my world to deal with this. The problem is that it is indeed spreading so quickly, and healers are a rare, valued resource that my people are already lacking enough of."

I rubbed my neck. "Even if we could get Estreyer to agree to lend us some healers, they'd have to use the arrays to get here in time, right? I'm…worried about that. We've been doing it so far, but there's a good reason they were forbidden, right? A reason that I hinted at very strongly when I did that interview with the Estreyan reporters. We should get a better idea of how likely we are to bring along an eldritch being before we authorize further mass use of the arrays." That darkness I'd glimpsed on the other side of the broken sky of the god's realm had brought to mind the danger. Plus, it would seem pretty hypocritical to ask people to use the arrays after I'd publicly condemned their use.

Jacky pursed her lips and tilted her chair backward to balance on two legs. "I know Blaine did most of the inventing, but isn't it possible to make more of that orange serum stuff? The one we used on Chanelle, yeah?"

I shook my head. "NIX might have the information on it, but that serum was meant for use on Players. It didn't actually get rid of the virus, just made it so the Seeds could see and deal with it, without negative side-effects. Plus, the serum wouldn't fix the brain damage already caused."

Sam leaned forward, shaking his head. "No, Jacky's right! Obviously, the serum from before won't work. But we're not limited to that. Our problem is that the meningolycanosis is spreading too fast, right? If we can stop that, and the spread of the Sickness, there would be time for any damage done by it to be healed at a later date."

Zed frowned at him. "But how are human immune systems supposed to deal with the virus? That's still a problem. A huge one. A lot of people have already been infected."

Silence fell for a moment. I looked between the two of them. "What would happen if you were to be infected, Sam? Would your body recognize it as a threat, then? I know your Skill becomes increasingly efficient at healing anything it considers a wound or a poison."

"You're saying, we might be able to find a way to kill the meningolycanosis in normal humans, by studying my body's response to it?" Sam said slowly. "I might be able to overcome it, but we'd want to test some on a blood sample first, I think."

I nodded. "Without Blaine, we probably can't make use of that ourselves. But NIX might be able to. If they could mass-produce a cure to the meningolycanosis, at least, we might be able to mitigate a lot of the devastation. I'm sure we can convince them, with a sufficiently impactful visual aid. We'll make sure your Skill can handle it first, and if so, you can do a live demonstration."

Gregor nodded wisely, his arms crossed across his chest. "I'm not an expert, but I'm pretty sure people create this thing called immunoglobulin with other people's antibodies."

I had no idea what immunoglobulin was, but I wasn't a child genius, so I tried not to let that bother me.

Zed raised his hand. "Uhh, don't forget, we have to stop the Estreyans from killing people directly, right? They're going after all the infected people. We can't just waltz into a city full of people going crazy and expect them to wait while we inoculate all of them."

"Not as things are right now," I agreed. "But there's no reason we shouldn't be able to expect that. In fact, I want those Estreyans on the ground *helping* us inoculate and heal people." I turned to Torliam. "Do you know what the hierarchy of command might be, among the invaders? Obviously, they're beholden to Queen Mardinest. And they've had some way to receive updated information from her. But with how reluctant your people are to send anything through the arrays, I assume there is someone in charge here on Earth. Someone the others would defer to, without needing confirmation from her. Maybe someone who has the authority to command the whole force? Maybe...even some way for me to contact Estreyer directly?"

His smile widened as I spoke. "Yes, there would be a warrior given command of the others, and a line of succession should the first die in battle. The commander is likely in charge of one of the destroyers."

"Is there any way to know which one?"

Torliam shook his head. "Not for us, unless we were to contact them and ask."

"But they have ways to contact each other?" I said. "If we were to access one destroyer, we'd be able to communicate with the commander of the whole invasion?"

"Yes. And with evidence of what we have achieved, I know no Estreyan who would not be willing to listen and...parlay, is that the word? They would parlay with us." He lips quirked up into a smug smile.

Adam rolled his eyes, but didn't say anything.

"We'll need the humans to agree on the terms of the peace, as well," I said. Sure, they'd been mostly on the back foot the entire time, but I didn't want them retaliating against any healers we possibly convinced Estreyer to send, or against Estreyer itself.

Adam tapped at his link. "Humans are so divided, who can we speak to that has the power to negotiate on behalf of the whole race?"

"There isn't anyone like that," Gregor said. "At best, we'll be able to meet with delegates from all the major countries."

Torliam said, "My mother also does not rule the whole of Estreyer. However, the rulers of other lands have never attacked Earth, and likely have much less ire against its people. They will still be interested in the cure, and willing to bargain with us for our help against the Sickness."

"Even more reason we have to be absolutely certain to protect that little stick," Adam said. "If they find out anyone with Seeds can use it, there's no reason for them to listen to us. And something so valuable can easily become a weapon, by the very act of withholding it."

"You are correct," Torliam said, nodding his head grudgingly toward Adam. "We will need to employ a bit of misdirection and perhaps a few lies about the requirements to use it. I doubt any of my people would dare to risk the loss of the cure, if they are sane. We would only need to point to an enemy and make an accusation, and the entirety of the world would tear them apart and lay their ashes at our feet."

The idea of power like that was…pleasing. If only it didn't come with such an equally heavy burden. "Perhaps, with careful examination of the situation, and the ways that Earth provoked Estreyer, we can make our own leaders see reason," I said.

We talked for a long while, laying out plans and routes of attack. "We'll head out in the morning. Well, morning such as it is," I said, looking out into the perpetual darkness through the cabin window. "It'll be good to see the sun again. A proper bright, yellow sun."

Chapter 33

There is in God—some say—A deep, but dazzling darkness.
 — Henry Vaughan

AT FIRST, we weren't sure where to go to find a destroyer, and Adam had discovered that the human leaders had long ago left their plush offices for more secretive and secure locations, so it's not like we could just walk up to them and demand a meeting.

But we knew where the most recent outbreaks of the meningolycanosis were, and that was the key. "That's where we need to be," Adam said, pointing to the map on his link. "They're not managing well. Which means the Estreyans are going to be coming, and the EDF will be there soon after to try to keep them from setting up another quarantine bubble and flattening the city into slag and bones."

Adam tried to hire a plane to get us back off Ellesmere Island, but even private flights were basically nonexistent, now. So we loaded up and went back to the boat owner's house, again.

The man had repaired the damage to his front door from Jacky's attack, and set up reinforcing bars around the frame to keep the same thing from happening again. A new peephole allowed him to see those outside without ever opening the door.

"Do you want to do the honors?" I said, turning to Torliam.

"I want to do it," Zed said, grinning. "Can you imagine the look on his face when he sees us again?"

Torliam ignored him, stepped forward, and knocked politely.

I kept Wraith extended through the tiny openings around the doorframe and into the house within, just in case.

It turned out to be a good idea, because when the old man came to the door, he peered out through his new peephole. He jerked back with a harsh gasp of surprise.

"He sees us," I said.

Jacky turned to Adam. "Umm… Did you remember to actually pay him for the first time?"

Adam was silent for a couple beats too long.

Torliam turned to him, an incredulous look on his face. "An honest man always pays his debts!" he muttered, before turning back to the door. "Err," Torliam cleared his throat and raised his voice to be heard through the barrier. "Hello again—"

The old man fumbled with the pocket of his thick robe, then pulled out a gun that looked like it belonged in a museum.

"Shields!" I yelled, the word bursting out almost before I made the conscious decision to speak.

Adam blinked, then jerked a hand toward one of the ink cartridges at his waist.

Torliam's hand was already rising, blue glow flowing outward and around us with a distinctly superhuman reaction time.

It was barely enough. The man pulled the trigger, the gun let out an ear-shattering *bang,* and the metal ball slammed right through the door and into Torliam's shield, where it compressed like slightly warm chocolate pressed into a pan.

Torliam stared at the bullet suspended in front of his face. His eyes followed it as it fell to the ground.

"Now I'm glad I let you go first," Zed said, also staring at the bullet.

Torliam turned to glare at him. After a couple seconds of awkward silence, he huffed, then turned back and ran a hand through his dirty blonde hair dismissively, making sure it settled smoothly to his shoulders. Then, he raised an arrogant eyebrow, lifted his foot, and kicked down the door, tearing the reinforcements out of the wall, along with the entire doorframe. It fell forward into the brightly lit interior, and he walked onto it, dramatically pushing his power-created shield before him and stopping the next five shots from the ancient gun.

The weapon clicked impotently. When the old man realized it was empty, he scowled, hauled back, and threw it right at Torliam's head.

It, of course, also bounced off the shield and fell to the floor.

"Whadda ya want with me?" he yelled.

"We wish to borrow the use of your boat once again," Torliam said calmly, taking up a disproportionate amount of space in the entranceway.

The man clenched his jaw a couple times, then seemed to deflate. He rubbed his hands across the grizzled stubble on his cheeks. "Oh. Thought you were gonna remove th' evidence o' where you escaped to. Shut me up, as it were."

"Escaped?" I said, narrowing my eyes.

"I ain't stupid. I can recognize a face bein' played on the screens as well as any other man."

Adam turned to me, a question on his face, along with an implied threat toward the old man.

I shook my head in response. "Did you tell anyone our location? I hear there's a reward."

The man snorted, but refrained from spitting on his own floor. He emphasized his words more, this time. "I ain't stupid. I kept my mouth shut and bought bullets for my grandpa's gun. 'Cept the gun didn't work out too well, did it?"

I couldn't help the little smirk at the edge of my lips. "That's true. And if you'd decided to collect on that reward, they would have killed you already." That last bit probably wasn't true, but I figured a little extra incentive not to rat on us to NIX or the Department of Defense couldn't hurt. "Go get dressed. The trip this time is going to be quite a bit longer."

The man grimaced and stomped away.

"Someone go guard him, just in case," I said.

"That went well, I think," Zed said, nodding happily.

Adam stared at him incredulously.

"Oh, come on!" Zed said. "Nothing went catastrophically wrong. One shield and a short conversation, and we've got what we came for. None of us are even injured!"

WHEN OUR CAPTAIN WAS READY, we went out to his boat and loaded it up, this time bringing our bikes with us instead of two big pallets of supplies. The boat ride took many hours as we navigated around the huge island and moved south.

I found Birch at the prow of the ship, lashing out into the air with little flashes of Chaos. Bursts of warmth wafted back from him, but whatever he was attempting didn't seem to be working. He flatted his ears and lowered his head, letting out a low whine.

"What are you trying to do?" I said, settling in beside him.

He pressed his nose to my arm, and my mind filled with an image of Chaos' black tendrils causing wood to burst into flame, and then the image of a fireball incinerating an evil-looking rat.

I nodded. I'd used Chaos to create fire a couple times. I'd used it to heat food and attack enemies once I got the hang of it, and, apparently, he also wanted to learn this technique. "Well, to make it easier, I think I should teach you a little bit of basic science first. Everything around us is made up of tiny little pieces called molecules, which are made up of even tinier things called atoms. They're so small that you can't see them, but you can still affect them to create change."

Birch stared at me, his cat features somehow expressing extreme dubiousness.

"It's true!" I insisted.

I taught him for a while longer, and then we moved onto practical exercises, creating short-lasting fireballs in the air in front of the ship. Since the boat owner knew about us already, and there was no one else around to see, I didn't feel the need for secrecy.

The smell of burnt sea air and the light of the pseudo-fireworks put us all in a good mood.

Birch put his nose to my skin again and, this time, sent me a thought I knew was straight from his imagination. He showed me myself, not recognizable by my facial features, but by my smell, the taste of my blood, the vague sense of my personality as he saw it, and two legs. I was surrounded by other, much smaller two-legged people, and, as I walked, I left behind a misty afterimage of Chaos, which bloomed into light like a thousand lightning bugs. The other two-legs smelled of awe. He sent me a sense of eagerness, and then pulled back.

I grinned and ruffled the fur on his head. "I guess that *would* be pretty cool, huh?" Feeling light and a little silly, I decided to try it. Letting Chaos waft out behind me when I walked only took a couple tries, and even that looked kind of cool.

Figuring out how to set it on fire without creating one large, Eve-shaped fireball was quite a lot harder. After a few experiments, I threaded almost invisible filaments of more condensed Chaos into the cloud, and at the tips of them, I heated the air in random pulses. It looked like I was shedding smoke and stars.

Gregor, Kris, and Jacky came over to cheer my antics on, while I tried to teach Birch how to create the same effect for himself.

The old man had been watching us since the beginning, in between puttering around his boat. His wariness seemed to have been replaced by obstinate pride and a heavy dose of curiosity as we spent more time together without killing him. Now, he stomped over with a scowl on his face. "What're you doin,' messin' around with light shows? You won't be killin' no aliens with them pretty sparkles. Damn flighty kids. Go back to practicin' your fireballs!" He waved his hands in the air dramatically. "Lethal attacks, that's whatcha need!" He stomped away back to the wheelhouse, muttering about how kids these days didn't have proper discipline, and we'd all get ourselves killed if not for him.

Finally, long after the sun would have risen were we nearer the equator, we arrived at the coast of the main continent.

We unloaded what supplies we had left and carefully moved our bikes down the worn, shaky ramp.

"You goin' back south to keep fightin', then?" the old man asked, his weathered face set in a permanent scowl.

"We are going to stop the war," Torliam said, climbing onto his bike.

The man harrumphed, then nodded. "Good. If you need a ride again, next time don't be breakin' down my door. Just ask nicely." He turned to Adam. "No need to be transferin' credits to me. I'm just doin' my duty as a human member o' the resistance." He nodded like a proud aristocrat, then stomped back onto his boat without a backward glance.

Zed frowned, sharing a look with the rest of us. Under his breath, he said, "He's acting like he never tried to shoot us with a gun. We tried knocking and asking nicely first, both times!"

Jacky shrugged. "Well, we also broke down his door, both times. I guess it evens out, yeah?"

AS WE RODE south with an urgency that only allowed for short breaks, we kept watch on the news. We were unsurprised when the Estreyans moved on the same city we were headed to. I wasn't sure whether to be satisfied that we'd judged correctly, or horrified at what this meant for the city if we couldn't get there quickly and succeed in our mission.

By the time we arrived, the energy barrier already shimmered around the city like a soap bubble, stretching miles in every direction.

We rode slowly along the edge, hoping to run into an Estreyan patrol. Other than that, I didn't have any real plan to draw the attention of the Estreyans. I figured that, if nothing else, we'd encourage an investigation if we started attacking the barrier.

People had gathered on the inside edge of it. Some of them struck at it impotently and were thrown back. Then they noticed us and began to scream for help.

I wasn't wearing my helmet or my shemagh, and, along with the fact that the makeup of my ten-person group was now pretty iconic, many of them recognized us from the news. We quickly drew a moving crowd of hopeful, desperate people tracking our progress around the edges of the city.

They made me uncomfortable. I could smell their unwashed bodies mixed with smoke and a faint scent of rot that accompanied a lack of electricity. I was too familiar with that animal look of panic in their eyes. They'd been dragged into something horrific and deadly, and they wanted so desperately to live, they would do anything. But there were no Seeds to make them stronger. They had no way to fight back against the forces that had taken their lives and destroyed the world they once knew. I tried to ignore them at first, but finally the tension gathering in my shoulders was too much. I stopped, and turned to the growing crowd. I raised a hand for silence, and after a few seconds of increased excitement, they gave it.

"We are here to negotiate a ceasefire with the Estreyans," I called out. "I don't expect the barrier to be lowered right away, but we do have a cure for all those who have been bitten, or otherwise infected with the new meningolycanosis virus affecting many of your neighbors. After the end of this war has been finalized, you will receive treatment. I do not anticipate any violence between us and the Estreyans. Please, go home, and await treatment and supplies."

I continued driving, and once they realized I was finished talking, they exploded into sound. They shouted pleas or accusations and screamed questions. Perhaps I should have stayed silent in the first place, because my words hadn't done any good. The people on the other side kept following, scrambling to keep up with the slow roll of my bike.

It turned out there was no need for me to draw any extra attention, as we encountered an Estreyan ship patrolling the inside of the barrier after a little while longer.

The crowd members screamed and scattered, elbowing each other and running over those who had fallen in their haste to get away.

The ship turned toward my group, ignoring the escaping civilians.

I bowed, imitating one of the greetings Torliam had shown me back on Estreyer. Zed handed me the modified megaphone Adam had created, and I raised it to my lips. The crystal symbol of Voice came to life at my throat, lending my words power. "Greetings. I am Eve-Redding, and I wish to be taken to your leader. We have found the cure to the Sickness."

The ship floated there, its crustacean-like wings and tail lazily moving through the air. I couldn't see through any of the windows, but I was sure the people within were staring out at us. The ship sank nearer the ground, and a hole opened up in the side, spilling out five Estreyans.

A woman with bright copper hair led the others, stopping on the other side of the barrier, directly in front of me. "Please display the three gifts and the mark of Testimony," she said. When I showed her the Oracle's last gift, still unsolved, her eyes narrowed. "You have found the cure, you say, though the third gift does not yet crown your brow? Though you have escaped to Earth and abandoned your duties for the sake of the Earthlings, and have even allied with the enemy against us?" Her tone was cold and accusing. "Do you think to deceive us with talk once again, while the allies of the Sickness gather in secret to ambush us?"

"Are they all so idiotic?" Gregor muttered spitefully to himself.

I suppressed the urge to groan aloud. "You have been deceived, but not by me. The path to the Champion was always through Earth, but indeed, he was not *on* Earth. We have not shirked our duties, and we have not allied against you, merely protected ourselves when your fellow warriors attempted to use force as a means to hinder our quest for the cure. The attack by NIX was not of our doing."

She continued to glare.

I sighed. "I can prove the truth of my words. If I am lying, you will know it immediately, as I would not be able to cure the Sickness. I am not lying. I can check you and all your warriors, and if any of you have been infected, whether the signs have become apparent yet or not, I can cure you."

Her glare faltered, then. "In return for healing, what do you wish?"

"Take me to the leader of the invasion's forces. There is much to do, to stop the spread of the Sickness and end this foolish war."

She hesitated for a moment longer, but the lure of healing for the Sickness, which might be festering inside any of them, unknown, proved too much temptation. With a nod from her, the remaining four Estreyans stepped forward and placed what looked like stones against the barrier at precise points. The barrier shimmered, and a hole opened up between the stones.

"Come through, if it pleases you, Godkiller," the woman said.

I did, and my teammates followed, walking beside our bikes.

"I must see the method of this cure, before you are given access to our ship, Eve-Redding. I mean no disrespect, but I cannot go against my orders without *significant* justification."

"That's fine. Who do you want me to examine first?"

She gestured to one of the warriors. "Jarrel has been exhibiting some...erratic behaviors. I have hoped it was only the results of battle-stress, but in my heart, I worried."

The others stepped away from him, and the man she'd pointed to moved forward hesitantly. He bowed. It was the bow of deep respect that Torliam had shown me and told me that I should probably never use unless I was meeting a god, because it would undermine my supposedly high social status.

"I must draw your blood," I said. "Give me your hand."

He hurriedly stripped off his armored glove and knelt on one knee as he held his palm up to me.

I drew the lance from the sparkling band woven around my left forearm, and solemnly pierced his skin with it. With the first drop of blood, that familiar light rushed into my mind. "The Sickness is within you," I said.

He shuddered looking up at me with quiet desperation. "Even so, you can heal me?"

I smiled, hoping I looked benevolent and powerful. "Do not fear." I closed my eyes and fed power through the lance, letting it re-write his damaged sections, till the language of his body was a continuous whole. "It is done."

He took a deep breath, his cheeks flushed and eyes wide. "I can feel it. I am cured! The day of prophecy has come!"

His fellow warriors hesitated for only a second, before pressing forward around him and talking over each other. "Eve-Redding, please examine me as well, I beg you!" "I am worthiest of your benevolence, Godkiller." "I also fear the Sickness dwells in me. I will grant you any boon you wish, if you will but heal me."

Their leader snapped at them to show honor and stand back, and they complied reluctantly, staring at me like starving dogs in front of a steak they weren't allowed to eat. Then, she gave me the same deep bow of ultimate respect. "I am the captain of this humble ship," the woman said, straightening and meeting my eyes. "My name is Milan, of the line of Drethel."

I bowed in return, less deeply than she had done to me. "Well met."

"You and your companions wish to be taken to Commander Levier? He is the commander of this city's destroyer, as well as the war force here on Earth. He reports directly to Queen Mardinest."

We'd gotten lucky, then. I wasn't going to complain, as it didn't happen often enough, as far as I was concerned. "Yes, take us to him."

THERE WAS silence as they escorted us onto the ship, which was much larger than the scout ship, *Lady Ladriel*, that Torliam had once owned, but many times smaller than the gargantuan destroyers. Then, one of the Estreyans, who had been eyeing us silently the whole time, burst out, "Have you really discovered the cure to the Sickness? Did you find the Champion? Is he returning?"

Captain Milan turned to him with a severe frown, but I smiled, and she didn't reprimand him.

I spoke loudly, letting my words travel to those looking on with curiosity. "We have indeed discovered the cure. We also found the god. He has been in a hidden realm, using his strength to slow the spread of the Sickness. He remained there to continue his part of the fight." I remembered the crumbling sky, and hoped my words were true. "But he imparted on us, on the Seal of Nine, the means to cure the Sickness before sending us back from his realm."

One of the others muttered, "Is this really happening? I must make an offering of thanks to the gods."

We came into a larger room where more Estreyans waited, fully armed.

"Stand down," the captain said. "It is truly Eve-Redding, and it seems she has succeeded in her quest. No harm shall come to her or hers. Set a course for Commander Levier's ship. The godkiller and curer of the Sickness wishes to speak with him."

There were gasps and shared looks all around, followed by excited mutterings and deep bows.

"My father has the Sickness, we believe," a woman said. "He has displayed early symptoms only, as of yet, but has been preparing his affairs before turning himself in to be cleansed in death by fire. Can you cure him?"

"There are many people who have been hurt at no fault of their own," I said. "Not only your fellow Estreyans, but the people of Earth as well. I have many, many people in need of healing. But," I paused, looking around the room. "All those who come to me for healing will receive it, as long as I have strength." Voice pulsed subtly in the air, and the Estreyans shivered. The Sickness was so hated that protection against it would earn me a good amount of loyalty, even if these warriors were supposed to be sworn to the queen. "I will examine any aboard this ship who wish it for signs of infection. Even if the symptoms have not yet begun to show, I can eradicate it from any of you that it has hidden within."

Jarrel confirmed my words and my ability with exuberance, and the rest fairly fell over each other offering me and my teammates seats, and then argued over who would be checked first. Under the captain's strict orders, they formed a line, every Estreyan on the ship waiting for my attention, including herself.

My teammates ate the warrior's food while I worked.

The Estreyans knelt before me, one by one, a hand outstretched to be pricked. The lance showed me their design and came away clean of blood every time. Most of them were healthy. But I found a few that had the Sickness, in varying degrees of progression. Those who had it, I told. And then I healed them.

By the time the ship stopped its leisurely flight toward the middle of the city, I had finished with the ship's crew. Some of them had cried, or were crying. Some had sworn their eternal allegiance to me, or offered me a payment of whatever valuable thing they owned. One had even tried to get me to agree to take his child as a ward, to grow up in my household and become a loyal warrior or servant to me.

I accepted the loyalty, and turned down any other rewards, forcing myself not to turn away from the expressions of gratitude. It wasn't right, that these people should ever have been so desperate as to react like this in the face of hope. Estreyans were supposed to be strong and proud. I had wanted their loyalty and admiration. I had wanted to bind the people to me, so that they would give me power by the force of their belief. But watching as a grown man sobbed, falling to his knees as he thanked me over and over... It made me feel like a horrible fraud.

The destroyer opened up a port in its side, and the ship we were on slipped into it, settling down on a floor made of rippling alien material.

"I will take you to Commander Levier now," the captain said. "And I thank you, Eve-Redding. If you need aid, you may call on me. On any of us."

"I may need your help shortly," I said, smiling ever so slightly. "I'm planning to stop the attack on the Earthlings and supersede Queen Mardinest's power. If she is not cooperative, I will remove her from her throne. Is that going to be a problem?"

"Queen Mardinest?" Milan said, frowning. "Is she not your ally as well?"

"I thought she was, too. But I was a threat to her power. She aimed to...*remove* that threat, disregarding our search for the Champion."

Milan's mouth tightened. "I see," she said, the words pregnant with meaning. "No, it will not be a problem. I know where the loyalty of my people should lie."

Torliam turned to me, his eyes heavy with the significance of the captain's words. Estreyans valued their honor. They did not take the decision to commit treason lightly.

Chapter 34

A man may die, nations may rise and fall, but an idea lives on.
  — John F. Kennedy

THE DESTROYER SEEMED EVEN BIGGER on the inside than it did from outside. Captain Milan escorted us through the massive structure that had been carved out of a still semi-sentient alien creature.

Guards stopped us along the way, some of them seeming hopeful and awed when they saw me, others demanding proof of my identity or shooting me angry scowls.

"I know Queen Mardinest must have sent some communication to your forces about me," I murmured to Milan. "Whatever it was caused the last squad I tried to talk with to attack and attempt to capture me and my team."

"We were given false information, it must be," the captain said, her voice hesitant, eyes searching my expression as if she were afraid of my anger. "She said that you were eschewing your duties to Estreyer, abandoning your search for the Champion in order to save your people's lives. We were commanded to capture and return you to Estreyer."

I snorted. "We were forced to escape Queen Mardinest partly so that she did not have us murdered in our sleep, but also because she refused to let us continue our search for a cure, especially if that search led us to Earth. Do you anticipate this causing dissension between me and your commander? I do not wish to find myself attacked and imprisoned before being able to speak to him properly and explain what has happened."

"I do not believe so. If anything were to happen, I will fight by your side." She nodded to me, then to my teammates.

"Let us start the conversation with the cure," Torliam said. "That should forestall any hasty actions on his part."

"If they don't listen, I'll open the Veil," Zed said.

The captain swallowed and paled, giving him a sideways glance. "Let it not come to that. We will kill them with blade and bow if we must. Commander Levier is stubborn, but he is an honorable warrior, and deserves a clean death."

Zed frowned. "Okay…?" He looked to Torliam in question.

"There are stories of the other side of the Veil. Souls are said to be trapped there forever, tortured without the ability to die. Stories talk of ghosts, evil things coming through from it, and various tales for the purpose of frightening the listener. This has no correlation to your Skill, I believe."

The captain shook her head dubiously. "Nevertheless, I implore you, do not send him to his death through the Veil."

Warriors from the destroyer soon formed themselves into a moving barrier of suspicion around us, and our now much larger group entered the command room quite dramatically.

The commander looked me over carefully, then his eyes flicked to his captain, standing beside me.

"Commander Levier, I bring you Eve-Redding, of the line of Matrix, the destroyer of the Sickness." The captain bowed, flourishing an arm out toward me.

The man sneered, and did not bow in return. "Has Eve-Redding fooled even you, Captain Milan?" He turned to me. "Or perhaps you have realized your duty and wish to surrender now? Have your Earthling allies turned against you, so that you need our protection once more?"

Beside me, Captain Milan stiffened, and her hand went to the sword at her waist. "Eve-Redding has found the Champion, and is now able to cure the Sickness. I have seen it with my own eyes. Things are not as you believe them to be, Commander."

Around us, people started to murmur, some with disbelief, others with hope.

"Well met, Commander Levier," I said. "I come to negotiate the end to this unnecessary war and the wanton destruction and death it has brought with it. We have succeeded in finding the Champion, and he has bestowed upon us the knowledge and the means to cure the Sickness."

"These words are convenient. You wish us to fall back in the war against the Earthlings, now that it is clear for all to see that they cannot stand against us? Many have claimed to know of the cure before."

Milan announced loudly, "It is true. Eve-Redding examined each of my crew, including myself, for the Sickness. She found four infected!" She paused for a second, waiting for that to sink in. "She has cured them all!"

Levier sighed gustily and raised his hands again, motioning sharply to his own crew, who were growing louder. "Peace," he ordered. "Let us talk," he said, turning to me. "Though my doubts are many, I will be the first to rejoice if you prove them wrong."

We moved to a private room and sat around a table, me with Milan and my teammates, and Levier with warriors of his own.

"Queen Mardinest has ordered your return to Estreyer, and I have seen the evidence of your collusion with the Earthlings myself. Good warriors have died, because of you," he said.

I explained again what had happened, and my innocence in NIX's surprise attack. I wanted to ask why they were so indignant about being attacked while they were holding an entire city hostage, but managed to refrain from doing so. People liked to imagine themselves the hero, and accusing them wouldn't gain me loyal allies with any ease. "Queen Mardinest does not believe that a cure even exists. We were to stay close to her, waiting for one of her people to slit our throats in our sleep if we went against her. We were to act as a sort of... figurehead, a mascot to secure her rule. This war is only another tool to that end, and it has cost the lives of millions, *millions*, of innocents."

The commander listened, occasionally interjecting a question, his expression intent, but his reaction to my words mostly unreadable. His warriors, on the other hand, were not so stoic. I could see their expressions changing as I spoke, doubt and fear and hope mingling in a strange cocktail of emotion.

"The humans knew of the Estreyans' existence, and they were preparing for war. But they did not plan to attack preemptively. They thought they would be invaded, as they have been, and dabbled in powers they did not understand in the hope that they might be strong enough to protect themselves," I said. "They were not purposefully cultivating the Sickness, rather a virus that can disguise itself or fight back against the power of the Seeds. The Sickness is insidious, and had hidden, riding along with that virus and lying dormant in the humans till it could spread."

"Still, whatever their intent, the results of their actions are clear to see. They cannot be blind to that, and their evil natures are obvious to me as well," Levier said.

I nodded. "It was incredibly *stupid*. It was also deplorable, to experiment with such things on children of their own kind. I myself was captured by them, forced to grow stronger or die. It is ironic, is it not, that if not for them, I would have never found the Champion, and the cure would still be lost to both worlds?"

The commander clenched his jaw, almost glaring at me. "I have yet to see proof of this cure." He held up a hand, stopping Milan from speaking. "Captain Milan is no liar, but she may have been deceived. I will require a demonstration before my own eyes."

I smiled. "I am happy to provide healing to every one of your warriors. I have no need to hide or deceive. However, once the truth is clear, I will accept no more disloyalty and dissension. I was innocent, brought into all this against my will, just as the people of this city have had nothing to do with NIX, the ones behind this. Yet, they now struggle with a virus which carries the Sickness and spreads among them. They are being killed like bugs in a trap." I leaned forward, clawed fingers straining against the table before us. "I will not stand for this to continue. I will have peace, and cooperation between both halves of my bloodline. In return, there will be healing for both worlds." I let Voice give gravitas to my words. "The Sickness must be stopped on all fronts. It is the enemy of all that lives, and I will not allow fighting amongst us mortals while it still stretches a single tendril of insidious death on either world."

The table vibrated subtly under my hands with the force of my words, the compulsion of my will acting to bend the world to my delight.

Commander Levier let out a shaky breath. "If you have truly fulfilled the prophecy, I will do as you bid, Godkiller."

AS I PROMISED, I checked every person on the ship, healing those who needed it. Even though I ate enough for three large meals over the course of twice as many hours, by the time I finished healing the lance had drained so much power from me that my legs trembled with the effort of supporting my weight. I had a throbbing headache to accompany my weakness, and was barely managing to hold back my irritability. However, seeing as the world was falling apart, I didn't have time to relax and take a break before moving on to the next diplomatic mission.

The Estreyans had apparently been inspired by NIX's use of the Shortcut to access Trials and their world, and had brought their own Shortcut to allow the military to maintain communication with Queen Mardinest instead of using an array. They wouldn't be reporting to her anymore, not until I'd had a chance to use the Shortcut myself. The thought of her face when she saw me again almost made up for my fatigue. Still, I had other tasks to complete, first.

After giving my commands for the immediate halt of all hostile action and for the rest of the invasion's forces—those not guarding the array they'd come through in Antarctica, that is—to assemble above our current city, I went out to meet the human military.

They had stationed an advance force about thirty miles to the west of the city, no doubt planning their doomed rescue mission in the hope that somehow they could get past the barrier. And who knows, maybe if one of NIX's Players had the right Skill, they could. I'd bet Queen Mardinest's warrior Ichi would be able to circumvent the quarantine bubble. How rare were Skills like that?

I was shaken out of that line of thought when a distinctive flicker appeared on the road in front of us.

A Player ran to meet us, growing a hedge of brambles behind him, so thick we couldn't even see through it. The thorny growth extended across the road and quickly stretched hundreds of meters in each direction.

I lifted a hand to signal my team members and the Estreyans running alongside our bikes to stop.

In the couple seconds the Player bought, a handful of others arrived to back him up, and the military camp behind him began to scramble. "*You* again," the Player said, and in his mouth, the words were a curse. "I won't let you sabotage the resistance any more. If you want to get past me, you'll have to kill me like you did Kilburn and Ridley."

I held back a grimace. "I won't pretend I'm sorry about what happened to Kilburn, but it really was an accident. I understand that you might hold some animosity toward me, but I've just negotiated a ceasefire with the Estreyans. Seeing as the fate of the world is at stake, I really think your bosses are going to want to talk to me."

Commander Levier had come with us to join in the inevitable negotiations with the Earth Defense Force. He moved to my side, glaring at the Player as if he hadn't been just as hostile only a few hours before. "Eve-Redding, there is no need for you to bow to the desires of an Earthling. Give the word, and your escort will open the way for you."

The Player's scowl only grew more intense, but I waved off Levier's offer. "I don't mind waiting. I'm sure it won't be long."

Sure enough, after a few minutes of communication via Windows, the Player scowled even more angrily, if that was possible, and created a hole in his hedge so we could pass. He and the other Players closed in around our group as we moved, glares and weapons trained on us unblinkingly.

To my surprise, he didn't lead us to a hastily erected military tent, but a small underground bunker. It wouldn't stand up against a destroyer's attack, but it was obvious the military had built it for exactly the purpose of preparing for action in the nearby city.

The Player led us to a room covered in wall-mounted screens and stiffly introduced us to a sharply dressed but haggard-looking General Price. He then stepped aside, but didn't leave.

General Price looked up from the screen in front of him, glaring at me with a look that seemed less about personal feelings and more about the hassle I represented. "Eve Redding. They tell me you've negotiated a ceasefire with the aliens." His eyes flicked to Commander Levier, who stood just a little behind me.

"Yes," I said. "We're here to discuss Earth's peaceful surrender, and the interspecies relief efforts going forward."

GENERAL PRICE WASN'T HAPPY, but he also wasn't stupid. Within an hour, the leaders of the EDF, which consisted of several people from NIX and their foreign counterparts, as well as the political and military leaders of almost all of Earth's other countries, had been contacted.

Within another couple hours, a mass teleconference had been arranged. More screens had been brought in, till the walls were almost entirely covered with devices meant to display the people watching and listening to me.

Commander Levier, Torliam, and Adam stayed in the room with me, along with General Price and a couple of his men. The rest of my team and the Estreyan guard Levier had assigned me stayed outside, guarding the bunker or resting, because there simply wasn't enough space for all of them inside. My other team members preferred not to spend hours trapped in a hostile political meeting, anyway.

I stood in the center of the room and spoke, turning occasionally so I got a chance to see everyone's reaction, since Wraith wasn't very good at deciphering screen displays. I gave a brief explanation of the actions and decisions leading up to the war, for those who were either unfamiliar or self-deluding. "The only thing standing between Earth and continued decimation is me and my team," I said. "It's in everyone's best interest if we can set aside grudges and work together. If Earth will accept peace and cooperation, we can provide help combating the spread of the meningolycanosis, as well as healing for the additional plague that has been using that virus as an infection vector. Hopefully, we'll be able to prevent the advance of a global pandemic." I looked pointedly to one of the screens, which displayed a man labeled as NIX's director.

"Now see here, you traitorous scag!" Another man snapped, slamming chubby hands on the table in front of him, as if he could intimidate me physically through the camera. "If you think you can threaten us with this, think again! Earth is a noble and proud planet, and we won't be downtrodden by anyone who uses unprovoked attacks and blackmail as negotiation tactics. Humans won't be bowing down and serving the whims of these…Estreyan bigots. We'll have fair terms for any ceasefire, or we'll keep fighting till the last man!"

I resisted the urge to roll my eyes. Was the man being deliberately obtuse? I wondered if it would be easier just to have someone track him down and kill him. Could we replace him with someone less consumed with their own importance? Even if the politician had gone into hiding, Torliam's Tracker Skill would surely be able to find him. I considered saying as much to the man's face, but held back. Without my own physical presence and the pressure Charisma could bring to bear, any threat wouldn't be as effective. Plus, if all the others realized how little regard I had for them, it would undermine their trust in the negotiation process and make everything harder.

Instead, I scraped my claws gently on the armor by my side, the motion drawing eyes. "I think you've misunderstood. What we're willing to offer is already extremely generous. Resources and relief efforts for those left destitute by the war, the type of healing you've never seen before in your life, and the possibility of collaboration with a society so technologically advanced the things they can do seem like magic."

I turned to Commander Levier beside me, who was either unable or unwilling to hold back his sneer of disgust toward the humans. "Or, we could destroy any ability for Earth to access or contact Estreyer again, and leave. Estreyer is in need of my team's services quite desperately, in fact. I'm sure they would rejoice if I returned to them immediately and didn't bother with mitigating the devastation here. Truthfully, I can't think of *anything* Earth has to offer worth the resources they'd be expending if these negotiations go as I had hoped. Really, the only reason we're even having this meeting is that I'm part human, and sentimental."

Levier nodded. "Indeed. I believe many of my people will be

desperate to convince you of such. Perhaps, if you wanted to ensure the survival of your race and save a number of innocents, we could allow them to immigrate to Estreyer. They would be treated fairly, with your name to shield them."

That caused a lot of grim stares, uncomfortable shifting, and a bit of distraction as people talked with their aids and considered my not-so-subtle threat.

"We are absolutely interested in cooperation," a woman said, throwing a glare toward a screen of her own, which I assumed displayed the tactless politician who'd irritated me.

Someone else spoke up. "I agree. However, we can't ignore the fact that millions of lives have been lost during the course of this attack, and billions more put in imminent danger. While I understand this is an unfortunate but unavoidable result of global war, I do have concerns about the populace's willingness to set aside grudges and cooperate with those they've come to detest. Truthfully, I worry about not only the civilians, but also those who might be in charge of these cooperative efforts between our two worlds. Perhaps a gesture of goodwill would be appropriate, as a sort of…apology?"

I stared at the man.

Adam scoffed. "Just say it outright. You want a bribe, a payoff, some blood money to grease the wheels a little bit?"

"A bribe? Certainly not! I meant an allocation of resources, perhaps technology, to show what benefit you might bring to offset the damage you've done, and mitigate hostility. I'm sure it would make all this easier if we didn't feel like we were being threatened into cooperation, but rather brought into a beneficial partnership. You may speak about your capabilities all day, but hard proof would be much more likely to sway the people in this meeting, I have no doubt."

Levier turned to me. "They wish us to come begging to them, bearing gifts…for the purpose of convincing them the worth of our further gifts?" He turned a hard stare back into the cameras. "Perhaps you should come bearing gifts, to convince us to have mercy on your worthless race."

The meeting didn't get any easier from there. Eventually, all the major countries agreed to the peace and varying levels of interplanetary cooperation, but along the way we had to deal with more requests for reparations and access to Estreyan military technology, supposedly to ensure an attack like this one wouldn't happen again. Not all the people included in the teleconference were idiots. In fact, most of them weren't, but those that were seemed to speak loudest and demand the most attention. If the Estreyans, and thus myself, hadn't been holding nearly all the cards, it probably would have been even worse.

Even so, when I demanded that the leaders of NIX and their counterparts in the other countries revealed their actions to the public, as well as the names of those who condoned and aided them, the meeting devolved again into anger, threats, and outright denials.

"Perhaps the results of allowing so much power without any oversight will be the catalyst for change in how our society is run. There's a saying, you know. Don't do anything you'd be afraid to have reported in the news the next day."

My words were no comfort, and in fact seemed to only stir the cauldron further. But by that time, I'd run through my very last drop of patience. "That's non-negotiable. For those of you who decide to refuse, I'm still not decided if it would be better to kill you, or just expose the truth on your behalf."

NIX's leader hadn't spoken very often during the meeting. Now, he leaned forward. "A threat like that might convince people to just remove its danger altogether and take our chances with the war we're already fighting. If you try to destroy the public's trust in its leaders, it will destabilize our society and send us into ruin just the same."

Commander Levier and Torliam both stepped forward, placing themselves deliberately and protectively in front of me.

Adam glared, muttering something about hacking into his accounts and ruining his life.

I indulged myself in a wolf-like grin, showing too many teeth. "The problem with that thought is, it's entirely impossible for you to kill me. I can travel through alternate dimensions." That was stretching the truth so far away from Zed's real ability to let the team travel through the Other Place that it was a blatant lie. Still, it sounded impressive. "You could bomb this place till the rubble escaped the atmosphere and I could still walk away and find you."

Torliam glared at the white-haired man on the other side of the screen. "You also seem to be confused about your people's strength.

Eve Redding is beloved by my people. If it were known that you even *spoke* such a threat to her wellbeing, there would be no one to restrain us. You would force us to take your threat *seriously*. Your world struggles to stand against our warriors now. You will be crushed like bugs under a force a thousand times stronger, when every warrior able to slay a monster finds a balm for his outrage in the blood of your people. You know not the power of the dragon you poke."

I kept scraping my claws against the armor at my sides, my bones almost *itching* with the desire to be anywhere else. I really was not cut out for politics.

I DIDN'T WANT to meet Queen Mardinest with any trace of weakness, so I forced myself to sleep a few hours before gathering before the Estreyans' Shortcut with the rest of my team and the delegation. Besides us, Commander Levier and a squad of Estreyan guards were coming, along with a small group of the less abrasive humans I'd spoken to during the negotiations. They'd been rushed to the city on high-speed personal flights from all over the world.

While we gathered in front of the metal sphere surrounded by orbiting rings, one of the escorting Players glared toward us, not bothering to disguise the loathing in her eyes when she saw me. She looked familiar, but I couldn't place her at first, until I noticed her nose, which resembled Commander Petralka's. She was the girl I'd fought with the second time we attacked NIX, when I'd broken the Shortcut and then been manipulated into joining their organization.

Torliam leaned in a little to murmur near my ear. "If you wish, we might demand they replace the girl with someone more respectful."

I shrugged. "It doesn't really matter. She's only coming along as decoration. It's not like she'd be able to do much if Queen Mardinest set Ichi on her, for example."

"Her insolence could undermine your authority."

I let one corner of my mouth curl upward. "I don't think much could undermine my authority, when I have the cure."

That was evidenced by the scurrying eagerness and sideways looks from the ship's crew when they thought I wouldn't notice. My team's armor had been cleaned and polished while we waited, and we looked impressively imposing.

Commander Levier's eye caught on a warrior in the corner, who held a drink and a platter of snacks, literally ready and waiting to rush over if I indicated hunger or thirst. He sighed, rubbing his eyes. "That is true, Godkiller. If you gave the word, I suspect half my warriors would abandon their service and follow after you."

Gregor reached up and grabbed my hand. He snorted, looking around. "Only half? I'd say at least eighty percent of them feel some sort of sycophantic hero-worship toward you."

Kris frowned at him. "Gregor! Stop being rude," she murmured.

Birch seemed to feel that the whole situation was quite normal, but also was apparently under the impression that *he* was the most important person in the room and all the fuss was on his account. He pranced over to the crew member with the platter of food and made a demanding noise.

The Estreyan didn't even hesitate, kneeling to the ground and placing the platter in front of the growing winged cat.

Jacky reached out futilely, as if to stop him, but Birch had already started snapping the snacks up. She lowered her arm belatedly. "There's cheese. He's going to be farting later."

Adam glared at her. "Don't complain. You're not the one who he always tries to gas in the face!"

One of the human politicians looked between my group and Birch. "Is it—" she cleared her throat. "Is that your pet, Ms. Redding?"

"No. He's one of the team." I raised an eyebrow. "He might look like an animal, but that's just because he's an alien. Birch is sentient, telepathic, and understands both English and Estreyan."

"Oh," her eyes widened, and she stared at him with barely restrained curiosity. "Do you think he'd communicate with me?"

I shrugged. "If you ask nicely, maybe."

She looked around, then sidled over to the creature, with the Player scowling and following close behind her.

Birch was disinterested and even distrustful at first, but she cajoled him with effusive praise till he deigned to touch his nose to her hand and communicate directly into her mind.

This delighted the woman, but put her guard even more on edge.

Birch bared his teeth at the Player and swirled a warning gust of air around them.

The woman found this even more thrilling, and then turned to scold her escort for the girl's lack of diplomacy, before coaxing Birch to come back to the main group and introduce himself to the other foreign dignitaries and politicians. At first, they were wary, but, after the first couple people exclaimed in delight when Birch did a trick with one of his Skills or showed obvious intelligence, most of them warmed to the creature.

I frowned. "They love him. I should have just let him deal with the peace negotiations! We could have gathered them all in a room and let them pet him, and it would have been over in an hour."

Zed grinned widely, bouncing on his toes. "We should get him a little badge! It can say, 'Diplomatic Envoy,' or something, and we'll send him out to all the official events and meetings so we don't have to go."

Gregor sneered at Zed. "Idiot. How's he supposed to wear a badge? Obviously, it should be a collar or a harness."

Zed squinted down at the boy doubtfully. "Why don't we just ask Birch what he'd prefer?"

They devolved into childish bickering, and I grinned, a little of the tension I'd been feeling released.

The crew finished coding all of us into the Shortcut, and the orbiting bands swung faster. With that familiar vibration through my bones, we returned to Estreyer once again.

Chapter 35

And this too will be swept away.
— Marcus Aurelius

APPARENTLY, the Shortcut technology needed to connect to a "place of power," which is why they were usually used to transport people to Trials, where the gods' power acted as the necessary anchor, regardless of distance. However, a group of the most talented arcane technologists was able to create anchors at different places of power, like the huge caverns beneath the city where Torliam had once broken the blood-covenants NIX forced on him.

That was where we appeared.

The humans didn't fare very well with the sudden disorientation and nausea, and, even after they'd recovered from that, they struggled under the increased gravity on Estreyer. Still, they were awed at the glowing crystals, the symbol-carved circle under our feet, and the gigantic stalactites and stalagmites jutting out and throwing dramatic shadows everywhere.

Even Estreyan signals had trouble reaching so far beneath the Earth, but we were still able to use one of their datapads to access the information network. Specifically, we searched for news of Blaine.

It had been reported as the assassination it was, which surprised me. However, apparently someone had run with our "allies of the

Sickness" scheme and blamed this shadowy group for his death. Queen Mardinest had supposedly been investigating it, but had found no leads.

With the escort of Estreyan warriors and Players, our group moved out of the circle and toward the bowels of the castle. We startled some servants as we traveled higher, and Commander Levier sent them scurrying for some of his fellow royal warriors who would have more insight into what was going on in the palace.

Either Queen Mardinest had some way of knowing the Shortcut had been used or one of the people we encountered informed her, because she met us just as we reached the ground floor.

Her eyes widened as they tracked over me, my team, and the other smaller people who were also obviously humans. She eyed her own warriors. She hadn't been contacted in many Estreyan days by that point, which had probably alarmed her. Even so, she glared and looked down her nose at us. "Was she captured, or has she surrendered?" she asked, looking at me though she was obviously talking to Commander Levier.

Before he could answer, I spoke. "Neither. I return triumphant."

Her eyes widened, then narrowed again. "Let us go to my war room. We may speak freely there." Her gaze lingered on Torliam, who stood just behind me, and then she turned and strode off down the hallway. She had guts, I had to admit.

Gregor glared at her back, then looked up at me. "Are you going to kill her? She had Blaine killed, right?"

"I think she probably did. We'll have to do some investigating to find out for sure, in case I'm wrong. If she's responsible, I'll make sure justice is meted out."

Gregor frowned harder, not satisfied with my words, but he didn't say anything more.

I didn't like it either, but I could work with a blackmailer who really disliked me, since I didn't have the resources to easily replace her. I couldn't work with a murderer, but I also wouldn't have Torliam's mother executed without proof, no matter how strained their relationship was. "Will you be okay, going to the spot where it happened?" I asked. I was sending the rest of the team, besides Torliam, to the array where Blaine had been murdered, so Kris could check for a spirit and they could get some sort of closure, or something. I wanted to go, too, but the time crunch was too great. Someone died of the Sickness pretty much every minute. I had to stay and talk to Queen Mardinest.

He scoffed and looked away. "Of course I'm going to be okay. I'm more worried about *you* getting assassinated if you stay here by yourself."

I ruffled his hair, grinning when he jerked away and scowled at me. "I've got Torliam, and a whole squad of Estreyan guards are staying with me. I'll be fine."

He didn't seem convinced, but turned to leave with the rest of the group.

Zed gave me a pointed look back over his shoulder. "Be careful, Eve."

I only nodded.

Escorted by a group of guards who took their jobs so seriously it was almost comical, Torliam and I followed the queen to her war room, the same one I'd met her in to negotiate when we first arrived at the capital. The human diplomats were shown to a nearby chamber to wait.

Mardinest stood at the head of the table, her hands on the back of the chair placed there. She watched my guards, as they spread throughout the room looking for hidden enemies, then stationed themselves in every corner and by the door. "Have you deceived even my warriors, then?"

I almost felt bad for the vindictive glee I felt, except I was too full of said glee to *actually* feel bad. "No. You were wrong. Your son had not been acting as a fool all this time, I am no more a charlatan than you, and your people have chosen to serve me based on *proof.* We have found the God of Shaping and Molding, and discovered the cure to the Sickness." I stayed silent to let my words sink in.

"Proof?" she echoed, her voice faint.

Torliam laid his hand on my shoulder. "Eve has examined hundreds and cured over a dozen people now, including the ones you knew of. It does not matter what stage the disease is in, or if symptoms have shown themselves. If someone has been infected, she can cleanse them."

Seemingly anyone with Seeds could do the same, with the help of the lance, but we were trying not to advertise its purpose. Plus, it was more satisfying to see her expression, this way.

"Have you come to dethrone me, then? To execute me for heresy?" Her words were more demand than the fearful plea I'd been secretly hoping for.

I sighed. "Perhaps not. I require the Estreyan people to make some rapid changes and shifts in resource allocation, to help mitigate the damage that has been done on Earth, as well as prepare society for the reality of a cure and the process of slowly spreading that healing throughout the populace. It is not so simple as a shot or elixir I can distribute en masse. You may not have believed, but from your words when you threatened us, I gathered your desire to safeguard Estreyer is genuine. If I am right, and you truly have the best interest of the people at heart, and not simply your own pride, you will agree to serve me. What could be more important than the eradication of the Sickness? Dethroning you would only make my job more difficult. We would have to find a replacement and deal with possible power struggles from the other powerful families."

Her hands fisted at her sides. "My duty has always lain with the people. I have honor. Even were you to tell me I must be flayed alive in the streets and whored out to animals, if this would mean the Sickness would cease to exist, I would agree a thousand times." She stared at me defiantly.

I let the silence stretch for several long moments, then I moved to stand in front of her and took her hand in my own. She did not flinch as I pricked her with the lance. "You are free of the Sickness," I said simply.

She swallowed a couple times, then pulled her hand back and watched as the small incision I'd made healed under the power of her Resilience. She bowed deeply. "I will serve you loyally in all matters, Eve-Redding, godkiller, life-bringer." More titles, huh.

I was skeptical.

Torliam nodded with satisfaction, and then we got down to the important business of planning out the immediate changes and Queen Mardinest's efforts to organize the people on my behalf.

Once all the high-level planning was finished, Torliam and I moved to leave, followed by my guards.

"Eve-Redding," she called out.

I stopped and turned to face her again, one eyebrow raised.

"I have searched for the murderer of your human follower, but have not found them. If you have more information about these 'allies of the Sickness' who were endangering you, it might prove useful. I have some suspicions, but I can find no proof."

My face settled into an expressionless mask. "And where is Ichi, then?"

She paled. "It was not I who ordered your human follower's death. It is true, Ichi has disappeared, but he was a warrior of loyalty and honor. He would not have done this without my approval."

"I don't believe you. But don't worry, I won't kill you without making sure you're guilty." I left without looking back again. I already had people assigned to watch her and the goings on in the palace, to make sure she was doing her part in the necessary preparations. Plus, I couldn't be confident she wouldn't try to move against me or blackmail us again. If she tried to cover up her involvement in Blaine's death after this, that would be the quickest way to implicate herself. If it really wasn't her, then we probably had a bigger problem. Who else would have wanted us dead?

THREE DAYS LATER ON ESTREYER, while not even a complete day had passed on Earth, I stepped into the center of the city's coliseum, followed by my team and guards. Despite the short period of forewarning, the surrounding stands were packed. It seemed as if every man, woman, and child in the city, as well as a few intelligent creatures, had come to listen to me today. Those who were not able to find seats crowded into the walkways, and when those were full, they surrounded the outside of the coliseum where large screens had been placed to broadcast my announcement live. Those who weren't able to make it in person waited in front of public-use screens or their personal ones at home. According to Queen Mardinest, who had been somewhat pale-faced when she told me, industry had stopped for the day. No one was traveling, no one was working, and it would likely be impossible to find someone in the city who hadn't yet heard about my triumphant return.

I was the first to admit that I could be a bit prideful, slightly arrogant. But I wasn't planning a big show or a cocky speech. Really, with what I was about to do, it would be hard to find something *more* impactful. My new ability would speak for itself, and, once I provided proof of the cure, I would be leaving most of the difficult stuff to Queen Mardinest.

I walked out of a tunnel opening onto the floor of the coliseum, then up onto the performance platform. It took a while for the screams to die down. When they did, I said a couple short sentences about having found the lost god and being given the method to cure the Sickness, which were beginning to feel repetitive already.

Once again, I had to wait for the shouting and people throwing gold and flowers at me to cease. I signaled to one of my guards, and they brought out a child from the tunnel.

The girl was heavily bound and gagged, like a deranged patient from an insane asylum.

The guard removed the gag, and she screamed mindlessly, spitting out dark clots of blood and staring around with eyes that were corpse-like and obviously blind. Her veins stood out, dark against pale skin, her limbs were skeletal and covered with bite marks where she'd managed to try to eat herself, and her stomach was grotesquely distended, as if she carried a child, though I knew she didn't. The screens displayed close-ups of the blatant signs of advanced Sickness. We would have held this display earlier, but for the difficulty in finding the perfect counterpart to make my announcement even more dramatic.

This girl would have been killed by now, normally. Her parents had seen my broadcast aboard the passenger ship when my team escaped from the palace. She'd just started to show signs of the Sickness at that point. Rather than turning her in, they'd hidden her away in their basement, hoping I would succeed before their child died, despite their fear the Sickness might spread to them.

My guard held her still, and I drew the lance out of its place between my left forearm and the armband wrapped around it.

I pricked her in the neck. My eyes fluttered with the rush of information, and I was almost overwhelmed with the sum of all that was wrong in her. It was surprising she was even alive, let alone struggling against her bindings and screaming. I funneled power through the lance, letting it gush out of me as quickly as it could be channeled into her.

Under the eyes of hundreds of thousands, maybe millions of people, her skin lost its papery quality and the black veins receded. Her belly shrunk. The film of blindness melted away. When I was finished, she was a too-thin girl trembling within her restraints. But most importantly, her gaze was lucid, and everyone watching could see the emotions fly across it. Disbelief, joy, relief. She cried, and a nation rejoiced.

My guard took her away, and I turned back to the crowds. "Since a time before history was recorded, the Sickness has ruled. Now, it is time for change. The humans are devastated and struggling against the same enemy our people have battled so long. These events were set in motion due to unnecessary fear, and Earth has joined Estreyer in fearing for the continuation of their world. But now, the cure to the Sickness had been found. We are honor bound to set things right, for them as well as ourselves. I have spoken with Queen Mardinest, and we are implementing new laws and policies to facilitate rapid healing and complete eradication of the Sickness, with those most worthy and most in need being the first to receive aid. The fight before us is as arduous as any that has come before, and I must go, to fight back against our enemy's spread on the front lines. Queen Mardinest will answer further questions."

I waved, and she walked out of the tunnel, taking my place while I escaped. Healing was limited, since there was only one lance. Those who had useful abilities or influence, and volunteered their services on Earth, would receive priority healing for themselves and their families. Following them, children in the later stages of the Sickness took precedence. There would be no more killing or burning of those with the Sickness. Instead, the infected would be made comfortable and safe to themselves and others, as much as possible. We had to mitigate the spread on Earth, and, once that was complete, we would slowly chip away at the numbers under the sway of the disease. It might be a task of years.

Hopefully, Mardinest could handle the backlash, the desperation, and the inherent danger of such extreme societal upheaval. I was only glad I didn't have to be queen.

I RETURNED to Earth with the team, letting some of the diplomatic envoys from Earth remain behind to help Queen Mardinest, as well as act as a line of communication to my home planet.

Kris hadn't found anything that seemed to be an imprint of Blaine, but they'd still had a small funeral ceremony for him and came back a little morose.

We helped to set up our new base of operations, housed in a huge building that had once been some sort of medical research facility where the staff lived on-site. It was actually one of the few buildings still quite intact after the invasion and subsequent riots, and many of the employees had still been safely barricaded within, desperately trying to find a cure for the meningolycanosis. They were resentful of our taking over their building and opening the lower levels to the public. Then they met Sam and learned about what he could do, and they couldn't have been more courteous, all while salivating over the chance to experiment on him.

Everyone worked frantically to get everything set up. We had medical staff and emergency volunteers coming in from all over the world, but we still lacked enough resources to really put a dent in what the city needed. I understood that we weren't the only place in the world that needed help, but this was the place where I was close enough to actually *do* something. "We need generators and oil, and I have to have buildings cleared out and prepared for people who've lost their homes. A place to sleep should be the least we can provide," I insisted, talking into the camera of my new link.

The person displayed on its snapped-open surface shook his head. "Miss Redding, if you're able to find local volunteers to help you clean out buildings, that will be fine. But I can't promise a shipment of cots and blankets that large until next month, at least. It's not that I don't understand what you need. But I have a hundred people around the world asking for the same thing, and some of them are in places even worse off than you. I just don't have it to give. Ask for donations from the civilians."

The call cut off, and I growled aloud, throwing my head back in frustration. The ground floor of our new base was huge, with a gymnasium, cafeteria, and recreational area. People were camping out in the gymnasium and the edges of the cafeteria, but more came every day, and soon, we wouldn't have the resources to even keep them clean and well-fed. We hadn't even started bringing in large numbers of the infected yet, since we didn't have enough places to contain them.

The city was still under Estreyan quarantine, and they created openings in the bubble for any supplies or workers coming in from outside. It just…wasn't enough.

With little other option, we organized those who'd come to volunteer as well as those who had simply hoped for food and protection. We set them to clearing the nearby buildings for emergency housing and securing what resources they could, from foodstuffs to clothing to medical supplies. Basically, we looted, with guards from either of the two worlds' militaries to keep our looters protected from *other* looters and the local gangs that had quickly grown popular for the "protection" they offered.

Queen Mardinest had sent a group of Shortcut engineers to Earth, the last use of the arrays before we had them shut down again for the literal safety of the world. They'd brought a ton of precious metals and jewels, steeped in power from close proximity to a god. With a lot of skill and a little luck, they'd be able to set up an anchor point on Earth, so people from Estreyer could travel here through their own Shortcuts. The process was extensive, but I looked forward to getting some more help. I'd specifically requested healers and people who could spontaneously produce clean water. Volunteers were abundant, since everyone was desperate to have me check them for, and possibly heal them and their families of, the Sickness. In fact, Queen Mardinest had reported a lot of bribery and underhanded dealings from people attempting to bump themselves up the waiting list.

The Estreyans raided a local cattle farm and flew back a batch of terrified sheep, which Sam first used his Black Sun Skill on, then killed with his Harbinger Skill, after destroying their ability to feel pain. Thus, he got a double charge to his healing, and we got meat.

As soon as the scientists were able to create a successful counter to the meningolycanosis via Sam, we went into mass-production, not only at our facility, but anywhere around the world with the resources to do so. I had news of the inoculation blasted over every inch of the city. Volunteer military and medical forces went out, injecting those already infected and giving the serum as a vaccination to those who were not. It wouldn't stop the spread of the Sickness if one of the "wolves" were to bite a healthy person, but it would stop them from going immediately crazy and biting ten more people themselves. We implemented a policy that anyone who received the latest version of the serum had to be checked for the Sickness, as well. We enforced this by having the injectors also create a tattoo upon administration, which would be removed once they were cleared by our facility.

We brought as many people in to be inoculated and checked at the same time as possible, but we didn't want the "wolves" to continue spreading their disease out in the city, so we also dropped off boxes of the serum injectors throughout the city for people to just take, with loud warnings about follow-up treatment. Those we brought in, we checked immediately, and then sent them to Sam, or one of the few Estreyan healers who were part of the invaders' force, or even a human medic, depending on the type of injury they'd sustained in addition to the brain damage. Really, with some of the things these people had done to themselves while mindless, we were working miracles, feeding and watering them, and then putting them to work.

At first, a lot of people resisted when they found we were working with the Estreyans. Then, the first of NIX's confessional news reports came out. "While our actions were radical, they were also necessary, as shown by the alien response. As soon as the state of emergency has been lifted, I will be stepping down from my position. I hope the people of this great nation can understand my actions were for the greater good, born from the desperation to save us all from total anni-hilation."

We had to force them to adjust their confession several times before approval so that they didn't leave out the more heinous crimes, like experimenting with biological warfare on kidnapped children. We allowed them to plead the justifications of their actions as they wished. People could decide for themselves whether NIX had been in the right. And they did.

I found it somewhat depressing that the response was so divided. Some people marched on the capitol in protest, while others commended NIX and those who had aided them for doing the right thing, even if it wasn't easy. However, the first confession led to others, as well as investigation into the details of NIX's actions. Players came forward and told of their kidnapping and blackmail. Journalists speculated about how things could have gone differently, if they had been handled with diplomacy instead of warmongering. Everyone wanted a public statement from me or my team members, but we were too busy.

The lance was in use twenty-four hours a day, seven days a week. We rotated healing shifts to check as many people as possible. "Move over one station to get the tattoo removed, and then go to one of the healing stations," I said to the woman I'd just checked. "The cut on your foot is infected."

The woman nodded, tightened her too-thin shawl over her shoulders, and looked around, half-lost, before following my instructions and moving to the tattoo-removal station. She'd been brought in after one of the inoculation teams found her wandering the streets. She didn't remember anything coherent since being bitten a couple days before.

"Next!" I called, and a dazed-looking boy came forward. I offered him a cup of filtered water, which he accepted gratefully. By this point, I didn't bother talking to the people I checked any more than I had to. It wasted time I could be using to heal the next person.

Adam sat beside me on one of the folding chairs. "Your shift's almost over. You doing okay?"

I nodded, pricking the boy's hand and finding faint traces of the Sickness. I overwrote them swiftly, then directed him on to the tattoo removal station after giving him a second cup of water. He was dehydrated, but not injured. Finally, I turned to Adam. "I'm okay," I said. I had one of the longest shifts besides Torliam, because whatever power fueled the lance's healing, I either had more of it, or used it more efficiently than the other members of the team. "I'm getting better at this all the time." I called, "Next!" We were lucky. Many of the people infected with meningolycanosis didn't have the Sickness, and of those who did, it was usually in a very early stage, and easy to eradicate.

I went through the routine with the middle-aged man who sat down. Water, pinprick, no Sickness this time. I waved him on. "How many, so far?" I said, trying to keep the weariness out of my voice. I knew Adam had checked the numbers before coming over to me.

"One-hundred fifty, for you. Total of two-hundred eighty so far today."

"That's it? Next!"

"That's more than most of the rest of us can manage. And we're getting faster."

"It's still not fast enough. That's only a few thousand people, so far. We have tens of thousands to see, if not more." I waved the next person in line over to the chair in front of me. "Maybe we could shave off some time, if we changed up the way we're doing it. Line them up and go to them, instead. No water, have them prepared ahead of time by one of the medics. A few seconds add up, over the course of thousands of patients."

Adam nodded, slowly. "We should try it." He didn't say what we were both thinking, though. The lance was too slow. Healing one person at a time was an unsound prospect, logistically.

YOUR MENTAL ACUITY HAS INCREASED!

"Sam's been healing people's brain damage since before the sun rose this morning. I'm worried he'll actually end up just passing out at his station." Adam's tone was more serious than I'd have liked.

"Overwork? Do you think I should force him to take a break?"

When I waved for the next person, Adam grabbed my hand and gently pried the lance out of it. "I think you should *both* take a break." When I opened my mouth to protest, he pointed at the link on my right arm. "Your shift's already over. Go. I sent a Window to Jacky. She's on her way to start healing, and I'll fill in for a couple minutes in the meantime."

I stood, stretching weary muscles. The fatigue from fueling the lance was both mental and physical, somehow. In a way, we were lucky to have access to such effective training. Normally, I wouldn't level up so much unless I was fighting my way through a life and death situation, straining my body to its limits. On the other hand, in a way, I *was* fighting through a life and death situation. I just wasn't the one in danger.

I looked at the people in varying levels of catatonia who waited in the huge lobby for us to check them. There were more of them now than when I had woken that morning. We were falling behind.

Sam sat at one of the tables, his hands submerged in a bucket of yellowish-green goo. It writhed and bubbled strangely, almost as if it was alive. I mean, it was alive, technically, but not in the same way an animal was. It sprouted into crystal, then melted down again, the color changing to an eggy white and letting off a burnt smell.

He withdrew his hands, washed them in the rigged-up sink, then dried them on a rag. "They're seeing if I can offload injuries into bacteria and algae. It doesn't work very well, but it's something. I've been experimenting to try and find what will get me the most charge to the healing side of Harbinger. This Skill…it isn't *meant* for healing. Sure, that's what I've been using it for. But its purpose is to learn how to hurt people, and then do it *better*." He tossed the rag into the bucket of similar ones in the corner, then turned to me. The edges of his sclera flickered for a moment, darkening inward. "If I could just use Black Sun on these people, I'd be able to get the charge I need. Half of them are catatonic from the brain damage. They wouldn't even notice, and they'd be fine once I healed them."

"I understand what you mean, but I'm worried about unintended side-effects. These people…they're already desperate and depressed enough."

He let out a huff that was half-laughter, leaning his head backward and pressing the heels of his hands to his eyes. "I know. I'm just so tired I don't have the energy to…"

He was too tired to care, I finished silently. "Well. It's time for a break."

He lowered his hands. "No, I can handle it, Eve. There are almost a dozen more people waiting in line for healing."

"And one of the other healers will handle them, or one of the human medics, or—" I held up a hand to stop him from interrupting. "Or they can wait. I'm pretty sure your bedside manner would not be improved by Black Sun sucking the will to live out of your patients. You and I *both* need to rest. I just got kicked off my own station by Adam. Let's go. A little sleep, and our Seeds will have us rejuvenated enough to start chugging again."

Sam sighed. He threw a look toward the people waiting for his help, but nodded.

The Estreyan guards assigned to each of us followed as we left the healing and processing room, which was basically the whole bottom floor of the building we'd taken over. The higher levels held barracks for the medics and soldiers, the lab, administrative and organizational staff and data, quarters for people waiting for more extensive healing procedures, and quarters for my team and the Estreyans who'd remained.

I fell into my bed and was asleep seconds after my head hit the pillow.

Chapter 36

I hold within my hand
   Grains of the golden sand —
   How few! yet how they creep
   Through my fingers to the deep
  — Edgar Allan Poe

EARLY THE NEXT MORNING, I got up and decided to go out with one of the patrols to help distribute supplies and cases of the serum to the more desperate areas of the city. A single lane of the main roads had been cleared forcibly, pods and other obstructions bulldozed to the sides, so we were able to make decent progress.

Chanelle, Zed, and Gregor joined me, along with two of our Estreyan guards, who I'd noticed bragging about their job to the other warriors. We rode out in a convoy of military and transport pods.

Chanelle smiled as we bumped along, looking out the window at the dirty, litter-filled street. "This is pretty wonderful."

Zed raised his eyebrows high. "Is that what you call it?"

She kicked at Zed's leg, and he jerked away dramatically to avoid her. "I just mean…we're helping. I'm okay, I can think again. I'm healthy, and I may not have a Skill anymore, but I'm still stronger than before I became a Player. I'm actually able to *do* something now." She turned to me and waved vaguely to the city. "It may look ugly now, but we're going to help patch things up. We succeeded. It's a very good thing."

I looked out the window. "I guess it is. Things can get better." The thought settled in my mind like a warm blanket.

While we drove, the spotters looked for infected, and the civilians called out tips to help us find them or asked for help and supplies. We stopped frequently to pick up wounded, drop off cases of serum, and talk to people who had info about the spread of the infection.

A little over an hour later, we stopped in the center of a market-place-like square and unloaded a few more cases of serum and some basic supplies like food rations and bottles of clean water, as well as a limited supply of antibiotics and things like insulin. This was a known drop-off point, so people had gathered in waiting, and came forward to get what they could before we ran out.

Many of the people offered thanks, but just as many were too focused on grabbing what they could and leaving quickly, and a good number of others wore accusing glares and muttered among themselves.

"You don't have any more food?" one man yelled, his arm held in a sling across his chest.

One of the team leaders said, "Sorry, this is all the food we've got, this time. But there's plenty of the anti-meningolycanosis serum, and we brought some sanitary wipes and baby formula, too."

"We need food!" the man said, his voice rising to the edge of a yell.

"This water will be gone by tonight. There isn't even enough for all of us to get a single bottle!" another yelled.

I frowned as I realized they were right. I turned to the inoculation team member beside me as we unloaded the remaining boxes of supplies. "Do we have more, back at the base? People need access to clean water, or things are just going to get worse."

She shrugged uncomfortably. "Relief resources are stretched pretty thin. This isn't the only city where the water isn't running anymore. Roads are shot to hell, how are the transport pods even supposed to get here? And even if they could, the Emergency Management Department doesn't have the money to get everyone what they need. They ran through the budget weeks ago, trying to keep people alive while the aliens were still busy killing us all." Her voice tightened as she looked up at the Estreyan standing beside the convoy and scanning for trouble.

I sighed, closing my eyes for a minute and rubbing chilled fingers against my forehead. I'd known the problem was big. I'd known I didn't comprehend everything that would need to be done to get Earth back on its feet, but I kept being reminded how utterly screwed our current situation was.

"And you aren't even trying to do anything about the gangs," Arm Sling yelled, to the nods of several of the other civilians. "They're taking control of the streets, stealing from the rest of us honest folk and making it generally unsafe to even leave our houses."

"Those of us that still *have* houses!" someone else shouted. "Cause your damn aliens destroyed some of ours!"

Arm Sling pointed his good arm at me. "Don't think we don't know who caused all this in the first place. We have eyeballs. You're *one of them*! I've never seen a human looking like you."

"You betrayed your own people!" one of the others yelled.

Those who weren't angry, or at least weren't brave or stupid enough to voice that anger, quickly withdrew with their supplies, while others pressed in closer. Anger has a way of feeding off the anger of others, building up like a fire jumping from tree to tree.

My Estreyan guard for the evening stepped forward, placing herself in front of me. "Back!" she called in heavily accented English. "Get back!" There was a threat in her tone and on her face.

I didn't think the threat was helpful, but how, I wondered, were you supposed to defuse an angry crowd? I doubted anything I could say would change their minds or make them feel better. My instinct in the face of a threat was to attack. But these people weren't a physical threat to me, and hurting or scaring them wouldn't make them see reason. They were just frightened and in need of someone to blame, and with my obvious role in stopping the war, the friendliness of the Estreyans, and my not-completely-human appearance, I was a natural target for their blame, their anger. "It is alright," I murmured in Estreyan.

"You must not be allowed to come to harm," my guard retorted, her eyes scanning the crowd, and even the rooftops, as if she expected an ambush.

Arm Sling wasn't deterred, though some of the others had hesitated when she stepped forward. The sound of her alien language seemed to egg him on. "You've got some nerve, coming out here like you're so kind and noble, helping us poor people of the city. But we're not fooled!"

"Dirty alien!" someone screamed from the back. "Fuck you! My son died!"

My guard drew her staff, runes written along its surface glowing to life as she stepped forward menacingly.

The crowd broke, then, scattering into the streets and alleys surrounding the market.

The inoculation team leader sighed loudly. "And there's the downside to having the super-powered people come out to help," he muttered. He raised his voice and called out, "Let's head back. Keep your super-senses…*thing* active, Redding. Now that supplies are unloaded, we've got space for a few more infected, if we pass them on the way."

Zed was scowling as we loaded back into the pod, followed by the female Estreyan guard. "Idiots. Can't they see we're trying to help? In fact, we're pretty much the only reason they're not all dead right now, or about to be mauled by rabid neighbors."

Gregor snorted. "People are stupid. You'll find yourself becoming stupid, too, if you care too much about what they think."

Chanelle fiddled with her tranquilizer gun, then sighed and leaned back. "Not all of them are like that. They just…" she shook her head.

"People aren't always rational," I said. "And they do have some valid complaints. I understand that we don't have the people or the time to police the city against crime, but maybe we can get some more supplies for them, at least? Some portable water filters might be a good start. One of the group told me that part of the problem is the availability of transportation and resources, but the other part is money. I wonder if companies would be willing to take Estreyan currency in place of credits. I have plenty of the former."

"Other-worldly precious metals probably wouldn't be unwelcome, if you could get them to agree to sell to you on a line of credit. But let me reiterate. People are stupid. Helping them more isn't going to make people any smarter."

I shrugged. "Well, I make a good face to hate. I think I need a PR manager to run some sort of campaign for me." I lifted my hands in the air, waving as I captioned an imaginary news header. "Eve Redding, Super Likable and Not At All the Reason Your World Got Attacked by Aliens. Also, She's Trying to Help."

Zed raised his eyebrows again, stared at me, and then snorted very deliberately. "That's why you're not in the news industry," Zed said. "That's a horrible news header."

"She is on the news, all the time," Chanelle said. She elbowed Zed and wiggled her eyebrows jokingly. "I saw her on the news this morning."

Gregor squinted at her incredulously, then sighed deeply. "You're not funny. Please…just don't."

I grinned. "Well, if you know so much about PR, why don't you show me how it's done?"

Zed raised his hands in the air. "Eve Redding, Superhero, Saves the Day Again."

Our Estreyan guard, who had been silent up till then, shook her head. "No, no," she said slowly, the English still awkward in her mouth. "Much simpler, make fear and respect in same title." She held up her own hands. "Eve Redding, Godkiller." She grinned, nodding eagerly as she looked around at us.

My teammates and I shared a look, then burst out laughing.

"Even better!" Zed crowed, extending his hand toward the Estreyan for a high-five, which she hesitantly returned, but only after he explained how high-fives were supposed to work.

A FEW DAYS LATER, I drove my bike back to the base through the darkening streets. I'd come from inspecting the anchor point the Estreyans were working on. They were interested in my power, Chaos, and the fact that I'd gotten it directly from a god's physical manifestation rather than as a Bestowal. They'd grown very excited when I told them how I'd eaten some of Behelaino's Seed core, and they had me push energy into a few crystal orbs, similar to what I'd done to the Yggdrasil tree or the healing lance, in the hopes that my proximity to a real god's power would give them the "weight" needed to bind the anchor spot to reality. Or that's what I'd been able to gather from their jargon-filled technical rambling.

My Estreyan guard ran behind me, keeping up easily. Half the city had lost power, if not more, and there had been rolling blackouts for the rest of the city. When we arrived at the base only to watch its windows, as well as those of the surrounding buildings, go dark, I wasn't surprised. We had backup generators running on energy cells maintained by Adam and a couple of the Estreyans who had electrically based Skills, and they would kick in for the essential building functions soon.

What did surprise me were the news logos on the pods outside.

"Why are they here?" I said aloud.

My guard shook his head. "I do not know, but I will not allow any harm to come to you. If these humans present a threat, only say the word and I will kill them."

I rolled my eyes. "Reporters are a hassle, but they don't deserve to be killed just because they're nosy."

"If you change your mind…"

I opened my mouth to respond, but cut off as a familiar Window popped up in front of my face. Another quest.

INSPIRE AWE
WHEN ENTERING THE LOBBY, USE THE EFFECT YOU
PRACTICED WITH BIRCH TO CREATE THE ILLUSION YOU
ARE COALESCING FROM FLOATING SPARKS OF LIGHT.
COMPLETION REWARD: INCREASED REPUTATION WITH
REPORTERS AND THE PUBLIC
NON-COMPLETION PENALTY: MORE DIFFICULT
INTERVIEW, INCREASED LIKELIHOOD OF PUBLIC
CRITICISM

I stared at the quest, reading it through a couple times. I sighed deeply.

Instead of going through the glass doors of the front entrance, which were locked at night, I moved to the side of the building. My guard and I slipped in quietly, and I explained what I was about to do.

He grinned eagerly and nodded, placing his fingers to his lips in the universal gesture for silence.

I walked, barefoot and silent as always, to the door leading to the lobby. Inside, reporters with cameras shining like little spotlights talked to the refugees about the building's loss of electricity, the living conditions, people's opinions of my team and the Estreyans, and whatever else the public was interested in.

I reached out with thin filaments of condensed Chaos from around the corner of the doorway, heating the air and create a few sparks of floating light while I stayed hidden.

At first, only a couple people noticed the bright sparks in the darkness. As I added more and more, letting them float around gently, my audience grew.

The reporters turned their cameras in my direction, capturing the phenomenon with excitement and speculating it was some sort of superhuman power by one of the aliens who stayed in the building.

I kept extending invisible threads and lighting their tips till the whole doorway shone like a blazing, multi-faceted fire. When I was sure no one would be able to see me through it, I stepped forward, let the motes draw toward me till they outlined my form, then shot them outward to reveal myself beneath.

I walked into the room, letting a few threads stay lit, their tips following behind me like fireflies.

People's mouths dropped open with gasps or shrieks of surprise.

"The power should be back on soon in all the essential areas," I said. "It doesn't take long for the backup energy cells to kick in, so don't worry." I turned to the reporters. "Are you here for an interview?"

They tripped over themselves to get to me.

Welcome to the Earth Defense Force message boards.

You are currently logged in.

You are viewing thread: "Interview with Eve Redding"

ORIGINAL POSTER "COLLEGE BRONY" SAYS:

This interview was broadcast live last night. Check it out *here*. A group of reporters went to Redding's relief center just as one of the rolling blackouts I'm sure we're all familiar with by now hit. They caught her…doing something that's hard to explain. I'll leave it to you to decide what you think happened, but personally I think she's able to turn her body into light and vice-versa. What this means about the rules of physics, I don't know.

She asserts that she is indeed human, but due to a distant ancestor from a few thousand years ago…when the aliens supposedly visited primitive Earth, by the way, she was captured by that NIX organization that just did all the confessional press releases. They experimented on her and were able to give her alien superpowers, which she's using for good, etc, etc.

I was actually impressed by how effective her relief center is. I'll admit, I was biased before. I only watched the interview to see her get torn a new one by the reporters, but after I heard what she had to say and saw the proof of what she's doing for San Mateo, I changed my mind.

She's barely twenty or something, and here she is, making our whole military and government look like incompetent fools. Sure, a lot of people died while she was gathering whatever leverage she used to blackmail the aliens into compliance, but I can't blame what happened to Mordsmouth on her. She did her best, and gave those people a chance to escape that they wouldn't have had otherwise.

I'm not too proud to say I was wrong. You're welcome in my city any time, Ms. Redding.

POSTER "NOT JAMES BOND" SAYS:

Hahaha, did you see the look on her face when they asked her if she was a shapeshifter hiding in the form of a human woman? Hilarious!

POSTER "NINJA PIRATE WARRIOR" SAYS:

I told you guys that theory was ridiculous.

POSTER "ALL YOUR BANDWIDTH ARE BELONG TO US" SAYS:

I don't have any beef with the Redding chick, but I gotta say her whole "look" is seriously intimidating. No wonder the aliens took one look at her and decided to make peace instead of war.

On a more serious note, I still want a proper explanation for how this whole effing shit-grenade of a situation got started in the first place. We get a peaceful scout mission from an alien and just assume they're an enemy? *BOOM.* Oops?

POSTER "ME-FOR-PRESIDENT" SAYS:

Official story is, they thought it was an experimental ship from another country, and by the time they'd shot it down, it was too late.

Of course, that's total bullshit. You've seen their ships. No one on Earth is building something like that. What really happened is some people got trigger happy, or maybe even greedy, seeing as they captured one of the survivors to experiment on.

The idiocy is astounding.

Of course, that's not even getting into how they covered it up as terrorist attacks and started preparing for interplanetary war under the table.

BTW, anyone know where I could commission a costume like hers? I live on a farm, will pay for work with potatoes.

POSTER "ALIEN77" SAYS:

This is what I've been saying all along, sheeple. Wake up! The government is corrupt. We need to overthrow the system and start ruling ourselves. We're never going to have real prosperity and control over our lives till we have freedom. I'm talking anarchy. Don't gasp in shock and outrage. Look around you. Think about your life over the last few months. Anarchy is the answer. We need to take our fates into our own hand, just like this Redding chick.

Though, to be clear, I'm not at all convinced by half the things she said. I still think the aliens introduced that plague on purpose as an excuse to wipe us out. If you stop listening to the obvious surface agenda of all those news broadcasts and put the underlying pieces together yourself, it all makes sense.

Especially if you think about how dependent we are on the fish people now, since without their help the world economy would fall into a devastating depression.

POSTER "SERIAL-PESSIMIST" SAYS:

Alien77, you know they're not fish-people, right? That's just what their ships look like. They're perfectly normal-looking, just much larger than humans.

POSTER "ANTHROPOLOGIE-4-EVER" SAYS:

I want to know where these Estreyans originated from. How is it possible that an alien race looks so similar to, and is supposedly even able to reproduce with us humans? Are there more humanoid races out there? Was that a winged cat? Why does Redding have scales on one of her arms? Is that a mutation from the experiments, or do a lot of Estreyans carry non-standard traits like that?

POSTER "CHASE123" SAYS:

I hadn't realized how tall she was, before now. I'm digging the Amazonian look. I wouldn't throw her out of bed for eating crackers, if you know what I mean. Wink, wink.

POSTER "POP-TARTS LOVER" SAYS:

You're an idiot, Chase123. I'm more interested in her super-powers. As far as we know, each of them has their own powers, and some of them even have more than one. Is it possible to give everyone these powers, or do you have to have an alien ancestor?

POSTER "BAY-BAY-BACON" SAYS:

I've drawn a fan-art story about Eve Redding, her flying cat, and the very buff, mild-mannered reporter who is tasked with covering the story of her adventures. *Cough Cough* You get the idea. Not safe for work. Find it _here_.

Chapter 37

I have seen the dark universe yawning
　　Where the black planets roll without aim,
　　Where they roll in their horror unheeded,
　　Without knowledge, or lustre, or name.
　　— H. P. Lovecraft

A FEW DAYS LATER, my popularity had grown, but it hadn't done anything to mitigate my exhaustion or relieve my growing sense of desperation. Every day, hundreds more infected were added to the queue of those who needed to be checked and possibly healed with the lance. Despite working twenty-four hours a day and speeding our process up to be as efficient as possible, we were still falling behind. If it continued, things would spiral out of control.

The main upside to my new popularity was that I'd been able to get a couple companies to agree to supply the rescue and relief efforts, in exchange for future payment of a few handfuls of Estreyan precious metals—which seemed much less *precious* on Estreyer than they were on Earth, thank goodness—and agreeing to endorse their brands in various ways.

We'd examined the god's artifact to see if we could figure out how to replicate its effects, but, except for the fact that the lance was mixed with Seed organisms, as if they'd been folded into the metal in trace amounts, we didn't discover anything we could use.

I felt a sudden flash of greed for the power inherent in a piece of the Seed core of the God of Shaping and Molding, but tossed the thought away as quickly as it had come. I didn't know how to extract them. Even if I did, I wouldn't know how to use them to do what was necessary, even *if* I even managed to live through the process of assimilation. The lance was literally made to fight the Sickness, so I should let it do its job.

I joined Torliam on his shift to inspect those he healed, still hoping to find a way to discover if the Sickness had infected someone without using the lance. That way, we could save time by only using it to heal instead of examining everyone. Unfortunately, I wasn't able to sense the signs of the Sickness when it was subtle enough that it hadn't yet started deteriorating the body.

YOUR FOCUS HAS INCREASED!

I waved the notification away with a vague hand motion, then rubbed at my eyes, hoping to alleviate the headache building behind them.

After his healing shift ended, I took the godly artifact from Torliam. I inserted it absently between my armband and my skin, my eyes tracking over the huge crowd of people I needed to heal during my session. I jerked when the pain registered, then looked down to my arm. The lance was stabbing into the soft skin of my inner elbow.

I drew it out, then stared at its tip as it absorbed the bloody smear. I laid it flat against my forearm. The head of the artifact extended to my palm. I reached out and grabbed Torliam by the elbow before he could walk away. "Torliam." When he turned to me, I showed him the lance, measured against my forearm. "It's grown longer."

He stared down at it, and after a moment, said, "This is very curious."

I grabbed blindly for an empty seat and tossed myself onto it. "Why would it be growing? Do you think it's getting stronger? Maybe that's why the healing has been going more quickly." I didn't wait to listen for an answer, instead sending my awareness into its metallic form.

I focused as hard as I could, till I could sense the vague vibrations of its molecules, but I didn't find anything that stood out as strange. So I pushed some power into it. The lance lit up in my mind like the bodies of our patients did. Instead of showing me a language-blueprint, it showed me itself, and all the places where cracks ran through it. Not really cracks, more like slices. Places where pieces of the puzzle fit together.

I pushed more power into it, till the sounds of the room around me and my own body fell away. My hand trembled, the surge of power and focus still not enough. The edges I had seen were visible as the lance shivered, but nothing happened.

Torliam's hand wrapped around mine, and I gasped as the lance lit up like a star with his power.

It burst apart.

I didn't even have the mental capacity to breathe while my awareness was so focused on the artifact, now a swirling mass of metallic petals, each pulling at my consciousness equally, forcing me to split my attention. It hurt.

They shot forward and sliced right into the dazed civilians.

I restrained my horror, and they jumped in varying levels of fright, but calmed when we all realized they weren't actually injured.

Each of their bodies bloomed into illumination before me. With another thought, I healed those who needed it. The drain on my power was bigger than I'd been prepared for, and I forcefully cut it off when I realized I was about to pass out.

The petals exited the civilians' bodies, more like light constructs than actual matter, and reformed in my hand, just like when the lance had first appeared at the feet of the god. "You'll have to finish," I half-slurred, turning to Torliam.

He scowled down at me. "Damnation, Eve. Is it possible you could pass even one day without forcing others to worry for you?"

"I'm just a little tired," I said. "I think it's worth it, since we just found a way to heal multiple people at once."

421

ONE OF OUR guards brought me a platter loaded with food, some of which was available in the mess hall, and some of which looked like they may have brought it from their own ship's supplies as a treat for me, since it was actually appetizing.

I sat in the corner and ate constantly for almost an hour, ignoring the looks of amazement from the humans who happened to notice my gluttony. The rest of the team was assembled, and a crowd of our volunteers gathered as well, curious about the excitement on our faces.

Torliam was able to reproduce my success, except with many more petals, and proceeded to heal the entire crowd at once. His face grew a little paler and he panted while the lance reassembled in his hand, but he turned an exuberantly boyish grin on me. "This will make a difference," he said simply.

Sam's smile was almost woozy. "You just healed almost as many people as we got through the whole of yesterday." He paused, then sighed. "We…are going to need more healers for the brain damage and the original bites, even disregarding the other wounds they manage to give themselves."

I nodded. "The Shortcut anchor should be finished soon. Maybe a week longer. We'll get more healers in the first batch of people."

Torliam handed the lance to Adam. "This method of use requires a significant amount of strength, but we must all practice till we are able to do so."

Over the next few days, we had to work out a new system for the healing. It required even more calories than we'd been consuming before, and a mid-day nap. We'd all taken on two shorter shifts instead of a single longer one, and we seemed to actually be catching up on the number of people who needed to be cleared of possible infection.

We still hadn't made any progress on duplicating the lance or even truly quantifying its effects. One of the scientists we'd pulled in to help augment our limited knowledge had said, "It doesn't make any sense. It's more like reality is being *warped* than any sort of cellular modification or regeneration."

Despite the deep resentment between my team and their organization, NIX sent a Thinker to our base to try to help.

Gregor snorted at the man after listening in to his initial report.

"You barely have any real knowledge about *Skills* that aren't from a Characteristic Trial. You don't understand Seeds. Your information isn't even relevant."

I agreed we may simply not have a good enough base understanding of how Seeds worked in the first place, and put in a request for some theoretical experts from Estreyer.

Still, the ability to heal dozens of people, hundreds if you were Torliam, at once was a huge relief to me. I had time to keep working with Chaos and studying chemistry. I read about synthetic drugs and wondered idly if Chaos could create such things given enough power and control. That would really help Sam and the healers, given our short supply of just about everything.

I even spent some of my spare time before bed working on the Oracle's last gift, which I was a little surprised hadn't been necessary to find the cure to the Sickness. I wondered, if I solved it now, would it show me cryptic visions of something I already knew?

I'd taken to experimenting on fish, since they couldn't scream when Chaos didn't work exactly as intended, and the ones I killed were waste-eaters from the polluted river and inedible anyway.

I could now fuse together broken bone with some accuracy, but working with nerves was like trying to build the Eiffel tower out of limp spaghetti. Nerves were complex in structure, and, unlike bones, I couldn't just fuse them together easily and be done with it. Chaos didn't bend itself to delicacy well, and kept overpowering my attempts at change.

My frustration only made things worse. Once, after a dead fish threw itself off the table in front of me when I messed up, I picked it off the floor and hurled it across the room with a shout of aggravation.

Unfortunately, the door opened right at that moment, and the fish almost hit Adam in the head. He ducked, then looked over his shoulder to the splattered form on the wall behind him. He turned his gaze back to me, eyebrows raised high.

I plopped back down into my seat and looked away, refusing to allow any embarrassment to leak out. "It was being difficult."

"The dead fish? What did it do to you?"

I poked at another smelly specimen on my desk and refused to meet his eyes.

"You know…" he said, walking over to me, "I can walk just fine. See? You don't need to drive yourself insane learning how to heal fish spines."

I looked at him.

He crossed his arms and smirked down at me. "Legs aren't everything. Someone famous said that, I think."

I STILL WANTED to keep training in the hopes of healing Adam, but his lack of reliance on me made me feel a little better. He picked up a fish, rubbed with disgusted fascination at the slime covering its body, and, without warning, threw it at me. "Payback," he said simply.

Within the next two seconds, we devolved into a fish-fight, lobbing them at each other like they were throwing knives. By the time we ran out of ammunition, both of us were covered in bits of raw flesh, and the room looked and smelled like the inside of a very messy meat factory. I walked around and disintegrated all the pieces I could find with Chaos, which was a good exercise in control since I didn't want to destroy the walls and floor.

Adam went to take a shower after watching skeptically as I used Chaos to get rid of the fish on myself, and I, still grinning, walked toward my quarters.

I passed a large group in the mess hall, shouting and laughing as they played some sort of game. Human civilians, Estreyans, and members of the military had gathered, along with my team, and none of them seemed to care who was who.

Zed sat at the edge of the room with his eyes closed and his legs crossed. Surprisingly, when I stopped in the doorway, he opened his eyes and looked right at me. He grinned and hopped up, jogging over to me. "I think I'm getting the hang of this Perception thing!"

"Oh?"

He nodded. "I'm starting to see more types of cracks, out of the corner of my eye. These are…different. It's hard to explain what they look like. Colors, maybe, that don't exist in the real world. I can't touch them so far, and I can only see them half the time, but I'm wondering if maybe they lead to different versions of the Other Place. How cool would that be?"

I pulled up his Game information through my VR chip. The augmentations NIX had done to him were obvious in his levels, which were closer to those of an early level Player than a normal human.

PLAYER NAME: ZED REDDING
TITLE: ONE OF NINE
SKILLS: VEIL-PIERCER

STRENGTH: 18
LIFE: 19
AGILITY: 15
GRACE: 11
INTELLIGENCE: 23
FOCUS: 9
BEAUTY: 11
CHARISMA: 9
MANUAL DEXTERITY: 15
MENTAL ACUITY: 18
RESILIENCE: 17
STAMINA: 21
PERCEPTION: 20

His Veil-Piercer Skill popped up with "Planeswalker Class" when I focused on it. I grinned. "You've got the weirdest power."

He gaped in mock outrage. "You literally have the power of Chaos, Eve. You shouldn't throw rocks when your own power is a glass house."

I squinted at him. "I'm pretty sure that's not how the expression goes."

"You're just upset because you didn't think of it first!" He stuck his tongue out at me, and I resisted the urge to pinch it between my claws.

"Little brothers," I said, letting it be a curse and an endearment both.

On my way up to my room, I ran into Kris, or rather, she, riding atop the shoulders of an Estreyan and ordering him to run "faster, faster!" almost ran into me.

He skidded to a stop when he saw me, power flaring as his Skill stopped Kris from flying off or smashing her face into the back of his head from the sudden change of momentum. He gulped, eyes darting back and forth as if looking for some way to hide from my sight.

I laughed. "Kris, did he lose a bet with you or something?"

He relaxed subtly, perhaps reassured by my lack of anger. The Estreyans who'd stayed behind on Earth all seemed somewhat awestruck by myself and the team, which manifested itself in different ways, many of them awkward.

Kris shook her head, the rising pink in her cheeks betraying her chagrin. "He was telling us stories about how they used to ride into battle on eight-legged horses, and…" she looked away, "it sounded fun."

Gregor burst out of the wall, turning from Shadow back to his corporeal state while in the air, screaming a war-cry as he descended on Kris and her Estreyan "mount."

He slammed into the side of the man, whose power flared again, softening the impact.

The guard grabbed Gregor's arm and lowered him safely to the ground. "Err, Godkiller, this is not—that is—I did not—"

Gregor rolled his eyes and huffed. "She's not going to get upset at you, doofus. I don't know why everyone's so scared of her." He turned to me. "We were playing. And Bobbus here was guarding us, while facilitating our…stress relief. Right?"

Kris nodded. "Yes. Stress relief."

I raised my eyebrows high, fighting against laughter. "That makes sense. Have you seen Birch?"

No sooner had the words left my mouth than the ceiling tile above us blew away in a sudden gust of wind. The tailos burst out from the opening, roaring, his wings spread open wide as he swooped for Kris.

Bobbus ducked, and Birch overshot, zooming into the hallway behind them.

"Oh, there he is," Gregor said, pointing needlessly. I could hear the quaver of suppressed laughter in his voice.

I turned to Kris. "You'd better run. It seems like you're outnumbered." I nodded at Bobbus. "Carry on, mighty steed."

THE NEXT FEW days passed in a rush of satisfying work and semi-permanent happy exhaustion. The Estreyan Shortcut engineers believed they had successfully created an anchor point on Earth. After some small tests, the first group was coming to help us and be healed by us. I felt that everything was finally going well.

I rode out to meet them and make sure Earth's customs and import operations went smoothly. I lay in the armored back of a pod while a human soldier drove and an Estreyan guard rode in the passenger seat. The Estreyans would be coming back to the base for processing and healing once the initial security checks were completed. I laid my head back and closed my eyes, knowing I would need all my energy for the healing ahead.

I slipped into another dream.

The pain woke me. I jerked half upright, gasping as the cold mud I was half-submerged in resisted my attempts at movement. I was lying at the edge of a lake. Mud completely covered my lower body, and I'd been buried with not much more than my face exposed.

I lurched against it till I tore myself free, most concerned with figuring out what hurt so bad. I cursed when I reached for Wraith and nothing came. I shoved at the mud on my arms, searching for cuts or broken bones.

Instead, I found white-rimmed craters in my skin, oozing pus and *moving*, my skin wriggling along with fresh agony as it tore. I watched as a pale, fleshy worm crawled past one of the craters, its body passing by underneath my skin, forcing more pus out.

For one second, then two, I stared in unbelieving horror. Then it overcame me, and I scrambled uselessly, my limbs jerking, spasming free of my control as I instinctively tried to get away from the bugs. But they were inside me. I felt them everywhere, all over my body. Some bit at me, some scratched and stung, and some burrowed within me.

I screamed.

The shrieks of horror burned down to whimpers and moans, but I regained some control of my body and tore at my clothing and my skin. I reached my forefinger and thumb into one of the holes in my opposite wrist, pinching a fat worm and drawing it out of myself. I smashed it to pulp against the ground and kept going. I clawed at my shoulders, raking away at the group of bugs biting my skin.

I threw up from pain and revulsion, and maggots spilled out, writhing helplessly in my stomach acid as it pooled and mixed with the soft mud.

I dug into the holes they'd created, ripping and tearing at myself when I felt them move out of my reach, hiding under my skin. I was sobbing, screeching anew at each fresh wave of terror and disgust, heedless of the scene I was making.

Finally, some spark of reason made its way into my consciousness, and I unleashed Chaos. It tore at me haphazardly, at first, and then I pressed its smoky tendrils into flames, and burned away the infestation within me. My skin melted off and turned to ash almost as quickly, and my abdomen writhed as the bugs attempted to escape the cleansing flame.

I stopped, when I was sure that all I felt was pain, and no more movement. I fell forward against the burnt patch of ground underneath me, my bloody hands screaming as muscles and tendons contracted and pressed against the dirt, only half-protected by patches of melted skin.

I gasped for breath dizzily, my body trembling. Tears stung my cheeks. It hurt, so badly.

It was worth it, for the bugs to be gone. At least the pain was my own.

I took a moment to compose myself, and then reached for Chaos again, this time trying to regrow what patches of skin still remained into a whole, uncompromised organ. I would never have been able to do this in real life, but this was a dream. I was in my mind. "I control everything," I mouthed.

Some of the organs in my abdomen were a little worse for wear, but none were completely gone. With concentration, I was able to fix what was missing by replicating what was still intact. More or less.

My skin felt stiff and stretched too tight around my joints when I moved to stand, but I couldn't bring myself to care. I stood, naked, in front of the lake that I only realized at that point was filled with blood instead of water. I clenched my fists and screamed at the sprawling mansion before me. I felt my face twist into a snarl of absolute rage. "No. More." I said, my voice sounding alien to my own ears as it grated out of my throat.

I moved to the edge of the coagulated, stinking lake, and scooped up a handful of rusty mud. I made sure there were no bugs, no worms wriggling within it, then smeared it on my arm. I didn't have any open wounds, but Chaos still responded to my call, burning at the mud and leaving behind a crude vambrace of metal. I repeated the process again and again, till I wore crude plate armor over my whole body, then plunged my hands into the ground. I pulled them back with sharp metal claws attached to my hands by gauntlets.

Chaos was all I needed, if I used it correctly. "No more," I whispered again. Then I screamed, "Come out! It's time for you to face me and die!"

Something in the center of the lake caught my eye, a slight brightness that looked like light shining beneath the surface of the blood, almost completely obscured. The lake rippled outward from that point, and a hand rose out from the blood. It slapped flat on the crimson surface like it was solid ground and pulled. A body climbed out of the stinking liquid. The thing that wore my face stood, dripping, and below her the blood froze, spreading outward till a solid pane of crystalized blood-red ice covered the lake.

The wind blew, fluttering a few strands of loose hair around my face as it pressed against my back and on toward her. I let out a few filament-fine strings of condensed Chaos, and from their tips, I created a fine powder that floated away easily. I was exceedingly careful not to get any of it near my own body. "How are you getting in my head?" I called, my words bouncing strangely off the surface of the frozen lake. If the wall hadn't kept her out, the ash tree grove around the inside of the wall should have.

She laughed. "I never *leave!*" She attacked first, using an explosively fast cord of condensed Chaos, faster and stronger than my own version. It smashed into my armored arm and knocked me away. The whip of woven Chaos bounced back from the force of the attack and fell apart.

I hit the ground and rolled, then threw myself back to my feet. I shook out my left arm, which had gone numb from the impact, and felt a grim satisfaction when I saw the armor was undented.

She raised an impressed eyebrow. "I meant to cut off your arm. I hope this means you're getting better."

"I've spent a lot of time thinking about how to kill you. This is my dream, my mind. I can create mithril here if I want. And if I say mithril is an unbreakable metal that returns kinetic energy, then that's what it is." It wasn't perfect, obviously, or my arm wouldn't be numb and I wouldn't have been tossed to the ground, but it was proof of concept.

She smiled widely, bouncing on her toes a little. "Good girl. Why don't you show me what else you've got?"

I stepped forward onto the surface of the lake, growing more thin cords woven from filaments of condensed Chaos, till they waved around my body like an obscuring aura of darkness. "You're going to a lot of trouble to get me to kill you," I said. "What is it you're so desperate to teach me?" The delicate branches snapped out with a loud crack, spreading through the air around her even as my power bent itself to producing heat, turning them into a weave of white-hot tendrils. They danced in a fractal pattern that gave her no room to evade, no place to escape to without facing heat strong enough to melt a line right through her body.

The ice around her cracked as it melted with abnormal speed.

She pulsed out a shell of Chaos and, as it touched my cords, it negated them. "I'm trying to teach you how to *win*," she snarled.

Even as she spoke, I sent more corded tendrils at her, this time going for density instead of heat.

She waved a nonchalant arm at them, and her shield of Chaos exploded outward once more. This time, it wasn't enough.

I grimaced and bore down harder, pushing power into Chaos till its filaments were tighter than lead, packed so tightly their weight grew beyond what real-world elements could match. I crushed down on her, but before I could squeeze her to a pulp, the weakened ice beneath her cracked, and she shot down into the lake of blood.

I took a moment to breathe. There was no way that would actually kill her. I kept an eye on the lake around me, ready for her to crawl back through the collapsed area, or even burst through the ice somewhere else.

Only a faint glimpse of light warned me.

I spun around to find her behind me, a couple tiny motes of light like white fireflies disappearing so quick I could almost have believed I imagined them.

She was no longer covered in blood like she should have been. She had also, for the first time, lost some of her resemblance to me. Her face had grown more angular, the eyes sinking inward as her jaw widened. The slit of her mouth stretched farther across her face, like a carnivore, allowing greater range of motion.

I threw myself back, jumping meters across the pond in a move Jacky would have been proud of. "Teach me to win against what?" I called, watching her for any hint of an attack.

She grinned, her lips spreading much too wide across her face. "You really are just so stupid. Is my purpose not obvious? Did you really believe I could simply remove your consciousness and use your body to end all this? If the gods could have done that, they would have long ago. I exist to teach you who and what you are, so that you might have some chance of winning the great war."

I narrowed my eyes. "You're...a piece of the God of Knowledge?" For what other reason could she have access to the light motes that were his Seed core?

The edge of her lips spread even farther apart, till the smile was half her head. "Did you think the Fear Trial was so easy to conquer? Your terror runs deeper than that, and my larger self could but postpone its true cost to allow you to receive the promised rewards. After all, at this point, you're our only hope. Unfortunately, you're useless."

"I already found the God of Shaping and—" my words cut off, as the wind picked me up and threw me, slamming me down on the ice.

I lashed out with Chaos, a veritable tsunami of power rushing out from me and crashing toward her.

The air shimmered strangely, like a mirage, or a distortion not so dissimilar to the one that had taken us to the god's realm. Between one moment and the next, she'd avoided the rush of Chaos, and stood before me again.

She pointed. The air shimmered again, this time in the shape of a dark sphere around me. It looked like a bubble made of black oil.

The not-Eve's expression was somber, for once.

The bubble darkened, and the world inside it began to distort. It wasn't a twisting or tearing, but an *erasure*. I didn't know what it was, but I felt instinctually that it was very, very bad.

Now barely visible through the bubble, a tear slipped down my counterpart's face.

"No!" I said. The word bursting from my mouth like a gunshot. It was a refusal. A command. A statement.

The bubble popped.

The not-Eve laughed, swaying on her feet. "What did you do?" Her voice slurred a little as her features grew even more angular and inhuman. She swiped at me with her claws, but I stepped back and avoided the attack easily.

"The humans have created a synthetic opioid called carfentanil. I can't create it in the real world, but here… It was the first thing I did, as soon as the wind started blowing toward you. I wanted to inject it directly, but I never managed to land a penetrating blow. Still, it looks like the dust was enough. It's lethal in very small doses." I watched her with morbid fascination. The feeling of bugs crawling under my skin flashed in my mind, and I shuddered, pushing it away again. She had to die.

She jumped toward me with sudden speed, her jaw swinging open wider and wider. She slammed into me, one clawed hand grabbing my wrist and crushing it, as if the armor was made of potato chips.

The other hand reached for my throat, but a cord of Chaos grabbed her wrist and ground down till bone cracked and blood spurted.

The creature straddling me didn't even seem to care. She leaned forward, maw opening as wide as my skull as she tried to engulf my head.

I strained backward and thrust my free hand upward, slamming her jaw closed so hard her head snapped backward. I kept pushing, then lunged forward and bit down on my counterpart's throat, sinking my blunt human teeth into her flesh with sheer force.

The skin vibrated as she attempted to speak. "You're—"

I jerked my head back, tearing the flesh. Blood sprayed.

She disintegrated, along with the world around me.

I blinked, and when my lids opened again, I found myself looking at the smoking wreck of the pod I'd been riding in.

Chapter 38

Out of the night that covers me,
    Black as the pit from pole to pole,
I thank whatever gods may be
    For my unconquerable soul.
— William Ernest Henley

"EVE-REDDING, ARE YOU WELL?" my guard asked, hurtling over to me and slipping her hand under my shoulder to help me sit up. She was missing three of the fingers on her left hand, and the stumps seemed to have been cauterized.

I looked around, eyes widening.

I sat in a crater a couple meters deep. A group of soldiers and a few Players surrounded me, guns trained on me and Skills primed for attack. The pod I'd arrived in looked like someone had taken a giant potato-peeler to it and then set off a bomb inside. The human driver who'd been chauffeuring us lay on the ground a few meters away, his tongue bulging out grotesquely and his skin blue as if from suffocation. He was quite dead.

YOUR CHARISMA HAS INCREASED!

Rather than please me, the notification made me shudder. "What happened?" I croaked.

"You went fucking crazy!" one of the Players said.

My guard glared at him. "You seemed to be sleeping," she said, "but you used your *blood-borne* abilities to attack. I realized something had gone wrong when your human driver fell asleep and then suffocated to death. I believe someone may have been attempting to assassinate you, Godkiller. These humans wished to kill you to stop you from causing further damage or harm while you fought in your sleep."

Damn it. How was I supposed to explain this? And what if it happened again? I'd killed the other Eve, but I knew from experience that didn't necessarily mean anything in the dream world. What if I hurt even more people next time? With our disrupted, chaotic sleep schedules and the absence of more dreams, my teammates had gradually stopped bothering to guard me while I slept, which might have been a good thing, if this could happen. We'd even optimistically wondered if the dreams were somehow caused by the Sickness, which seemed to be supported by the fact that Torliam's Tracker Skill led him to *me* when he tried to find the person who'd attacked me in my dreams. Obviously, we'd been wrong.

I climbed to my feet. "I'm fine," I reassured my guard. "Sorry about that!" I called out to the wary people surrounding us. "Someone attacked with a long-distance Skill that put me into a coma. I was fighting off their control, but I had no idea my attacks were manifesting outside my body. I'm sorry for your colleague's death."

I knew that wouldn't be the end of it, but there was no way the humans could do anything antagonistic to me right now without offending the Estreyans, a whole ship of whom were about to teleport into the air less than a mile away.

As if the thought was a trigger, the Shortcut anchor, a tower shaped like a double helix which glowed faintly even to my physical eyes, brightened. A ship appeared beside it, and the air rippled outward from its form, kicking up dust and buffeting my body as it rushed past.

The ship swung around the tower, moving fast. It wobbled, then jerked.

Dread welled up in my chest. That wasn't normal. Either the Shortcut had been calibrated incorrectly and caused a malfunction, or something had gone wrong with the passengers inside.

The ship's nose dipped and its stingray-like form hurtled toward the ground. It jerked again before hitting, leveling out for a skidding crash-landing rather than total head-on collision with the ground.

I took a step toward it, but a vice-like grip on my arm yanked me to a stop. I turned to my guard to explain that I might be needed to help. "People are probably hurt—"

She squeezed harder, as if trying to break my arm, and her eyes rolled around wildly as her eyelids fluttered. Black veins crept up the side of her neck, even as her skin paled and thinned. Her lips grew a tint of red at their creases, as if she'd bitten her tongue and blood was filling her mouth.

She opened her mouth to let out a choked sound, putrid breath spilling out around suddenly blackened and bleeding gums. She squeezed harder.

I let out a stifled scream and pushed Chaos out from my arm, disintegrating her hand even as I yanked away.

She didn't even cry out in pain, simply drawing her staff from its sheath on her back and swinging it at me. The bright red glow of her power surrounded it. If I hadn't ducked, it probably would have decapitated me.

"What are you—" I dodged again as she shrieked and lunged at me.

She had the Sickness. Somehow, she'd been infected with the Sickness, and it had progressed to the point of causing madness within seconds. What the *hell*?

She wasn't the only one. In the crowd, a couple people had started attacking those around them.

The link wrapped around my arm lit up with a call, and I almost ignored it, except that I saw it was Zed on the other end. Why wasn't he sending me a message through the VR chips, like we usually did?

I condensed Chaos fibers into a tightly wound cord and lashed out with it, cutting off my guard's legs at mid-thigh. Another application of power cauterized the wounds with a sizzle. She wouldn't be a threat to me anymore, but if I could get her to the lance in time, I could still save her life.

I answered the call.

"*Hello*? Can you hear me?" Torliam's voice screamed out.

"You don't need to scream. The links transfer sound just fine, no matter how far away we are."

Torliam was panting, and I heard screams in the background.

More adrenaline filtered into my blood, preparing me for danger.

"Run. Escape," Torliam said. "The Sickness is…" there was another loud noise, and his voice was muffled. "Chanelle is crazed. They are coming after the lance. I will protect it, but you must not return, for your safety!"

With a final screech that made my ears ring, the call cut off before I could question him.

Then a Window popped up.

—ONE OF THE GUARDS JUST GOT KILLED. HE STARTED JERKING AROUND AND THEN HE GRABBED ME, AND TWO OTHER GUARDS KILLED HIM. I HEAR SCREAMING FROM DOWN BELOW, AND I THINK SOMETHING BAD IS WRONG. PLEASE COME BACK QUICKLY.—
-KRIS-

—THERE'S A RIOT ON THE GROUND FLOOR. I'M SUPPRESSING THEM, BUT THOUGHT YOU MIGHT WANT TO KNOW. THEY SHOW SIGNS OF THE SICKNESS.—
-SAM-

I turned and ran for the nearest pod, yanking the driver out of his seat. I sent a Window to the rest of the team.

—I'M ON MY WAY.—
-EVE-

I DIDN'T NEED my superior senses to hear the screaming as I neared the building, which had been the closest thing to a safe haven for me and the team over the last few weeks.

People had rushed out into the streets to escape, both civilians

and military, and had been followed by what seemed, to all reasonable examination, to be people horribly infected with the Sickness. The infected jerked about, screamed, and stumbled on rotting legs. They were attacking others. A group of them piled on a woman in medical scrubs, and bore her down to the ground, already eating at her. A military man shot at them with his gun while screaming with mindless fear, but even as they died they didn't seem to care.

My eyes watered as the smell of fecal matter, pus, and rotting meat coated my nose and throat. People were rotting from the inside out.

I pushed my awareness outward, letting Wraith get a good catalogue of the moving bodies within my range.

Sam fought at the base of the main stairwell on the ground floor, wading through infected people like a force of nature, one man against a veritable swarm. Every movement dropped another person, with a single moment of eye contact or touch of his skin enough to send a member of the crazed horde slumping to the ground, unconscious. He was holding them off, keeping them from going up the stairs. They piled up around him in a mountain, then climbed over the bodies of their comrades and kept coming.

Most of the infected tried to get past him, but a few of them had made it to the auxiliary stairwells and were heading upward unimpeded.

Kris, Gregor, and Birch were a few floors up, in the barracks with their guards, one of whom seemed to be dead. They all moved frantically around the room. Something was wrong, there. Birch was using Chaos, which only confirmed my worries.

Even higher, Zed, Torliam, and Chanelle were on the top floor, within one of the labs. They were far from alone, as that seemed to be where all the infected were attempting to go. A group of them were attacking, but Torliam held them off.

Jacky and Adam were both rushing up the stairs, probably heading toward them.

During the few seconds it had taken me to find my teammates, a surge of power blew out a row of windows on one of the middle floors, as an Estreyan guard's power expelled a writhing mass of infected humans. I didn't hear the crunch and splatter as they hit the ground, because the sound was covered by all the other noises of extreme panic and destruction.

Sam was okay on his own, and Zed and Chanelle had Torliam to protect them, but I was worried about the kids and Birch. Going through the building would mean fighting off a horde of infected along the way, which would probably slow me down. A fire escape wove up the face of the back wall, but a few infected were climbing it, too, and the kids were on the opposite side of the building from it.

I eyed the sheer glass and metal wall nearest me, then shoved down the accelerator and rammed my stolen pod into the crowd. It threw a few bodies out of the way and bumped over a few more before the press of the crowd stopped it. Then, I blew a hole in the ceiling with Chaos and climbed out, avoiding the reaching arms. Before the infected could climb atop the pod, I hurtled myself off, landing behind the closest group and weaving toward the building. "Move!" I bellowed, and Voice slammed my command into the throng like a hammer. People stumbled and fell in an effort to make a path for me.

I brought out those woven strands of Chaos as I reached the building, punching them into the metal struts between the panes of reinforced glass. With those ready-made handholds, I scuttled up the side of the wall, continuing till I reached the level where the kids and Birch seemed to be fighting frantically. Another of their guards lay on the floor, probably dead, but I'd been distracted and missed what had happened.

I broke the window beside me with a whipcord of Chaos, then scrambled through with minimal care to ensure I didn't cut myself. I found a male and female guard fighting infected in the hallway. They killed them, then rushed over to me, talking over each other as they expressed relief for my wellbeing and their opinions on the sudden, explosive resurgence of the Sickness.

I waved away their words. "I'm here for the kids. Block the stairway with anything you can find. There's some furniture in the rooms that should do the trick, as long as none of the infected trying to get past it have Seeds. Hurry, they're coming quick." Before they could respond, I'd moved onward.

The two of them had a quick argument, and then the male guard followed me while the woman slammed into a nearby room and drew the furniture out of it with what seemed to be telekinesis.

Before I could open the door to the kids' room, the male guard grabbed my shoulder to hold me back. "It is not safe. I will go first," he said, with the least amount of deference I'd ever heard from him. He slammed the door open and stepped in, only to receive a knife through the stomach.

Gregor stumbled as he returned to his corporeal state, his eyes bloodshot and his fingers spasming around the hilt of his knife.

The man dropped to his knees, pressing on the wound to try to keep his innards from spilling out.

"Eve!" Kris screamed, riding atop the back of the remaining Estreyan guard, who I recognized as her playmate, Bobbus.

I took in the scene quickly. Three guards were down, now. One looked like he'd been crushed by a garbage compactor, but the other two had vicious knife wounds. Birch stood protectively in front of Kris and her guard, and Gregor was pale. The muscles in his face spasmed, and he leapt toward me, turning to Shadow with a stutter, instead of the smooth transition he normally achieved.

I dropped to the ground, already rolling away before he touched the floor again.

"I'll kill you!" he screamed.

I dodged to the side and sent a Window to Sam in the same motion.

—GREGOR'S INFECTED AGAIN. IT'S BAD. I NEED YOU TO GET UP HERE AND PUT HIM TO SLEEP. ASK ZED FOR A PATH.—
-EVE-

Anything I did to truly incapacitate the young boy would surely injure him, since I couldn't stop him from slipping into his Shadow form otherwise. "What happened?" I said to Kris.

"I don't know," she sobbed, directing Pinocchio to trip Gregor as he returned to his corporeal state.

The boy growled and twitched on the floor for a moment. "Hate you, hate you, *hate* you!" he shrieked, before he was a living mass of darkness again and sank through the floor, seeming to get stuck halfway through before disappearing.

Kris' guard stepped deliberately away from the walls, keeping up a constant scan of his surroundings.

Kris spoke in a rush, looking around frantically as she waited for her murderous little brother to reappear. "One of the guards went crazy, and then Keremisha and Bobbus killed him. People were screaming everywhere, and Torliam ran past and said for the guards to stay here and protect me and Gregor, and not let anyone in. But then Gregor said he was going to go see what was happening. He went Shadow and left even though I told him not to. When he came back he was all weird, like Chanelle got when the Sickness was making her insane, and then he attacked Keremisha and killed her, and he was trying to attack me and Bobbus, and then you came."

Gregor leapt through the wall behind me, and I slammed myself into the ground as his knives gained corporeality with him, right where my neck had been a split second before.

He hit the floor and rolled painfully, clumsily. His arm jerked, and one knife sliced a thin line across his thigh. He hissed in pain, and took a gulp of air, as if he'd been drowning. "I'm going crazy," he said. "The Sickness got me, you better run—"

A grey rip opened in the air above Gregor, and Sam spilled out of it, falling onto the smaller boy in a way that would have been comical, if not for the circumstances.

Sam got up, and Gregor didn't.

My stomach lurched, but Sam reached down and picked him up, handing him to Bobbus. "He's asleep. Keep him safe."

The guard nodded. Swallowing visibly, he took the knives out of Gregor's hands.

Zed hopped out of the rip, panting. "Hey Eve. Sam said he needed a hand, so I went to help. We got barricades in place down there. I thought about tranquilizing the horde, but I don't have enough non-lethal rounds. They're going to break past the barrier if they keep pushing."

Sam turned to me, and only then did I notice the blackness of his eyes. "We need to get up to Torliam. He has the lance. Chanelle has also been reinfected. Or she relapsed." He spoke those last words with a grimness that made my jaw clench.

Zed's hands ran over his guns and ammunition in a repetitive pattern, as if reassuring himself with their presence. "Torliam's on the top level with her. He was trying to heal her when I left, but not making much progress."

I nodded. "That level has blast doors and quarantine rooms. If we can get there, and take out the mob already attacking them, we should be safe."

We ran toward the stairwell. This time, I went first, but I was careful to watch out for danger, and I kept Wraith active and searching. I slowed as we reached the top level, wary of more deadly surprises.

I entered the main lab area with claws extended and Chaos ready to lash out.

Torliam was crouched down within one of the reinforced-plastine quarantine rooms, the lance in his hand and jabbed into Chanelle's arm. He had a blue shield spread out through the interior of the small cell, giving a second layer of protection to the both of them.

It was necessary, because both Adam and Jacky seemed to be doing their best to break into it, along with the other infected humans milling through the room. Both of them showed the obvious signs of the Sickness, and they moved with the infected humans in an odd sort of synch. Like they'd studied group tactics together, and found a way to attack as a mob without any individual being a hindrance to the others. It was a creepy kind of organized chaos. I remembered the vision the Spire had shown me of a similar crowd turning to look at me, as if each person was a part of a singular whole.

"Oh, *shit*," I whispered, my eyes watering again from the horrible stench. That was a third of our team, turned against us.

***

"ZED, get Gregor in there with Chanelle and Torliam," I said. "The rest of us need to stop the attack."

Zed pulled Gregor from Bobbus' arms and into the Other Place, while Sam waded into the crowd, knocking people out with a touch.

The guard hung back a little with Kris, but had no trouble knocking small groups of the infected into unconsciousness with concussive blasts that had them bleeding from the ears.

I lashed out with a weak wave of Chaos toward Adam and Jacky, who were the biggest dangers, but also able to take more damage than a human, which meant I didn't have to worry about killing them accidentally.

A few more people who'd already been on one of the upper levels before Zed and Sam had blocked off the stairwells ran up behind us, but Bobbus took care of them well enough.

Adam attacked me with a bolt of lightning, but I had enough practice noticing the signs of building electricity to throw myself out of the way in time. The bolt was weak, anyway, and he stumbled after channeling it, bloody spittle dribbling from his mouth.

Jacky grabbed one of the infected people closest to her and literally threw them at Sam, the body slamming into the boy and knocking him backward. With him out of the way, she sprang forward, hammering her fist down on the reinforced plastine of the small quarantine cell with enough force to make the whole room shudder. The clear wall cracked, but didn't shatter.

Zed dropped Gregor inside that room, next to Chanelle, who was still jerking on the ground.

Torliam's face was white with strain, and he said a few words to Zed that I couldn't hear.

I sent a Window to both Sam and Zed, while sprinting toward Jacky to stop her from breaking through the wall.

—Take out Adam and Jacky. Use the Other Place if you need to, but I need them out of here.—
-Eve-

Once they were out of the way, I'd be free to use lethal measures on the rest of the horde if it became necessary. I lashed out at Jacky's lower back, hoping to hit her in the spine.

A human woman launched herself in between us, intercepting the blow. My fist smashed into her chest.

The sound it made was mostly *crack* and a little bit of *crunch*, but I tossed her to the side without pause. She'd be fine, or she wouldn't. I didn't have time to care about that right now.

Birch darted around at Jacky from the other direction, lashing out at her with a Chaos-misted gust of wind.

She dropped to the ground and kicked out at him, sending him sliding into the waiting arms of the crowd.

One of the infected had been a soldier. He had a gun by his side that he hadn't been using, but now he raised it.

I swept a loose whip of Chaos out at ankle level. Enough to break, not enough to sever straight through.

The humans in a swathe around him fell like cut wheat, screaming as their flesh twisted and their bones shattered. Sam could heal them when this was over. Bullets punched holes in the ceiling, and then I cut the soldier's hand off with another lash of power.

Adam waved his hand and blood poured out of a jagged slash on his arm. It spun, forming into a crimson drill that sprang through the air even as Jacky ducked out of the way, though I knew she couldn't have seen it coming.

It bored into the plastine, sending chunks and peeled-away strips flying outward.

Torliam's blue shield held, but his shoulders hunched forward protectively. He looked up and met my eyes. He shook his head, sweat dripping down his pale face.

The veins in Chanelle's neck were blackened. Even as I watched, they writhed upward into her face. She arched her back and black vomit spilled past her lips.

Torliam returned his attention to her, turning her head to the side and digging his fingers into her mouth to clear her airways and keep her from choking.

I saw an eye appear, hanging in mid-air. It looked around, and then Zed's fingers poked out of empty air and threw wide an opening to the Other Place. Together, he and Sam reached forward and grabbed at Jacky and Adam from behind. They pulled their two infected teammates back through the rip, and Zed closed it as quickly as he could.

The removal of the two most dangerous aggressive elements on the battlefield had taken less than a second.

The rest of the horde twitched as one.

Chanelle arched as if being shocked by a defibrillator, then went limp. Her body broke apart into a mound of dark, leggy forms. Bugs. They collapsed outward for a few seconds, as Torliam stared in shock, and then they drew back together.

He threw himself back across the cell, grabbed Gregor's limp form and released the reinforcing barrier. He broke a few more chunks out of the wall, then climbed out with the boy in his arms.

Alone in the ruined cell, the bugs coalesced into a humanoid form and an outer shell settled on it. Tiny bugs turned into skin and cloth, arranging their carapaces and then spreading with color as they locked together, creating a complete camouflage of almost artistic perfection.

Chanelle sat up.

Chapter 39

That is not dead which can eternal lie. And with strange aeons even death may die.
 — H. P. Lovecraft

BUG-CHANELLE STOOD and climbed out of the jagged hole in the quarantine cell.

"Torliam, get Gregor into another cell," I said sharply.

He complied, locking himself inside with the unconscious boy and the lance. He would protect both.

None of the remaining infected even looked at him as he passed.

Chanelle looked around with bright eyes and a casual air. Her clothes and skin all had faint indentations in their surfaces, but they still might have seemed almost natural if Wraith couldn't sense the lack of heartbeat or breath from her body.

I attacked to kill. No hesitation. Chaos flew forward, wrapping around her and tearing her body apart, eating right through it.

She disintegrated, little pieces falling to the ground where she'd stood.

I stepped forward, frowning. The disintegration, I'd expected. The wiggling of the pieces remaining? Not so much.

The hair on the back of my neck rose up as little bugs wriggled to their feet, some of them missing legs or chunks of their bodies. They skittered around mindlessly, searching for cover.

In the corner of my eye, I saw dark movement. I looked up.

Bugs streamed across the floor, seeming to appear out of thin air. They coalesced into a form, building into a mound that turned humanoid surprisingly quickly.

I wondered if I was somehow dreaming again. Because how could this be real? We were on Earth, and things like this didn't happen on Earth, outside of dreams.

The outer shell settled, color spreading across the tiny bugs that made up her skin and clothing as they locked themselves together again.

She, I only then realized, was touching Bobbus.

Kris had had the good sense to toss herself backward and away from both of them, luckily.

The guard's back arched.

The creature wearing Chanelle's form stepped behind him and used him like a shield, or a hostage, as the Sickness ate at Bobbus with vicious suddenness. His eyes rolled back in his head as his stomach distended and the skin split from the stretching.

Then, the creature tossed him toward me.

Another body threw itself forward, tackling Bobbus away from me. It was the female guard that I'd set to barricading the stairwell. She must have followed us at some point. She snapped her fellow guard's neck with a twitch of her fingers, then tossed his body away with her Skill. "Are you harmed, Eve-Redding?" Her voice cracked with the strain.

I waved my hand in a calming motion toward the woman, then looked to Chanelle, who was smiling calmly. "Who are you?"

Chanelle smiled even wider. When she spoke, the voice of a man came from her throat. "You don't even know who you've declared war on? You vowed to eradicate me from existence. Ring any bells?"

Blood rushed through my head, the sound of my own heartbeat almost overwhelming in my ears. "The Sickness?" I whispered.

He laughed and held his hand up, letting bugs crawl up his palm and form into a lance, almost indistinguishable from the one we'd received from the God of Shaping and Molding. "Yes, though in the old tales, I am called Pestilence. You've gotten cleverer, godling. Learning to create is a big step. But you'll never be able to cleanse faster than I can destroy, and you've made too many mistakes." He crushed the lance, and it turned back into a mass of bugs, crawling out between his clenched fingers.

I lashed forward with Chaos, letting it spring out of me without moving a muscle to announce the attack. My mind spun with the revelation. The Sickness wasn't a disease, not like we'd thought. It was a being. Like a god. A *sentient* being.

He fell apart again, not even bothering to dodge. It didn't matter, apparently, as once again bugs crawled out of the walls and from the air itself, and there he stood, unruffled.

I was afraid. "What do you want?" I tried to make the words a demand—confident, angry—but my voice cracked.

He waved a hand.

With that casual gesture, the guard who'd thrown herself in harm's way to save me was infected. Her arms and legs withered away, her tongue stuck out grotesquely, swelled, and turned purple along with her veins. She died, her body slumping like a mush-filled balloon, stinking goo spilling out of her orifices.

Pestilence's smile shifted into a snarl, like a flash of lightning across Chanelle's cherubic face. "My power is greater than even the so-called Champion's. Do you think *your* will can stand against me? Without a piece of his conviction, you cannot even resist the tiniest fraction of my influence."

Without warning or signal, every sick person within five meters threw themselves at me.

I lashed out with Chaos, and Zed shot tranquilizer bolts through a rip near the wall, while Sam stumbled out of that same rip and returned to putting people to sleep, his body steaming with the sudden change from cold to warm.

Birch held one wing a little gingerly and some of his feathers stuck out haphazardly, but with a warbling yowl, wind cut across the room like a scythe, first slamming into the heads of the infected, then rolling off the far wall and heading back to swipe their feet out from under them.

While I fought, I yelled to Kris, who'd pressed herself into a corner. "Get out of here. Find one of the guards to protect you and *run.*" I hoped at least one of the Estreyans was still alive. Judging by the sounds of fighting down below, I thought there must be.

When the wave of attacks died down, I whirled around frantically, looking for Pestilence. I found him at the edge of the quarantine room where Torliam was futilely tending to Gregor, as well as Jacky and Adam. I pushed my Wraith Skill out as far as I could, searching for the glow of power that would give away where Pestilence's strength was held, an actual weakness that I could disintegrate. I found nothing, not even a hint of power in the already reforming body halfway across the room.

Pestilence thrust his arm against the plastine wall, and the appendage collapsed as the bugs lost structure. They coalesced from nothing on the other side of the barrier and Torliam's shield, reforming his arm before I could call out a warning. The appendage reached forward and tore the lance from Torliam's grip, so fast and inexorably that my brain could barely process what was happening before it was already over. Pestilence's hand reformed attached to his body, and the lance was in it.

Zed cried out in dismay and shot a steady stream of familiar bullets, the ones Blaine had created that folded and twisted in on themselves in a way that defied physics and hurt my eyes. Zed must have been saving them for an emergency.

Pestilence was gone by the time they reached where his body had been. The bugs reformed a couple arms' lengths in front of me, on top of some of the bodies I'd felled in a ring around myself.

The horde of people stopped attacking again, just standing there, facing me creepily.

Pestilence held up the lance, as if examining it in the light. "I've been watching you for a long time, when I was able. I saw faintly out of the eyes of those who'd fallen more deeply under my influence, and followed the talk of your progress from ear to ear. It was really quite amusing, how the mortal gods led you on such a merry adventure, trying once again to create the being that could lead to my end. I'll admit, I did have a few moments of concern, and I even set myself to destroying the Spire. But look, all you have is a little toy. I needn't have bothered."

Torliam's power lashed through the air like a giant pincer.

Pestilence scattered and reformed, unperturbed. He looked to

Torliam and smirked. "Oh, did you think this was a *cure?*" He laughed. "A cure doesn't exist. This is merely a temporary counter to my influence. Your Champion, that puny god, thought he would shield himself within another realm, but my power comes from a greater source than his. Even the most powerful of your mortal gods cannot defy me. They run from me, or fall to my influence. And you, so helpfully, brought me with you as you searched for a cure. For I am part of you." He whispered the last sentence, his words twisting into an echo that tickled the inside of my ears and made me want to claw it out.

The remaining infected turned toward me, those who'd been downed but not killed rising again, no matter the severity of their injuries.

Still in the corner, Kris waved her arm in a wide arc, the tendons in her neck straining. Half of the mindless horde fell to the ground, like puppets who'd had their strings cut. SI realized she'd done something similar to me in the Yggdrasil Trial, but I hadn't recognized the utility of the ability.

Pestilence blinked once, and then twice, the semblance of Chanelle's face losing all expression.

Torliam burst out of the quarantine room, a shield rushing to cover Kris as he sprinted with superhuman speed toward the Sickness' manifestation. He roared, lashing out with a spear of sky blue that pierced right through the spot where Pestilence's heart should have been.

I lashed out with Chaos, even as Torliam's blue-girded fist smashed through his head. "Kris, run!" I screamed. I sprinted forward, throwing myself over downed bodies and bowling across the infected who still stood, eerily motionless.

Kris was running toward Zed, who'd opened a portal for her halfway between the hallway and the quarantine room.

Birch created a burst of wind behind the girl that sent her flying toward safety. It wasn't enough.

Pestilence reformed, arm already outstretched, pointing toward her.

I sent cords of condensed Chaos lancing forward, so quickly my eye couldn't follow them, and heated the air so fast when they reached him that it exploded inside him, sending bugs bursting outward.

Pestilence reconstructed himself in the same spot, almost faster than he'd been ripped apart. His hand still pointed at Kris.

Zed shot at him over Kris' head. His bullets moved too slowly through the air.

Kris buckled. She fell.

I wrapped her in a shell of solidified Chaos strands, their black filaments pulsing with all the power I could give them. I did the same to Pestilence, but crushed inward with that shell, squeezing and disintegrating in equal measure, making sure not the tiniest bit of a single bug escaped destruction. When there was nothing left inside, I set the entire structure alight with the black flames of remaking that I'd used to cleanse the God of Knowledge.

Kris screamed. Her head jerked backward and then forward, cracking against the floor. The impact didn't stop her, as her limbs contorted into impossible positions.

Near the door to the room, bugs appeared from nothing, forming on the ground and flying through the air. I knew I hadn't missed a single bug, so whatever allowed him to reform his body would not be so easily stopped.

I released the ineffectual shield and dove toward her. I hit the tile and slid into her, then grabbed at her arms, pulling her closer and trying to keep her from breaking herself to pieces.

Zed screamed, turning to the newly reforming bugs and blasting them apart, one bullet after another.

Torliam's power filled the entire room with a glow of blue mist. Around me, the infected screamed as he crushed them to death, even as he tore at Pestilence's body desperately.

But that wasn't Pestilence's body, was it? He'd said his power came from somewhere greater than that of the gods. I sensed no Seeds in him, no glow, no point of weakness. So how were we to defeat him? The only possible way we lived through this is if we ran away, so fast he couldn't find us, hiding away from the eyes of any who carried his influence, his disease.

Kris gasped. Her eyes locked on mine, and then rolled back in her head. Her veins blackened and withered. Her head jerked forward and she bit into my forearm, blunt teeth sinking deep with the strength of her gnashing jaw. She convulsed again, tearing a chunk of skin and a little muscle away.

She left a couple teeth in me, loosened from her swollen, blackening gums. Another gasping breath, and she screamed, the sound gurgling out around the blood and meat in her mouth.

Pinocchio tugged frantically at her arm.

I turned, searching for the lance.

Pestilence walked up from behind me as if reading my mind, holding the artifact in Chanelle's small hand.

Zed stopped shooting, and Torliam ceased his own attacks. The decoy pile of bugs in front of them stopped trying to form into anything and scattered mindlessly.

Pestilence laughed again, like he thought he was clever. He held up the lance. "You thought to free my people? *Savior*?" Suddenly he was snarling. He clenched his fist, and the lance crumbled into dust.

Beneath me, Kris' body relaxed, slumping down onto the cold tile floor. No breath, no heartbeat, no life.

Pestilence leaned forward, putting his familiar, almost-seamless face too close to mine. "You thought to make my people *rejoice*?" He howled the word like it was a curse. "Now they lament." He reached forward and slammed his hand into my head, knocking me backward.

I felt the skin on my forehead warp and crinkle like old papyrus, crumbling off me in little chunks.

Zed screamed like an animal, no longer bothering to shoot. He ran forward, gripping his gun like a club.

Jacky's body rose from the ground where she'd been laid in the quarantine cell, unconscious after Sam's attention. That didn't seem to matter, as she sprang forward with superhuman speed, fairly flying through the air. She grew, then used her fists to smash through the plastine. It shattered easily beneath her reinforced blows.

Torliam spun toward her, lashing out with his power since he was too far away to stop her physically.

She grew, gaining a couple more feet in a tenth of a second, and jerked around Torliam's shield with a zig-zag. She stumbled in a way she wouldn't have if healthy, but still met Zed at full speed. Her black-veined arm swung around and crashed into him, snapping his ribs like candy-canes.

His movement was completely arrested, for a single moment, as he bowed forward around her arm. Then, he flew backward and smashed into the wall with a wet thud like a bursting watermelon.

"Die." The Sickness said, smiling gleefully down at me. Then he disintegrated, leaving not a single bug or faint trace of his presence behind.

I stared into the air where Pestilence had been for a couple heartbeats, then looked down, to what had once been Kris.

***

I BLINKED.

The drought spread through my face. My veins burned, my skin flaking away behind it. My eyelids fell off, so that I couldn't block myself off from the horror, even for the space of a blink.

There were sounds around me, maybe voices, but it was like they were in slow motion. I couldn't understand them.

A hand gripped my arm, and I looked up into Zed's face. I knew he was talking because his mouth was moving. "Please don't die, Eve. Don't die. Just tell me how to help you, tell me what to do."

Sam's hand was on the back of Zed's neck, and I could hear the shifting and joining of my brother's bones as he healed. Still, he was hurt. He shouldn't be moving.

Torliam's huge body collapsed onto its knees beside me.

The sound of my heartbeat sped up as the world came back into focus. "Are you alright?" I said, looking up at Zed.

His jaw clenched so hard it looked like he might break his teeth, but he nodded.

Torliam grabbed my other arm and helped me carefully to my feet.

I turned to Jacky and found her standing still, gnawing on her own hand. "We need to restrain them, so they don't hurt themselves," I murmured.

"What about you?" Zed said.

I would have blinked, if I could. "Restraints won't work on me. Chaos, remember?" I looked down at Kris' body again, and carefully walked around it, moving toward Jacky.

At my request, Zed, Sam, and Torliam helped me bind up our

remaining teammates so they didn't hurt themselves if the hunger got too bad.

I knew they were all dead, or as good as. Same as me. I was only prolonging what little time we had left.

Torliam started talking, but I couldn't concentrate on his words. "Can you use Chaos to heal yourself? To burn away the infection, as you did the god's?" His skin looked so healthy, despite the faint layer of sweat and grime.

My mouth watered.

Zed put his arm on my shoulder to get my attention, and I lashed out at him, almost scoring him with my claws.

I glared at him, chest heaving as my breaths came faster, hissing through my teeth like the anger hissed through my veins. "Get back," I snarled. I knew I didn't actually want to hurt him. Or to eat him. Even though I could feel my insides dissolving for the need of more energy, more power. I could get it if I ate him, I knew. I stepped backward, trying to convince my anger that it would be sated if I moved away, instead of toward him.

Was there nothing I could do? No one who could help us now? Where was the God of Shaping and Molding when you needed him?

THE REMNANTS
FIND THE REMNANTS AND CONVINCE THEM TO LEND
THEIR AID AGAINST PESTILENCE.
COMPLETION REWARD: ANOTHER WEAPON IN THE
GREAT WAR
NON-COMPLETION PENALTY: DEATH

I almost laughed. Torliam had searched for the Remnants already, and found nothing, as if something was blocking his Skill. And even if we could find them, how long would it take? I could feel the Sickness spreading through me, too rapidly to resist. I wouldn't be there to meet them. But maybe they could help the others. "Find the Remnants," I said to Torliam through the numb vestiges of my lips. "They can help."

Zed was crying.

I held back a vicious snarl and threw myself toward one of the plastine quarantine rooms. The smartglass pad by the door beeped and accepted the vicious poking of my fingers as I coded it for no release. "If I break out, kill me," I said to Torliam.

His face was white beneath the tan and the beard. He said something, but I still wasn't listening. Couldn't focus.

I stepped forward, and the door closed behind me. At first, I paced back and forth. But the rage was strong, and all I wanted was to rip the building apart around me. To go out there and tear the flesh from their worthless bodies so that for once it could do something useful by sustaining me.

So I turned and tucked myself into the corner, sliding down till my raw face pressed painfully into the armor over my knees.

I hid away from the light and sunk into myself to try and escape from the pain, the hunger, and the hatred.

I drifted into the world of my mind, standing in front of a familiar stone wall and wearing a body no longer my own.

I blinked.

THE STONE of the dream construct wall looked like it had been mortared together with iron and had started to rust. Or, more morbidly, like it was bleeding from every crack. The wall stretched up and around, and I knew that it had no gate. I'd built it to be impenetrable, not to let things in and out.

I thought about cutting a door through the wall with Chaos, but decided against it. Instead, I dug my fingers and bare toes into the cracks and lifted myself. The lack of claws made it a little more difficult, and without my superhuman strength and endurance, I was panting by the time I made it to the top.

I stood, and looked out over the structure I'd created so long ago in my mind. The Sickness was here, too, though it had taken the form of a creeping mold that ate away at the grounds and structures like a particularly tenacious acid, reducing them to little more than dust and blank death.

Some of it was eating at the wall beneath me, and I let forth a wave of Chaos, hoping to disintegrate it. That didn't work, so I urged my power to burn, instead. The stone burned, melted, and was eaten by the black flames, but the creeping mold of the Sickness remained, unperturbed.

I stood and watched as my mental world died, knowing I would die along with it. A section of the sprawling, Victorian-style mansion crumbled and collapsed into dust. I thought I heard a scream, but I didn't know if it was within my mind, or without.

There were splotches of darkness on my skin. I tried not to look at them as they spread.

I watched, still, as another section gave way, falling in on itself with a poof of blackness, as the grey mold billowed out. This time, though, a tiny mote of light escaped. One of the last remnants of the unpleasant gift Knowledge had bestowed on me.

I realized then that the mold wasn't mold, as it turned and swarmed after the mote of light. More bugs. Tiny, devouring *bugs*.

I threw myself off the top of the wall, uncaring for the way my ankle buckled or my joints screamed in pain at the impact all the way up my spine. I ran toward the mote of light as fast as I could, trying to keep the ankle from rolling beneath me.

The mote flew towards me, but the great swarm of bugs followed along behind it like the hand of death.

Before I could reach it, they swallowed it up.

I fell to the ground in despair as the cloud dispersed, more of the bugs landing on me in little patches of darkness. I brushed at them, but it did nothing. It was as if they were part of my skin, now.

A familiar sensation reached out to me. Torliam. He lent me his rage, as he had done once before. I sucked it up like I was made of thirsty earth, twisting and feeding on it till it became my own.

I screamed out my rage, my despair, my desperation, and scratched mercilessly at myself, wishing for my claws, for the scaled toughness of my left arm, for my *strength*. This weak, soft shell of a body wasn't *mine*!

I looked out on the destruction of my mind, and, like an echo through mist, I heard a voice, maybe a memory. "Do you know how gods fight with each other?" It spoke in my voice, even though it was Knowledge's construct that had said the words.

The thing that had been crumbling inside me as my hope and my willpower died… It stilled, and turned to focus on those words.

The Eve construct had been preparing me for this moment. I'd thought it just didn't realize I'd already succeeded, but, on the contrary, it knew I *hadn't* and was teaching me to fight Pestilence's true nature.

I turned my mind to the memories of the dreams, reaching with desperation for any clue I could use.

In the first dream, I'd learned how to use Chaos' black flames voluntarily, and healed myself.

In the second, I'd transmuted stone into air. She'd said the more important question was who *I* was. *What* I was. She'd said that even when I was dying, she still wanted it more than I did. She'd made the empty threat to take over my body if I kept dying.

In the third dream, I'd once again healed myself, created a sword out of stone, and caused an explosion. She'd said Chaos was more than some Skill. It was the tiny piece of the goddess of Khaos, living inside me. She'd asked me then, how gods fought with each other. She'd said I couldn't beat her not because of her body or her Skills, but because she *still* wanted it *more*.

In the last dream, I'd wanted it more. I hadn't been desperate, I'd been determined. Intent. She'd told me she was teaching me to win. She had created that bubble of death, and with a single word of conviction, I had popped it. I wished, now, that I'd let her finish that last statement before ripping her throat out. Maybe it was important.

Still, I think I understood what she'd been trying to teach me. Pestilence wasn't a disease, it was a distortion of the world. The lance had acted as an extension of the Champion's willpower, negating that distortion. It wasn't healing. It was *re-writing*.

And I wasn't a powerless human. Even Pestilence had announced it plainly. It had literally been in front of my face the whole time, if I cared to look. "I am a godling," I whispered. "The progeny of Behe-laino. Khaos." I pronounced her name with the distinct "K" and "H." "I am descended of the line of Matrix, and carry the blood of a god twice over." Not a human. Not a human…anymore. I had power.

I let Chaos flow out from my body, feeling no need to bleed to access it. I let it burn black. It ate into my flesh, yet still seemed impotent against the black decay of Pestilence.

I gritted my teeth. The Sickness might be strong, but it was a *lie* that nothing could stand against it.

"This body belongs to me," I whispered with burning lips and tongue. "It is *mine*. This mind belongs to me. You have no power here." I burned the spreading growths away. "You will not win. I *refuse*." I burned my own weakness away.

Then, like I had done before, in a situation not so dissimilar to this one, I turned the cleansing flames outward. They rushed to my command, unhesitating and gleeful, brutally efficient. "My will is like the ocean," I said. My voice echoed, not needing any crystal to add weight to it. "It is like the void. It has no end to its depths, no banks to its shores. You will cease to exist," I said, snarling at the creeping blackness, "because I command it so." I set my mind to a belief so strong that either I would break, or the world would bend to my command. "You are no part of me."

The world bent.

Chapter 40

They are all gone into the world of light, and I alone sit lingering here.

— Henry Vaughan

I BURNED AWAY THE SICKNESS, and the decay, and the gloom. When I was finished, I barely stayed to admire the gleaming beauty left behind. "I wake," I said. It was a command.

I opened my eyes again, to once-sterile plastine walls. Now, some parts of the quarantine cell were covered with ash, while other parts were completely melted away. I rose to my feet, taller now, and used new hands to force the remains of the door open. My eyes caught a bit of my reflection in the melted-smooth plastine. The dark honey-comb scaling had spread over more of my body, leaving only a few sections of plain skin behind. The armor I had once worn was gone, leaving me protected by scales shaped a little like feathers. They over-lapped my body almost stylistically, providing modesty and gathering thickest where I would have worn metal armor before. I flexed new muscles, and the scales shifted and fluttered, angling to catch the light.

My clothes and armor were burned away, but it did not matter. Humans were the only creatures who wore clothes. And I wasn't really human anymore, was I? One look at my once-again remade body and anyone would know that.

I looked for the others, but did not see them. Except for the body. That was still there, but had been moved to the other side of the room and laid with her arms across her chest, holding Pinocchio.

The corpses of the other infected were piled in the opposite corner. My scales fluttered in disgust as the rank smell assaulted my nose, coating the back of my tongue and lingering. The sun still shone through the bullet holes in the ceiling, but the light looked different, now.

Had the others gone to find the Remnants? Were they even still alive?

Then a familiar rip opened in the world, and Zed stepped through, dragging Gregor's body with him. No, not Gregor's body. Gregor. The boy's lips were blue, and his blackened veins stood out against pale skin, but he was breathing.

"Hurry. We need to get them warm quickly, before the Sickness has too much time to progress," Zed said.

"Isn't this more cruel, in its own way?" Sam's voice filtered through the rip, though I couldn't see him. "They are dying."

"Birch says Eve's going to wake up okay. Just like she did with the God of Knowledge."

"He is an animal, telepathic or not. And even if she does, without the lance, she can't do the same for the rest—" Sam's voice broke off as he stepped through, carrying Jacky over his shoulder. The black orbs that sat in his face in place of eyes turned toward me.

Torliam's voice filtered through the opening. "He may be an animal, but I, too, feel her fighting. Have you not seen the power rolling off her? If there is any in this world who can defeat the Sickness, it is her."

Zed turned to follow Sam's gaze, while Torliam stepped through behind Sam, holding Adam's unconscious body in his arms.

"Eve?" Zed said, staring up at me.

Birch burst out of the Other Place, hurling himself at me and forcing me to catch him in my arms. He let out little high-pitched sounds, both excited and whiny, and licked at my face, his tongue rasping against the faint scales on my jawline and at my temple.

I squeezed him gently, letting my fingers sink into his fur and feathers, their softness a balm to the jagged edges inside me. I set the cub down, then took two steps forward, and took hold of Gregor. The boy's skin leeched the warmth from my own, so soft and malleable compared to me. I was careful not to hurt him, since I couldn't retract my claws anymore. I pushed my awareness into his body. Without the lance, the Sickness wasn't highlighted, but its effects were obvious throughout. I'd had enough practice to recognize them.

How was I to do this? How did the lance work? If the Sickness wasn't an actual illness, but the effects of that *thing's* influence... The lance was the Champion's counter-influence. Negating Pestilence's *will*. Still, I wasn't confident in my ability to burn away Gregor's entire body without killing him. In fact, that seemed impossible. He was a human.

"Ah," I said aloud, as I realized the answer. I took a single claw, which tipped the end of a too-long finger, and sliced it against the palm of my hand. Blood flowed sluggishly, and the wound started to heal even as I watched, but it was enough. I pressed my hand to Gregor's mouth and tilted his head back, then massaged his throat to help him swallow.

Where my blood flowed, so too did my power, for my life was in my blood. I flushed my power, my influence, and a tiny portion of the Seed of a godling through him. I enforced my will through it. The Sickness would be eradicated, destroyed. Its influence would *cease to exist*.

He returned to health, though his body was still morbidly cold. Dangerously so, if his vital signs were any indication.

"Warm him," I ordered, handing him off to Sam, who stared at me silently, Black Sun filtering the weakness out of him. He turned off the damaging Skill and pressed his hands to the boy. "Being cold isn't an injury itself, but I can make sure it doesn't kill him. Birch, can you do that thing Eve does and heat a blanket or the floor tiles without setting them on fire?"

Birch, shivering himself, let out an uncertain mewl and then spilled Chaos from his mouth, carried like mist on a weak swirl of wind. It slipped into the floor, which glowed red-hot and then melted a little. He coughed, then hung his head, ears drooping sadly.

Torliam wrapped the boy in a cocoon of his power and held him floating above the spot so he could absorb the warmth without being burned. "Is he...healed?" Torliam said, the words almost a whisper.

"In a way," I said, wincing as I bit my tongue. My teeth to the sides of my incisor seemed to have grown more pointed, and even my molars were sharp and almost jagged. "He was not sick. Rather, poisoned, or infested with a parasite, and I have removed the attacker."

I turned to Adam, and then Jacky, and did the same. I knew this didn't make them safe, truly. Keeping them healthy was a constant, low-level drain on my power, as Pestilence willed the Sickness to overtake them, and I willed the opposite. If Pestilence came after us again directly, I didn't know that I could stand against the full weight of his influence.

I stood, staring at Kris' body. I walked over to her and tilted her face upward.

She was stiff. Intellectually, I knew it was rigor mortis, but I shied away from the thought. I cut my palm again and forced my blood into her mouth. At first, my thoughts of rejecting the Sickness didn't work. I changed tactics and just tried to heal her. It took a while, and I burned through much of my remaining strength. But though I was able to force her flesh to re-form and the obvious signs of the cause of her death to recede, it was not healing. I was only playing with meat, because there was no life in the body.

I stood and turned to the others, who were watching me.

Jacky had awoken, and, despite violent shivers, she stared between me and Kris with unblinking desperation.

"I don't know how to bring something to life," I said. My voice broke. "I'm sorry." My hands hung uselessly at my sides.

Jacky let out a choked sob past her uncontrollably chattering teeth.

Torliam moved closer, hesitantly at first, and then leaned forward and hugged me.

I realized I was as tall as him, now. The warmth of his body seemed to thaw something in my chest. I closed my eyes and tears ran down my cheeks.

Zed stepped up and grabbed my hand, holding it between both of his. "It's not your fault."

A faint sound of movement came from behind me, and I spun violently.

Kris' hand had moved, falling away from Pinocchio.

The wooden, four-armed puppet wiggled again, and her other limb slumped away. Pinocchio crawled off her chest and stood beside her, looking at her face. Then, it lifted one hand and wiggled the fingers experimentally, before turning to us. It waved.

Jacky's voice was high-pitched and almost disbelieving. "Kris? Is that you?"

The puppet nodded.

KRIS, in Pinocchio's body, pantomimed how she'd died, felt herself blowing on the wind, or maybe dispersing, then tossed herself into the little puppet. She'd fallen asleep from the strain and only now awoken. When we asked her if she could put herself back in her body, she hesitated, shrugged, then shook her head, which we took to mean that she didn't know how, or maybe was afraid to try it.

Jacky cried, muttering "thank you" over and over to herself as she looked at Zed walking around perfectly fine, and Kris, not fine, but at least not…precisely dead.

Adam woke next, and then Gregor. Neither of them reacted well to the memories of what they'd done under Pestilence's influence.

We were able to calm Adam with relative ease, with the assurance that Kris had housed herself in Pinocchio when her body was destroyed, and that he no longer had the Sickness or needed to worry about losing control of himself.

Gregor wasn't so easy to mollify. The boy grew hysterical immediately upon waking, and didn't seem to comprehend our words when we spoke to him, or maybe he didn't believe us. He flailed about with heart-wrenching sobs, struggling away from us when we tried to calm him or hold him, and beating his limbs against the floor until they bruised.

I was about to have Sam sedate him forcefully when Kris moved away from her empty human body, shaking her head disapprovingly at him.

She walked over to her brother and punched him in the stomach with one of her four wooden arms. The blow wasn't hard, coming from a two-foot body with little weight behind it.

Even so, it snapped the boy out of his frenzy. He stared at her. "Pinocchio? Why are you moving? Is Kris still alive?" He looked over her head to the corpse near the wall. His eyes brightened as he noticed the lack of outward injuries or signs of the Sickness on her body.

She crossed both sets of arms over her chest and tapped her foot on the ground.

"We've been trying to tell you," Jacky said, kneeling beside the boy and gripping his shoulders. "Kris put her spirit inside the puppet's body. Eve healed her real body, but it didn't…" she cleared her throat. "Well, Kris is the puppet, now."

Gregor stared at her new body, rubbing the tears away from his face. "Is Chanelle in another body, too?"

Jacky and I shared a look of dismay.

"No," I said. "Chanelle is dead. Pestilence… Whatever it did, it got rid of her body, too."

Adam cleared his throat, still a little hoarse from his mindless screaming as part of the horde earlier. "Was she…that thing, in disguise all along? Pretending to be human?"

I shook my head. "I don't think so. Maybe he was there a couple times, when she had one of her attacks, but she was just Chanelle most of the time." Just a girl who'd done her best to seize the little moments of joy, despite the hopelessness of her situation. Who'd been so delighted to have a second chance to live. Someone who'd believed in me, trusted me. China's sister, who I'd promised to save.

Torliam placed his hand on my shoulder, drawing my attention back to the real world. He didn't say anything, just squeezed slightly.

My scales shifted a little under his hand, but he didn't seem to care.

Suddenly, Gregor scowled at Kris. "How do you know for sure it's her? What if Pinocchio is impersonating her!?"

The puppet's jaw dropped open.

Gregor pointed at it dramatically. "I'm going to interrogate you. I'll ask you questions only Kris would know, and if you're trying to trick us…"

Kris made a writing motion, and Gregor ran off toward the other end of the room, uncaring about the putrid corpses piled up in the corner.

Kris tried to follow him, but, after a few meters, her steps grew clumsy and she stopped, clutching at her chest.

Jacky was beside her in a moment, hands clenching in useless panic. She picked the wooden puppet up gently. "What's wrong!?"

Kris pointed back toward her human body, jabbing her finger toward it clumsily.

Jacky fairly sprinted across the room.

As soon as Kris got close to her body, she stopped clutching at her chest plate and her movements grew smooth again. Obviously, there was still some sort of connection to it which allowed the puppet body to function. I imagined it might become just an empty puppet if taken too far away from Kris' original body.

Gregor ran back to his sister, holding a marker and a small white-board. Tears rolled down his face again, and his voice had risen with panic. "What's wrong with her? Is she dying?"

"She needs to stay near her body," I said, careful to avoid another accident with my reshaped teeth.

He stopped crying with a few deep breaths and some sniffles, but his deep frown remained. "This isn't safe. What if she gets separated from her body? We have to find some way to get her back inside it."

I hesitated. "Maybe…the Remnants can do something to help. Right after everything, I got a quest to go to them for help against Pestilence." I certainly did not want to experiment with the child's life myself. It was too dangerous.

Torliam rubbed his face. "I have been searching for them already, and my Skill has found nothing."

"There should be a way," I said. "Maybe the Oracle's third gift has a clue. I still haven't been able to solve it, though, and I don't feel any closer than when I started."

Zed cleared his throat, looking around pointedly. "Guys, you think maybe we should go somewhere less…filled with bodies? We should check on the Estreyans, too. They didn't all have the Sickness to start with, right? So some of them have probably survived. Maybe they can help us."

WE FOUND A PLASTINE BOX ABOUT KRIS' size, placed her inside, then filled it with ice in the hopes that preserving her body would pay off later. Jacky insisted on carrying it with her, strapped to her back in place of her pack, with the puppet riding in her arms.

We came upon a couple infected still alive in the halls, and Zed killed them with a bullet to the head before they could even look at us. "Don't want them reporting how miraculously *alive* the rest of us are to their boss, just in case he's watching this place," he said.

We reached the edge of the stairwell leading down to the ground floor, and I motioned for the others to stop with a raised hand. "There are a lot down there," I said. "Why don't you take us out of the building through the Other Place? That'll be a lot simpler."

Zed complied, and we stepped into the deathly cold of the grey alternate world. As soon as the opening closed behind us, a weight lifted off my shoulders.

My eyes widened, and I turned to look at the others, examining them for any change. "Pestilence's influence just stopped."

Adam and Torliam both scowled, almost identically. They rounded on me and spoke at the same time. "Has he been attacking you all this time?" "Explain yourself."

My scales rippled with irritation. "The Sickness is a product of his influence. You can't *heal* it, you can only negate it. That's what I've been doing. But as soon as Zed closed the opening to the real world, the tug against my willpower just…disappeared."

Zed looked around. "That…actually makes sense. Sam and I noticed that when we dragged Adam and Jacky in here to stop them during the fight that they stopped acting so crazy. We thought the Other Place was just draining them, but when we brought them and Gregor back in after you locked yourself away, we noticed they didn't seem to be getting any worse while they were inside. That's why we tried to keep them here while you were burning yourself and that whole quarantine room into mush. Maybe Pestilence can't reach in here."

That could be game-changing information. If we could find a way to replicate the effects without the deadly cold, we might be able to save a lot of people.

We hurried down through the empty halls of the building and moved a few blocks away before returning to the normal world.

When we exited, I looked around in horrified disgust. Even here, there were bodies and crazed, dying people.

I watched through the window of one of the buildings we'd set up as a temporary shelter as a woman in a floral nightdress set fire to an empty crib, cackling madly through split lips.

On a street corner, a man nibbled daintily on a small leg, which had been torn off at the knee.

I smelled the ash and saw plumes of smoke rising from fires all over the city, and klaxons once again screeched out a warning to those people who could still manage to care about their own safety. Perhaps those who hid inside would live, if those with the Sickness did not tear and burn down the city in their consumptive rage and delirium before succumbing to death, or if Pestilence didn't decide to spread his influence further as he continued the charade of disease.

"The Champion must have been defeated," Torliam said. "When his realm was disturbed, I thought it so unlikely that another god would be attacking him. Yet, what is this, if not for his death?"

Adam gritted his teeth, shuddering. "All this time, he'd been holding back...that *thing*. Now it's free to do what it wants. The world is going to crumble."

"I thought you couldn't kill a god?" Zed said. "Just...disperse them? So he's going to come back, right?"

I frowned. "I'm not so sure. Maybe you can't kill them, but I have a feeling, if you were powerful enough, you could make them...cease to be. You'd just have to change the universe into a place where they didn't exist. And even if that's not possible, it might take a very long time for what's left of him to gather enough of his power to affect anything. Also," I paused, tilting my head to the side as I searched for the best path toward the Shortcut anchor, "I think Pestilence might not be a god, per se. I can sense Seed power. He didn't feel like any god I've met, and none of the people under his influence feel like a Skill is focused on or affecting them. Even if the bug-body was a decoy, there should have been some flare of power that indicated Pestilence's control over it."

Zed's eyes narrowed, then widened. "What if he was just hiding whatever powers him in another realm?"

I turned, leading us down the clearest path. "Do you know something we don't?"

"I told you how I've started to notice other cracks in the world besides the ones to the Other Place, right? These cracks have different colors, and I can't touch them, yet. I'm pretty sure there's some sort of…entrance, in his chest. I would notice it sometimes, when you guys destroyed the bugs forming his body. It's not a rip, more like a line, or a point." He shook his head, fingers clenching reflexively around the grip of one of his guns. "It's hard to explain it, when you can't see what I can. But it makes sense, right?"

"It does," I said. "We're gonna need you to keep focusing on your Perception, if you're the only one who can see it. It would also explain why the God of Shaping and Molding was hiding in that hellscape realm all this time."

Adam's head was on a paranoid swivel, his gaze traveling all around as he searched for danger like a character in a horror film. "Is the god definitely dead? If he's still out there, he'd probably be our best bet to make it through this alive."

"I will search for him," Torliam said. His eyes went blank for a moment. When they regained focus, a frown grew between his brows.

I sensed the glow of Seed power flare within him as he fed strength into the Skill.

He turned, slowly, till he was facing me. "I do not believe he is alive. Or if he is, there is no path to him. When I strained for a different answer, my Skill pointed me, with the slightest of tugs, toward *you*."

Chapter 41

You must do the thing which you think you cannot do.
— Eleanor Roosevelt

I TILTED my head to the side, then nodded. "We can probably use that pod," I pointed. "It's still running, and there are enough seats for all of us."

Adam looked to the pod, then to me. "Wait. You're just going to let that statement fly by? Why is Torliam finding you when he looks for the lost god?"

I waved my hand for them to follow, then crossed the street to the empty pod and climbed inside.

The others packed in behind me.

As I drove off, I explained. "Well, it's in the prophecy, isn't it? I'm one of his *distant* descendants. I don't know if I have any of his Seed organisms in my body or not, though if I do it's probably a minuscule amount. However, I am a godling."

Torliam nodded, but the others stared at me in confusion.

"When I swallowed that piece of Behelaino's Seed core, she said it would give me the chance to 'ascend' and called me a godling. Some of you were there for that, remember? I'm *not* a god, but Chaos isn't a Skill like most of the ones we have. It's the direct power of the god, and I guess it makes me kind of similar to one of their physical manifestations."

Sam leaned forward, looking out over my shoulder. "Does—does this mean you made a blood-covenant with them when you healed them? Do you need to do that with the rest of us, too?"

I shifted my grip on the steering wheel, which wasn't sized for people with extra-long fingers tipped by claws. "It is a one-sided blood-covenant, like what we had with Torliam before he had it broken. It might give you access to a little more power than you'd normally have, and you might have some extra awareness of me. I hope that's not a problem. I figured you guys wouldn't mind, if I could save your lives."

Torliam's face was carefully expressionless, but Jacky, Adam, and Gregor weren't worried about sharing a blood-bond with me.

"I might need to give the rest of you a little blood, too," I said. "Even if you don't have the Sickness now, it'll help me counter Pestilence's influence if he comes after you."

Gregor's voice was small, coming from the back seat. "Do you think he'll come after us again?"

"Definitely," Adam said, before anyone else could respond.

Gregor hunched into himself, and Jacky sent Adam a threatening glare.

Adam scoffed. "Do you think it's better to lie to him? He can handle it. We're all going to have to do the same. It's not like we can just hide in the Other Place forever. If you haven't noticed, the conditions there aren't exactly conducive to *life*."

The thought of Pestilence showing his face again filled me with a volatile mix of emotions that set my heart pounding. My fingers flexed, squeezing into the steering wheel and leaving an impression of my hand in it. My lips had curled back from my teeth without my conscious intent.

Zed noticed, but didn't comment on it, instead saying, "Why did Pestilence even come after us in the first place?" He looked to me. "With the Champion out of the way, he's so much more powerful than us, there's no way we could have stood against him. Even with the lance. He didn't need to confront us. He didn't *need* to destroy it. He chose to."

I replayed the thing's words in my memory and felt my mind start to rush, as it did when the universe was a puzzle just starting to slot together in front of me. "Because we were a beacon of hope, still. Futile as our power was against him. Because the Sickness isn't only physical." I turned to Torliam, my gaze boring into his own as I willed him to understand.

He nodded slowly. "It brings only ruin. It is despair. It is hopelessness. It is the loss of all that ties the mortal world together. And yet, we brought hope."

Sam settled back into his seat, his eyes shadowed but not black. "He needed to attack because he was afraid of what would happen if he let us keep going."

I laughed, the sound sharp and biting. "It was a preemptive strike. It's true, he will come back again. Because we didn't die. And he was *lying* when he said he couldn't be defeated. We've all seen the evidence, and we already have a quest to work with the Remnants against him. The lance isn't our only answer."

Gregor's fists clenched so tightly his knuckles turned white. "It killed Chanelle because it was afraid? That's why Kris is…like this?"

I slowed the pod to a stop as we came to the edge of the hastily erected encampment around the Shortcut anchor.

"We're going to retaliate, right? We're going to find a way to kill him for good, so he can't ever hurt us again, right?" The boy leaned forward, almost pleading with me. "We *have* to."

I grinned back at him, showing too-sharp teeth. "You don't have to convince me. I'd want to kill him, even if he ran away from us and pleaded for forgiveness."

"It will be justice," Torliam said.

Zed grinned, his fingers trailing over a spot in the air that seemed just like any other to my own senses. "Let's not pretend. Eve doesn't really *get* justice. This is about revenge."

"Hatred is a strong motivator," Sam said. "Pestilence has made a mistake."

I agreed. I looked out onto the strewn about bodies of Estreyans and humans alike, catching faint glimpses of Skill effects going off in the distance. More than just my appearance had changed, when I remade myself. I didn't know if I'd taken another step down that sociopathic spectrum Kilburn had accused me of being on, or if I'd just somehow broken under the stress of so much despair and the following rage. It might even be some side effect from acknowledging myself as a godling instead of a human. Whatever it was, it was cold and predatory, and filled with a hatred that swirled like ice and fire inside me.

I PULLED up the quest Window again, looking for any extra clues I may have missed in my distraction the first time around.

THE REMNANTS
FIND THE REMNANTS AND CONVINCE THEM TO LEND
THEIR AID AGAINST PESTILENCE.
COMPLETION REWARD: ANOTHER WEAPON IN THE
GREAT WAR
NON-COMPLETION PENALTY: DEATH

It wasn't much to go on, but I shared the Window with the others.

Adam twirled three-dimensional ink in the shape of a small snake between his fingers, absently making it disappear and reappear with sleight of hand. "They must have done something to block even pseudo-scrying Skills like Tracker. If Torliam can't find them, what other options do we have? They've somehow managed to stay unrevealed until now, and I'm pretty sure even NIX wasn't aware of them, or they would have been capturing people to harvest Seeds from or experiment on."

Torliam's jaw clenched.

The ink snake whipped around faster as Adam closed his eyes. His lids fluttered, an indication that he'd activated his Hyper Focus Skill to work on the problem. After a few minutes, they snapped open. He turned to Torliam. "Didn't you say the effectiveness of your Skill is based on how familiar you are with whatever you're searching for? What did you ask the Skill to find, *specifically?*"

Torliam's eyes widened, and his expression lacked the usual antagonism when he returned Adam's gaze. "I searched for the Remnants, I believe."

Adam smirked. "So why don't you try looking for Eve's mother and father, *independent* of their association to the organization that calls itself the Remnants?"

Torliam wasted no time, power flaring as he set it to work. Less than a minute later, his smile stretched across his face like a self-satisfied cat. "I have them. East and slightly south. Not far, but not near either."

I let out a low chuckle of satisfaction. "Well, that was less difficult than I thought it would be. Now let's see if there's anyone we can get to give us a quicker ride."

I drove the pod slowly through the encampment, avoiding the putrid, dead bodies. Many of them had died to wounds, but just as many had died from Pestilence's influence itself. When its effects grew too much for their bodies, they simply collapsed in a puddle. Like Kris...

Soon, we came upon a mixed group of humans and Estreyans fighting back against the infected trying to exit the downed ship. An Estreyan with copper hair, who I struggled at first to recognize as Captain Milan past the dirt and grime covering her, lead the resistance group.

Above them, a fighter ship flitted around, picking off the remaining infected and attacking the wings of the downed ship when they moved despite the damage already done to them. It looked like they'd purposefully broken the ship's wings so it couldn't fly away, but it was attempting to leave anyway. I shuddered to think what damage Pestilence might have caused if his minions had managed to commandeer it.

I didn't expect to be able to completely avoid all infected from now on, but I also didn't want to advertise Pestilence's failure to him. It was likely he'd soon realize I wasn't dead, but we needed time to prepare before we faced him again. Hopefully, it would be enough to keep Pestilence out of the truly valuable information about any future plans.

I had Adam contact the fighters with a parrot ink construct.

They almost destroyed it out of distrust before it could reach them, but Captain Milan held out a hand to stop them, her eyes narrowing.

When the parrot reached them, it spoke in my voice, repeating the words I'd spoken as it inflated to its full size, like a balloon. "Not all hope is lost. The Sickness is stronger than we knew, and wears a body to walk among us, the same way the gods form a physical manifestation. Yet it has failed to remove the threat to its existence. The godkiller lives, and continues to fight against it. Captain Milan, bring those you are able to save out of the city, and meet us with the ship at the junction of roads."

Her eyes widened, as the people around her started chattering with excitement, confusion, and distrust.

The parrot, now completely deflated, disintegrated. With our message received, we left.

A few hours later, the skirmish around the Shortcut anchor died down, and the scarred fighter ship flew to the junction where we waited, settling down warily a few hundred meters away.

Captain Milan exited the ship, and I got out of our pod, walking toward her slowly so she had time to examine me and notice all the features that had remained the same about my body, as well as the Voice symbol and the Oracle's two gifts.

"It's me," I said simply. "It's going to be alright. We have a place to go, and some people we hope will help us beat the Sickness, who goes by the name Pestilence, by the way. We'll find a way to kill him for good, so that he can't come back and do this again."

"Truly?"

My scales shifted, catching the last light of the dying sun. "Truly."

She bowed to me. "I will follow you, Godkiller."

PACKED aboard the fighter ship were the people Captain Milan and the others had managed to save. Quite a few who'd come through the Shortcut as volunteers, but hadn't had the Sickness, had been rescued or fought their own way out. Many of them were families of those who'd volunteered, and a good number were still children. There were some Players, and even a few human soldiers.

The weight of the living cargo was enough to slow the medium-sized ship, as it had never been meant to be crammed so full of people, but it was still faster than any pod we'd have been able to find, and could fly toward our destination in a straight line instead of needing to follow the half-destroyed roads.

The groups that formed, including our own, were sporadically loud with chatter and gravely silent, as we tried to distract ourselves from the missing voices and, in doing so, only reminded ourselves of them again.

Many of the passengers stared at me when they thought I wasn't looking, whispering together about my appearance. I wondered if I should be embarrassed or offended by this. I probably would have been, not so long ago. I might have even been disturbed by the further deviation from the body I'd once worn. But now, I felt oddly detached from them and their opinions. It was obvious that they would stare, because I was so different from them. I couldn't even bring myself to care what they thought.

Torliam directed us to the middle of the ocean, and, with a little trial and error, we got close enough to the island for it to appear past whatever Skill-based obscuring barrier they'd erected. Despite their protections, we'd found the Remnants with ease compared to the God of Shaping and Molding.

Adam scoffed. "What is this, Atlantis?" Then he went silent, frowned, and shook his head. "No way."

The ship lowered itself to the water and tentatively slipped past the barrier. As we passed through, a wave that felt like sinking through warm jello played over my body.

Two of the Remnants met us on the beach, one holding up a hand to stop us from continuing on.

The other had both his hands pressed to a glowing crystal orb raised on a pedestal, similar to the ones in the cavern beneath the palace, or that the Shortcut engineers had used to make the anchor tower. He frowned, and I felt a glow of power from him. Behind us, the view of the surrounding sea disappeared, replaced by an all-encompassing, roiling fog which stretched beyond the spherical barrier in every direction.

I stepped out of the ship along with my teammates and Captain Milan, eyes roving and Wraith searching for danger.

"Welcome," one of the Estreyans said in smooth English with barely a hint of an accent. "Our *scryer* saw you were coming, and had us prepare accommodations for those who have been rescued. Please, have them follow me."

Captain Milan's eyes narrowed, and she made no move to bring them out of the ship.

He smiled. "They may stay in the ship if they wish, but now that we have once again shrouded the island, you wouldn't be able to fly away even if you wanted. We have food, baths, and a place to sleep. Why not come?"

The other Remnant turned to me. "Are you Eliahan's daughter?"

Zed snorted beside me, and I resisted the urge to do the same. Instead, I said simply, "I am Eve Redding, of the line of Matrix."

That was apparently enough for him, because he bowed and they both started walking away, with a motion for us to follow.

After another moment of hesitation, Captain Milan called for the people she'd rescued to follow as well, and they spilled out of the ship, trailing after us like a long, blobby tail.

The beach opened on to a single-lane, paved road that wound over the island like a snake. We passed houses and shops and community buildings. The idea that this Estreyan village had hidden here on Earth for who-knows how long was somewhat surreal.

As we walked, the villagers shouted to each other in a language that seemed to be a mix of formal Estreyan and accented English, word spreading almost faster than we traveled. We arrived at a large stone hall and were taken to an open-sky courtyard at its center, where there was a large, flat basin of water.

The refugees were led on from there, and Captain Milan went with them to make sure they were safe and had everything they needed.

"Your families have been eager to see you," the guard said. "I will bring them. Our leader will grant you an audience shortly."

Zed and I shared a quick look, and then turned to Sam, whose smile seemed a little unsure. "It's strange, to think about my family," he said. "It's been so long since I've seen them. It almost seems like their son is a completely different person than me. I barely remember who he was."

I could understand the sentiment.

A young couple and two people who were probably their parents came over to us, looking around as if searching for someone. They all had fair coloring, and the woman, the *mom*, I realized, was short and still somewhat cherubic-looking. Despite their similar coloring, their eyes traveled over and past Sam without stopping.

My heart sank, and I took a deep breath to brace myself. "Hello," I said, stepping forward to meet them.

The grandparents startled obviously, but the parents were a little more contained.

"Hello," China and Chanelle's father said. "Are you…"

"My name is Eve Redding. I was friends with your daughters, both of them."

"Was?" the woman repeated in a faint voice, her lips already starting to tremble.

"I thought Chanelle was still alive," her father said, gripping his wife's hand and tensing as if the news was trying to crush him into the ground.

"She passed away only a few days ago," I said. "There was a massive attack by a non-mortal being." I cleared my throat awkwardly.

"Were you there?" her grandfather asked. Unlike the younger two, who made careful and constant eye contact, he and his wife ogled at my 'deformities' blatantly.

"I was."

"Was it quick? Did she suffer?" her mother asked.

Should I tell the truth? That just seemed cruel. I didn't think Chanelle would want to impress the full horror of her gradual deterioration, recovery, and horrifying death onto her family. "She didn't suffer."

While the four of them asked me more questions, some of which I blatantly lied about, another group of people I could only assume were Sam's family hurried over to my teammate, drawing him away and into tearful hugs and platitudes.

The rest of us tried not to watch. Jacky didn't have family of her own, and Gregor's only remaining family had either been assassinated or was encased in the body of a wooden puppet.

A haggard-looking man with grey stubble covering his jaw stood in one of the paths leading to the little courtyard. He looked at Adam, Adam glared at him, and with a nod and a sad quirk of his mouth, the man turned around and walked away.

My mother walked out of a side door, striding confidently. She seemed completely unsurprised to see us. She spared a quick, almost twitchy smile for Zed, her eyes pausing on him for a few seconds. Then her eyes turned toward me, and looked me up and down deliberately. She pressed her lips together. "I see that you didn't take my advice."

My scales shifted.

Beside me, China and Chanelle's bereaved family members seemed to sense the tension and withdrew, clinging to each other for support.

Torliam's eyebrows rose as he looked at my mother, and then his expression hardened.

Zed just sighed, looking away from her with a faint wince on his face.

My jaw clenched, and I stood straighter, the scales at my sides shifting subtly in agitation. "Did you know what was going to happen?"

She scoffed out a fake laugh. "How could I possibly know you'd turn into…that?" She waved me up and down. "No. But I knew you were involved in something dangerous, both for yourself and for the world. And I have access to the news channels. It seems I was right, hmm?"

"Silence yourself, woman." Eliahan's voice rang out from the entrance to another hallway.

My mother's look of self-righteous censure morphed into a fullblown scowl.

Eliahan was accompanied by a wizened old man and a tall woman, whose hair was so dark a black it gleamed blue in the sunlight. The woman led the trio, and she sighed, tossing a look to Eliahan. She turned back to the rest of the room and asked the humans to leave. "You will have further time to reunite with your children when we are finished here. But for now, I must speak with them on urgent matters." She spoke in English, and held a kind of authority that reminded me of Queen Mardinest, but less vicious and more calmly self-assured. "Is it time our aid is needed?" she said, looking at me.

I laughed angrily. "Is it time?" I repeated mockingly. "Pestilence is now free of whatever shackles the God of Shaping and Molding had placed upon it. It attempted to kill us, and succeeded in killing a ton of other innocent people, along with one of my teammates. One of my other teammates placed her spirit in the body of a puppet to avoid that same fate, and the world is pretty much deteriorating at the rate of a rotting carcass. Which is what the entire population will be, soon." I took a deep breath, feeling the rumble of my anger in the air. "I think it's well *past* time."

"I understand your anger, but we have done what we must. We could not leave this place to fight with you. The fate of our worlds is much more important than the loss of a single battle, or even the lives of many. We have bought you time, experience, and a second chance."

I bristled, but kept silent.

"I am Ester, once of the line of Matrix." She paused to let the fact that we were at least distantly related sink in. "We are the Remnants, and we have fought against Pestilence since the days before the arrays were closed and we became trapped here." She walked to the basin of water and looked down into it, eyes distant with memory. "You are not the first to find the God of Shaping and Molding. My people and I discovered him, and though we were not meant to put an end to this, he accepted our aid and what power we could funnel to him. He created this place for us. We have hidden, and we have lent our power to the Champion without ceasing, and we have waited for the spark of prophecy to be born among our children with the humans." She shot a repressive glare toward Eliahan, then.

My anger had gone from a roar to a simmer, but none of it had disappeared. "Even if you had to stay here, that doesn't mean you couldn't have warned us. You could have *said* something about Pestilence. Maybe if you had, we wouldn't be in this situation right now."

She shook her head. "If we had told you anything more than we did, you would be dead." She looked up from the basin, her own eyes strangely reflective, as if they were mere films over deep pools of water. "The eldest of us was but a child when we became trapped on this forsaken planet, but she was chosen for the mission because she had been granted a Bestowal by the Oracle. She has some ability to see the future, though only one path can be made clear with each attempt. She has searched ceaselessly, since we first became aware of your existence, and the answer has never changed. In every future where you came to us for aid, having *survived* Pestilence, you are angry at us for keeping this secret and leaving you to fail. We were told by the god himself when this island was created for us that one day, when the spark-of-hope found him and convinced him to aid them, despair would follow hope, the world would fall, and only in this darkness would we once again have a chance to eradicate the source. Our scryer found no path that would allow you to survive long enough to do this, if all was made clear to you before the right time."

My scales settled down as my anger lost its outlet.

QUEST COMPLETED!

AFTER THE INITIAL MEETING, Ester took us to her home and brought some of her people to examine Kris while we continued to talk. Ester had a big open room on her ground floor that looked kind of like a dojo, but with Estreyan symbols and designs burned into the wood floor over most of the room.

The Remnants she called were happy to help, and, rather than showing consternation at Kris' condition, seemed quite fascinated, almost excited.

"So, can you fix her?" Gregor demanded, arms crossed over his chest.

They shared looks with each other before speaking. "There is nothing *wrong* with her. She is not broken, merely sub-optimized." The speaker turned back to Kris, who sat in her puppet form atop her chilled human body. "Her Seeds should have been transferred along with her spirit, if she wanted her new body to continue functioning properly."

Gregor scowled. "You're supposed to put her spirit back in her *old* body."

The Remnant huffed at him, as if amused. "Well, I can't do that. But I can keep her alive by helping her form a Seed core within her new body."

One of the others cleared her throat. "If the problem is that the new body is…less than aesthetically pleasing for the housing of a young girl's spirit, I can help with that. I have some prowess with physical transmutations. She'll be able to do everything she could as a human, once I'm done with her. I'll even make her look the same."

Kris seemed okay with that, judging by the double thumbs-up she shot to everyone.

The group got to work setting up Kris' body and the puppet within a couple of the symbolic circles burned into the ground. They started cutting shallow symbols in the human corpse's skin and brought out a few more of those crystals that seemed to be used for a lot of their non-Skill based extraordinary exploits. Supposedly it was technology, but really it looked like magic to me.

While we watched and waited, we talked with Ester, who was my...great-great-great grandmother or something. "So, do you know how to actually *fight* Pestilence?" I said.

She sighed wearily. "We do not. His power is not like our own. From what we could glean from the ancient texts, which were old even when our people lived on the old world, Pestilence draws power from the void, the *breaks*," and here she used that same Estreyan word I'd heard before, which had no equivalent in English, "which exist in the emptiness of the space between worlds. Its body is an anchor point, similar in concept if not execution to the anchors used for the teleportation devices I believe your kind have dubbed 'Shortcuts.'"

I nodded. "We guessed that."

"Truly?" She sounded surprised.

"My brother is the Veil-Piercer," I said. "He can see cracks in the world, and when he opens them, it creates a portal to...another realm, I *think*. Maybe an alternate dimension of some sort. It seems that within that realm, the Sickness does not progress. Pestilence's influence doesn't reach there. Zed has been training his Perception, and he believes he can see a different kind of connection in Pestilence's chest, when his covering of bugs is destroyed. We assumed he was hiding his core in another realm."

Excitement took over Ester's stoic features, and she leaned forward to grab my forearms. "Do you know what would happen if you were to bring Pestilence himself into this other realm? Tell me more about these cracks in the world."

Zed cleared his throat and nonchalantly opened one to show her, instead.

Chapter 42

There is only one sin and it is: weakness.
— Swami Vivekananda

ESTER WAS FASCINATED by the Other Place, as well as the different colored cracks Zed saw, but couldn't touch. Before the first group of Remnants she'd called could even finish with Kris, she'd sent for others to work with Zed. "There is no time to waste," she said, smiling widely and pressing her hands together despite the cold still wafting off her from her trip to the emotion-draining realm.

Their research was postponed for a little while, when the people working with Kris finally finished their preparation. The little crystals glowed, smoke curled up from the symbols on the floor, and Kris' dead, human body arched.

At first, that seemed to be all, but then the crystals flared brighter and the air above Kris' chest started to shimmer. The sheen grew till it was filled with a small but obvious sparkling ball of Seed material, darker than the Seeds Torliam had once provided NIX, and oh-so-faintly purple.

Once they had drawn all they could, the tiny Seed core floated over to Kris' new body, where the chest plate had been removed. It settled in her chest, and they worked quickly to put the puppet back together.

Then, the woman who'd promised she could "transmute" Kris's body moved to stand over her, hands waving through the air like she was sculpting invisible clay, or maybe playing an exotic instrument.

The puppet's wood grew skin-toned, then morphed, till the joints weren't bare and the structure looked like a real body. Kris grew hair and her features extended from the wood and refined till they looked delicate and human.

In a few minutes, she was a miniature version of the child she'd once been.

I expected her to grow at that point, but the woman lowered her arms and stepped away. "There," she said with a nod, her tone satisfied.

Kris stood up, examining her new body with consternation. "I'm...tiny," she said, her voice high-pitched due to the size of her voice box.

The woman frowned down at her. "Well, yes. But you're quite lovely, now. I never promised I could make you huge. I can transmute things, I can't simply take matter from the ether."

Kris stared up at her, mouth falling open. After a couple seconds, she rallied. "I have *four arms*."

"Well, you can still unscrew the second set, if you want. I made sure you didn't lose that modular exchange ability." The woman grinned with pride.

APPARENTLY, there wasn't much to be done about Kris' new body. Ester informed me that making her mostly human again was already pretty much a miracle, with what Skills they had available to them. Perhaps someone on Estreyer could help, but she doubted it, unless they happened to have the perfect Skill, or we found two people with a Skill combination that could work together.

Apparently, the Remnants were the greatest masters of arcane technology around. A lot of their knowledge had been lost to their home-world in the time since the network of arrays had been locked. The Shortcuts were the height of the technology that remained, and the Estreyans barely understood those. Ester strongly advised against trying to use Chaos to make Kris bigger, without extensive research into the possible repercussions.

Though Kris had been upset at first, she responded with surprising maturity for a child barely in the double digit years and said she was just happy to be alive, no matter how small she was.

Gregor quickly decided that having his older sister be smaller than him came with distinct advantages and lorded it over her until she punched him again.

After less than a day to check out the situation, Captain Milan had talked to Ester, then contacted all the other Estreyan ships still on Earth, letting them know where to come for refuge. The moderately sized island was bustling with people. The refugees settled in alright, but many of them were traumatized by the sudden reversal of hope to despair, and more than a few of them blamed me for it or thought that I'd deliberately lied when I said I could cure the Sickness. One woman, fresh claw marks from a human running down her face, tried to spit on me as I walked past.

At first, I bristled, my new scales rising up a little like a cat puffing up in anger. But I took a deep breath and let the anger settle back down inside me. Her dislike wasn't unfounded. In the eyes of the Estreyans, I had either betrayed them or simply failed so horribly they had lost faith in me, even learned to hate me.

I let her be and moved on to keep preparing for the final battle. My new body had come with an increased level of control over my Skills, once again. Chaos, specifically. I found a small bird that had been injured falling from the nest. I picked it up and let Chaos burn at its flesh. I used a combination of understanding what I was trying to do and a measure of steely willpower that forced the remade bird to be healthy and whole even if the laws of nature wouldn't have allowed it otherwise.

When it didn't die, and in fact seemed just fine, the seams around my healing invisible even to Wraith, I went straight to Adam. "I can heal your back," I announced abruptly.

He looked up from the fractal ink tattoo he'd been sinking into his own shoulder. To my surprise, he didn't brighten at the good news. "Are you sure? This isn't just as simple as putting me back together. You need to overcome the force that keeps normal people from being able to heal an injury from a god's attack, too."

I rolled my eyes. "I'm resisting Pestilence, and even the God of Knowledge couldn't do that. I can do it."

"I'm getting by just fine with the ink latticework under my skin."

I waved a hand. "This won't stop you from using that to move around if you want to, or if I fail to heal you properly. But if this works, it will mean you can keep moving even if you're down to the last drop of Skill power or for some reason don't have access to Animus again, like what happened during the Yggdrasil Trial. Really, what are you so hesitant about?"

He swallowed a couple times. "I just…this has become normal for me. I've wanted to be healed since it happened, but when you offer it so suddenly, it's somewhat nerve-wracking." He chuckled. "Well, that's stupid. Let's do it. Do we need Sam or anything?"

"Err…that's probably a good idea." I should have thought of that ahead of time, but I'd been too excited.

Adam smirked at me, obviously reading the chagrin in my expression. "Let's go find him then."

We did find Sam, but we also happened to find Zed, Gregor, and the group of Remnants Ester had set to investigating his Skill and the Other Place.

"We did it!" Gregor yelled, running over to me.

"What did you do?" I caught him in my arms and shifted him around so he could ride atop my shoulders as I walked over to the cold rip hanging in mid-air, which the research group was stationed all around.

"We figured out how to measure the signs of the cracks. Not just the ones to the Other Place, but the ones Pestilence uses! And if we can measure them, these Remnant scientists think they can set something up that will *react* to them. We can trap Pestilence in the Other Place, and once he's there, we'll be able to kill him!" the little boy announced.

THE REVELATION that the Other Place was basically a battleground created to give us an advantage against Pestilence's regenerative ability gave an impetus to our planning strong enough to hurl us forward.

The Remnants had found that their bodies didn't react nearly as well to the Other Place as ours did. We speculated that bearing one of the Seal of Nine symbols somehow helped, because, despite how enthusiastic they were about training, it didn't seem to get any easier for them, and every time they entered we had to worry about them passing out within. It had been the same for Chanelle and Blaine, of course. While the rest of us built up a resistance to its effects, they'd seemed to constantly suffer.

The warriors might not have been useful, but the intellectuals set to creating something that could affect Pestilence via his connection to whatever extra-dimensional void he'd stashed his source of power in, and the rest of us started training our resistance to the Other Place's draining effects.

I knew the coming fight would be difficult, if not impossible. I spent the time I wasn't training working on the Oracle's third gift. But no matter how much I wanted it, I couldn't get it to fit together. I tried crying and bleeding on it again. I got up in the middle of the night to work on it. I had my teammates try and help me. All to no avail.

To my surprise, Ester wasn't concerned by my failure at all. She laughed. "The gift of the Oracle is to give one a vision to help one on the path, *when they need it*. If you do not need it, why are you so desperate? We know how to kill Pestilence now. Maybe one day, you will face another difficulty, and need a vision to guide your way. Save it till then."

I didn't stop trying to solve it, but I didn't worry about it so much after that, and spent more time determining concrete things I could change to affect the outcome of the battle directly. While the physical Attributes were important for any fight, I knew the true merit of the winner would be dependent on that thing my Attributes only measured indirectly through Charisma. I needed willpower created from a strength so powerful it would mold the world to my wishes. I would have to do more than control my own body and mind, this time.

Ester told me how to strengthen myself in that way, when I mentioned my uncertainty. "A godling grows stronger the same as every other being. Through hardship."

I found that distinctly unhelpful at first, but realized that the answer might actually be simpler than I thought. It was possible to acclimatize oneself to the Other Place, to build up a resistance to its draining effects over time and with practice. How were we doing that? Sure, our Resilience grew a bit from the actual cold, but my Charisma also leveled up sporadically after spending too much time in that version of reality. Thus, a somewhat reckless plan was born.

Alone, I stepped through the rip Zed had created, my back close enough to it that someone could reach through and pull me away if things went pear-shaped.

I let a few faint, misty tendrils of Chaos spill out of my palm. There was a subtle sense of tension, of tightening, in the air around me. The hair on the back of my neck rose, and I knew I was being watched. I set Chaos to vibrating the air a few inches above my skin, just enough to warm it.

The world darkened in the distance, as if it was a stage and the spotlight had been turned on me.

I pushed a little harder, and a small ball of air burst into flame. Something inside my chest loosened at the rush of color and life the warmth brought.

Darkness rushed in around me, sucking at the fire with a hunger so great it was palpable in the very air. The flame dimmed, and the color leached out of it, along with all but the tiniest amount of heat.

My eyelashes frosted over, and I choked as that same hunger pulled at my body, trying to draw the life from me as if it were sucking the marrow from a stew bone. I resisted, taking away the warmth and power and holding it within, imagining my skin as an impenetrable barrier. "Are you hungry for the taste of fire?" I called out, my voice rough as my lungs and throat struggled with the frigidity of the air.

The watcher responded, the darkness of its presence concealing the world beyond a radius of a few feet as it swirled around me.

Wraith stretched out, but could not sense its edges.

"I am hungry," it said to me, with an echoing voice that sounded like a whale singing from the depths of the ocean. In its echo, I caught the idea of a form so vast I couldn't quite comprehend it. I was like a speck of dust in the eye of a cosmic whale.

"I have an enemy," I said. "I will bring it to this place to fight it."

"You wish your enemy to be weakened? For me to devour their life instead of your own?"

I hesitated, and, rather than agreeing, explained exactly who and what my enemy was, to the best of my knowledge.

I caught the echo of acknowledgment, perhaps understanding. "So you must destroy its physical form, and ravage the connections to its power, so that it may not exist again. The boy can do it, if his fingers can learn the touch."

The boy could do it? "Do you mean Zed?" I said.

The cosmic whale shifted, and I caught its amusement. "Is that what you call him? The one whose fingers can reach me here, from your own realm? The one who brings me warmth and travelers to pull from? Yes," it said, suddenly echoing back firm confidence, with an undertone of slithering slyness. "I can pull at your fire and life less, when you bring the thing here to kill it. Do you want anything else?"

Slowing the rate that the Other Place weakened us would be a huge boon. I hesitated, before agreeing, though. "Can you do anything else that might help?"

"It is not alive. There is nothing for me to take from it. Though if you wish…I might offer you the adversity to grow stronger."

I shifted, my eyes narrowing. How did it know that's what I'd come to ask of it?

It pulsed in a way that felt like laughter. "I heard an echo of your question in the air. That *is* what you want, is it not?"

I did.

"What will you offer me in return?"

I thought carefully before answering. "Fire."

"Yes. Light, energy, and life, in its own way. You will give me one day of constant flames, and I will ease the burden of my realm on you while you fight."

There was that *slithering*, again. I thought carefully before opening my mouth to speak. I looked at the darkness around the patch of grey I stood on. "What is one day, in a place where the sun never rises and never sets?"

The cosmic whale laughed.

WE HAD a small celebration when I healed Adam's legs.

Sam very carefully numbed Adam's body from the mid-back

down, which was a kind of torture in itself due to the way Sam's Skill worked, but not as bad as the burn of Chaos would be. Then, he used Black Sun to give Adam lethargy and apathy, which really didn't work as a substitute for anesthesia, but at least allowed him to relax.

Before starting, I put my hand on the sides of Adam's lower back, around where the wound still gaped open, a little raw and only having avoided infection because of Sam's Skill. I pushed Wraith into Adam's flesh, cataloguing everything that was wrong, and building a model in my mind of what it should have looked like instead.

I took my time thinking the procedure over, planning the steps, the transformation, and cementing the idea of Adam's healed back in my mind. He was missing some muscle-mass and bone, and though I could forcefully take it from something else, like air, it was easiest to cut a chunk out of an animal that was roughly the right size. When I was ready, I let Chaos bubble up out of my hand and start to burn. Then I let it eat up the chunk of meat and dropped the flames into Adam's wound.

Despite Sam's ministrations, Adam screamed, and his arms scrabbled at the slab of smooth granite he lay on.

Torliam hurried to shove a rolled-up wad of cloth into Adam's mouth so he didn't break his teeth with the clenching and grinding. I remembered when he'd done the same for me.

I set my will to making Adam whole again. It took a few minutes.

He kept screaming, but, as I worked, his legs started to twitch and jerk along with his arms.

When I had finished, he lay on the rock slab limply, a sheen of sweat covering his body. He spat out the wad of cloth in his mouth. "Sam, I need an antidote for the numbness. Next time, I'll just take the pain straight up, that way I don't have to deal with both."

I pulled up Adam's Attribute Window to check that nothing obvious was screwed up.

PLAYER NAME: ADAM COYLE
TITLE: ONE OF NINE
CHARACTERISTIC SKILL: ELECTRIC SOVEREIGN
SKILLS: HYPER FOCUS, ANIMUS, BESTOW

STRENGTH: 28

LIFE: 27
AGILITY: 68
GRACE: 21
INTELLIGENCE: 49
FOCUS: 37
BEAUTY: 12
CHARISMA: 12
MANUAL DEXTERITY: 35
MENTAL ACUITY: 40
RESILIENCE: 19
STAMINA: 25
PERCEPTION: 11

When he sat up, able to hold himself without bracing on his arms, and jerked his legs around a little, I let out a sigh of relief, and the others burst into cheers.

Adam managed to stand for a few seconds, his legs trembling under him, before he had to sit back down again. He'd lost a lot of muscle to inactivity, and though I'd replaced a portion of the loss in his back, I hadn't done so to his legs, simply made sure his nerves worked correctly. It would take time for him to walk and run again, but with practice he'd be as good as new.

We set up a little bonfire and ate fish that Kris had tugged out of the sea by forcing their spirits toward her. If she tugged slowly enough, the spirits weren't ripped directly out of the fish's bodies, but were drawn physically and inexorably toward the surface, just like they were caught on a line.

We stayed up late despite the fatigue that had built up throughout the day, because that bonfire was a spot of light in the darkness in more than one way. When we left it, we would have to sleep, and face the reality of our situation. Three of our number would never celebrate with us again, and the nightmares made true rest difficult.

THE REMNANTS HAD BEEN free from the Sickness before the Champion fell, but, after that, we had brought in the refugees from

489

the downed ship and the encampment around the Shortcut anchor. Some of them showed symptoms, which progressed more rapidly than normal.

I avoided the infected like the literal plague. Partially, this was because I didn't want to give Pestilence such an obvious opening to find and attack me again, if he didn't already know where I was. But it was also because I felt guilty, knowing that I could probably help those people if I decided to enter into a blood-covenant with them. Sure, my power would quickly run out if I attempted to keep too many people healthy against Pestilence's will, but I could do more than I was. Even so, the thought of sharing my blood with strangers made me shudder. I had a faint sense in the back of my head for the rest of my team, now, since I'd given a drop of blood to each of them. It wasn't nearly as strong as the connection I had to Torliam, but, in its way, it was intimate. I didn't want to feel that with strangers. I sympathized anew with Torliam for his own forced blood-sharing.

Still, the whole thing weighed on me, until I had an epiphany. I burst into Torliam's room and started pacing the floor in front of him. "I just realized something," I said.

He watched me pace, but didn't respond, perhaps waiting for me to explain myself.

"Pestilence feeds off the idea that we can never win. He made it obvious he wants our despair. But what if it's not just that? What if he *needs* our despair? What if our despair nourishes him? Think about it. He's always been cultivating this sense of the inevitable, for the last few thousands of years. 'If you try to escape your sick world and build another, I'll just follow you. There is no cure. And if you happen to find one, I'll destroy it in the most cruel way I can think of and leave you to slowly die.' But!" I spun, pointing at him.

He blinked slowly, the corners of his mouth twitching upward.

"I realized something new," I continued. "Perception molds…no, perception *is* reality, in a way. I reframed the way I thought of myself, and I changed. Or maybe I'd just been holding myself back all along because I lacked imagination." My voice lowered as my thoughts trailed off the path I'd been taking. "I did, after all, use Knowledge's greater understanding of how my Skill worked to burn out the Sickness once before, even if the Champion *was* still weakening Pestilence at that point."

"Yes?" he said, raising an eyebrow. He waved his hand to me, as if the motion would clear my brain of whatever fog was distracting it.

"The point is, I wouldn't have been able to save Gregor, Adam, and Jacky the way I did, before I remade myself and acknowledged the idea that I'm not the Eve I once was. It was my perception that I was a godling and that I could do it that *allowed* me to do it. I'm not normally one for the flowery, feel-good, do-gooder heroism. But in this case…hope might literally be a weapon. A sort of poison that actually does make Pestilence's victory less inevitable. I think that's why he's so set on crushing it. I think that's why the prophecy is about *finding* a spark of hope, when all seems lost. So we either need to figure out how to heal people without the lance, or find another way to give them hope."

Torliam remained silent.

I grimaced. "I mean, I could be wrong. But why is it that I can affect the world with pure willpower, the gods can, and Pestilence can, but normal people are out of luck? That doesn't make *sense*. Sure, maybe the average mortal wouldn't be very powerful, despite their Seeds, but even if individual power is weak, a huge mass of people working together to change something should have some effect. I think the population has been working *for* Pestilence, believing in the inevitability of defeat, and we accidentally converted them to our side, and that's why he came after us with such prejudice.

Torliam rubbed at his newly trimmed beard. "I am skeptical whether the hope of mortals will actually weaken Pestilence, or simply enrage him. Either way, we could use this to our advantage, but I am not sure what might cause the people to feel enough hope to be useful, at this point. As you said, much of my people's optimism was likely crushed when the moment of reversal and despair was so critically timed to follow their moment of greatest hope."

I stopped pacing. "What if we don't just try to make them *feel* better? What if we give them the impetus to actually make a difference? If we could give them something an individual could do to actively fight back against the Sickness, wouldn't that transform the landscape of the whole battle? Until now, it's been running and hiding and killing each other to try and stay safe. I think there might be a way to change that."

Torliam's eyebrows rose. "Alright. Your words hold sense, but *how* would you do this?"

I grinned at him. "I made a bargain with the Other Place. Fire, in exchange for it draining less of our strength during the fight. What if we could do something similar, but on a much, much larger scale?"

He paused, as if arrested. "You would have the people make offerings to the place beyond the Veil?"

"Well, more or less. They can't exactly send over an actual fire, especially not fire fueled by Chaos itself. But they could send over something filled with *energy*, right? Because that's basically what the Other Place wants. Even if I'm wrong about hope undermining Pestilence's odds, a better bargain with the Other Place is a concrete advantage."

Torliam stood. "The crystals! The ones we use to hold power for our devices and our Shortcuts. Every Estreyan can push power into them with a small bit of blood dropped onto the surface. The larger ones are rare, but the small ones are everywhere, like your human batteries. It might not be Chaos, but with enough of them, you can call down lightning from the heavens and fold space itself. What is that, if not energy?"

Chapter 43

Fear cannot be banished, but it can be calm and without panic; it can be mitigated by reason and evaluation.
— Vannevar Bush

I TALKED to the cosmic whale of the Other Place again, and it was pleased to offer greater forbearance in draining us in exchange for more energy, in the form of Estreyan battery crystals.

So I had to go back to Estreyer. I was able to do so, because one of the ships that had joined us carried the invading force's Shortcut. But I *really* didn't want to.

I stood before the ball with its floating, orbiting rings, feeling faintly sick. My fingers trembled, and I felt like I had to pee, even though I knew I didn't. I didn't want to face Estreyer again, after my sensational failure. If I hadn't been filled with a profound, roiling hatred that bubbled up when I sat still for too long and demanded I destroy Pestilence down to the last atom, I probably would have found some excuse not to go.

But I *did* have that hatred. It was a more competent motivator that my own selfishness had ever been. It didn't care if I was afraid to face the people I'd let down and didn't know how to convince them to help. My hatred was happy to sacrifice even me to the flames, if it would mean I could destroy Pestilence too. And in the face of his death, what was a little trepidation, a little humiliation?

I wondered—if this hatred was ever spent, would I be left empty? What could remain, when now it filled my soul to the trivialization of all other emotion?

Beside me, Zed knocked his shoulder into my arm and threw me a small, reassuring smile.

On my other side, Torliam didn't touch me, but his tone was a little too nonchalant to be convincing when he said, "Some may be foolish and wish to blame us for what was not our fault, but once they learn the truth, many of them will do all that is in their power to aid us. Those that do not are not worthy of saving, in any case."

I took a deep breath, made sure my new scales and their involuntary reactions weren't giving away my internal emotions, and nodded to the Shortcut operator.

The floating bands spun quicker and quicker, I heard faint music, and then we were standing in the cavern beneath the palace, barely nauseous.

Zed and Torliam came with me while the others remained behind to train and prepare. Zed, because he could provide me with protection by literally pulling me out of danger and into another world, and Torliam, because he was an Estreyan native, powerful enough to fight against other Estreyan warriors, and his mother was queen.

We'd only been walking away from the glow of the orbs that surrounded the arcane circle for a few minutes when Queen Mardinest greeted us.

She must have had some sort of alert set up on the Shortcut itself, I thought inanely.

She'd obviously run to meet us. Her skin was pale and drawn, with bags under her eyes. She'd come without any guards and stood blocking the path alone, panting wildly. She drew the knife at her waist immediately, brandishing it with a sure grip. "How dare you come here again, you honorless scum!" She spat on the ground, glaring at us.

Torliam stepped forward, snatching his mother's wrist and holding it aloft.

She struggled against him, her other fist punching into his side in rapid succession.

Torliam winced and grabbed that arm, too, grunting out, "Mother, it is not as you think. We have not betrayed you, or the people," before she could resort to kicking him.

She panted, glaring at him. "If you do not unhand me, I will be forced to fight against you seriously. Step back."

He let go and took a big step away from her, sidling close to Zed for protection in a way that was almost comical, since my brother was so much smaller than him.

She glared at all three of us. "Explain. You have but moments before I lose my patience and call the guards to have you executed before the crowds as payment for the people's suffering."

I felt calmer now than I had before we left. "Use that Skill you told me of so threateningly. Smell the truth of my words as they carry through the air," I said challengingly. "The Sickness is not a disease. It is the influence of a being called Pestilence, who is sentient and powerful, and much like the gods of this world. The Champion has been fighting against him until now, and that is why Pestilence struggled to spread his power among us. Pestilence has now defeated the Champion, and this is why he is able to kill swaths of people within days."

She paled dramatically. "You lie."

"I am telling the truth, and you know it."

Her fingers convulsed around the hilt of her knife, and she let her arm fall to her side limply.

"Pestilence came after me and my team. He tried to kill us. He tried to kill me. And that was a *mistake*, because he *failed*. If he had been content to continue on as he had been, we might have never been able to eradicate the Sickness, without the God of Shaping and Molding to hold him back. But instead, he wanted to crush us completely. He revealed himself. We learned his true nature, and we have a way to defeat him for good. We can kill him, and when we do, unlike a normal god that will simply reform, he will lose his access to the realms of mortals, his power cut off and trapped at its source, the *breaks* between worlds." I paused. "This is not a battle that I or any of the Seal of Nine fights alone."

She scoffed. "Do you wish to ask more of my warriors to fight and die by your side, as they did the last time? I cannot ask that of them again."

I shook my head. "We have a weapon to defeat Pestilence, and we don't need the blood of warriors to wield it. I doubt they would be able to survive its effects, since its use depends on the Seal. What we need is power to run it, and every man, woman, and child on Estreyer can contribute to that easily."

I'D THOUGHT we would put together another press conference or an announcement in the coliseum, but Queen Mardinest laughed raggedly when I suggested it. "I think you do not understand the situation here on Estreyer. If your presence was announced, it is likely we would have to deal with several assassination attempts. I was forced to send your human peace delegation back to Earth after the first attempt of that nature was made on one of their members. Oh," she said, seeing my expression, "some of the people still hold faith in you. But those who have lost faith feel betrayed in the greatest way imaginable. An oathbreaker of such magnitude is anathema. No, we will record your message. You will explain that you have grown fully into your role as a godling," she raised a derisive eyebrow at my surprise, "and tell them what you told me of Pestilence and your plan to defeat him. My power has been greatly diminished, but I still hold some sway with the people. I will place my honor beside yours." She turned to me, her eyes narrowing. "If you fail to defeat the Sickness, do not come back alive."

We followed her plan, and I was back on Earth by the morning, the whole trip much less hassle than I'd been anticipating. Admittedly, I'd encountered very few people during that time, but none of them had tried to spit in my face.

With one more-or-less-ally acquired, I went to the humans next. Their understanding of non-mortal beings and powers that broke the rules of physics as they knew them wasn't as good, but they felt less *personal* resentment toward me as the cause of all their woes. When I told them that the cause of the disease was a recently discovered single member of a *third* alien race, hostile to both humans and Estreyans, and which was actively perpetrating and maintaining said disease, it was easy enough to understand. When I told them I had a way to kill this alien, they asked me what I needed from them.

The Shortcut anchor had been built on what used to be a huge mall parking lot adjacent to a city park. I had them clear away the encampment they'd built there, with as much secrecy as possible, then evacuate the citizens from the surrounding area. Security cameras were shut down. Then, the Remnants came in and got to work, building an arcane circle around the Shortcut anchor, where we would be receiving a *huge* shipment of fully charged crystals of various sizes soon, hopefully.

We asked for human weapons that didn't require electricity to work. We went into the Other Place and set up our battleground. We had more weapons and armor made, catered to the Skills they would be used with. Those Estreyans who were here on Earth, and still wished to work with us, helped with the creation of our battle-plan.

After a couple weeks had passed, we went into the Other Place for one last training session. We could only prepare so long before Pestilence decided to take the initiative again and come after us on his terms, and that would be a disaster. None of us wanted to find ourselves dead in the night, in our beds, without any chance to change anything. I already couldn't sleep for the tension and the nightmares, and it only grew worse.

I let out a deep breath and watched the water particles within freeze instantly into minuscule fractal snowflakes, too small for the normal human eye to make out. "Is everyone ready?" I asked, looking at my teammates past the dancing branches of condensed Chaos that wove through the air around me.

The dust flakes that the Other Place seemed to produce had grown a lot heavier in the time we'd been training within. Now they fluttered down like thick grey snow, though they still disintegrated immediately upon touching anything.

Adam looked up from his ink constructs, arcs of lightning playing across his skin. "Are you seriously asking that? What will you do if someone says 'no?' It's not like we have a choice here. It's kill or be killed."

"I'm ready," Kris said in her doll-like voice, riding atop one of her new marionettes so she didn't have to look up from the perspective of someone only two feet high. She clenched her fist, and the bugs darting around dropped from the air and ceased their movement, whatever tiny spirits had been inside them ripped mercilessly out of their bodies.

I wondered what I would do, if some of us died tomorrow. I knew Adam's words were true, but would it be worth it, even so?

I pulled up my Attribute Window and ran my eyes over the numbers that defined my worth in a fight.

PLAYER NAME: EVE REDDING
TITLE: BEARER OF TESTIMONY
CHARACTERISTIC SKILL: SPIRIT OF THE HUNTRESS,
TUMBLING FEATHER
LEVEL: 38
SKILLS: COMMAND, WRAITH, CHAOS, VOICE

STRENGTH: 30
LIFE: 81
AGILITY: 37
GRACE: 31
INTELLIGENCE: 34
FOCUS: 30
BEAUTY: 18
CHARISMA: 40
MANUAL DEXTERITY: 10
MENTAL ACUITY: 31
RESILIENCE: 73
STAMINA: 43
PERCEPTION: 45

Once, when I'd first started as Player, I might have been astounded at the combined value of those numbers. Now, I knew how lacking they were. I could only hope that the nine of us together would be able to match up against Pestilence.

The Summoner, the Gale, the Gifter. The Tracker, the Struggle, the Shadow. The Black Sun, and the Veil-Piercer. We were *meant* to do this, right? The gods had been preparing us specifically for this fight. I'd originally thought the greater Trials had been completed when we successfully got the nine parts of the Yggdrasil tree to grow, but obviously I'd been wrong.

The Other Place darkened at the edges and contracted around us as the cosmic whale announced its presence. "Have you many stones of energy for me? You will not last against Pestilence even with all your training, if you do not give me another source to pull from as you battle him. Even cut off from his true power, you will need to destroy his body many, many times before he is weakened enough for his existence to be erased from the realms of mortals."

Gregor snorted at the swirling darkness around our little clearing. "We have a small mountain coming through, according to Queen Mardinest. Just wait. You'll eat until you get fat."

The whale thrummed with amusement, and a bit of wistfulness, but beneath it all was the ever-present, ravenous *gluttony*.

THE NEXT DAY, we set the last bits of the trap. We were as rested as we could be, with the nightmares and the constant stress. We'd gathered a few city blocks away from the Shortcut anchor to wait. The cloud cover was thick and heavy, rolling cumulous masses that hung inert and oppressive above us. Snowflakes drifted down from them lazily, as there was no wind to blow them about. They melted when they touched the ground, and I was reminded of the dust falling in the Other Place.

Adam's link displayed the news. Specifically, it showed the broadcast of the press release we'd filmed just hours earlier.

"…Symptoms caused by attacks of this third alien race, which is hostile to all life forms," the link spoke out in a slightly tinny voice. Part of the press conference was to illuminate the unknown, as knowledge was a natural counter to fear. "We have multiple teams working to recreate the cure, and expect to be successful soon." The other part was just to forcefully alleviate that fear, so that whatever benefit Pestilence got from it would be lessened. The broadcast went on to warn civilians to stay away from the part of the city we were in, as we were fabricating some very energy-intensive, potentially destructive weapons specifically meant to be effective against the third alien life form. We'd had as many people as possible evacuated already, but I knew we hadn't found all of them, and some had refused to leave.

On Estreyer, a similar news release meant to threaten Pestilence was being broadcast, while they gathered the last of the Seed-charged crystals. Any moment now, they would be sending them through the Shortcut.

"Do you think this will work?" Zed said, scanning our surroundings restlessly.

Estreyan warriors, those Remnants with a battle Skill, and a smattering of human soldiers were hidden in the buildings around us.

Our location and some false details of the operation we had planned had been leaked. Anyone determined enough would be able to find us rather easily, hopefully without being tipped off to the trap. With the announcements we'd made, I was sure he would come. When he did, no matter which direction he came from, someone would be there to attack and slow him down. We wanted to make it as difficult as possible for him to reach the Shortcut anchor, mostly so that he didn't suspect the trap. Just for that, people who'd volunteered to hold him off would probably die. But we needed every advantage we could get. The trap *had* to work. "He'll come," I said, my voice a little softer than I intended, as the words enhanced my trepidation.

Jacky fingered her new gauntlets with the spiked knuckles, clenching her fists and watching as the interlocking pieces shifted. The gauntlets were Gregor's idea, and were designed to expand along with her fists when she grew. They were also filled with a few dozen doses of poison that Sam had created, and would release some of that poison whenever she punched something with enough force.

The poison Sam had developed didn't just put people to sleep or paralyze them. Well, actually, it did *both*, but it put them to sleep so they wouldn't have to experience the agony and fear associated with the nerves along their spine being dissolved. Their bodies were literally incapable of movement after the poison did its work, but, as long as they didn't panic too much, they would continue to breathe and their heart would continue to pump. It was a precaution against Pestilence's ability to control the bodies of those he had tainted directly, despite otherwise-debilitating injury or unconsciousness, as well as insurance against the chance that he might have been holding back when he attacked us before.

Behind us, the Shortcut anchor glowed, its double helix form lighting up the heavy fog and reflecting off the packed clouds above.

Then the crystals arrived, appearing in a small mountain that let off even more light as the displacement wave rolled outward. I sensed a few spatters of still-warm blood over some parts of the mound. Had Pestilence tried to stop the transfer?

We busied ourselves, drawing lines and symbols on the ground in black tar. It would activate an effect for as long as it burned, or that's what we had purposely let slip, anyway. The symbols we drew didn't actually have any meaning, but they were close enough to seem like they might. We'd made it very clear–to people we didn't really trust–that the focal point of this experimental ritual to kill Pestilence was at the Shortcut anchor, and that if something happened to it, or the crystals that had just appeared around it, everything would be ruined.

I heard the gunshots first, coming from a few blocks to the north. There were crazed screams from Pestilence's minions and a cacophony of noise from the world-bending effects of Skills being brought to bear on them.

A few of the landmines we'd planted exploded. I winced, knowing some people wouldn't be walking away from that.

I didn't sense Pestilence among the horde. All of them had heart-beats and seemed to be made of flesh. Where was he?

I spun around, as bugs flowed up from the gutters and out from the walls of the abandoned buildings around us. They rushed together, climbing atop each other's bodies till they formed a mound, and then a humanoid body.

Chapter 44

And when this dust falls to the urn, in that state I came, return.
— Henry Vaughan

MY HEART POUNDED and chemicals rushed into my bloodstream till I felt light-headed. I released a haze of Chaos threaded with branching tendrils, letting it hang around my body as an immediately ready shield or weapon. I forced my breathing to slow. I was ready for this. I *was*. "Zed, Sam, kids, go protect the ritual circle," I ordered. "The rest of us will hold off Pestilence."

The four of them ran, and Jacky, Torliam, Adam and I grouped together, with Birch growling continuously at my feet.

The facade of Chanelle's body smiled at us.

A soldier stationed in one of the nearby buildings braced his gun on the windowsill and shot Pestilence.

His body rippled and splashed with the spray of bullets, bugs bursting and showering down around him. His leg buckled, but before gravity could act on him, the bugs had already rematerialized to fill in the hole and stabilize the appendage.

At a gesture of his fingers, and the soldier fell back from the window, dead.

Jacky was growing already, and would quickly surpass Torliam and me in size if she continued. A product of the fear, no doubt.

I understood. My own hands trembled, and my armored scales were flexed and angled toward Pestilence to better protect against attack.

His head turned to watch as the others ran ahead. "The girl looks smaller than I remember, and..." he counted on his fingers. "How are there still nine of you?" His eyes tracked to the lance tucked between my armband and the scaled skin of my forearm. "So you had a backup. That was clever of him. But obviously not clever enough, because you were too stupid to just give up."

I'd created a replica of the lance out of heated metal, using Chaos to shape it. It was good for nothing but ornamentation, but I hoped it might hide the truth of exactly how we'd survived. I didn't want him getting too wary too early. I took a deep breath and mocked him back, like we'd planned. If anyone was to draw special ire while we were distracting him, it should be me, because I had the best chance of surviving his retaliation. "I think we're a bit cleverer than you counted on. Or maybe you're just weaker, because we're not dead, are we?"

He grinned and pointed brightly to his own face. "One of you is!"

"Fuck you!" Jacky said, spitting towards him.

Pestilence twitched an eyebrow, then made a motion toward her with his fingers.

We all tensed, but rather than an attempt at infection, he was apparently directing his already-infected minions. A body 'popped' into place beside her, dagger already swinging for her lower back.

Jacky twirled, her gauntleted hand smashing into the side of her attacker's head and slamming him to the ground with a caved-in skull. The knife never even had a chance of making contact.

A group of Remnants rushed out from around the corner where they'd been gathering, standing between Pestilence and the Shortcut anchor. We attacked at the same time.

A woman pointed and said a word I didn't recognize, neither Estreyan nor English.

Pestilence's body quartered as if someone had sliced him straight through in the shape of an 'X'. He was rebuilding even as his bugs sloughed away.

Adam released a flock of darting birds that he'd prepared ahead of time. They dive-bombed Pestilence, and the explosives inside their stomachs—specifically created with his blood as the ink while he focused on doing as much damage to Pestilence as possible —exploded.

Bugs went flying in all directions, their pulverized pieces raining down through the air.

Half of Pestilence's body turned into goo from one of the Estreyan warrior's Skills, and I reached out with a wave of misty Chaos, disintegrating the top layer of the street and everything around Pestilence for a good five feet, including his body.

He didn't bother to fight back or continue to withstand our attacks. Instead, he reformed half a block down, in the direction of the Shortcut anchor. He smiled, and called back, "Really? Did you learn nothing the last time?" His voice still made me twitch, when I heard it coming from the visage of my friend. He turned his back to us and started to walk away.

I nodded sharply.

Torliam's power rushed forth to create a huge glowing wall across the street in front of Pestilence. "We will not let you pass. You have destroyed enough."

Behind us, the mass of infected Pestilence had brought with him swarmed up the street, falling to attacks from the surrounding buildings as they came, but unconcerned for their own safety.

Torliam released another wall of power, this one slamming down from above and crushing half the horde into the ground.

Adam shot an ink prison toward Pestilence. It grew into a bubble and chomped closed around him, cutting right through the inhuman creature's arm, which had been outstretched toward Torliam's barrier and too far away from the rest of his body.

Many of the infected he'd brought were human and slavering with the meningolycanosis. Despite the extra strength the disease afforded them, they wouldn't stand a chance against us. But others retaliated with Skills, or pushed back against Torliam's crushing force with sheer strength.

I dodged as one of their hands extended toward me like the snapping tongue of a frog. I severed it with my claws as it passed.

Birch let out a burst of wind all around us, and the half-rotting minions fell backward.

That was one of Pestilence's weaknesses. Sure, he could create endless minions and turn your allies against you, but the mind control went along with a certain level of physical degradation, a little less finesse with the Skills. Not anything like a shambling zombie, but just enough that it could make the difference between getting your head chopped off and being able to duck, as both Torliam and I did when a ball of red fire appeared above our heads and exploded.

Torliam shot a lance of power at the perpetrator, and she went down and didn't rise again. Not all of our enemies would receive the relatively humane treatment of Jacky's poison. After all, if we lived through this, Sam would be able to heal *her* opponents.

The group of Remnants ran past us, holding off the horde as best they could so we could focus on Pestilence, who was still inside the ink prison.

It imploded into a sphere of spikes, and Pestilence once again fell apart. He reformed on the far end of Torliam's barrier, turned to wave at us, and then ran away, forcing us to sprint after him before he caught up with the rest of my team.

His body was destroyed by several attacks along the way, from the people meant to hold him off from the anchor. He ignored most of them, but when someone was particularly effective, he stopped to point, subsuming them with his disease and overriding their will.

Those people burst into the streets to fight us, slowing us down. Others, once allies, turned on them to keep them from harming us and sabotaging our chances against Pestilence. I reminded myself that they had volunteered for this, knowing the risks.

We caught up to him without much effort, but when I lashed out with Chaos, Pestilence fell apart with a teasing smirk before my attack even reached him.

I looked around, but his body didn't reform. "He's going for the anchor!" I snapped, already sprinting ahead. My claws dug into the cracked pavement of the street as I hurtled forward, screaming at myself mentally. The others were there, and without me, there was no way they could stand up to the Sickness on their own.

The elaborate tower came into view, surrounded by glowing crystals that my teammates spread over the ground like a thick layer of gravel. The majority of the arcane circle carved into the pavement was still visible, but the most important parts near the center had thus been obscured.

Pestilence's body reformed even as I ran toward them.

I screamed out a warning. "Zed, behind you!"

It was too late. Pestilence's hand coalesced already around the back of my brother's neck, fingers seeming to sink into his skin as the bugs lost their shape from the pressure of his grip.

Zed's eyes went wide, and he gurgled as his veins blackened, crawling up the skin of his cheeks.

Pestilence drew his hand back down, and my brother crumpled.

<hr>

"NOW!" I snapped. I stopped, still a hundred feet or so out from Pestilence, but well inside the circle, as were the other members of the team.

A quarantine bubbled popped to life around us, thick enough to distort sight through it, and buzzing audibly with power.

As Pestilence looked around in mild surprise at the barrier sphere that had surrounded us, less than a hundred meters or so from end to end and all the stronger for it, he moved away from Zed, who twitched futilely on the ground.

I could feel the faintest hint of my brother's panic and horror, like an echo in the back of my mind.

Zed stood up, but the motion was jerky, his skin pale and beaded with sweat.

I stepped forward, with Jacky and Torliam at my back, while Sam ran to the edges of the barrier, downing the few infected Estreyans that had managed to keep up with us and get trapped inside with their controller.

Outside, Pestilence's minions attacked the barrier with flashing Skills and fancy moves if they had them, or tossed themselves bodily against it and were thrown back if they didn't.

The people we'd stationed in the city converged on us as well, knocking out everyone they could in the hopes that the unconscious would be able to last long enough for us to kill Pestilence.

"And now I guess you're trapped in here with us. Don't worry, we'll make sure to kill you quickly." The words felt inane coming out of my mouth, but I made sure to put as much real hatred into them as I could. The barrier had been specifically created to keep him from simply abandoning his current body and reforming himself outside it. If he wanted out, he would have to do it the hard way.

"Trapped?" he repeated, his tone almost sing-song. He shook his head. "On the contrary, if we were trapped, it would be *you* who were stuck in here with *me*. But I'm not trapped at all."

Zed sprang toward me, and I ran to meet him, as Pestilence's body shot toward the edge of the barrier, faster than he'd ever displayed the capacity to move before. As fast as Jacky sometimes moved when she pushed her Struggle Skill to the max, combined with her ability to manipulate gravity upon her own body.

I dodged a few of my brother's bullets, their trajectories easily projected with his slow and jerky movements and even worse aim. He was obviously meant to be a distraction as Pestilence escaped, but I didn't mind. *I* wasn't fast enough to stop Pestilence, anyway.

Jacky sprinted forward, using both her Skills to chase after Pestilence.

He stopped at the edge of the barrier, looked back to me with a broad grin and a twinkle to those light blue eyes, and pressed his hand against the buzzing wall. He didn't seem concerned about Jacky tackling him at all.

As the first bug began to coalesce from the nothingness of the air outside the bubble, I sidestepped Zed's lunge and grabbed him around the back of the neck, like Pestilence had just done.

The subtle buzzing that had been brushing against my senses, power waiting to be triggered into action, *snapped.*

There was a single moment of weightlessness, and then we were falling. Me, my team, and Pestilence. Along with a huge half-sphere of concrete and dirt, and every other thing that had been inside the barrier bubble when the hidden teleportation circle was activated by Pestilence trying to leave.

The mist from the cloud around us was almost chokingly thick, but it quickly cleared as we fell back down toward the ground. The gigantic chunk of falling earth and asphalt let out a booming, multi-tiered crunch as it collided with the Other Place version of itself.

I collapsed with the impact, more than a little rattled. I was careful to cushion Zed's landing since, with his physical control impaired by the Sickness, he might not be able to do it himself. I lay there, my clawed hand pressing into my brother's neck. I squeezed, just until the tips of my claws broke the surface of the skin.

He let out a half-growl, half-shriek, like an animal, and scrabbled at me, trying to get a grip on the gun he'd dropped when we landed.

I forced my fear for Zed to transform into rejection. "No." My voice reverberated and strength streamed from me like water from a sieve. The black veins receded from his skin, and he let out a shuddering sigh of relief, then looked up and closed the gigantic rip in the sky above us.

Our teleportation into the sky, along with half the parking lot, had cleared a huge section of the artificially thick clouds. Clouds which Birch, Torliam, and an Estreyan with hydrokinesis had created to hide the gigantic opening to the Other Place.

Pestilence threw Jacky off, but she'd already done her job, clinging to him and enforcing gravity to make sure he didn't somehow manage to escape our little trap by literally floating away or something.

I pushed to my feet and hauled Zed with me.

Pestilence looked around at the frigid, grey world, for the first time showing *real* surprise on his smug facsimile of a face. His eyes landed on Zed, whole and healthy again, and widened further. "What have you done?"

I pulled the fake lance out of its sheath and crumbled it in my hand, like he'd once done. I didn't bother to reply further, darting toward him. I wreathed my clawed hand in Chaos and swung for his blonde, pigtailed head.

Pestilence didn't seem overly concerned, till he started to fall apart to avoid my blow. Instead of disintegrating and reforming somewhere else, he shifted and stumbled as if he'd lost his balance or tripped over the air, half-crumbling.

Chapter 45

All goes onward and outward, nothing collapses,
  And to die is different from what any one supposed, and luckier.
  — Walt Whitman

WHATEVER PESTILENCE HAD BEEN EXPECTING, failure to discorporate wasn't it. But even as my fist swung through the air, his expression hardened. He turned, fist meeting my own clawed hand in an inhuman blur of speed. The force was enough to snap my arm backward and shatter something internally, and it blew my whole body away as if I'd just punched an airburst bomb.

Adam and Torliam both encased him in shields to keep him from coming after me, and Sam darted to my side. The crunching in my shoulder as it fitted back together sounded like a concrete mixer without the background noise of the city to drown it out.

Pestilence blurred into action within the shields, his fist smashing into first Adam's, and then Torliam's with a speed and force like a jackhammer. He was free in less than thirty seconds.

Torliam threw a spear of power into his chest, and it gouged a hole right through it. But that hole quickly refilled with bugs, and Pestilence didn't seem overly bothered, or in fact, injured at all.

He turned toward me, batting away Zed's physics-bending

bullets. They had been Blaine's, and I knew the man would approve of their use against Pestilence. Of course, I'm sure he would have been *happier* if any of them would have actually connected. "I commend you for your cunning," Pestilence said.

Adam gave a quick signal via a Window, and we all closed our eyes for the half second it took him to call a lightning bolt. It struck directly through Pestilence's body, bursting the thing apart like a watermelon hit by…well, a lightning bolt.

There was something painfully *off* about the space that remained, without the bugs to fill it, but I couldn't actually see or sense *anything* there until the bugs wiggled back to occupy his humanoid form. "You've cut me off from my source of power," he called, projecting his voice like an announcer at a circus. "But I know this place must be weakening you already. My reserves are large. Do you think it was smart, to trap yourselves in here with me?"

None of us responded. We weren't here to talk, or gloat over our perfect plan while accidentally giving him hints to use against us. We were here to kill him. And because of our deal with the Other Place whale, we had time to do that, at least until it had run out of crystals to feed off.

Jacky rocketed by, but Pestilence barely even flinched as her fist took a chunk out of his torso. Her attack should have done more damage, but, apparently, he was putting more power into keeping his body together than he had before, out in the normal world.

"Is your plan to die here, and by doing so entrap me? Because…" he shook his head as if scolding a puppy who'd had an accident, "all I have to do is wait for this place to be discovered again by someone else, and I'll be free. I literally have all the time in the world."

Around us, the sediment that looked like ash swirled heavily, obscuring vision at longer distances and disintegrating as it touched us. It was like we stood in the center of a grey snow globe.

I lashed out with a grasping maw of Chaos that shot forward and engulfed him from every direction. I set it to burning, willing my power to do what it did best. Destroy.

It took a while for Pestilence to reform after that, and the rest of the team kept up the bombardment of attacks, keeping him from rebuilding enough of a body to move away from us. We got into a kind of rhythm, one attack after the other so there wasn't space in between for a response.

Zed shot him, and could now hit him.

Gregor swung his new weapon, an extendable staff with blades that could protract and resheath themselves from its surface. He switched back and forth from Shadow to corporeality like a strobe light, the tip of his staff cutting through Pestilence so quickly the air sung with its passing.

Birch opened his jaw and spilled out Chaos, which rode the wind to Pestilence and turned into small fireballs like we'd practiced.

Adam channeled a slow and steady stream of electricity out of the two large energy cartridges strapped to his back. It wasn't as dramatic as a lightning strike, but the damage was continuous, bugs frying into little crisps when they managed to form past the rest of our attacks.

"Die," I whispered, Voice carrying my words on the air and pushing against Pestilence as he tried to reform. Even more bugs fell to the ground, perfectly fine except for the fact they were now dead.

Sam kept the void of his black eyes trained on the place where Pestilence's head would be, if he managed to remake it past our other attacks.

The blue glow of Torliam's mist crushed any bugs that tried to crawl in from farther away.

Kris kept her marionettes in reserve, since they would be damaged by our attacks if they tried to get close to Pestilence, but she glared at him with a hatred that was backed by terror, her tiny hands clenching atop the grip of her four-legged, metal mount. She tried to kill the bugs by ripping out their spirits, but they didn't have any.

Jacky kept back as well, except for throwing pieces of rubble at the spot where he would have been, where the air looked wrong and hurt if you stared for too long.

Pestilence responded to our barrage by rebuilding himself even faster, too fast for us to stop, too fast for us to *see*. He reappeared five meters away, snarling. There were obvious cracks in the facade of Chanelle's face. He held up a finger, as if he'd had a realization. "Actually, I don't need to wait for someone else to find this place. I only need to wait for *you* to die." He shot forward, moving so fast he lost pieces of himself from the force of the air pressure against his body. The bugs left behind immediately succumbed to the cold and died.

I tried to jump back, which helped lessen the effect of his cracking blow to my jaw. Still, my head snapped back, and I flew a few meters before Torliam's power wrapped around me and gentled my fall to the asphalt. I counterattacked with Chaos even as I rolled to my feet, a spear of darkness that exploded into black flames as soon as it entered Pestilence's chest, engulfing him from the inside.

I poured on the power as I bought the single second the others needed to join their attacks to my own. We had planned for this. Trained for this.

Our barrage broke even faster, this time.

—IT'S TIME.—

-EVE-

I lashed out with the branching cords of Chaos, cut his body in two, and then set the entire street on fire with the force of an explosion.

We ran away, scattering into the nearby buildings.

I could feel the attention of the Other Place as it turned its hunger on the fire, but it kept to our bargain and didn't draw at it any more than normal.

Pestilence made it out of the mixed black-and-orange flames, more cracks in his facade showing themselves. His head swung back and forth as he looked for us.

I watched with Wraith from inside a nearby building, keeping the others updated through a shared Window. It seemed likely that he'd have some way to sense targets for his power, living things that could be corrupted, so we implemented the plan immediately. We were on a time limit in any case.

While the rest of us stayed as still and silent as physically possible after running away from an intense fight, Gregor rustled a bit within his building. The tip of his staff peeked out above the edge of a windowsill.

Pestilence's head swung toward him, and he shot off, jagged grin stretching his mouth wide.

Gregor entered his Shadow state, even as Pestilence crashed through that same window onto the boy.

Pestilence swiped for him, but his hand went straight through Gregor's dark form.

I breathed the tiniest sigh of relief, and remained hidden.

Gregor raced away, but Pestilence easily kept pace with him, attacking again and again despite the outward lack of effect.

I bit my lip. I knew Gregor's Shadow form could only take so much disruption before it started to seep through to his physical body, and then caused the Skill to give out completely.

The boy led him into the depths of the building while Adam crept through from the other side, on a course to meet them.

Pestilence stopped and simply pointed to Gregor.

I squeezed my eyes shut instantly, fighting back against his will as he tried to kill the boy the only other way he could.

Gregor jerked and almost fell, but I poured my power into negating Pestilence, sweat beading on my brow and freezing before it could fall, and Gregor regained his composure and kept running.

Pestilence seemed to give up and returned to attacking physically with a scream of rage. As Pestilence's blows grew more rapid, Gregor stumbled, then turned, swiping out toward him with his staff, its tip extending as it swung.

Pestilence jumped backward to avoid a blow that never actually turned corporeal, and that gave Gregor the tiny opening he needed. The boy brought his foot down, excluding his shoe from his Shadow state, and letting it drop onto the concealed pressure trigger at that spot in the floor. He turned, and raced away, for all appearances looking as if he'd gotten scared and swung, failed to do any damage with his weapon, and instead lost his shoe before realizing his failure and running off again. That is, if you weren't familiar with Gregor, and you hadn't been one of the people painstakingly rigging the building a week before. We hadn't needed to even come into the Other Place to do it, because once something was stationary for long enough, the Other Place replicated it. We'd had the military rig the trap up and disguise it, and then we'd kept anything that could possibly disturb the building far away.

Gregor wasn't more than two meters away before the spark hit, and the napalm in the floor burst into flames. He made it to the door before Pestilence, and dropped the lever on the other side, releasing the steel blast doors that had been suspended over both openings to this inner, reinforced room.

Pestilence realized his mistake, then, but Adam had reached them. He slapped a multi-layered, complexly woven ink shield mixed with blood and diamond dust over the doorway.

The blast door on the other side of the room fell, as Pestilence pounded futilely against Adam's shield, and within slightly over a second, he was trapped within, with thousands of gallons of napalm and the oxygen tanks in the corner.

Within, Pestilence screamed again, and then his voice was swallowed by the flames.

The walls of that inner room were heavily reinforced, and, as Pestilence's body was being continuously destroyed by something else, we had time to regroup outside the building.

I extended a hand for Gregor to high-five, and he grinned up at me proudly.

"Is this gonna be enough to kill him?" Jacky said, frowning as she slapped her fist into her palm over and over.

"If it is, that'll be a waste of all our other plans," I said.

Zed shook his head. "The Remnant scientists said I would probably be able to see the weakening of his connection, once he used up a certain percentage of his power. Judging by the tiny amount of damage we did to him back there, I don't think this is going to be enough, either."

Jacky grinned. "I guess that means I still might get to punch him, no?"

Despite our preparation, Pestilence wasn't trapped inside as long as we had hoped. The high heat of the napalm fire, combined with the pressure of the exploding oxygen tanks, weakened the metal reinforcements of the walls. He burst out a few minutes later, still on fire, spots all over his body now dark and wriggling with the insects that formed him, rather than showing the fake skin veneer. As he moved, bugs sloughed off, and the napalm with them. He stopped when he reached the outside of the building, a few dozen meters from where we were. He stared at us for a moment, and then, instead of attacking, darted off into the cover of another building.

I shared a look with the others. "He's not stupid. He knows our plan is to wear him down."

Sam looked toward the spot where he'd disappeared, then moved to follow. "Does he also know he has no chance to escape? The Other Place only extends so far until you reach that edge of hungry darkness, and we have two Skills among us that can keep track of him wherever he goes."

Kris stared intently at the mini-map of his location I was sharing with them. She twitched her fingers, and one of the marionettes she'd stationed around the Shortcut anchor cut Pestilence off.

Literally. It cut his head off his body, then his torso off his legs. Then it stomped around within the mass of bugs.

Pestilence reformed and destroyed it like it was a toy, but every little bit counted.

Adam's fingers twitched restlessly. "How much time do we have left?"

My jaw tightened. "Not a lot. We'll have to start paying up directly, soon. If this becomes a drawn-out battle of attrition, we don't have the advantage. The only way *he* loses is if we kill him. *We* can just freeze to death, once the crystals are out. My bargain of a day of fire won't make enough difference to matter, beyond that."

A building a couple blocks away shuddered as Pestilence set off some of the landmines we'd planted.

We ran after him, darting through the swirling pseudo-ash of the Other Place.

PESTILENCE WAS FAST, but he didn't know this section of the city like we did, and he wasn't able to sense us from ten blocks away and adjust his course correspondingly.

When we got close enough, Adam Animated a flock of lightning birds, born from greater control of his Skills, which allowed him to combine Electric Sovereign and Animus when using blood as the medium. Electricity arced between them as they flew together, chittering like the sound of a hundred android songbirds, but way more disturbing.

They caught up to Pestilence and flew around and through him, small branches of lightning arcing between them with that high-pitched sound as swaths of smoking bug carcasses exploded or fell to the floor half-cooked.

Another of Kris' marionettes came after him once the birds were snatched out of the air and crushed to death.

Zed sniped at him with a small rocket launcher, complaining that the Other Place didn't allow him to use guided missiles.

At that point, Pestilence dropped all semblance of being human. He darted toward the Shortcut anchor, just a dark, humanoid mass of bugs moving faster than should be possible, shedding pieces of itself under the friction of the frigid, ash-filled air.

We ran to meet him, hurrying even faster when we realized he was attacking the crystals scattered at the base of the anchor. He stomped and crushed them under feet morphed to be cartoonishly large. He looked up as we arrived, a dark scar in his face widening in what might have been a smile. "I figured out what you did, how you're still functioning," he explained in a conversational tone, his voice made of the drone of bugs chirping and rubbing their legs and wings together at just the right frequencies.

A shudder rolled through me just at the sound of it, something in my hindbrain telling me it meant danger and a painful, slow death.

The broken crystals flared with light as the energy escaped them. He wasn't destroying the energy, but I watched with Wraith as the air greedily absorbed it. He was simply spending it faster, so that we would lose its protective buffer.

We lashed out at him, and he dodged, zig-zagging to make it more difficult to catch him with an attack strong enough to stop him. It meant we couldn't easily trap him with another constant onslaught of damage.

"I know what this place is, Eve. When you're dead, the others will be without your protection. I know exactly what you are, what you've done to safeguard their puny little lives. You can't last against me. When I'm finished, your brother will open the Veil *for* me."

Marionettes rushed in from all around, throwing themselves sacrificially at Pestilence for the chance to arrest his movement.

Kris trapped him, just long enough for one of Zed's anti-physics bullets to rip him apart and Torliam to enclose him within a shield.

Sam caught Pestilence's eyes, or the dark spot of wriggling bugs that would have been eyeballs on a human, but the creature laughed, completely disregarding the flare of cold power. Sam shook his head. "Black Sun won't work." He rushed in as Torliam crushed Pestilence like a bug inside a fist.

Jacky followed Sam, whooping with excitement and growing even larger.

As Pestilence reformed, Sam swept his hands through the bugs a single time and ran away.

None of the bugs were even dead. The ones he'd batted aside rejoined the whole again. Two seconds later, the spot where Sam had touched started to crumble, the bugs losing their grip and spilling out from the body like water. The effect spread, and, with a curse and a swipe of his hand, Pestilence destroyed his *own* body, letting the entire mass of bugs fall away and starting anew, free of whatever spreading agent Sam had introduced.

Jacky stepped in where Sam had been, braced herself, and kicked right up between Pestilence's legs.

The boys winced.

Birch caught Pestilence's disrupted, half-floating form in a gust of wind and slammed him away from the crystals.

Pestilence landed at the edge of the rubble we'd created by crashing a gigantic island into the Other Place.

Jacky followed, raining blows on him with her huge limbs, moving faster than anything that size had a right to, fast enough to make the air whistle and her attacks blur. She kept growing, and started screaming as she continued, pounding a crater into the ground around the two of them as the earth gave way under the force her rage.

Adam released a couple tentacled ink constructs, these ones also releasing electricity, but, instead of a more damaging attack, the suckers on the underside of their tentacles basically acted as a taser.

When there was a break between Jacky's attacks, they intervened to keep Pestilence trapped, along with a responsive blue barrier from Torliam.

Meanwhile, the rest of us watched, unable to intervene without fear of getting in her way or hurting her with overflow from an attack.

Struggle eventually gave out, and, as Jacky shrunk, Torliam swept in and snatched her away, and the rest of us stepped back in to take her place.

After a couple more minutes, the crater she'd pounded had only grown. We attacked without pause, not trying to match each others' pace, simply destroying Pestilence as quickly and as completely as we could.

I panted as I lashed out with more lightning-quick branches of Chaos, tightening around the tiny ball of bugs that was all Pestilence had managed to rebuild, and then exploding into a ball of black flames. I squinted through the blizzard-like storm of grey sediment swirling through the air, that ashy fuzz heavier than it had ever been before. It still disintegrated immediately upon contact with a solid, but it was impairing our visibility.

I spared a moment of concentration for a glance at the dimming crystals behind me. "How much longer?" I yelled to Zed, my voice hoarse with the cold. This wasn't the most I'd ever used Chaos before, but it was a lot, and I'd spent a huge amount of energy directly negating Pestilence's will when he tried to infect Zed and Gregor. I was growing tired, and the crystals were running dry.

Zed shook his head grimly, the lack of answer enough to sink my hopes.

Pestilence grew desperate soon after, the spot where he began to reform, the central locus of his body, jerking around spastically.

The rhythm of our attacks faltered, a beat just a little too long opening up between Torliam's crushing barrier and Birch's exploding Chaos-fireball.

Pestilence darted out of the crater, straight toward me, too fast to dodge. His hand smashed into my neck and clotheslined me. He bore down till my head cracked into the ground, pushing his will against mine. "I made a mistake, the last time," he said.

For half a second, I felt dizzy, as his power flowed into me and tried to subsume my body and my will, but then it was gone again as Pestilence avoided an attack and was forced to release me.

I rejected his influence, negating my bleeding gums and the skin at the base of my jaw that had started to literally rot off the bone.

Pestilence turned his head toward me as he dodged my team-mates. "I should have turned you, and set you to attacking the world you loved. It's not enough for you to die. The mortals need to *see* their heroes fall." He cracked a hand ineffectually through the space where Gregor's jaw would have been, if he were corporeal, and received a knife through the back of the knee as the boy retaliated, lettings his daggers shift into their physical state for only the instant it took to attack.

The black contours of Gregor's face split into the ghostly image of a vicious smile.

Pestilence stopped attacking or retaliating against any of the others then, only dodging their attacks if moving wouldn't impede him from attacking me.

I lashed out as viciously as I could, pushing myself faster and harder as I felt the drain of the Other Place start to take real effect. Still, I started to falter. And though Pestilence was growing weaker, he began to gain the upper hand, noticeably. Several times, I escaped a crushing blow or grapple only with one of the others' help. I tried to keep my body heated, warming my own blood with the faintest whisper of Chaos, but something about the Other Place ate at you with more than just physical cold.

The outcome was inevitable at that point, I suppose.

I lashed out with a horizontal cutting wave, and Pestilence ducked beneath it, pushing himself forward and up at me.

An ink barrier from Adam blossomed to life between my opponent and me.

I turned to leap away, but I stumbled, my limbs reacting just a little too slow. "Animus," I blurted, letting the ink wings spring to life at the base of my shoulders. Before they could complete a single flap, a hand reached around from behind and grabbed my chin.

I tried to fling myself around to face Pestilence, but his hand pulled faster than my body moved, and it was too strong for the muscles of my neck to resist. I felt it, as my spine cracked apart at the force, severing the nerves.

Light flashed and lightning crackled, and his hand disappeared.

I fell to the ground, completely limp. I blinked, and waited for death with a mental cry of anguish, but it didn't come.

Pestilence dropped down to straddle me.

Though I couldn't feel his body atop mine, I could see him out of the corner of one eye, and I could still sense the whole battlefield with Wraith.

He pressed his hand to the side of my face, grinding my head into the ground.

I *could* feel the Sickness, as it burrowed into me. It overpowered what resistance I had left, and, somehow, I felt it as I started to rot apart.

<hr>

Chapter 46

<hr>

Be careful when you cast out your demons that you don't throw away
the best of yourself.
— Friedrich Nietzsche

SOMEONE SCREAMED. It wasn't me, but I almost wished it was.
That would have been some sort of outward resistance, at least.

Instead, as my team went crazy with their attacks, turning Pestilence into an empty space once again, I lay on the ground and lost
the battle of wills.

I was still, as something else filled the space where the thing that
made me, *me* should have been. Hunger and pain and hatred pushed
me out.

Zed came into my field of view, and our eyes met.

The piece of me that was still aware, from somewhere in the back
of my consciousness, saw it as he realized I was gone.

His eyes deadened, and he said my name, though the word was
lost in the chaos of screams and attacks around me.

Some of those attacks were hitting me, I was pretty sure, but I
knew if I were myself, I wouldn't care as long as they could save me
from the Sickness. But I wasn't myself, and so if they didn't save me
from the Sickness, I knew I would kill them. They had to die, because
I was hungry.

But the Other Place sucked even that from me, and, since the madness was not my own, I did nothing to try and keep it from being devoured. I wasn't *pleased*, exactly, to see it go, but I felt somewhere deep inside that it was a positive change.

Zed screamed something to the others that I didn't quite catch the meaning of in my distraction, ending with, "I'll tear it apart!"

The attacks stopped, and Pestilence reformed above me.

Maybe that was the plan, because as soon as he did so, he was gone. Jacky had tackled him. She wrapped her limbs around his own, arching back and immobilizing him, even as she began to scream, her blood curdling and turning rancid in her veins, under the force of Pestilence's will.

I frowned, the tiniest twitch of my eyebrows, as I watched them with Wraith. Within me, something tiny sparked, and caught, and I remembered hatred. It filled me up, a comfortable sensation, spreading warmth through my limbs and giving me the energy to keep fighting. Strength poured out of me as I resisted Pestilence's influence, and the hatred just gave me more.

One of Adam's arms was bare of ink, the fractal tattoo that he'd worked so painstakingly to rebuild wrapped around Pestilence like a living thing, pulsing tendrils grabbing at any part that tried to wiggle away and squeezing them back into the center.

Why weren't they attacking him? Just a little more, and he would lose the power to maintain the connection. Just a little more, and he would be banished forever, back into the nothingness from whence he came.

Torliam's blue mist crushed Pestilence, and Jacky beneath him, into the ground.

Pestilence jerked spastically against them, bugs falling off as he spent his power against my own. His limbs began to crumble.

"You are no part of me," I mouthed silently, and yet the words still weighted down the air with my will.

Zed was there, then, screaming raggedly. He plunged his hands into Pestilence like his chest was an empty space. Then he began to *rip*. I could feel it, as Pestilence tore and snapped, whatever was holding him together breaking apart. Not just the bugs, but the space where he existed, the locus where the thing beyond met the world here.

I caught one last glimpse of Pestilence's shocked face, and then he disintegrated.

He did not reform. Where he had been was not an empty space, but an ink-spill patch of darkness, unlike any of the other rips Zed had ever created. I averted my eyes, lest they be tainted.

The *otherness* left me, and I felt stretched out and deflated, like a used balloon.

Zed stumbled back, turning to look at me.

Jacky rolled over and crawled away from the oil-spill of darkness hanging in the air, more than a little beaten up, but free of the Sickness.

I looked back to the darkness, maybe by accident, maybe by instinct. Once I did, something wouldn't let me look away, as if my gaze was magnetized.

Zed's voice filtered through to me, strangely loud without the sounds of battle. "Are you alright?"

Before I could answer, if I *could* even answer, the world shivered. Not physically, like an earthquake, but like reality experiencing a glitch.

Zed turned back to the rip, following my gaze.

It bulged.

He reached for it, probably to close it.

It was too late. It exploded outward, as *something else* reached back through.

I LOST my sense of space and time. I looked upon the eye of something not meant to be seen. Something changed. Something moved. Then it was gone, along with the jagged, black rip in reality. Had Zed closed it?

I was relieved, for a single moment, until the world began to shriek and swirl as it collapsed in on us.

Adam snapped out a huge ink shield, and, as it crumbled inward, he used the other sleeve of tattoos, letting the fractal surround us. It pulsed against the pressure, and then it crumbled, too.

Sam dropped to his knees beside me, his hands on my neck. His own bones crunched as the injury transferred to him. He started to slump over, but caught himself even as his body slotted back together and the nerves reattached themselves. "Can you move?" he screamed to me, the sound almost lost to the hunger of the cosmic whale as it sucked at us and everything around us.

I could, but the *pain* of my ruined body held me back from doing so, now that I could feel it again properly. Whatever they'd attacked Pestilence with while he was trying to kill me—it felt like I'd been crushed by a stampede of demon-buffalo while being flayed by angry wasps. I tried to ignore it, reminding myself that I was a godling and could remake as many bodies as I needed. Pain was temporary. It was hard to convince myself of that, while experiencing said pain.

Zed stumbled toward me, his hands flailing at the air but not finding purchase, as the cold drove him to his knees.

Torliam pushed against the edges of the blackness, but his glow was consumed even as he released it.

Gregor pulled Kris' tiny body to him, curling around her in his corporeal form to provide her protection.

Birch screamed out a ball of Chaos that burst into a single instant of colorful, illuminating flame. It was absorbed almost immediately, but the feeling of it as it alleviated the deadness in my chest gave me an idea.

I let what power I still had burst out of me, exploding into flame as I set the air afire. "Wait!" I screamed, the sound deadened by the near-vacuum.

The swirling around us slowed as the cosmic whale turned its eye on me, though it still sucked at the warmth and color and power I produced, almost faster than I could create it.

My lungs heaved.

I felt the echo of its anger toward us. "Please," I whispered. "I will bring you fire, in exchange for our lives."

"What could you give, that would be worth your lives, when this has been done to me? All that I have gathered, the fruits of aeons of hunger and struggle, *gone* in an *instant!*" Despite the rage in its words, it pulled back a little, and my flames expanded.

The heat spread farther, a little more oxygen making it to me. "Our lives, taken now, are worth less to you than the energy and heat I could bring. I will give a thousand Earth-days of fire."

It drew back, still circling us predatorily.

Time stretched on interminably, and my heartbeat started to stutter.

"Agreed." Its single word held a depth of meaning, and it drew away.

The fire petered out, but it lent enough heat to the world for Zed to stumble to his feet and open the Veil.

I felt arms, more than one set, wrap around me and carry me out.

Chapter 47

Having become a god, he became a demon.
— Ilium Troia

THE WARMTH of the normal world *burned*, but it returned life to my limbs.

We lay in the crater where most of the mall parking lot had once been. There was a strange distortion hanging in the air above us. Not like an opening to the Other Place, and not like that jagged blackness that had appeared when Zed tore Pestilence apart. Looking at the new distortion felt like hearing the taste of purple, and that's about as much sense as it made.

YOUR CHARISMA HAS INCREASED!
YOUR LIFE HAS INCREASED!
YOUR PERCEPTION HAS INCREASED!

Once Sam had regained some of his energy, he healed the worst of my injuries, sobbing tearlessly with each new hurt absorbed. He had to throw up a couple times, but I didn't say anything, because a few tears slipped down my own face in grateful relief for the cessation of pain. If my Life Levels and my healing factor hadn't been so high, I probably would have died already.

Our healing factors were similar, actually, but my power was exhausted. He could have left me to fix my body on my own, one way or the other, but it would have been a long wait filled with agony for me. He couldn't even use Black Sun to mitigate his response, because it didn't work in conjunction with the healing part of Harbinger, not if he wanted the person he healed to remain non-suicidal.

I was grateful.

When I was repaired enough to function on my own, he did the same for the others, but we stayed in the crater for a while longer. Exhaustion made the climb to the top edge seem impossibly daunting.

Kris sobbed, crawling over to me and wrapping her tiny arms and legs around my scaled torso. She buried her face in my neck, and I patted her back soothingly as I stared up at the sky.

Birch sat in Adam's lap, and, for once, didn't do anything mean to the boy.

Torliam lay back and fell asleep, and he looked totally and completely at ease.

Jacky fussed over Gregor, and he smacked her hands away when she tried to ruffle his hair, but then held her hand and tucked his head into the dip of her stomach. "We're safe, now," the boy murmured.

Adam, hands trembling and his face set in a scowl, made an ink parrot and sent it out to ask for help.

Not long after, a group of Estreyans peeked their heads over the edge of the crater, glancing warily up at the distortion hanging above it.

"We won, you idiots," Adam said. "Hurry up and get us some stretchers or something. I'm too tired to walk."

They returned soon after, exclaiming about the sudden absence of the Sickness in everyone who had been infected. There was no need for healing, no period of lag. One moment, they were rotting apart and attacking with crazed disregard for their own safety, and, the next, they were whole.

They had waited, hoping for our return, for some sign that this was permanent.

People squeezed my fingers in thanks as they lifted me onto the stretcher, bowed so deeply to us their noses almost touched their knees, and murmured about the end of the Sickness as if afraid talking about it too loud would break the illusion.

Was it over, then? I searched inside myself as they carried us out, flying us to the island of the Remnants for recovery. I wondered if I would be empty. Instead, I found my rage unspent, coiling within me like a sleeping animal. Yet now, there was nothing to expend it on.

TIME PASSED.

Not all was well, though things were on the mend. Many of Earth's leaders were angry, bickering with each other and the Estreyans. Some angled for more reparations, others to destroy any goodwill the civilians of their countries might feel toward me or the Estreyans. Others were just afraid of something like the attack and the Sickness happening again, and handling that fear poorly.

In turn, the Estreyans had little respect for the humans, and made it clear.

Despite this, both worlds seemed to be healing, and I thought the chance of total separation between Estreyer and Earth was unlikely at this point, as was further war.

People from both worlds visited the other using the Shortcuts. The transfer could not be permanent, and would forcefully return what had been sent after an alignment or two had passed between our worlds. Still, it was enough to allow people to gain a greater understanding of the other side, and with understanding came acceptance and, if not camaraderie, at least a lack of fear.

Word spread quickly that the Sickness was gone for good, and Pestilence was dead. Reporters from both species were rabid to know how we did it.

I wondered, too.

Zed sat beside me and explained, as best he could one day. "His center was all wrapped up with these connections to somewhere else. Just like there are cracks in the world. But when I reached into them…I didn't open the cracks. I tore them apart. Like they were lines drawn on a piece of paper. I tore the lines in two. I destroyed the cracks, and I guess that killed Pestilence, because he didn't have a *real* body, anyway. He was only a manifestation of the power those connections allowed him to draw on."

I didn't quite understand. That worried me, because I thought something more may have happened, beyond the destruction of Pestilence. The strange distortions scattered around both Earth and Estreyer weren't *normal*, though they didn't seem to be malicious.

They were places where physics was broken. The more learned or the incredibly stupid of both our species had been examining them with a combination of rabid scientific fascination and fear. A couple people had died, or disappeared, walking into them, and one man who'd been drunk and touched one on a dare from his buddies claimed to have gained the ability to communicate with fungi and bacteria.

The military had blocked most of them off for the safety of the population, and to study them. Some people insisted they were a sign of the end of times, and blamed me and my team.

Time passed.

Jacky laid her head in my lap and told cheesy, dirty, stupid jokes till I choked on laughter, not at the jokes, but how amusing *she* found them.

"These are good jokes!" she insisted. "Here, how about this one, yeah? 'My dog used to chase people on a bike a lot. It got so bad, finally I had to take his bike away.'" She snickered, then continued. "'What's orange and sounds like a parrot? A carrot!' 'What does one saggy boob say to the other saggy boob?'" She paused dramatically, then answered herself. "'If we don't get some support, people will think we're nuts!'" She clutched her stomach and guffawed in my face.

I pushed her off my legs, and she fell to the floor, still snorting through her laughter. "You're really *not* funny," I said, unable to hold back a snicker.

She pointed a finger up at me. "You're laughing! I *am* funny!"

I tried to deny it, but I couldn't, because I kept giggling when I looked at her flushed face.

Time passed.

We went back to our old base at Blaine's house and had an informal remembrance-ceremony-thing for our dead teammates. It had rained, and as we stood at the edge of the forest, where the air smelled green and fresh, the world was beautiful for once. I cried, and tried to hide it, and Adam rolled his eyes and told me to get over myself, but he wrapped an arm around my shoulders in a hug and sniffled more than a bit himself.

The nightmares grew less frequent.

We returned to Estreyer and were lauded as heroes. Our faces adorned every screen. People had donated so much wealth to us that we would still be rich if we lived for ten lifetimes. Queen Mardinest wasn't exactly pleased about it, but she simply sniffed when she saw us for the first time after our return, and said, "I am glad you were not frauds."

We searched for an answer to Kris' diminutive body, and thought we'd found it, only for her to throw herself across the room to avoid the pain as she started to grow. She said something in her heart, which was now really just a floating Seed core inside her chest cavity, had felt like it was tearing. The Remnants said they would research to find a solution, now that both worlds were connected again and they could go home, but no answer had come from them yet.

We dealt with a few less-than-pleasant people, even on Estreyer. Someone tried to steal the Oracle's third gift, which still lay unsolved. Though I kept it a secret, in the back of my mind, I knew that some part of me wanted to need the third gift. Some part of me wanted another enemy, something to bring me purpose, to connect me to life in such a vibrant way again. The rest of me, the *smarter* part of me, hoped it lay as a loose band of sparkling loops for the rest of my life.

Zed's eyes started to crinkle at the edges again when he smiled.

Still, there was a sort of separation between us and the rest of the world. To the humans, we were alien. To the Estreyans, we were godly.

Time passed.

I took time every day to visit the Other Place with Zed's help, burning anything the whale wished, till my power was exhausted, only to return the next day and do it again. At the rate I was going, it would take me many years to pay back the debt of energy I owed it.

One day, as I played with the flames as I created them, shifting an orange bloom into a bright purple flower, only to have it devoured by a crashing wave of blue, the cosmic whale of the Other Place laughed at me.

When I had first returned to it, the space on the other side had been reduced. Before, I might not have been able to tell the difference between the Other Place and the real world if only judging by how big it was to my normal senses. Now, it stretched only a few meters in every direction before abruptly dropping into darkness.

As I fed it flame, the ash-like snowfall would grow heavier, dissolving into the ground and the environment. Ever-so-slowly, the Other Place grew again, each little flake formed from the absorbed energy and replacing some of the lost mass.

The cosmic whale, which I imagined to be the sentience of the Other Place, or Blue, as I had taken to calling it, after it found this description pleasing, swirled around me as I repaid my debt to it, one day at a time. More and more often, as its anger toward us mellowed, we would talk.

"The day of darkness comes," Blue said, one gigantic eye looking down on the flames from beyond the black edge of the reflected world.

"An eclipse," I said. "The Estreyans are holding a big party."

"Perhaps you will need my help again, then?" Its voice held the slither of characteristic slyness and a blatant measure of greed.

The fire faltered. "What? Why?"

"Keep burning," it ordered. "You are not tired yet."

When I complied, it swirled around me a few more times watchfully before answering. "I have not seen you use the last Aspect of Chaos. If you require my help again, *Zed,*" and it said the name with ire, "shall not rip into the void with his clumsy fingers. You will learn yourself."

I swallowed, blood rushing in my ears. "Do you know something? Is something bad going to happen?"

The swirling slowed, and the impression of the gargantuan eye pressed closer. "Are you not meant to fight against the Abhorrent?"

"We were. I was. But we killed him. Or at least—banished. Is there some way for him to get back here again?" My voice tightened as I spoke, and the fire died down as I lost concentration.

Blue's temper pounded in around me like the beat of a giant drum. "You killed Pestilence, you foolish morsel. Now, if you will not continue to bring me life, *get out.*"

The realm contracted, receding in around me till I found myself stumbling out of the rip Zed had left open for me.

I tried to go back through, but there was nothing on the other side, no replica of my immediate surroundings, just a jagged pane of darkness and the faint impression of Blue's form receding into the distance.

I ran for the palace, sending a mental Window to the others as I went.

People bowed to me and called greetings as I passed.

I blew past without acknowledging them.

Torliam met me in the throne room, and, as the sky darkened in midday, the sun being blotted out by the joint efforts of the double moons, the others arrived as well.

My fingers trembled as I fumbled with the Oracle's third gift. As the day turned into night, its pieces fitted together. I held back a sob.

My hands shook as I settled the multi-banded crown on my head. It writhed and tightened, weaving through my hair and settling on my brow. Then came the pain, as it injected its contents into me.

YOUR CHARISMA HAS INCREASED!

I fell into the vision. When I finally opened my eyes, with blood in my mouth and my team's grim faces all around me, I bowed my head and let angry tears run down my cheeks. They flowed into my mouth and dripped off my chin, sliding into my scales. "We were wrong," I choked out. "Pestilence is not the Abhorrent. He is merely one of its Aspects. One of nine. The *first* of the greater Trials."

THE STORY CONTINUES in *Gods of Smoke and Stars: A Seeds of Chaos Adventure*

This side adventure is fun but not a critical read, and comes before the conclusion of the story in *Seeds of Chaos Book V: Gods of Ash and Amber.*

Also by Azalea Ellis

Seeds of Chaos Series (Complete)

Book I: Gods of Blood and Bone

Book II: Gods of Rust and Ruin

Book III: Gods of Myth and Midnight

Gods of Smoke and Stars: A Seeds of Chaos Adventure—Available free to newsletter subscribers

Book IV: Gods of Ash and Amber

A Practical Guide to Sorcery Series

Book I: A Conjuring of Ravens

Book II: A Binding of Blood

Book III: A Sacrifice of Light

Book IV: A Foreboding of Woe — Coming Soon

Codename: Moonsable (Patreon Exclusive Sidestory)

The Honeymoon Suite (Patreon Exclusive Novelette)

The Catastrophe Collector: A Practical Guide to Sorcery Series

Book I: Larva — Coming Soon

More books may have been published since you purchased this copy.

Here's a Quick Link to All my Books.

About the Author

I'm the type of person that often has a wacky, shocking, or silly–but totally *true*–story to tell about my life.

(Like the time my brother and I were chased through a secluded strip of woods in the middle of the city, for over a mile, by a naked man with an erection.)

(Or the time a trucker threw an open bottle of pee out his passenger side window without looking right as I was walking by. You can guess what I got splashed with.)

I've got an active imagination that tends toward the outrageous and the macabre, which led to me being voted "most likely to borrow someone else's car to transport a dead body."

I write books about things that interest and excite me. I'm always in the middle of teaching myself something new, and if I'm not over-whelmingly busy I tend to get antsy. I believe that the impossible is only so if we believe it to be so. Therefore, nothing is impossible.

If you'd like to get updates from me, both about my books and about what I'm up to from time to time, the newsletter is the place to be, as I tend to be very scarce on other social media.

https://www.azaleaellis.com/newsletter/

For more information:
www.azaleaellis.com
author@azaleaellis.com

* 9 780999 675014 *